By Harvey Swados

OUT WENT THE CANDLE
ON THE LINE
FALSE COIN
NIGHTS IN THE GARDENS OF BROOKLYN
A RADICAL'S AMERICA
YEARS OF CONSCIENCE
THE WILL
A STORY FOR TEDDY—AND OTHERS
THE AMERICAN WRITER AND THE GREAT DEPRESSION
RADICAL AT LARGE
STANDING FAST

STANDING FAST

STANDING FAST

Harvey Swados

DOUBLEDAY & COMPANY, INC., GARDEN CITY, NEW YORK
1970

Library of Congress Catalog Card Number 73–121957
Copyright © 1970 by Harvey Swados
All Rights Reserved
Printed in the United States of America
First Edition

To
BETTE AND SANDY

What grows out of the free acts of countless men and comes upon us like an overwhelming tide of events is no mere tide of events. Every individual acts in it as a free agent. However powerless he may feel, no one is wholly powerless. We may quail before the course of history as before a relentlessly rising tidal wave, and we may be swept along. But we join in building dikes, and men have been able to stand fast. History differs from the tides of the sea. Those tides are mute. History speaks, and we answer. The very union of men is no mere natural phenomenon but an event animated by their freedom. However minute a quantity the individual may be among the factors that make history, he is a factor. He cannot attribute it all to a tide of events of which none is his doing.

Karl Jaspers.

PART ONE

1. NORM

Slanting between the red-brick ranks of apartment houses and business buildings of Upper Manhattan, the sun struck Norman on his bared head, finding its way also to the wooden platform from which he addressed the street-corner meeting. He gripped the railing tightly, taken by a kind of exhilaration.

"They lied to us," he cried, "all of them! Stalin, Chamberlain, Roosevelt! If I had said a week ago that Stalin would make a deal with Hitler, you would have laughed at me. Now I tell you that we cannot rely on Stalin or Chamberlain—or Roosevelt—to fight fascism for us."

"So who do you suggest?" An aging, unshaved man with a shriveled right arm peered up at him anxiously, more worried than challenging, from the front of the crowd.

"Ourselves!" Norman spread his arms wide in an all-embracing gesture. "When Molotov said that fascism is a matter of taste, he did more than give Hitler the green light. He taught us something we should never have forgotten: to rely on our own strength as a class."

"On our strength?" The graying man waved his newspaper incredulously at his neighbors. To judge from his accent, he was probably a German refugee. "Wiz us," he persisted, "wiz us you're going to stop ze Nazis?"

"With international solidarity. The workers as a class have nothing to gain from fascism."

"Tell it to ze German vorkers."

Norman had been prepared for the usual assaults from the

Stalinists, but the Pact had silenced them. On this sunny September afternoon almost everyone was willing, perhaps even anxious for a new explanation of what still left them stunned.

Nevertheless the skeptical refugee was not entirely wrong. He stood among children on roller skates, slowing to stare at the orator on the little platform, gaping at his flag and his fervor as they might have at a sidewalk pitchman. Beyond them, women shoppers glad of an excuse to linger on the summer street, high school kids licking ice cream suckers, their unformed faces curiously neutral; and worn-out working people and shopkeepers, in flight from other shores like the heckler, or from long hours at the sewing machine, the lunch counter, the punch press. What could the concept of class mean to them? Were they prepared to think of themselves as the bearers of incalculable possibilities?

Raising both hands, he brought them together, symbolically uniting himself with them. "When our comrades pass among you, put your names and addresses on the sheet they carry, and we will be happy to keep you informed about our activities and our program of mass action for peace and against fascism."

Sy and Bernice had been standing in the middle of the crowd, their upturned faces absorbed. No longer children, after the depression years at home and the alcove arguments at City College, they were still not quite adults, not when you looked down at their transfixed worshipfulness. It was flattering, but just a little silly, and Norm was glad to see them bustle hopefully with their literature bundles and interest sheets.

They were a smallish, rather intense pair, both with shell-rimmed glasses and sweet doglike dark eyes. If they lacked humor, life had not given them much to laugh about; it was more important that they were decent and loyal. When they held each other by the hand, the history major and the sociology major, they could touch you not only with love but with envy.

Norman leaped off the platform and began to fold it up. Some of the youngsters hastened to help him; whether or not they understood what he had been saying, they were at least ready to give him a hand. In a way you could say the same thing about Sy and Bernice, even though they swore fidelity to Norman's faction. He had the uncomfortable feeling that with all their knowledgeable talk about the need for an American radical party, and a real break with the traditional fixation on Russia, they were smitten with him as a dashing figure, more glamorous than the Marxist logic-choppers with whom they had grown up.

Still fresh from Mexico, where he had been first pick-wielding archaeologist and then pistol-toting bodyguard to Trotsky, he possessed for them the added attractiveness of having gone to college out of town, in Ann Arbor, of having played football there, of having his own place on 113th Street. They could not possibly have understood that he still felt trapped in the middle-class and had been attracted to the revolutionary movement as a possible way out of experienced middle-class agitators like himself, whose principal working class like Sy and Bernie, would have invested him with an additional appeal: the man of quality voluntarily disassociating himself from his origins in order to better serve their common ideal.

"I leave these to you," he said to them, rolling up the American flag and stowing it in the folded wooden platform, "to put back in the branch office, along with the literature. Have you got the key?"

"Somebody will be there," Bernie assured him. "We made arrangements beforehand."

"Did you dispose of many papers?"

Sy nodded, pleased. "And I made three good contacts, thanks to you. Your talk was great. You know how to get through to people."

"It won't last very long, without a follow-up. By the time they finish their salmon salad, they'll be wondering whether to play cards or go to the movies. My speechmaking has a limited effect."

But so did his belittling of his speechmaking. Sy replied anxiously, "You'll be there tonight, won't you?"

"You still want me to talk to the downtown branch?"

"We've publicized it," Bernie said seriously. "Everyone's expecting you, to hear about your experiences in Mexico."

It was nearly five; his father would be waiting. "Suppose I come by your flat," he said to Sy, "about a quarter to eight." He could as easily have gone directly to the headquarters of the downtown branch, but the warmth and contentiousness of the Glantzmans' Lower East Side flat were as attractive to him as the obligatory visits to his father's Riverside Drive apartment were tedious.

Sy was pleased. Loaded down with literature, he shook hands somewhat awkwardly and then turned to help his girl friend with the dismantled speaker's platform. Norm waved farewell to them both and hurried off to the 175th Street station of the Independent subway.

He had to change after one stop, at 168th Street, for the Seventh Avenue. Here, beneath the Presbyterian Hospital complex, he joined the walking wounded of the great city and its bastard civilization: invalids returning from treatment of banal or exotic complaints, visitors to the afflicted, sniffling relatives, and the motley mass of workers coming home from a sixth day of work downtown—or leaving home, carrying night lunch in brown paper bags, for name-less labor in deserted office buildings or sheeted and eerie depart-ment stores. Even if they had not yet been affected by the new war declared in defense of an obscure territory, they were neverthe-less abstracted and unsmiling, enfolded in the private problems that bore on them more heavily than the far-off Nazis.

It was already too late, he was realistically convinced, to keep America out of war, no matter how many committees were formed, no matter how enthusiastically Russia's admirers now embraced isolation. The trick would be to transform what had been learned from the betrayals and the miseries of the Thirties into a new movement that would do what no one else was doing: fight on the one hand against the war and the obviously inevitable military dictatorship and postwar depression, and at the same time against the fascist poison that had already infected the isolationists and the Stalinists.

The odds were that it was a hopeless effort. But did that make it wrong to try? You had to do what was indicated by history, as well as by logic and passion. Most painful was the quality and insufficiency of his own comrades, an ill-assorted handful of in-experienced middle-class agitators like himself, whose principal asset was their stubborn refusal to concede that radical politics would end with the ending of the Thirties.

They proposed to attract to their side Communists whose sensibili-ties were still live enough to be shocked by the Nazi-Soviet Pact; Socialists who also refused to make common cause with racists; trade-union militants who did not propose to quit fighting, simply because they might embarrass the Administration; and young ideal-ists like Sy and his girl, overwhelmed by the clarity and inner logic of a Bolshevik Leninism, that, like Catholicism, seemed incon-trovertible once you accepted its first premises—but too humane nevertheless to follow blindly the dictates of the old man in Mexico, much less the tyrant in Moscow.

It was not much—a little group of Akron rubber workers, a roomful of Chicago students, a couple of old militants on the Mesabi Iron Range, some second-generation Wobblies here and there —but it was what they had, and it included people who were not simply more good than bad, but in all honesty, he believed, far ahead of their contemporaries in intelligent self-sacrifice and dedication to principle.

At 72nd Street he took the steps up to Broadway two at a time, still almost childishly pleased that he could reach the street faster than anyone else, without being winded. Heading west, toward the Hudson, he turned north on Riverside and breasted the river wind before his father's stately apartment house as the sun was already slipping behind the Palisades on the Jersey side.

The building had been his home, too, for a brief period after his return from Mexico. There had been plenty of space for the two of them in the four and a half-room apartment, but as soon as he had broached the idea of his taking a room farther uptown, near Columbia, his father had been more than receptive. Why not? At fifty-three Milton Miller kept an oily-nosed Turkish mistress in the very same building, one flight below in 4D, and although he visited that slothful but voluptuous woman three meticulous evenings a week, it was undoubtedly a nuisance to have his grown son hanging around, picking up the telephone even when it was Zoraina who rang, answering the doorbell and the downstairs buzzer too, grabbing the mail, watching his comings and goings like a jealous wife.

Nevertheless Milton, who had buried two wives already—Norman's mother and an almost as dim second one—had made his own fortune as a factor to textile jobbers, and was not about to throw any of it away on things like separate establishments—no matter how convenient that would be for all concerned—without imposing conditions. He was determined to show that he had not forgotten the value of money just because now he had a lot of it, and to reassert his authority over a son who was pushing twenty-five and still not settled into a profession.

"Listen," he had said, mouthing his Antony y Cleopatra, in the shrill piercing voice that made it impossible for you to do anything else, "put it out of your mind that you're just going to use me as your friendly neighborhood bank."

"What do you want, interest?"

"Funny. I want only your own good. You've got no mother, I've got to be twice as careful. You majored in archaeology at Ann Arbor, fine. You were crazy about it, you persuaded me you should go to graduate school. Fine. Then you had to do field work in Mexico. Fine."

"We've been through all this."

"All of a sudden," his father went on inexorably, "you're not on a dig. You're moved in with that crazy old man, guarding him, taking your life in your hands every minute."

"That didn't cost you a penny."

"Heartache it cost me. How many sons you think I've got?"

"I never did find out."

"Wise guy. Now he converted you, I'm supposed to support you while you run around and make propaganda for him. This country was pretty good to me, and I'm not going to let you—"

Hastily Norman reassured the patriot, righteously indignant in Palm Beach suit and silk socks rolled to the ankles. Teetering in his two-tone black and white summer bucks, his father demanded from him a commitment that he would indeed register at the Columbia School of Journalism as a graduate student, in earnest of his desire to enter a new profession.

"You can't spend your life being an agitator. You've got to have a profession."

It did not seem possible to Norman that his father could really believe that the war would spare him. Perhaps he thought—Norman did not really want to find out—that the magic of a "profession," even a semi-respectable one like journalism, would confer enough prestige to warrant a commission, if not protection from the hazards of an infantryman's existence. It was clear that he wanted to be able to say to his friends that his son was on the road to becoming a professional man. Since this did not seem too much to ask in return for support with few questions about his daily life, Norman had agreed, especially since his comrades, already preparing to form a new party, had regarded this as an excellent device, freeing him to work for them as publicist and propagandist.

Now that the war in Europe had actually broken out, however, Norman was somewhat less than sure himself about the bargain.

He intended to take this up with his father and thereafter with some of the people in the national office.

Milton Miller was standing in the doorway of 5G, fountain pen in one hand, cigar in the other, when Norm stepped off the elevator. "You're a little late."

"I hurried." Norm smiled reminiscently, thinking of how disgusted his father would have been if he had been among the crowd of spectators in front of the soapbox on Fort Washington Avenue. "The bank isn't closed yet, is it? I see you're just making out my check."

"Boy are you a comedian. Maybe you ought to audition for the Eddie Cantor show instead of being a perpetual student."

"Then you'd take me off the payroll, and how could I become a professional man?"

His father, already bending over the big family-sized checkbook that he favored, probably because it made him feel not so much businesslike as patriarchal, declined to answer. Certain payments that he did not wish to have on record he made in cash; if he paid his son by check it was no doubt because he desired proof that although his son was of age he was still classifiable as a dependent on Form 1040. Well, why not take advantage of the tax allowance?

Milton's attitude toward the Internal Revenue Bureau wasn't nearly as shocking as his taste in clothing and household furnishings. The apartment was a disaster, and each time that Norman came back to it, no matter how briefly, he congratulated himself on having gotten out from under. Brocade chairs lined the stippled walls like sentries. The baby grand Steinway of dead wife number two, its never-lifted lid draped like an odalisque with a fringed Spanish shawl, served as showplace for a gallery of photos, ranging from Norman's overstuffed and artificially tinted grandparents on his father's side to Norman himself in cap and gown. Every time he glanced in the direction of that unsmiling, unforgivable dummy he felt himself as dead and buried as his grandparents, all of them survived by the indomitable widower, still undertaking, along with the weekly gift of money, to do good works.

"Here, stick this in your pocket. Why do you look so down in the mouth?"

"For openers, there's that little war that started since I was last here."

Milton Miller laughed readily. "Hitler got you down too? Listen," he begged, "that bum has finally bitten off more than he can chew. He's bluffed himself into a corner."

"You sure of that?"

"I'll make you a little wager. First time those armies meet—if they ever do—you'll see what a hollow shell Germany is. The Czechs or the Polacks are one thing, but just let him come up against a first-class fighting force, like the French and those fortifications of theirs—"

"Then what?"

"The Krauts'll starve. He's got an exhausted labor force, and what's more he hasn't stockpiled food for a long war. Time," he announced, as though it had just come to him, "is on the side of the allies."

The line sounded familiar. Norman's eye wandered over the pile of magazines in the wrought-iron rack beside the wing chair. Back issues of *Harper's, The Nation*. His father prided himself on being "forward-looking," as he called it, and did not hesitate to pass off as his own the dubious estimates of the liberal journals of opinion. This daring had often confounded his more motheaten associates in the textile industry, but it only depressed his son, who kicked himself for having compounded this fashionableness by sending his father the beaten silver mask from Taxco and the straw baskets from Xochimilco that hung on his father's wall with a kind of magnificent pointlessness as proof that, if nothing else, Milton really had sent his boy to Mexico to dig for pots.

"I doubt that you're right," he said to his father. "But even if you are, I doubt that time is on my side."

"Meaning what?" His father squinted suspiciously through the cigar's fetid smoke.

"Meaning that sooner or later they'll catch up with me."

"Who will? Jesus Christ, can't you be clear? Specific? To the point?"

"The U. S. Army, that's who. You never saw a more draftable specimen than me."

Round-shouldered from protecting his money, enemy of every form of physical culture, Milton glared at the fullback's frame which Norm kept in shape at the 63rd Street Y. "Ridiculous. Besides, once you have a profession—"

"I won't have one in time to be made a general, or whatever

they'll do with people like Walter Lippmann and Elmer Davis. So I've been turning around in my mind the possibility of going to work in a defense plant."

"Already you want to welsh on your agreement. I tell you one thing: no journalism school, no checks. Finito."

"But I won't need them if I'm working, right? Besides, I'd have thought you'd be pleased with the idea that your only son was tucked away safely in a defense plant, making tanks or airplanes."

"You think you'd be safe from the draft there? Workers like that are a dime a dozen."

"So are graduate students. I just thought I'd broach the subject. After all, if I can't talk to you . . ."

Mollified, his father buried his cigar in a beanbag ashtray, alongside four of its fellows already dead earlier in the day, and patted Norman on the arm. "I suspected you were down in the dumps the minute you got off the elevator. Don't worry, kid, you stick with your studies and don't get sidetracked—and I'll stick with you."

How far? All the way into basic training, a movie comedy father and son team? Or would Milton confine himself, as seemed more likely, to one more recital of his own adventures in 1918 as con-man and general all-around fuck-off artist in the Quartermaster Corps?

Norm sighed. He was about to make some innocuous comment preparatory to leaving when his father suddenly remarked shrewdly, "You know what the trouble is? You've got big ideas about the war, but you're not sure whether you can get anybody to listen. That's why you won't even talk to me about them. If you want to go work in some Goddamn stupid factory it's not to save your skin. It's because you've got that Trotsky dream of saving the world."

"What's so bad about saving the world?"

"I say it's bullshit. And not because I'm a right-winger, you know that. I just look at it realistically. I say to myself, twenty years the Communists have been in business in this country, the Socialists longer. Where did it get them? All these years you had millions out of work, hungry even, did you see a revolution? I didn't, and don't tell me it was because I was too busy making money to notice. A revolution I would have noticed."

"There are historical reasons—"

"Sure. And there's going to be more reasons why you won't do any better. Listen," he confided, "I'd be on your side if you had one chance in a million. But you haven't, and in your heart you know it. Wait"—he held up his ringed hand to forestall further objections—"don't say anything more, and I won't either. It's something you've got to get over. Maybe it would have been better if you'd gotten it out of your system with those radicals when you were an undergraduate—I used to congratulate myself that you stuck to your schoolwork when I read about those kids running around with the protests and the petitions."

"Of course, it's just possible that my ideas are more substantial, since I came on them when I was already mature."

"Yeah yeah. Mature. I think to myself, maybe it's worse that way. Like with love, you know what they say, no fool like an old fool? All I'm saying now is, don't tell me about it. If you feel like you have to do it, good luck to you—but like with the girl department, keep it to yourself, okay? Tell you what. Let's hop into the old Chrysler and drive out to Sheepshead Bay. We can get ourselves a seafood dinner at Lundy's, steamed clams, lobster, the works. What do you say?"

Embarrassed by the father's generosity, but even more by the revelation that he was not champing at the bit to descend to 4D, Norm shook his head quickly. Too quickly. "I'm sorry, but I've got an appointment."

"Not a date, huh?" Milton Miller asked with heavy irony. "An appointment?"

They shook hands, almost formally. "See you next week." "Right, next week." "Take it easy." "You too."

Back on the Broadway-Seventh Avenue, released from a physical presence as strong as the smell of cigar smoke that clung to him as though it had been painted on his skin like iodine, Norm found himself wondering what his father would be doing if he did not go down to 4D. Nibbling on that lobster all alone? It did not seem likely. But he had grown so accustomed to the mental picture he had painted for himself, of his sharp-eyed father lolling at ease in Zoraina's never-seen seraglio (always multicolored in his mind's eye, a cross between an oppressive, windowless Turkish carpet store and a halvah factory), that it was hard to imagine him elsewhere, playing cards with friends say, or God forbid spending an evening alone in 5G surrounded by silence and the keepsakes of dead wives.

Distracted, troubled by the check in his pocket from someone whom he could mock but not scorn, he almost overshot 14th Street. Just before the subway doors closed, he leaped out and got on a crosstown BMT train headed east. At Union Square, still uneasy in his mind, he was disoriented, paused on the sidewalk for a moment, momentarily unsure of his direction, and gazed about him.

Yes, there they strutted, across the way, high above the last heedless shoppers, behind the second-story showcase window of a cut-rate furrier—the two models who personified for him both the surface pretense of New York and the senseless strain that lay behind it. Posturing and pirouetting like mannered showgirls, they twirled briskly to display their furs, crossing each other's path at fifteen-second intervals with the inhuman precision of trains controlled by a dispatcher at an electrical panel. Just as precisely, they smiled, coldly, like streetwalkers. But even at this distance, the sweat trickling down their cheeks and furrowing their stage make-up was plainly visible.

Ducking his head, Norm hastened over to the national office. His comrades rented a corner building in the warehouse-secondhand bookshop area south of the Square. The street floor was occupied by a plumbing-supply house, its unwashed windows half-concealing a clutter of pipe joints, elbows, and upended water closets, their dangling guts corroded and mute, as if dug up from some extinct civilization like the shards he had hunted with such assiduity only a year or two earlier.

Above this midden heap of almost-junk, the windows of the upper three floors were covered with exhortations to Build Socialism and Vote For Workers' candidates. Already faded and curling, the posters, with their promises of a happier future, attracted scarcely any more attention from people too intent on their own miseries to look up and read portents and claims than did the fly-blown plumbing reminders of a hydraulically functioning past.

The interior of the building was alive, though, from the moment you pulled open the scarred door and felt the rickety steps vibrating underfoot in sympathetic rhythm with the mimeograph's clockety-pockety-clockety. At the first landing, a hefty young man nodded to him between shouts into the pay phone, doodling on a plaster wall already adorned with graffiti. Norm continued to climb, past the second floor where boys and girls in their teens sang and

argued among themselves while they filled bundle orders and cranked
the mimeograph. Past the third floor too, where he himself had a
desk for his journalistic works. On to the top floor, where the
national leadership, in somewhat more remote austerity, surrounded
by maps of the United States and the warring world and by ancient
posters of the Russian Revolution, met to plan and to scheme for
their few thousand followers.

Here you had to watch your step—not only because the floor
was actually giving way here and there, threatening to drop the
leaders down onto the heads of the writers like Norm, who strove
to publicize them and their ideas, but also because one man watched
another: rumors of a split, the plague of every radical group, rent
the air, and those who were already working to build a new party
from elements of this one were narrowly watched by the loyalists.

Norm stopped first in the cubbyhole office of Comrade Hoover.
The bald, saturnine Negro, veteran of three earlier socialist groups
and early organizer for the steelworkers and then the auto workers,
had declared himself for those who planned to build a new party;
but because he never stooped to personal attacks and still retained
certain connections within the labor movement he had a wide
respect on all sides.

Hands locked behind his head, Hoover regarded Norm quizzically.
"Well," he said, "what's on *your* mind?"

"Don't you want to know how the street-corner meeting went
uptown?"

"Not particularly. I've been told that you do a good imitation of
Dworkin."

Norm flushed. At the same time he had to laugh: Who didn't do
a good imitation of Dworkin? Their brilliant leader's brain, tongue,
and arm moved like cleavers, chop, chop, slicing through the
stupidities that he destroyed with relish, his ruthless wit terrorizing
the opposition within the movement and humiliating the hecklers
without. Only a few, like Hoover, could sit back and assess Dworkin
coolly—and even Hoover had chosen to associate himself with
Marty Dworkin's faction, seeing in it the hope for a new radicalism
freed from the crippling attachment to rigid dogma.

"Is Marty here?"

"He's with a man from *The New Yorker*. The way the kids are
hopping downstairs, you'd think the barricades were going up on
14th Street."

"Well, you can't blame them. That'll be a good break for us, an article in *The New Yorker*."

"A good break my *foot*." Hoover tilted back in his scarred swivel chair. His bald brown skull caught the light from the dusty window; the back of his head rose alarmingly, as if it had been squeezed in a vise. Even atilt and at ease, he was a man of great force and dignity; unlike Marty Dworkin, the dapper debater, with his hairline moustache and wicked grin, it was difficult even to think of him, much less to address him, by his first name. True enough, Marty was the public figure, the theoretician and writer, even the international figure; but when you thought of him or spoke of him, respect was almost always mixed with mockery.

With Hoover it was different. Neither witty or fiery, he was upon occasion sardonic, as in his deliberate choice of nom de plume. And far from being a cafeteria intellectual or street-corner hotshot, he was dismayingly tough, he knew the labor movement. For a small organization, he was as precious as money in the bank.

He said coldly, "Now Dworkin is sitting there with him, *chatting*. And all those brats downstairs are hopping up and down because some *jour*nalist is going to write us up for a comic magazine."

"A good press won't do us any harm with the middle-class liberals."

"The only thing that will do us any good with liberals or anybody else is re*sults*." Hoover scowled and passed his palm over his skull, as if it had hair worth smoothing down. "What I can't seem to get through you guys' heads is that all this talk-talk, all these sessions with journalists, won't amount to a hill of beans. Not unless you speak with authority as revo*lu*tionary workers' leaders."

Hoover's surface anti-intellectualism was alarmingly like that of certain self-styled Bolsheviks—except that in his case it was not a fake hardness or hatred of mental accomplishment. Indeed he was a man filled with quiet but intense admiration for the genuine accomplishments of novelists as well as mathematicians. What he detested was pretense and bombast. What he dreamed of—if you could think of such a man as a dreamer—was a community of people who thought, decided, then acted, without further ado.

With suspicious kindliness he concluded, "Now I know *you* mean business, unlike some of these *dent*ists' and *milli*ners' sons and daughters we're stuck with, playacting at being revolutionaries. They

wouldn't know a barricade from a barroom. And they're the ones
Dworkin caters to, with fancy names like the locked-out generation."

"That's what I'm here to talk about, with you and Marty. I'll
make it short: I want to get into the labor movement."

"Have you got guilt feelings too?"

"Maybe. That's not important. Now that the war has started, I
have a greater sense of urgency. I have to be where the action
is, working in a shop where I can contribute something more substantial than—"

"More substantial? Do me a favor, will you?"

Norm nodded, and leaned forward, hopeful of a special assignment.

"Spend a little time *learn*ing, before you run off with a red flag
in your fist and your feet going every which way, like Charlie
Chaplin in that movie." Hoover scowled. "If there's one quality
this outfit is short on, it's humility."

Hot-faced, Norm protested. "I don't think you have any reason
to accuse me—"

"I'm not accusing. But there's people like that all around you. Your
first responsibility is to show them what *dis*cipline means. You don't
have to tell me that we've got to get some of these young blow-
hards into the shops, and let them use their big lungs in union
meetings. But we've got to do it in an orderly fashion, and we're
not going to strip the national office of people with skills like
yours. Who's going to put out the paper, the youth? They don't even
know how to give it away, much less sell it, much less edit it. When
the time is ripe, you'll hear from us."

"In the meantime . . ."

"In the meantime I thought you were serious about becoming a
labor journalist. Well get on with it, man. And if you've got heart-
burn, talk with Lewis, not me."

He had been hoping too to discuss an article with Hoover before
sitting down to write it up for the paper, but now he felt himself
definitively dismissed, and he left the office with no further talk.

Two doors down, Dworkin was chatting, as Hoover contemptuously called it, with the man from *The New Yorker*. The door was
ajar, and the journalist's hands alone were visible, holding a pad on
which he jotted as Dworkin spoke.

"Yes," Marty was saying, "I did run for mayor against La
Guardia. It's my contention that I was counted out, by some eight

hundred thousand-odd votes. If I had the resources I assure you that I'd demand a recount."

The man across the desk laughed, and in that instant Norm was filled with jealousy. Not that he wanted to be sitting there, chuckling at Dworkin's familiar repartee. But he knew that he was competent to write just such a story, and others too, that could move and stir the conscience of far more readers than he could ever reach in the small circulation revolutionary press.

Maybe Hoover sensed this, that he was torn between throwing himself into an activist's life and becoming a successful writer—a radical writer, a crusader, but still a non-participant in the battles of his time. It was embarrassing to think in these terms, much less to talk in them, at an age when he should have already made his decision, but he could not free himself of the contradictory pulls.

Comrade Lewis was hunched over a sheet of figures in the office adjoining Marty Dworkin's. A large pudding-faced man with the soft hands of an esthete, he was neither agitator nor theoretician nor working-class leader. Exactly what had propelled him into a position of leadership was not clear to Norm, except that he was constantly involved in figures; it was said that he had once been an accountant and even now knew more about the market than most people on Wall Street. He met the bills, raised the money (or told others how), and organized the fund drives for party press and organizers' field trips. Uninteresting work, but essential; and he was almost as highly valued by Dworkin's faction as was Hoover.

At Norm's entrance he held up his hand and pressed the backs of his fingers to his lips in sign of silence. He murmured, "Let's not disturb Marty and his visitor," arose, and reached for his hat, a conservative but oddly elegant summer straw. Then he hesitated. He said very softly, "I'll meet you at the Automat," and sat down again.

Norm retreated from the office and the building. He was already halfway through his frankfurters and baked beans when Comrade Lewis came up to his table bearing a tray with the mixed vegetable plate and a foaming glass of milk.

"Have you ever observed," Lewis asked, while he arranged himself, "that when the air bubbles subside, what you are left with is approximately three-quarters of a glass of milk? Scientifically calculated to gyp the poverty-stricken—who are so transfixed with pleasure by what happens when they drop their nickel in the slot that it never occurs to them to complain."

"How about all the Horn and Hardart cocktails? Ketchup and a glass of water to make tomato juice? The customers get even."

"They don't get even," Lewis said with finality. "If they did, the Automat would have gone out of business . . . I hope I didn't discommode you by driving you out of my office. It wasn't simply Marty's visitor—it's getting difficult to talk frankly there. Too many ears."

"I thought so. In any case, I'll be brief. Now that the war is on, I won't be able to accept money from my father like an undergraduate, pretending to go to graduate school while I work for the movement."

Comrade Lewis was far more attentive than Comrade Hoover; he was all but courtly over his carrots and boiled potato.

"The future is as uncertain for us," he said, "as it is for you. Just as you have to take into account your own psychology under pressure of the outbreak of war, so we have to take into account what our resources will be, if we have to go out on our own and form a new party. And that was hardly the sort of thing I could discuss with you in the office. There are already too many people up there who will be calling us traitors for not submitting to their worn-out dogmatism."

Raising his head, he nodded to a stocky young man with protruding eyes who was just coming off the cafeteria line, carrying his tray and the evening paper. The young man squinted at them through his thick-lensed glasses as if considering whether to join them. Then he nodded briefly and headed for another table.

"You know Harry?" Lewis remarked.

"Not well. You don't mistrust him, do you?"

"Comrade Drang?" Lewis chuckled—but did not make clear whether it was the question that amused him or the party name Harry had chosen as a substitute for his family name, Sturm. "We count on him as we do on you. He accepts the fact that he is both a chemist—a technician—and a party functionary. Why can't you?"

"I'm a technician as you call it only by courtesy. Harry can earn a living as a chemist. Do you think that *The New Yorker* would hire me as a working journalist?"

Lewis glanced at him slyly. "One day they may."

"But not now. It's hardly enough, that I can do an acceptable job of turning out a four-page agitational paper. Besides, with all due respect to Harry as a chemist I can't see him in a shop, talking to workers. But I can myself. In fact I think I'd be better at it than at what I'm doing now. Happier, too."

"That could be. And perhaps it will be. But for the moment you'll have to subordinate your personal preferences to our needs. If we can hold the youth, and attract more, we'll have the forces to colonize certain industrial areas. If we sent you, alone, we'd be all but throwing you away, at a time when we really need you here. If you set an example of revolutionary discipline to the youth today, they'll be all the more inclined to follow you a year from now."

"A year?"

"Perhaps less. But remember"—Lewis leaned forward and tapped him on the arm—"first things first. We can't move vigorous young people into the shops until they really understand just what we ask of them. Take Sy." Lewis observed shrewdly, "He admires you very much. We may ask him to go into industry, especially when the defense program picks up. But our immediate perspective is that he be elected as a delegate to the Madison convention of the American Student Union in December. That may sound modest to you. But after their disillusionment with the Stalinists and with the outbreak of the war, radical students are ready for what Sy can bring them. We count on you in the weeks ahead to help him mature sufficiently to carry out our plans."

Lewis's plea was simplicity itself. Nor was it easy to quarrel with it when he himself was of two minds.

Norm found himself wondering, after he had said goodbye and stepped out into the darkening street, what people like Lewis did of a Saturday evening, if they were not at the national office or addressing a meeting. Were there wives? Record players, perhaps? He had a vision of Lewis seated in the half-gloom, smiling in concentration as he filed his nails, tapering the corners, while Stokowski conducted Bach. Hoover no doubt sat hunched over a book, underlining in pencil, pausing from time to time to jot a note on a filing card. But Marty Dworkin was unimaginable apart from the press of politics, the stab at an opponent, the parrying of an attack, the preparation of a polemic or a public statement. And yet people said that he had an absolutely separate life somewhere in the suburbs, children, a darkroom where he developed his own pictures. Pictures of what?

He took a bus, changed at Grand Street, then left the second one for the Glantzmans' tenement on Senator Street. He always approached Sy's home with a sense of anticipation that he would have found difficult to explain to Sy, who would have laughed, perhaps even with bitterness, and charged him with romanticizing the squalid bickering and political squabbling from which he hoped, like his older brother, to flee. Nevertheless Norm's spirits rose when he clambered up the cabbage-smelling steps to the Glantzmans', and he could only contrast this with the way his heart sank when he ascended the elevator to his father's.

He rapped at their door and was greeted by the Russian-accented voice of Sy's mother. "Come in, come in, it ain't locked!"

He pushed open the door and stepped directly into the kitchen. The linoleum, its old mosaic fading into reddish blotches, was still covered here and there with the Yiddish papers, the *Vorwärts* and *Freiheit* from the day before, scattered like ice floes from the stove to the living room.

Mrs. Glantzman was scrubbing pots and pans in the washtub. A somber, heavy-breasted woman who seemed always to be grimly working, she raised her head for a moment and gave him a smile, all the sweeter for its rarity. "You came in time for a glass of tea," she said. "Don't say no. I baked strudel, the kind you like, with the walnuts inside."

"You know my soft spot."

"Why I shouldn't?" She stood before him in her characteristic flat-footed stance, her features as familiar as if he had known her forever, not young, not yet old, the heavy nose flaring beneath the unhopeful eyes, the graying hair escaping from a net, the heels of her slippers crushed beneath her weight. If not for a certain querulousness, amounting at times almost to a plea for pity, she could have been considered a handsome woman. What was deeply moving to Norm was not so much that she was overworked—maybe it was simply an article of faith that work was life itself and relaxation, death—as that she was disappointed.

Sarah Glantzman and her happy husband, cheerfully baiting his younger son in the parlor, were of the socialist generation that had assisted in the birth of the unions in the industries in which they both still worked. Not long after their marriage the socialists (Sarah's garment workers) and the Communists (her husband's fur workers) had split, initiating a sporadic fratricidal war that was mirrored within the family. Norman, unused to having a mother, much less one with a mind of her own, was a fascinated, at times even an envious spectator of the family battles.

Baruch Glantzman faithfully followed his leader Ben Gold to Union Square on May Day, not just because his job (when there was work) depended on it, but truly because the Soviet Union had become for him that spiritual homeland for which his heart had yearned ever since he had cast off the faith of his fathers, marching down Seventh Avenue on Yom Kippur, flaunting sandwiches with his brother atheists.

But Sarah, transformed into a skeptic by the pressure of those small daily events to which her husband was impervious, set her face solidly against the split squads of the Communist opposition in her union hall. Suffering from her husband a lifetime of sneering scorn, she had settled into an existence built on the consolation of her co-workers at the dress shop, her cooking, and the raising of her boys, to whom she had transferred all the bounty of her heart.

The older boy, Sid, having thrown himself into the Young Communist League with the hearty approval of his father, had been courteous to his mother only because she was his mother, and in the autumn of 1936 made his escape to Spain. Writing home infrequently, he did not let them know until the wound was all but healed of the dum-dum bullet that had torn away a substantial section of his forearm. He had come back silent but restless, only to take off again as soon as he had gotten a workaway card from the National Maritime Union.

There remained Sy, to whom his brother never spoke when he was in the house, and on whom his father dumped all of his pent-up venom as if he incarnated the ubiquitous capitalist enemy. It hardly helped him to know that his mother saw in him her ace in the hole, the last card she could play in a game in which all the other cards seemed to have been stacked against her. If she was silently grateful for his rejecting the politics of hatred espoused by the other two, she had lately grown fearful that he in his turn was committing himself to a life that would deny all of her sacrifices and all of her aspirations. This contradicted her own socialist convictions and she knew it—she was not a stupid woman—but she could not help herself. She could not keep from hoping that, like hers, Sy's brilliant convictions would weather down, fade into simple personal preferences, much as one casually decides to vote for one mayoral candidate over another, and so would not hinder his escape from a life of obscure poverty.

Looking now into her desolate countenance, aching-eyed like an unmilked cow, Norm saw not only the impossibility of her situation, but the aggravating effect that he himself was bound to have upon it. And yet he could not bring himself to play the hypocrite with her. "Well," he said to her, "what do you think about the war?"

"I don't want to say anything," she replied somberly. "Glantzman"—she nodded toward the husband she always referred to by surname—"he's rubbing his hands together. Go in, maybe you can keep them from fighting. Here," she extended the cookie sheet, "take a strudel. Take, take. I'll bring in some tea in a minute."

Norm walked on into the parlor. There, seated in the sunken, lopsided mohair armchair that was his very own throne when he was not bending over his workbench stretching muskrat skins, was the foolish father, before the curtained window beyond which loomed the fire escape that led down to Senator Street.

"Here comes another one," announced Baruch Glantzman by way of greeting. He spoke not to his son, who stood to one side, his face queerly contorted, but more to himself, ticking off his son's friend as one more thick-headed enemy of progress. "You gonna give me the same song and dance about Stalin letting us down?"

Norm permitted himself a smile. "I never felt that he was lifting us up," he said to the older man. "There's no more workers' power in Russia. Workers don't make deals with fascists."

"No, huh? You don't think so?" Baruch Glantzman grinned slyly. He was small and crabapple-hard as his wife was large and soft-bosomed. In his self-satisfied shrewdness he was not unlike the credulous shoppers preyed on by pitchmen, easily convinced that the shoddy goods, the patented apple corers and handrolled linen handkerchiefs fetched out of cardboard cartons with one eye out for the cop on the beat, were in reality fantastic bargains, enhanced by the fact they were hot merchandise. Secure in his broken-down armchair, in his stained and defeat-smelling tenement flat, he screwed up his small red-veined eyes and demanded confidently, "What do you know about the woikers? You ever woiked in a shop?"

"That has nothing to do," Norm said stoutly, with a confidence that he did not feel. "I do know——"

"You do know nothing. We always got to make deals with the

bosses, even when we got a whole country, a sixth of the world, until the time when there's no more bosses anyplace."

Trembling, his son demanded, "Supposing you drew the line at making a deal with the worst enemy of the working class, the worst enemy of the Jews? Supposing you swore you wouldn't?"

"Swore, swore." His father waved his disfigured hand, swollen with calluses from the shears he had been clutching for so many years, until the long layoffs. "You can't get it through your thick head that protecting the woikers' state is not like playing stickball on Senator Street."

Sy was pawing furiously through the pile of *Daily Workers* that lay at the old man's feet. For one irrational moment Norm thought that Baruch Glantzman, simply by way of emphasis, would lift his foot and kick his son in his thick head. He recalled suddenly, in the flashing speed with which a dream arrives, Sy recounting his mother's determination to buy arch-support shoes—and his father's sneering comment, "Go ahead, baby yourself. In the Soviet Union the women go without shoes to build socialism."

Then Sy was erect again, gripping a paper and reading from it in a tight strained voice: "The whispered lies to the effect that the Soviet Union will enter into a treaty of understanding with Nazi Germany are nothing but poison spread by the enemies of peace and democracy."

"So what?"

"You believed it yourself, a week ago."

"I believe in my party now, like always. They couldn't let us in on it beforehand." He pressed his palms together and rotated them gleefully. "What a brilliant move! Last month the imperialists were pushing the Nazis to attack the woikers' state. Now they're turned against each other, they'll wipe each other out, and Russia will live."

"Russia will live," his son parroted angrily, his voice rising, "and we'll be dead. Is that what you want?"

"Dumb head, don't you think Russia will be in it sooner or later? Meantime they'll build up, Stalin gained them time, that's the mark of a genius."

"You call it genius, to start another war? Millions of people will die and you'll sit there, my own father, rubbing your hands together!"

Now he had gotten to him. Norm perceived now what he had not observed before, a zigzag blue vein swelling and thumping in the temple that shone pale as death under the fringed lamp. The old man lifted his thickened fingers again and opened his mouth as if he intended to say something in reply, but no words emerged.

Sarah Glantzman came in from the kitchen bearing the tea things and a bowl of strudel. "Seymour," she said, "take the *tchainik,* and —" Suddenly she stopped, then cried out hoarsely, "Glantzman, *Glantzman!*"

Dropping her armload on the card table, she threw herself awkwardly on her husband. He had slumped in the chair, his mouth drawn down to one side, saliva drooling from it in a slow string. His eyelid hung down, frozen in a roguish wink.

Frantically, his wife massaged his hands, calling to him by his last name, calling him back from the dark hole into which he had fallen.

"Seymour," she gasped, "go down by the drugstore, call the society doctor. Call my sister in Buffalo, call collect, don't be ashamed, don't stand there like that."

In the doorway her son hesitated. "What can she do?"

"Her boy will know."

"Irwin's not a doctor, he's a dentist."

"You want I should go down? Go already, quick!"

The door slammed. Norm approached the stricken man and knelt beside his wife. He whispered, "I think he's . . ."

She raised her eyes from her husband and glared at him impersonally, as if she were looking not at him but at something beyond him and beyond his comprehension. "Politics, politics," she said. "It's going to kill us all yet, politics."

2. FRED

Fred was bending over his desk, checking off the papers he had just corrected for his Freshman English quiz section, when the rat tat tat on the hallway door made him lose count.

"Don't get up, Fred," Bea said. She had been sitting behind him, in their one easy chair, sewing up an open seam on a T shirt. She was at the door before he could complete the count and stuff the test papers into the briefcase she had bought for him for his twenty-fourth birthday.

Not that Bea was eager for company. Quite the contrary. She was so anxious for him to get on with his dissertation that she intercepted and discouraged callers. Most of them admired her for it, as well as for her selflessness in seeing her husband through graduate school. Fred himself did not know how to tell her—much less anyone else—that there were times when this put a deadly pressure on him to be "productive" and "creative."

At this very moment he would have liked a bit of a break between his teaching chores and his dissertation, but the determination in Bea's tread announced otherwise.

As soon as he heard Vito Brigante's gravelly voice, though, Fred pushed back his chair and arose. Bea would not be able to discourage the painter that easily.

"Hey, Vito," he said. "You look a little mad at the world tonight."

In fact Vito always did. He had been an amateur boxer during his student days in Hutchinson High and thereafter had put himself through art school as a club fighter, a fair welterweight. But it

wasn't punches that had damaged him (actually he was marked only
by scar tissue above the eyes, which gave him a falsely threatening
demeanor) so much as growing up poor and parentless.

By turns cocksure and uncertain, believing in himself as a painter
but ashamed of his ignorance and social awkwardness; he had been
a Communist of sorts when Fred and Bea had first met him at a
party for the Spanish Loyalists. Now he had broken with them,
infuriated by the Nazi-Soviet Pact because he simply hated fascism
and wanted no deals with it. As a result he had been dropped by his
entire circle; friendless and frustrated with no outlet for the nervous
energy that he did not burn up in his studio, he had taken to dropping
in on Fred and Bea. He admired Fred as a "professor" (distinctions
of rank were too complicated for him), and he was not put off by
Bea's protective attitude—it was possible he didn't even notice it.

"It's always got to be somebody," Vito said raspingly. "If you're
not mad at somebody what's the good of being alive? Listen, I'm
not interrupting you or something, am I?"

Fred ignored his wife's sidelong glance. "I just took care of tomorrow's classes. What's on your mind?"

"I didn't mean to stay. I'm on my way to the Elmwood Music
Hall, so I thought I'd drop in. They're going to have an America
First rally. I want to see if the same faces show up that were at
that beer garden the other night. You folks want to go, maybe?"

Bea winced. "Fred is really very busy. He has to deliver his
thesis to Cornell . . ."

"How long are you going to be there, Vito?" Fred asked.

The artist hunched his muscled shoulders. "Half an hour, maybe
an hour at the outside. I don't want to shoot the whole evening on
those bums."

"In that case," Fred said, "I'll join you. I could use the fresh air,
it'll clear my head for my dissertation. Coming, Bea?"

"Thank you, no."

Vito had invited him only three nights earlier to observe the
German-American Bund rally at a Genesee Street beer garden; he
had declined, under pressure from Bea. Under pressure, or because he had been afraid of getting banged up? Vito had a taste for
trouble, he had joined the Jewish War Veterans picket line outside
the beer hall, and in no time was embroiled in a slugging match
with a crowd of uniformed Nazis. The cops had dragged him away,
and sent him home when they recognized him as the ex-pug.

"You see that?" Bea had said triumphantly, showing him the story in the paper. "How would it have looked if you'd been mixed up in a brawl like that?"

"Maybe not so bad." He had never gotten involved with the Communists, except at occasions like parties for Spanish relief, but now that they had given up picketing Nazis, he felt doubly guilty at not being involved. His father, an old-line Social Democrat, had come to Buffalo from Germany just before the outbreak of World War I to practice medicine, and marry a simple girl, one of the city's quarter of a million Poles, who saw her original homeland smashed to its knees and occupied by the Nazis.

"For my family," he said to Bea, "I should have been there."

"For your family it was better that you were here, working for your degree. Would it help your family or your career to wrestle in the streets with those bullies? How long do you think you can go on working for eighteen hundred a year?"

What she meant was, how long do you think I can go on working instead of having a baby? And, do you want to turn out like your father, rolling his own pills to compete with doctors who wrote out prescriptions, dreaming away the dismal days in his dusty half-empty office, while his bovine wife retreated to her own dream-world of movie magazines and chocolate creams?

Unlike his father, though, he was very ambitious. Beatrice knew that, but she couldn't reconcile it with the restlessness that came over him when he read the papers or watched the newsreels. That she saw as a threat to his career if not to their marriage, and she looked upon it—maybe correctly, how could he be sure?—as the only tie uniting two such different people as Vito and himself.

"All right," he said to Vito, "let's go." He plucked his raincoat from its hook on the hall door and pecked at Bea's averted cheek. "I won't be late."

"I'm tired," she said flatly. "I'll be in bed." Which meant, take off your shoes when you come back.

When they were out on the street Vito said, as if it had just occurred to him, "Say, I hope Beatrice won't be mad at me for dragging you away."

"If she is she'll get over it."

"Yeah, but when you find somebody that sticks up for you like she does, working and all the rest of it, you want to treat her right."

Vito's words sounded more dutiful than laudatory. *He* hadn't married early, *he* didn't have to account to a wife when he wanted to drop his work and take to the streets. But then he added, as they hurried ahead into the teeth of the wind that blew off the lake, "I should have stayed in the studio myself tonight. Now that I'm making signs for a living instead of collecting my forty-three eighty from the WPA every couple weeks, I don't paint enough. But even when I'm working and it doesn't go right, I feel like maybe I'm on the wrong track, I'm not sure which way to go. You know what I mean?"

"I think so," Fred said cautiously.

"I look at my work and Christ, it stinks. Is it because I'm in a rut, because of the social protest stuff I've been doing the last couple years? Or is it just because I haven't found a new way yet? You take a man like Burchfield, all these years he's been doing those marvelous delicate trees and flowers, and at the same time he does those brutal street scenes. He goes his own way, and you think anybody around here realizes how good he is? You know how many years he's been designing wallpaper for a living?"

"That doesn't seem to keep him from doing his own work."

"He's found his way," Vito said. Before subsiding he added simply, "Not me. Not yet."

But when they got to the Elmwood Music Hall the lights and the gathering crowd enlivened him once again. "Christ," he said, "look at all those poor slobs! Still looking for a hero, Lindbergh or somebody, to take them to the promised land."

"They're not bad people." Fred stood with him on the corner, observing the couples, mainly middle-aged, hurrying on into the hall. "All they want, most of them, is to stay out of the war."

"You mean you can tell by looking at them?" Vito was almost scornful. "There's enough poison inside that hall to kill off the whole city."

If Vito was right, he still made no move to join the picket line that was forming on the sidewalk just before them.

"All right, let's keep moving," a policeman urged them, his nightstick extended. "Either you go on inside or you keep moving."

Vito jerked his head at Fred and led him across the street. "No point in messing with those guys all over again."

"How come you didn't jump onto the picket line?"

Vito folded his powerful arms and stood spreadlegged, watching the latecomers hastening on into the building. "Even if these people are poisoned, what have I got to say? That we ought to go to war and start dropping bombs? It's different when things are clear-cut. I was right here on this spot four, maybe five years ago, when the fascisti hired the hall to celebrate Mussolini beating the Ethiopians. A big night for all the paisanos, the Italian consul gave a pep talk, the blackshirts were singing *Giovanezza* so loud you could hear them all the way downtown."

"What were you doing?"

"Picketing. My first experience, I lost my cherry that night with my Uncle Rocco. His wife, Zia Concetta that brought me up, she was scared. No politics, she kept saying, no politics." Like Bea, Fred thought. "But old Rocco, he was a big Garibaldista. They're against the workers, he said about the blackshirts, they're against liberty, they're a bunch of shit."

"What did he do, your Uncle Rocco?"

"For a living? He played the bull fiddle with the symphony, and gave lessons. Fifty cents a lesson. But he had the whole family against him on the fascisti thing, all except me. We're marching up and down, right over there where those pickets are, and Uncle Rocco is yelling at the top of his lungs *Abasso il fascismo!* and all of a sudden the bulls come down on us like the charge of the light brigade. They're clubbing us, people are yelling. It was my baptism, so I dropped my sign, quiet, like I'm throwing away a cigarette, and I stroll around the corner like I'm minding my own business. When I turn around to look, nobody's after me in the confusion, but I see them dragging Uncle Rocco off to the Black Maria."

Vito paused, mulling over the recollection. He unfolded his arms and spread his hands wide. "What am I going to do? I can't go home and tell Concetta. They take Rocco away, I can't stop that. But I find another picket who got away too, a guy I didn't know before, and he says to me, 'Come on, we'll go over to the precinct house and see what's cooking.'

"When I got there, it was my first experience with a Communist. Their organizer Will Henry had been leading the picketing. You know him?"

Fred shook his head.

"Big black fellow, buck teeth, yellowish eyes. He sat for me last year, I did his portrait. Always laughing and good-natured even though the cops pull him in every week and work him over. That night they had Will in the back room and they beat the piss out of him. The sound was terrible, even outside where I was. My Uncle Rocco they had sitting on a bench, by the desk sergeant, so he could listen. When it was finished they said to him, 'Go on home and play your fiddle, and next time you want to play politics remember what happened to old Will.'"

By common consent they started to walk away from the hall, heading back up Elmwood Avenue toward Fred's flat. Fred was thinking about the big-handed old bass player, the next thing to a father to Vito. "What did he do?"

"Rocco? He went home with me. He died the year after that, from cancer. But I was impressed by the guts of that organizer, I said to myself, Look at the way he goes and gets himself beaten up, for what? for some people five thousand miles away. So the next time I bumped into the Communists, on the WPA, I was ripe for them."

"No one ever set *me* such an example," Fred said. "Besides, my father always warned me off the Communists. Well, I think I'd better head back to the apartment. Maybe I can still get some work done."

He was uneasy lest Vito kid him about being henpecked, but instead Vito agreed readily. "Yes, let's call it a night. I'm going up to the loft and paint out some bad canvases. I always get satisfaction out of that."

By the time he got home, Fred felt like doing some more work. But no light leaked through beneath their door, so he took off his shoes and, carrying them in his hand, tiptoed in. It was not late, but Bea had made sure of his punishment by turning in earlier than usual. He mouthed her name and waited for an acknowledgment. Nothing.

Cursing to himself, he slipped into the bathroom, put on his pajamas, and when he had finished with his toilet brought back his face towel to the desk. Draping it carefully over the student lamp, he set to work. Behind him, from the opened studio couch, came his wife's soft breathing, so slowed down, so profoundly metronomic, that it seemed impossible she could be disturbed by the scratch of his pen, much less aware of it; yet he knew that she was, and he hated himself for going on as much to please her, to show her that he appreciated her sacrifices, as to progress a bit further toward the acceptance of his dissertation.

Finally he felt that he had done enough—for himself, for her, for whatever purpose. He switched off the lamp, folded up the towel, and came to bed with the blind caution of an uncertain intruder. When he had slid between the sheets, shivering a bit, he was all but overcome by the furnace heat emanating from his wife's body. With a convulsive movement she flung her sleeping leg over his; she seemed unconscious of the change in position.

She must have been moving about earlier, for her rather prim high-necked nightgown had ridden up, leaving her naked to the hips. Not just warmed, but aroused, Fred slid his hand very lightly along the fleshy part of her calf, around and over her kneecap, then up her long warm thigh. Although she did not otherwise respond, the tempo of her breathing quickened and he knew that she was awake. He cupped her buttock, then slipped his fingers between lips already wet and swollen. Bea freed herself from his hold by pushing lightly against his chest, and twisted out of bed with a sigh that might have come from either passion or resignation. She began to grope through the drawer of the night table for her diaphragm.

Fred turned away to free her from the embarrassment of his presence while she squatted awkwardly with the slippery contraption. She was seemingly a long time at it, and by the time she had rejoined him his own eagerness had faded. But he bent conscientiously to his plunging task, and as they heated each other, first cautiously then ardently, he had the hope that everything could be lovely anyway, that they could go on loving each other as they had in those first afternoons of secret discovery in the woods outside of Ithaca.

It was only a day or two later that he was invited by a student-faculty group to moderate a discussion panel on Art and Society, one of those programs that were always being undertaken on college campuses. He accepted, on condition that he be permitted to participate in the selection of the panelists; it did not occur to him that Bea would be annoyed.

"Why do you have to waste your time on that stuff?" she demanded.

"What do you mean by stuff?"

"Running around, contacting people, making arrangements." She checked herself, he could see it; it took self-control for her to keep from adding, "When you could be working on your dissertation." Instead she simply said, "What good does it do you?"

Annoyed, he replied without even stopping to reflect. "I don't want to be just a professor."

"*Just* a professor? What's wrong with that, all of a sudden?"

"Nothing." He did not want to sound sullen, but he feared that he was not succeeding. "I just can't see myself spending my whole life in Buffalo, teaching freshman comp, with an occasional course in Elizabethan lit if I behave."

"Who says you have to stay on once you have your doctorate? You were grateful enough when you got the appointment. There weren't that many instructorships lying around loose. If it wasn't for the fact that you did your undergraduate work here, and your father—"

"All right, all right." He cut her off before she could go on. He didn't need Bea to remind him that his father had not been too proud to plead among those whom he knew at the university for an assistantship, anything, to give his son a start.

"Maybe we ought to talk a little," Bea suggested, as she hooked her stockings to the girdle that she always wore for the weekly visit to his parents'. "I mean here we are, I work all day and you teach all day, and I cook supper and do the dishes and you work on your thesis all evening. And we never stop to ask where we're going. If we could just stop for a few minutes and talk a little. . . ."

Fred remained stubbornly silent all the way to the bus. "Talking a little" sounded too much like "having a little talk," which had been his mother's clumsy euphemism for sex education (after he had already pillaged the gynecological and obstetrical texts in his father's bookcase). It was only when Bea made him tell her that he was inviting Vito Brigante to be a panelist on the discussion program that she succeeded in forcing him into a dialogue.

"What can he have to offer an audience of academics and intellectuals?" she demanded. "He's a lost soul, that man."

"What you object to is that he occasionally takes me away from my desk."

"I don't know what you see in him, why should I deny it? If he has to walk the streets, it's because he's got no friends, he's in between girls, even his family doesn't like him. I don't see what you can do about all that, aside from feeling sorry for him."

"I don't feel sorry for him. I admire him, I think he's a man of principle. You're just being snobbish about somebody who isn't educated and can't help me in my career."

"Oh come on! Vito's talented, sure, and he's at least as ambitious as you are." She twisted about on the straw bench and
looked at him hard. "But you both want something more. You
don't want to be 'just' a professor, he doesn't want to be 'just' a
painter. You both want to be famous before you're ready for it—
it's people like you that the leftists are always on the lookout for."

"Now I'm a sucker—me of all people. The Communists never
got to me in college or in graduate school. And you know perfectly
well that Vito dropped them when they showed what they really
were."

His disgust was genuine; nevertheless he was uneasy with the
sharpness of her attack—it was too sharp, too disassociated from
him, as if she were not his wife but an acquaintance standing to one
side and watching him operate. She said to him, almost coldly,
"You were simply too busy at college to mess with the Communists.
Besides, what did they have to offer you? As for Vito I grant him
his integrity, but he's all emotion and no head. Now that you're so
close to the degree, though, now that everything but the dissertation
is out of the way, you're getting restless. And you won't talk about
that."

"Let's get off," he said roughly. "We have to transfer."

In his father's house it was better. At least stolid mama was
proud of him, she approved of everything about him, his tweed
jacket and slacks, his short haircut, his popular lectures. And dad,
rubicund and jocular, carving with neat surgical precision the roast
that he could not really afford, was delighted to discuss the panel.

"Art and society!" he said. "Now there's something timely and
yet perennially interesting. You haven't forgotten, I hope," he demanded of his son, "what Lessing wrote in the *Laokoon?*"

Back in the bosom of his family, enjoying his mother's peasant
cooking, more savory than the slapdash boiled dinners that Beatrice threw together in a state of dull fatigue, arguing German
esthetics with his father (who should himself have been a professor
rather than a general practitioner), Fred was happy. Happy for the
moment anyway, cheered on by his parents and the sense that he
was fulfilling their expectations.

But by the end of the evening impatience set in, as he always
knew beforehand that it would. It was not so much the simplicity
of his parents that grated as it was their poverty—and their acceptance of it. No, not me, never, he swore to himself (if not to

Beatrice, for fear that she might then accuse him of something else): the rooms above the office; the hopeful glancing up at the falsest sign of life below, as if they were running a penny candy store instead of the professional quarters of a man of science; the pinching on light bulbs, toilet paper, butter, collars, socks. . . .

Angry with capitalism for what it had done to his father, angry with his father for not doing anything about it, Fred bent to his Crashaw, piling footnote upon footnote, even while he knew in his heart that it would not be enough for him, not even if in the end it fulfilled Bea's small dream. Meanwhile he lined up his people for the forum.

Vito was reluctant, particularly when he learned that he would be sitting on the platform with a philosophy professor and a music critic—even when Fred assured him that the professor was a bore and the music critic a piano teacher with a brother-in-law who was an editor.

"There's nothing to be nervous about," Fred assured him. "All you have to do is talk from the heart. You don't even have to prepare anything."

"Easy for you to say. I never did anything like this before. It's not my game, Fred."

He tried another tack. "You've performed in front of bigger crowds than we're going to have. And with less clothes on, too."

"You want me to talk or fight? I'm not in shape for either."

In the end the painter agreed, not merely with misgivings, but with palpable fear. When he came out to the campus, it was a blowy bleak day in late autumn, the few trees on the vast expanse of lawn were already bowed and leafless, and when Fred looked up from his desk in the corner of the office that he shared with two other English instructors he saw at once that Vito would be out of place.

His friend had declined to wear a topcoat—did he have one?—but was instead zipped into a brown horsehide jacket from which the leather had been scraped here and there leaving bald spots, as though he had been doing not just roadwork but felling trees. His chinos and work shoes were clean but stained with ineradicable traces of oil paint. Even his shaving bore the defiant scars of a razor wielded like an ax, with little dried clots and blurs of blood strung out across his neck above the wiry black hair that curled up to his throat and through the open collar of his corduroy shirt.

"Good to see you." As he arose Fred was conscious not only of his height but of his well pressed jacket and slacks. "The others must be over in Haines Hall already. Shall we go?"

They had a good turnout, perhaps several hundred, and not all of them students or faculty. Among the non-academic faces, he observed, as he led Vito onto the platform to join the others, were some of the off-campus intellectuals (like his college classmate Irwin Metzger, now a full-fledged dentist) who turned up at performances of the Theatre League and the Cinema Club, and at the Friday evening lecture series of the Museum of Natural History.

He went over the ground rules with panelists and audience, and decided on the spur of the moment, since there were no objections, to open with the philosopher, get him over with, go on to the music critic, and save Vito for last.

What happened he might have foreseen. The esthetician attempted to define the terms of the discussion, as if such patently "reasonable" discourse would enable them all to come to an agreement, in the course of one afternoon, as to what constituted art— to say nothing of society. Bobbing his bald head enthusiastically, as if he were ducking for apples, the philosopher came up at this Halloween season only with clinkers, putting half his hearers in a stupor and inciting the others to a great crossing and recrossing of legs. From where Fred sat, the swinging legs looked as if they too were fighting off sleep.

He decided to take things in hand. He tried a few pleasantries to recall everyone to the problems at hand before bringing on the next speaker. At first he was uncertain, but within a few minutes the faces before him were relaxed and laughing. Quickly he introduced the music reviewer, a shaggy anecdotalist with a repertoire of moldy stories about temperamental artists. Paderewski, de Pachmann, Percy Grainger were trotted out, leaving everyone confused as to what all this had to do with anything and eager to hear Vito Brigante.

Vito was a disaster. Fred introduced him, gracefully, he thought, making clear that Vito came to the campus as an authentic artist, grappling with the problems that concerned them all. One problem that Vito had not grappled with, as he himself had warned Fred, was that of explaining abstractions with words. In the space of fifteen agonized minutes he contradicted himself innumerable times, pleading on the one hand for the right—in fact the necessity—of the artist to be allowed to make his own mistakes, and on the other for the artist to align himself with the forces of social change. And because he could not even put it that clearly, he flailed his arms as if in search of the clarifying words that eluded him, just beyond his fingertips. When he had finished he was dripping.

Observing the rivulets running down his neck, which were surely stinging the unhealed shaving cuts, Fred was tempted to pass Vito a handkerchief. But he could not do it without calling attention to Vito's discomfort, so he patted him on the back, and announced that the floor would be thrown open for discussion after he attempted to synthesize the positions of the three panelists. He had been making notes as they spoke, but he hardly found it necessary to refer to them as he wove together what they had been struggling to say.

Then he surveyed the audience, searching for the hands that, if he guessed correctly, were those of the most articulate and animated. Irwin Metzger, he saw, sat with arms folded, his full lips pouting, looking rather bemused.

But no matter whom he recognized, the question was addressed to Vito. Worse, they were not questions, but assaults delivered in spite and fury. They attacked Vito not for his confusions but for his refusal to associate himself with "progressive" forces. They addressed Vito not as an honestly confused artist, but as a tool of reaction.

The word had been passed among the faithful that Vito was a traitor, an anti-Soviet element, and they had come out as a squad to cut him down. After the first one or two, Fred thought that he could spot certain familiar overheated faces and tried to avoid giving them the floor—but too late, they clamored, they grumbled aloud when he did not recognize them.

"Did you really withdraw from the artists' union, or were you expelled for antisocial behavior?"

"What right do you have to appoint yourself as a spokesman?"

"When you were fighting as Kid Vito you were disqualified for thumbing. Did you think you were setting an example? Or showing what was in store for people who disagreed with you?"

Not without difficulty, Fred regained control. He insisted that he would entertain questions directed to the first two speakers only. But by then it was too late; the room was alive with local arguments, laughter, angry byplay; there was no point in bringing back the philosophy professor or the music reviewer, since no one wanted to hear them again anyway; and Vito was sweating furiously, his skin gone blotchy, his fists jammed into the pockets of his leather jacket.

So Fred thanked each of the speakers, referred to the "unexpected liveliness" of the discussion, and drew some general conclusions about the need for dialogue between artist and concerned citizen. But he was unprepared for the most flattering result of all, the crowd of faculty and students who clustered around to congratulate him.

So many strangers clapped him on the back and shook his hand that he was close to losing his composure. But not quite: his only real disappointment was that Bea had not left her typing table in the dean's office to see for herself that he could do something besides preparing lecture notes and grading papers.

When he had finally freed himself, he took Vito in tow. "Let's get the hell out of here. I was thinking about a beer."

"Something stronger," Vito muttered. "Those bastards really put me through the wringer."

"I couldn't be more sorry."

But was he? That was what troubled him as he led his friend out onto the darkened campus, away at last from the hooters against whom Vito had been all but defenseless.

Vito was ready to brush it aside. Beyond his depth as he had predicted, he was too miserable to see that the afternoon had been a kind of triumph for the moderator—and unable to complain at having been exposed, against his better judgment, to ridicule. Even while they sat in the bar and drank boilermakers, Vito was talking about getting back to his easel, working from the human figure, doing something that might turn out to be a mess, but that he had to try anyway.

I didn't mean for him to suffer, Fred said to himself. At the same time, he began to feel a certain relief that Bea had not been there. It would not have been beyond her to observe, in her acid way, "But he certainly made you look good, didn't he? The contrast didn't hurt you, did it?" And how could you be sure that something of the sort hadn't been passing through Irwin Metzger's head as he sat silent, arms folded, face expressionless, in the fifth row? And my own head, he asked himself, what was in the back of my own head?

There was no point in self-punishment. Already he began to see what he might do next—a series of open meetings, maybe a radio talk. Vito hadn't been badly gored, only scratched, and to hear him now maybe he was right, he might even paint better after this assault.

"They're fools," he said to Vito. "Fools. All they did this afternoon was to isolate themselves even more."

Vito wiped his mouth with the back of his hand and climbed off the bar stool. "The hell with them all. I'm going to order a hero sandwich to take out, and head for my studio."

They caught the Main Street trolley and rode back into town together in a silence that was not uncompanionable. It was Vito who got off first; from the streetcar window Fred watched him hurry off into the night, bandylegged, combative, fists crammed into his jacket pockets as always, neck bunched into his shoulders against the gathering storm.

3. BIG BOY

Now that he had a personal decision to make, one that in the end would have to be his own, no matter how many people volunteered advice, Big Boy was suddenly confronted with the realization that aggressiveness did not equal decisiveness. He had never been a reflective person, but up to now he had felt no need for reflection. When something had to be done, he felt it at once, sometimes even beforehand, almost instinctively; if he had a choice, the particular course that he selected seemed inevitable and therefore unquestionably right. Even his reading—limited mostly to newspapers because of time pressures and his own slowness—was a process of choice, of picking out those items which he needed to know about: skipping the front page stories of Russians fighting Finns someplace up near the North Pole, and concentrating on how John L. Lewis and Sidney Hillman and Philip Murray had frozen Harry Bridges out of a CIO vice-presidency. He was a New Orleans warehouseman and a union organizer, and he knew what he needed to read.

But he did not know whether he ought to go to New York. It was not the union that wanted him to go, it was the Communists, an unknown quantity to those he occasionally consulted—his mother, his aunt, and such rare confidants as Little Bobby Winton. Bobby was scared, but envied him the free ride and the chance to see Harlem. His mother was scared, but envied him a visit with her sister Emma, the preacher's wife, up in Buffalo, which Granny visualized as right next door to New York. "In fact," she asked him shyly, "it's in New York, ain it, Clarence?"

None of their reactions responded to his problem, which went beyond living it up in Harlem or visiting mama's sister in Buffalo. What he had to decide now was whether to commit himself—and that meant committing at least some of those who followed him— to a kind of politics that went way beyond fraternal clambakes and church suppers. If he took up the offer to talk to that meeting in Manhattan, to sit on the platform, have his picture taken and his name in the papers, he would no longer be the same person. But he was uncertain as to how he would be changed, and whether for his own good or his own ill, whether for the good of the union or the hurt of the union, and it troubled him deeply.

After all, it was only recently, when he was already in his mid-twenties, that Big Boy felt that he had found himself. Until then he had banged around in Houma, run errands for the Cajun fishermen after dropping out of school, worked in the same shrimp cannery as his mother, pushed a dolly in the French Market after his father died and they moved to his aunt's in New Orleans, played basketball until he got too musclebound and thick in the thighs, and hustled coffee sacks in the L&N freight yards.

None of it meant much one way or the other, beyond putting money in his jeans, until he discovered one day, more or less by accident, that he was a leader. The boss of the warehouse in which he had been working, a sloppy little fellow named Perrodeaux, told them—didn't ask them, told them—they'd have to work overtime for three nights in a row, unloading, at straight time. It hurt extra bad because this was just before Mardi Gras, when they all had a chance to work on the parade floats and make some folding money.

"Mist' Perrodeaux," he said suddenly, surprising himself as much as any of the others, "we ain stayin in."

"You ain what?" The little pusher stared up at him, shocked.

"No sense us losin out just because you busy. This our bes season too. You don pay us what we can make on the Mardi Gras, we ain comin in."

"What you mean, we? You don have to come in, Big Boy. You can quit right now, that'll be fine with me."

"You fire me, you firin everybody, Mist' Perrodeaux. That the way you want it?"

The words were out before he had even given them a second's thought, but even as he uttered them he knew that his instincts had not failed him. The men around him, frozen stiff as if they had been locked too long in a reefer, were staring at him with a mixture of fear and hope. Not one would dare to contradict him, much less to rat—he was a head taller than the biggest of them—and besides he was speaking *for* them not against them, saying what they had all wanted, but lacked nerve, to say.

The boss too suddenly shrunk. He had always been timid but noisy, like a terrier that yapped at your heels but was ready to run off the minute you raised your foot. Nobody had ever raised his foot before, was all. Now, surrounded by a circle of somber black faces, Big Boy's the blackest and grimmest of all, he seemed to have grown closer to the ground, like a hedgehog or a turtle, suddenly conscious of his aloneness and insignificance.

"No reason to get all fired up," he said, tugging at his already loosened tie. "No reason we can't talk this over man to man, an work somethin out. I wouldn want you fellows to suffer on account of the season."

That night Big Boy had rounded them all up one by one, from their homes and from the bars, formed them into a club, and elected a committee headed by himself to deal with Perrodeaux. At the next meeting of the club, they voted for him to get in touch with the CIO; at the third meeting—a victory celebration, paid for with part of their raise—they unanimously made Big Boy their president and authorized him to begin talks with the white warehousemen and refinery workers.

Some members were uneasy about his talking in terms of partnership with groups of white workers against the bosses. Big Boy answered them calmly. "If I kin talk to white boss I kin talk to white worker. Ain scared of one, ain goin be scared of the other. Besides—they need us on their side as much as we need them on our side. Maybe more."

He was proved right soon enough. The club became a provisional local, then they were issued a charter by the International. The news spread to the whites as well as to the blacks, like the word tapped out on jungle drums in the Tarzan pictures, so that when he hit some little crossroads town in Terrebonne Parish, to say nothing of Iberville Parish, they'd be out waiting for him—not sullen or suspicious, but reaching up to slap him on the back, offer him a smoke, buy him a Dr. Pepper, gather round and listen while he made his pitch between gulps of soda, waving the bottle for emphasis.

When they hired a hall, the white workers sat to one side of it—

but they came. And they joined up; they weren't too proud to stand up and address him as Brother Hull.

It was like being on a month-long jag, a year-long jag, only never hung over. Jumping out of bed fresh after four hours' sleep, he would lay out in his mind the schedule for the day ahead while his mother and his aunt buzzed around, praying and cautioning and stuffing his lunchbox . . . There were setbacks here and there, warehouses where workers closed their faces, drifted away when he began to talk, shook their heads and muttered about white man's union. But where there was half a chance, they called for an election, and in the days before the balloting, while the bosses were frantically trying to set up fake unions, clubs running with free beer that the workers knew would dry up after election day, Big Boy was all over them like a tent, banging on the table at the Elks', pounding on the lectern at the AME Church, bagging them on the way home, or on payday at the bar, or following them into their kitchens and talking union over the soup until they caved in and signed their names, those that could write, on the dues authorization card.

And so he built an organization, of city black men and former plow jockeys, men who hauled sacks and loaded boxcars and squeezed sugar and pushed dollies and guided forklifts and drove trucks—men who discovered that they were needed and that the more they organized the bigger and taller they stood, like Big Boy himself. Men twice his age, old enough to be his daddy, listened hard, discussed their problems with him, deferred to his judgment, voted for him, and so moved forward when he moved forward and succeeded when he succeeded.

Even though he was not by nature reflective, there were moments, particularly when he shaved before the little cracked mirror over the kitchen sink, wincing from the smart of the witch hazel on his jaw bumps, that he stared at his heavy, even glum, face and marveled at how it had the power to move others. Despite his upbringing, despite Granny's nagging, he was not particularly interested in religion, but simply recognized that he must have gotten his gift of gab from the father he could barely remember—and who knew where *he* had gotten it from? Not from heaven, more likely from some African prince. What was more, he knew—almost as you know, without the need for warning signs, which streets you can safely walk and which you cannot—that if he had not had the backing of the CIO and the International, he would be exactly nowhere. He would be the head of a club of black men with no power to translate their desires into reality.

He had no specific hunger to enter the white man's world, nor even any particular envy of it, and in fact what went on on the other side of Canal Street, all the way out to Newcomb College, on Freret Street, where his mother worked as a charwoman, was of no special interest or significance to him. He had too much to do right where he lived—and worked. But the labor movement was not just the white man's world; it was quite simply that access to it—and to the power and the glory that lay beyond—was controlled, like everything else, by white men.

So a series of delicate maneuvers began between him and a couple of the most militant of the CIO activists, each feeling the other out like kids at a high school dance, in an effort to find out each other's attitude and intentions. Big Boy did not bother much with girls—he had no time for them, except for the most rudimentary purpose—but it did occur to him (he wished he could say it to someone) that there was something ridiculous, something artificial, in the early stages of his connection with Rudnik and Driscoll, the CPers on the waterfront—like the sharped-up boys and girls sizing each other up along Basin Street on a Saturday night.

More and more though, as all the official white men got more patriotic (everybody was waving the flag now that the war had started up in Europe), Rudnik and Driscoll got tougher about the workers' rights. At labor council meetings, in negotiations, and in their private talks with him, they pushed aside the official labor patriotism about "defense."

"Listen," Rudnik said one day, sinking his teeth into a hamburger in a Bar B Q restaurant where he and Big Boy met from time to time, "you're no dope. You're gonna get just so far with pure and simple trade unionism."

"I don know as I follow you," Big Boy said cautiously. He wiped the top of his Dr. Pepper bottle before putting it to his lips. Even when Rudnik and Driscoll didn't use long words, they had a way of being mystifying—like girls trying to make you think they had some special secret that fellows couldn't understand.

"I mean that if we want the CIO to do the things it's supposed to, we can't stay out of politics. What do you think the war is? Politics. The bosses are tryin to drag us in for the same reason they're tryin to bust our unions. That's boss politics. What I'm talkin to you about is working-class politics. There's only one place where the workers have got the power. There's only one country where the leaders are honest enough to stay out of the war and let the imperialists destroy each other."

It sounded clear enough, all except for the last part, and that didn't make too much difference anyway, because it was over across the ocean. What counted was muscle right here. And for that, he could not deny, Driscoll from the CIO and Rudnik from the International were solid as cast iron. They were the ones who got him another organizer when he needed one, they were the ones who moved on the white workers when they got restless and started up the old Jim Crow, they were the ones who brushed aside the patriotic propaganda around the CIO when it came time for strike votes or moving in on warehouses storing material for the new army camps popping up like mushrooms. And they were the ones who saw to it that Big Boy himself was supported not only by his own ranks, but by the labor press, by the CIO itself, and later in big national papers like the *CIO News* and the *Daily Worker*. It was something, to see your name spelled out in a newspaper published all the way up in New York City—and not just for stealing chickens, either, but for what you were trying to accomplish.

Big Boy's mother was dubious. This he more or less expected, and he tried to make clear to her, in terms that she could understand, his tightening connection with people like Rudnik and Driscoll.

"You got nothin to be scared about," he assured her. "They're just stickin up for me, is all."

"I ain scared for myself," his mother replied. She fixed him steadily with her tired eyes. "How come you so sure they goin keep on stickin up for you? Sposin they quit? Then what you goin do? Seems to me you better off stayin with your own."

"I kin take care of myself," he said a little truculently—it was his usual manner. "Been doin that for a long time now."

It was somewhat more serious when Little Bobby Winton, his oldest friend, almost the only person who had stuck close to him for ten years now, expressed reservations paralleling those of his mother. For when Bobby did speak, it was not with the nervous voice of the older generation. He had thrown himself into the organizing drive from the earliest days, long before it became respectable and—what was more—relatively safe. His jalopy was always available, so was every cent in his jeans, so was his time without stint, so was his attentive ear. Rudnik had been sounding him out too, occasionally giving him a paper to read, or a leaflet, and inviting him to sit in on some of the same sessions to which Big Boy had been asked. But Bobby had hung back, like a girl uncertain of a persistent suitor's intentions.

"I just don know why that cat so anxious to be friends," he said to Big Boy one day on the way back from Lake Pontchartrain, where Bobby had driven to see about a roadhouse bartending job. "Be different if I was after *him*."

Bobby's cynicism was disturbing. It sank true, plummeting deep to the weakest point of Big Boy's own self-esteem. He knew in his heart that he was susceptible to flattery, publicity, and the kind of buildup that made sense only for a Joe Louis or a Louis Armstrong. On the other hand, without the resources and the organization of the white man (of the special, rare white man like Rudnik or Driscoll at that, who picked him out for their own reasons), where could he go?

"If it works out for both of us," he said to Bobby, biting down hard on a wooden match and then throwing the pieces away, "what's wrong with it? You an me, we got a solid local, men they never thought to organize, maybe never could have, without us. I'm not sayin they just want the dues, but they want the membership, don't they? It gives them more meat in the International and in the CIO, right? What you so suspicious about? So they aimin to sell us their politics, I know that. It's like a preacher tryin to get you to join his church, he don just want you to throw your money in the basket, he wants your soul too."

Bobby had been hanging over the steering wheel. At these words, he turned, his face twisted slyly. "You ready to pray where Rudnik prays? Ain't you got enough trouble already, just bein black? I ain goin borrow more, gettin mixed up in that communism stuff."

It was easy for Bobby to say. He wasn't a leader, he had no responsibility, he was satisfied to do what Big Boy decided and not ambitious to strike out for power on his own. If he wanted to lead and not just follow, he'd talk differently.

But in the course of time, despite all this talk, everything seemed to work out slow but inevitable, like the sun coming up, so that it wasn't a matter of a conscious decision on his part to tie in with

Rudnik and Driscoll. One cup of coffee led to another, one bar b q sandwich to another, a public meeting led to a private meeting, a caucus to a fraction, and almost before he knew it Big Boy was thinking of Rudnik and Driscoll and their group not as white leaders but as his friends, not as his friends but as his comrades. Until the big question, of going to New York.

Still he was busy with his job (he had to eat, there wasn't enough money in the union treasury to put him on the payroll fulltime), as well as with the endless details and calls and snap decisions involved in running his own local, and he felt, as you sense your best friends' intimate lives—whether miserable or marvelous—following their course independently of you, that there were all sorts of things going on among the white comrades which he was not told about. Dates, discussions, documents—all these, he knew, were a part of the other lives of Rudnik and Driscoll in which he had no share, no invitation to participate.

But, he figured, what he didn't know wouldn't hurt him; the part of them that was white was a matter of indifference to him. What he did know was that in crucial areas of his own life Rudnik was becoming indispensable. Or rather, not Rudnik himself so much as the network which fanned out behind him to the CIO office, the regional director, the labor press, the local papers.

"It's backing," he explained to Little Bobby. "We can do what we done before all by ourself, but we can do it better with backing. There's thousands of white workers we got to have alongside of us, an I can't get but some of them to go with us. Rudnik an the others got ways of reachin them, long as we all. . . ."

"Pray in the same church?"

"You see anythin wrong in what they been tellin us?"

"No," said Bobby slowly, "I guess not."

"Well, as long as it's like that, I don want you lookin at me like I was . . ."

"How'm I lookin at you? Like you was what?"

"You know what I mean. Like all I wanted was to get my name in their papers. Now listen. They goin have a big meetin up in New York, biggest meetin since the Scottsboro boys. Remember them?"

"I guess."

"Same people runnin this show. For labor and Negro rights. Rudnik an Driscoll want me to go as a delegate."

Bobby stared at him. "Where you goin get the money to go up there?"

"They want to *send* me. Pay my way."

"Hoo—ee. Ain bad for a lil ol boy from Houma. You gonna go?"

"I'm thinkin. I'm thinkin."

It was then that Bobby Winton made his envious remark about Harlem, Sugar Hill, the Savoy. Bobby could not know that it was a far more effective deterrent than shrewd skepticism or recalling those only too recent days before the war when Rudnik and Driscoll had been superpatriots. Nor could his own mother know that her lonesomeness for her sister, married for a second time to a Bible-punching Buffalo preacher, and her hope that he might see her, made him far more reluctant to go north than her fear of his association with white strangers.

In the end though, none of this added up to anything. Certainly not when you measured it against the daily more apparent evidence that if he did not go, if he did not support those who supported him he would condemn himself to a future which, however satisfactory it would be for Bobby Winton, would put an end to his own hopes.

He borrowed the Winton family's leather valise from Bobby, cut a piece of clothesline to supplement its rotting straps, and began to stow away shirts, socks, and underwear with the meticulousness of a good warehouseman. He was going.

4. BILL

The minute that Margaret opened the door for him, Bill knew that
something was wrong. Actually he had guessed it as soon as they told
him at the candy store across from the plant that his wife expected
him at her mother's. It wasn't the first time Margaret had left a
message for him there, since it was a kind of communications center
for militants of the rubber workers' union; but she hadn't ever asked
him to go clear across town to her mother's apartment. Mrs. Rodenko
would still be working at the real-estate office, unless something had
happened to her, and her younger daughter, Vera, would be at the
dime store, selling lipsticks and face powder.

Margaret kissed him warmly. But she was distracted, she did not
ask how things had gone on his shift. Instead she took him by the
hand and led him toward the kitchen, explaining in her quick, clipped
way, "Vera's inside. I wanted you to get here in time for us to talk
before mama gets back from work."

He knew better than to ask what was up; small as she was,
Margaret was both firm and close-mouthed, self-assured and decisive, and talkative only when she had something worth saying.

Besides, he could see for himself from the moment he stepped
into the kitchen. Vera was sitting at the table, her face and neck
blood red, all the way down to the opening of her sweater. Her
eyes were swollen, and she was clutching a glass of milk with both
hands, as though her very life depended on its being there, between
her rather clumsy fingers. At nineteen, Vera was considerably taller
than her sister, and she had always struck Bill as coarser, from her
thick and almost kinky hair down to her broad, mannish hands and

feet. Even her customary silence seemed to him to stem more from sullenness than from reserve.

Whatever poise Margaret had managed to teach her was gone now. Vera looked as though she had been crying for hours already; the tabletop was littered with damp crumpled handkerchiefs; a drop of moisture hung from the end of her nose. As he looked down at the girl who did not even glance up, much less greet him, and watched his wife comfort her, he knew—just as if he had always known—what was wrong. But why hadn't he known it before? Why hadn't Margaret told him—or if she hadn't known, why hadn't he been able to guess it himself?

The answer to that had something to do, he thought glumly, standing with folded arms before the two girls suddenly become strangers to him in their sisterly solidarity, with the humorlessness that people were always kidding him about. It wasn't that he was self-centered, he honestly didn't think he was, but rather that he thought of everything in terms of what it could mean to the movement. Margaret knew that he would do almost anything to see her through law school; his own sacrifice of a college education, his sticking in the shop with his old man, came from faith in what Mrs. Margaret Zivic would be able to do for the movement as a labor lawyer rather than from belief that a wife in the middle-class would be able to lift him out of the working class. For him the workers' movement was something he had learned at his father's knee; his father in turn had brought it with him from the mountains of Serbia to the rubber town of Akron; it was as natural to subordinate your personal life to the demands of the movement as to fight Hitler, Stalin, Mussolini, or Harvey S. Firestone without regard to personal advantage or loss.

"Do you want to tell him, Vera?" Margaret asked her sister. "Or should I?"

"Never mind," he said. "You're pregnant, kid, aren't you?"

Vera did not speak. But she nodded violently, jamming a handkerchief to her nostrils as if she were trying to stanch a nosebleed.

"Now," he said, with a firmness he was far from feeling, "we've got to sit down and talk this out rationally. We've got to keep cool. That's number one, isn't it?"

"Number one"—Margaret spoke so fiercely that her words were almost a blow—"is for Vera to understand that we're not going to leave her in the lurch."

"Wait a minute," he said. "I think Vera knows that. That's something we ought to take for granted."

"I just wanted her to hear you say it. Now sit down, Bill."

He straddled a red leatherette kitchen chair. "How far gone are you, Vera?"

"Too far. Too far, too far!" She bit her lip and started to sniffle. "If mama knew, she'd die."

She began to weep again. It struck him that in all the time that he had known her, he had never once seen her cry. Always she had been withdrawn and secretive, but concealing whatever lay behind with a kind of adolescent toughness, surliness even. It made him feel a little helpless, but he persisted anyway, groping for the right language.

"When you say too far . . ."

"She's not sure," Margaret explained, "not exactly. But it looks like it's too late to do anything. She should have come to me, but she didn't. She tried on her own, but nothing worked. Well, there's no point in yelling at her for it. What's done is done."

"Can I ask a couple of questions?"

Vera said nothing, apparently she was incapable, but Margaret nodded.

"Listen, Vera," he said to his sister-in-law, "are you in love with this guy?"

She shook her head wildly.

"How about him?"

Vera sobbed shudderingly. That means no, he thought grimly. What have we gotten into here? "Would he be able to marry you anyway?"

"What do you mean?" she asked painfully. "What do you mean? Do you think I'd marry somebody I didn't love? Somebody that didn't love me?"

He was on the verge of an angry retort, but he choked it back. At a time like this she was talking about love? "Well," he said, "with or without love, you're going to have that baby, aren't you?" The question was somewhat rhetorical, so without waiting for a reply, he turned to Margaret. "Maybe we'd better talk to Dr. Elkins."

Margaret put her small hand flat on the table between them. The gold band on her third finger caught the pale cold light filtering through the kitchen curtains. "That's out," she said. "I know what he does with girls. He sends them to that home for unmarried mothers.

How could Vera stay there for five or six months? You think mama wouldn't find out if she was there?"

"In other words, you want her to leave town."

"Not alone."

The two words fell more heavily between them than had her hand, a moment earlier, when she had said flatly, "That's out." A chasm opened, and he recoiled, almost instinctively. Just as he had begun mental calculations—borrowing from the credit union, taking out a loan on their furniture, cutting back on everything in order to be able to send Vera a little money every week—he saw that what was being demanded of him at his family council was something that went far beyond any sacrifice of a dollar here or a dollar there.

What hit him with the force of a blow, as he stared into his wife's green eyes, glittering with determination behind her tortoise-shell glasses, was that they seemed to gleam with contempt for his conservatism, his fear of change, his satisfaction with things as they had been. It was ironic that he, who throughout their courtship had lectured her on the overriding obligations of the social revolution and his determination to remain free from bourgeois commitments, should now be the one to shrink from any sudden alteration in their circumstances.

"We've got a few weeks in which to work things out," Margaret said. She seemed to sense that he was waiting for her to set out the plans which were crystallizing in her mind. "After that it's going to start to show. I think the first thing is to decide where. Once we've figured that out, we can make plans."

"I don't see why Vera couldn't move to Cleveland, or Chicago. I'm sure some of the comrades would take her in. We could go to visit her, she could tell ma that she's got a job there."

"No. I'm not sending Vera away alone. What she's facing is tough enough without being deserted."

"Hold your horses," he said. "The way you talk, you're going to throw everything away simply to settle a temporary problem. You're going to drop out of law school and leave town for something that's going to be finished within four or five months."

"Have you got a better answer?"

"Maybe I will if you give me time." Disregarding Vera's sniffles, he added, "You did spring this on me kind of suddenly."

"I'm not going to accept any solution that involves deserting Vera at a time like this. Or breaking my mother's heart. To say nothing of your parents—your father may be an old fighter, but he's damn conservative about things like babies."

She was implying, he was practically certain, that this held true for him too. "I thought," he said stubbornly, "that law school meant a lot to us both. To you."

"Vera means more. Losing a semester won't kill me. I'm young, I can make it up."

"That may be. But how am I going to explain your packing up and going off with Vera?"

"You won't have to. There won't be any problem, if you come along."

Once she had said it, he knew that this was what she had been leading up to, and he felt suddenly strangely calm. At least now everything was out in the open. Margaret arose, leaving him with Vera, and said coolly, "I'm going to put on some coffee."

He supposed that he should say something to Vera, but at that moment her arms slid forward across the part of the table vacated by her sister, and she allowed her head to fall forward too, as if it were a burden too heavy for her to hold up any longer. Cradling her face in her forearms, she half sat, half lay quietly, only her curved back rising and falling with her jagged breath. He reached out awkwardly, not used to touching her, and began to pass his hand back and forth slowly over her coarse thick hair that felt under his palm like the mane of a frightened restive mare.

He had never foreseen anything at all like this. If he had ever paused to reflect on their common future beyond the months immediately ahead, he had supposed that one day after her graduation from law school Margaret would bring up the possibility of their having a baby. And if he ever thought of anyone else invading their privacy, it was his mother-in-law, one day in some distant future when she might be old and tired. What Margaret was asking of him now was that all of a sudden he undertake responsibilities neither of them had foreseen when they had decided to get married. She talked very tough, but what she was really saying was, Take care of us.

He wanted to turn on her, to say in reply: This wasn't part of the bargain, this wasn't what we used to whisper to each other last year when we went walking by the river. They had a common outlook, they knew who they were and what they wanted. In a world that was falling apart, they were going to hold together. They had made a compact, sometimes with words, sometimes with embraces. They had prided themselves on being different from the anxious striving young couples of Akron, made prematurely middle-aged by nervous ambition, egged on by their desperate fear of falling back into the working class from which their parents had pushed them at such terrible cost. He and Margaret planned that he would stay in the shop, not simply to put her through law school and into the practice of labor law, but to put him in a position where his seniority and his militance on the shop floor would earn both respect and leadership— not for himself alone but for the movement.

He twisted about in his chair and said to Margaret, "On account of this mess, you're asking me to pack up and say goodbye to Akron. Never mind my parents, never mind that I was going to run for shop steward. But the fact that I've got roots here means something to the movement. And I've got more than just an obligation— the movement is my life."

It was a little melodramatic, maybe it hurt Vera and only made her feel worse, but he had to get it out. Margaret seemed to understand. She glanced across from the stove where she was waiting for the coffee to perk and said calmly, "I was coming to that. I'm in the movement too, you know. So is Vera. But we're not just faced with a temporary family crisis. The fact is, right now Vera doesn't want to give up the baby. Maybe she'll change her mind, but if she wants to keep it she's got the right to. To me that's as basic as the fact that it's the workers who have to change this rotten world."

"Vera," he demanded, honestly bewildered, pleading with her averted face, "how are you going to take care of a baby?"

She swung her head, still cradled in her arms, from side to side, the heavy mop of her hair falling first to the left, then to the right. Bill lifted his hand uncertainly, then brought it to his mouth; he began to rub at the stubble of his beard, thickest around his lips, but there arose to his nostrils from beneath his watch strap the acrid odor of hot rubber. It was only an hour since he had left the shop but already it seemed to him that he had left it far behind. Would there be nothing left to him of his years there but the memory of this smell, which arose to him in the dead of the night when he tossed about on the pillow and flung his hand across his face?

Margaret brought the coffeepot to the table, with three cups. When she had set them down, she reached out and grasped him by the left wrist, almost as though she guessed the message it was transmitting. She said to him, "We're going to do it together. The three of us. We'll take care of the baby."

"And what about my job? What about the movement?"

"First comes this baby. Socialism begins at home. We're in the movement together and we're in this thing together. You don't mean to tell me that we can't afford Vera's making a mistake? Christ, we're not that old. We'll move, you'll get a new job, we'll join another party branch—and if we have to, we'll start a new one."

"Just like that. It isn't only the six-hour swing shift, Margaret, even though there's no other city where I could get a job like that. It's my seniority, my roots in the shop—even the Stalinists can't mess with me, they know my old man too well, they know me too well, they know I've got the guys on the fourth floor behind me. You don't just throw something like that away."

"No, you don't. Not any more than you throw law school away. But we've got a whole new ball game here, Billy. At a time like this we have to shake off all our old habits and make plans for a fresh start."

"You think I'm conservative by nature, don't you? Well, maybe I am. I was just settling in for the long haul, and I didn't count on anything disrupting it, short of Hitler or the draft. Is there something wrong with my being built for endurance?"

Margaret seemed to sense that his anger (maybe she even thought of it as petulance) was a sign of hesitation rather than of absolute refusal. She said teasingly, as she poured him his coffee, "I know all about that endurance stuff. You and Lou Gehrig."

"When Gehrig left the lineup last spring," he said stubbornly, "he took along a record of twenty-one hundred and thirty consecutive games. That's going to stand for a long time, and I think it's something to admire, getting out there day after day in good weather and bad, in good health and sickness."

"Sure, sure." Margaret seated herself between him and her now motionless sister. "But I bet Gehrig was never faced with what happened to Vera, or he would have ended his streak a lot sooner. It's one of those things, that's all. If it makes you feel any better, blame it on Hitler. This fellow was a sailor, and he was—"

"Oh, stop it!" Vera cried in a strangled voice. Raising her head, she licked her swollen lips and demanded of her sister, "Why don't you drop it? Why don't you leave him alone? He's right, he shouldn't have to suffer on account of me."

"I didn't say that," he protested. "I didn't say anything like that."

"Well, it sounded like it," Margaret remarked sharply. "Why don't you give a little bit? What happened to Vera could have happened to me, why pretend otherwise? How do you know you haven't just been lucky? That sailor was going off to England, where the submarines are, and he gave Vera a hard-luck story."

"She could have said no."

"Like I did to you? Who are you kidding?"

He jumped up, agitated, feeling the flush rising to his forehead. He had never spoken of sexual matters to Vera, but that didn't mean that Margaret hadn't. How much had Vera known about them? Hadn't she been asleep, like her mother, when he and her sister, right here, up against the stove . . . Christ, there Margaret sat, sipping coffee with cool refinement, fingers curled gracefully. Was she the same person who had grappled with him in such gasping wildness, right here, slipping to the floor, cursing under her breath while she tugged at his zipper with furious eagerness . . .

He turned about in confusion. "I don't want you both to get the impression that I'm not on your side. I've just been weighing the thing out loud, is all. If we decide that it's best for us to leave Akron, we'll leave Akron. Period. But we'll have to have a damn good story ready, the three of us—not just for mom, but for my folks too. There's no reason for them to suffer."

"I promise you they won't!" Margaret cried joyfully. She took him by the head and kissed his cheek. "When I get done, sweetie, they'll all be wondering why we didn't make the move sooner."

By God, he thought, they probably will; women were as good at inventing and improvising ways out of trouble as they were at getting into it in the first place. "Listen," he said, to show them that he too was not unresourceful, "I'm going to talk to Dworkin. He gets here in five days, you know."

"I know. We hired the hall, didn't we?" Suddenly wary, Margaret released him. "You don't mean that you're going to ask him for *his* permission, do you?"

Somewhat stiffly, he reminded her, "Marty's on a national tour. He's familiar with the situation in every industrial center where we've got people. He should have some practical information—I don't mean necessarily about where we'll be in a position to establish the new party. I mean a city like Buffalo, maybe, where I could land a job in a defense plant, and you could get into a decent law school, and Vera could—"

To his astonishment, before he had even finished the sentence Vera fell to her knees before him, and while he was thinking to himself, Mary Mother of Jesus, what will I ever know about women, she had pressed her tear-blotched face to his hands and was kissing them fervently, this girl who had never once kissed him other than dutifully ever since she had been sixteen and he had made love to her big sister on this very spot where now she knelt before him, kissing his hands and weeping, weeping, weeping.

5. JOE

When Joe came up the walk to the back porch there was Uncle Jerry, sitting on the back steps and whittling, his handsome profile stern with concentration under the purple fuchsia that grew up against the screen door. It was a picture to keep in your mind, that bent head just turning silver, the firm lips slightly puckered as he dug the blade of his penknife carefully into the beechwood that he would never get around to finishing, any more than he ever finished the other scraps that he left for his sister to dispose of after he had passed out.

Uncle Jerry glanced up from his thumb, which was guiding the back of the penknife blade. "How's things in Westwood?"

"About the same. Mom back from the store yet?"

"Give her another ten minutes. But your sister's inside, listening to the radio. Pauline seems to get a lot of pleasure out of the radio, doesn't matter much to her what's on."

Joe set down his books and dropped to the step beside his uncle. "What are you carving?"

"It just might turn out to be a totem. Indian friend of mine, when I was working up north in the logging camps, taught me all about totems. Kwakiutl, he was. Highly intelligent man. You learn about the Kwakiutls in those anthropology courses of yours? It's anthropology you're majoring in, isn't it?"

"Yes, but I'm getting awfully sick of fraternal relationships in primitive societies. It doesn't seem to have anything to do with what's going on in the world."

"I knew you'd get interested in politics sooner or later," his uncle remarked, not without satisfaction. "You haven't got my side of the family's blood for nothing. Last time I tried to tell you about Upton Sinclair's campaign, you only cared about basketball."

"I've been growing up. Anyway, I've still got the EPIC button you gave me."

"Old Upton really put the fear of God in the upper classes. But he didn't have it in the oratory department. When it came to power and magnetism nobody could touch TR. He had, what we call, greatness."

Uncle Jerry had put down the block of wood and tossed his knife from hand to hand as he spoke. "I warrant you'd have been keen on Old Teddy too," he went on in his old-fashioned rhetorical way. "It doesn't seem possible he's dead these twenty years."

The refrain was not only old, but very familiar. But ever since he had met up with a merchant seaman at the Public Library who had incited him to read *Looking Backward* and *The Iron Heel,* Joe found his uncle's reminiscences fascinating. If Uncle Jerry garbled the past, at least he made it seem more alive than the history professors at UCLA.

"I don't understand," he said to his uncle, "how you can be high on Teddy Roosevelt when he was such a jingo. You used to rave to me about Gene Debs."

"I don't take that back," his uncle said solemnly. "Not for one little minute. Ever tell you how your grandfather, your mother's daddy and mine, had the honor of serving as brakeman on Gene's Red Special when he made his greatest transcontinental compaign tour? He introduced me to Gene personally and we sat down and talked, just like you and I are now. That was the kind of man he was—and don't forget I was a kid, I was working as a candy butcher, I'd just dropped out of high school."

"But later, when Debs went to jail for opposing the war, TR was itching to get us into it."

"That was what the people wanted, Joe. You can't buck the people, and when Gene tried to, why, he went down to defeat. But look at the things he was pleading for, and look at what TR accomplished while he was in the White House. That's the test—fighting for the little fellow, for the underdog, against the big operators back east. Conservation, water power, railroad regulation, you never saw the like of it until TR came along. And there's something else that you can't put into words, because you can't see it in the laws or anything

like that. I mean the spirit of the man. He was no quitter. He was
a fighter all the way."

"You mean you wouldn't say that about Gene Debs?" Joe asked
maliciously.

"Who said I wouldn't? It's just that he wasn't practical."

His uncle's confusion was almost comical. Joe pressed him tact-
fully: "But what did Debs *look* like? What was it like, talking to
him?"

Uncle Jerry turned slowly and brought his face up close to Joe's.
He was only about five feet eight, half a head shorter than Joe, so he
raised himself on his palms to bring his eyes on a level with his
nephew's. As he began to speak, Joe caught the delicate flowerlike
odor of gin that emanated from his lips, mingled, as it almost always
was, with Sen-Sen. "He gazed at me just like I'm looking at you,"
Uncle Jerry said solemnly, his faded blue eyes, the color of well-
washed jeans, fixed on him unblinkingly. "And he talked in that
flat Indiana way, flat and squeezed out. But you were important to
him, even if you were only a kid, a candy butcher like me. He
cared. He wanted to know what your job was like, what you wanted
out of life. He had this sharp, kind of long face, but there was
nothing hard about it. He was like a friend that wanted to know
what he could do for you. That was what socialism meant to him,
Joe, don't kid yourself. It wasn't book learning like you get at
college. He cared, that was it. And he didn't want to see you pushed
around."

How could Uncle Jerry hero-worship two such different men? Until less than a year ago, Joe would have put it down to booze. The
very notion of socialism had seemed boozy, just one more of those
nutty religions that flourished in California. His uncle was right,
Joe's own cult had been basketball, that and doing well at college—
at least until Fred, the Wobbly seaman, had buttonholed him. After
that it was inevitable, with the war deepening and the Germans invading Norway, that he should have gotten involved in the student
movement. Now he wasn't sure about anything.

Uncle Jerry was now no longer just a lazy bum, but a source of
information about Grandpa Dwiggins, a socialist railroad man,
and about the other threads that led back from a confusing present
to a romantically radical past.

"I really do enjoy talking with you about the old days, Uncle
Jerry," he said impulsively.

His uncle reached out and squeezed his kneecap. "I enjoy being here with you. And Pauline. And your mother. My favorite sister," he observed vaguely. "Besides, who knows what the future's got in store for us, now that the war is heating up? You watch and see: I won't be too old and you won't be too young, Joey. There's going to be fighting ahead for us both."

This feckless man, too weak and woozy for anything other than odd jobs and living off a younger sister long since abandoned by her husband, dreamed of escaping into uniform in the mindless but spirited manner of his poorly remembered idol, Teddy Roosevelt. But this war was too serious for Rough Riders, even socialist Rough Riders. Soon he would be leaving the house himself, but he hoped that his journey, wherever it took him, would lead him toward Debs's railroad train rather than TR's horse.

"I'm going to get a Coke and say hello to Pauline," he said, and added casually, "Care for a drink?"

"Not before dark, son," his uncle replied with perfect seriousness.

Inside, the house was his mother's, from the plaster birds nailed on the dinette wall to the Gainsborough reproduction in the front hall and the waxed fruit in the dining-room table's cut-glass bowl. There was no sign in the Spanish-style bungalow of his presence or for that matter of his uncle's, not even in the glass-doored bookcases on either side of the fireplace, with their shelves of H. G. Wells, Will Durant, Eugène Sue, and E. Phillips Oppenheim. Just maybe, if you dropped in as a stranger, you might feel that those books could reflect something of the taste of the long-absent Mr. Paul J. Link; so with the Mission furniture in the dining and living rooms, rather massive for such a small house. But it didn't *smell* as though men lived there, or ever had. As he peered through the gloom (the venetian blinds were slanted down, as always, against the slash of the Southern California sun), it occurred to Joe that if he were to walk out tomorrow and never return—which was more or less what he had in mind—there would be no evidence, aside from the few *Field and Stream* magazines at his upstairs bedside, and the barkentine in a bottle that Uncle Jerry had once given him, that he had ever lived in this house.

His sister Pauline was sitting in the darkest corner, under the bridge lamp with the fringed shade. An unopened magazine—it was the new issue of *Field and Stream*—lay on her lap, and she was listening to Scattergood Baines, her eyes unfocused and her mouth half open as though she was having difficulty breathing.

"Hello, Pauline," he said loudly, over the soap opera.

His sister looked up, happiness coming over her face as she recognized him standing there in the arched hallway. His heart contracted; his return was one of the landmarks of her day. But within hours after his departure she would not know where he had gone—or think to ask.

"Hello, Joey," she said, in her slow singsong. "Dja study good in college?"

"Sure did. You didn't go to the store with mother, did you?"

Sometimes Pauline went along—not to wait on customers, which frightened her, but to work in the back of the shop. She loved repacking gloves and stuffing tissue paper into purses until they were properly puffed out, crouched in a corner and so absorbed in her little repetitive tasks that she had to be taken by the arm and reminded that it was time for lunch.

Pauline shook her head, still smiling vaguely. "I guess I didn't get up fast enough."

"Go ahead and listen to your program. I'm going to get washed up for dinner." He needn't have replied at all, for Pauline was no longer attending to him; her neck drooped toward the console radio, like a long-stemmed lily groping for the sun, and as he headed for the bathroom she had already forgotten his presence.

It was Pauline, his mother had insisted more than once, who had been the cause of his father's taking off, leaving her with a rumdum brother and two babies, the older one retarded. The birth of Joe had been no consolation, since it coincided with the discovery that little Pauline was feebleminded.

"He was gutless, Joe," his mother had told him, when he was fifteen. "I don't like having to run your father down. But you're old enough so I shouldn't make up stories."

Never sending home a dime, in fact moving to Las Vegas, Paul J. Link had forced Lettie to become bread-winner as well as mother. Absorbed in the daily grind of raising the kids and running her ladies' accessories shop, she had ignored the rumors that he had returned to California, especially since he had never bothered to write, much less see for himself what had become of his family.

It was Fred the Wobbly seaman who had set Joe to thinking about his old man, pushed out of his consciousness ever since the kids in the play yard had taunted him about being a virtual bastard. But once he questioned what he had been taught in school, the very values by which his mother lived, he began to wonder what his father was really like. He and his mother were good friends, bound together by adversity and by concern for Pauline, and always would be; but while she had made it clear what his father was not, she had never given him any idea (nor could she) of what his father was.

On the day that he was asked to be a delegate to the American Student Union's convention in Wisconsin, Joe went to the library and looked up the name of Paul J. Link in every California telephone book. It didn't take long: his father was listed as a rancher in Camarillo, less than two hours to the north, so close that it was spooky how they could have lived all these years without ever seeing one another. Or maybe they had, maybe he and his father had brushed up against each other on a bus or in a movie, or had sat next to each other at the Hollywood Bowl, and never known, never known . . .

It would be cruel, he thought, as he sloshed water on his face, to tell his mother that he intended to look up his old man. Enough that he would be going all the way to Madison—she was shrewd enough to know what that implied. But when he heard Lettie's old Plymouth coupe coughing to a halt in the driveway, Joe felt himself losing his nerve. He wiped his dripping face hastily and trotted on into the kitchen to get a Coke and ice cubes from the refrigerator, and the gin bottle from the broom closet, where Lettie tried to hide it from Uncle Jerry. Already she was kissing Pauline. He got out the vermouth and began to pour.

When she came into the kitchen, tossed her purse onto the table, and began tiredly brushing stray hairs back from her forehead, he said cheerfully, "I'm mixing a nice cold martini for you. Coke for me and Pauline. Uncle Jerry seems to be on the wagon, for the moment."

"Why are you being so nice? Want to borrow the car?"

"Drink up and I'll tell you what. The thing I want to know is, are you in good enough financial shape for me not to take a Christmas job?"

"We're all eating, aren't we?" His mother glanced at him warily, drink in one hand, cold meat loaf in the other. "Are you going to spend the next three weeks studying?"

"I was thinking of taking off for the San Joaquin Valley day after tomorrow, right after my last class. I want to see for myself what's going on with the cotton pickers' strike—you know, you heard about it on the radio."

"The Okies, you mean." His mother's tone was carefully neutral.

"That's right."

"Figure on being gone long? Tulare isn't all that far."

"I thought I'd hitchhike up and look around for a day or two." He took a deep breath. "What I want to do, mother, is head east from there. They've asked me to be a delegate to the Student Union convention in Madison over the holidays."

Now his mother's face, long and freckled like his own, began to betray her. "So you are getting in deep with the Communists."

"Not me. I've been on the other side ever since I joined the ASU. But I don't deny I'm interested in socialism—between what's been going on in California and what's happening in Europe, it'd be funny if I wasn't—wouldn't it?"

"But it's so"—his mother groped through the air with her bread knife—"so *uncharacteristic*. Why, you never even used to read the newspapers, except for the sports section. When I think of your old friends, Pete, Skippy . . . your girl friends, Pattie, Verna . . . They'd be flabbergasted, simply flabbergasted."

"You're talking about people I haven't seen in years. All I used to think about was fun and games, it's true. Then there was the business of becoming an anthropologist, but now it seems to me that that was childish too—it was a little more glamorous than basketball, that's all. Maybe I was simply slow in maturing, but now I'm more and more concerned with our future."

"Leave mine out of it, brother." His mother spoke flippantly, but she was clearly shaken. She had always been good to him, some people had even told him that she deliberately spoiled him because of her great confidence in him and her hope that unlike his father, he would stay, tied to her not just by gratitude, but by closer bonds. Now she seemed to be deliberately restraining herself. "I've got enough on my hands in this house without Communism."

But the moment she had said this, she seemed to realize that she had gone too far, with her insistence on something he had already denied. She added hastily, "Don't get me wrong, Joey, I couldn't care less whether you go Communist, Socialist, whatever you want to call it. God forbid I should turn into a nagging mother. You

know something? I voted for Sinclair, as well as for Olsen. Of
course I couldn't tell my customers, but . . ."

Joe winced. The more she tried, the harder she made it for him.
Next thing, she would be bringing Pauline into it. Was this what
had made his father flee?

"Mother," he said, "I know you're not narrow-minded. After all,
we come by it honestly. Not just Uncle Jerry, but your own father—"

She interrupted him bitterly. "How would you know what it cost
my mother and me—yes, and Jerry too, poor man—to have my
father running around peddling his papers and waving the red flag
instead of staying home and looking out for us? You think we had
a respectable life, just because it was respectable to vote for Debs?"
She stopped short, biting her lip.

After a moment she began again, speaking lightly, smiling even,
"The only people who can afford to be radicals are the ones who
have arrived. Like those people in Hollywood, the actors and the
writers who can do whatever they damn please, thumb their nose
at the world and nobody cares. Take out some more ice for me,
would you, Joey? And put the Coke away? I'm going to make a
pitcher of lemonade, Pauline loves lemonade."

Tugging at the ice tray, his head averted, Joe muttered, "I'm
going to have to find my own way, and I know you won't try to
hinder me. Not many sons can say that, can they? But I don't want
you to suffer for anything I decide that I have to do."

As he straightened up he was startled to feel himself being gripped
and turned about by his mother. Although she was a tall woman, she
stood on tiptoe to stare directly into his eyes. "That restlessness,"
she groaned, peering at him searchingly, "that restlessness . . ."

Then she pressed him to her, her face hot against his neck, in
order that he should not see her eyes, which had suddenly filled
with tears. Never, never before had she forced herself on him, as
he had sometimes observed (with a queer constricted feeling) Italian
or Jewish women doing with their sons. He was stricken speechless.

"Listen," she said, her voice muffled, "you do what you think
you should. Just as long as you believe it's right. Pauline and I'll
make out. But this war . . . I want you to promise me . . ."

"What?"

"Nothing, nothing." Suddenly she was pushing him away, laughing as she reached for her apron. "You're too damn skinny, you

know that? Go call Jerry and Pauline for dinner, I'll see if I can fatten you up a little before you run out on us."

He was determined to see his father before he did anything else. Two days later he packed a bag and stuck out his thumb on Route 101, not long after his mother had left for the shop; within a couple of hours he was wandering around Camarillo, what there was of it, looking for Paul J. Link. But nobody seemed to have heard of him. It wasn't until he thought to ask at the post office that he found out that his father's place was out on Route 34, up toward Moorpark.

Trudging along, after the first lift had dropped him in the middle of noplace, a mile or two short of his goal, Joe told himself that he mustn't outstay his welcome. No matter how much his father urged, he'd have to leave within a few days; if necessary, he'd cut short the trip up Route 99 to the striking cotton pickers. The houses thinned out, the sidewalk ended, but then at last there was his name, LINK, lettered haphazardly in black across a gunmetal mailbox, lopsided on a two by four at the roadside. Beyond it stood a grove of lemon trees.

Passing through the sagging gate, Joe threaded his way through a scattering of greenish lemons that lay rotting on the ground, some of them burst open on the blotchy brick walk that meandered from the road and the postbox to the frame house, whose outlines were barely visible behind the rather stubby fruit trees. The air was spicy, almost rancid, from the citrus. Joe paused at the front door, his hand on the discolored brass knocker, his heart thumping painfully in his breast. Supposing there was no one at home? Could he just sit out here and wait? Perhaps he should have phoned first? But that was ridiculous, he could no sooner have picked up a telephone to introduce himself to his father than he could have to President Roosevelt. But what should I call him—Dad, Father? Nothing sounded quite right. Finally, cursing himself, he raised the knocker and let it fall heavily.

The silence was enveloping, strengthened by the sun that hung overhead as if behind some vast blanket. It was *too* quiet for the place to be empty—the absence of sound was more like what descends upon a house whose occupants, angry and enraged with each other, have fallen into a sullen silence.

But then there came a scratchy shuffling, as of sandpaper being drawn randomly across a board, and the door swung inward. Out-lined in the darkness was the figure of a woman with bleached hair.

"Yeah?" she demanded incuriously. She stepped out from the darkness, encased in a wraparound house dress and shower clogs; she wore no stockings on her pale and hairless legs.

"Is Mr. Link home?" he asked.

"What's on your mind?" she retorted. "You selling something?"

"No, no. It's nothing like that. I'm . . ." He swallowed, the saliva went down the wrong way, and for one long terrible moment he could not go on. "If I could just—"

From behind the woman came a masculine voice, deep and rasping. "What is it, Melba? Magazine salesman? You came to the wrong house, bud." He stepped forward as he spoke, a tall man, tall as Joe himself, with lank straight dark hair that fell across one side of his head like Hitler's, and a potbelly that went oddly with his narrow frame, pushing out the braided belt that more or less held up his baggy trousers. His white shirt was buttoned to the neck, but he was tieless, and he needed a shave.

"I'm not at the wrong house," Joe said, somewhat more boldly, "not if you're Paul Link. Because I'm Joe, your son. I don't guess you'd recognize me, but I'm not selling magazines, I just came to . . . well . . ." But here his resolution failed him and he could do no more than gesture.

"Whatever it was you came for, you better come on indoors. And close the screen door before the goddam fruit flies get all over everything. Melba," he said to the woman beside him, without introducing her, "put up another pot of coffee, will you?"

She shuffled to the back of the house in her clogs, and he mo-tioned to the corner of the vestibule, by the umbrella stand. "Drop your bag there," he ordered. Joe complied, followed him into the darkened living room, and stood hesitantly on the Mexican sisal rug, his hands dangling, until he was nudged to the green plastic couch. "Go on, set down. Melba'll have some coffee for us in a minute."

Then his father seated himself before a bridge table littered with papers, and took up a cigar which he must have been chewing on when the knocker fell. Scowling at its moist end, he puffed it into life, his thin lips pursed, then explained, "I was working on my year-end figures."

"I hope I haven't disturbed you."

"I'll get back to them. What's the difference, I got nothing to show for my work, the government takes it all away anyway."

Joe did not know what to say, but since nothing else was forthcoming, he nodded sympathetically.

However, his father made no effort to pursue the subject. Instead he said abruptly, "So you're Lettie's boy."

Yours too, Joe was on the verge of retorting, but his father was scowling, and it struck him for the first time that his father was probably as uncertain as he as to how to proceed.

"You're a good size." His father rolled the cigar back and forth across his fingertips. "Kind of scrawny, but you'll fill out. How old are you?"

"Going on twenty."

"Got a job?"

"Part time, here and there. And summers. I go to college, to UCLA."

"Still in the same house, are you? You and Lettie and the dummy?"

"She's not a dummy! Pauline is slow, that's all. But she can talk, she's no trouble, and everybody likes her."

His father shrugged. "Is that all? Just the three of you?"

"Uncle Jerry stays with us from time to time."

"That free-loader. That parasite. Long on talk, short on action."

"He does like to talk."

"Big bag of wind. Well, if it's money trouble, kid, I—"

"Oh no," Joe said hurriedly. "Mother's been doing pretty well with the store, all things considered. Business'll probably pick up, too, Southern California's bound to be a boom area once the defense contracts start to spread around."

"Defense my ass. War, you mean. We're going to—" He was interrupted by the return of Melba, who shoved the papers into a pile on the corner of the bridge table, then set a coffeepot on it and two mugs, and turned her back, all without saying a word.

"How do you take it?"

"Black." Actually he liked milk with his coffee, but he did not see any; and he was afraid not only of putting Melba out, but of giving his father trouble.

But when his father filled a cup to the brim and shoved it at him, Joe was hard put to swallow without choking or making a face. The coffee was not only bitter, but sour, as though it had been standing around too long, heated and reheated time after time; it had a taste like the smell of the half-rancid lemons outside on the path.

"They're going to get you, kid," his father said, rinsing coffee around in his mouth as though it were toothbrush water. Maybe it loosened up the cigar taste? "Don't think they won't. First comes the draft, then they drag you off to the war."

"Oh, I know!" Joe said eagerly. He thought he must sound like a fool, but this was his first chance to talk seriously. He went on in a rush, "I don't kid myself about that. My mother doesn't understand though. It's hard for her to see why I've suddenly gotten interested in politics. The fact is, I'm more concerned with the antiwar movement than I am with college. You know what I mean, don't you?"

His father, his face furrowed, muttered something he could not catch. Then he ground out his cigar butt and said, "What's all this stuff with movements. You'd be better off keeping your nose clean and trying to make a living until Morgenthau and his crowd shove you into the Army."

"Why should I toss in the sponge? I don't mind telling you, there's plenty of students want no part of the war."

"Students," his father said scornfully. "Bunch of Commies. You see them trying to stop the Russians from gobbling up Finland? That's the only goddam country ever paid its debts, but you think the college boys care?" He added irrelevantly, "Girls and good times."

"At least we're trying to do something. As a matter of fact, I'm on my way to the national convention of the American Student Union."

"Now what do you want me to do about that?" his father asked. "Pat you on the back? You want to save your skin, don't make out like you're a hero in the bargain."

"It's not just my skin," Joe persisted. Looking not at his father but at the worn rug that lay in the shade between them, he felt that maybe they might at least have in common the fact that they both wanted no part of the war. He went on doggedly, "When the CIO was getting started, I never paid too much attention to it. Maybe I was too young. But now I think that if the anti-war people and the students and the labor movement can get together—"

"The labor movement! Christ I hate that word. Where'd you

pick up all this crap, from that dumb drunk uncle of yours? Don't you know who John L. Lewis's stooges are, big fella like you, college boy? Bunch of red agents, that's what. Don't you know what they've been doing right here in the state of California?"

"As a matter of fact, I thought I'd try and find out—I'm going up to the San Joaquin Valley, to see what's been going on with those cotton pickers in that strike."

"I'll tell you what's been going on. Commie agitators stirring up the Mexicans and Okies so you can't get a goddam day's work out of any of them. Think that's funny, like in *College Humor?* Not to somebody that's been knocking himself out trying to make a go of it."

"All I said was—"

"I heard what you said. Those brain trusters never taught you at college that it's the same Jew crowd behind both Lewis and Roosevelt, no matter how the two of them pretend they're feuding. You know why? Because the professors are hand in glove with Morgenthau and the Jews to drag us into the war and turn the country over to the CIO." With real satisfaction, as though he had invented the phrase, he repeated it: "Hand in glove."

"I guess . . ." Joe cleared his throat in order that he might go on, and was almost surprised that it was not blood risen to his mouth. ". . . you and I haven't got much to talk about."

His father clattered cup into saucer and flung back his head in an oddly youthful gesture, to get his straight black hair out of his eyes. As though he were discussing the weather, he said neutrally, "I didn't go to see you. You came to see me."

Joe hated himself for sitting there, still, on the sofa, as though he were nailed to it, but he could not gather strength or breath to rise and flee. At last, though, he was able to pull himself erect. Looking down at his father seated before his coffee and his columns of figures, he said, "That's true. Now that I've satisfied my curiosity, I'll be on my way. And you can get back to what really matters to you."

These words seemed to touch something in his father that had hitherto been beyond his reach. He too arose, his long, defeated countenance darkening with concentration. "Now wait a minute," he said. "I didn't mean it that way. Let me get Melba to fix you a sandwich."

"That's all right. I'm not hungry."

"It's no trouble for her, it'll only take her a minute."

"I've got no appetite."

His father hitched up his trousers. "Then let me give you a lift downtown. I can run you back to the bus terminal, or wherever, in my pickup."

"Don't bother. I can go the way I came."

As he walked to the front hall to retrieve his bag, Joe could feel his father's breath on his neck; he was afraid to stop for fear they would collide, but at the door he had to turn once more.

"I thought you were coming to put the bite on me, see," his father said, his voice somewhat shrill with uncertainty. "And I'm in no position—"

"Neither am I."

"Then don't go off mad." His father barred the door. He held Joe's arm in a surprisingly strong grip while with the other hand he dug deep in his pants pocket.

"Here." He fished out something and pressed it into Joe's free hand. "It might bring you luck. Everybody can use a little luck."

Joe pushed open the screen door with his shoulder and went on out with his bag before him, not looking back. When he was halfway down the walk his father called after him, "Keep your nose clean, kid!"

All the long way back to the highway, he did not unclench his fist, nor did he shift the bag from one hand to the other. Only after he had stood for some time at the intersection, alone, waiting for a ride to Route 99, did he open his hand.

A silver dollar lay there, wet from his sweat. As he stared down at it, and at the deep circular groove that it had bitten into his palm, the odor of lemons seemed to rise to his nostrils, dilating and prickling them.

He lifted his arm and flung the coin away with as much force as he could muster, and then, as he felt the tears coursing down his cheeks, he rubbed his palms along his thighs and pressed them to his wet face, rocking slowly back and forth at the side of the road, waiting for someone to come along and drive him away.

6. IRWIN

Sleet spattered the windowpane and the radio droned on with its dopey dance music. Irwin lay back in his dental chair and slowly turned the pages of *Native Son,* savoring as he read. A terrific book, the best writer since Steinbeck. With his free hand he explored the interior of his mouth, using a pick from the porcelain platter on his round swivel tray; with his foot he tapped on the chair's corrugated rubber pedal in time to *Begin the Beguine.* The telephone rang.

Absently he reached back for the crank to tilt the chair forward from horizontal to vertical. Then he arose, finger between the pages, dropped the pick, and lifted the phone at the alligator desk set that his parents had given him on his graduation from dental school. "Dr. Metzger speaking."

"Doctor, I'm calling to find out have you got time, I can make an appointment. I've got such a toothache, my head is splitting. But don't tell me you can make it right away, understand? Say in three, four days."

"Oh mother," Irwin said wearily. "There's nobody here. You don't have to always play that game with me."

"It's not a game. Believe me, nobody respects a dentist, a doctor, if he isn't busy, all the time busy."

"But there's nobody here to impress."

"How was I supposed to know? Believe me, as soon as you start to do a little better, you're going to have to get a girl." She amended rapidly, "I mean a nurse. It makes a bad impression, like you can't afford it, when you answer the phone yourself."

"I haven't got a big enough practice for one yet." To change the subject as much as to encourage her, he added, "But I've got two new patients scheduled for tomorrow. One is just a toothache, a cavity, but the other is maybe bridgework."

"See?" his mother cried eagerly. "What did I tell you? The word gets around that you know your stuff, you got nothing to worry about. Pretty soon, you'll be so busy I won't even be able to talk to you on the telephone."

That'll be the day, he thought. "So what else, mother? Is there anything else before I hang up?"

"Of course. There came a telegram for you from my sister Sarah's boy, Seymour. Sy Glantzman," she added. His mother had a habit of supplying unnecessary information. "You know, from New York."

"I know, I know. What does it say?"

"'Harry and father arriving Buffalo Terminal five eleven grateful regards Sy.' You know what he's talking about?"

"It's a fellow named Harry Sturm, a friend of Sy's. He just got a job in Niagara Falls. I promised Sy I'd pick him up—him and his father. In fact I think I'd better leave now, the weather is so miserable it'll take me a long time to get out to the terminal."

"All right, you'll be careful with the car, yes? And wrap up good with your muffler. Maybe next week it's spring by the calendar, but this is the real pneumonia weather."

After he had hung up, Irwin cleaned his cabinet shelves (not that there was much to clean after mixing amalgam for two fillings and reading Richard Wright all day long), examined his face in the closet-door mirror (his teeth looked fine, like an ad, but at four-thirty he already needed a shave), shrugged into his overcoat and scarf, buckled his galoshes, slipped *Native Son* under his arm, snapped off WKBW, locked his door with its fresh gold leaf, IRWIN METZGER DDS, and punched the elevator button.

The icy wind lashed at him from the foot of Main Street as if it were something alive, pricking his eyelids, drying the mucus in his nostrils. From out of the grayness, lights were popping on here and there on both sides of the street, shop windows suddenly sparkling in the snow, neons gleaming dully in the perplexed and turbid air. Moving sidewise, like a crab, turning only one cheek to the sleet, Irwin made his way to the parking lot and paused on the whitening cinders to fumble for his key ring.

The door of the wooden shack opened and the attendant emerged, a great hulk of a man, a Negro in a plaid mackinaw and woollen seaman's cap, with a huge flattened nose and an air of controlled power about him. "Can you find your car all right?" he asked.

"Sure. I'm a regular," Irwin said, not without pride. "You're new here, aren't you?"

"Temporary. I come up from Louisiana. They said there was work out at the steel mill, but I ain't been called yet."

Swinging the car up Main Street and over to Broadway for the drive out to the terminal, Irwin found himself wondering about people who came to Buffalo from elsewhere. All his life he had dreamt about moving away, and he never had, not for college or dent school. A few of his high school classmates had been able somehow to go to out of town colleges, in the depths of the depression, and two of his friends at the university had made it to New York. But almost all the people he'd grown up with were stuck here just as he was. "Getting away," that was what they sat and talked about, he and Fred and all their crowd, night after night.

But at the same time there were men like that attendant, and Cousin Sy's friend Harry Sturm, coming here from places like Louisiana and New York. What he wouldn't have given five years ago, a year ago, to settle in New York instead of Buffalo. Or to wake up in New Orleans, sipping an absinthe on Bourbon Street and exchanging glances with a beautiful Creole.

Now people were coming to Buffalo instead of leaving it, because for the first time in ten years jobs were opening up. Driven by the war instead of the depression, others would be leaving, he was sure, traveling to places they had not chosen and in some cases had not even heard of, to live more deeply than they had ever been able to here. And perhaps to die too, far from home.

Peering through the windshield, past the wipers that were sluggishly pushing the slush back and forth, weakening a little with each rotation, Irwin felt that he too was going to be starting a new life, perhaps not in another place, perhaps not in the profession that he had fallen into only because no medical school would have him, but in some inner region unknown to his parents and those acquaintances who knew him, he was painfully aware, as a somewhat mournful and idealistic young dentist who loved music and was shy with girls. The long stillness of the last decade, when he had not dared to fall in love, to picket the Italians in Ethiopia or fight the Moors in Spain because he had to make good in college and dental school and justify his parents' sacrifices—all this, he felt it in his bones, was coming to an explosive end. Who knew but that this fellow Harry Sturm, the metallurgical chemist, if that was what he was, might be the agent of change?

Irwin respected both of his New York cousins, the brothers Sy and Sid, and tried not to be swayed by their mutual detestation. Their parents' poverty only served to remind him of his own good fortune in having been born to the sister who had escaped the family blight by marrying an out-of-towner. Their doctrinal differences only underlined the intensity of their politics, and diminished them no more than did the fact that they were both younger than he, for he had to envy the pitch of their lives, so much more exciting than his own. Sid had already fought, been wounded, perhaps had killed fascists; and Sy, despite his youth, was already going seriously with a girl, probably even sleeping with her. Withal, it was Sy to whom Irwin felt closer (Sid's politics chilled him), and Sy's friend whom he looked forward to greeting.

He parked the car, traversed the cavernous Roman terminal to Track 11, and spotted his man leading his shrunken father slowly up the ramp. The younger Sturm had a prognathic lower jaw, and in consequence a faulty occlusion: his pronounced underbite and hanging lips reminded you forcibly of a mastiff. His blue eyes, suddenly alight with recognition, bulged menacingly behind thick-lensed glasses. He ascended impatiently, with the rapid bouncy walk of the small man who compensates for his lack of stature with great physical self-confidence. His faltering father, not simply aged but tremulous, was shivering as if with an ague.

It was therefore to the father that Irwin hurried first, extending his hand. "Welcome to Buffalo."

"Simon Sturm," the old man introduced himself. "I didn't know we had friends here."

"This is Dr. Metzger, pop," Harry said in a sharp, decisive, Bronx-accented voice. "He's the cousin of my friend Sy. You've forgotten, I told you about him. You didn't have to meet us, Irwin —we could have taken a cab."

"I'm glad I did. Your father looks chilled to the bone," Irwin said, but before he could say more, Harry Sturm had added, out of the corner of his mouth, "He's got Parkinson's. Also diabetes."

Disconcerted, Irwin led the way to the baggage counter, where

Harry retrieved three very heavy, rather ancient suitcases, and a bulging bookbag tied around with twine.

"Let me give you a hand with those," Irwin said. "Is this all?"

"I shipped my books and journals in cartons, by Railway Express. I must say," Harry panted, staggering forward with the two largest valises, "this is very kind of you. Sy wasn't exaggerating when he said you were the best of all his relatives."

Irwin was embarrassed. "Well," he said, "it must be rough coming to a strange town in the dead of winter. Even the porters are disappearing, now that the steel mills are reopening."

"War is the health of the state, eh?" Harry said, with a peculiarly grim gaiety.

"Unemployment is letting up at least. Where did you say your flat was?"

"On Linwood. Is that far?"

"Not too terribly. Here's my car, let's put the bags in the trunk. Did you rent sight unseen?"

"I was up here for a day, for a job interview, and I picked it out of the classifieds. Pop and I aren't particular about furniture. As long as he has his radio and a little view . . . I won't be home much anyway, except to make meals for him. He can still watch out for himself, in all the little things."

"I think you'll be comfortable in the back seat, Mr. Sturm," Irwin said to the old man, "when I get the heater going again."

"Don't worry about me." Simon Sturm was a long while getting into the back, making his way awkwardly around the folded-over front seat. "I've got to take a back seat, you know. Got to get used to it."

"I'm afraid the city's giving you a poor welcome. But the spring and summer are pleasant, cooler than New York. You'll see."

"Makes no difference. My son's career comes first. I'm indoors all the time now anyway."

On the way back downtown, Irwin glanced at his passenger, snug, incongruously dapper in his fitted fly-front overcoat, ignoring his huddled father and looking out with lively interest at the gray grimy city reluctantly freeing itself from the long clutch of winter.

"I understand you don't know many people here," Irwin said. "I'll be glad to do whatever I can. . . ."

"I'm going to take you up on that, Irwin. Sy may have explained to you about my having a master's in physical chemistry, in electrophoresis."

"I thought it was metallurgy."

"Not quite. I did my master's thesis on electrophoresis of proteins—but I won't bore you with that. I'm interested in doing some teaching. I'm not sure yet whether my job will give me time to go on with my Ph.D.—the plant is in Niagara Falls and it'll take me an hour each way—but in any case I'd like to teach, maybe a course in inorganic, a couple of evenings a week." He leaned over and added confidentially, "I've got to keep the two of us going. What with the medical aspects, my expenses aren't small."

"I understand."

Harry took a black briar pipe from his overcoat pocket and proceeded to load it. At once, the pipe, clenched by that protruding lower jaw, seemed absolutely a part of him. "The only fellow I know personally at the university," Irwin said, "is just an instructor, and in the English Department at that. But we're good friends, and he'd probably know whom you ought to talk to."

"Very good," Harry said decisively. "The sooner the better. What's his name?"

"Fred Vogel. He's doing his doctoral dissertation on Crashaw."

"What's that?"

"An English poet, Catholic, some time after Shakespeare. You'll have to ask Fred for any further information. He's very clever, a good speaker, he won't be an instructor forever. His wife, Bea, works at the university as a secretary. She might have some suggestions herself."

"Sounds promising. How about tonight?"

Irwin had been thinking about a week or so later, after they had settled in. "Why, sure," he said. "I'll ring up the Vogels when I get home. If they're free, I'll come by for you right after supper."

"I'll be ready." Harry clamped his teeth on his pipe. "Once I hang up our clothes and fry up a couple hamburgers for me and the old man, I'll be ready."

Irwin was pleased to be able to explain to his parents, at dinner, that Cousin Sy's friend was enterprising and vigorous as well as a devoted son.

"That being the case," his father said, attacking a chop with his small sharp incisors, "you'll invite him for dinner some night."

"And the old man too," his mother added. "If he can get out. It's a shame, two men living alone like that."

"You got a girl lined up for him? Maybe for the old man too?"

"Don't make fun."

"And don't you waste your time making a match for Harry—he's got no time for girls. Better concentrate on me instead—I'm more ready for it than he is."

"Irwin," his father said, "your mother asked you not to make jokes. She wants to see you settled in your profession before you settle down. As for me, I'd rather see you with a nice girl than—"

"I know—than in the Army. But supposing I wind up with both? I'll see you later."

Harry Sturm was bundled up and ready when Irwin arrived. He gestured cheerily with his pipe and came trotting down the walk to join him.

"Is it much of a drive to your friends?"

"They live out on Elmwood. A car is more necessary here than in New York. It can be a long cold wait between buses. Maybe you ought to think about—"

"I have." Harry smiled pleasantly. "Getting a learner's license is on my agenda for tomorrow, along with getting the phone hooked up, opening a checking account, et cetera. I've already scanned maps of the city and the Niagara Frontier area. Maps are a little hobby of mine."

Irwin tried to make small talk, but Harry made you feel guilty if what you said did not have a practical purpose or impart information. Harry did remark, "By the way, I have regards for your mother from the Glantzmans. Your Aunt Sarah has a very hard life, you know."

"She always had to work."

"Not only that. Her husband is a sour old fanatic. All he did was trade in the religion of his fathers for a newer model."

"He's harmless. He takes that stuff about the happy Russian workers at its face value. If it wasn't Russia, it'd be something else."

"That doesn't make him any easier to live with. Sid is a thousand times worse. If he had state power, he'd stand you up against the wall."

Even though he did feel much the same about his Uncle Baruch and Sid, Irwin did not want to appear disloyal. After a time he

said, "Now this is Elmwood Avenue. We simply go straight out
from here."

"Where you live, that's the old middle-class neighborhood. And
where we're heading, that's the new middle-class? Where do the
industrial workers live?"

"It isn't quite that simple. The city is divided more on ethnic
than on economic lines. It's true, you wouldn't find working people
living along Delaware Avenue, or Bidwell, or Chapin Parkway.
But it's easier to define one section, say, like the Twelfth Ward,
as colored, and one like Cold Spring as Jewish. And the Germans
live mostly off Broadway. There's a tremendous Polish population,
not just in Black Rock, which is practically a separate town, but—"
He broke off. "What I mean is, while most of the Poles are working
people, their middle-class lives in the same neighborhood. You
see?" he asked uncertainly.

Harry puffed imperturbably. "And where the Jews move out, the
Negroes move in."

"That's right. William Street used to be the big Jewish shopping
center, but they've started moving all the way to the Hertel section,
and so—"

"And so the Negroes have moved in. Yes, I've already done
a little reading, in addition to checking my maps."

Disconcerted, Irwin fell silent. What did this have to do with
chemistry, with colloids and evening classes?

As if he had anticipated this too, Harry said, "It's not simply
a matter of acclimating myself. I'm convinced that we're on the
brink of vast social changes. Once we're in the war, this city's
going to be a key production center. A year ago my firm wouldn't
have let me in the back door. Now they need me. Same with the
Negroes and the unemployed. They're going to be absorbed into the
working class. They're going to become part of the labor movement."

Like the big Negro in the parking lot, Irwin thought.

Suddenly Harry shifted ground. "Have you been looked up by a
fellow name of Bill Zivic? He's a rubber worker from Akron, moved
here some time ago."

"I don't think so."

"He too is a friend of Sy's."

"No," Irwin said more positively. Emboldened, he demanded,
"Harry, how do you come to know Sy, anyway?"

"He and I have been involved in the same political movement.

So has Bill. The fact is, there's going to be a new party born from it, very soon."

"A new socialist party?"

Harry replied quickly, "Don't you think we need one?"

"I don't know. I call myself a socialist, but that's not the same as getting mixed up in politics, is it?" He raised his gloved hand and gestured at the modest apartment house on their right, sharply outlined by the street lights now that the sleet had slacked off and the night sky had cleared. "Here we are."

Like his mother with her incessant matchmaking, Irwin was eager that Harry and Fred, two very different men, should take to each other. Fred liked himself, but with reason, he was smarter than most, and too diplomatic ever to rub anyone the wrong way; while Harry, who was also self-confident—you felt it at once—got at you directly, imposing himself on you.

Harry, his bullet-shaped head enveloped in the fragrant smoke of his sandblasted bulldog pipe, his eyeballs popping, stood with legs apart, expectant, pounding his fist into his palm like a salesman calling on a hot prospect. No sooner had Bea Vogel opened her door than he was inside, pulling off his scarf, pumping her hand, making himself at home as if he had known the Vogels forever.

They were impressed. Despite his hornrims and elbow patches, Fred was inclined to be deferential to those who were from the big city born and bred. He was even willing, Irwin observed with a little surprise, to accept from Harry unsupported comments that ordinarily he would not have allowed to go unchallenged.

Harry went directly to the point. Indeed, he gained the academic information he desired at once, and moved on so rapidly to talk about the war that Irwin began to wonder which had been the ostensible and which the real reason for his desiring to meet the Vogels.

Bea resumed her work at an ironing table in front of the bookcase, and Fred stretched out his long legs to show off the argyles Bea had knitted for him. Bea listened politely, Fred intently, to Harry's self-confident analysis. It was his belief that the United States was going to try to emerge from the war as the world's greatest imperial power. But he had no particular sympathy for Russia, which he also characterized as imperialist.

"All these imperialist wolves that you're talking about," Fred laughed, "look more like reluctant dragons to me."

"Don't kid yourself." Harry puffed grimly on his pipe. "We're in for a blood bath."

"Well, I read in *The Nation* not long ago about the Englishman who said, 'The war isn't lost, it's just mislaid.'"

Harry was the only one not to laugh. "That kind of joke only serves to distract people from the fact that none of the rulers really wants to fight fascism. They're using the popular fear of fascism for their own ends. That goes for them all—English, French, Russians, Americans."

"The FBI did arrest seventeen Christian Fronters," Fred observed.

"And then we balance it by sending Browder up the river for four years? So we perpetuate the myth of the government as being above the classes."

"Aren't we getting a little off the subject?"

"I don't think so. We're going to be asked to swallow mobilization—M Day—then all-out war, while they go on using the Negroes as they do in the Navy—as potwallopers and bodyservants. Would you say that the Negroes have a stake in the so-called war against fascism?"

Fred said earnestly, "I'm not arguing for us to get into the war. I think we ought to do everything we can—"

"To do what? To help Chamberlain, short of war? To keep America out of war, along with those isolationist committees loaded with outright pro-Nazis?"

"Then what do you suggest?"

"Aha." Harry was on his feet. "If you're serious—and I take it that you are—then there are things we can do, there is a program we can argue out. What would you say to our forming a discussion group, a Marxist club to examine current issues? We could assign topics, present papers, invite guests for an open discussion. If we could get hold of some centrally located place, maybe in an office building, a room perhaps or maybe a studio—"

At the word studio Fred snapped his fingers. In another minute, Irwin marveled, he's going to think the whole notion was his. "I've got an idea," he said. He turned to Irwin. "You know Vito."

"Vito Brigante? I've met him. I heard him at that panel you organized."

"He's got a studio in a crazy old building down on Franklin Street. There must be others available in the building."

"Is he reliable?" Harry asked.

"The most unreliable man I know," Fred laughed.

Bea was suddenly very busy with the neck of the blouse she was ironing; Irwin remembered the talk that she, like many others, had once been involved briefly with Brigante. "He's a painter, worked on the WPA arts project, but now he's got a little sign-painting business. He used to be a Communist, in fact."

"When can we get hold of him?"

"We'd have to go bang on his studio door."

"Tomorrow? Let's make a date. How about you, Irwin?"

Pleased to be included, Irwin said, "We could meet at my office in the Brisbane Building and walk over. Then afterward I could drive you both home."

"You'll want to come to our meetings, won't you?" Harry asked Bea, who was still bent over her iron.

"Frankly, I doubt it." She straightened up and looked coolly into Harry's eyes. "My horizons are a little narrow. My main interest is in Fred getting his Ph.D. I can't think beyond that."

"Perfectly understandable. Crashaw, I believe Irwin said? Thanks to you, Fred hasn't taken Crashaw's couplet *On marriage* to heart." He quoted: *"I would be married, but I'd have no wife, I would be married to a single life."*

The Vogels gaped at Harry, calmly touching a match flame to the bowl of his pipe.

"Not bad for a chemist," Bea said flatly.

Pulling himself together, Fred demanded, "Harry, do you know Hayman's *A Mad answer of a madman?"*

"I'm willing to learn."

"One asked a madman if a wife he had. A wife? quoth he—I never was so mad."

"Ha ha," Bea said, and yanked the plug of the iron from the wall.

"Very good." Harry chuckled. "Very good indeed. Maybe I went into the wrong field. There are some lovely formulae, but I've never heard of any funny ones. Unfortunately, though, no matter what our own desires are, the world is pressing in on us."

"And you think you can press it into the shape that you want? You and Fred? And maybe Irwin?" Bea's tone was almost openly scornful.

"I think it's worth trying. Especially when I think of the alternative. Anyway, why shouldn't Fred be free to work on Crashaw and teach, and the rest of us to live our lives without having to go to war, or to starve between wars?"

"Hear hear." Fred raised his coffee cup. "If you want to run on that platform, Harry, we'll all vote for you. Even Bea, I bet."

And so the evening ended, on a note of high amiability. On the way back to Harry Sturm's flat, Irwin could not refrain from asking how he had managed to bone up on Crashaw almost without notice. "What a performance! It reminded me of those *Reader's Digest* stories about great insurance salesmen. I don't know who was more surprised, me or the Vogels. Why, when I told you about Fred, this afternoon, you didn't even know who Crashaw was."

"You must have misunderstood," Harry insisted blandly, and in the end Irwin had to drop the matter.

Maybe that was the most unsettling thing about the man. Harry loved secrets and secretiveness despite his professed hatred of secret diplomacy and of totalitarianism. Yet he was both quick and tremendously informed; what was most impressive about him was the air that he communicated with every gesture of his square thrusting head, his bulbous commanding eyes, his stabbing pipe stem, of confidence in the power of argument. Life could not be completely without prospect as long as people like Harry Sturm turned up to persuade you that there was still a future worth fighting for. Even the idea of looking in on Vito Brigante became, Irwin thought before dropping off to sleep, not just another way to pass an evening, but a rendezvous filled with exciting possibilities.

Fred and Harry arrived at Irwin's office within minutes of each other. When he came out into his waiting room after extracting an impacted wisdom tooth for a saleslady from his father's store, they were already deep in political discussion.

"I haven't had so many people in here at once since I opened the office," he said. "It makes me feel like a success."

Harry waved his arm to take in the pine table and chairs, the piled-up copies of the *New Republic* and *Time,* the carefully selected Kollwitz prints, the X-ray cubicle, and the glittering equipment of the office beyond, with its glass-doored cabinets and framed diplomas.

"Very nice setup you've got here," he said. "Must have cost you a pretty penny."

"Not me. My father. He went into debt to get me started. I'll be a long time paying him back."

Harry surprised him by remarking, rather heavily, "Sometimes you never can, you know," and Irwin had a sudden vision of old Simon Sturm, sitting alone in the flat on Linwood Avenue, staring unseeingly out the window at the strange landscape, the radio blaring behind him unheard.

"What are you complaining about?" Fred demanded. "Better to be indebted to your father than to your wife."

The waiting room was suddenly an uncomfortable place. Fred seemed to realize it too, for he went on quickly, "Come on, let's go."

Vito Brigante had his studio in one of those ancient red brick loft buildings whose sooty windows and rust-caked dangling fire escapes bespoke a kind of permanent depression, a defeat accentuated by the accumulated debris of the years. The minute they stepped inside the dim and dusty hallway, it was painfully familiar to him, all of it, from the building directory with its crazed glass and tumbled letters to the sloping stairway and sagging banister, the shuttered and sometimes shattered doors of leather goods repairmen, dressmakers' findings wholesalers, junk jewelry jobbers, mail drops for notions advertisers, strength and health parlors, and offices of semi-bankrupt glassblowers' union locals—and the abandoned rooms, doors hanging on their hinges, exuding an odor of must, of the hides of small animals, of taxidermists' chemicals.

As they mounted the steps past the second floor, the sound of a radio came to their ears, replacing the fading sounds of the street below. When they arrived at Vito's floor, it was clear that it was the artist himself who was tuned to the Benny Goodman Quintet. "In that case," Fred pointed out, "why should he object to our barging in?"

In fact he did not. He flung open the door at Fred's knock, one paint brush in his fist, the other clenched between his teeth. Looking at the three of them with some surprise, he demanded, "What in Christ's holy name is this, a delegation?"

"We came to ask you to turn down your radio," Fred said.

The tendons flickered in his hairy arm, braided with veins, as he grasped their hands in turn. He wore a striped sailor's jersey and a pair of chinos down the front of which he had wiped his hands and brushes so many times that they stood away from his thighs like tubular canvases. On his bare feet he wore sneakers without laces.

"We've met once or twice before," Irwin said hesitantly.

"I've been meaning to see you about getting my teeth cleaned. But I've been busy and broke."

"Harry Sturm is my name," Harry said. "Fred thought that you might be able—"

"Yeah, well, look, I've got a model here that I'm paying good money, and I just want to do a little more work before I start to shoot the shit."

It was then that Irwin saw, at the far end of the loft, a brunette sprawled out on a broken studio couch, one leg of which had been replaced by bricks. While they stood in the doorway talking she was attempting to cover herself with the shawl which had been draped across the back of the couch; but before she succeeded, he caught a glimpse of a bare breast and belly, and the misty shadow below the belly. Her legs were long and shapely. Irwin swallowed.

"Supposing we come back later," Fred suggested.

"No, no, that's all right. Why don't you all park on the army cot, I'll be with you in a little while."

"Hey, what is this?" the girl cried out as they filed in. "I came here to model. Let them go the Palace if they want to see a burlesque show."

"Relax, Carmie," Vito urged her. "These are respectable citizens, college professors and what not. Fellows, face the other way, will you please? We're being modest tonight."

They squeezed themselves onto the rickety cot with its stained army blanket, still in their overcoats, squatting in a row like three blackbirds on a telephone wire. They faced the wall against which Vito had stacked some of the showcard color signs which he did for a living: Spring Topcoat Fiesta, FIRE SALE EVERYTHING PRICED TO GO (flames licking at the lettering), Loblaw's Will *NOT* Be Undersold. Completely ignoring them, Vito was already absorbed in his work once again, stabbing at the large canvas which they could only glimpse obliquely, and singing loudly in rough tune with *Avalon* while he worked. Above the sink, in which lay a sock, an empty coffee can, and several brushes, hung a broken mirror. Irwin glanced up at it, and his heart almost stopped beating.

Reflected in the glass was the girl on the studio couch, one arm crooked behind her head, the other resting idly on her raised hip. She was naked once again, sullen-faced and pouting a little. Her body was so richly curved, so voluptuous, that Irwin was dazzled and awed. He had experienced this confusion before—of being at once worshipful and sensually aroused—while cautiously circling the Maillol nude in the court of the Albright Art Gallery. He was embarrassed to the point of wishing he could look elsewhere; but his gaze kept returning to the broken mirror and the pale flesh framed within it, lighted from the side and above by a bulb partially shaded with a green metal reflector. The girl's heavy breasts, with their surprisingly tiny, tight, and virginally pink nipples, were tautly hung; between them began a shallow channel which ran down to the shadowed cup of the navel; her belly dipped rather than swelled, for her waist was seemingly tiny as a child's, its narrowness accentuated by the power and majesty of her upthrust hip; and at the fork of her thighs, even smoother than the Maillol nude's and bluish-white like skim milk in the harsh light, the coarse pubic curls glistened thickly, as luxuriant as the black hair tumbling carelessly across the satin pillow on which her head rested. Staring, Irwin found himself fantasizing over the flesh of her cool calf, curving down like Maillol's marble, but alive beneath the smooth flexion of her rounded knee. Dry-mouthed, he dreamed of stroking it, cupping it in his palm while he put his lips to that rising breast and his other hand ran free.

Suddenly the girl's dark, almost sullen face, which had been all but devoid of expression, as though she had been thinking of nothing beyond the texture of her haunch beneath her own fingertips, came to life. Her lips pursed, and from between them the pink tip of her tongue darted out, quick as a snake's fangs, once, twice, three times.

"Hey," Vito exclaimed. "Don't do that—I'm working on the mouth!"

"Then tell that guy to quit looking like that. How can I hold a pose with him staring at me that way?"

With a start Irwin realized that he was the one about whom the girl was complaining. Desperately, while his companions grinned, snug in their overcoats, their wives, their politics, and Vito coaxed the girl back into silence, he attempted to transfer his gaze elsewhere and to ignore the taunts that seemed to lie behind the laughter and the casual talk. But no matter where he looked, his cheeks flaming, he felt that his gaze was tangibly false and artificially fixed.

At last, hating himself for his weakness, he allowed himself to look into the mirror once again. Although the girl was in precisely the same position, it seemed to him now that her body arched more proudly than it had before. Perhaps it was merely that she had stiffened almost imperceptibly, under tension? What was beyond question, though, was the set of her face, with its large sensual mouth and short, soft, almost blurry nose; for while she no longer stuck out her tognue, it was at him, Irwin, that she was looking, with an expression at once haughty and scornful.

He wanted to leap to his feet and flee from that mocking glance, but he had instead to sit there miserably, sweating from his scarf to his woollen socks, his eyes fixed on the diamond pattern of his brogues, until at last Vito tossed his brushes into a turpentine jar and muttered, "We'll call it a day."

He wiped his hands on an oily rag, and the girl disappeared to dress behind a moldy screen, half-collapsed beneath its rusty hinges. Fred rose. "Do you mind if we look, Vito?"

The artist shrugged. Away from the easel, he seemed despoiled of the intensity that had possessed him. With the voice of a simple, weary artisan, he said, "Look, what do I care. Go ahead and look. All I got to say is, it's not done yet."

Irwin was relieved that the center of attention should be shifted from the girl, and from himself, to her portrait; but he was astonished to see that it bore no resemblance to the recumbent body he had been staring at so avidly—or indeed to any human form.

"I'll be damned," he muttered, gaping at the red, pink, violet slashes of paint across the expanse of canvas. There *was* a figure, you could make it out if you looked hard, but what was it doing? And why?

"You said it," the girl agreed, as she reappeared from behind the screen. She shrugged back her long dark hair over the upturned collar of a trenchcoat which she was buttoning over a turtle-necked sweater and plaid skirt. "He yells at me to shut up, he's working on the mouth, and you can't even find it, for God's sake."

"You're getting paid, aren't you?" Vito growled.

"Yeah, when?"

"As soon as Loblaw's pays me. If they're good for the money, so am I. What do you want me to paint on my own time, another post-office mural?"

"It certainly is startling, Vito," Fred said. "You've been looking at Picasso, I suppose."

"I've been looking at a guy called Gorky, if you want to know.

And he's been looking at Miro. But what's the difference? The thing is, I'm moving toward something new, see. I don't even know what the hell it is myself."

"You seem to be moving away from social involvement," Harry Sturm remarked, pipe in his teeth.

"I don't know what that means any more." Vito yanked a sheepskin jacket from a nail on the wall and threw it over his shoulders. "You think it proves anything, painting kids with big eyes and swollen bellies? Or workers with big muscles? I don't. I think it proves something to paint. That's why I do it. I'll tell you something —what'd you say your name was?"

"Harry."

"I'll tell you, Harry." Vito jabbed his index finger at his painting in progress. "I think good painting is a hell of a lot more radical than the crap the lefties are handing out."

"Depends on which ones."

"Yeah, yeah." Vito shook his head from side to side, derisively. "I got burned once already, when I was with the WPA. Down with war and fascism, the comrades told me. Bunch of bullshit. Stalin cracks the whip and they all fall down."

"I'm going on home now, Vito," the girl said. She was no longer sullen, but almost shy. "See you Thursday, same time, okay?"

"Wait a second, Carmie. We're all going out for a coffee, why don't you come along?" He slapped his forehead with the heel of his palm. "I never even introduced you! Carmela, this is Fred Vogel, he's a literature professor at the university."

Fred held out his hand. "I'm just an instructor. Carmela, this is Dr. Metzger, Irwin Metzger, and Harry Sturm. He's just arrived from New York City."

For the first time, the girl smiled. Her teeth were as white and regular as Vito's, and her rather sultry eyes took on life. She was tremendously attractive; Irwin tried hard to put out of his mind what she had looked like, naked and lolling, before she had dressed, put on high heels and bundled herself into the belted trenchcoat; he couldn't keep from swallowing as he took her startlingly small hand and felt the smooth grating of her fingernails against his palm.

"I'm sorry I upset you before," he heard himself saying. "My car is just down the street. I'd be glad to take you home afterward."

"What do you say, Carmie, let's go." Vito pulled her by the elbow. "He can drop us both off. I live not far from her, I moved back in with my aunt again after they threw me out of my rooming house. Maybe I'll move in here if I can fix it with the super—nobody's supposed to live here according to the codes—but he's crazy like a bedbug."

"I wanted to talk with you about him, Vito," Harry said, falling in step with the painter as they left the building.

The girl too had fallen into line between Fred and himself. Irwin, his hand on her elbow as they descended to the street and entered the coffee joint on the first floor of the building next door, was caught in confusion between his interest in her and in what was being said by the others. Squeezed into a booth with Carmela, her thigh pressed against his, he felt that he should follow the conversation between Fred and Vito, seated opposite them, and Harry, who had pulled up a chair and from his position at the edge of the table dominated them all.

"You can't get me excited about a discussion group," Vito was saying to Harry, "whether you argue Marxism or marbles. That's all that ever went on in this town—a lot of talk and no action."

"Supposing I told you that I wanted to combine analysis and action."

"What kind of action?"

"Mass action—against war and against fascism."

"Sounds a little familiar. But you haven't even got any troops. You expect three people to do something about Hitler and Mussolini?"

Carmela, her head cocked, was saying to him insistently, "I said you look kind of young to be a doctor."

"I'm sorry," Irwin apologized to her for the second time. "I was distracted. I'm not really a doctor, I'm a dentist."

"Even so."

"I just graduated last June. My office is downtown, near Kleinhans. But it's not easy getting started, building a practice."

"I bet." Her eyes narrowed, and she nodded sympathetically.

"One man," Harry was saying, "can move masses. I can tell you exactly why your CP never got anyplace with the workers of this town. They twisted a great idea to fit the needs of Russian foreign policy. Can you blame the workers for being disgusted?"

"Are you implying," Fred asked, "that workers get more disgusted than other people? Doesn't that endow your workers with mystic virtues?"

Harry said patiently, "Simply because of the conditions of his life and labor, the worker stands at the heart of the productive process. Unlike ours, his attitude is crucial, and his conclusions are decisive."

"I heard all this from the Communists for years already," Vito mumbled as he bit into a cruller. Irwin was thinking that he had heard this, too, from his cousin Sy; but it was less easy to argue away when you heard it from the lips of someone else. "You mean to tell me," Vito asked, "that you can crack the workers when the CP couldn't?"

"Sooner or later," Harry responded, "the workers will turn to those who have been consistent."

Irwin lit the cigarette that Carmela was extending before him. She held his hand for an instant, as if to steady the flame that he offered. Emboldened by her touch, he asked, "Are you a full-time model?"

"Oh no." She expelled smoke nervously. "I never did it for anybody except Vito—that's why I was so jumpy when you fellows walked in. I mean, how does it look? It's different with Vito, he always lived in my neighborhood, I know him from when I was practically a baby. But my father, he's a punch press operator, he's been laid off for years. And my mother works part-time, nights, practically for nothing doing short order cooking in a beer parlor. So I've got to bring home whatever I can make."

"You think you can do singlehanded," Vito hunched down into his sheepskin jacket, "what whole armies haven't done, OK, more power to you. I'll talk to my crazy super, Easley Edwards, and we'll see if he can rent you a meeting room. But don't count me in your club."

"I won't count you out either. I don't count anybody out with a conscience and a skill. You go ahead and paint the way you want —but don't tell me you'll turn your back on me if I can show you a dedicated movement that's built on truth instead of lies."

"Well, maybe," Vito grumbled. "Right now I'm too tired to argue with you."

"What's it all about?" Carmela asked Irwin.

"Well . . ." When you stopped to think of it, she was what they were talking about—even though she didn't know it—and they treated her as though she wasn't there. ". . . Harry wants to start up a discussion club, to talk about Marxism."

"What's that?"

"I'm not too sure myself." Encouraged by the look of relief in Carmela's eyes, he added, "It's got to do with persuading people to get together and make socialism, instead of wars and depressions."

"It'll never work."

"Why not?"

"People are pigs."

Shocked, Irwin could not attend to what the others were saying. The remains of his coffee, cold in the cup before him, reflected the mud that lay silted in his own mind. Sadly, he asked her, "What'd you take up in school, Carmela?"

"I took a commercial course. You know—typing, bookkeeping. What a laugh."

"Why do you say that?"

"Because they only want experienced, that's why. The only time I got taken on after I said I was experienced, I should have known what was coming. The office manager chased me around the desk all day, till I quit." Her face darkened. "Pigs."

"How do they expect you to get experience, by magic?"

"Don't ask me. I worked in the dimestore, Kresge's, before Christmas. Sometimes I get some homework typing mail order envelopes. And when Vito asks me, I model for those crazy pictures. He's a good guy, he's my paisan." She leaned over to whisper in Irwin's ear, "But sometimes I think he's a little nuts."

Dizzied by the smell of her flesh, Irwin could only return the pressure of her leg against his; he wanted to press her hand with his, but he was afraid that the others, even though they were engrossed in their discussion, would notice.

"So now you know the story of my life." She drew away with a short laugh. "Not much to show for nineteen years, is it? Same for my whole damn family. Sometimes I wish I was dead."

Irwin recoiled. "You mustn't say that."

Carmela seemed a little mollified. "As long as you don't hold it against me, what I do for Vito. If he was a different kind of guy, he never would of let you come in tonight."

"I understand. Besides, there's nothing wrong with modeling, it's just as worthwhile as typing."

Then they all piled into Irwin's Mercury, Fred and Harry squeezing into the back seat, although they had to be dropped off first. Camela sat up front, next to him, knees together, leaning forward, warming her hands at the heater. Vito had lapsed into silence, seemingly sunk in thought, barely saying goodbye to Harry and Fred, but when he opened the door to be let off on Niagara Street, in front of a darkened clam bar, he said, "Say, you think that guy Harry is on the up and up?"

"What do you mean?"

"He didn't even say what the name of his outfit is."

"I gather it's just getting started."

"If he really wants to do something, maybe we all ought to give him a hand, right? Thanks for the lift. Carmie, say hello home, I'll have the dough for you Thursday."

"That's okay."

With a wave, he disappeared into the night.

"I'm right around the corner, practically," Carmela said. "Turn right, I'll show you the house. Boy, this is a nice car."

As he swung the wheel around, Irwin said quickly, casually, "Carmela, how would you like to work as a dental assistant?"

Carmela said nothing until he had stopped in front of the two-family house that she had indicated. Lips parted, she sat staring at him. At last she said, "Do you mean it?"

"You'd have to wear a uniform, answer the phone, make appointments, make out the bills, keep the books."

"But I haven't had any experience. Not to speak of."

"And I haven't got any patients, not to speak of. That's why it'd have to be part-time, at least for a while. But I'm going to do better, I'm sure of it. Once I build up a practice . . . What do you say? Would you be interested?"

"Would I? And how!"

"Supposing I call you up when I've figured it out, about the hours and what I can afford."

Carmela shook her head ruefully. "They disconnected the phone. But Vito knows how to reach me, by the candy store, how's that?"

"Fine. We'll be in touch."

Carmela paused, her fingers on the door handle. "Say, what kind of a name is Metzger? Is that German or something?"

"Yes. But actually," he cursed at himself, "actually I'm Jewish."

"Oh. I kind of thought so. You know something? My mother

always says Jewish boys are the nicest kind, sober and steady. And I think so too." Her laugh, with its hint of mockery reminding him instantly of the way her tongue had darted out at him, drifted back over her shoulder like perfume as she ran out and on up the porch steps, her full hips swaying beneath the trenchcoat. At her door she turned for an instant to wave farewell. Then she was gone.

I knew things would happen, he said to himself when finally he lay in bed, I felt it in my bones. To calm himself he began mentally composing a letter to his cousin Sy, who had stopped off, excited, on his way back from the Students' Union convention after Christmas. I'll tell him about Harry, he thought, and the way he's bulldozing us, and about Vito, and Carmela . . . but then it all ran together, Harry's insistent pressures and Vito's jabbing at the canvas and Carmela's body . . . and he gave himself over to dreams.

PART TWO

1. BILL

Bill had mixed feelings about spending a Saturday afternoon with Harry that he might better have spent with Margaret. But there was almost no other time when they could get together, since he was working second shift at the airplane factory.

Although he had not gotten home from the plant last night until one-thirty, he had arisen early this morning to do the weekly shopping with Margaret, pulling a neighbor kid's wagon the three blocks to the A&P and back. Vera was much too big now for that kind of chore, and anyway he enjoyed being alone with Margaret, even if only while they roamed the canned goods department together, checking the prices of Ann Page against Del Monte peaches. Now he would have liked to be on the sofa with his head in Margaret's lap while she studied and they listened to the Metropolitan Opera on the Texaco broadcast.

Still he was anxious to hear what Harry had to say, and as he approached his house on Linwood (a real middle-class neighborhood with a big lawn and an oak tree in front, and an awninged upstairs porch, far more expensive than anything he himself could possibly afford) he was also rehearsing in his mind the excuses for stalling Harry one more time, until Vera should have had the baby. But Harry was not at home: as he pressed the upstairs bell the downstairs door opened instead and he was greeted by a very tall, very fair girl, with a cluster of freckles running along the upper part of her face.

"Excuse me," she said, "but are you Bill?"

"That's me. Why?"

The girl smiled and brought out a key from the pocket of her skirt. "Would you let yourself in? Mr. Sturm had to run a few errands—he's such a busy man—and he thought his father might be sleeping and not hear your ring."

At the head of the stairs he rapped, and this time heard a weak voice from the interior calling out, "Come in, come in."

It was Simon Sturm, who sat huddled at the far end of the living room, near the front porch, his legs tucked in behind a steamer rug, an afghan around his sloping shoulders. He was dressed as if for a reception, in a heavily starched white shirt and a brocade tie with a loose, wide, old-fashioned knot. Bill had only met him once before, and it seemed to him that in the interval the old man's head had both shrunk and darkened, as if it had been left out in the sun too long; jutting from its sides like great handles, the ears too, thickly tufted with whisks of gray hair, seemed to have grown larger and more pendulous, drooping uselessly like an old woman's breasts.

"Do you remember me, Mr. Sturm?" he asked. "Bill Zivic."

"I know. My son told me you were coming."

"Well, we're both newcomers here," he remarked with awkward joviality. "How do you like the town?"

"To me it makes no difference. I could be in Timbuctoo." The old man raised his mottled trembling hands from his lap and exposed his palms, as if to display their emptiness. "All day I listen to the serials, the news. I read the paper a little. I boil myself an egg. Sometimes I look out from the porch, but to me scenery is scenery. You know, I used to be a painter and a paperhanger, first-class decorating. But always inside work, I never stuck my nose outside except to get on the subway. What difference does it make now, where I am?"

How awful, Bill said to himself, to be so out of it; I'd rather be dead. What was the sense of rotting away, no longer wanting to achieve anything at all, not even able to recall anything more substantial than the living rooms you'd painted and the bedrooms you'd papered? Why not fold, cash in your chips?

"Don't you miss New York at all?" he prodded, wondering whether he was being kind or cruel. "How about your friends?"

"What's to miss?" Simon Sturm turned down the dry wrinkled corners of his mouth. "When you're sick like I am, nobody wants to hear about your troubles—everybody wants to tell you their own. Who needs it?"

Stricken more by this desperate bravado than by earlier intimations of self-pity, Bill replied, "I'll listen. I mean it."

"Another time." It was Harry, standing stocky in the doorway, pipe in his teeth, a sack of groceries under his arm. He set down the sack and gestured toward the front porch. "Pop, you'll excuse us if Bill and I leave you for a while."

Without waiting for his father to reply, he pushed open the screen door. "William, let's sit down out here."

"How've you been?" Bill asked him.

"Busy. Lively and busy. There's a lot to do in this town."

"Have you started with the girl downstairs yet?"

Harry removed the pipe from between his teeth and gazed at him seriously. "What for?"

"To recruit her, of course," he replied with mock seriousness.

"Anne? If you knew her you wouldn't ask that. She's thoroughly bourgeois. Genteel, plays the piano all day long, has one or two students. Her parents are nice landlords, not inquisitive, although they're very friendly, like most small-town people."

Bill was annoyed by the patronizing tone of these last words, worse even than Harry's solemnity about the girl downstairs.

"You know of course why I wanted to see you." Harry had lowered his voice. He fixed Bill with his prominent blue eyes. "It's high time we exchanged information. I have a little news—but I also have to send a report to the national office."

"What's your news?"

Harry leaned forward. "The split in the movement is decisive. The new party will be functioning within the month."

"Under what name?"

"The New Party. And none too soon. Now we'll be free to recruit for an organization we believe in without reservations. The policy of colonizing industry with youth leaders should be helpful for us here. We're scheduled to get Irwin's cousin, Sy Glantzman, and his girl friend Bernice something or other. Do you know them, by chance?"

"I don't know many of those New York kids."

"These two are hard working and serious. They're getting married shortly, and graduating from City College next month. And if we're lucky, we may even get Norm Miller."

"The writer? That's real news. How come?"

"There are hints . . ." How Harry loved to mystify, to remind
you that he was privy to all sorts of decisions made by only two
or three men and communicated to him confidentially! ". . . that
if we can demonstrate our capacity to grow, they'll see to it that
we get more comrades like Norm. Besides, let's be frank—Marty
wants to try to place key people like Norm in defense plants wherever possible, so that we won't be decimated by the draft before
we're fairly started."

"And this student, Sy, if he's going to be married—"

"Well, we don't know how long that will protect people, do we?
Meantime don't underestimate him. I understand he did a first-rate
job at the ASU convention last winter, recruited a terrific guy from
the Coast who's already working for us, joined the Sailors Union
of the Pacific. With Sy and his wife, you and your wife, and Vera
as well, we'll have the basis for a stable branch here. I'm fairly
certain that Fred Vogel, out at the university, if not his wife, will
come in as soon as we're chartered. By the way, Fred and Bea are
friends of my landlord's daughter, Anne Schuyler, but as I told
you, she's no particular prospect."

"What about the dentist?"

"Irwin? A very nice chap, every obliging—but let's face it, William,
at bottom he's a petit-bourgeois type."

What was Harry himself? Maybe his father, neat but shriveling
like a plant that insisted on dying despite daily doses of sun and
water, had been a socialist housepainter in his day; but the room
in which he withered was completely foreign to an American
workingman's idea of home and hearth. Its glassed-in bookcases on
either side of the fireplace were crammed with chemical handbooks
and abstracts, and Russian classics, including books on nineteenth-
century revolutionaries whom Bill had scarcely heard of; its stippled
walls were decorated with framed prints of anatomical drawings
by Vesalius and Leonardo.

"Irwin's friends may come along—they're excited about the idea
of a new party. But Irwin"—Harry paused to relight his pipe,
then shook his head—"I think we'll have to classify him as a
sympathizer. It's better to be realistic, don't you think? The best
thing Irwin can do for us is to flourish in his dental practice. Now
let's hear about you."

Bill said slowly, "It hasn't been easy, integrating myself into the aircraft industry. I'm not complaining, I just want to make things clear. When you work in rubber, you have a certain pace, you have ways of learning what's going on, either on the shop floor, or in the elevator, wherever. But aircraft isn't like tire building, it's all horizontal, the shop stretches out forever, no elevators, no connection between departments, the noise never stops."

"And the workers?" Harry looked at him keenly.

"Fortunately for me I got hired at the plant with a union contract—if I'd been taken on at the other one, I'd be spending all my time bucking the company union. As it is, I can function in the UAW without any trouble, I even have hopes of being elected a steward in the wing department—I work as a riveter, you know, on the leading edges in the wing department. But . . ."

"But what?"

"These men aren't like the Firestone workers. They have no tradition of militancy, or even of organization. The union was handed to them on a platter, they've never had a strike action, much less a sitdown. They don't even have a background of building airplanes."

"Things can change. Workers learn under the pressure of events —faster than my students at the university."

"I'm just trying to explain to you that I can't be like I was in Akron, I don't get the same response in the shop. The work is harder, the men are slower. Does that explain anything? It hasn't been easy for me to acclimatize myself."

"That's why I was hoping that you'd be able to give me a hand," Harry said. "Later on, as you get more involved with the affairs of your local, you may have even less time for party building."

"Don't worry about that. Our leave of absence is strictly temporary. When you're ready to launch the New Party, Margaret and I will be ready to pitch in."

On that note they parted. They had spoken not so much to each other as at each other, and Bill was somewhat uneasy about the light in which he could be put by Harry's report to the national office. But that was beyond his control until he and Margaret could rejoin.

Vera was already at term. Hurrying home from Harry's, he thought wryly that he was more like a father-to-be than an expectant uncle. Except . . . would a father put such a burden on

his baby? The poor little thing, maybe at this very moment preparing to plunge into the world, helpless and handicapped from
the start, was already being looked on by himself, his wife, and the
girl who carried it, as the bearer of their deliverance from an
oppressively unnatural situation. It was strange to think of the birth
as an end rather than a beginning.

And yet of course it would be a beginning too, of a sort. Not
just for the infant, but for him and Margaret, engaged in an enterprise they had undertaken in a spirit at once adventurous and
solicitous. Once the baby was born, the adventure would be finished,
the solicitude no longer necessary, either for Vera or her mother.
But then what? Would everything arrange itself in some mysteriously
simple way? Presumably, Mrs. Rodenko would go on in her innocence, toward a peaceful old age, undisturbed by any intimations
of irregularity in her daughters' lives. Vera would give up the child,
last evidence of a mistake of sorts, and go on to another life. He
and Margaret would be liberated from the foolishness of feeling that
their flight had been motivated only by noble self-sacrifice, and
would go on to pick up the threads—law school, the shop, the
movement.

But supposing stubborn Vera, driven by imperious need, should
refuse to give up her first-born? It was a possibility that until
now he had not even dared to broach to his coolly planning wife,
engrossed in arranging their lives and reassuring the folks in Akron
that all was in order—not even in the dark of the night when they
lay whispering together, listening to the tossing girl in the next
room as her belly troubled first her conscience and then her very
dreams.

What was more, he could not suppress the horrible suspicion
that Margaret herself was not what she had always seemed to be,
that she was no more predictable than the most wildly irrational
of girls. It was no longer unthinkable that she should propose to
him that they keep the baby, perpetuating the presumably temporary dislocation of their lives, compounding the deception prac-
ticed up to now with such a multiplicity of lies that all of their
lives would become the most endlessly complicated of nightmares
from which there would be no possibility of awakening for the lifetime of their parents—if not of the child itself.

When he arrived at the dark, cramped apartment that was all he
could afford, his grim speculations appeared absurd and quite un-

founded. Panting from his haste and his fears (one driving the other, like a set of pulleyed gears), he rapped nervously at the door—and was met with a kiss by his relaxed and smiling wife, aproned and floury.

"We're baking a couple of pies with the rhubarb you bought this morning," she said gaily. "First of the season!"

They weren't simply having fun, the two sisters. Sitting with them in the kitchen while they took the pies from the oven and prepared the dinner, he discovered that this was a ceremonial, one of an entire series of preparations for the period when Vera would be in the hospital. Part of it was no doubt a practice that Margaret had learned from her mother, perhaps even in her earliest childhood, when Mrs. Rodenko had worked in the kitchen until the last moment to stock up against the time when she would have to lie down in the bedroom and give birth to her second child. But for the rest he could see—if Vera could not—that this was also a kind of game, like mud-pies, deliberately contrived by Margaret to distract her younger sister from the terror of what should have been but now could not possibly be a beautiful experience.

Wrapped in his own gloom and unease, watching the comings and goings of the two as if he were a stranger, he thought that he could see something else as well, something that they were attempting to push out of sight while they pored over the smeared cookbook and bent over the stove: Each envied the other. You couldn't tell it by so much as the littlest quickest glance of an eye, yet he was positive nonetheless that Margaret was envious of Vera's great globe, within which the baby had already dropped—and that Vera, no matter how she had earlier procrastinated, until it was too late *not* to have the baby, was eaten with jealousy of Margaret's narrow waist and quick darting freedom of movement.

Still, their dinner was normal. Wonderfully so, if you considered it as one more stage in the long wait for the overdue arrival. Margaret wanted to hear about his discussion with Harry. He played down both Harry's request for help and his own desire to get back into politics, instead he talked about old Simon Sturm, Harry's father. But even as he described the tottering paper-hanger, he was assailed with doubts—would they, would Vera, see the old man as an analogy to Mrs. Rodenko in Akron, lied to and abandoned? God damn it, he said to himself, why can't I carry things off more easily?

The doorbell rang. He scraped back his chair. "Sit still, both of you," he said. "I'll get it."

He wiped his lips with his napkin as he unlocked the door and pulled it open. His father, Frank Zivic, stood before him, slanting cheekbones shining as if they had been polished, razor marks still clear and sharp from the morning, posing for a photograph: In his Sunday suit and stiff black shoes, cap in hand, gray hair greased so that the separate strands stood up and away from his forehead like so many spikes. Bill blinked. He could not stop his eyelids from fluttering while his eyes registered the momentarily frozen presence.

"Surprise," his father said shyly. "We decided to surprise you for Easter." He stood still, as if uncertain of his welcome, then raised his arm and pointed over his shoulder with his cap. "The three of us."

Da tree of us. The achingly familiar accent shook him as though his father had stepped forward and kissed him.

"Pa!" he said. His throat was convulsed. "Pa!"

His mother and his mother-in-law stepped out from behind Frank Zivic. His mother, a head taller than her companion, carried a valise and a bulging shopping bag; his mother-in-law, a basket of presents, an armload of groceries. Struggling forward with their burdens, sweating in their coats, they surrounded him, breathing heavily, straining to kiss him, wanting to be embraced.

"Billy," his mother said, "you look so skinny. You don't like your job, you work too hard?"

"Where's Margaret?" his mother-in-law asked. "Where's Vera? Did they go out, are you home alone?"

Retreating, his voice failing him, he mumbled, "Pa, ma . . . I didn't expect . . ."

"A surprise," his father repeated, "a surprise. Ma was afraid you wouldn't be home. I said, 'We'll find them.' We made it in no time, the old Pontiac is great . . ."

Bandylegged on the mat, cap still in his stubby hand, his father suddenly stopped. He had heard something, and he stood stock still, his head cocked oddly, as if he were expecting to hear it repeated, like a bird call that he might then imitate.

"Where's the girls?" he demanded. "What you standing like that for?"

"Pa," he said. "Ma. Let me try to explain."

They pressed on him, sweating in the silence, waiting for him to go on. But he could not, and as soon as they grasped that, they pushed him aside as though he were a bellboy or a real estate agent who had misled them. Storming through the room, they made for the kitchen, from which Bill could now hear the panting, the sounds of struggle that had alerted his father.

He hastened after them, trying to pull them back from the kitchen doorway, where they had piled up, tall woman, small woman, bowlegged man, still toting their gifts and presents, like figures in some low comedy.

"Come back!" he cried, his voice all of a sudden returned. "Give me your coats! Put your stuff down!"

But it was too late to stop them, just as it had been too late to forewarn the girls. With a thrill of terror he saw his wife leaning out the kitchen window, halfway onto the fire escape, the bare skin of her thigh shining white as she strained away, tugging at her sister, who cowered out of sight.

Then they were all shouting at once. Bags fell to the floor. His mother-in-law was first at the window, clawing at her older daughter.

"What's the matter with you?" she demanded sternly, as though her girl had let the milk boil over, or spilled the sugar. "What's the big idea?"

Margaret swung about, one hand still on her half-hidden sister, two red blotches high on her cheeks. "It's Vera. She's scared, mama, she's upset."

"About what? About what? Vera, you get back in here before you hurt yourself. Now come on!"

Vera showed her face, pale, puffy, and swollen, in the open window. "I wasn't going to hurt myself, mama. Honest, I wasn't going to jump or anything like that."

"Then what are you doing out there? Are you crazy or something?"

"I guess I was going to run away."

Bill's father turned to him. "Say, what's going on here?"

Before he could answer, the three women were at the window, tugging and hauling; Vera stumbled on the sill, tumbled into the room; they all fell back, first to give her space so that she would not collide with them, then—as she arose and displayed her outline —in a kind of parody of awe.

Margaret grasped her mother by the arm as if to draw her even further back. "We couldn't tell you, mama. We didn't want to hurt you."

"Hurt me? Hurt me?" His mother-in-law's voice rose up and up. She turned to his mother. "Look at her! Look at that sight! That's what we came to see! That's why we saved up our money! That's why we got time off and bought presents . . ." She turned back on her swollen daughter. "Presents we brought you! I should hit you on the head with them!"

Then everyone began to talk, argue, cry, plead. Or at least the women did; stealing a glance at his father, Bill was startled not so much by his pallor and new misery as by his withdrawal. Their eyes met for an instant; by unspoken consent they backed out of the kitchen.

"Sonny," Frank Zivic said, and stopped, after having uttered the long-unused word. He cleared his throat. "Why didn't you tell us?"

"I couldn't." Lying, he blurted, "On account of her mother."

They talked. The old man tried, so desperately that the tears started to Bill's eyes, to bridge the thirty-six years that lay between them like some yawning bottomless canyon. But everything he said, all his pleas, came down to what still did not seem possible: We would have understood. Not when you heard the hiccuping sobs and anguished cries in the kitchen.

And why should they have been expected to understand? That was what Bill could not bring himself to utter, even in kindness and love. It would be like condemning his parents to consciousness of their age and condition, their painful limitations, their inability to adapt to a world different from the one in which they had honeymooned in the Macedonian mountains, a generation ago.

He had known it earlier, he realized, but never until now with such hurtful clarity. Before he had left home, when they both worked in the same plant and belonged to the same local, he had interpreted this only as physical weariness on the part of the father he honored not simply for his principles but for his past; he had endured flogging, freezing, a war, blacklisting, a depression. He was entitled, after the sitdown had won a measure of security, to enjoy that security, to sit home with his feet on the hassock and his hands gripping the Akron *Beacon-Journal,* while his son slogged off to the union meetings and undertook also to build almost from nothing the movement that would carry their family's bred in the bone socialism to American factory workers.

Now he knew that it was not that simple; under the hammer of the years something had broken in his father that could not be mended. What was more, he had a sudden fearful foretaste of that inevitable accident, age, striking him down one day in his turn. Moved perhaps more by this prevision of his own impotence and withdrawal than by his father's hopeless demand, he stepped forward and embraced him.

"Anyway, pa," he mumbled into his father's shoulder, "we meant well."

"I didn't say you didn't." The old man held him off, one gnarled, knuckly hand upraised. "Listen. How come all of a sudden it's so quiet in there?"

"Maybe they're making up."

Struck with guilt at having left Margaret not just to mediate but to battle for a decision that now appeared not just wrong or pointless, but (to use his father's word) "crazy," he hastened to the kitchen doorway.

It was an odd sight: the two older women still in their coats, and hats too, with little feathers in them, his mother's with a hatpin jabbed through it into her bun and out again—Margaret still in her apron, with the two red splashes still high on her cheeks—all three of them now grouped in a half-circle about Vera, who had fallen into a chair, slumped so on the bottom of her spine that her chest seemed to have sunk down into the great mound that heaved up before her. Her eyes, vacant and glassy, floated in fluid; her mouth hung open, pouting but pursed, as if she were silently saying "Ow."

Margaret glanced up. "Willie," she said, "her pains have started."

"All right." He pretended to a great calm. "What's the first thing we do, call the doctor? I think I'd better call the doctor."

"Shut up," his mother said to him. "Stop talking so much. We're timing the pains."

Behind him his father said, "Where's the phone? We better call the doctor."

"We haven't got one. I'll go next door."

"Wait," his mother-in-law said. "What about the hospital? Have you got a reservation? Who's going to take her?"

"We haven't got a car either," he said. He added defensively, irrelevantly, "How could I keep a car and feed three people on fifty cents an hour?"

"We can call a cab," Margaret said. "That's what I figured on doing anyway."

"Listen, what's the matter with my Pontiac?" Frank Zivic asked. "I can take her, that's no problem. You go call the doctor in the meantime."

"Pa, you'll need me to show you the way. You can't go wandering around with her in labor. Margaret," he said, "you go next door and call the doctor."

Vera pressed the heels of her hands onto the chair, on either side of her hips, and pushed herself erect. "I don't want to go without Margaret. Margaret, don't leave me." Her face contorted; she wedged her knuckles into her mouth.

Margaret glanced at her watch. "Bill, go call the doctor. Tell him they're a little more than ten minutes apart. Don't worry, baby," she said to her sister. "I'll stay with you. We'll go together."

Her mother started to cry in a high monotone. "What about me? You ran away once, you going to run away again? Now? Of all times? Isn't it bad enough what you did, you have to turn your back on me now?"

"Listen, I can't take everybody," Frank Zivic said. "I mean, look at her. She's got to be comfortable in the car, she's got to have some room. Mama," he said to his wife, "explain to Fannie, somebody's got to stay here. Worst comes to worst, I can make two trips. I'm not tired."

Margaret jerked her head. "Bill," she said, "go call."

When he came back his father, cap on his head, was already holding open the door for him. Behind him Margaret, an overnight bag gripped in her hand, was half hugging, half leading her sister across the room.

The ride to the hospital was agonizingly long. But not for his father, who seemed pleased to have the sisters instead of the older women in the back seat. "I got thirteen point two miles to the gallon on the way up from Akron," he told them. "I keep her at a steady forty-five on the highway, that's the secret. Especially for an old car. I just did a ring job on it myself."

When no one answered, he fell silent, gripping the wheel with both hands, making the turns very slowly, so as not to jar Vera. She was groaning audibly now. Bill wished that his father would go faster but could not say so; Margaret was trying to distract her by talking about their mother, reassuringly.

"If anybody can handle her, my mother-in-law can."

"At a time"—Vera gasped—"like this . . ."

"She's here and that's all there is to it," Margaret said. "What's done is done."

It was not that simple. Nothing would ever be that simple again. What was more, as he and Margaret helped Vera out of the car and into the hospital, leaving his father to park the car, he could feel—without either of them having to say anything—that Margaret knew this as well as he. Better, maybe, for the whole idea had been hers, and its sudden stunning failure, its essential foolishness even, was something she would have to cope with. He almost felt sorry for her.

They tucked Vera into a wheelchair after signing her in. As she was being rolled away, Margaret turned to him swiftly. "Wait here until I get her settled. They'll probably want to take her to the labor room after that."

"Your mother—"

"I told ma where I keep the sleeping pills. If they worked for Vera, they'll work for my mother." Suddenly she flung her arms around his neck and pressed her head against his, her face against his, with such force that their cheekbones collided. "Christ," she whispered, "I'm so sorry." Then she ran down the corridor and into the elevator after her sister.

When his father arrived, they sat together on a maple bench, waiting. Here too Frank Zivic looked out of place, his box-toed shoes pointing dead ahead on the hospital floor as though nailed to the waxed linoleum tiles. In funeral blue, his tie awkwardly knotted, that horrible grease on his gray hair making it stand up from his forehead as if in shock or wonderment, he looked even more ill at east than the expectant fathers who leafed, unseeing, through old magazines.

Actually however he was not. He said comfortably, "Well, Billy, I bet you didn't think a couple hours ago that you'd be sitting with me in this here place."

"Pa," he said, "believe me, I didn't want it to come out like this. But I couldn't think of a better answer for them."

"It's not the end of the world."

Startled, Bill looked up. His father was smiling—from one side of his mouth only, but smiling nonetheless.

"This isn't the old country," his father said. "You shouldn't have let the girls get you in such a panic. Nobody was going to run her out of town."

"We couldn't take a chance. Look at her mother, she's in hysterics."

"What did you want her to do, sing a song? It's her baby girl. No husband to talk about it with. No husband for Vera. But she'll get over it. When she quiets down she'll want to take care of Vera."

"If I'd been sure of that last fall, pa, I never would've left Akron."

"That ain't the worst thing that could have happened either."

Once again Bill stared at him. When they had packed up and left town, his father characteristically had said very little. It had led him to believe that his father thought him a damn fool; now he was not sure. He asked: "What do you mean, pa?"

"I told mama, you were better off going away and making a start on your own life with Margaret. What did you have to be in the same shop with me? Or even in the same town with your mother-in-law? I didn't know it was Vera, but I knew it was some monkey business. And I figured to myself, whatever it is, let them go work it out someplace else. What do you look so surprised? How do you think your mother and me left the old country?"

Bill felt very close to his father. Maybe he was just being kind, but even that was more than he had a right to expect. If his father could talk like this to the two women who had stayed behind, maybe things could work out. This was no time to whine about the inconveniences that the deception had caused him. His face burned when he thought of what he had let slip about not being able to afford a phone or a car. The man at his side had not been able to afford a car until he was almost fifty years old.

Yet it was his father who broke the silence, saying uneasily, "Margaret's been gone a long time. Maybe we ought to get back to mama and Fannie—they don't know what's going on."

"Margaret said to wait for her."

His father arose as if he had been rebuked and began to paw clumsily through the pile of magazines on the table in the corner. He took up a copy of *Life* magazine, sat down again, and stared at it hungrily while he turned pages, with the concentrated fascination he customarily gave to mechanical, political, and union problems.

"Hey," he said after a while, "did you see this about Bertrand Russell? I didn't read anything about it in Akron."

Bill stopped gnawing at his fingernail. He had bitten out the skin on his little finger, which now began to burn and bleed. Sucking at it, he said, "About him being fired from City College for moral turpitude? Why should they print that in Akron? Who cares there?"

"Me," his father said. "I think it's terrible, they treat a great man like him that way. And just because he's an atheist, or he don't believe in marriage. I never believed in God, did I? They could of done it to me."

Confused and embarrassed, Bill replied, "You're right, pa. But those politicians always cater to the most backward elements. La Guardia is supposed to be a big liberal—he never lifted his finger for Russell. You think he's going to get all those Catholic voters mad at him for one lousy little philosopher?"

"Just the same I think it's terrible. In a free country—"

Margaret was hurrying toward them, heels clicking on the corridor floor, skirt swinging. Her hands were made into fists.

"What is it?" he asked her. "What is it? We've been waiting here forever."

"Listen," she said rapidly, "I'm scared."

It was Frank Zivic who put his arm around her. "Tell me, Margaret," he said.

Her eyes were glittering. "The baby is presenting itself wrong. The nurse says they've got to do a version."

Bill was not sure what she was talking about. But as he took her stiff, still clenched hand, he felt something start up deep within himself, a trembling fear of the absolutely unknown and unforeseeable, that begans to vibrate in time with the pulsation in his wife's wrist.

"They're going to have to use forceps. The head . . . The baby . . ."

"Why didn't they tell us?" His angry voice was unnaturally loud. People looked up. He demanded again, whispering, "Why didn't they tell us?"

"They didn't know. Not without X rays. Billy, I'm scared. I want mama."

He glanced up into his father's eyes.

"She ought to be here," his father said. "If we could reach her on the phone maybe."

"It's too late. They're asleep next door already. And how would she get here?"

"I'll go," Frank Zivic said. "I'll bring her back. Except I don't know the way."

"Billy," she said, again using his parents' pet name, "you go with pa. Hurry up."

"No," he said. "I'm not going to leave you here."

"God damn it," she said, "we can't just walk out of here."

"I'll stay. They won't let you or me in there anyway. I'll stay, just in case. You go with pa, show him the way, and bring back your mother. And mine. Don't stand here arguing with me. Go ahead."

He no longer knew, standing there alone, if he had done the right thing. So many wrong things had been done already that now, at midnight, he was incapable of judging. This last decision had sent his wife on her way feeling that she was going home to her mother at least, no matter what lay like a stone in her mother's heart or in her mind. Better, he thought, than having her sit here shivering and hating herself.

He was not surprised when after some time a man in white, pink-faced and oddly pink-eyed too, approached him. "Are you the, uh, husband?"

"Zivic is my name. I'm the brother-in-law."

"I was discussing with your wife."

"She's gone to get her mother."

"Well, it's finished." The doctor looked down, suddenly fascinated by his rubber-soled white buckskin shoes. When he looked up his eyes were swimming. "I'm afraid . . ."

Bill wanted to talk, he wanted to say something encouraging. Instead he stood clammily silent.

The doctor seemed almost angered that he was not being helped. He said abruptly, "We lost the baby. There was no other way."

Bill felt a roaring in his ears, as if the doctor had been shouting at him through a bullhorn. He put his hands to his ears and discovered that he was hugging his head. "How is she?" he asked. "Why don't you say anything about her?"

"She's very worn out. That's understandable. But she's a young and healthy person—she'll be all right. They're taking her back to her room now."

"Now look," Bill said, and stopped.

He and the doctor gazed at each other for a moment, and then the doctor said, "It's up to you, if you feel that you want to tell her. But you shouldn't stay for more than a couple of minutes. She's going to need rest."

"I think maybe my wife . . ."

"That's up to you. But once she's under sedation she shouldn't be disturbed for some time."

"Well." Come on you stupid shit, he said to himself. "I guess I'd better go up, all right?"

They proceeded in silence to the empty elevator, which smelled of floor wax and disinfectant. The doctor closed the door and manipulated the controls. Without a word they ascended, got off, went down the corridor, proceeded to a room with a rubber strap extending around the door handle from outside to inside. There the doctor left him.

There was a night light at the bedside. Vera lay flat, her head sunk into the pillow, her eyes that had been staring glazed at the ceiling rolling about in her head to follow his sound as he approached. He tore his eyes from the mound that rose from the middle of the bed. She still looked pregnant.

"Hello kid," he whispered. "Rough time, huh?"

Her shallow slanting Slavic eyes, long and dully shining like white radishes, followed him as he seated himself beside her. She drew back her cracked and parched lips; her teeth were still caked with clotted blood from biting down; that was one part of her they had neglected to sponge.

"I forgot to tell you before, Vera, when I got back from Harry's. After that there was so much excitement . . . There are Indian women, they look like they just came in from the reservation, on all the street corners downtown. They're selling daffodils, the first spring flowers. I'll bring you some tomorrow."

Unspeaking, she blinked. Water ran slowly from her eyes, downward, into her ears. He searched fruitlessly for a handkerchief, then found some paper squares on her night table beside the water glass with the bent tube protruding, pointing toward Vera. He patted her temples, wiping them dry, then blew his nose.

"The baby," she whispered hoarsely. "I know about the baby."

"The main thing," he went on, as though she had not uttered the words, as though he were reading lines that had been written for some silly play, "is for you to rest up and get your strength back."

"It's crazy," she whispered. "Isn't it crazy? What I put everybody through? And for what." Then she said something unintelligible; he could not make out any words, it was as if she were talking in her sleep, and he was frightened that she might have gone out of her head. But she twisted her neck, urging him closer, and he leaned forward until she had no need to do more than make the words with her lips, tongue and bloodflecked teeth.

"I'll make it up to you. If it takes me the rest of my life, I'll make it up . . ."

He offered her the bent straw, but her head fell away from him, and her eyes were closed. A nurse was standing above him, a silver metal tray in her hand. She jerked her head silently toward the door; he stumbled out blindly.

The hospital seemed utterly devoid of life. The elevator arose slowly in response to his command. Empty save for him, it descended slowly, in absolute silence, and deposited him once again in the long bare corridor. A nurse sat humped over her chart; with her rounded back and unblinking gaze she might have been some giant Oriental cat, carved from granite. She did not move or acknowledge his presence as he passed.

He continued on through the front door to the three shallow steps leading down to the sidewalk. There he paused, breathing in the sweetness of the April air. From the lawn before the hospital, and the foundation plantings, arose the odor of freshly turned earth and life rising anew. For a few hours more it would be still, hushed and quiet like this; and the next day—this day, really—he would not have to go to work, bury his head in the trough of an airplane wing, smash his brains against the blast of the incoming rivets. It would be a respite.

Next to his foot lay a small bundle of papers still tied with twine, morning papers tossed there by the passing truckmen for hospital patients and staff. It was the news section of the *Courier-Express;* no doubt the rest of the Sunday paper, funnies, fillers, lay elsewhere waiting to be stuffed with the latest news. He bent to look: the German armies were invading Holland. The frontier had been crossed. The war now moved to the west.

With a sigh he slumped to the steps. He sat there, awaiting something, the dawn maybe that could not be too far off. When he heard the approach of his parents, his wife, her mother, the four of them hurrying toward him across the dark empty street, mouths agape, panting, questioning with their eyes before they could breathe words through their mouths, he arose heavily and stepped forward to meet them all.

2. SY

Sy looked forward with dread to having dinner with his brother. Still living under the same roof, they saw each other seldom. Sid was away at sea most of the time, Sy himself had been busy with his last year at City College, his impending marriage, and the formation of the New Party. Neither of them was usually home of an evening—certainly not together—and even if they were it would have been difficult to talk freely in front of the old man, more confined than ever, since his stroke, to his sagging throne before the window and the fire escape.

So they had agreed—with the active encouragement of their mother, hoping against hope for a fraternal reconciliation—to meet in neutral territory, a second-floor Chinese restaurant on 14th Street. They had also agreed, tacitly, that they would not argue politics but would confine the table talk to family problems.

"You think that will help?" he asked Bernice, somewhat rhetorically. "Watch and see. He'll find ways to show his contempt for me."

"You don't know that for sure," she replied earnestly. "Give him the benefit of the doubt. After all, you don't know when you'll see him again."

"I've got a feeling it's going to be once a year. An annual occasion, like a class reunion or a company banquet. Ugh."

They were sitting side by side, waiting their turn in the office of a doctor, a distant relative of Bernie's, who would take their blood and guarantee its purity—a funny but useful wedding present. Across the room an elderly peasant woman sat with legs apart, breathing hard through her open mouth, groaning quietly with every exhala-

tion. In the corner an old man, shrunken into himself like an over-
baked potato, coughed inconspicuously into a soiled handkerchief.
Beside him a young girl, her face knotted into sudden ugliness,
waited for the summons, fists on her knees like a fighter awaiting
the bell.

The outer door opened. A red-faced mother, streaked with sweat,
the back of her summer dress sticking to shoulderblades and buttocks, came in off the steaming street clutching a wailing reluctant
boy with a makeshift bandage on his arm. Dragging backward, the
boy tripped unseeing over Sy's outstretched feet.

Throwing down the dogeared *Consumer Report* he had been
using as a kind of shield against his surroundings, he arose. Alarmed,
Bernie looked up from the New York *Times* which she had folded
lengthwise, subway-style, in order to read about the latest Luft-
waffe raid on London.

"Are you all right?" she asked.

"I'm not sick. I'm just sick of waiting. Can't we just leave our
blood and go away? In a little bottle, like a specimen?"

"It won't be too much longer."

"Neither will I." Feeding on her whispering plea, he added aggressively, "I can't hang around here all day."

Stung, she tilted her neck like an embattled swan. "Oh no? That's
funny. I thought you were resigning from your executive position
at Macy's in order to get married."

"I'm only on my lunch hour." Why should she rail at him because
he had been wrapping parcels ever since graduation? Was he angry
because she had taken her degree to Klein's and gotten a temporary
job selling brassieres? Hadn't they agreed to work until the last
minute before marrying and leaving for Buffalo? Coldly he said,
"I have an obligation to go back and finish the day."

"Please don't let me keep you." She bit her lip. "I can't walk out
on an appointment, but you go right ahead—I can always use the
blood test for another occasion."

Enraged, he slammed out of the office. Didn't she know what
he had been going through, running back and forth between her
and his mother, now burdened with a drooling invalid? Did she
think it had been fun placating his mother all these months while
Sid was off at sea? Promising her that not only his shipping job at
Macy's but his factory work in Buffalo were temporary expedients?
That when things opened up (that magic phrase, *when things open*

up, had been a part of the family's vocabulary ever since the Crash, for over ten years now) he would assuredly use his bachelor's degree in history to escape from the ranks of the hopeless and the downtrodden?

Oh, she knew. As he walked, sticky with sweat and shame on the boiling summer streets, he knew in his heart that she knew, she felt what he had been through, she understood how painful it was going to be for him to sit opposite his brother in that restaurant. That was one of the reasons he loved her; and it was humiliating to think of how he was going to have to get his blood test elsewhere, and apologize to her, and explain the unexplainable. What kind of a way was this to get married?

What Bernie didn't understand (how could she, eager as she was?) was that, now that it was actually upon him, he was terrified of marriage.

Terrified, and depressed. Suddenly his life seemed to be proceeding on a course that was not just logical, but dreary. Could this be all there was to it? In his pocket burned a thick letter, a packet really, from Joe Link, whom he had met in Madison and walked the streets with, dredging out his hesitations one after another, overmastering them, until Joe had first capitulated, then enlisted with passionate enthusiasm. The letter was postmarked Suva, wherever that was, over some beautiful stamps. It dutifully recounted his political discussions in the fo'c'sl, his hope of being elected deck delegate, his estimate of the social aggressiveness and racial backwardness of his fellow-members of the Sailors Union of the Pacific, and his encounters with odd radicals on the waterfront in Sydney and Brisbane. But it also hinted of stranger adventures in Honolulu and Kobe, with whispering women willing to teach him tricks he might never have learned in Los Angeles.

Joe was going to try to sign on with a coastwise line when he got back from this lengthy voyage, in order that he might make all the ports between Pedro and Anchorage, familiarize himself with conditions, become better known and so better able to function within the union. He didn't say so directly, but he would have liked someone willing to make these ports with him, to share his adventures and help him with his organizing.

Why should it be out of the question? Was that all that was left from now on, to say no? He had never done anything, never been further from home than that Wisconsin trip, never picked up strange girls or posted letters from Suva. Now it looked as though he never would.

It gave you a sick, trapped feeling, and maybe the worst of it was that there was no one to admit it to. He could not even acknowledge it to Joe; their friendship was too new, and Joe might misinterpret it as a slur on Bernice. Which was not what he meant at all.

But it was not true either that he had had to plead with her to marry him, or that he could not wait to be married, as Norm seemed to think. Norm envied him, no doubt about it. He had admitted it, half jocularly, when Sy had asked him to be a witness at City Hall. Sy had sensed an equation between Norm's envy of him and his own envy of Joe Link in the South Pacific. Unless he was crazy, Norm also harbored a carefully concealed resentment of Bernie. Sy had been both friend and disciple (again, a relationship now repeated, in reverse, by himself and Joe Link), and now all that was gone. It was not logical, to envy someone for getting married at the same time that you resented his fiancée for interrupting your friendship; but it was understandable.

The proper person to have discussed this with should have been his older brother. But, Sy thought angrily, as he wielded the little hooked knife on the twine tying the last of his cartons in the shipping room, it made no more sense to take up such things with Sid than it did to engage him in a political discussion.

He said goodbye to the shipping room crew with whom he had been working ever since the beginning of June. The handclasps and good wishes gave him more of a pang than he would have thought possible—it was strange how quickly your life became intertwined, in a variety of small ways, with those of the people who earned their livings alongside you. Then he had to get a blood test (he still grew hot in the face when he thought of Bernie sitting in the other waiting room and attempting, when her turn came, to explain his absence), and at last, after hanging from a strap and staring at Miss Subways—*Anna Girardi* (a sausage of her hair dangling over her forehead) *is a comptometer operator in a Broadway bank, but has dramatic aspirations and dreams of acting in a play of Sidney Kingsley or Lillian Hellman*—he was mounting the steps to the Golden Dragon Restaurant.

He was five minutes early when he pushed aside the beaded curtain and entered this Chinese Switzerland, this neutral territory favored by various left political factions, each convened in its tacitly exclusive alcove for discreet discussions over the egg drop and the sub gum. It did him no good, though; Sid had arrived even earlier. Seated in a window booth, he examined a newspaper with studied patience, a glass of water his only solace. At the sound of Sy's approach he glanced up confidently; armed with the righteousness of the early arrival, he beckoned needlessly with a crooked index finger.

Cursing to himself, Sy greeted Sid; doubtless he would have been sitting here securely, studying the NMU paper, *The Pilot,* even if he himself had arrived not five but thirty minutes early. The paper—Sid put it aside with elaborate casualness—was opened accidentally on purpose to a page of convention photos. Sid himself was quite clearly visible in the corner of one picture, listening intently to a hulking Negro identified as *Clarence Hull, N.O. longshore leader.*

It was not very subtle, particularly when you thought of the other advantages that he enjoyed, in addition to his early arrival. He was older, more self-assured, more worldly, and he had pa—foolish though he was—on his side. Most important, he bore on his bare right arm the stigmata of the certainty with which he had accepted the consequences of his commitment. Flesh and bone had been scooped out by the fascist dum-dum bullet that had burst there in the fighting before Teruel, leaving a deep channel, an ugly maimed forearm.

Like any infirmity, the arm drew your eye despite your desperate efforts to look elsewhere. Ordinarily that left you with the shameful secret satisfaction that your own arms were whole; but the wound with which Sid had returned from Spain almost two years ago remained as a silent ugly reminder of his demand not for pity but respect.

After the wound had healed and mama's tears had dried, Sy had asked him whether he was aware of what the Communists had done to the anarchist workers of Barcelona while he was spending his blood for them. A gangling freshman, pamphlet-proud and theory-ridden, Sy had been a pushover for the returned veteran. With one thrust of his punctured and puckered right arm Sid had sent him sprawling. "You spit on my comrades? You, you little City College shit?"

So the wound had never faded for Sy, even though perhaps it had for the man who bore it. Sid was wrong, but he had earned his wrongness, and if the wound was still a weapon and not simply a souvenir, that was not of his conscious doing.

Squeezing in across from him, Sy was pleased to see Sid fold up his union paper and tuck it away. "So how was your voyage?" he asked.

"Recife is a good port town. Beautiful canals, something like Venice and Amsterdam."

"Was your Spanish any help?"

"They speak Portuguese there." Sid smiled, but only with one side of his mouth. "And for what I was buying, I didn't need Portuguese."

Sy was suddenly haunted by a jealous vision of Joe Link prowling through the palm-lined streets of Honolulu and Sydney.

"Never mind all that," his brother said, waving exoticism aside and gesturing to the waiter. "Let's get the same soup, that way they'll give us a tureen. And then two different main dishes, for variety. We'll start with the won-ton, it's like kreplach, you like that. Then how's about one pepper steak and one pork fried rice, they're both filling."

Assuming indifference, he shrugged. But his heart was beating rapidly; he was angered by the continuing assumption of the rights of the first-born, and uneasy about what would come next. He remarked rather harshly, "Well, at least we can agree on dinner, especially if you do the ordering."

Sid did not rise to the bait. Instead he busied himself with making a bed of rice for the pepper steak, and soaking everything liberally with the varnish-like brown sauce in the glass bottle before him—that, and commenting on Van Lingle Mungo's pitching prowess. To show that he kept up, even though he was just back from Recife, he even found something to say about the latest young literary sensation from the South. Carson McCullers, wasn't that it?

At length Sy could stand it no longer. Snapping an almond cookie in half, he demanded, "Aren't you going to congratulate me?"

"You mean about getting married? Well, you're not married yet, are you?"

"I will be soon enough."

"You're a little young. Aside from the fact that this is hardly a suitable time for you to pack up and walk out on the folks."

"What would be a suitable time?"

"You know what I mean. Ma has her hands full."

"When won't she? Pa is never going to get much better. I talked it over with the doctor while you were gone. If there was something I could do to help her, I wouldn't leave town. Besides, it strikes me that you're in no position to talk."

"That's different."

"It always is, when you're the oldest."

Stubbornly, darkly, his heavy brows coming together in annoyance, Sid persisted. "I don't see what you're going to do in Buffalo."

"Irwin Metzger says things are opening up there, in industry."

"In industry? What about your college diploma? You going to paper the wall with it?" He sounded as though he were on the point of adding one more spiteful question: After all the sacrifices the family made to see you through college?

Sy answered, "Nobody needs historians. Not like they do riveters."

"Great future in riveting," Sid remarked sardonically.

He was tempted to ask since when socialists thought in terms of personal success, or of rising from the working class. But Sid himself had been unable to go to college because of the depression; who knew how much that had hurt him? Rather sulkily he said, "Don't worry about me reneging. I've already promised ma I'm going to send her money every week."

"That's all right. Between us, she'll make out." For the first time Sid's voice softened. He said with something more than politeness, "I should have invited your girl to join us."

"Bernice probably would have preferred for us to see each other alone anyway."

"Ma says she's a good girl."

"I like her."

"You'd better do better than that." Then Sid spoiled it all by adding, "Don't be in a hurry to get her pregnant. Like I said, you're a little young."

"Well, even if I am, she's mature."

"Yes, I figured you'd think that."

Sy glanced up suspiciously from his teacup, but Sid seemed intent on his chocolate ice cream, spooning it up rapidly, then jamming a whole fortune cookie into his mouth, as if he were anxious to finish and be on his way.

At the cash register Sy extended a dollar to Sid, already busy taking advantage of the last of the restaurant's offering—a toothpick and a mint. His brother stuck the toothpick into the corner of his mouth and demanded, "What's that for?"

"My share."

"Oh no." Sid shook his head. "Oh no. Save it for your honeymoon." Then he relented. "You can pick up the check next time, all right?"

As they descended the stairway together to the sidewalk where they would part, Sy was sweating, from the tea and from thinking about shaking hands in farewell. On the street he said, "Ma worries about you and those torpedoes. Maybe if you could get a coastal run instead of—"

"My luck has been good so far." Sid made an odd little thrusting gesture with his maimed arm, fist clenched and twisting as if to say, Screw the world. "Yours should be so good with your wife."

Sy was about to express his thanks, and had even half-extended his hand, when his brother added, "Who knows, maybe when you get into a shop you'll learn who the workers' real leaders are. And you'll develop a sense of responsibility. Take care!" With a wave of the arm, Sid wheeled and walked off.

On their wedding day, Bernie's parents cried because they were not invited to the wedding, his mother cried because they were going away, his father sat immobile, grinning maliciously—but whether because he did not believe in the institution of marriage or because the stroke had left him frozen in a grin like those stone-dead Pompeians forever fixed by lava in the similar attitudes of sleep or birth, it was impossible to say.

The brief ceremony was as matter of fact, and practically as painless, as the extractions which his cousin Irwin did half a dozen times a day. Shaved, pressed, and bursting with good health and good spirits, Norm stood at his side; Comrade Hoover, grave, ageless, brown hands folded quietly before him, stood beside Bernice. The gray little man who married them expressed no surprise at the unusual quartet, but went through the official words rapidly and left them to their own devices. It occurred to Sy that Hoover might have done a more impressive job of it.

They stood under the archway of City Hall, blinking out into the hot summer sunlight. Suddenly he realized, like a patient cut from under and probing with his tongue for the missing tooth, that it was over, finished, he was married! He felt giddy and lightheaded, but the others were looking at him worriedly.

"Seymour," Bernie asked, her fingers on his arm, "what is it? Are you all right?"

Hoover, his summer straw once again clamped to his skull, his large eyes heavy-lidded, was surveying him wordlessly. It was Norm who spoke up. "Doesn't marriage agree with you?" He added vulgarly, "You look like the morning after instead of the morning before. There's no blood in you, boy—your face looks like a flophouse bedsheet, all gray and wrinkled. I'm going to have to buy you a drink."

At that everything came loose in him, and he started to laugh. "No, no," he said, "I'm buying! I'm the groom! Bernie, we did it!"

In the Brass Rail, Hoover, hat in his lap, sipped primly at a whisky sour while Bernie drew her Tom Collins happily through a straw. Norm was toasting him, bottoms up, pleased with himself. "Now," he said, "you've got a little color in your cheeks."

"Bernice," Hoover was asking politely, "aren't your parents a little put out at not being here?"

She turned quite red. "I explained to them," she said, as she would have to an inquiring uncle, "that we were just having a civil ceremony, and that since Sy's father couldn't get here . . ."

Hoover turned to him. Relentlessly he demanded, as if he were just now becoming aware of the enormity of the situation, "What about your mother?"

"My mother never believed in the institution of marriage."

"She married your father, didn't she?"

"Only pro-forma."

"Like you just did."

"Not exactly. My folks were bohemian radicals, the way people were in the early days of the Russian Revolution."

Hoover reached back into his mouth for a piece of gristle. "I don't mean to criticize them, but no child of *mine* would get married without me there. Parents let their children run too loose nowadays."

Norm winked at them. "Hoover," he said, "I'm glad you're not my old man."

"Who said I'd want you for a son?" He turned to Bernie. "What's all this about you two hitchhiking to Buffalo?"

"We want to save the bus fare. We'll need the money to live on while we're looking for work."

"You can call me old-fashioned, but the idea of young ladies hitchhiking does *not* please me one bit. I bet your folks don't know about this, do they?"

Again Bernie blushed; she was not good at lying. She glanced helplessly at Sy, but before he could reply Hoover was lecturing again.

"You'd better keep an eye on this girl, Sy. Don't accept rides from drunks or dis*rep*utable characters. Now Bernice, I want to say a word about Buffalo. Harry is trying to do everything at once, and besides, the man isn't an organizer, he's a con*spir*ator. You'd think Buffalo was the *Bal*kans, or Si*ber*ia. As for Bill, he's solid, but he's been busy with his union. Right now he's in San Francisco as an alternate delegate to the UAW convention. They're finally ready to take on Ford. So you're going to have to take charge of literature. That includes *New Labor* and *New Socialist* bundle orders, and all correspondence pertaining thereto."

"If they want me to, you mean."

Hoover's long arm swept downward impatiently in its characteristic scythe-like gesture. "Never *mind* that. You just take over, you hear?"

A little drunk, Sy sat back and surveyed his three companions. Norm was laughing silently in that way he had, his broad powerful shoulders shaking, as if it was all too much for him; their mentor, the granitic organizer, was passing his brown hand across the shining dome of his intimidating skull; between them Bernice, his wife, no longer dressed like a college girl, wearing the little wedding corsage that he had rather timidly offered her, pinned to the shoulder of her new summer dress, sat with hands folded quietly in her lap while she nodded politely to the men around her. Was she thinking the same thing that he was? Tonight would be the last night that they would sleep apart from each other. Tomorrow they would have put everyone behind them, their parents, Norm, Hoover, everyone; and they would be alone together on the road.

At dawn, then, they had their rendezvous. Pockets filled with Hydrox cookies, cheese sandwiches and peaches in a paper sack, they walked across the George Washington Bridge—as Bernice said gaily, "Like kids again, like going on an overnight hike." Except that they carried two heavy valises, filled with their clothes, their Modern Library Giants, their photographs of the folks, and the few wedding gifts tucked in among underthings and sweaters.

By nightfall they found themselves in Geneva, at the border of an innocent blue lake, perhaps halfway to their destination. They were bone-weary from walking, waiting, and jouncing high above the highway in the cabs of diesel trucks.

Slowly they strolled the leafy streets. Here and there the sidewalk heaved angularly, like the deck of a pitching vessel, forced away from the earth by the massively bulging roots of guardian elms, but otherwise the town lay evenly on either hand, its long cool lawns stretching away to the columned porches of leisurely, many-roomed white houses, birthplace and shelter for generation after generation of the quietly secure.

"It's like a picturebook," Bernie whispered. "I didn't know people really lived like this."

"America. Did you think it was all skyscrapers, Grand Concourse, and slums?"

"But it's so beautiful. So stable. Don't you wish you'd grown up here, roller skating, or pushing a box scooter?"

Sy paused to shift the bags from one hand to the other. "Just because there's no dirt, you think there's no misery? Behind every one of those little discreet signs—Tourists, Guests, Visitors—there's a woman sitting by the radio and knitting, waiting for a salesman to drive up and rent the best bedroom. Without the salesmen they wouldn't be able to keep up the fire insurance. They might even have to turn the place back to the bank."

"In your own way," Bernie said, as she touched his cheek, "you romanticize as much as I do."

"How would you like to stay in one of these houses tonight?"

"I'd love it."

"Pick one."

Her eyes shone. "That one." She pointed across the street. "With the blue porch ceiling and the rockers with the cretonne cushions."

"Come on."

He led her across and up to the shallow, freshly painted gray porch steps, avoiding the sprinkler that was flinging a fine spray across the front walk. It was more modest than its colonnaded neighbors—perhaps that was why Bernie had chosen it—but geraniums grew from white-painted pots on either side of the steps, the parlor curtains had been crocheted by hand, and the clapboard glowed with an almost glassy pallor. Sy drew the screen door toward him, and twisted the keylike nipple of the round metal bell in the center of the front door. He felt Bernie's warm uneven breath on the back of his neck.

"It's all right, you know," he said, glancing around at her flushed and expectant face and then at her new wedding band. "We're all legal now." Actually it was his own arms that were trembling a bit, no doubt from carrying their bags.

Then the door opened, and a heavy-breathing elderly woman was peering at them nervously over the top of her spectacles.

"We'd like a room," Sy said. "A nice airy one, if possible."

"Of course." The woman's voice was uncertain and quavery. "I was doing the dishes, generally I hear people pulling up in the driveway . . ."

"We left our car to be greased." He gestured at the valises on the porch. "I didn't want to leave the bags in it."

"I don't blame you, what with the things that go on . . . Won't you come in?"

They stepped into a cool hallway, redolent of roses. Sy said, "Could you tell us what you charge?"

"It just happens that you have your choice this evening, I mean the front or the side bedrooms upstairs. They're all two dollars . . ." She inclined her neck toward them anxiously, as if afraid that these words might cause them to flee. ". . . if that's all right with you?"

"Certainly. If we could just put the bags away and wash up, I'd like to take my wife out to dinner."

"I'm afraid I can't offer you dinner. We eat early . . . I haven't shopped . . . But my sister and I serve breakfast," she added hastily. "It starts the day off right. It's fifty cents extra. For both, I mean. If that's all right—"

"Sounds fine." Sy bent over the hall table to sign the guest book.

"I'll leave the kitchen door open. Would you remember to snap the lock after you? The picture show is next door to the G&R restaurant." She peered at what he had written. "From New York, are you? You don't look like you've been married very long, if you don't mind my saying."

Bernie said tensely, "We haven't."

"It's so nice to be able to travel," she said with open wistfulness, "while you're still young enough to be able to enjoy it. My sister and I were taken to Sweden when we were just girls, children you might say. It was the homeland. But now Christine can't even get downtown on her own what with her arthritis, and we sit and worry how we're going to keep our heads above water."

She would have gone on, but Sy began to fear that Bernie would become so involved that they would wind up rocking with her on the front porch. So, after carrying the bags upstairs to the waxed, crisp, immaculate front bedroom, he led Bernie away from the house and the lonely woman and her invisible sister.

They ate at a diner, counting out their change beneath the formica counter. Then, at Bernie's insistence, although she was drooping with weariness, they walked on through the town. "It's one thing to go roaring through here in a truck. But when will we ever be here again, the way we are now?"

She was too shy to define it further, but they understood each other; if she wanted to put off returning to the upstairs room, that was her right. Finally he led her to a green bench at the north end of Lake Seneca.

There, with the rising moon casting a sheen over water scarcely troubled by late-drifting canoes, with the willows around them waving like whisks languidly sweeping the fringes of the lake, and at the far end the theatrical green-black pines rising into the dark, they half-listened to the little night noises, the moonlight bathers diving and surfacing, and the splashing of the idling boaters. Bernie rested her head on his shoulder.

A few feet away, a couple drove up in a convertible, its radio blaring *Blue Room*. Startled, they arose from the bench by common consent. But before they could leave the news announcer came on and they stopped, bound to the bulletins like true city people. They acknowledged, waiting, the words that returned them to the world beyond the lake.

The voice was adding up, as though recapitulating a ball game, the night's score of Nazi bombers shot down over London, for across the sea the worst of the night was already over and the tally was already being made, the subtraction of downed planes from devastated buildings and those buried alive.

"Mexico City," the voice continued, modulating with pleasant confidence from disaster to tragedy. "Leon Trotsky, exiled Communist chieftain attacked earlier today by a hatchet-wielding assassin, has succumbed to head injuries."

Bernice began to cry. Sy had a sudden hateful vision of his brother, gloating, so delighted by this latest murderous demonstration of the omnipotence of his all-wise leader that he could scarcely maintain the fiction that the dictator was innocent of this most outrageous murder of all.

He thrust his arms roughly about Bernice, feeling her tears and her saliva through his summer shirt, as her parted lips pressed trembling against his breast.

After a time—the young people in the convertible had driven away—Bernie subsided. She leaned back limply, handkerchief to her nose, muttering, "It's too cruel, it's too savage."

"That's the way the world is. The Old Man knew it, even if we didn't."

"You really believe," she said wonderingly, in a tone he had never heard before, "that I don't *know*. I've been sitting here, thinking of my grandfather, my *zayda*. He died long before I met you, I never spoke to you about him." She paused to swallow. In the light filtering through the window, he could see the muscles in her throat working. "I was twelve, I stayed home that summer to keep house for papa while mama was up in the mountains with the baby, the one that died later. The two of us would go up to visit them every weekend.

"It was a terrible, terrible summer. The heat was like some big, slimy animal. At night it crawled over your naked body. The depression was getting bad, people were too tired and sweaty even to argue about what was coming next. My *zayda* used to sit out in front of papa's laundry with a newspaper over his head, saying hello to people, making the customers a little cheerful when they brought their bundles into the hot store. He was so sweet, sometimes he'd have green leaves for me, in a little paper bag. And when he didn't have any, and I'd tease him about it, he'd pull out his leather change purse, as long as a stocking when he unrolled it. He'd unsnap it and fish out new pennies for me.

"One afternoon late in August, I think today is the anniversary, he fell forward off his chair as if he'd been hit on the back of the neck. His forehead struck the sidewalk with a terrible noise, like a hammer against a boulder. But that wasn't what did it, because even though the ambulance came right away, there was nothing they could do. He was already dead.

"Papa had to make all the arrangements. There was no telephone at the farm where mama was staying, we had to send a telegram and she couldn't come back till next day. So I had to clean the house and get it ready for the undertaker and the relatives and the

condolence visitors, while papa was taking care of the business part.
I even baked some cookies, he told me to have stuff to eat for the
company, after the funeral. The kitchen window was open while
I was dropping the chocolate chip cookies on the sheet like mama
had shown me, but it didn't bring a breeze, all it brought was
papa's voice clear down at the end of the block, yelling at the man
from the burial society who was trying to gyp us on our family
plot. I was crying so hard I couldn't see to get the temperature
right on the oven.

"Later, when the undertakers brought *zayda* back and laid him
out in the parlor, they had to pack him in ice on account of the
heat. All night long, while the relatives were in the dining room,
waiting for the funeral, the coffin was dripping and dripping all
over mama's good rug and onto the hardwood floor. And I was on
my hands and knees under the coffin, mopping it up as best as I
could with a sponge and squeezing the sponge out into the toilet
when nobody was in it. All the time, all night, I was crying, partly
for *zayda*, but partly because for the first time I was frightened
of him. I was positive I could hear him moving around in there
over me, trying to get out, while I was underneath on my hands
and knees mopping up the pools of ice water that dripped down
onto the floor like blood, making a stain that would never come out."

At length they arose from the bench and walked slowly back
to the solid clapboard home of the Misses Andersen, on the street
where people were not axed from behind or bombed from the sky
and blasted from their basements, but died peaceably in the beds
in which they had been born. No one was abroad, save for an
elderly gentleman in an old-fashioned summer suit like a tropical
planter's, with a rolled-up newspaper under his arm. He was
whistling thinly, out of tune, an old air, *Turkey in the Straw*
perhaps, but he stopped as he approached them, as if the noise
might give them offense, and tipped his Panama politely in passage.

"I like it here," Bernie said. She added, not defiantly, but with
a kind of sadness, "I don't care what you say."

Sy did not attempt to answer. He was more sick, still, with the
news than he dared admit. Upstairs at last, they moved about in
silence, tacitly taking turns, Bernice first, in the immense old hall
bathroom. When he returned to their room, Sy discovered that his
bride, in a pink nightgown, her bare toes curling beneath it, had
not gone to bed to await him, but was leaning on the windowsill

in the darkened room, her hands cupping her cheeks, staring out through the thicket of maple leaves at the moon slowly riding through the sky. He moved to her side and went to embrace her.

She shuddered, despite the warmth of the evening. Clasping her upper arms with her crossed hands, she turned blindly away from the window and moved over the hooked rug in her bare feet until she had reached the turned-down bed, on which she lay as still as if she had been walking in her sleep.

"It isn't death we're celebrating tonight," Sy whispered. "I feel as though I'm born again. And it's all because of you."

"No, no." She smiled, suddenly. "It's because you brought me here, to this town, this street, this room, this bed." She flung back her arms. "Even the mattress, the pillows, feel just as I dreamt they would. Fresh and sweet and soft."

She raised her body from the bed, then, just enough to lift up her nightgown until it was gathered under her arms. Quickly she pulled it over her head, tossed it to a chair and fell back with a little laugh of pleasure, her hair loose on the pillow. In the uncertain light of the swiftly riding moon her body was incredibly blue-white, rich and opulent as milk carelessly spilled, but touched with pink and in the havened shadows darker and more mysterious than the night.

She extended her arms and he fell forward, feasting on her flesh as her eyes closed and everything else in the world was washed away in the flooding channel of his mind, his heart, his soul.

3. JOE

Stepping out of the hotel into the raw cutting rain of a Pacific
Northwest January, Joe shrank turtlelike into the upraised collar
of his peacoat and buttoned the uppermost flap so that he could
tuck his chin inside. He checked his watch against the clock in the
front window of the Vancouver *Sun,* across the way. Nerves. His
watch was right—he had just made sure in the hotel lobby. And if
it was five minutes off?

All that mattered was that the trusteeship should be framed and
ready. He hadn't enjoyed letting it out of his hands, but it had
occurred to him that the more official it looked the easier things
would be, and so he had taken it to a picture framer. The shop
was only a few blocks, and when he pulled open the front door,
as dusty as the old prints haphazardly displayed in the window,
he was cheered once again by the friendly tinkle of the bell that
swung to and fro over his head as he closed the door behind him.

"Oh, yes," the shopkeeper smiled in the gloom, inclining his
bald head with the courtesy of a scholar who enjoys being disturbed by an acolyte, "it's ready for you, young man." He reached
under the counter and brought forth the document, neatly framed
now in sober black. "Does that suit? Shall I wrap it well, against
the rain?"

Joe thought for a moment. "Suppose you just put it in a paper
bag, could you do that? And could you tell me if there's a
pawnbroker nearby?"

The pawnshop proved to be in the direction in which he was
going anyway, toward the waterfront. He studied its window, the

broken-stringed banjos, tarnished silverware, loving cups, steak knives, wading boots, then strode in decisively.

The pawnbroker, who did not come out from behind his wicket, gazed at him speculatively, then at the paper bag under his arm, as if trying to appraise it even before it should be drawn forth.

"No no," Joe said. "I don't want to pawn anything. I want to buy a thirty-eight."

The proprietor brought his hand to his mouth. "Well," he said slowly, dropping his hand to the counter, "I've got just one Smith & Wesson."

"Let's see it. If the price is right, you've got a sale."

The man unlocked the cabinet behind him with a key on a chain and drew forth a parcel wrapped in flannel. "Kept in nice condition," he said, unwrapping it. "Oiled and everything."

Joe picked up the revolver and broke open the chamber. "No bullets."

"Of course not. Do you think I'd keep a loaded gun—"

"But that's what I want."

"Not here you won't get it. I don't sell live ammunition." The pawnbroker's tone was righteous.

"You afraid somebody might get hurt? What are you selling the gun for—demonstration purposes only?"

"Ammunition can't be sold without a license. My license is a broker's, just for pawning and redeeming merchandise."

The man was a bore. Besides, it was getting late. Joe haggled with him for a while, more because it seemed expected of him than because he really wanted to, and in five minutes he was out of the dismal shop with the gun in the right-hand pocket of his peacoat and the framed charter under his left arm.

He counted off the blocks, turned left, crossed the wet glistening street, hardly glancing up at the second-floor window painted with clasped hands and the circular motto, *SEAFARERS INTERNA-TIONAL UNION*, entered the building, and mounted the stairs. He pushed open the smoked-glass door, also painted with the union emblem, and went on into the main hall. A sailor with a white peaked cap cocked over one eye was sitting alone on a wooden fold-up chair, his feet on another, reading the *Sun*. At the sound of Joe's entrance he rolled a match from one side of his mouth to the other, but said nothing.

"Anybody home?" Joe asked.

The sailor inclined his head toward the rear of the hall, his one earring glinting. Joe followed the direction, walking the length of the hall without haste to another door. This one was unmarked; again he pushed it open without knocking.

Inside, a young man was bending over a chair on which he had placed his right foot; he was polishing and buffing his shoes with considerable care. At the desk to his right two men were seated, playing rummy. A heap of shiny Canadian quarters lay between them; each had his own pile of coins, but they shared a glass ash-tray. They were drinking bottled ale.

The older of the two card players glanced up incuriously. Purple shadows lay around his eyes; his skin was sallow; he looked as though he had trouble with his bile. He said, in a deep, husky voice, "Don't you believe in knocking, sailor?"

Even though it was very wet, Joe did not remove his cap. "My name is Joe Link," he said. "I'm here on the authority of President Lundberg."

The baggy-eyed man turned wary. "You don't say."

"I'm lifting your charter."

The younger one spoke up, his voice reedy and querulous: "You and who else?"

"Harry Lundberg." He tossed the official authorization on top of the playing cards. "By virtue of his constitutional authority, he's putting this Local under trusteeship."

"Quit joking, son."

Joe took three steps to the wall, yanked off the framed charter which hung between the pictures of King George and President Roosevelt, and turned to face them. The sailor with the shoe cloth still bent over his foot, but his mouth hung open. The two card players gazed at him apprisingly. At last the older one arose. His chair squealed.

"You just put that back where you found it. And get the fuck out of the hall before I throw you out."

Joe did not answer. He shook the framed trusteeship from the paper bag under his arm and hung it in the place of the charter. "As of now I'm running this office."

Now both were on their feet. The sallow one jerked his head at the shoe-shining sailor. The three confronted him, closing in step by step.

"Let's come to order." Joe drew his hand from his peacoat and waggled the revolver at them. "Any old business?"

They fell back, startled, almost awed, by the sudden materializing of a weapon. The reedy-voiced card player said nervously, "Say. What the hell is this? You barge in here like some kind of a, I don't know what, a wild man, waving a gun at us like a hold-up man. What's the big idea? If you're from the International, why don't you behave like a union brother?"

"Because I want your books, brother. Because the per capita payments don't jibe with the book members. Because sailors have been beefing to the International that people have been selling books up here."

"We never—"

"From now on the International will decide whether you ever. *Comprende?*"

The second card player said righteously, "That's a fine way to take over, at the point of a gun."

"You didn't give me much choice." Joe waved the pistol at the telephone on the desk. "You want to call the police? Help yourself."

The sallow man reached out to the desk, but instead of picking up the phone he pulled a Life Saver from a roll that lay among the scattered cards and popped it into his mouth. Chewing hard, he said, "How long is this here going to go on?"

"As far as I'm concerned? Until every single sailor on the beach gets to ship out of this port in his proper rotation, without paying ice. Until the ordinaries are issued trip cards without having to pay under the table. And until the membership elects some new officers. But it's going to be up to the International—I'm only serving as trustee."

"For Christ's sakes," the man burst out in honest frustration, "you don't hardly look old enough to vote. Let alone be a trustee. I'm going to call Harry. I'm going to see what's behind all this."

"Not on this phone. From now on, spend your own money on long-distance calls."

"And I'm going to call a meeting of the book members. Then we'll see—"

"Go right ahead. But I'm chairing all meetings from now on. And I'm appointing the sergeants-at-arms. And I'm changing the locks on the doors. Now take your cards and beat it. I've got work to do."

The two crammed the pockets of their raincoats with their quarters and their cigarettes. The younger man, last one out, eyed him curiously over his shoulder as he closed the door on them. Joe sat down heavily behind the desk and let out his breath. His hands were shaking. "Jesus," he said softly. "I did it."

He began going through desk and cabinet drawers methodically, taking inventory, making a list of what he had been told to look for and find. When he had everything before him, he dragged over the rickety typewriter on its rusting stand and began to type out a letter to the International, pausing only to ring up a locksmith. Beyond the windows it had grown quite dark; he had to reach up and snap the chain of the fluorescent tube.

He worked steadily. When he felt that he had done sufficient for the day, he switched off the light and stuffed the essential records into the brown paper bag that still lay on the floor beneath the framed authorization on the wall. The sailor who had been reading the paper was long since gone; empty, the room looked like a rehearsal hall, waiting for human voices, laughter, the sound of pounding feet. Joe shrugged into his pea jacket, tugged at his cap, slammed the door behind him, and hurried down the stairs to the drying street, sudden hunger gnawing at him.

On the off chance that mail might have followed him, he stopped in at the main post office and was rewarded. Nothing from his mother, but a letter from Buffalo, from *Box 45 Gen'l Deliv,* which could only be Sy. Warmed, he thrust it into his pocket, next to the slick steel of the thirty-eight, and doubled back to a restaurant in Chinatown.

He took a seat in a booth facing the front door, hung his peacoat on the hook behind his head, and persuaded himself not to open the letter until the waiter had brought both soup and tea. It was a thick letter, written small on folded-up sheets of ruled paper, and he was deep in it, fist on his forehead, when a shadow fell across his plate.

He looked up. It was not the waiter, but the shoe shiner, the sailor, who had left the SIU office with the two goons. Cursing his carelessness, he measured the distance from his hand, with nothing in it but a soup spoon, to the unguarded pocket of his peacoat, but hesitated as his eyes met those of the young sailor.

"Relax. I just want to talk."

Joe wondered if his relief was mirrored in his face. "Take a load off your feet." He folded Sy's letter and stuffed it into the breast pocket of his denim shirt. "Want some tea?"

"I just ate. I was walking by, and I spotted you through the window, reading your mail. What'd you say your name was?"

"Joe Link. Out of San Pedro."

"Call me Pete. I don't know if you realize who you tangled with this afternoon."

"I know their names."

"They happen to be two of the toughest characters on the front."

Joe put down his spoon and stared into Pete's rather watery blue eyes. "How tough are you? Do you shine their shoes, or just your own?"

Pete did not stop smiling, but he wiped at the corner of one eye with a finger suddenly rigid and accusing. "There's not many guys I'd take that from. You got a hell of a lot of nerve for a guy your age."

Joe bent to his soup again without answering.

"I been saying to myself, How come? What's in it for him?"

"You tell me first," Joe said, "who sent you to talk to me."

"Nobody."

"What about your buddies, the card players?"

"You mean, up at the hall? That's easy. The one with the big circles under his eyes is my uncle. He got me on as a workaway, he fixed up my papers. I sail as an oiler, I'm on the Alaska run, lots of overtime. What would you do if you was me, spit in his eye just because he runs the union like a family business?"

"You don't see anything wrong in that? How about the sailors that haven't got any uncles?"

"You're lucky my uncle didn't throw a chair at you. Don't tell me you're some kind of Boy Scout, going for merit badges. Boy Scouts don't carry guns. Are you going to tell me what's in it for you, or do I go on back to Uncle Wally?"

It really was time to talk. Even as he began, elbows on the table, leaning forward and fixing Pete with his eyes, Joe could feel that little thrill that came whenever he started to talk union, to talk politics. Nothing could touch it, making somebody see things your way, especially when you knew that from the long view it was incalculable, like starting an avalanche by pulling out one stone that had jammed up others behind it. It was never just one man—or if it was, that one man was a social force, as important to reach as any mindless crowd.

They sat in the restaurant until nine-thirty. Then they walked, Pete showing him parts of the city he would never have gotten to know otherwise. Like many young men who pride themselves on their cynicism, at bottom Pete was searching for something in which to believe. Because he had been deeply impressed by Joe's coolness, he was ready to concede that it was not simple greed or strongarm tactics that had animated him, but a disinterested desire for justice that was both puzzling and exciting. By the end of the evening Joe was certain that, at minimum, Pete would not betray him. How much more he could expect would depend on other factors, some beyond his control—how well would those watery eyes stare down the uncle? It was well after one when Pete dropped him at his hotel.

By the weak light of the rusty old floor lamp, the only one in the room, he reread Sy's letter. The club (the term Sy habitually used for the New Party) was pleased with the speed with which Joe had established himself in the SIU, but cautioned against his getting separated from the ranks; Hoover would be in touch. As for Sy himself, he had gotten an assembly line job with no difficulty, in an unorganized aircraft plant; Bernie was working part time too, the city was ripe, the CIO was growing fast, the Buffalo branch of the club was firmly established, but based unfortunately on middle-class people like Fred (last name not given), a dynamic English teacher at the university. Harry, their organizer, was very effective with people like Fred, less so with workers. Dynamic but neurotic, was the way Sy described him, completely uninterested in girls except as possible converts. Despite her good looks, he paid no attention to his landlord's daughter, a very intelligent girl named Anne Schuyler, a beginning piano teacher with serious aspirations. "Reason I mention her is that she is now in Vancouver, consoling her aunt, a widow, who just lost her only child in action in the Canadian Navy. The family was worried about her, so Anne went out to stay with her: Mrs. Leslie Renfrew, the Ferns, Lagrange, Victoria, B.C. until the worst wears off." The implication seemed to be that he would do a number of people a favor—perhaps himself as well—if he looked her up.

He turned off the floor lamp and fell asleep almost at once.

At seven he awoke refreshed and eager. He copied the Schuyler girl's address into his memo book, and by seven-thirty was at the union hall, to claim the mail and supervise the changing of the locks. It was good to see the expressions on the men's faces as they came in to have their books stamped and got official receipts. Lundberg didn't have wings, true; nevertheless he had sent Joe up here because he saw in him not only a nervy kid but a trustworthy radical. Lundberg could dump him as quickly as he had picked him up—Joe didn't need Sy to tell him that—but in the meantime the union leader was giving him the opportunity to talk to all the Petes, on the beach as well as aboard ship.

It pleased him when Pete dropped in, toward noon, elaborately aimless, and asked very casually, "You going out for lunch?"

Settled down in a sailor's hangout with sandwiches and mugs of hot coffee, he was more direct. "My uncle's hiring a lawyer."

"Better than if he tried to break down the door. He hasn't got a leg to stand on."

"I'm not bleeding for him. I just thought I'd keep you posted."

"What do you say to giving me a hand around the office until you ship out?"

"You mean it?" What he meant, it was clear, was, Do you trust me?

"I'm no office worker, I'll drown in all this paper work unless I get some help."

"My uncle might think I was doing it to help *him*."

"Let him. I've got no secrets, Pete. All I want is to run a clean hall until I get the word to clear out."

Two days later, ready to test the boy, Joe turned over the office to Pete and took off for the island ferry, across the Georgia Strait to Victoria.

He had felt that it would be simpler to take a chance on the girl's being in than to phone ahead. At worst, he would have a sailor's holiday, a long ferry ride. But after he had disembarked at the pier below the great ivy-covered pile of the Empress Hotel and stopped for a bite of lunch, he began to wonder if he might not have done better to make some formal arrangement, perhaps for her to meet him in Vancouver. The provincial capital was not to his taste: its formal prettiness, its green, green lawns and shrubs, everything raked and tended, its fake Tudor and secondhand Victorian homes fenced off with clipped hedges, were all too like the desperately pretentious suburbs of Sydney and Brisbane where a few months earlier he had tried to make some sense of the phony formality with which the provincial strivers had copied, from a world away, English county towns that had never been theirs.

He had been far more at home in the Australian and Canadian pubs, with the men who stood up at the bar arguing politics and asserting no matter how profanely or primitively their class interests, fighting over the future instead of fawning over the past like those who built museum-houses in memory of an England that no longer even existed.

Then why was he proceeding up the walk of this terribly English terribly middle-class villa? Partly from politeness, but more from loneliness. Rationally he had scorned the middle-class, but some part of him yearned for everything that went with it—the pots of ivy, stucco, flagstones, girls in sweater sets, phonograph albums of operatic arias, baby grand pianos in bay windows . . .

He was so absorbed in these rueful reflections, and with the nagging uncertainty of how deep his radicalism really went despite his having become, once and for all, a workingman, that he hardly heard the music until he was reaching for the knocker.

He peered through the bay window to his right. A straight-backed, very fair girl was seated at the piano, in profile so that he could observe the precise attack of her large hands as she went on with the Schubert. He withdrew his fingers from the knocker. It was an Impromptu, but which? His heart beating as he listened, he discarded the early three; it was one of those from the Opus 142. And so well played that it wrung his heart, bringing to him in an instant what he had been scarcely aware of having missed in bleak union halls and aboard sloppy rustbuckets crawling back and forth across the Pacific.

When the girl had finished she bowed her head over the piano as if acknowledging applause, or herself rendering homage. Her straight blond hair fell forward like a shawl, almost concealing her face. He lifted the knocker and let it fall.

Startled, she arose and then disappeared as she crossed to the front hall. When she opened the door her lightly freckled face was quizzical. She surveyed his white cap and peacoat with frank curiosity.

Before she could say anything he introduced himself, removing his cap. "You're Anne Schuyler. My name is Joe Link."

She laughed. "Should I know you?"

"No, but you will. We have mutual friends. The Vogels of Buffalo—"

"Are you from Buffalo?"

"No. My friend Sy settled there not too long ago, and he wrote me—"

"I know Sy, and his wife Bernice. Come on in, won't you?" She took him by the hand unaffectedly and drew him through the front hall into the room where she had been playing. The furniture was covered with sheets, and two barrels of books stood in the middle of the bare floor. "Aunt Flora!" She called out to a woman bending over in a darkened corner not visible to Joe from the walk. "We have a guest, a friend of friends from Buffalo. Mr. Link, my aunt, Mrs. Renfrew."

"I was eavesdropping," Joe said as he shook hands with the older woman, who was closer to sixty than to fifty, entirely in black, and ravaged looking. "It's been a long time since I've heard that Schubert. It's Opus 142, I know that, but I just couldn't place which one."

"The second. You must play too."

"I gave it up in high school for basketball. In my part of Los Angeles, basketball was more manly than piano."

"Anne has been giving me great pleasure, Mr. Lincoln," her aunt said. "She's been playing for me every day."

"Not playing, Aunt Flora. Just practicing."

"Isn't she modest? Mr. Lincoln, you must have some lunch."

"Thanks, I've eaten."

"Then tea. Just sit here with my niece while I bring things in. It won't take long, in spite of the mess. Anne is helping me move up to Vancouver in a day or so—I'm taking a war job there."

"I'd help her," Anne explained when her aunt had gone, "but it gives her something to do. I think it's marvelous, that she's going to work in Vancouver. She's been in a bad way. She lost her husband in the first war, before they'd been married very long. He left her with a little boy whom she raised by herself—that's the one that was torpedoed recently, leaving her absolutely alone."

"It's very decent of you to come all this way to help her out."

"Not as decent as you might think." She looked at him candidly. "I was very damn reluctant. I'm not all that crazy about Buffalo, but I was just starting to get students and I couldn't see . . . Well, here I am. At least I'm a voice in the house. When she doesn't need me, I go for long walks. It's a different world for me."

"How about my coming along on some of those long walks?"

Without hesitation she said, "I'd love that. Except that I'll be in Vancouver."

"So will I."

Her breast rose. "Do you live there? Or what?"

"I just got to Vancouver, on union business. I'll be there a while, a few weeks maybe. How about you?"

"That long too. Depending on whether Aunt Flora can settle into the other atmosphere comfortably." She was not looking at him now, but at her long fingers, ringless and tapering, twined quietly in her lap. They had established something; he could still feel the warmth of those fingers that had drawn him into the living room. By the time her aunt returned they were talking quietly, as though they had known each other for a long time.

Anne's aunt was pathetically eager for him to stay. "There's no ferry back to Vancouver before morning. I won't hear of your stopping elsewhere than here, after such a trip."

Something beyond hospitality, a kind of yearning anxiety, made him uneasily resistant to her appeal for him to take over, if only temporarily, the role of her dead sailor son. He temporized: "I'll visit you both after you've moved to Vancouver."

Once back in his Vancouver hotel room, he took the gun from the drawer where it lay next to Sy's letter, went out to the street, and dropped it in a trash can in a deserted alley. Then he hastened to the nearest phone booth and telephoned Anne.

"I want to see you again as soon as you've moved," he said. "Will you call me up if I give you the office number?"

"Of course."

Her simple directness made him lightheaded. He felt airborne. He said abruptly, "Something happened when we met."

"I know."

"Even before we met. While I was standing outside listening to you."

"Joe." She spoke more deliberately now. "You're very lonely."

"I didn't know it showed. But then so are you."

"All the more reason for us not to be rash."

"I'm a believer in spontaneity. We'll talk about it at great length."

Her laugh, high and clear, as musical as her playing, sustained him for the day.

By afternoon he had almost forgotten the absurdity of his own histrionics.

In the days that followed, he and Anne walked for miles through the mists and soft rains of the northwest country that was rapidly becoming a part of them, of the couple that they were becoming. When the weather was too bad, they were forced indoors, occasionally to a movie. They stood in line for *Fantasia*—he liked it, she thought it was vulgar. They talked endlessly.

"Tell me what it's like," she demanded, "going to sea."

For the first time, he was able to explain, as he had not been in his letters to his mother or even to Sy—the lust it aroused in you for traveling to new places, the blue monotony of chipping paint or standing watch in an endless sea, seemingly lost in time and space, and the talk, the talk, the talk, sailors' substitute for sex, liquor, and the daily trials of shoreside life.

Anne listened more than she talked. "For me," she said, "playing the piano is a form of conversation. I'm not too good at the other kind. If you want, you can take that as a confession."

"I'm grateful to you for having that much trust in me."

"But you've got what I don't. You're a fantastic talker. I think you could sell anything to anybody."

"There are principles, yes, that I want to sell very hard, I make no bones about that. One thing I like about you is the way that you listen."

But she hadn't meant quite what he thought. She paused—they were strolling among the thousand year old Douglas firs in Stanley Park—and confronted him. "I begin to get the feeling that for you talk is a way of making love. Maybe even a substitute."

Her face was half-shadowed by the giant trees. But then she lifted her head and the sun struck through the needles, lighting her deep brilliant eyes. As he reached for her she seemed to topple as though she had been felled. He had to catch her as he kissed her; her mouth opened as if to cry out, not just to kiss, and she clutched his thatch of hair like a drowning soul, despairing, trying to pull him down with her, or perhaps to save herself. She was tall, very nearly his height; there was more of her, he felt, half-swooning in the sunlit glade, lost among the giant trees, than he could possibly have imagined.

Gasping, they broke free.

"Not a substitute," he said, after he saw that she did not intend to say anything more. "A way of making love, yes. I thought you'd sense that from the start."

"It makes me uneasy. Can you blame me? I'd have felt safer if you'd just dragged me up to your hotel room." She twisted about desperately. "What do you want out of me?"

"Everything."

"All that talk about seafaring, labor, Marxism. What's it got to do with me?"

"Don't you know?"

"I don't want to know. You're so young. I'm going back to Buffalo. You're going back to California, and to all those girls in Sydney and Auckland and Honolulu. Why didn't you just try to make me and let it go at that? It wouldn't have been hard, but I'd have made it seem that way, to please you. Do you want me to sit in Buffalo and mope for you, is that what it takes to satisfy you?"

"I wanted to make you fall in love with me."

"Well, you've done that already," she said angrily. Her eyes were filled with tears. "That was easy, you didn't even have to exert yourself. Now I intend to get over it."

"But why? Don't you *like* me?" He felt like a child asking his teacher if he had a chance for the Honor Roll. "I wanted that first of all."

"You caught me at a susceptible time."

"It would have happened to us at any time. I'm committed, to my politics and to you. And in both cases it's for good."

She stared at him. "I think maybe you're crazy. You're such a romantic! And I don't know anything about your politics. All I know is a little music."

"And a little love."

"Yes, yes, if you insist. But I ought to try to get over that."

"I won't let you."

"How are you going to stop me from shopping around for someone who talks less and stays home more?"

"I'm going to write you long passionate fascinating letters. And then one day I'm going to turn up. Buffalo isn't nearly as far as some of the cities I've already been to. Now do you understand me a little better?"

In the last days of their stay in British Columbia, Joe was encouraged to believe that in fact she did. At least, once he had told her of Uncle Jerry and his incoherent progressivism, and of his mother and her lonely struggle to make a home for him and poor Pauline, Anne found it possible for the first time to talk to him about her mother, about music school and the dream of concertizing, even about a failed love affair. And her questions to him became not simply polite but pressing. What did he really want? Was he honestly satisfied to serve as strong-arm man for a squarehead union boss? Didn't it bother him, to have given up college in exchange for a life that by his own confession was a mixture of monotony and mindlessness?

"Monotony," he said, "even loneliness, is a small price to pay for what I'm learning about the working class. And from them. I believe with all my heart that there is no way out for any of us without a revolution led by the workers. Without them we're nothing. If I survive the war that we'll soon be in, I don't want to settle for my little groove, my little job, my little house. I want to be a part of history, I want to make history."

It was hard for him to tell whether Anne was digesting this, or simply rejecting it; and he did not want to ask her. Above all, he did not want her to try merely to please or placate him.

"As for college, at the end it meant something to me only because I was involved in the student movement. As long as it had possibilities it held me—once they were through, I was. At its peak, the American Student Union had fifteen thousand members. Right after the Nazi-Soviet pact the ASU collapsed, went down to less than two thousand, like letting the air out of a tire. Finished just when I was getting started. But the labor movement! The UAW is organizing Ford, the SWOC is organizing Little Steel, they need people like me. I'm desperate to learn, at sea I read all the time, but I want to teach while I'm learning. I get less from a professor at a blackboard than from a worker at the point of production. That's the great value of Marxism—things fall into place."

Not for her, that was too much to ask. What he hoped for was her respect. He tried in every way. He took her to see the new Chaplin film, *The Great Dictator,* and he asked her whether she thought Hitler could be treated as a figure of fun. She was reading *For Whom the Bell Tolls,* so he gave her the New Party's pamphlets about the Stalinist sellout in Spain. She asked him about his girls in Hawaii, New Caledonia, New Zealand, and he talked instead about the Australian radicals he'd met and the way they'd called him matey (pronouncing it mighty, which made him feel like a killer) and argued with him over so much steaming tea that he feared his kidneys would burst.

"Did you ever see those movies of the German and Russian

soldiers in the first war, fraternizing between their trenches at Christmas in no man's land, hugging each other and weeping? They were learning that it was their officers and their rulers who were the real enemy. When you go to sea you learn the meaning of international solidarity, if nothing else."

"What you're saying is that travel is broadening."

"Damn it, no. Or anyway, I'm saying more. Several months ago I was in a grogshop in Honolulu with two of my shipmates. We got into a discussion with a group of Negro messmen at the next table, potwallopers on a battleship tied up at Pearl Harbor. They were bitter at being deprived of any opportunity to learn a trade, like the white enlisted men.

"I said, Don't just bitch. Organize. My own shipmates, including one cracker who couldn't see sleeping with nigras in the fo'c's'l, pitched in. They told them from their own lives what misery seafaring used to be before the union, how much stronger ten men were, even under naval discipline, than one man begging like a puppy dog for table scraps. It worked both ways, do you see? Not only on those Negro messmen, but on my shipmates as well. They all saw that they had more in common with each other than with their officers or with racism."

"But what did you achieve?"

"How do you know, when you plant a seed? At the end of that afternoon in the Tropical Bar the future wasn't the same for any of us there—and what's more, none of us could have been a worse human being when we broke up than when we began. Incidentally," he added, "do you know who came over from that bar to join in the discussion? Sy's brother Sid, with some of his shipmates, off an NMU ship. He didn't identify himself, but I knew right away who he was."

"I never knew he had a brother."

"He's a little older than Sy, a little heavier, and his right arm was chewed up by a German dum-dum bullet in Spain. As soon as I noticed his arm and heard his line, I knew who he was." He laughed briefly. "I've got enough trouble with reactionaries without messing with Communists, so I never did bother to introduce myself. Now here's the point of the story, to really answer your question. A little while ago the Navy, I doubt that you noticed it in the newspaper, threw out thirteen messmen for organizing a protest against Jim Crow. They didn't list the names or say who or where, but isn't it more possible that some of them were the guys I was talking to in that Honolulu bar?"

"It's also possible that now they're more miserable than ever, unemployable, with dishonorable discharges."

He stared at her, uncomprehending. "Wouldn't you want them to have fought for their rights?"

"I can't be so cavalier about other people's lives."

So she resisted. She was fascinated, yes; but, he feared, more by him than by what he believed in. Tossing alone on his hotel bed, he thought wryly that he was in the position of the middle-class maiden who wants to be loved not just for her body but for her mind as well. Still he was determined that she must consider the depth of his commitment as something in its way parallel to the depth of his love.

They went walking in the park, beyond the great totems and on into the woods, along a footpath high above the Capilano River. Holding hands, they inhaled the pungent aroma of the pines which by now he had come to associate so intensely with Anne Schuyler that it seemed to flow like an emanation from her fingertips to his own. He had the feeling that forever thereafter it would be her own perfume for him, or some secret scent that her body exuded.

"I have to leave tomorrow," he said. "I'm glad I'm the one that's leaving first. Walking here alone and thinking of you back east in the snow wouldn't appeal to me."

"I'll be there soon enough." She added grimly, and somewhat tartly, "At least when I leave it'll be my decision, and not because somebody else is pulling the strings."

Stung, he demanded, "What do you mean? My job is done here, that's all. Now I have to ship out within the next two weeks."

"I'm sorry." She faced him, the freckles high on her cheeks and across the saddle of her nose darkening as her color rose. "What it comes down to is that you're going to keep on going to sea." Was that what ate at her? Was she still mourning the Canadian cousin she had hardly known?

"Despite all the fun I've had out of it—despite the fact that it liberated me from white shirts and Saturday nights—I don't want to spend my life at it. Partly because of you, partly because seafaring is too marginal. I don't want to be on the fringes of the labor movement, I want to be in the heart of it. But that's not for me to decide on my own. It's for the Party to say."

"I see," she said coldly. "I'm touched that I enter into it."

"You're going to have to understand about the Party. It's important—"

"For me to understand you. I know. But what I'm trying to understand is myself. Not you. I'm trying to figure out how I ever let myself in for this."

"I knocked at the door. It was my fault. Now listen. Never mind the doctrine, or what differentiates us from the Communists or the Socialists or whoever. What matters to me is that thanks to the Party I'm more of a man. Whenever you're away from the piano for a day, two days, you're miserable, aren't you? Because you've submitted yourself to the discipline of daily practice."

"Because I *want* to."

"Exactly. Because you understand that the road to mastery is submission to discipline. When you lose yourself in the music, you've gained something. The piano is your instrument, the New Party is mine. So when it suggests where I ought to go or what I ought to do, I listen—even though it's still so small that no one else can hear it. That's something I want to change too."

"In other words you're just another soldier."

"No more than Sy and Bernie. They went to Buffalo for the same reason that I'm going back to sea. The people who give us the assignments are the ones we've picked to be our leaders. That doesn't diminish me. I'm more than just Joe Link, I'm acting out history. If there wasn't a Party I'd have to invent one."

"Oh, you're so so persuasive!" she cried angrily. "You're so sure of yourself!"

He was winning, he knew it—her scorn was not for him but for herself—if only he could control his tongue and remain silent.

"How I'd love to hear you admit, just once, that you don't know all the answers! Maybe I haven't read the books you have, or had the experiences you have. All I ever did was practice and go to the conservatory. But I'm older than you are, don't forget that."

"Eleven months, isn't it?"

"To me you're a child. I've gone out with men thirty, thirty-five years old. Married, some of them were, too. And I've been in love." She was glaring at him, her breath frosting in little vanishing puffs, her hands clasped as if she were singing rather than speaking. "Well?" she demanded. "Have you?"

"Not really. Not until now." He added stubbornly, "But I always knew I'd be ready for it when it happened."

"Ready for what?"

"Ready to be a lover. Or a husband. For me finding the right girl was like finding the right cause. Worth living for, worth dying for." He felt himself flushing. "This is the only thing that's hard for me to talk about. To explain to you why it's you that I love."

"Oh my God," she groaned, "what have I let myself in for?"

The tall, poised, cool girl was weeping in his arms, her cheek hot against his neck. They clasped each other, alone together on the Capilano suspension bridge, swaying as if in terror of the frail structure and the chasm directly below.

"For me," he said, stroking her hair. "For me. And every time I think of you until we're together again, it will be like this, with the green water down there and the pine needles underfoot and that smell, as if it was Christmas morning and we were children on our knees under the tree. You're the most beautiful Christmas present I've ever gotten."

She arched her neck so that she could look him in the eyes while he continued to hold her. Her lips were pressed tightly together, but she was trying to smile.

"You're going to give me a hard life, aren't you, Joe?"

"I'm afraid I am. But I promise you one thing: you'll never be bored."

4. NORM

"Cold?" the fat man in the ripped plaid lumberjacket repeated, as if personally offended. "Cold? This ain't nothing compared to the 1919 strike. That winter was colder than a witch's tit. You young guys, you're always bitching. It's practically spring, for God's sake."

When Norm laughed he could feel the skin stretch across his face. Inside his sweat socks and steel-toed work shoes his feet were turning numb. Fortunately the picket line kept moving, even if slowly, so that he could stomp with every step, and at each turning, before it curved around to cross the entrance gates of the steel plant, he snatched a quick delicious moment at the fire blazing away in a trash barrel, fed from time to time with barrel staves and lashings of kerosene.

The street lights were weak, as if with the banking of the mill's fires the city of Lackawanna had run out of money or power, or wanted to dim the bitter scene. The only real illumination (aside from the flame leaping from the can at the corner) came from the pale floodlights of the mill itself, almost a hundred yards back from the gates—and at that, they were only maintenance lights, kept on for the convenience of skeleton crew and supervisors. There was no moon. Even the stars were obscured by the smoky haze that still hung over Lackawanna despite the fact that Little Steel was quite closed down. In this all but total darkness, with the shadows jumping to life only as the bundled picketers paused and then reluctantly passed the infernally tempting flames, their low chants and white mingling breaths disappearing quickly into the night air like fluid poured into a dark bottle, the scene was at once ominous and somberly impressive.

How else could it appear to a supervisor gazing out on his men gone wayward and meanly intractable, like rebellious children inexplicably and frighteningly out of hand, refusing to respond to promises or threats? For Norm it was pure pleasure. Even the 10-degree cold was inspiriting, fresh as the frost that had caught at his lungs when he had dug his cleats into the frozen turf, getting away fast, the distant roar whipping past his ears as he charged ahead under the spiralling football, knees pumping, chest hurting, charging the receiver to hurl him to the ground. Best of all was the certainty even as it all began that you were not going to lose. It made bearable the funereal pace of the line of march, the dismalness of the scene, the absence of cheering spectators. The enemy were going down, and they knew it.

But, of the fourteen thousand men who had walked out of Bethlehem early this morning, exactly one belonged to the New Party; all who had so much as heard of its program could meet comfortably in the tavern across the way; while those who had been influenced by it could get together in the phone booth at the back of the tavern. The workers were on the march, but toward what front? and under whose leadership, when they had won this skirmish? If we had twenty people in steel, he thought, even ten . . . but the party had decided, probably wisely, to concentrate in new industry, where hiring was open, and there were greater possibilities in unions like the UAW. Later on they would have to try to reach the militants in steel.

In the meantime, he was not supposed to be identified with the New Party. It had assigned him to what radicals called opposition work, which meant trying to win over, after having let himself be supposedly won over, by those already affiliated with other radical groups. It was not to his taste, but it had been the only condition on which they had allowed him to leave New York. Sy and Bill walked the picket line only fifty feet ahead of him, representing their respective UAW locals, wearing their dues buttons on their caps, and serving as emissaries not from the socialist movement, but from other workers who had either succeeded in or were attempting to organize aircraft workers.

And Harry, Comrade Drang, was standing off across the street, his steaming pipe clenched between his teeth, clapping his gloved hands from time to time to bring back the circulation. He knew that it was Norm's job to write up the strike for *New Labor;* he was simply taking notes on his own. He intended to present an analysis of Little Steel to the Political Committee of the Party, in the form of an article in the Discussion Bulletin. Deep in the English tweed overcoat he had bought in Canada, its collar turned up against his ears, his eyes popping, he seemed remote from the conflict. Still, his stamina was admirable. He had already worked all day in the lab at Niagara Falls, gone home to feed his father, run out to teach his college course—by the time he pushed aside his typewriter he'd be able to snatch only a couple of hours' sleep before crawling out for the hour's drive to the chemical plant.

Suddenly the fat man directly in front of Norm began to shout hoarsely. Waving his arm, the torn fabric of his lumberjacket flapping like the wing of a crow, he called to a dark figure on the other side of the galvanized wire fence, silhouetted under the lights like a figure on a stage, or in a dream.

"Hey, Stosh! I see you, you bastard! Don't think I don't see you!" He turned to Norm, stung by a kind of happy fury, his broad peasant's face red with rage and cold. "I know the son of a bitch. Twenty years I know him." Then he bellowed, a bull ready to charge the fence, "Nineteen nineteen you lost your leg, watch out you don't lose the other one now!"

The figure at whom the shout was directed raised his clenched fist in an obscene gesture, then hobbled off to the shelter of the guards' shed. Under its bare bulb he hesitated bleakly, an Ahab in navy peacoat and knitted watch cap, then stumbled away into the obscurity of the night, the peg below his stump grating on the cinders with awful clarity.

"Nineteen nineteen he lost his leg, the dirty scab," the fat man cried out, not to Norm but seemingly to the world in general. "Let him come out here, we'll get rid of the other one this time!"

Norm shivered. He was about to question the striker when they were both caught in the blinding headlamps of a car bearing down on them from out of the blackness. In the instant before impact, it struck him that the sedan must have reached the gate with its lights off, waved on perhaps by the one-legged man and his allies on the wrong side of the plant entrance. But there was no time to think, the car was between them like a steel wedge, a metal ram aimed by its tight-lipped driver at the mill beyond the newly opened gates.

"Ayee!" the fat man screamed in a sudden soprano yelp, like a trod-on dog. He went down, out of sight, as the car rolled forward, then stopped, halted by a reformed wall of strikers' bodies.

The pickets surged forward, Norm in their midst, and began to rock the car rhythmically from side to side, slowly at first, then more rapidly, pressing against the heavy mass of the huddled men trapped within. A police whistle blew, long, high, hysteric. On the other side of the muddy, frosted vehicle pickets were carrying off the fat man, his leg dragging. With the right side of the car unblocked, its occupants scrambled out in terror and ran off, this way, that, followed by a clot of strikebreakers from another car stalled behind it, leaving its door dangling, running awkwardly in their bulky overcoats, lunch pails banging, sandwiches spilling to the sidewalk, desperately seeking sanctuary.

Norm took off after them, legs pumping, thighs icy against his whistling corduroy pants, tearing off the cardboard placard from his picket sign as he ran. Without breaking stride, he rounded the corner behind the bar, and after one block was running down a street of company houses, before an endless row of spindly wooden porches that dwindled miserably into the night like some dread imagining of Charles Burchfield. One glance over his shoulder assured him that the police, swinging their nightsticks to free the cars, had not followed the strikebreakers.

He was gaining on the most laggard of them. At the first intersection he fell upon the scab as he stumbled over the curbing. They tumbled to the gutter and rolled across a clump of frozen horse droppings, a memento of the morning milk wagon. Frightened, gasping, his nose running, the fleeing man swung out ineffectually, and at last managed to push himself erect. He sheltered his head in his arms to protect it from the blows of Norm's stick.

"Stay away from the mill." Norm flailed him about the shoulders, not viciously, but swinging back and forth as though he were beating a carpet. "Don't come back till it's over. Don't take the bread out of other people's mouths."

The man sobbed something in a strange language. Disconcerted, suddenly embarrassed, Norm sent him on his way with a not unfriendly push and made for the one he really wanted, the driver, who had slipped on a patch of ice and was retrieving his ear-lapped cap from where it had fallen.

He was a big-bellied man, moving uncertainly onto the sidewalk and then into the shadows of one of the row houses. Norm found him cowering there, pressed against the peeling clapboards.

"Don't hit!" he pleaded, gloved hands before his face.

Norm tapped the stick against the exposed belly; when the driver lowered his guard, he cuffed him lightly. "What do you mean, don't hit? You could have killed us. Supposing I took you to the station-house and had them book you for assault?"

"We was just trying to get to work."

"Through a picket line? You broke the old man's leg—I ought to break yours."

"I won't go back."

"You better not. I find you there, I'll break you in half."

"I promise, mister."

Norm shrank back from the older man's fear. How could you hate when you were confronted first with an uncomprehending foreigner, then with someone older, defenseless before your youth and your strength? "Oh Christ," he said. "Go on home and stay there until it's over."

He flung down the stick and turned back to the mill gate.

Two nights later, the strike already over and won so quickly that even the local leadership was hardly prepared for it, Norm went up to Harry's. Old man Sturm had retired, you could hear the radio playing in his bedroom, and Harry was padding around in his stockinged feet, his hair standing on end, an Oom Paul pipe hanging all the way down to his collarbone, putting up a pot of coffee for the two of them.

"A bit more comfortable here than in Lackawanna, eh?" His bulbous eyes glowed innocently. "Those picket lines can be power-fully cold."

"I enjoyed the exercise."

"With a weapon?"

"I could've gotten hurt without it."

"You also could have gotten arrested for assault. That wouldn't have done anyone any good."

Norm was tempted to observe that standing on a far corner didn't do much good either; but he restrained himself. "You have to take your chances sometimes. It was important to discourage the scabs from thinking they could crack the picket line. My picket captain was pleased, I'll tell you."

Mollified, Harry poured coffee.

Norm yawned. "I was up till 4 A.M. knocking out a piece for *New Labor*. I sent it off with a great cartoon by Vito. What a find he was!"

Harry smiled complacently. "Finding him was simple—the trick was to re-educate him. He's a goodhearted chap, but politically primitive. And I think he prefers to spend his time on those meaningless paintings."

"Maybe he's a genius, who knows? His cartoons are even more brilliant than my articles. So what difference does it make if he spends more time in his studio screwing than painting?"

Harry looked disapproving, and even more so when Norm went on, "What about you? Haven't you set up a soviet at Electrochemical yet?"

Harry smiled a bit mechanically, just enough to show that he could take a joke. "I have more than enough to keep me busy."

"I'm sure."

"I did consult with the NC about whether to involve myself with that Stalinist technicians' union. They agreed that it's a hopeless task and that I'd do better to consolidate my professional position, to hold on to the draft deferment. Then I have to continue with my teaching. And there go three evenings."

"Of course."

"Somehow, in addition to our branch meetings, preparing educationals, and sending reports to the NC, I have to squeeze in my theoretical work—to say nothing of the parallel organization, about which I needn't say anything to you."

These last words, innocuous in themselves, were punctuated . . . by . . . the ominous and . . . rhythmic . . . banging of Harry's pipe against the ashtray as he endeavored to dislodge the dottle from the bowl. Successful at last, he gave the pipe a final tap against the heel of his hand and glanced up at Norm with a pleased smile. The parallel organization was an imitation Party, like a wax model, which had to be ready to come to life, complete with telephone numbers, post office boxes, and new party names for those members who would stick after the day of repression, when they would be declared illegal. Preparations for going underground were beyond the ken of rank and filers; for Comrade

Drang they were meat and drink. How many evenings, Norm wondered, had Harry already devoted to the happy task of constructing false identities and new means of communication for them all?

Tired, he told Harry about the occasional evenings he had been putting in with the NAACP as a volunteer, helping them plan a mass meeting featuring A. Philip Randolph, who was talking of a march on Washington. "I've been delegated to bring it up before the CIO Council for their backing."

"What are your chances?"

"I'm a new boy. Aside from the fact that I was just elected to the Council, I'm not even a regular delegate, just an alternate. But with luck I'll wind up with a resolution—and the credit for it."

"Never mind the gags." Harry stuffed his pipe. "We daren't let the workers and the Negroes get ahead of us. They're moving, Norm, they're moving. Who'd have thought the SWOC could crack Little Steel the way they did? Fanny Perkins said the steel strike was called too suddenly. Too suddenly! Before she knew what hit her, Bethlehem caved in, and the workers have got the protection of open membership."

"The workers are joining the CIO, not the Communist Party. Or ours. Not yet, anyway."

"Isn't your perspective one of radicalization of the masses?"

"Oh boy, what a mouthful! All I'm saying is that the American workers are just getting around to what the Europeans did a generation ago."

"It doesn't follow that they'll recapitulate the European mistakes. They're capable of leaping beyond transitional stages—the sit-down strikes prove it."

"Believe me, their attitudes are strictly middle-class."

But Harry was not as anxious to argue as he was to hear what Norm had been accomplishing—if anything—among their adversaries. Dutifully he enumerated meetings and contacts, but he could not refrain from adding, "I'm not crazy about doing opponents' work. I didn't pick it, when I was sent up here. I don't enjoy pretending to be what I'm not, or hiding what I am."

"You couldn't hide it for long anyway. Too many people in New York, if not here, know you as a contributing editor of *New Labor*. It's just a temporary expedient, until we can get someone else to take your place. Then you can function as you want."

"That's the story of my life in the Party."

"Sorry. I'll recommend that you be relieved of opponents' work. But in the meantime I suggest that you steer clear of socializing with our people. Why lose the contacts you've made, by being tagged prematurely as one of us? That would mean all your work has gone for nothing." Harry fixed his bulbous eyes on him so benignly that Norm half-expected him to go on, "Now we wouldn't want that to happen, would we?"

He said innocently, "I doubt that anyone saw me come up here, Harry."

"I wasn't referring to that. If anybody was watching this house my father would tell me about it."

"Don't you want me to have Irwin fill my cavities just because he's Sy's cousin? I doubt that my contacts are watching his office, if they're not watching your house."

"I'm not talking about Irwin either." Harry smiled hard. "I refer to Vera."

Norm forced himself not to reply in heat. He said quietly, "I don't want the Party patrolling my love life."

"No need to look at it that way. As a supposed non-Party person, you've got a special responsibility. Vera does give out the paper at factory gates. She's known. In fact, she wants to be known. Besides, you know as well as I that Bill is functioning openly and actively as one of us, in the shop and in the union. And Vera lives with him and Margaret."

"She won't live with them much longer. We're going to set up light housekeeping." Once he had said it, Norm felt better. He rose, reached for the leather jacket he had flung over the corner of the couch, and added reassuringly, "Don't worry, Harry. It's not going to limit my effectiveness. Who knows, it might even make me more effective. How can you tell?"

Was he mistaken, or did Harry flinch? Thinking about it on the way back to his rooming house, walking the cold quiet streets to which winter still clung like a lover reluctant to take leave of his mistress, he could not make up his mind whether he had really gotten to Harry.

Several evenings later, sitting with Vera in the booth of a quiet tavern on Elmwood Avenue, he took it up once again. "Harry should be doing what I'm doing, and I ought to be out in the open, agitating."

She looked at him uncertainly, then dropped her eyes. It was not in her to question decisions that had been made in New York; she was not only loyal, she was humble. Her humility went oddly with a seething dissatisfaction that had drawn him to her from the first. She had been not only muffled to the ears against the onrush of winter when he had encountered her on his arrival in this raw city four months earlier, but withdrawn in spirit too, to the point of shyness, sullenness almost. Nonetheless she was for him, she was what he wanted; and he could not rest until he had her out of that shell, out of those clothes, and into the shelter of his arms, naked and weeping, ashamed of her uncontrollable passion.

He had never been comfortable with middle-class girls, even those who threw themselves at him. Just as he had fled the endless theorizing and the tiresome theological certitudes of his intellectual friends at Ann Arbor for the uncomplicated pleasures of the football field, so he had turned away from their girl friends, whose middle-class aspirations were only imperfectly masked by a temporary cosmetic, a superficial jargon of rationalistic idealism. The mask was too artificial, the true aspirations too basic and too painfully obvious. What he wanted rather was a kind of girl that he sometimes feared existed only in his fantasies—quiet, deep, committed. A working-class girl loyal to her roots but ready to risk everything for the rebellion that she craved as dearly as he did.

But now that he had found her, a girl absolutely free of affectation and of personal ambition, a girl who worked like a dog in a factory not because it was currently the thing to do, but because her sister needed the money to get through law school, a girl who got up uncomplainingly before dawn to distribute their paper to other workers . . . he was confused by her temperament, which accorded neither with the artless simplicity of her self-sacrifice nor with his earlier fantasies.

Looking into her eyes, seated so close to her that he could reach under the table from time to time to caress her legs, Norm tried to discover in that dark restless glance some clue to the tormented uncertainties that afflicted her increasingly as he undertook to plan for their common future.

She wore her abundant brown hair, coarse as an animal's, drawn straight back from her forehead and gathered at the nape, with a severity which made her look years older. What was more, when he commented on it she looked gratified, as if it pleased her to learn that she had succeeded in making herself less attractive to him.

Her forehead was large and glassy smooth, furrowed only when she narrowed her oval eyes in an effort to assimilate his dismaying explorations into the turmoil of her inner life. Her rather broad and sensual nose was short and flattish in the saddle (the only point of resemblance to her older and smaller sister); her fleshy mouth seldom curled up at the corners. There were times when he could elicit a smile from her only by indulging in the broadest horseplay, like imitating Bela Lugosi: Permit me to introduce myself, the name is Count Dracula . . .

On impulse he said, "If you wore a babushka you'd look like a Transylvanian peasant girl. That neck is worthy of Dracula's teeth."

"My grandmother in Akron still wears a babushka. If you said Dorothy Lamour instead of a peasant girl, wouldn't that be a more impressive compliment?"

"I do want to impress you." He bent forward quickly and imprisoned her ankles between his hands before she could withdraw. "I also want to caress you."

"Not here." She squirmed unhappily. "Not in a bar."

"Why not? Everyplace, and all over." How he loved her legs, all the way up, especially the backs of her thighs, where they melted like butter into the meat of her behind. But it was curious, how she had gone to bed with him so readily, in an almost comradely way—and yet wept from what he could only attribute to prudishness. She had panicked at the thought that her sister and brother-in-law might find out, when Bill and Margaret made no bones about having slept together long before their marriage.

"It is nice to be wanted," she said, flushing. She pleaded for him to release her legs until at last he did. "There's nothing nicer. But you won't feel that way about me for long."

It was painful, the way she kept returning to this. And why? He had not been in Buffalo long enough to earn a reputation among the shopgirls as an inconstant cocksman. It was not he whom she mistrusted, but herself. She was afraid to admit that she loved him, and in consequence belittled herself and her desirability.

"What are you afraid of," he demanded, "that I'm going to fall in love with a movie star?"

"It's not that." Vera knotted her hands and then, with an effort, unclasped them. "It's just that I'm nobody in particular. Not beautiful, not especially intelligent."

"Very special. That's what you are. You're what I want. I can't seem to persuade you what that means to me."

"It's not that I don't believe you." Her voice was low. "You're so honest. You're even unspoiled in spite of the fact that girls turn around to look at you. Who am I? I'm not good enough for you. And sooner or later you'll find it out."

Her voice was near the breaking point. Her strange Slavic eyes were suddenly filled with tears. Who would have thought that such a big girl, quietly capable, always uncomplaining, responsive to endearments and unashamedly eager in lovemaking, would be so prone to tears? In bed they flowed more readily than in a barroom, trickling down her sloping cheekbones, disappearing into the channels of her ears, soaking his pillow, and all from causes to which even when he pressed her she could not put a name.

"I won't find it out." He forced himself to be funny. "I refuse to. I insist on being hoodwinked. I'm a sucker for Slavic broads from Akron. Come on up to my place."

"I can't, tonight." She compressed her lips and touched a handkerchief furtively to her eyes. "I have to iron, so Margaret can study for her midterms. Bill's out bowling with the shop stewards."

"That's what I should be doing, instead of sitting in some bar trying to make a girl that's trying to ditch me."

"You're crazy." Despite herself she was smiling at last. "But you're right, you know. That's just what you should be doing."

A thought struck him. "You wouldn't be trying to shake me off for political reasons, would you?"

"I don't know what you mean."

"I was wondering whether Harry hadn't persuaded Bill to make you stay away from me on account of Bolshevik discipline, or some crap like that."

"No, no. Bill just said that I should be careful."

"Well, we won't have to worry about that nonsense much longer. I've asked for a change from the national office, and when it comes through you and I can do as we damn please. You know what that means?"

Her face was shadowed by the hand on which she rested her forehead. She licked her lips. "I just wish I could make you see . . ."

"Let me do that, all right? Let me be the one to do the worrying, all right?"

"Answer me one thing. What'll you do when you get sick of me? What'll you do then?"

"I'll run away. Will that suit you?" My God, he thought, I wish I could handcuff her to the bedposts, she gives me a perpetual hardon, and yet she worries that I'll get sick of her.

"Promise me something. Promise me that you'll never stay with me only because you feel sorry for me."

He was about to say something funny again, but her straining stare, almost electric in its intensity, made him pause. "Why yes," he said soberly. "I promise you that."

Early in April he found himself standing with Bill Zivic at the entrance to the Peace Bridge, with the word DETROIT chalked on his overnight bag. The police chased them, so they walked over into Canada, and no sooner were they on the other side than they flagged a ride all the way across Ontario to Windsor.

Their driver, a luggage salesman eager for company, squeezed them in among his samples and talked to them continuously for five hours while they drove past the severe old red brick farm houses, porchless and austere, along the drab roadside, and past the ricks and narrow curing sheds of the low grade tobacco farms, glittering, after much rain, in the brisk spring sunlight.

It was not until they had been dropped off at the Ambassador Bridge, and were walking up West Fort Street to the downtown area, that Norm and Bill finally had the opportunity to talk to each other alone. But after the long siege with the salesman neither felt much like talking. The truth was that aside from politics—and the two sisters—they did not have a great deal in common. With his rimless glasses, his eternal khaki work clothes like a gas pump jockey (all that he needed was his first name embroidered over the left breast pocket), his well-honed pocket knife, his businesslike little wife in law school, Bill was as charmless and unexciting as the town from which he had come. He was far superior to the run of brothers-in-law, he was loyal to his wife, his family, his union, his class, he stayed out of your way, there were even moments when he was sensitive and perceptive. But he was so dogged!

They had both taken several days off from the shop, delegated by Harry to attend a three-state conference of active party workers.

The strike wave was spreading while the party branches completed the plans for the meeting, but no one had been able to predict that on the day that they were to get together in Detroit all of Ford would be out on strike, eighty-five thousand strong.

The city was a carnival. Sober-sided Bill, always older than his years, could not help grinning like a kid, as if he'd won a prize. They had to elbow their way down Woodward Boulevard through crowds not just of women shoppers but of men wearing their CIO buttons like sprigs of holly and smiling proudly, as though they were taking their wives on an Easter parade instead of being out on strike.

"Buffalo wasn't like this when we won in Little Steel," Bill said. "Here, the auto workers dominate the town. It's like the rubber workers in Akron. This takes me back to that freezing day when I watched my old man and his buddies march out of Firestone after the first sitdown."

A wave of laughter rolled up and down the sidewalk. Everyone rushed to the curb, jostling and gesticulating in such numbers that Norm could barely glimpse the wobbling, ancient Tin Lizzie wandering erratically along the broad avenue, belching smoke. It was bedecked with CIO posters.

"Jesus Christ," cried the man next to him, "old Henry must be having a heart attack!"

When they got to the loft where the Detroit branch had its headquarters, everybody was talking UAW and Ford strike. "Seven thousand goons Bennett had," a hairy little lawyer was saying happily. "Did it do him any good? A whole private army, and it melted away when the workers hit the bricks."

The strike was all but won. Final negotiations were going on, a face-saving operation, so that the union's victory could be presented as a "compromise." Another member of the Detroit branch, a grinder at Ford and himself on the strike committee, was in agreement with the little lawyer that the corporation was on the verge of signing. As soon as it caved in, the workers would take to the streets. It was hard to get down to the other problems that they had come together from Flint, Akron, Toledo, Cleveland, and Buffalo to discuss. Bill made a cautious report on the Buffalo situation which filled many of the others with envy. When they finally broke up late at night Norm went off with a young couple from Wayne University to sleep on their living room studio couch.

In the morning he was up early. He wanted to get in a quick visit to the Rivera murals in the Art Institute. Ever since his days in Mexico, he had been impassioned by the Mexican muralist revolutionaries. Wandering through the public buildings of Mexico City and Cuernavaca, he had gazed at the gleaming garish walls and at the sandaled peasants and workers as they stood before those giant walls, on which the beaked silhouettes of their own ancestors, their similars, had been immortalized by a generation of obsessed painters. Now he looked up at the band of paint that curled around the walls like some monstrous gray guts coiling and uncoiling ticker tape, sheet steel, automobiles, and dominating everything, goggled auto workers, swollen, heroic, and heavy with the seed of the future in their loins. And there came to his mind not the thunder of the streets outside or even the tremor that must have shaken the inner sanctum of the Art Institute when this commissioned subversion was unveiled, but the very first day that he had spent with the Old Man, just after staring at the murals in the Ministry of Education. The bright bowl on the table between them caught the sun. Natalia brought oranges, papayas, fruit knives, as the Old Man chopped at him, eager to make his point, to be listened to, in the somnolence of the Coyoacán afternoon . . .

Then he had to run, because already he was late. He transferred trolleys for the long ride out Michigan Avenue to Schaefer Road, where he was to rejoin Bill and the others. He found them all arguing and laughing in front of a drug store, and he persuaded the Ford committeeman to show him the Miller Road overpass at River Rouge where the famous battle had taken place, where Walter Reuther and Dick Frankensteen had been beaten by Bennett's thugs.

But before they could get all the way there, the Ford strikers came pouring through Dearborn, down the middle of Michigan Avenue, singing *Solidarity Forever* so loud that surely the Canadians could hear it on the other side of the Detroit River. Thousands of them, row upon row, rank upon rank, marching not like soldiers or even like Rivera's militant proletarians, but raggedly, like yesterday's strollers, chanting the song that most of them had lived all of their lives without even hearing until this day.

He wanted to be judicious, professional, as he took notes for an article, but it was very hard, for his eyes were filling with tears. If only Vera could be here! He wished desperately, as he stepped

off the curb and swung into the line of march, that her hand were
in his, vibrating to the thudding feet in their thousands, liberated
from their own nothingness, delivered from their long years of
stupefying labor, fulfilled at last, discovering themselves and their
precious humanity in this swarming singing mass . . .

Throughout the spring months Norm waged what he came to
think of as a two-front war, against Vera's irrational fear that he
would drop her when he found out that she was not good enough
for him, and against the Party's insistence on his playing a role
which went against his grain. He won both battles, but not exactly
because he was right.

Vera was not strong enough to insist on a life without him, not
after she had begun their life together by sleeping with him. She
could not persist indefinitely in pleading her unworthiness, as if he
were some nobleman bent on marrying beneath his station; not
when things went so well with them both in bed and out. In the
end, not without foreboding and a countenance more gloomy than
radiant, she capitulated, even though she defined their wedding as
a further sign of her weakness, her inability to protect him by
renouncing him.

As for the Party, they were not insistent on his doing opponents'
work; in fact the whole idea was dropped as fruitless, which gave
him to wonder.

What he had not foreseen was how little difference these victories
would make. It began to appear that he was not going to be easily
satisfied by getting what he immediately wanted—and perhaps not
even by gaining what he ultimately wanted (if indeed he knew).
Maybe it was because they were so young, he thought, that people
like Sy and Bernie could still think as though all would change with
certain victories for themselves, their party, or their class. Four or
five years made a difference.

Now that he was entrenched, like Sy, in an aircraft plant, now
that he was deep in the daily round of meetings and caucuses, he
could not keep from thinking (and from confessing to Vera) that
the great issues would be decided not in his shop, or even in the
controlling echelons of the UAW, but—after all of his efforts to
arrive here—elsewhere; perhaps across the sea. "It's possible," he
said to Vera, "that the big victory over Ford was the end of some-

thing rather than the beginning. It's possible that soldiers, not workers, will change the world."

Vera's face darkened. It was not his heresy that she feared so much as his restless yearning to be where other victories were to be gained, victories that would involve not one more contact, one more subscription to the paper, one more member, but conquests over fascism itself. She could see that while he went on with his work, as riveter and revolutionist, it did not suffice. It was not all that he was, any more than being a married man was all that he was. It was not an entire life, and she took to switching off the radio while they had dinner in their little one room apartment— as if mere silence could insulate them from the intrusion of another world.

But it pleased her to be accepted as a daughter-in-law by Mr. Miller, the frightening factor, just as she was touched by the shy kiss her mother gave Norm during their honeymoon weekend in Akron; and their life together seemed well-favored. Among their joint assignments, the long-range work with the NAACP particularly pleased her because it captivated Norm, appealing to his sense of the bizarre.

The Buffalo chapter was still debating, rather pathetically, it appeared to Norm, Randolph's threat of a march on Washington. Fortunately the members liked Vera, perhaps more than they did Norm himself; indeed, he suspected that some of the older people were relieved at seeing her with him, for they had looked on uneasily whenever he sat next to Miss Wilbur, a pretty young schoolteacher, or walked her home after a meeting.

One morning a school in the Negro neighborhood burned to the ground. Suddenly the chapter had an issue, an immediate issue far more pressing than discussions about a possible march on Washington. The school board tried to keep the Negro children from turning up in white schools by assigning them in batches to other Negro schools, some of them far from their homes. It became a matter of applying pressure to the board, preventing it from taking advantage of a near-tragedy to seal the Negro children off from the whites.

It was the sort of situation Norm welcomed, pushing these timid middle-class laggards, showing them that they needed a spelled-out radical program for longer-range issues, but that they could both enlarge and tighten their ranks for struggle on the larger issues by fighting hard and winning those at hand.

He and the Reverend Matthews, a tall, lean romantic with a black shiny face and whitening sideburns, were named to investigate, lay plans for a counter campaign, and set forth the case of the Negro community to the school superintendent. For long hours he sat in the Reverend Matthews's study, a wretched lean-to attached to the back wall of his Cedar Street church, smelling of kerosene, old books turning brown, and the sweat of inconsolable parishioners. At the entranceway Mr. Matthews's stepson, a gangling soulful-eyed adolescent named Hamilton Wright, seemed always to be lurking. Ham played the piano at the services, but something in his glancing stare gave Norm the uncomfortable feeling that the boy did not admire his step-father—or by extension his associates.

When they had determined the line that they would take with the superintendent, they found themselves in polite disagreement as to who should present their case. Matthews was eager for Norm to accompany him, and accepted his refusal only reluctantly and fearfully.

"If only we had some connections with the Negro working class," he complained to Vera, "we could stiffen up these guys' backbones. Even that kid Ham mistrusts them. Let's just hope that they'll learn something from the experience. If they win any sort of concession at all, maybe we can use the momentum to get them to back a strong campaign for the march on Washington."

At the next branch meeting, Norm presented a report on this situation. There was very little discussion. Everyone was preoccupied with other matters—Fred wanted a panel on war propaganda; Harry was hot to interpret the mysterious parachuting of Rudolf Hess into Scotland; Margaret and Bill wanted to analyze splits in the ruling class on the war. "We have to clarify for ourselves before we can to the workers in the shops," his brother-in-law said doggedly, "how it is that Allis-Chalmers, where the UAW has concluded one of its fiercest strikes, holds forty million dollars in defense orders, while at the same time its president plays a leading role in the America First Committee." Even Sy wanted to explore the Stalinist management of the big UAW strike at North American Aviation out on the Coast, where six thousand men were on the picket line, and three thousand Federal troops had been called in.

Norm suspected that Sy's interest in this particular crisis arose from his correspondence with Joe.

"For God's sake," Norm said angrily, "go ahead and decide the future of the whole human race, but at least give me a reaction first on relocating kids from that Negro school."

Harry gazed at him benevolently with his fishlike eyes. "We all feel that you've done good spade work—"

"Very funny."

Harry flushed. "That was not meant as a joke. I don't make racial slurs. I for one feel that you shouldn't go too far out on a limb. FDR is so worried about the possibility of a march that he's calling Randolph to the White House. He may buy him off, right?"

"And if he does," Sy said quietly, "Randolph will cave in, Norm."

"But he'll be under pressure from back home too."

"From whom? From your preachers and barbers? As it is, they're scared by Randolph's socialism."

Norm shrugged. He was not too surprised to have Sy taking the floor against him, with Bernie sitting there knitting, nodding, lips pursed. No doubt they were more right than wrong, but it was no fun to be reminded that what you were knocking yourself out doing, when you could have been home resting after bucking rivets all day, was inconsequential. It was all a question of perspective, really, whether you sat in the White House and genially urged a Negro not to upset your war preparations, or whether you sat in the 12th Ward and worried about your child getting run over on the way to a broken-down ghetto school.

The school year was nearly over when the superintendent finally met with Reverend Matthews. Tremulously he presented his case, backed up with figures painstakingly collected by Miss Wilbur and her subcommittee. To his astonishment and gratification his position was supported by the superintendent.

As soon as Norm learned the good news he said to Matthews, "You must call a victory meeting. We can use it to crystallize community sentiment." He was thinking of the projected march, and Randolph's forthcoming visit to Buffalo, which would be the occasion itself for a mass meeting; but it also struck him as tactically sound to give the leadership an opportunity to blow their own horns, and preach the power of organized pressure to their constituents.

Reverend Matthews agreed. Two nights later he presided at a songful celebration from the pulpit of his crowded church while his

lanky stepson leaned fervently over the keyboard of the upright
piano.

"I'll bet you," Norm whispered to Vera in the last pew, as the
reverend prepared to make a triumphal entry from his upstairs flat,
"this is the biggest turnout he's ever had."

It was predominantly a female gathering. Comfortable Negro
matrons clasped purses and packages in their ample laps; here and
there a husband and father, ill at ease in shirt and tie, shrank into
himself against all the femaleness. Miss Wilbur was radiant. When
Reverend Matthews descended the stairs, his well-kept orator's hand
happily caressing the rounded wooden ball of the newel post, everyone rose and remained standing until he had mounted the platform
and raised his arms over the lectern, pale palms forward, sleeves
falling back from his white starched cuffs.

"Brothers and sisters," he said in a voice that was pure honey,
"I bear glad and happy tidings."

"Praise him!" cried the woman on Norm's left, with sudden happy
abandon. "Praise him!"

"We have presented our case. We have offered our earnest appeal. We have petitioned for justice. And we have prayed for our
children."

"Yes, Lord!"

Norm felt Vera's uncertain gaze upon him. He sat quietly, arms
folded, not looking at her, as the pitch of the preacher's voice rose.

"Our presentation was strong. All thanks to Coretta Wilbur, and
to Mr. and Mrs. Miller, the white brother and sister, recently married, who sit so modestly in the last pew."

Vera clutched her purse tightly. Everyone was staring openly at
them both. Norm permitted himself a smile of acknowledgment to
those he knew.

"Our appeal was heartfelt, our petition was powerful. Most of all,
our prayers were effective. Our prayers were heard."

"Yes, Lord!"

"In September next, your children and mine will go to the proper
schools, the schools closest to their homes, without regard to race or
color. While their new edifice is being erected, they will study in fine
surroundings with fine well brought-up children."

"Praise be!"

"Let us send them to school with hair combed."

"Hair combed!" More voices took up the response.

"Teeth brushed."

"Teeth brushed!"

"Faces washed."

"Faces *washed!*"

The room was rocking now. Perspiring freely, the Reverend Matthews passed a handkerchief around his face and under his clerical collar.

He cried out: "Shirts starched!"

"Shirts starched!"

He slashed forward with both hands, as if clearing a path. "Pants pressed."

"Pants pressed!"

"Shoes shined."

"Shoes shined!"

He ducked like a boxer sliding under a punch, hands in front of his face in anticipation of the response, teeth clenched, lips parted. "Dear brothers and sisters, can I overemphasize this? Can I over-insist that our precious children be sent forth smelling as sweet and fresh as they smell in the nostrils of the Lord?"

"Praise the Lord!"

When they were able to slip away at last, Norm and Vera stood uncertainly on William Street, hands interlocked, the black faces and the laughing voices slipping by them unceasingly, like music on the soft summer air. Ignored as if they had suddenly ceased to exist, they had become invisible, wraiths, nothing more, to the passersby.

At last he said, "We don't amount to much, do we?"

She tossed her head. "Don't be depressed. Those children are going to be happier this fall. Isn't that something?"

"You're right." He took her arm. "But it's disconcerting, how you can work for a goal, and achieve it, and then discover that it doesn't mean what you thought it would. With hindsight you can explain it all, how social forces like mysticism or nationalism reasserted themselves and swamped you and all your bright ideas. But what good is hindsight? It's fine for historians, but supposing you're committed to making history instead of writing it?"

A newsboy, a wizened black man with a soiled canvas change bag sagging from his middle like a kangaroo's pouch, was selling extras at the entrance to a noisy gin mill. His voice pleading as the preacher's, he held the *Evening News* uplifted in one hand while he folded papers and made change with the other.

"Hitler invades Russia," he called out in a monotone, over the sound of the juke box. The inflection neither rose nor fell. "Hitler invades Russia, Hitler invades Russia."

Norm glanced at Vera briefly, then lowered his eyes quickly as if she might discover something dangerous in his look. Her fingers had tightened convulsively on his arm. Wordlessly, they turned away from the music and walked off into the night.

5. BIG BOY

When Big Boy clocked out of the warehouse he slammed the shed door to behind him with such force that the window panes rattled.

"*Hoo—ee!*" Little Bob scuttled out beside him in mock alarm, his pinched black face shiny with sweat. "You bang that door a little harder, they goin hear you clear downtown."

"Let em. Bad enough I got to rassle them sacks of sugar all day long, without that bunch of handkerchief heads turnin on me."

"Maybe you askin too much, Big Boy. They join up because in union there is strength. You preached that, I preached that, a couple other brothers come along, pretty soon we got our own local. But then you—"

"You givin me old history." Big Boy wanted to be patient with Little Bobby, but something drove him, some force within him pushed past his oldest friends, even when he knew that it would be to his own advantage to bank the fire which did not seem to consume others as it did him. And the midsummer heat was oven-like. He passed his hand over his face. "I don need old history. I need to get downtown before Father Gaudet leaves the CIO office. You goin give me a ride, or do I have to take the bus and the trolley?"

"You know I'm goin give you a ride. Don I always? But you got to listen to me for a minute, that's the least you can do."

Out in the lot, Bob unlocked the door of his old Pontiac. Big Boy slid onto the torn velour front seat with a sigh. He bent over and unlaced his hightop steel-toed shoes, thirteen triple E; you couldn't get them any bigger, yet every night he had to open them to give his tired feet a little air and a little stretching room.

"Well I'm listenin," he said, as he put his feet on his metal lunchbox. "You want to lecture me now, Bob, you got me trapped."

His companion backed cautiously out of the graveled lot, waved to a group of their fellow workers just emerging from the trucking ramp of the long, low, all but windowless warehouse, jounced over the freight car tracks, and headed onto the highway for downtown New Orleans. Finally he said, "If anybody was ever on your side, Big Boy, it's me. Right or wrong?"

"So?"

"When I tell you you can't expect to turn everybody around overnight, why you get so sore? You actin just like when you bought your first jockstrap. But you ain fourteen, you almos twice that old."

"It ain me turned around overnight, it's the union leadership. Ever since Russia got attacked by Hitler, they singin a different tune. Before, it was militant this militant that. Now they want us to lay down with the boss like the lion with the lamb. You know somethin?" He swiveled about and jabbed his friend in the ribs, hard. "They won be satisfied till they got us over there fightin their war for them."

"You forgettin somethin. It was you sold everybody on the Union and the Leadership. They was scared an suspicious, an you tol em the Union'd sweeten their pay an get em conditions. Now they got the little extra sugar an they got the conditions, maybe not heaven but closer than they ever been, you start tellin them no, they shouldn't trust the Leadership no more. Maybe they just can't learn fast like you. Doesn mean they won't learn. Man, you talk about the Communists. You can't turn people on and off like they was faucets, Big Boy."

"I'm trying to tell them what's right." His throat tightened. "From experience."

"They got to learn from experience too. No reason why they goin follow you like you was the Lord Jesus. When they see you're right, the International's wrong, they'll stick with you. You know that for a fact."

Big Boy slapped his fist into his palm, slowly and rhythmically. At last he said, "Maybe I do. But by that time they ain goin have no Local no more. They goin have some stooge runnin it out of San Francisco."

Bob slowed down as he slipped into the rush hour traffic. It was plain that he was not going to attempt to carry the argument any further.

"Listen," Big Boy said, "you drop me off up here on the corner an I'll catch the trolley downtown."

"Naw, I'll run you on over to Camp. I got to go out to the Quarter later myself. Goin make a fin tonight, servin drinks at a gamblin joint out on St. Peter."

Big Boy took a cigar out of his buttoned shirt pocket and, after Bob had declined it silently in accordance with their usual ritual, jammed it into his mouth without lighting it. Arrived at Camp Street, he bent over for his lunch pail and opened the door. "Keep it loose, Bobby."

"You too. Be good, man, you hear?"

Big Boy strode over to the office building and went on up to the CIO headquarters. The secretary had already gone home, but Father Gaudet was waiting for him, sitting on the edge of her desk, feet dangling.

"You're going to trip over those laces, Big Boy." As the priest rose to shake hands the top of his close-cropped graying head came up from the newspaper he had been reading. Although he was six feet tall, it reached only to Big Boy's nose.

"Forgot to tie em up after Bobby dropped me off. My feet hurt a lot. Anybody else in the office?"

"All gone home." The priest's face sobered. "How'd it go at your lunch hour meeting?"

Big Boy shook his head. "I got to watch my words. They got stooges planted, both the company and the International. So it's better if I just talk to one here, one there, two here, two there. On the loading platform, by the fork lift, in the boxcar, on the ramp."

"I'm sure you know best."

Big Boy smiled sourly. "They don think so. I mean my own guys. They stuck their necks out when I told em black an white had to unite, but now that times are good they jus soon relax an let somebody else worry for em. They can't see that the International's goin to sell em down the river, come contract time."

"How about Bobby?"

"He's all right, him and one or two others. They're more farsighted, they can see what's comin. But even they keep tellin me, bide your time, man, don get too far out in front. They're forgettin already how we wouldn have a local here at all, if it wasn for me gettin out in front. That's where I got to be—I can't operate no other way."

"There's times when you have to. I learned that in my first parish. My bishop was hard as nails, and when I tried to buck him head-on I got my nose bloodied. So now I pick my spots, and I get to work with the CIO. Which is what I want to do."

"When I come up here today I was countin on you givin me a hand. Way you talk, sounds like I better look someplace else. You change your mind about the war too, Father, along with the Union and the Communists?"

"I didn't say that, Big Boy. In the long run, the change in the party line is going to help us swing the workers. They'll go our way, once we show them they can have democracy and autonomy in another CIO union. If we try to move too quick, though, they can charge us with dual unionism, or union busting. I don't want to see the warehousemen and the refinery workers abused by the Communists. I've been called a lot of bad names for that already. Redbaiter, ACTU fink. But why should we expect the workers to snap to, as if we were a couple of straw bosses?"

"Yeah, well, you know," Big Boy took the unlit cigar from his mouth and examined its moist end, "maybe you feel like you do because the Church don like Communism an all that. That's your business. But you ain here long enough to know why I feel like I do. After I organized my home Local, I went on down the river an organized all them other places, big an small. So they took me up to New York, year before last, an set me on the platform in a big convention in Manhattan Center and introduce me, Brother Hull the big rank an file organizer from the Deep South, everybody clappin like mad. They take me all roun New York in a Chevy convertible, pushbutton radio, sweet talkin me all the way. They call me a Neegro Leader and promise me the moon, I mean, man, there's no limit—if I string along. An I want to tell you somethin, I may be a country boy, but down in Houma we know when we smell dead fish. Sure enough, the day after Hitler attacks Russia, they tellin my Local to pull in its belt for the war effort. They ain worried about conditions for my membership, they fixin to run em from the top just like the white boss always done, only they call it somethin else.

They call it Comrade. Well I'm here to tell you, Father, I ain goin hold still for that jazz. They took me for some kind of hick, tell me one thing one day and somethin else the next day. You think I ain got no pride?"

"That's exactly—"

"Not exactly." Big Boy knew he was being rude, just as he had been harsh with his oldest friend, but it wasn't anything he could help. Didn't anybody know how he had been hurt? "When Stalin make the pact with Hitler, bang, the line done change. Now it done change again. First time, my boys say, Great, now we goin get some of the gravy, Union talkin tough, we don want to get mixed up in no war, just want a piece of the profits. Now they change again, bang. Boss goin crap all over us, Union goin say, that's the way it's got to be, fellows, we got to ship them goods out to Russia. An now how do I know you're not on their side, I mean sayin to yourself, I got to sit on Big Boy so he don get in the way of the war effort?"

Father Gaudet's glance was almost cold. "You have my word. I don't give it easily."

Big Boy stared hard at the older man. "That all you got to say? That why I come up here tonight? How about us gettin a little practical, like cuttin my boys loose from that outfit?"

"From what you yourself tell me, I'm thinking that right now the main thing we can do is to prepare the men for an alternative, for another union. Then when they do get disgusted with the International leadership they'll be ready for action. No point in leading a parade, is there, when we haven't got anybody to march behind us?"

"I got em to march behind me when there wasn't no protection for em at all, when they had no Union, and the only reception committee was in the jailhouse."

"They were ripe for the union then. They're not ripe to leave it now."

"I guess what it boils down to is that I am. Maybe the union's too small for me, and N'Orleans is too." Big Boy shoved the cigar back into his mouth. The juicy end had dried out, and he had to roll it about between his lips to moisten it. "Maybe if I was a believer like you, Father, I'd be a patient man. But I'm in a hurry. I got to have action or I get no satisfaction."

They shook hands. Twisting his head wryly, the priest made for the door, saying over his shoulder, "Better let me get clear of the

building before you go on out. We don't want the wrong people seeing us together and drawing the wrong conclusions. Slam the door
behind you."

Big Boy waited until he could see Father Gaudet through the dusty
venetian blinds, in his sober black suit and stained Panama hat,
marching across the street with his swift athletic stride. Then he too
left the office, the cleated tips of his rawhide shoelaces clicking along
the floor. At the corner he stopped to buy an enchilada from a
pushcart vendor and walked on home somewhat more slowly, ruminating as he munched. Maybe they were right, all of them, for one
reason or another, and he was wrong. But hadn't he been right, less
than two years earlier, when everybody said he was nuts, he was
taking his life into his hands trying to organize the warehousemen?

So what, he thought, if it is me after all? If it is, it's on account
of something I can't control any more than you can control a hungry
tiger after it's been provoked. I crave action, he said to himself. If I
can't get it here, maybe it's because I already did my job here and
now it's time for me to move on.

Deep in thought, licking the last of the enchilada from thumb
and index finger, he did not see the light turn red, took one extra
step, and bumped into the soft behind of a white girl who had
stopped at the intersection, Bon Marché shopping bag in hand. She
was pale and slack, shrunken within her red white and blue striped
dress like a child hiding inside a flag. From the back her bare arms
were putty-colored, as if she had embalming fluid for blood, but
when she turned and glanced up at him in annoyance, the color
rose to her cheeks after all. Her plain sweaty features were distorted with anger and fear, and she was muttering unpleasantly as
she hastened away from him, once the light had changed again. Big
black buck nigger, that was what she was thinking, the skinny little
bitch with the gold crucifix bouncing up and down on her scrawny
chest.

Maybe everybody else is right, he said to himself, maybe I ought
to be more flexible. Or more tame. Well, if he was wrong, best thing
would be to leave town. And if he was right? Same answer. Let
Bobby stay with the Local and try to hold out against the International. He'd learn, they'd all learn.

His mother and his grandmother were fussing in the kitchen as
usual when he pulled open the screen door in their court down at
the far end of the Quarter; but he couldn't complain, he was hun-

gry and it smelled good. It was poisonous, though, being continually surrounded by women—it made no difference whether they were big like his mother, or small like his grandmother. It made him want to break out sometimes, it drove him to spend his nights talking union.

Tonight, perhaps because of the bitter mixture of defeat and rebellion seething within him, it was different. After he had washed up and kicked off his shoes and stuck his head down during Granny's mumbling the supper blessing, his mother proceeded to read a letter from her sister Emma up in Buffalo while he wolfed down his sowbelly and collards and the old lady scoured out his lunch pail.

"Times are changing, she says," his mother said, looking down at the ruled paper through her steel-rimmed glasses. "It may be God's Will that man should be fighting again in Europe—We pray that our boys will never have to go again, but anyhoo (*she always write anyhoo,* his mother interpolated, *always has, always will*) it looks like on account of the war the De-pression is licked. Thank the Lord. Six men on the block went off the welfare this week at last, one got a political job with the Sanitation, one got a taxi license, and the other four all got called back to the mill in Lackawanna. And the bestest news is that Ham is going to work out there too, night shift, while he finishes last year high school."

Big Boy raised his head from his plate. "What mill she talkin about?"

"Steel mill. Emma told me more than one time, half the folks that come up from Miss'ippi and these parts work in the steel mill."

"Strikebreakin, more than likely." He ran his tongue around his mouth and reached for a toothpick. "White boss bringin em up to scab on white man's union."

"Not no more," his mother replied emphatically. "They all in the same union now. Just like the sugar workers, like in your union. Ain no Jim Crow in that union, the way Emma tells it."

"That'll be the day. Still . . . they're all in the CIO." He added thoughtfully, "She says they're callin em back, does she? Even a young kid like Ham gettin hired?"

"Hitler say he don like us," his mother replied obliquely, "but seem like he doin us a power of good right now. Where you say you was goin tonight, Big Boy?"

"I didn't."

"Well how's about you comin home early for a change an gettin

a decent night's sleep? Your Granny and I goin to the Ladies
Auxiliary tonight, an when we come home to an empty house we
just sit an worry."

"You ain comin home to no empty house tonight, cause I ain goin
out."

"You what?"

"You heard me," he said, a trifle impatiently. "Go on along, ma,
I got some thinkin to do."

When they had left, he shaved at the kitchen sink, because it
gave him something to do, and then he sat down in the parlor which
had been like a doll's house for him ever since he had grown up.
Maybe that was one reason why he could never stay put in it, but
always had to be out where there was room to wave his arms while
he argued.

What am I leaving, he thought, if I go? The respect of the men I
organized. Even the International couldn't simply go around him,
they would have to deal with him if they ever hoped to sell their
politics to the members. But once they knew he had their number,
once they were certain that he would not go along with their line,
they would be as efficient in cutting him down as they had been in
building him up. At best he would be a small time leader with a
small time following, defensive and harassed. He had to break
through, to the heart of heavy industry, if he was ever going to be
any more than that. For a time he had thought that the Communists
would be the ones to hold the door open. Even now, if he would only
go along, he could be a big man. But on what terms? It stuck in his
throat that his own men should not see what was being asked of him.
Better to throw it all over and make a fresh start, quickly, before it
was too late, while the men were moving into the mills, and their
minds were not yet frozen over with fear and gratitude.

Beyond the window, Lil Green was singing on someone's phonograph, *I've had twenty years practice in the art of love, twenty years
practicin, Lord above, and I know how to do it . . .* Then a confused cluster of excited white northern voices, tourists' voices: *This
is the street, I'm sure it isn't, How would you know, The boy at the
hotel said this was where the action was, Action? Looks dead around
here . . .*

Man, he thought, I know how to do it.

6. IRWIN

It was the endlessness of their aisles, Irwin thought, that made furniture stores so unsettling, gave you such a feeling of displacement that after half an hour you lost any sense of the world outside —to say nothing of the impossibly tiny and confined home you had left behind, like a snail venturing forth from the underside of a grape leaf to explore an endless vineyard that glittered all the way to infinity.

He remembered vaguely that it was chilly outside, autumn had arrived. Here, even with topcoat and scarf hung on his arm, he was sweating profusely. But he could not be sure whether it was because he was padding through all these overheated plantings of mohair, velour, frieze, velveteen, sateen, broadloom, or whether the sweat burst forth from some deeper spring, some guilt at having invaded this monstrous ladies' powder room, surrealistically overblown, windowless, borderless, macrocosmic.

If he had been alone, boredom might very well have succeded guilt, and then given way—when his darting eye revealed to him no boundaries, much less exits, from the vast mushroom fields of plush sofas—to the mindless panic of the trapped. But his bride all but skipped before him, humming with pleasure, pointing out further-off delights as in a country garden, squealing as she flung herself onto this couch, rubbed her palm across the napped curve of that wing chair, or ran ahead to open a massive book of Technicolor swatches, chained in place like some medieval hand-illuminated manuscript.

Under the pendant fruity clusters of brass chandeliers, in the sallow glow cast by the scalloped and fluted glass shades of torchieres as nicely spaced as a Bavarian pine woods, Carmela bloomed. Laughing up at him, she tugged at his sleeve until he fell beside her into the mushy embrace of a down-filled sofa as yielding as a tub of tepid water; flashing her taut and shiny behind, she leaped up, hastening forward on flimsy spike heels to admire fragile telephone tables, machined reproductions of pre-Alexander Graham Bell craftsmanship, now and then bearing—as in some crazy dream—not telephones but Chinesey porcelain lamps with pagoda-roofed shades dangling over their shiny-bellied Buddhas.

"Irwin!" she cried. "Aren't these beautiful?"

"Um," he replied, gratified by her happiness even while he shrank from the bulbous proofs of her bad taste.

The trick, he saw, was going to be to steer her past the acres of iridescent living-room suites, formica kitchen sets embossed with gilt stars and sunbursts, oval dining-room tables rigidly squared off with cute colonial place mats and Oneida Community silver services. Armed with an introduction from his father to his father's lodge brother, part-owner of Shulman's Select Furniture, they had come hoping for a rakeoff on a box spring and mattress. Who could have foreseen that to reach the simple security of the bedding department they would have to traverse these treacherous fields of *chazerei* that tempted his eager bride at every turn?

He hadn't married her for her taste, but for her . . . well . . . how could he explain to anyone, let alone to his outraged parents, that yes he thought of her behind all day, but also of her mouth, her teeth, her smile, and above all her invulnerability. It was hard enough trying to explain it to Carmela herself, so hard that sometimes he despaired, and flung up his hands. Now he followed her meekly through mazes of hideousness, hoping only to get her safely to the bedding department with his checkbook and his self-respect unscathed.

"Irwin!" his father had cried out in honest anguish, his forehead beaded not just with summer sweat, but with the ooze of parental terror, while he pleaded on behalf of Irwin's mother too, locked weeping in her bedroom. "Can't you see she's out to hook you? What her name is, what her background is, I couldn't care less. I'm not proud like your mother. I'd be willing to stake you, it wouldn't make any difference to me that she was on home relief and her whole family with her. But you can take one look—"

"You wouldn't even take that one look if she was Jewish. Maybe mama would, but you'd be happy, wouldn't you, if it was a nice Jewish girl that was keeping me out of the draft?"

At these words his father's face, always small and seamed like a hardball, shriveled even more. "That's the way you're trying to make us swallow it. Right?"

"All I ask is, don't hate her because she made such a terrible mistake, being born Italian. She's not asking me to turn Catholic or anything like that."

"Big hearted. Who hates? Just wait till you—"

"I know. Wait till we have our first fight, she'll throw it up to me."

"You think not? You think your parents are crazy? Wait and see."

Then Irwin played his trump card. "I want to tell you something, dad. I want you to think about it. Carmela is willing to become a Jewess. It's not me that asked her, she's the one who brought it up."

"Why not? Once she's got you hooked, it doesn't hurt to play the game for a while. What kind of fool are you? What kind of fools does she take us for?"

Nevertheless the concession softened his father—as he had known it would, or he would not have lied and said that it had originated with Carmela, instead of with himself. And compared to what he went through with his parents, Carmie was easy when he told her what it involved. After all, to put it crudely, her parents were the lucky ones, not his. He was the nice sober Jewish boy, he was the good catch (as to this, it was galling to think that, pickled as they were in the salt of their prejudice, his parents were perfectly right) while she was only the girl lucky enough to work for him, and lucky enough for her boss to have fallen for her. Besides, it was no big deal, learning some rules about children, circumcision, and cooking. Compared to the terrifying alteration of turning yourself into a Catholic, it was a bagatelle.

Carmela caught on. She gave off a bitter scent of frustration, pungent as perfume, arising from her having been deprived of certain vague benefits to which even she herself could not give a name. She had recognized this, had known in fact just how to capitalize on it. The guilt that she aroused in him for having had a happy childhood gave the color of truth to his parents' distorted picture of her as a would-be parasite, and tormented Irwin almost as much as his unfulfilled desire for her.

From the moment she first slipped into the starched white uniform that enwrapped her voluptuousness without concealing it, like cellophane tautly sealing a freshly baked cake, she must have known that her presence in Irwin's office (first thrice weekly, then daily, as his practice grew) could only be a sexual irritant, like Spanish fly or a hand rubbing at him even during business hours.

He didn't have to chase her around the office, like Groucho Marx after Thelma Todd, for her to sense, practically from the start, even before he told her, that he was desperate for her. Any girl, he supposed, could tell that easily enough; for someone like Carmela, it was an ordinary hazard of existence, like looking both ways when you crossed the street, and one that you could use to your advantage. Fred and Harry, along with Sy and his wife and all the others, he thought bitterly, could argue the position of woman in capitalist society until they were black in the face and never come as close to it as Carmela did. She got there instinctively and—what was worse for him, since she held him in some awe as she did not the other men who had run after her—bluntly.

"What else would I have to offer?" she asked him by way of definitive reply to his miserable plea that she sleep with him.

"Carmela, I don't understand you," he had lied. "Do you think you'd be wearing a sign afterward?" And then, when she shook her black mop of hair silently, "Do you think I'd tell people?"

"People would know." Her voice was more weary than stubborn, almost as though she were talking to herself rather than trying to placate him. "I'd know. It would make me different. People can tell, once you're different. And after that," she repeated, "what else would I have to offer?"

"You hold yourself pretty cheap if you believe that. You've got fantastic looks, vitality, intelligence—"

"Baloney," she said brutally. "I haven't got a dime. I haven't got any clothes. I haven't got any family, or any education. I don't even know how to talk right—you think I can't see your face when I don't answer the telephone right for you?"

The more she said, the more it hurt—but worse than that: the more he wanted her. He practically groaned aloud at her next words, even though he had no faintest idea whether they were really "true" or whether she was inventing them for the occasion, or even merely repeating a phrase that had become utterly devoid of meaning.

"I still want to get married in church in a white dress."

"Oh come on."

"You think that's corny? Then tell me what else I've got to look forward to. I'm not like your fancy friends, college teachers and scientists and piano players . . ."

Was that the time he had interrupted her complaint with false re-assurances? It was impossible to remember, for she always countered automatically with the pat phrase, each time he attempted to pass her double warning lines at the waist or the thighs. But it made no difference overall, for she had goaded him into making a choice—either dropping her, firing her, putting her out of his life as schoolboys were supposed to exorcise their erotic dreams with cold showers—or capitulating. Finally he had done just that. Gritting his teeth, he proposed, "How would you like to get married, even if it's not in church or in a white dress?"

She had flung herself on him, knocking the breath out of him, mashing those wonderful breasts against his chest, tugging at his hair until the tears started from his eyes, kissing him hotly, her tongue speaking for her inside his mouth. Passionate? She became more than passionate: she became reasonable. Her parents would understand that she could not have a church wedding; they would even settle for an elopement, if the idea of a civil ceremony with both sets of parents in attendance should be too much for the Metzgers to swallow. And finally, yes, she would go to a rabbi if that was what you had to do, she would study and learn to do the things Jesus' own mother had done, why not, it was all in God's eyes, that was what counted, wasn't it?

Slowly his parents had thawed. Not melted, not to the point of being decent to her—what could you expect, he asked her, once you understood that the Church had hung over them like some foul shadow for as long as they and all their ancestors could remember—but thawed to the point of ceasing the suicide threats, resigning themselves, even allowing one stiff living-room visit (the first time they had ever seen her out of uniform, so to speak).

Eventually, it was not unreasonable to expect, they would come around. After the first child was born. Particularly if it was a boy. That was the point at which the gates of benevolence would open wide and the parental arms would enfold them all in a forgiving embrace. Meanwhile there were concessions, such as the phone call to the lodge brother with the furniture store, and the hoped-for rakeoff.

Carmela, hot-eyed with a passion to possess, roaming these erotically overheated aisles with the avidity of a nymphomaniac suddenly given the freedom of a steaming boys' gym, had to be restrained and steered to the rakeoff department without being insulted. For she was tender in her sensitivities, which marriage had only increased, along with his appetite for her.

Sighing, Irwin took his wife's hand, plump as a child's but red-nailed, and passed it under his arm. "We really don't have time for anything other than the bed today," he said. "Besides, it isn't just a question of filling the apartment. Someday we'll have a house, it won't be too far off, and I'd like to furnish it with antiques, wouldn't you?"

Pausing for a breath, Carmela absorbed the idea. "Antiques? You don't mean just old stuff? Secondhand?"

"Oh no." He groped for the words that would impress and distract her, transport her beyond the cheesy opulence. It was not easy. "I was thinking of the really beautiful things, tables, chairs, that not just anybody can buy. They're expensive, but if we look carefully, and get one at a time . . ."

"Such as?" Carmela demanded suspiciously.

"It depends on what we decide." The bedsprings and mattresses now hove into view dead ahead, heaped up like some rosy vision of a safe harbor; he steered her carefully. "Supposing say you decide on Chippendale or Hepplewhite. Or maybe the house will call for Early American. We might even want to mix different periods— you can get away with that in the right kind of surroundings. I've seen it work, haven't you?"

She was afraid to confess ignorance. "I guess so."

In a moment she was poking and prodding among candy stripes and rosebuds, searching for the combination of tension and yielding that would suit them.

"We want to sleep better," she explained to the salesman. "We want something soft but still firm, you know? So we can wake up in the morning feeling fresh and ready to go. How about this set here—do you mind?"

Before the salesman could invite her to be his guest, she had flung herself down on the mattress and boxspring, coat flaring open as she landed on her back. She bounced once, gasping with pleasure, arms and legs wide, skirt flying up above her knees, beyond her stocking tops, the rosettes of her garter belt tight and brilliant against the wide whiteness of her thighs.

"Wow!" she cried. "Irwin, this one is great!"

Blushing, he averted his eyes not only from his wife but from the salesman until she had adjusted her skirt and raised herself on her elbows, breathing hard. Even then, her breasts still heaved from the sudden exertion.

"If you like it, Carmie," he said, "it's yours."

These early weeks and months of marriage were not quite what Irwin had expected. Their honeymoon had been a violent and prolonged voyage of sexual exploration across the mattress of Room 758 at the Hotel Taft in mid-Manhattan, occasionally interrupted by heavy meals and Broadway shows. Carmela's sexual proclivities were unpredictable, even after they had returned to the furnished apartment which they gradually began to fill with their acquisitions: At times, when he wanted to relax with a Woody Guthrie album or an article in *New Labor* (which he now not only subscribed to, but subsidized), she railed against him for being unromantic or even undersexed. At other times, if he went to approach her at night, she would not even put aside her apple and *Redbook* magazine, or if in the morning, would mock at him for being piss-proud. "Go to the john with that!" she would command imperiously. "You don't need me, all you need is to make pi-pi."

Even more unsettling were her moods, which came upon her without recognizable warning and lasted sometimes for an hour, sometimes for the better—or worse—part of a week. Presents, brought home in tiny boxes (earrings), medium boxes (shoes), or large boxes (roses, a vase), sometimes worked so well that he earned the heady sensation of being raped in return, but at other times were hurled to the floor with a curse.

"What do you know about women?" she would cry. "What do you know about the blues? Not a goddam thing!"

It was true. He had never really lived with any woman but his mother, and except for the boxes that she had stacked and hidden in her closet like dirty books he might never have known that she menstruated. The matter was never discussed in his presence, and he had only the vaguest notion that his mother's temper varied with the time of the month, for to him as well as to his father (who made no bones about it) she was more or less a perpetual or permanent *kvetsch,* her complaints intensified by external provocation rather than by any inner mechanism.

With Carmela, he never knew. "When my period is coming, I want to cut my throat," she informed him in one of her more placid moments. "Or yours." But how was he supposed to calculate the approaching storm and so forearm himself, when for him the calendar was simply to pay bills and keep appointments? Besides, it seemed to him sometimes that her suicidal or murderous mood arose long before it should have, or just after the previous one had worn off. A puzzle.

Anyway, her moods went beyond the moon; maybe, he guessed, all the way to the stars. Often she wanted the things that money could buy, but lost interest in them once they were hers; or hungered for friends, but questioned their sincerity when they made overtures to her. She was ambitious, but not for anything specific; lustful, but not easily appeased. He loved her, he grew more sure of that as his bewilderment grew; but it was disconcerting, how she seemed to be learning so much more about him than he about her.

Mixing the amalgam for a filling, he would step away from his patient while he nudged mercury into silver with his glass pestle, and peer hungrily into the anteroom, only to find Carmela whistling in amazement at the billings and his soaring income from the mouths of defense workers long unemployed and with teeth long neglected.

Making out a check for the New Party or its press, he would discover that Carmela had been at the checkbook first, making penciled subtractions in the margin of how much he was throwing away on Harry (whom she found a bore) and his screwy politics.

"If you liked your work more," she said one evening as he was shrugging into his coat before picking up Fred Vogel, "you wouldn't have such a need for so many friends."

This struck him as the kind of half-ass insight that Carmela might have picked up from the column of a lady playwright or politico in a homemaking magazine. He decided against making this point and in favor of placating her.

"You may be right," he said. "I'm not crazy about dentistry. But I'm as good at it as the next fellow, so I'm not gypping anybody. Besides, what's wrong with having friends? When I was a kid I never had very many (this was not exactly true), so it's nice for a change."

But Carmela, when she was not jealous of his friends, was uneasy with them. Apart from Vito, who was a link that bound her to her native past, and with whom she remained on terms of whispering intimacy, the others of their circle were distasteful to her in varying ways. It made no difference to her whether they were old friends, like Fred and Bea, and his cousin Sy and Bernie, or new ones like Harry, the Zivics, and the Links. Harry was "creepy" and Bill "too serious"; Margaret was "too smart" and Bea "too cold." Anne was a "piano player," which meant an upper-class type with advantages Carmie had been denied and stigmata—a quiet presence, a subdued voice—which would never be hers.

It complicated their lives, for if she did like one member of a couple, say Joe the open-faced Californian, whom no one could dislike, then Anne made you feel like she was slumming. Cousin Sy and Bernie she did not regard as friends, since they were "just relatives" and "all wrapped up in the Party," anyway. Fred was all right, a regular guy considering that he was a college professor, but since his wife was a frost . . .

Only with Norm and Vera Miller did Carmie feel genuinely at ease. Norm she openly admired not just because he wrote things that "really got printed" (after all, was *New Labor* a "real" paper?), but because he was a gorgeous hunk of man; while Vera, a strange one, slant-eyed and withdrawn, imperceptibly became Carmie's confidante. This was baffling. Irwin tried to think: What could they have to say to each other? What did they have in common? He decided finally that it had to do with their both having grown up in poor immigrant households, and with their both being less than comfortable with their husbands' friends.

Whatever the reasons, he was grateful. Particularly since he suspected that his friends were being kind to him about Carmela. Neither outraged by her, as were his parents, nor patronizing her, which would have gone counter to their principles, they gave him tacitly to understand that they understood her reluctance to enter their lives.

In a way, his situation paralleled Fred's. Bea was actively annoyed by Fred's new enthusiasms, which were hardly what she had envisaged when she had gone to work to see him through graduate school. Her resentment, Irwin thought, was superficially like Carmela's: she detested sitting on the edge of boring discussions of the recent UAW convention in Buffalo and the Byzantine struggle between the Lewis and Murray factions; or of the federal prosecution of Teamsters Local 458 and its Trotskyite leaders in Minneapolis.

In any case, the noninvolvement of the two girls—who otherwise had practically nothing to say to each other when they had to spend an evening together—served to revitalize his friendship with Fred. For a time he had feared that they were growing apart, since Fred was engaged with surprising wholeheartedness in the branch's organizing work, while he himself stayed clear of any commitment beyond contributing money or attending an occasional discussion meeting in someone's home. It was funny that of them both, Fred should have been the one to join up. He had always cultivated an amused, quasi-esthete style, mocking at Irwin for being so emotionally uncontrolled and (as Fred liked to put it) "overwhelmed by the underdog." But then, Fred's pose was one of many—depending on the occasion he played pipe-smoking academic, library-loving intellectual, or slippered homebody—and it was hard to know whether this new enthusiasm was not just one more. He spoke with a fervor that Irwin shared of the probity and intellectual distinction of his new leaders, and of the chance they were affording the country to break loose from the politics of cynicism. But how much did this have to do with the post-partum blues that had settled on him after he had gotten his Ph.D., and how much with discontent in the hearth?

For several weeks now Fred had been carrying out the assignment that Bernie had given him, to distribute *New Labor* from door to door along a particular block on Cedar Street, in the twelfth ward. As a college instructor, she felt, he would be less conspicuous there than in front of the auditorium at a UAW convention, or at a factory gate guarded with cops and buzzing with observers from other political groups. And maybe he would be effective in talking with contacts. The technique, like making friends for a breakfast food or a vacuum cleaner, was to ring the doorbell, explain, "We're giving out this labor paper free for several weeks, so you can see if you like it, see if you don't agree that it's got news you won't find anywhere else," return the second week with the next issue and a reminder, and try the third week to obtain a subscription and thus the name and address of a potential convert.

These hours passed in the doorways of homes in the Negro section were profoundly educational in a way Fred had not foreseen, quite the opposite of the learning experience that supposedly took place at the university. "It's very humbling, Irwin," he said, "to find such courtesy in an oppressed minority."

Actually, Irwin suspected, the courtesy was just more of the same old shrewd darky talk contrived to distract social workers, rent collectors, salesmen and other intruders, but he had no way of proving it, not when he himself sat home with his guitar and his record player. He suspected too that, as the weather grew nastier and his reception more frigid, Fred wasn't having quite such a transcendent experience, pounding the sleety pavements with a bundle of three-cent papers which brought to uninterested domestics and WPA workers the news that Marty Dworkin had won his fight to get on the ballot for the New York City mayoralty campaign.

Only the week before, Fred had rung a bell, was greeted by a toothily grinning colored girl, and then disappeared within before Irwin's eyes, while he sat waiting in the Mercury with the heater going. Some moments later, Fred had stumbled out, his face aflame. "Jesus Christ," he muttered as he fell into the car, "Jesus Christ."

Only after long silence was he able to tell what had happened: "That girl said, 'Come on in the kitchen, we're all just sittin aroun.' She took me by the hand, led me to the kitchen, where five or six girls were drinking coffee, reading movie magazines, doing their nails. They made me sit down, they gave me a cup of coffee, and they said, 'What you sellin, white boy?' I started talking about jobs for all, open the defense plants to the Negroes, thirty-hour week, thirty-dollar minimum, God knows what. Whatever came into my head. 'Man,' they said, 'sounds great, I'll buy some of that.' I passed around subscription cards, and they were all laughing, I didn't know what was going on until one of them said, 'What you goin buy from *us?*' That was the first I realized they were all in housecoats and wrappers, when they started opening them and grabbing at me. One of them threw herself on my lap, all open in the front, with nothing on, and began unbuttoning me, shoving my papers all over the floor. 'Come on, white boy,' she said, 'you'll be my first tonight, first one is the bestest one.' I was dripping sweat, I was trying to pick up the goddam papers, they were cackling and yelling and smearing me with nail polish . . . Irwin, if you tell anybody, I'll kill you."

Irwin accepted his friend's admonition. But he could not help but wonder, now that another week had passed, what new foolishness Fred was courting, while he waited out in the car, with Artie Shaw to keep him company.

Suddenly there was Fred, over a block away but walking toward him eagerly, coat collar turned up, cheeks aflame again, the last of his papers flapping in his hand. Irwin folded up his own paper and tossed it into the back seat to make room for his friend. In a few minutes Fred would fold himself into the car and they would go off someplace for coffee and conversation before returning to their wives and their separate lives; Irwin would try to find out, without being rude, if things were all right with Bea, and Fred would want instead to talk politics.

But what was politics? If he was uncertain as to who had been right at Kronstadt in 1917 or at Canton in 1927 or even as to which faction was which within the UAW, Irwin was sure nonetheless that the decent and intelligent members of Sy's group were more right than anyone else about the world, the war, the country. But what were they trying to tell the Negroes? And what did it all have to do with American politics? These Negroes were Americans, after all and above all, not just an "oppressed minority" or whatever else Fred and the others called them in the effort to get them to pay attention. And their conception of politics was probably closer to other Americans—a great game, a show among other shows—than to those of the intense believers for whom it was a way of life.

In an instant there came to him, like one of those fleeting dreams which tells a complete tale within a matter of seconds, while you are turning over, the long-forgotten but suddenly bone-bright memory of his own introduction to American politics. He had become, for a brief spell in the fall of 1928, the lieutenant of Hank Knobloch, biggest guy on the block. It was Hank's whim to upend a campaign cap of white cheesecloth, imprinted VOTE FOR AL SMITH in green, and have Irwin fill it, using a barrel stave, with horseballs dropped by the nag that dragged the Hall's Bakery wagon down Brunswick Boulevard. "Who you for?" Hank demanded of the first unsuspecting kid, while Irwin and the others cut off his escape. "Al Smith," said the strange boy on the chance that this was the correct answer. "Then wear this home!" cried Hank, dumping the cap over the kid's head and sending him weeping down the street, followed by the jeers of those who, like Irwin, were themselves afraid to be ashamed.

But Fred had arrived. He pulled open the door of the Merc and clambered in. "What are you sitting there shaking your head for?" He clapped his hands, teacher calling the class to order. "Wake up!"

"I was daydreaming. Where should we go?"

"Just drive. Listen," he said excitedly, "I have had the most fantastic experience!"

Irwin started up the car. "Who'd you meet this time, Lena Horne?"

"I've been banging on doors and having them slammed in my face, when all of a sudden a big gangling boy opens the door and says, You the man from *New Labor?* Come into the parlor, my cousin wants to talk to you. So I go on upstairs, it's over a church, feeling a little uneasy. I was thinking of, you know, last week. But no, there's the cousin, an enormous fellow, built like a fullback, black and solemn. Four or five men are sitting around him. I get the impression they've been having a conference."

"Poker conference?"

"They'd been talking about something serious. When I came in, they broke off. They took their cue from him. So he says to me, You got a pretty interesting paper there. I try to explain how it's edited in the interest of the working man, and he says, 'You think we could get something about us printed in here? About conditions in the mills? In Lackawanna?' I could see by the way the others deferred to him that he was a natural leader."

"Did you get his name?"

A little embarrassed, Fred laughed. "I was so excited I almost didn't." He patted his breast pocket happily. "But I've got it on a sub. Clarence Hull. Big Boy, they all called him for obvious reasons."

Irwin was impressed despite himself. "What did you tell him?"

"I said I was pretty sure we could get a story into the paper. He said, 'I want to get some publicity about conditions so we can shake up the membership and the leaders of our union.' I didn't want him to see how excited I was, so I got out of there in a hurry. Even though he's apparently come up from the South not long ago, and he'd never heard of us or our paper, he seems to be pretty sophisticated politically." With evident relish, Fred repeated himself: "He's a natural leader. And I'm not equipped to handle him. He doesn't want to talk to a college teacher like me—he needs someone who's working in industry himself—maybe Joe—or maybe" (by now he was ruminating aloud) "we could even bring Hoover up from New York for discussions with him. It isn't just one man I reached today—it's an entire group!"

Well, better to be euphoric, even to the point of self-delusion, than to fall into a cathouse—or to stumble home in tears with a

hatful of horseshit jammed over your head. Besides, Fred was entitled to feel excited about the results of his doorbell-ringing, when
he had so comparatively little to cheer him on at home. "Be glad,"
Fred said, when their talk had turned to private matters, "that you
didn't marry a girl with intellectual aspirations."

Irwin attempted to protest: "But Carmie doesn't like politics any
more than Bea."

"Different thing, Irwin. Bea has all her hopes fixed on my academic advancement. Any distraction is a disaster. With Carmela,
all you've got to do is bring home the bacon." He added hastily,
"You know what I mean. As long as your practice keeps growing,
she won't begrudge you your other interests."

It wasn't entirely Fred's fault that he saw Carmela so superficially. He didn't really know her, and for that matter no one else
did either. Carmela's dissatisfaction, if that was the word for it, was
often manifest only in bed, in the dark of the night—and that was
something Irwin was not going to talk about with anyone.

In her daily behavior though, Fred was right: Carmela did bloom
as Irwin's practice throve, and there was more money to spend.
She was getting the hang of middle-class taste too, sloughing off
the aspirations of the poor, gliding imperceptibly toward those of
the educated, a sinuous proof that acquired taste was more important than "inborn" values. She moved from hints of Miami
Beach hotel vacations to talk of cottages on the Cape; she forgot,
as if it had never existed, her yearning for sets of World's Great
Classics and began to buy, one at a time, expensive Phaidon art
books (with Vito to tell her, thank God, what was good).

But beyond all that lay a discontent deeper than the ocean,
terrifying because it seemed to sink further and further below the
plumbable even as they adjusted their surface lives one to the other
as easily as two goldfish sharing food sprinkled atop the water. It
was almost as if she had married Irwin not for his charm, not
even for his moneymaking potential or his social status, but in a
desperate hope that he would introduce her to mysteries of whose
existence she was certain but was helpless to define—and as if, as
her disappointment intensified, she floated away from him into some
female fantasy world, her mermaid's tail twitching as she flirted
off, down, down, in search of the unfindable. At times, usually
after they had made love, she cried in her sleep. When he tried

to comfort her, after her piteous sobs had awakened him from his own depths, she would mutter something about the rottenness of her earlier life. "I dreamt I was thirteen again, and it was freezing, I was getting dressed in front of the kitchen stove, shaking all over, what would you know about that?" Or what was worse she would push at his chest as he strove to take her in his arms, muttering, "Leave me alone, it was nothing you would understand, why should I tell you?" she would switch around on her side, leaving him staring and solitary.

Nevertheless, as his appointment book filled, their apartment did too, with so many new possessions that they began to think of maybe buying a house in the suburbs. They even managed to arrange and carry off an evening that had loomed beforehand as agonizingly difficult: a meeting of both sets of parents in the apartment which neither had as yet seen.

Irwin bought both Bardolino and Mogen David wine, Carmela brewed both tea and coffee, her parents brought spice cookies speckled with anise, his parents brought home-baked strudel. They sat stiffly facing each other, initialed linen napkins lying in their laps like narrow white boxes, their voices rusty and harsh in the English that was still not quite natural to any of them. On the edge of the sofa, beneath the Breughel print of other peasants, Carmela's parents were dressed as for a funeral, but they did try hard, moving from the weather to the war in search of a topic; Irwin's parents did not look directly at them, spoke in monosyllables, and left as soon as the after-tea cigar was smoked down.

Angry with his parents, Irwin was inclined afterwards to pity Carmela's. He was surprised to discover that she did not share his pity.

"What the hell," she said, "it was harder for your folks. For mine it was an experience, they'll have something to talk about."

"They could have had something more pleasant to talk about than my mother's highhatting them."

"Oh, I don't know. It broke the ice. They don't get out much anyway. Believe me, they didn't know they were being highhatted. It was harder for your folks to come."

If he was disconcerted, Irwin was also grateful. "Let's throw a party," he said. "We haven't had all our friends here at once yet. It can be a kind of housewarming, what do you say?"

Carmela shrugged. "They all have such crazy hours. Some work
second shift, some work nights."

He was inspired. "We'll have a Sunday brunch. Then they can
drift in whenever they want. We'll have lox and whitefish and
scrambled eggs and vegetables, you know, platters of stuff, and
coffee and booze, and we can just sort of go on all day."

"Well . . ."

Then he found the key. "I'll get a girl to come in. A colored girl.
She can cook the eggs and help with the serving and do up the
dishes."

"It sounds nice."

Irwin was rather excited, he liked the idea of playing host, and
he splurged on delicacies, caviar and artichoke hearts, which Carmela had never tasted. He awoke early on the day of the party,
and was already laying things out when the specially hired maid
turned up. Carmela was sulky when he brought her some wake-up
coffee, but cheered at the sound of the girl working in the kitchen,
and was singing *Amapola* over the pastries by the time Cousin Sy
and Bernice arrived, first as usual.

Irwin was a little ashamed to think that there had been a time
when he had thought of Sy—and by projection Bernie also—as
somewhat righteous. Actually, he thought, as he pressed bagels on
Sy and black olives on Bernie, he was the one who had been stuffy.
Bourgeois in taste and outlook, he had mistaken their dedication
for dullness, and so had overlooked their sweetness. They cared
about people, that was clear to Irwin now; surely there was a
connection between this and the fact that they were in love.

The Zivics—now there was another question. Blinking behind his
eyeglasses, laconic, Bill looked like an intelligent mechanic, nothing
more. But Irwin had learned with his own two hands, doing root
canal work on him after lancing several nasty abscesses, that Bill
was a stoic, able to stand up to misery unflinchingly. A Bohunk
with guts, his fellow-workers called him, and with reason. He was a
man to have on your side, with one of those almost neutral, almost
changeless faces, very little flesh, and bones aslant—twenty years
from now he could hardly look much different—chunky, committed, clumping on down the road which he had been persuaded
took the right direction. His wife was freer, more effervescent, but
then she was not tied to clock punching. Margaret loved the law,

she was grateful to her husband and her sister for helping her through school, and she was going to make a good labor lawyer. She had a gayety, a charm, that her husband lacked, but at bottom was as levelheaded as he.

Irwin kissed her cheek, pleased with himself for learning. Margaret smelled not of perfume but of soap; her hair was so freshly washed that it was not yet dry, but it was short and carelessly combed out. Businesslike.

How different her sister was! Taller, heavier, more curved, sensual like Carmela, Vera was quite lacking in vivacity. She was slow, almost gloomy, with a somber heaviness around the eyes. A strange girl, and a strange wife for the quickest and most glib of them all, in a fast-talking group. Why, with his physical self-assurance, his eagerness to be in the middle of everything, had Norm chosen someone so withdrawn? And why had she exposed herself to such a risky husband? But of course the distances between himself and Carmela were even wilder. And he was determined, like grim death, to confound those who—he knew—were already predicting an end to his marriage.

He opened the door to Vito, his scuffed brown leather jacket zipped over a striped jersey. His stiff wiry hair was standing on end. He stuck out his callused hand. "Hiya, doc. I brought a friend." Flourishing his left arm like a magician producing a rabbit, the artist hauled a plump frightened girl into the room. "Name of Deedee." She looked no more than eighteen, but she had a big bust and a lot of make-up, lipstick painting her mouth even larger than it really was, and accentuating rather than concealing its vulnerability.

Before Irwin could try to put her at her ease, Harry Sturm was squeezing in between them, saying "We're a threesome, Irwin. Vito picked me up on the way."

Irwin wondered fleetingly if invaluable Vito, in addition to drawing cartoons for *New Labor,* was fixing Harry up with some of his extra girl friends, but it became clear that Harry regarded Deedee as a rival for Vito's attention, for he began at once, even while fixing himself a sandwich, to talk excitedly with the painter. Irwin took hold of the girl, who really did not appear moved by the conviction of the twenty-eight Trotskyist teamsters in Milwaukee, and led her over to Carmela and Vera.

The apartment was filling, everyone was eating and arguing, and they had gotten Carmie to bring out his guitar from the closet. But then the big Californian Joe Link came in, with Anne, the girl he was marrying, and was at once the center of a circle. Standing together, he and Norm made a remarkable pair, both long and rangy, with quick nervous hands. Irwin was suddenly conscious of his own lack of height, and of his spreading waistline. He glanced at Anne, who stood quietly to one side, composed but perhaps tense, her hands clasped before her.

"I won't play in front of a professional musician," he said, pushing away the guitar. "You think I want to look like a fool?"

"What's this?" Joe demanded, jaw bulging bagel and cream cheese. He gulped coffee. "Sorry we're so late," he said to Carmela. "You know, I work nights, and last night I was supposed to be off, being it was Saturday, but they're going on six days with the new Air Corps orders. Actually I was glad they asked me, since I haven't got much seniority and I couldn't turn down the time and a half. So anyway I slept late this morning."

Anne said, "I do wish you'd play. I'd love to hear you."

"We're still expecting Fred and Bea Vogel."

"So what?" Vito demanded. "Don't let that stop you. Fred must know your routine by heart anyway."

He dragged a chair into the center of the living room, cocked a leg on it while he tuned the guitar and then, with Carmela feeding him from a plate, he sang some of his favorites, starting with one or two of the old ones from the Carl Sandburg Songbag like "Willie the Weeper," and coming on down to "Los Cuatros Generales." Norm started beating time, then hunkered down on the hooked rug and began a kazatsky. Arms folded on his chest, flinging his legs straight out, right, left, he hopped through the crowd like a rooster after a hen. Joe was growling rhythmically, "Yah, huh! Yah, huh!" and Anne, blushing, caught the olive pits he aimed at her.

"Hey," Vito cried, "let me have a go at that guitar!" He began to bellow what he claimed were Venetian gondolier ballads. In the middle of it all, Fred appeared with Bea, shrugging out of his coat and waving.

"We would have knocked," Bea half-apologized, "but who would have heard us?"

"I thought you'd never get here," Carmela said. "You missed Irwin's recital."

"If I'd known things were going to get out of hand," Fred laughed, "I'd have set the alarm. Say listen, you guys"—he pulled them eagerly aside in the foyer—"this is as good a time to tell you as any. Bea's pregnant. We wanted you to know first, of all our friends."

"Well, I'll be damned." Irwin glanced at Bea, already digging hungrily into the plate of whitefish and eggs that Carmela had given her. Her face was puffy, her eyelids swollen as if she had been weeping, or perhaps vomiting, her waistline had thickened subtly. "I'll be damned."

"Is that all you can say? It could even happen to you."

"You know I'm pleased, Fred. I think it's great."

But even as he was kissing Bea, he found himself wondering what lay behind the planting of this seed, the consequences of which could be even more mysterious than its origin. A plain old accident, like the numberless accidents that populated the globe? A last convulsive effort to tighten the bond that lately seemed to be fraying like a worn-out rubber band? Or a calculated attempt to ensure a father's deferment, since seventeenth-century studies, if they got around to drafting husbands, would be ludicrously inessential?

Bea accepted his felicitations—and those of the others, once word spread through the apartment—with outward placidity. It was impossible to tell what was in her mind, and in truth Irwin did not really want to know. Once Vito had stopped bellowing in Italian, everyone started talking Jap negotiations, submarines, FDR. Babies went with war and politics, he thought sadly, and then, embarrassed by his own sentimentality, he made himself a drink, even though he was unused to bourbon so early in the day.

The party was coalescing into two groups, women in the kitchen-dinette, men in the living room, smoking, cooling down as the afternoon came on. One or two were already talking about leaving, the others had gotten down to local matters—Big Boy this and Big Boy that, a little confusing until Irwin realized that they were discussing the Negro steelworker Fred had accidentally flushed out. Joe had followed up; Big Boy was definitely a hot prospect, maybe because his idealism hadn't been completely used up by the Communists, maybe because he needed outside help, such as publicity in *New Labor*. "Maybe both," Norm said, and Harry cut in, "We don't have to psychologize. What counts is that he can open the door for us to the steelworkers of Lackawanna. I propose to urge the NC to send Comrade Hoover up here to meet with Big Boy and his followers."

Somebody said, "For God's sake, this is a party, it isn't a meeting, what do you want to do, Harry, call the question?" and somebody else said, "I heard it might snow and I haven't got enough alcohol in my goddam radiator. Let's turn on the radio and get the weather."

"Weather!" Carmela laughed. "All you can get on Sunday afternoon is the preachers and the Philharmonic." But she bent forward to switch on the set.

The announcer's voice had to compete with everyone else's, but then Carmela turned it up and what he had been saying, what had sounded so preposterous, was now in an instant a part of their altered lives, stopping them where they stood, beating in the air like the reverberations of a struck gong. "We repeat once again. Pearl Harbor has been bombed."

Music came on then, but no one listened. It was silence that they could hear instead, and dread that they saw, as they looked about almost furtively, searching for something in each other's eyes.

Harry was the first to speak. He yanked loose, as if it had been an aching tooth, the curved pipe that had been dangling from his lips, and said angrily, "What the hell, didn't we expect it? Didn't we predict it? Weren't we the ones to say it had to come?"

Yes, and to warn that it would go on indefinitely, bringing the most terrible devastation, the end of democracy and the imposition in its stead of what they were supposedly being called on to fight. And as Harry's words hung in the air like the announcer's, with no one to argue them or even to answer, Irwin saw with fascination the answers creeping over his friends' faces, stronger and more revealing than words. For it was not the brain but the blood that spoke, draining from the women's cheeks as if it fled to their loins, fear mingling with concern and even connivance—he could have sworn that a flicker of satisfaction gleamed for an instant in Bea Vogel's eyes—while the men, their features suddenly suffused with blood (all except for Harry, pleased that he had been proved right but annoyed that so few had paid attention), blood calling to blood, eager to be a part of the destructive process. Or so it seemed as he turned from Fred to Norm to Joe. Only Sy, stepping to his wife's side, and Bill, blinking rapidly behind

his steelrimmed glasses, did not have the look of men straining
to be off to the sound of bugles. And I, Irwin wondered, maybe
I am crazy? He walked slowly to the hallway mirror to examine
his plump civilian dentist's face, flushed still from his happy party.

"Well," he said, as he turned to the others, "the party's over."

PART THREE

1. JOE

Munching on a Clark Bar as he strode down Main Street, his unzipped jacket swinging free and the spring sun striking through his thin pullover, Joe found himself staring at the people on the streets as if they were there for the first time. All winter long, huddled in street corners waiting for trolleys, turning bent backs to protect their blue-white faces from the spitting slush spun out by passing cars, wrapped and withdrawn like peasants in some remote Russian village, they hadn't let you look at them, these peasant children of peasant immigrants, any more than they looked at you. They were featureless, rednosed men and women who worked to live, ate to fill up, saved to pay the rent, and resigned themselves to freezing six months out of the year.

Did they wait, like bears, for spring? He had once asked Anne, but she had laughed and called him a spoiled Southern California kid. She had grown up tobogganing weekends at Chestnut Ridge and ice skating afternoons on Delaware Park Lake. "I bet you don't even know the difference between hockey skates and figure skates."

"I'm willing to learn. I moved here voluntarily."

"No matter how long you stay, you'll think we're all a little crazy."

"Not exactly crazy. But hard for me to understand. This town is full of peasants from the frozen wastes—Polacks, Germans, Russians, Bohunks, Finns. They simply didn't have enough sense to keep going until they hit sunshine."

"There isn't enough room for the whole U.S. in California, you know."

"There's a correlation between politics and the weather," he insisted, fearing that he was not really funny. "You don't find the libertarians in the cold climates. Only the Czars and the Stalins, and the ragged peasants, grateful for the chance to get drunk and kill a few Jews." But then he thought of Herzen and the great Russian romantics, about whom Sy had been telling him only a week earlier, and he felt a fool.

"I suppose you believe the same nonsense about music."

"You mean you don't prefer Rossini to Sibelius? Or Verdi to Grieg? You actually like those frozen stiff composers?"

"You nut!"

And they had fallen laughing into each other's arms, as always. They had even gone bellyflopping several times with Sy and Bernie, on Flexible Flyers found in the Schuylers' basement, shouting to each other in the frosted blue moonlight, slivers of icy snow clinging to hair and mittens until they retreated indoors to argue sleepily over hot chocolate in front of a real fire. But behind it all, for him, had lurked a kind of melancholy. Not for friends or family such as would have affected Anne, had their situations been reversed, but for the sea, the waterfront, people who worked in the open air. Singapore fell, then Manila, places that he knew as well as this grim cold city that he had come to for a wife and a new life, and he struggled to adjust himself to the clockpunchers in a windowless factory surrounded with mountainous heaps of slush black as slag.

But then the weather turned around, after this endless first winter of the war, and he was touched by the miracle of spring. Suddenly he knew why the huddled thousands endured the long cycle of darkness, wind, and bitter cold. They lowered the windows in their cars, they raised the windows in their houses, Indian women sold jonquils on street corners, and the air was alive with scents that had never before reached his nostrils. Everything was renewed, and he strode the streets like a man reborn.

Comrade Lewis of the National Office was awaiting him in Vito's studio. Lewis was on tour, but apparently not anxious to be seen at the branch headquarters. He was seeing a few chosen people, one or two at a time; the very fact that you were summoned— even on a precious Saturday afternoon—was flattering.

He found Vito at the window facing the street, under the northern skylight, standing spreadlegged in pants encrusted with paint at the thighs where he had wiped his brushes. He had set out a group of his recent canvases in a semi-circle, and was showing them to a pale-faced, rather sensitive, almost soft man in a blue business suit and topcoat. Comrade Lewis. Joe shook hands quite formally with the national organizational secretary, who said to him with genuine enthusiasm, "You people have a very good painter here, do you know that? Very good indeed. I had no idea, just from seeing his cartoons."

Lewis wasn't simply being polite. Joe was a little embarrassed. Acutely conscious that he was lacking in the vocabulary of polite agreement, he mumbled, "A lot of people feel that way. I only wish I knew more about art."

Vito laughed. "The hell you do. It would only turn you into a suspicious character, kid."

He said stubbornly, "I mean it, Vito. I get the feeling sometimes that you're so far beyond not just me, but everybody around you, that it's—well, it must be painful for you."

For a brief moment Vito's face was bleak. Then he winked, his creased face twisted into a grin. "What the hell, we got the movement between us. That's something, ain't it? The workers' fight against the war, and all that? You two have got things to talk about, excuse me while I go out. Make yourselves at home." He snaked his leather jacket from the broken-springed couch and walked out whistling.

Lewis seated himself on the studio couch, crossed his legs, and motioned to Joe to join him. "I meant exactly what I said about him, you know. He's a very gifted man. His cartoons liven up our paper and all that, but it's a shame we can't make better use of him."

"What else—"

"Precisely. What else? We use actually the least of him, and he knows it as well as we. Vito's no fool. He wasn't in the Stalinist movement for nothing. Luckily for us, he knows we wouldn't abuse him." His voice turned a shade more personal. "But painting signs! In a decent society he'd be an honored artist. I know a little something about what he's after in this new work. He's reaching far."

Joe waited.

"Now to you." Lewis folded his white, rather plump hands around his knee. He had the face of a naturally courteous man, but Joe was somewhat taken aback by its anonymity—it might have belonged to a bank clerk, a civil servant, a teacher. It made you wonder, since it betrayed neither fanaticism nor passion, but merely politeness, why the revolutionary movement.

"We've given you more thought than you might expect."

"Because I'm not from New York? Not Jewish?"

"America is full of young men who are not from New York and are not Jewish. But they don't have your talents."

Joe was uneasy. Whatever he had expected from Lewis—whatever Sy and Harry had told him about this pale quiet functionary with a head for figures and an ability to lay hands on printing presses, hotel rooms, automobiles—it was not flattery. He demanded, "Is this why you wanted to see me? To butter me up?"

Comrade Lewis shook his head. "I have no time for that. You and I come from different backgrounds. I studied accounting, you studied anthropology."

"How did you know that?"

Lewis waved the question aside. "What unites us today is the belief that our group, although others may regard it as laughable or pathetic, has a tremendous potential, if only because we are closer to being right than anyone else. Correct?"

"Go ahead."

"We also believe that once we can get this across to the workers they'll turn to us. The little catch, the part that makes us seem ridiculous, is, how do we get to the workers? The answer is, not just with our press and propaganda, not just with Vito's cartoons, not just with faithful girls distributing them at the factory gates—but with cadres inside the shops.

"Now let me tell you why I'm touring the country. I'm not making speeches, I'm not even addressing open branch meetings. Every man to his own function. My job is to pull the cadres up tight, into a fist. One man here, two men there. But only those we can count on. Men who believe that we're right on the Russian question; that you can't support Stalin because FDR said we should for one specious reason, or Trotsky said we should for another specious reason. Men who believe that we're right on the war; that you won't beat facism by supporting Russian totalitarianism, or by bombing the German workers, that it will bring the American workers only a dictatorship like the one they're asked to fight. And afterwards a depression worse than the last one."

Joe stirred restlessly. "All this I know."

"We've selected this city as a concentration point for our meager forces. That's why we agreed to your coming here even at the cost of losing your excellent contacts on the Coast. I can't count on Fred or Vito, much less on Irwin. I have to count on the cadres. On Sy. On Bill. On you."

Why hadn't he mentioned Norm, or Harry? Was it a slip, or a deliberate omission? It was not a question you could raise. Instead he asked, "What is it that you want? What don't I already know?"

Lewis sighed lightly. "I want us to entrench ourselves in the factories. I want us to go into the services—where we'll have to start all over again, after having lost our bases in the shops and the unions—only when we have to. That means fighting for deferment, by obtaining the necessary skills, by raising families, by appealing 1A classifications. Above all it means showing the way, starting with financial sacrifices."

"Specifically?"

"By pledging, and paying, a sliding scale percentage of your weekly wages, a minimum of ten percent, and rising for skilled workers. I want your commitment to that, today."

"I'm willing."

"You've got to be more than willing. You've got to demonstrate to those you recruit that they won't be doing you a favor. That we are a fraternity of sacrifice. That our press can publish only with their money. That with them we can grow, right in the midst of this war, and become a force. A force," he repeated with satisfaction.

"In that connection," Joe said, "I've already requested the National Office to send up Comrade Hoover for discussions with our steelworker contacts. I figured a Negro comrade, an older man, could swing weight that I couldn't. Or any of the rest of us, for that matter."

"I'm aware of your request. This branch will have to assume responsibility for the entire financial burden."

"Why not? After all, we've got the prospect of bringing in a real leader, and an entire group of his followers."

"Hoover will come. Meanwhile, we have confidence that you can talk sense with Hull, just as you did with the West Coast sailors. The proof is not just in the progress you've already made with

Hull, but that you've so quickly been elected shop steward in your plant. It would be easy for me to assure you that you can move up in our party. That's no great feat for a clever man. After all, how many of us are there? What I am telling you is more important: That you have it in you to become a working-class leader of national distinction. That as the movement grows, you can grow with it." Lewis smiled. "You're the kind of person who could make good in a capitalist society as a salesman or a schoolteacher. Or an engineer. You've got brains, patience, and personality. You stick, and we'll move ahead together."

By the time they parted, Joe was somewhat bemused. It was reassuring to be told that you were effective: without masses of men following you, it was not easy to measure your progress as a professional revolutionary. Still the interview with Lewis had been disconcerting. Something in his praise, in his talk of the possibilities of the movement, was the least bit out of tune. It jarred; as he hurried home, he was reminded of how Anne winced when she had to listen to performers whose pitch wavered or who betrayed an insensitivity to nuances of timbre.

Anne was still busy with her last student of the day. Turning in at the side entrance of the apartment her father had found them, he could see her through the living room window, so intent on the struggles of the curlyheaded girl at the Steinway upright that she did not see him pass. Changing his clothes quietly in the bedroom, he listened with keen pleasure first to her low intense voice, singing in time to the child's irregular struggle with *Für Elise,* then to the clicking of her lead pencil against the music stand.

After she had dismissed the child, Anne joined him in the kitchen, where he had seated himself at the table, with pad and pen. She buried her face in his neck for a brief moment.

"I'm writing home. Uncle Jerry is still kind of shaken up by Tom Mooney's death, believe it or not."

"Tell them I sent that little present to Pauline, and let me get washed up. After seven kids in a row I feel like I've been heaving coal."

"Take your time. I'll be writing up grievance reports."

No matter how tired he was, or how many other things pressed on him, Joe never allowed himself to fall behind in writing up grievances. "Rule Number One," Bill had called it, from a longer experience in rubber as well as aircraft, in sober correctness about its importance if you wanted the respect of the men who had elected you.

He and Anne were meeting Sy and Bernie for dinner in a small spaghetti restaurant in the old Italian section behind City Hall. Working different shifts in different factories as they did, they could only get together on weekends. He had the feeling, strengthened now by the sight of his friend hunched into a rear booth with his wife, that Sy was prey to moods of isolation. The plant in which Sy and Norm worked, on different shifts—unlike the one in which Joe and Bill Zivic worked—was not a UAW shop; and while Sy was deeply involved in the auto union's effort to organize it and to break the power of the company union, he was even more deeply uneasy about his position in the shop if the UAW were to fail.

What was more, without the elixir of engagement in a militant union, Sy was thrown back onto the most gloomy reflections about the war, which now began to look as though it might go on forever —if indeed the allies could force a stalemate. He was not volatile like Norm, but the prospect of long dull years in an aircraft plant—or an army camp—with no hope of participating in any action organization larger than their own little group, could be depressing.

He and Bernie talked now, as they anointed their spaghetti, of the union election compaign at his plant, but with no real enthusiasm: the company was playing a smart game and the union was not. In consequence the outlook was poor.

"Tell me," Joe asked him, "is the draft hitting the men in your department?"

"Starting to. The new hires are getting picked off. And the company isn't putting up a fight with the draft boards. Instead, it's starting to hire Negroes."

Bernie and Anne were suddenly very silent, concentrating on sprinkling grated cheese over their spaghetti as if it were a difficult task, requiring silent application. He was taken with pity for them both, for he knew how the matter of draft deferment dominated their lives, and those of all young wives. He changed the subject; and it was not until they were on their tortoni and espresso that the talk once again returned to politics. Sy leaned across the table: "What did you think of Lewis?"

It was the same question Anne had asked him on the way over to the restaurant, but she was merely being polite, and relieved that she had not had to sit in on the discussion. To Sy, however, it mattered.

"I liked him well enough."

"Boy, are you diplomatic!" Bernie laughed.

That was one of the hardest things about the Party to explain to outsiders. The rank and file were proud of their leaders' special qualities—Dworkin's oratorical skill, Hoover's ability to talk to workers, Lewis's knack for operating behind the scenes. But they were quite free of that sickening sycophancy of the Stalinists, who had to make a nonpareil of every Communist leader in their waxworks. People like Sy and Norm not only laughed at their leaders' failings, they boasted of them almost as if they were building another kind of myth. Thus Dworkin was not only a great orator but a great windbag and one of the biggest loudmouths in the radical movement; Hoover was not only a fine organizer but a fine bullshit artist, a walking omnibus of cranky notions ranging from extrasensory perception to doubts of Einstein's sanity; and Lewis was not only a first-class manipulator but a first-class cynic, whose attachment to socialism ranked far behind his attachment to the bank accounts he had reportedly opened for the party in a variety of fake names and odd localities rivaling those of W. C. Fields.

"All I mean," he explained, "is that Lewis seems remote from what I believe in. I know how long he's been in the movement, but—"

"You're right. Nobody ever knew where he stood in a faction fight until the final vote was taken. The funny part is he practically always wound up on the right side, but that might be because he always goes along with Dworkin at the last minute. Lewis is an accountant, a goddam clerk."

"You sound like Lenin on Molotov."

"Except that Lewis is more than that. He's never been known to express an original idea, but in a funny way he has taste. Besides turning up on the right side, he has taste in people— which ones are going places, which ideas are going to make it. He's not a fool. Well," Sy concluded, "since we need him more than he needs us . . . shouldn't we be grateful?"

It was a question that Joe turned over in his mind occasionally in the weeks that followed, while he worked alone, cut off from almost everyone. He was in the fuselage department, usually on a ladder, holding a bucking bar against the rivets that his invisible partner on the other side of the aluminum aircraft shell smashed home at him with an air gun. Sometimes he held the gun and his partner the bar, but between the echoing roar of the rows of rivet guns, in the quiet intervals while they awaited the inspector, or a fresh supply of rivets, he wondered whether he was going to be any more fit to lead than Lewis—who in any case did not lead but rather moved with the leaders behind the scenes and whipped the rank and file into carrying out the leaders' decisions.

Already he knew, from his union activities alone, that even in the most democratic of institutions leaders were not simply people chosen by other people for a limited period and limited responsibilities, but determined men who imposed themselves because they loved power, or were obsessed by a belief that they ached to put into practice.

He himself had begun as humbly as you could in this vast bleak cavern, running for and winning the job of transmitting complaints about dirty toilets, insufficient smoking privileges, unfair time clock penalties. But he was under no illusions about his own selflessness, any more than were his opponents, who saw the steward's job as the beginning of freedom—starting with an hour or two a day away from the drudgery of work on the assembly line—and as the first opportunity to climb a ladder paralleling that of the group leaders and foremen (the latter closed to them because of their lack of schooling or connections with the front office).

As far as he was concerned his task was to prove to the men around him that he was trustworthy as well as intelligent. Once they accepted that, he would be able to move them on larger issues.

For him it was all one. The whole vast factory, the entire city, was a kind of on the job training program—you learned while you worked, what you picked up in political infighting you applied at stewards' meetings. And vice versa. In the dull work of repeatedly mashing down rivets to hold two pieces of metal together, you learned patience and the art of concentration—both would come in handy, in the army, or in jail. In his daily arguments, whether with foremen over time cards or suspensions, or with workers over Hitlerism ("Hitler gave us our jobs") or anti-Semitism ("You can't tell me the Jews didn't bring it on themselves"), he learned to proceed painstakingly, relating their self-interest to the ideals they had been taught in school or church so that they would come out the other end as better people—at the very least as men who saw the connection between what they wanted out of life and what they had been taught was good.

Inevitably, he made enemies. The Stalinist slate was supporting union surrender of double time pay after forty hours as a win-the-war measure. But even they found it difficult to make their usual epithets stick, and had to fight it out with him on the issues. On the day shift Bill, like himself, was publicly identified as standing for the same principles. If he too could get a transfer to the day shift, he would be able, he felt sure, to run for a plant-wide union position with a fair chance of success; already he had begun to discuss *New Labor* articles with certain shopmates to whom he gave the paper, and whom he invited to the open Sunday evening meetings in the new branch headquarters.

Working days would also help to make his life with Anne more like what they had both hoped it would be—and was not. For Anne the Party, the union, the contacts and the converts, all were her rivals. When he was home, he sat in the kitchen writing up the grievances of anonymous others while her own accumulated. Meeting followed meeting—the caucus, the stewards, the fraction, the branch—and when he made love to her he had to do it not in the leisurely dark as she would have preferred, but at odd moments, in the bright awkward light of morning, sometimes almost as an afterthought, when they were practically out of the door, she on her way to the library, he off to yet another meeting.

If she understood that he was not happy with this either, that in fact his own grievances were accumulating, she gave no sign of it. Finally he undertook to explain once more, early one Sunday evening, shortly before leaving (he had not yet told her) to introduce the newly arrived Comrade Hoover to Big Boy Hull. Seated before the voile curtains that bellied inwards from an occasional puff of wind, she folded her hands in her lap and inclined her head politely, as though she were at a lecture, while he told her of his hopes, describing the men who now accepted his leadership, and quoting an occasional passage from Marty Dworkin's article in their theoretical magazine, *New Socialist,* on perspectives for mass radicalization in the event of a long war.

After a time she stirred. "Are you trying to tell me that we're going to go on like this indefinitely?"

"I mean that there's a possibility of things going our way, if we can stick it out. Besides," he added stubbornly, "aren't you and I better off than if I were still going to sea?"

"I suppose one night out of seven is better than none," she laughed.

Conscious that he was being awkward and blundering, he said, "I'm afraid I've got to go out tonight. I have to pick up Hoover—"

She paled, and at once he stopped. She arose abruptly and went to the piano.

"Can't I explain?"

"As long as you're going out," she said over her shoulder, "I'd like to get on with my practicing." And she began to play.

Enraged, he leaped up and pinioned her arms from the rear, so that she could not go on. He cupped her breasts in his hands, and when she bent her head to bite his fingers, he wrenched her about, clamped his mouth to hers, and fell to the carpet with her. They struggled wordlessly, panting, flailing.

Her skirt was rucked up over her thighs. He caught a glimpse of her mound, dark and furry beneath the white nylon of her panties. Before she could conceal herself he tore at the triangle, ignoring her desperate writhing until it gave and she was exposed to him. He rolled over onto her, forced himself between her legs, and unzipped his pants. Wedging his foot against the scrollworked leg of the piano, he set to enter her, his teeth clenched, when to his astonishment she suddenly spread her thighs wide and clapped her heels over his hips, urging him on. Gasping, they fucked as if for the first—or last—time.

Afterward he dressed, his back to her. When he was tucking his shirttails into his trousers she finally spoke to him. "Now you're all set for the meeting, aren't you?"

He swung around. "You knew I had to go."

She lay on her back without moving, not trying to cover herself, naked on the carpet, tears trickling from her tight-shut eyes. "So you couldn't take a chance on my being asleep when you got back."

"That's not true!" He dropped to his knees beside her. She was trembling, her belly quivering, her hands clenched. "You know me better than that!"

"I don't know you at all." She swung her head violently from side to side. "This isn't the way I wanted to live. Not like this."

He covered her with his body. He whispered, "I chased you all the way across the country. I sit in the kitchen listening to you give lessons and thinking of how I want to make love to you."

She was weeping now. But she said, her head averted, "You'd better get up. You'll ruin your crease. And you'll be late for Hoover."

So he flung on the light windbreaker that Anne had laundered for him and as the twilight drew down he hastened angrily along the blowing streets, kicking pebbles out of his path on the way to the meeting which was now, even more than a moral obligation, a bitterly necessary proof of his independence.

Hoover's stay was being paid for partly by Irwin who—so Joe had learned from Sy—had pledged a weekly commitment on condition that it not become generally known, even within the branch which was paying the remainder. Hoover had spent the first day or so in tending to private business and settling down in his room (according to Norm he and his wife, a rather severe socialist schoolteacher who wrote a woman's column for *New Labor,* were used to long separations). Now he was waiting at the branch headquarters for Joe to take him to Big Boy's, where a group of black steelworkers had gathered.

No sooner had he mounted the steps to the branch headquarters than Hoover greeted him, almost curtly, clapped his hat on his head, and gestured him to lead the way to the street.

On the bus Hoover removed the hat and passed his hand over his glossy brown skull. He gazed out placidly at the Negro shopping district, the saloons, the notions and ladies' wear shops, storefront churches, Bar B Q restaurants, cut-rate drug stores and seedy pawn shops, gypsy fortunetellers, and forlorn Jewish delicatessens, reminders of an earlier ghetto. "Things are pretty quiet here in the Black Belt."

"As far as I know. You might check with Norm, he's been working with the N double A."

"I have already."

He was a little abashed. "Well, for an outsider he'd know."

"For an outsider." Hoover sounded hard and unrelenting. But then he went on, in a conversational tone, "I was in Detroit last month. There wasn't *any*body knew there was going to be riots in the Sojourner Truth project. No outsiders. No whites. The Negro workers knew, all right. They told me, and I knew. I'll tell you something else. There's going to be more and worse in Detroit before it's over. The black workers are banging on the doors of the war plants. When they get that steady pay check, they start banging on the doors for decent housing. At that point things heat up. One explosion means there's going to be more."

"What's the answer?"

"You've got to recruit black workers. You've got to fight racism in the shops. The workers learn solidarity in the plant. See to it they don't unlearn it on the streets. What else you think you're working in industry for? To stay out of the draft? To pat yourselves on the back that you're leading the workers? A leader is no damn *good* unless he leads. When do we get off this bus?"

"Next stop."

Big Boy was awaiting them with a group of steelworkers crowded into his aunt's little parlor. Joe counted six—it seemed like more because the room was small—and after shaking hands all around squeezed himself into a corner by the window. He was the only white, but the others, most of whom had already met him, were far more curious about Hoover, who greeted them all with a certain reserve, like an older relative come to visit.

On the faces of all—black or brown, clear or mottled, cloddish or alert—there shone one common element: respect. No doubt the way had been prepared for Hoover by his own column, which they had been reading in *New Labor*. Nevertheless these rough and awkward workingmen were as silent and solemn as if they sat in the church below, waiting for the Rev. Matthews to deliver his sermon. Looking up from their work shoes heavy on the worn linoleum of the living room floor to their intent faces, Joe felt the silence as deference for an older man, who had lived in their world but was in addition an educated person, a writer and speaker. But it was also a human response to Hoover's immense dignity, to the fumed-oak head that rose hairless and glistening as if sculptured above the starched white shirt.

He said calmly, "I didn't come here to make a speech to you men. Organizing is thirsty work. I came to find out about conditions in the mill. So you do the talking, and I'll pitch in when the spirit moves me."

"Can I get you a drink, Brother Hoover?" asked Big Boy. "A beer, maybe?"

"A glass of water would do fine."

"We was talkin," Big Boy said when he came back with the water, "about a lot of particular things. Small things, maybe so small you don want to waste time listenin."

"There's nothing that small." Hoover sipped at the water, then inclined his head politely. "Go ahead."

In a matter of moments they were talking freely among themselves, with Hoover occasionally interjecting a comment, little more. Joe himself tried, from the corner in which he sat, to observe both Hoover and the steelworkers among whom there might be possibilities for contacts beyond Big Boy himself. Although he had not discussed it with anyone, he had expected that Hoover would take advantage of the occasion to give the workers what they wouldn't hear from Big Boy, from their union, from their lodge, from their church: the basic message of the movement.

But no. Hoover never once went beyond the narrowest questions about washrooms, parking lots, tools, furnaces, time clocks. Toward the end of the discussion Joe fixed his attention on Hamilton Wright who was seated on Big Boy's right; he was the stepson of Reverend Matthews, and Norm had already had a few discussions with him. He had recently graduated from high school and gone to work in the mill. Much more fair than his cousin from the South, he had the smooth palish skin of one who can count Indians, or perhaps Orientals, as well as Negroes, among his ancestors; he spoke with eager intensity.

"Mr. Hoover, I got my hands full with my boss. I say to him, I got all these grievances to process, I can't let this drag on, and he just stalls me."

"Well, you know," Hoover's voice slowed to what was almost a deliberate drawl, "just *having* a boss is a grievance. Ever think of it like that?"

The room was silent. Ham Wright looked down at his knotted hands, uncomprehending, perhaps even disappointed, by the older man's reply. But then, as it sank home, he raised his head slowly. "Say," he said, grinning, "that's the truth. It sure is the truth."

And everyone in the parlor was laughing, nudging, clinking beer bottles in salutation, slapping their knees, stretching, chuckling. Hoover arose too, buttoned his coat, picked up his hat. He nodded slightly at Joe, and in another minute they were out on the sidewalk. Now I know, Joe thought: it takes a lifetime, twenty-five years, a quarter of a century of meetings, arguments, discussions, in saloons, lunchrooms, union offices, factory washrooms, to be able to compress all the complex gradations of struggle and despair into one simple observation made to sink like a plumbline, straight and true, into the depths of your fellow man's being.

Once out of earshot of Big Boy's house, Hoover said, "I could use a cup of coffee after all that jabbering."

Joe squinted at the older man. "Why didn't you take anything except water in the house? Big Boy's aunt would have been proud to give you some coffee."

"I wanted to concentrate," Hoover replied somewhat obscurely. "Now which way is the Y? Got to get my bearings."

"We turn left here and go on up to Michigan. Want to stop for coffee?"

"I'll brew myself a cup in my room."

"Doesn't it keep you up at night?"

"That's *poppy*cock," Hoover replied sharply. "*Su*perstition. You have got to be in control of your body, not let your body be in control of you. When I say to my body, Go to sleep, it goes to sleep. When I say Get up, it gets up. I don't need an alarm clock—alarm clocks are a sign of weak *char*acter."

While they walked to the Negro YMCA, Hoover lectured him somewhat impatiently on the spartan virtues. Joe was uncertain whether this ire sprang from revulsion against bourgeois decadence or from the younger generation as such, including even—or *especially*—the young radicals: "soft headed, soft bellied, soft living."

"They like to jabber in the cafeterias," Hoover concluded, "about this revolution and that revolution—but they're afraid to get out and do a day's *work*."

To Joe all this sounded oddly like the right-wing commentators who sustained his father, buried deep in his lemon groves. Hoover urged the young to straighten up, talk less, work more—but his grimness had a note that rang strangely. Joe wanted to invite him into the Y cafeteria—but feared he would be castigated by the older man as one more degenerate young hanger-on.

"You coming up?" Hoover gestured with his thumb at the elevator. Apparently conversation in one's room was more licit than conversation in the cafeteria; Joe hastened into the elevator.

But once he was seated on the wicker rocker, watching the gaunt-faced man heating the coffee on his single burner, then spreading jelly on the white bread with a tin spoon, he could not bring himself, even in his own mind, to mock.

"I want to tell you something, Joe," Hoover said in a businesslike tone, as he passed him a toothbrush mug of coffee and half-sandwich. "You watch your step with that Big Boy."

He looked up, startled.

"I know that type. He didn't kid me one *bit,* bringing the troops in like that to show me how much muscle he's got in Lackawanna."

What was all this? "Now wait a minute! You were the one who wanted to meet him. We were the ones who wanted to get in touch with his crowd."

"I'm not complaining about that. I'm talking about the *way* he did it. You've got to feel those things. How do you know those guys are the best militants in the mill? How do you know they're not just lackeys, looking for a leader? What do you know about his motives?"

"Well, I don't think—"

"You've *got* to think." Hoover sipped his coffee. "You looked around and saw all those black faces, and you said to yourself, boy, here's our chance to move in on the black working class. But how many of them have got the intelligence or the guts to move out on their own, without hanging onto Hull's coattails?"

"I didn't have much chance to find that out."

"You had as much chance as I did. Who asked the best questions? Who was the most serious?"

Joe set the mug on the floor. "I guess it was the cousin, Ham Wright."

Hoover nodded sharply.

"But wait a minute. If anybody was hypnotized by Big Boy, it was that kid. He was the youngest one there and the most dependent."

"Right again. He's a preacher's son, rebelling against his father, and Big Boy turns up with all the qualities his father hasn't got. But he's too smart to be anybody's camp follower. He's got too much curiosity. When he asked the right question, I made my pitch."

Joe gazed speculatively at Hoover, bronze and impassive in the pool of yellow light cast by the shabby floor lamp, his head bowed under the cracked shade with its crude and mercifully faded painting of a Venetian gondolier. How many lonely and confused black wanderers had sat in this split-bottomed wicker chair, slowly rocking, trying to bring their lives into focus? "There's just one thing," he said. "Do you mean I've been on the wrong track about Big Boy?"

"I didn't say that. But if you came up here for a pat on the back," Hoover said scornfully, "as if I was *Lewis* or somebody like that, you're knocking at the wrong door."

"I didn't want—"

"Big Boy has got real virtues. A kid like Ham Wright can see, the minute Big Boy sets foot in the mill, that he's got it all over the men around him in guts and leadership qualities. But right now I'm talking to *you,* not Ham, and I'm telling you Big Boy's an ambitious man."

"Is that bad?"

"Ambition is the curse of the world."

"But what would he be without it?"

"A cracker. Nothing but a cracker. That's all right, too. The thing is, ambition has got to be balanced by principles. I'm not saying Big Boy hasn't got principles. The Stalinists sold him down the river, and it hurt bad, because he wasn't willing to turn in his principles for a new set. But I'm not so sure about the next time around."

"You don't think we ought to recruit him."

"I didn't say that either. All I'm saying is, don't get hysterical about him, because he's looking for something from us that'll make him even bigger in the eyes of those guys he's moved in on and taken over." Suddenly Hoover gave him a cold grin. His fox-white false teeth shone in the lamplight. "Do I make myself clear?"

"Well . . . I guess I've got some thinking to do."

"And I've got some letter writing." Hoover pulled open the top drawer of the flimsy maple bureau and took out a fresh white handkerchief which he shook out and passed across his shiny temple, pressing it against his eyelids for a moment.

In that moment, before Hoover pushed the drawer shut, and as Joe arose to take his leave, he was startled to see the butt of a small calibre revolver protruding from among the neat piles of socks and handkerchiefs. In the space of an instant he was reminded of his own little melodrama in Vancouver. The very difference in their situations gave him a feeling, for the first time, that he could understand the man before him.

For it was Hoover the man, not some anonymous drummer or itinerant preacher, whom he saw seated alone in the split wicker rocker, pausing in his solitary journey through the hostile white world, after bouncing in grimy coaches with no ally in the enemy camp but the porter, himself wary and indrawn, or holding himself erect, always on the alert for challenge and betrayal, while others dozed in Trailways buses driven by tobacco-chewing tyrants. Sitting alone in the Y, he wrote neat careful letters to his wife, to the National Committee, to the Political Committee, alerting them on the strengths and weaknesses of Big Boy, Ham, Joe himself. Preacher's son, college graduate, doughboy, veteran of the Bonus March, hard socialist, black union organizer, student of astronomy in narrow iron beds. Alone with his hard beliefs—and a gun.

Joe rested his hand lightly on the astronomy text at the bedside and said, "I'll be on my way now. Thanks for the coffee and the conversation."

Hoover barely glanced up. He was already taking out pen and paper, already composing his correspondence in his mind. Absently he waved farewell; before Joe had closed the door he was bending to his task.

When he was once again on the street, he stood irresolute for a moment. Astonished by what he had learned, about himself and his facile readiness to pigeonhole people, but even more about the old revolutionist and his steadfastness of purpose, he felt that he would never again be able to forecast with any certainty the course of his own life if he in his turn were to be subjected to such an endless test of his fortitude. For the first time since he had left his apartment, hours earlier, he bethought himself of his wife, weeping naked on the carpet; he had put her out of his mind deliberately. Now he hastened home, anxious, fearful of what he might find, yet hopeful that passion could be translated into patience, and the long, long view.

2. NORM

During the final days of the union election campaign, summer came
in with as much suddenness as if a cosmic hand had turned up
the heat, and in the factory itself men walked the clamorous aisles
between the silvery ranks of fighter planes, handkerchiefs tied round
their foreheads, T shirts clinging to their chests and backs, armpits ringed with sweat. Their tempers rose too, not from the heat
alone, but from the intensity of the struggle between the two con-
tending unions, the UAW and the Machinists.

In the earliest days of the UAW's effort, before the war, men
had been afraid to wear CIO buttons, and the company had
sponsored its own "Independent" union. Since then both men and
management had grown more sophisticated. The company union
had been quietly liquidated; the workers, seeing that others around
them were organizing, had become more bold, decorating their
lunchboxes and auto bumpers with union stickers—and the AFL
had entered the scene with a well-financed and noisy campaign,
challenging the primacy of the auto union's drive among these
thousands of defense workers, few of whom had ever belonged to a
union.

Despite the heat of the campaign, and the heat of a summer
hardly tempered by breezes off the lake, Norm felt a chill deep
in his being. Strange people were dying—Tom Mooney, released
but lost in a world he had never made; Russian boys fighting hopelessly for Rostov, an industrial city he had scarcely heard of before
the Nazis claimed it as booty; Odell Waller, a Negro tenant farmer
who wrote, before they electrocuted him in Richmond: "You take

big people as the President, Governors, judge, their children don't never have to suffer. They has plenty money. Born in a mention nothing ever to worry about. I am glad some people are that lucky. In my case I worked hard from sunup until sundown trying to make a living for my family and it ended in death for me." And he himself was withering, drying up in a way that frightened him.

"Maybe I just like to be on the winning side," he said to Sy one Sunday evening after a branch meeting. Now that he had been transferred to the second shift (like Joe, still working nights at the other aircraft plant), he rarely saw Sy, except when he clocked in at the plant early of an afternoon and passed his friend at the station where he was already finishing his day's work.

Sy glanced at him curiously. "I never heard you talk like that."

"Why do you suppose I got such a bang out of the Little Steel strike? It wasn't even my strike, I wasn't a steelworker, but when I went scab-chasing I knew I was on the winning side."

"You'd have done the same in any strike situation. I know you too well."

"I wonder. I'm going to be twenty-seven in August. And I'm beginning to think the great days are over for me."

"What's eating you?"

"We're not going to win that election, Sy. You know it in your heart."

"Well, maybe we won't." Sy added stubbornly, "It won't be the end of the world."

"Or the beginning either. When the workers had empty bellies, they were ready to take all kinds of chances. Now that they're buying groceries regularly, they don't want to rock the boat. Out of the kindness of its heart, the company gives us a bigger raise than the UAW was able to squeeze out of the other plant, even with aggressive leaders pushed by Joe and Bill and some of those Trotskyite boys. These workers get the message fast. They're going to play it safe, not make the company mad, vote AFL. You know that in your heart."

"You said that already."

"For God's sake, we've been beating our gums at those guys over a year now, and where's it gotten us? They'd be just as pleased to have the war go on forever—as long as they don't get drafted."

"It hasn't started to pinch yet."

"One guy in my department said yesterday the war's good for

ten years—and I couldn't contradict him. Not even when I knew he meant, I *hope* it's good for ten years. The whole UAW line about equality of sacrifice is for the birds. The UAW has lost its punch, Sy."

"I know they're mishandling the organizing drive," Sy said. "But maybe our argument will make sense out in Detroit, once the ballots are counted."

At that point he had given up. Sy misunderstood, he was committed to the long view: This organizing drive was just a skirmish, you had to have confidence that after the workers had learned you'd been right, they'd listen to you. But supposing they wouldn't? Supposing the skirmish was a sign of something else, something worse?

Questions like that couldn't be raised easily, even with friends. Besides, friends would want to argue the matter logically when it wasn't a matter of logic but of . . . hunch. Or, to put it another way, your own unreasonable desire for a kind of action that wasn't tied to the prospect of an endless war. All he got by attempting to confide in Sy was a look of hurt. Sy did not want to learn that the man he had admired was weakening; it threatened his own determination to stick it out.

He should have been able to discuss his doubts with Vera, but it was unfair to whisper treason to the one comrade who had to be sympathetic because she was married to you. Besides, what right did he have to shake her, when she herself, behind the mask of stolidity that she wore for strangers, was already uncertain? All she had in the world was him, her sister, and the movement that had brought them together.

In addition to her Party tasks, Vera worked hard at a dull factory job, assembling small parts, but she smiled readily now, she even sang at the sink or over the stove, and there were moments when he caught himself feeling that she was stronger and more stable than he. Without the solace of Vera, cooking bohunk meatballs, punching him in the belly to see if marriage had made him soft, curling her toes into his when he sneaked into their skimpy three-quarter bed at half past one every night, life on the second shift would have been intolerable.

By the eve of the balloting he knew that the cause was lost. You could see it for days beforehand from the soundtrucks the workers responded to outside the parking lots, the leaflets they took and the ones they threw away, and worst of all from the way they began to back off when he approached, his belt peppered with CIO buttons and the UAW overseas cap perched on his head. They smelled a loser. They were going AFL, which meant essentially that they were ready to string along with the company, probably for the duration. Ten years? Twenty?

No matter how he turned it over in his mind, he could not dissociate the union balloting from his own situation. His friends would put the best face on it and say that at least now the workers would have an independent rather than a company union. Still, they had voluntarily turned down the toughest, most militant, and most democratic union. This was the first real defeat for the UAW since the days of its brilliant victories over Ford and GM. Was it, as Sy claimed, simply the result of a poorly run campaign against a paternalistic corporation and an unscrupulous rival? or was it a portent of something that none of them had foreseen?

In either case, he was in the soup. If he were slow and patient like his brother-in-law Bill, he said to himself angrily, if he were a chess player instead of a football player, things would be different. But he was what he was, and now he had no future in the shop. Or even in the city. The Negroes with whom he and Vera had worked had accepted him, in the first instance, as a UAW man, able to speak for them in the CIO Council. Now, suddenly, his union local no longer existed; he would no longer be even an alternate member of the Council. Of what practical use would he be to Reverend Matthews or Coretta Wilbur? Whites were no good for Negroes, no matter how noble their intentions or how sound their advice, unless they had muscle. To a lesser extent the same held true for radicals: you could talk yourself hoarse, but if that other path you kept pointing out was only a thicket of brambles and the worker rejected your directions, what else was there to say to him? How long could you wait for him to go your way?

Weary and unsure, he entered the apartment quietly so as not to disturb his sleeping wife. But he was no sooner at the sink, rinsing out his lunch pail, than Vera was upon him, arms around his neck, hands in his hair, kissing him.

"Hello, you sneak! Out tomcatting again with the boys?"

"Vera," he said, "what are you doing up at this hour?"

"I've got good news, guess what?"

Guess what. The kids on his block used to say that. Vera, still the kid sister, was probably waiting up to give him good news about Margaret and the bar exams.

"Bea Vogel just had her baby, a girl. Fred phoned me from the hospital, Bea was in labor all day long, poor thing."

"I guess we'll have to get them a present."

"You don't have to sound so grim."

She did not know what was on his mind, and he could not bring himself to tell her.

So he stifled his doubts, tried to pick up the pieces at the plant, signed up in the AFL and caucused with his fellow CIO workers. He even managed to maintain a relationship with his Negro friends, partly because of Big Boy, who had no roots in the Negro community as did his uncle, Reverend Matthews. Big Boy had concentrated his skill and energy on the mill, where he had rapidly built up a sizeable faction in the union, with a core of followers almost as devoted as his hero-worshipping young cousin, Ham. Now he was insisting—with some reason—that the branch do for him what the Stalinists had not. He wanted it to come to his aid in the 12th Ward, to sustain him as a new Negro leader, in fact to help him push aside his ineffectual uncle. Since Norm had the closest connections with the established leadership, Harry had more or less assigned him to the job.

He consulted with Hoover, he met with NAACP activists on his free afternoons before heading for the plant, but he had no stomach for any of it. No doubt the liaison work was important; the Party was growing, and Big Boy was part of its future. But even if he had been convinced—as he was not—of the morality of undermining Reverend Matthews in favor of his aggressive nephew, there were others who could do the job.

The thought did not help him bear more patiently his stupidly boring work. When Vera organized a Sunday beach picnic with Sy and Bernice, he decided to raise the entire matter with his best friends.

But once again he was put off, this time by something less foreseeable than the birth of a baby. When they had settled at a quiet spot on the Canadian lakeshore, he said to Sy, "How come you didn't invite your cousin today? We could have used up his gas ration stamps as well as yours."

"Irwin was busy," Sy said shortly. Then he took his wife by the hand and went running into the shallow water with her.

Norm turned to Vera, on her bare knees in the sand, meticulously spreading towels, caps, sun-tan oil, on the blanket. "You look charming with your face puckered up," he said, "but after a while I'm going to get tired of that frown."

"The thing is," Vera responded rather awkwardly, "Carmie and Irwin have been having some trouble."

"What kind?"

"It's hard for Sy to talk about it. He and his cousin are such good friends, and Irwin's parents fought like mad against the marriage, and now that it's getting unstuck . . ."

"Is it? With Irwin making money like he invented it? What more does that girl want?"

"Why do you assume it's Carmie's fault?"

He should have known better. Since his transfer to the night shift the odd friendship between Vera and Carmela had been growing thicker. It was only natural for her to side with Carmela. Like Irwin, Vera saw something in Carmela that escaped him.

Puzzled, he asked, "Are you trying to tell me Irwin's walked out on her?"

"They haven't broken up. It hasn't come to that. But Carmie is not happy. And so of course Irwin isn't either."

"Naturally." Vera glanced up in suspicion, so he added hastily, "What's it all about? Bedroom trouble?"

"I don't think so. At least Carmie hasn't said, and I don't like to bring up that stuff with women anyway. She feels that Irwin isn't accepting her into his inner life. She feels that he's keeping her as a kind of pet, to decorate his home, the way she used to decorate his office."

"Maybe I'm insensitive. But what can she bring to Irwin's inner life? If I haven't noticed any hidden talents, maybe he hasn't either. Maybe they're not there."

"She has aspirations." Vera was a little stiff now. "Or do you think only men are entitled to them?"

"I never said that."

"Only intellectuals, then? Or radicals? Carmie comes from working-class people, like I do. It proves nothing that she can't get interested in our politics—except maybe that Irwin didn't know how to go about involving her."

"I never held Irwin up as a model of anything. I simply like him, that's all. Now suppose you tell me what's happening to him."

"Well . . . She's been seeing someone else."

"I think that's positively shitty. Don't you?" he challenged her. "Don't you think it is?"

"I don't think it's right."

"I wonder if you'd be so polite if it was Irwin that was doing the running around."

"I'm trying to understand, don't you see? It's very sad."

"Does Irwin know?"

"I don't think so. It's someone from an entirely different world, a man without anything, not even any friends. All he has to offer her is sympathy and understanding. Actually, I don't think there's anything for Irwin to know, at least not anything physical."

After that Sy challenged him to a race to the raft, which he won easily, as Sy must have known that he would, and when they were on the beach once again, eating the ham and potato salad that the girls had prepared, he found that he had lost the desire to talk with them about what had been troubling him.

Besides, he began to sense that Vera was changing. As he grew more glum she became more cheerful. No, not quite. It was rather that, when they had first met, he had been self-confident and she unsure; whereas now, he felt himself daily more uncertain while Vera bloomed in the sunlight of their presumed stability.

Even while he was casting about for ways and means to disabuse her the postman resolved it for him by delivering his reclassification to 1A.

With the draft board notice in his pocket, burning there as though it had been written in letters of flame, he steeled himself for the explanations. But Vera had known all along, she assured him with supreme wifely reasonableness, that he had been disheartened ever since his union's defeat.

"I've felt for a long time," she said, "that you'd be happier in the other plant, with Bill and Joe, where you could work in the union, like they do, and become a real leader. I know how frustrated you've been, trying to influence unskilled women workers who are so grateful for their eighty-five cents an hour that they won't believe they were the cause of the CIO's defeat. But if you could lick the job freeze, if you could quit, then you could get taken on with Bill and Joe, and join their local." She sat up on her haunches and looked at him eagerly. "Wouldn't that be great?"

"There's one little thing you leave out of account."

"What's that?"

"The draft."

"But . . . assuming you could get a release, you'd have the same right to deferment at another aircraft plant."

"Who says I've got a deferment?"

She blinked.

He reached into his pocket and drew out his reclassification. "There it is," he said bluntly.

To his astonishment, Vera gazed at it with great calmness. She paled, yes; but instead of cursing, as he had half-feared, she permitted an almost sly grin to creep across her face.

"Wait a minute," he said confusedly. "You look glad about this. That's not what I—"

"I am no such thing!" She cut him off. "It's just that . . . come here, sit next to me."

He obeyed, and allowed her to take his hand in both of hers. After a moment's silence she said, "See, I sort of felt this was coming . . . and I . . ."

He had no idea what she was getting at. He was about to twist free from her grasp, which was becoming uncomfortably tight, when she burst out, "I'm going to have a baby."

He stared at her. She was trying not to look away. She continued to clutch him. He could feel her pulse beating.

"Norm," she muttered, "you mustn't misunderstand."

"How can I? Either it's true or it's not."

Her laugh was unnaturally high. "I meant that I didn't want you to think that I was tricking you in some way. I hate women who do things like that."

He felt numb. All he could think of was, Well, she's found a way to quit her boring factory job. It was a stupidly unfair thought, too stupid to utter. He remained silent.

"I was afraid if I asked you beforehand, you'd say No, because I wanted to have it just for your sake, on account of the draft, to keep you here, and not because I love you and want to have your baby." She finished in a rush. "Do you know what I mean?"

"I'm really not sure."

"It must seem like the worst kind of . . . I don't know . . . I couldn't think of any other way."

Now that she had released him, he arose. The numbness was

wearing off. Or maybe what he felt now was a different kind of numbness: a sense of bafflement, of inability to cope.

"I'm sorry," he said finally, "if I don't seem to react in the right way. I guess I don't know how."

Breathing hard as though she had been running, Vera said, "It's not too late. I mean, for you to say No. Please don't think I would have waited to tell you until it was too late. Even if this hadn't happened with the draft, I would have told you. I was just looking for the proper . . ."

Proper occasion, was no doubt what she had started to say before allowing her voice to trail off; but it wouldn't do. He was convinced that she was lying now, and that she had had no intention of telling him until it was too late, or until the draft would have forced him to suggest pregnancy as a way out. No wonder she had made such a fuss over the Vogels' baby.

"Do you really mean it?" he demanded. "If I insisted on saying No, would you—"

She nodded jerkily. But her eyes denied her, and then her speech: "The thing is, though, you could go to the board and honestly say it was on the way before you were reclassified. They'd see that, they couldn't say you did it to avoid—"

"You're such a child," he said wearily. "Do you think it makes any difference to them which night you got knocked up, any more than they care whether I'm a social patriot or a social revolutionary? They've got a quota to fill, that's all."

"Yes, but they're not taking—"

"You think they won't take Fred Vogel? Guess again. He'll go, baby and all. You picked one hell of an inspiration."

She flushed. "It was more complicated than that—although Fred hasn't gone yet, has he? Don't you believe me when I tell you it was because I've been so happy with you?"

How could he answer without being a brute?

"I thought about Carmie and Irwin too," she hastened on. "More than you did. Because to me it was so sad, that they should need each other so badly and yet be pulled apart. I didn't want that to happen to me, to be idle and useless and miserable— and to make you miserable in the bargain. Oh God," she cried out, the tears coming at last, "I wanted it for you, for you! I want everything for you! And if you don't want it, then—"

He knelt beside her. "But I do. Give me a chance, it's just

that I'm new at this." His voice muffled against her sweater, he said, "I don't know which of us is more foolish. I really don't."

"But you want it?" she cried gaily. "You really do?"

He nodded. She squeezed him hard. His ear was pressed to her belly, as if he were a doctor, a prospector, an archaeologist. "I want it all right," he said. "But without illusions."

"What do you mean?"

"I mean that I'll be going into the army just the same."

"But defense workers with dependents, with children, are being deferred. Most of them anyway. When you appeal your classifi—"

"I'm not going to appeal."

"You have to."

"Who says so?"

"Why . . ." She leaned forward, as if inspired, and grasped his shirtsleeve. "The branch, that's who. If you don't appeal you'll break party discipline."

"Not unless they order me to. All we've decided is that we don't volunteer, that we go with the workers—some to the war plants, some to the armed forces."

"But you're supposed to accept deferment when you're entitled to it. You have no right to decimate the Party."

"I'm not going to plead with my draft board. I'm not going on my hands and knees to those fat middle-aged flagwavers."

"Not even for me? For us?"

"I just told you."

She turned on him then, swinging her full, rather voluptuous body upwards from the studio couch as if to attack him physically. "You're ready to quit, just because of that lousy election. One little licking, and your principles are gone. You're ready to let them stuff you into a uniform and shove a gun into your hand."

"For me the election was only a signal."

"A signal? Of what?"

"Danger. Boredom ahead."

"And what about Danger, death ahead?"

"There's no point in dramatizing. I could very easily sit out the war in some barracks in Kansas."

"Not you," she said. "I know you better than that."

"Let's wait and see, shall we?"

"Me wait? Like this? Oh what a joke," she was laughing and weeping at once, "what a lousy joke."

Half exhilarated, half uneasy, Norm was certain only that Vera would not let him go off without a struggle. He was hardly surprised when Harry took him aside after the next Sunday branch meeting and informed him, pipe streaming short ominous puffs of smoke, that he wished to see him, alone.

"I can guess what's on your mind," he said. "Since I'm on nights, I suppose it'll have to be next Saturday."

"Too late. Let's make it now. As for Vera," Harry added, anticipating an objection, "I'm sure Margaret and Bill can see her home."

Harry had a horror of talking over important matters—and for him everything was an important matter—in public places, and emulated Hoover's scorn for the cafeteria-conversationalists. He preferred to meet in obscure ice-cream parlors or, as they did now, in the somewhat eremitical privacy of his own book-lined living room, his footsteps muffled by thick Oriental throw rugs that must have been his mother's, his voice heard by no one but his father.

"How are you feeling?" Norm demanded of the old paperhanger, who was clad only in a stretched-out, droopy undershirt and pajama pants.

Strum's voice came out rusty and mottled, like the hand which he extended. "The heat gets me. It's not as bad as New York, no, but it still gets me." His cheekbones shone in the light of the torchiere like those of a death's head; the puff of white hairs on his chest, above the sagging undershirt, bloomed in the lamplight like the milk pod of a dandelion. "Let me see, you're Sy's friend, aren't you?"

"You've got a good memory, Mr. Strum. Norman is my name."

"All the years I was in the decorating business, I never forgot a face. Well I'll leave you. This heat is bad for my asthma. It's supposed to be good for it, but I know better than the doctors."

Harry closed the door on his father. "Comrade Hoover was called back to New York. He agrees with me though that we have to straighten out your draft status."

"Have you got that much pull with my board?"

"Listen, no joking, we're going to be very hard hit by the draft before the year is over. If our cadres go, we may be knocking ourselves out in vain, trying to build a party. Already the NC has been hard hit. We're a young party, with young leadership.

We're more vulnerable than any other left-wing group. You can't just walk out."

"I'm not volunteering."

"You're not appealing."

"Harry, I'm in no mood to put off the inevitable. That's a personal decision."

"I'm afraid it can't be. This is a party directive, and I'm talking as the organizer. I need you here as long as possible to stabilize the younger elements, as well as to lay out a program for recruiting in the Negro community. In fact, that's the next thing I want to talk to you about, once we get this draft business out of the way." Harry smiled, hard. His protuberant blue eyes seemed to be fairly popping out of their sockets.

Fifty Harrys, Norm thought, and we could hypnotize the working class into socialism.

"I don't know if you had trouble at home, Norm, or what, to be so lackadaisical about such an important matter as staying out of the army. But since Vera's pregnant, I take it there can't be *too* much trouble."

It was incredible. The voice of the virgin, married to his sick old dad, his chemical engineering handbooks, his files of Marxist periodicals. Surely Harry must have had a mother once upon a time. How could he have lived this long with no conception of what went on between men and women?

"Harry," he said solemnly, "I think you're going a little too far."

"Forgive me. I just wanted to say that I'm sure everything will be all right. I'd prefer to use our precious time to discuss active party work in the 12th Ward."

He seemed to assume not only that he had made his point, but that Norm had accepted it; and he went on to other matters.

Vera was waiting up for him, lying awake with a book even though she had to be up at six-thirty. She had the grace to look guilty while he sat on the edge of the bed and threw off his shoes. When he was undressed and lying beside her, she snapped off the light and put her arm across his bare chest. "You're not angry, are you? I felt I had to tell Harry."

"It had to get to the Party one way or another."

"And he didn't persuade you."

"Well, persuade. He gave me an order. And I guess he assumed I'm going to carry it out."

"But you're not."

In the dark, on the pillow, he shook his head.

"In a month, two months," she began, and then stopped. "What a prospect. What a prospect! Back to Akron. My folks haven't even got any room for me any more, let alone for a baby."

"Now that Margaret's out of law school," he suggested, "couldn't you move in with her and Bill? He won't be drafted—his local would never stand for it."

Her laugh frightened him. It reminded him of the night she had announced her pregnancy. But there was something worse in it now, a kind of hysterical hopelessness.

"What's the matter?" he demanded. "Don't you think Margaret and Bill would be glad to have you back with them? They're very solid people."

"Oh, very solid." Was she laughing? Hiccoughing?

"Can I get you a drink?"

"Make it bourbon."

"Listen, did I say something wrong about Margaret? Have you told her? I bet she'll be jealous."

Vera leaped out of bed and ran to the bathroom. She locked herself in. After a while he knocked at the door but she mumbled, "Please leave me alone." For the next hour, until she crept out, he lay staring at the ceiling and trying without success to think of what he might say to comfort her.

When she crawled back into bed she muttered, "Thanks for not pointing out that I brought it on myself."

"Don't be so funny."

"Well, you could have reminded me that it was my own fault. *I* wouldn't have had your self-control."

In the morning she was sick, but she insisted on going to work, and their life went on, seemingly unchanged. Several days later, on his way to work, passing the fuselage department where the first-shift men were cleaning up, he caught sight of Sy's upflung arm.

He hastened over to the corner where Sy was already folding his denim apron and dropping it into his toolbox.

"Nine minutes until the bell rings," he said to Sy. "What's up?"

"I got called for my physical yesterday."

"Why didn't you tell me?"

Sy shrugged in some embarrassment. "I figured it was enough that Harry knew, without making a big noise about it."

"Well, how did you do?"

"I got turned down." Sy flushed. "Flat feet. Isn't that ridiculous? I never knew I had them."

"Don't be silly. It's great. Bernie must be delighted, and Harry too. What a break."

"Yes, I guess it is. Funny, the only thing that consoled my mother about my working in the shop and living away from New York was that it would keep me out of the army. So now this."

"Sy, with a 4F you could even wangle your way out of the shop."

Sy stared at him, puzzled. "Why would I want to do that?"

Norm realized that he had blundered. He said lightly, "To make your mother happy. How's she doing?"

"Considering my father and Sid, not too bad. I called her last night to tell her about the 4F, it took me an hour to get through, and when I did she was miserable. She'd just gotten a cable from someplace called Loch Ewe, that Sid had been rescued after being torpedoed en route to Murmansk. She'd never even known that he'd been torpedoed."

"You admire his Stalinist discipline, don't you?"

Sy blinked. "If I'm going to admire anything about him it might as well be that." He said abruptly, "I understand you're violating party discipline on the draft."

"That's a matter of—"

Sy held up his hand. He leaned forward so that the workers around them could not hear him. "Everything I learned in the movement I learned from you. You recruited me."

"True. And you recruited Joe. And Joe recruited Big Boy, and Big Boy recruited Ham, and Ham—"

"I'm serious. I'm not asking you for my sake—we hardly see each other, except to wave. I'm not even asking you for your wife's sake. But the branch needs you."

"If the branch's life depended on me it wouldn't be much of a branch."

"That's not the point. We have to set an example to the new people. They're going to vote to censure you at the next meeting, to discipline you for not following through on Harry's instructions. Why don't you go and file the appeal, Norm?"

He shook his head. "That's not for me. I'm sorry, Sy. Believe me."

"If you *had* to go, there wouldn't be anything we could do about it. But you make it seem as though you *want* to go, as though you don't care any more about all the things . . . Isn't there any way I can persuade you?"

"I don't think so."

"Even if I tell you they may vote to expel you? Or doesn't that mean anything to you either?"

"I haven't heard of any party branches where I'm going anyway."

"It's a moral issue, Norm. I'm going to have to vote with Harry. Do you want to fight Hitler, is that it? That I could understand."

He shook his head. "I don't believe in the war. I don't think they're really fighting fascism. But Sy . . . Where the dying is, that's where the living is. Not here."

Sy looked very solemn. "I want you to know that I'll always regard you as my friend, even if I have to vote against you. I hate the Stalinist way of breaking off personal relations when you have political differences." And he extended his hand.

Sy's eyes were enlarged and swimming. It was ludicrous, his solemnity, but there was nothing funny about it, nothing funny at all, any more than there was in Vera's going to Sy and pleading with him to help. At that moment Norm loved his friend as he never had before.

3. IRWIN

Peering down into the yawning mouth of his recumbent patient, zeroing in on the dark spot of decay, Irwin said firmly, "This is going to hurt a little," stepped on the pedal, and brought the whirring drill down, down until it had made contact, the victim squirming as the destroying needle burned away the corruption. My own little air raid, Irwin thought, turning it slowly in a spiraling motion to make sure that he had gotten it all. His buzzer rang.

"Rinse," he said calmly. The girl was supposed to buzz him only for personal calls, but he had not been able to bring himself to explain to her which people named Metzger he wished to hear from and which he did not. Miss Rogalski was not the kind of person you confided in.

A moment later, as he was altering the patient's head rest, the door opened. Miss Rogalski stuck in her starched blond head, square as a box, and said crossly, "It's personal, Doctor."

"Thank you," he said. He added, "I was aware of that," but she had already closed the door behind her, depriving him of the satisfaction of the last word. He glared at the phone on his desk. Who? If it was Carmela, he was afraid, wanting and not wanting. If his mother, he did not want—but she was as inescapable as the war.

It was his mother. "Did you have lunch with papa today?"

"You know I did."

"I couldn't reach him in the store, he was out on the floor." Lucky man. "You talked with him about Carmela?"

"He'll tell you."

"And the commission? He told you about that?"

"I'm terribly busy, I've got a waiting room full of patients."

"You used to complain because it was empty. I used to call you so your phone should only ring." And I used to ask you not to.

"I have a patient in the chair," he said briskly. "It was great to hear your voice, goodbye," and he hung up.

She would never leave him alone, never, never. When she could not get at him herself she sicked his father on him. But his father, like a terrier released from the leash, did not know quite what to do other than to yelp plaintively.

He had yelped through lunch, urging his son to eat heartily while saying things that ruined Irwin's digestion and caused the spinach to catch in his throat, halfway down, like long salty strands of seaweed. His father's head, much too small for his shoulders and the rest of him, was wrinkled with pain and disgust as he mouthed the atrocious rumors of Carmela's misconduct. "We're going through a difficult period, papa," Irwin had explained, and winced as his father angrily spat the end of his cigar onto the remains of his Caesar salad. "You smoke too much, papa," he said, but he was not thinking so much of his father's heart or lungs as of the disproportion between tiny head and huge cigar.

Just as his parents were learning to live with the humiliation of his disadvantageous marriage, they were humiliated by the gossip about Carmela's wildness, her refusal to go out with Irwin to visit his friends, her abrupt silences, the prolonged "shopping expeditions" from which she returned oddly empty-handed. Divorce— a device for bums, millionaires, and movie stars, and hence an added reason for horror when Irwin and Carmela had decided upon marriage—now became thinkable. Indeed, it was even proof of their being up to date, wasn't it? his mother argued, that now they were ready to admit divorce as a reasonable alternative not just for the riffraff but for the respectable.

Useless for Irwin to argue that he had no faintest intention of getting a divorce. Now that the unspeakable had been spoken about, his parents demonstrated their flexibility on yet another front: his military service. It too had been a dirty word like divorce, with the most improbable, illegal, and downright unpatriotic alternatives seriously suggested to him, but now—as photos of soldier sons began to appear on mantelpieces and mothers began to brag of their boys' brilliant progress in OCS—Irwin was being urged to be a go-getter, to show a little initiative, to secure the best possible deal before he was unceremoniously yanked off.

In fact, his parents yoked together the two crises. He could resolve both, they hinted, by securing a commission with a promise of service in some nearby base on the Niagara Frontier, and then, during the period granted him for settling his affairs, he could settle this affair forever by slipping off say to Mexico and returning as a single man, an officer and gentleman whose marital status could no longer be the subject of gossip. Indeed, his mother even envisaged the painless liquidation of his apartment (perhaps under a local anesthetic) and his return to the family home and the bachelor room which would await his weekend relaxation from the stern demands of military dentistry.

In a way, he himself had made this fairy tale plausible. Not necessarily by marrying the wrong girl, but by taking into junior partnership a club-footed young man named Stuart Kraft who was fresh out of dental school and without funds to furnish an office of his own. His mother had winced at the young man's affliction, but as she collected herself she came to think of it as a gift from God, a guarantee that Dr. Kraft would hold down the fort while Dr. Metzger was off at the front, tending the other afflicted. And there was something to that. Stuart was honest and capable, they got on well together, and they had already worked out an informal agreement whereby Irwin would receive a small percentage of the office earnings for the duration if he should go into service, and the partnership would be resumed with the peace.

But there was Carmela. One day she would agree that his plans were thoroughly sound, that Stuart was a nice boy, a real find, and the next she would shout, "What the hell do I care? You think it makes any difference to me what you do?"

It did, though. It made a lot of difference. If not, why did she always tell him that she detested so many things that he did?

"I'll change," he said to her, "I'll try not to upset you if you'll tell me what's on your mind," but that only infuriated her more.

"You wouldn't understand!" The old cry.

There were times when he was unsure whether the cry was wrung from her by contempt or by despair; because of his fear that it might be the latter, he held his peace, hoping that the calm which always followed these outbursts would one day become permanent rather than an interlude as unpredictable as the rages themselves.

It had reached the point where he was no longer certain to find her at home at the end of the day. Sometimes she would come home when he did, even a few moments later, her arms loaded, color high on her cheekbones, crying, "Wait till you see what I bought!"

It would turn out to be seating material for four chairs, petitpoint, needles, books of instructions which he knew she would never read. "I'm going to make all four different. Fantastic! A dog on one, birds on another, maybe fishes, a shepherdess. You can do anything!"

Or a portable kiln for doing ceramics in the kitchen, which upon examination turned out to require the kind of voltage available only in a factory.

Once he had suggested, tentatively, that she might like to come back to the office again, not full time, but to help out her successor, Miss Rogalski the blockhead. "Stuart and I could use you."

A mistake. "You could keep your eye on me, is what you mean. What's the matter, your mother been telling you stories again?"

His mother didn't have to. There were evenings when he sat alone, wondering, and Carmela drifted in toward midnight, hungry, raiding the refrigerator, filled with lassitude.

"I was over at the Zivics', keeping Vera company. Her belly's so big she can't even sleep right any more."

What was he to do, ring them up and find out if Carmie had really been there all evening? Chances were she had—but there were also occasions when he was even more certain that she had not been where she claimed, when indeed her excuse ("I was with my father's cousin Nettie, she's got cancer") was so listless that it did not defy verification, but rather hung in the air like a carelessly rinsed, faded undergarment, proclaiming her utter indifference as to whether or not he liked it.

She rejected his political sympathies, yet chose for a friend Vera Miller, radical and member of a lifelong radical family. Still he had to admit that this made sense: she turned away not from the bred in the bone dissidents but from his middle-class friends like Fred who had selected radicalism as one might choose a tie, or from those who had married into it, like Anne Link; Vito's cartoons she waved away as favors done for friends. "I know him," she said, adding illogically, "I posed for him. What he really cares about are the crazy pictures."

Irwin was willing to respect her judgment on the crazy pictures, as well as on his friends. All he asked in return was that she respect his, or at least allow him his eccentricities and his financial aid to those whom he admired. But this Carmela would not do. Instead she attacked what she called his "pretensions," a new word for her.

"Besides," she said finally, "you're not creative."

This was new too, and therefore alarming. Pressed to explain, she could only assert that his guitar-playing and his folksong collection were proof that something was missing from his life.

"Well maybe," he conceded. "But suppose they're just hobbies that I enjoy?"

This she would not accept. In her insistence that his lack of creativity was stifling her Carmela began to resort to a jargon which he was sure she had picked up outside the house. It was as if she had taken to wearing clothes which neither she nor he had bought, and it tended to persuade him that the worst of the rumors had some basis.

Still, there were those times when she was all that he had hoped for—fetching, gay, amusing, companionable—yes, even laughing at her own striving, her ludicrous effort to escape being "just one more Wop kid."

On the evening of the inconclusive luncheon with his father and the abruptly terminated conversation with his mother, Irwin guided the Mercury through the icy ruts to the apartment house garage, glancing up so see if the lights were on in their living room. Not that that proved anything: Carmie delighted in turning on all the lights on dreary winter days and leaving them on even when she went out. "My old man used to beat me," she would say proudly, "if I left the light on in the john after I was finished using it."

So he went on up in the elevator, not knowing whether he would be alone with Gabriel Heatter, Lowell Thomas, and the fighting in the South Pacific.

Not only was Carmela there, she was snapping her fingers to one of his folk songs on the Magnavox, spaghetti was bubbling on the stove, and as she tugged off his overcoat and threw his scarf around her own neck she gave him a hot kiss.

"Hello my baby," she said gaily, "how's my tired baby?"

"What's the occasion?"

"Don't ask. Talk less and make yourself more useful."

"Such as?"

She wiped her hands on her apron. "Open the wine. I got Bardolino, justa like you like. And clam sauce with the spaghet'."

Who could complain? They laughed their way through dinner, the clam sauce was marvelous, they made love on the couch without even going to the bedroom, and before they gathered up their clothing from the floor and fell into bed he had her laughing hysterically at the way he had hung up on his mother after his father, nagging at him about his commission, had made him choke over his spinach. The last thing she said before dropping off like a baby in the crook of his arm was, "Just the same, you shouldn't make fun of your parents. Not even if they say things to you about me. Don't tell me they don't, but don't make fun of them either."

And yet, two nights later, when he came home to shower and shave for the party for the latest draftee, Joe Link, at the Vogels', Carmela was not there. There was nothing in the apartment, no note, only his present for Joe, a foolishly expensive monogrammed toilet kit for a rich GI, lying gift-wrapped on the coffee table. He tucked it under his arm and drove off slowly, hoping against hope that Carmie would turn up at the Vogels' or might even be there already, helping Bea and Vera.

Everyone was very polite. They neither avoided him nor crowded around him—after all, his party would come in its turn. Joe, today's hero, was seemingly at ease, in command of himself as always, his arm often encircling his quiet wife. When Bea's baby awoke, she too joined the party at Fred's insistence and was given a fingertip of wine as a toast to her departing godfather.

Irwin sat smiling on the couch, chatting with his friends, trying to be cool each time he said something noncommittal about Carmie. Vera joined him for some time, her hands in her lap while she spoke of Norm rather than of his wife.

"Yes, finally I got a letter this morning. He's been on maneuvers, that's why I didn't hear for a while. In Louisiana. His outfit is in training for jungle combat. I'm keeping my fingers crossed. The doctor won't let me travel now, he says no. But afterward . . ."

Vera was not the only one who missed Norm, the fast talker.

And when you yanked Joe out of the room, no more deep laugh, no more big basketball player's hands waving as he talked, what an emptiness there would be, as if you had scooped some of the air from the room, some of the joy from their lives. Who will be left, he thought, gazing about him—Sy, me, the restless women? He himself would be going soon enough, but maybe Vito would be left to console them. "I'm 4F, I've got a crack in my ass!" Vito shouted, when someone asked him when he would be going to war. But this was only because, so Fred had informed Irwin in confidence, the painter suffered from a bleeding ulcer that he did not want to talk about any more than he wanted to discuss his pictures. Just at the point when Irwin thought he might squeeze Joe's hand in farewell and slip away, Vito had cornered him in Fred's study. There, surrounded by his friend's library and his framed facsimile of a Crashaw manuscript poem, he was trapped by the man who had struggled, cursing and muttering, to translate Carmela's flesh into immortality. "What's the matter," Vito demanded roughly, "Carmie giving you a hard time?" and when he mumbled some foolish words, the painter bellowed: "Take my advice and I mean it: Give her a belt in the mush."

It was a painful evening in every way. He found it hard to forgive Carmela for her absence, even after she turned up at the railroad station the following morning at dawn with a box of her mother's spice cookies for Joe and a hug for Anne, who, she said later, stood on the platform stonelike with the weeping mothers, not even waving after the train, saying only "Now I'm going home to practice."

One way or another he and Carmela made it up, or at least let it slide, as the winter days slid by. What right did he have to complain? The Russians were dying in unimaginable numbers at Stalingrad, but then so were the Germans, freezing with their fangs bared, like wolves impaled on icicles, and it began to seem as though the Nazis could be stopped at last. And while the blood sank into the snow, and he tooled between apartment and office in his heated Mercury, his father was working as he had never worked, indefatigably exploiting his connections in the Masons to ensure that Irwin would be stationed at Fort Niagara with captain's bars catching the glint of his probing dentist's drill.

Meanwhile he gave to the Party, he helped pay the rent for the branch headquarters, he contributed to a campaign fund for

Big Boy, running for City Councilman as one of the first New Party candidates between New York City and California. He even ventured to a Sunday evening social at the branch headquarters, impressed by the crowd of defense workers lindying under Vito's boldly lettered socialist banners. "We're rolling, Irwin, we're really rolling," Harry murmured over a paper cup of beer, and Sy, standing on his other side, added quietly, "You've got your share in this, you can be proud."

But he was not proud, he was lethargic. He listened to Harry, and occasionally to Hoover when he was free, and at times he even ventured to quarrel with their analyses; he took pleasure in the growth of the Party, in Bill's stature as a militant leader known throughout the city, in their careful nurturing of Big Boy and the foothold they were gaining among the Negroes; but he was not the man they were. Sometimes, when he surveyed his wife's face, frowning before her make-up mirror, furrowed over a restaurant menu, frustrated over a crossword puzzle before she pitched the paper away in despair, he too was in despair, for he knew that he would never be able to strike her, to rupture that glorious blue-white skin, bruise that elastic flesh, give her that belt in the mush as Vito had insisted he should.

If that was what she really craved it would have to come from someone else. And perhaps it did. Her absences grew more frequent as the second winter of the war ground on, the snow spitting from his skid chains as elsewhere it was crunched under tank treads. She stayed out later and later, no longer even troubling to tiptoe on her return, sometimes banging bottles about in the medicine chest, once or twice even jerking back the bedclothing as though she knew full well that he lay awake in the dark waiting for her, and falling on top of him, naked and demanding.

Demanding what? He could no longer ask her, not when her absences stretched out to days on end, any more than he could say why she chewed the polish from her blood-red nails when she did stay at home.

When he remained in the apartment, reading, listening to his record player, drinking bourbon against the moment when Carmela would crumple the crossword puzzle and throw the paper away, she would look up, as if the sound of the tinkling ice distracted her, and demand, "What are you drinking that bourbon for?"

"Because I can't get Scotch."

"You know what I mean. You ought to be ashamed. I thought Jews weren't supposed to be drinkers. A glass of wine, a little schnapps, right?"

"So they say. But I haven't been sleeping well."

"You must have a bad conscience."

It was preposterous. Crazy. But he fared no better when he ventured out. Where was there to go? Fred was eager to solve his problem for him, but that was precisely it: It would have been easier to hear about Crashaw, Irwin thought, and took to staying away, relieved at not having to face Bea, smiling at him with middle-class wifely solicitude over her baby's naked behind as it bounced, dimpled, on her blurp-stained shoulder. He suspected too that Fred, now that Crashaw and the Ph.D. were behind him, was unhappy with Bea all over again and wanted to confide as well as to advise. And he did not want to hear this either. Above all he did not want an equation made between Bea—who was sexless and a bore—and Carmie who—whatever else she was— was neither of those.

Sy was out—he worked nights. The women, the wives, seemed to lead their own twined lives, leaning on one another and growing together like vines, and mixing with the men mostly in the course of activities—such as the distribution of *New Labor* at plant gates— in which he could not participate. Only once in a while was there an evening's solace with Bill and Margaret, who made no demands, and once took him to Anne's to listen in silence while she played Scarlatti sonatas for them for an entire tranquil evening.

Besides, he had one foot in the army already, he had filed the papers, and he dared not jeopardize the commission. What was more, the people who were coming into the Party, and the Party members who were coming to the city for war jobs, did not engage him as had the earlier ones. Harry, with whom he had hoped he would have a good deal in common, was very taken up with these new people when he was not busy with his evening chemistry classes or the preparation of forums and educa- tionals for the war workers and professionals. Some of these he passed along to Irwin as patients.

One among them, a dour, cadaverous sheetmetal worker named Hunter—that was all, just Hunter—came to see him for a toothache late one evening toward the end of winter, when everything was at its worst and Carmie had completely disappeared. Hunter lived alone in a rooming house on Franklin Street and worked alone in an obscure machine shop. He waited his turn patiently, sank back at last into the chair after a quick glance behind him almost as if to be sure that he had not been followed, submitted quietly to the drilling and the filling, and insisted upon paying for the work at Irwin's full scale. Lonely as he was, Irwin was glad to see him go, so that he could shut up shop.

Cleaning up after him, Irwin thought he heard a strange sound in the waiting room. Had Hunter come back? Miss Rogalski, and Stuart also, were long since gone; he opened his office door for a look.

Vera Miller was sitting on the edge of the leatherette sofa, hands folded beneath her swollen belly, her cheeks reddened from the cold night wind, her abundant coarse hair escaping from a scarf drawn over her head. Her mouth was open and she was wheezing slightly. That was the sound he had heard.

"Vera, for heaven's sakes!" he greeted her as cheerfully as he could. "It's good to see you. I hope everything's all right—no emergency, I mean?" He dreaded doing extractions on women in the late stages of pregnancy; the anesthesia frightened him, and when he had to conceal his fright he felt it an encumbrance that kept him from functioning well.

"No, I'm all right." She looked at him anxiously. "Do you have a minute?"

"Of course!" To reassure her, he sat down beside her, folding his white jacket into a square and tossing it aside. "You just missed Hunter."

"Thank goodness. Bill says he's just lonely, but he gives me the creeps. I must say, we're getting some weirdos in the branch. First Hunter, then that hillbilly trio, the Smalls."

"I'm glad you feel that way. I was beginning to think it was maybe my fault that . . . Well, anyway, what do you hear from Norm?"

She undid her scraf and shook her hair free; a few drops of moisture fell to the floor. Snow again, snow and more snow. "He says he's fine, and I believe him," she said. "He's so rugged. He's lost eleven pounds, going on forced marches down in those swamps with full pack . . . He's en route to a POE . . . I think it's going to be Fort Ord, or someplace like that."

"Where's that?"

"California. I knew from the start, practically, that he'd wind up in the South Pacific. The baby is due any day. After the delivery, as soon as I can"—her speech was nervous and uneven—"I want to go on out there to be with him before he ships out, even if it's only for a little while. What I'll do is, I'll leave the baby with Margaret. When they're that tiny, brand new, all they do is sleep all the time anyway." She laughed tensely. "So they tell me."

"It must be rough, sweating out these last few days."

"It was almost better when I was working in that dumb factory. At least it kept me tired and I had the girls to talk to on the line. Now I'm trying to keep things going for Bill and Margaret—she's very busy, you know, in her law office, she brings home cases at night. So I do what I can for her, and later, she'll be helping me. But Irwin . . . what I really came to talk to you about is Carmie. She hasn't been home, has she? Not for a while?"

Irwin closed his eyes. "No," he said. "No, she hasn't."

"What's the matter with you? Haven't you even tried to find out where she's gone?"

"I suppose you think I'm a fool. Or something even worse. But it goes against my grain, do you see? Either she wants to live with me or she doesn't. It's too degrading for me to run after her and—"

"Irwin, she's pregnant."

He felt the blood rush to his head, hot, dizzying, as though he had been slapped. "You're sure."

"Oh yes."

He arose and began to pace about the waiting room until the burning had subsided, but when he faced Vera again he could not think of what he ought to say. Almost shamefacedly, he stood before her, rubbing his cheek, waiting for her to go on.

She said tiredly, "I hate to be here like this. To be the one to tell you, I mean. But it seems so awful to me, that the two of you should be so unhappy. You don't mind my saying that, do you?"

"No, no," he said hastily, "not at all. I haven't tried to hide . . ."

"I simply thought—well, what I would give, just for Norm and me to be together, even to fight, or yell at each other."

"I know."

"So I said to myself, I'll go see Irwin and tell him where she is and leave it up to him." She blew her nose. "She's staying with a man named Lindenbauer, Louis Lindenbauer."

Staying was a good word; it made everything sound so neutral, like a hotel. Stopping at a hotel, was the way the English always described it. Not eating, not living, certainly not sleeping. He said to Vera, "Who's he? I never heard of him." He forced himself to add lightly, "I suppose everybody else has except me."

"It's one of those crazy things. He works for Hall's Bakery, you know, the bread wagons."

"What does he do?"

She glanced at him, surprised. "Like I said. He drives a delivery wagon."

Sliced bread? Parker House rolls? He wheeled on her. "Are they in love? Are you trying to tell me they're in love?"

Vera looked almost shocked. "I don't think so. At least, she's— Irwin, I don't think she knows what she's doing at this point. I think you made it too easy for her, she wasn't used to anything like that, she's used to being told what to do."

"And she made it too difficult for me. That should have evened things out."

"I'm not trying to tell you what to do with your life," Vera said apologetically. "I'm the last one . . ."

"Just the same you think I ought to see her."

"Well . . . She's living, I mean he is, way out, sort of on the way to Niagara Falls, or Grand Island, I hardly know that section at all." She fumbled in her purse and brought out a sheet of paper torn from a five-cent notebook. "You know where Dunlop Tire and Rubber is?"

He stared at the paper, then at her. "But there's nothing there. I've been by there a million times. There's no houses there at all."

"It's not a house. It's a trailer camp."

Vera was sitting spreadlegged on the leatherette couch, wheezing, substantial as though she had been carved, but he had the feeling that she was out in the middle of the Niagara, like some northern Lorelei, beckoning to him to join her and Carmela; when he waded into the icy torrent, stones would smash against his shins, the current would catch him and fling him onwards, flailing and choking. But no, here he stood, warm and dry, the piece of paper in his hand, as though she had come through the snow to bring him the address of a sale on steaks, or tires.

"Come on," he said. "Let me take you home."

"You don't have to do that. I only came up because I didn't want to talk to you on the phone about it. I hate the whole thing."

"Me too." He shrugged into his overcoat. "Put on your scarf, don't catch cold at this point."

On the way down in the elevator he said to her, "You wait in the lobby by the swinging doors while I run over to the lot for my car. I'll toot when I get back, okay?"

"You don't have to do that," she said again. "I'll walk over with you," but her words were almost lost behind him as he ran out into the sleet.

They drove to the Zivics in virtually absolute silence. At one point, when they were waiting for a red light not far from her sister's, she turned to him suddenly. "I think she's sorry for him."

"What about me?" he demanded loudly. "What about me?" It was, he realized, the first time he had raised his voice since she had brought him the news. He felt a fool.

Vera replied mysteriously, "I think she's sorry for you too. But in a different way."

They said nothing more until he had walked her from the car up the icy path to the storm door, gripping her firmly by the arm. "You're not angry at me?" she asked. He could almost feel her great warm belly as she swung the door open, swaying awkwardly. Bea, Vera, Carmela.

"I'm grateful," he said. "Say hello to Norm when you write."

He sat in the car in front of the Zivics' darkened apartment for some time with the motor idling, until he began to feel a chill. From the glove compartment, where it lay buried under badly folded road maps, he pulled out a pint of bourbon. He took two long drinks, replaced the bottle, and studied Vera's little sheet of paper for a moment; then, mopping the condensation from the inside of the windshield with the back of his gloved hand, he drove off in search of the trailer camp.

It took a while. The weather was vile, and the dimout did not help. The trailer colony sat humped in the frozen mud, half-buried in stale snow like giant grubby toys left over from Christmas, left outside to rust until they could be raked up and thrown away in the spring cleaning. Toy lamps perched in their toy picture windows. Who in God's name would park himself in a potato field with a tube of bottle gas for an Ali Baba jug, a withered geranium in a pot for a tropical garden, a scalloped metal awning for a Provençal roof? It was hard to believe that real people, war workers most of them, to whom his friends peddled *New Labor,* lived in these imitation things. Hunting for Louis Lindenbauer, Irwin clumped through the halfheartedly shoveled alleyway that served as the trailers' boulevard, his ankles soaking, his feet filling with snow as he pounded at the wrong doors.

At the third one a slender man, his features indistinct, the light from within silhouetting his figure, said, "Yes, that's me. What can I—"

"I want to talk to you." Irwin proceeded up the steps and shouldered his way in, all but forcing the man to make way.

Lindenbauer backed up awkwardly. There was something wrong with his hip, Irwin saw at once; it jutted at the belt as if he had a hump, or a growth. What a job, he thought, climbing in and out of a breadwagon all day with that thing. It made him seem old, that dislocation and awkwardness, and in addition he was losing his hair; but as he backed into the light of the ugly little lamp in his window, Irwin saw that he had a young face. A young-old face. He was no more than thirty.

Carmela was seated beyond the lamp, before an ancient clumsy typewriter that would have looked more at home in a pawnshop window. On either side of the machine lay a stack of paper, one of yellow second sheets, the other of bond. Carmela wore a longsleeved sweater, slacks, snow boots, although the tiny room was stifling. There were circles under her eyes.

"Hello Irwin," she said.

"Who is this?" Lindenbauer demanded of her.

"This is the husband," Irwin said. "Didn't she bother—"

A curtain was pushed aside at the far end of the room and a woman emerged from the cubbyhole beyond, an older woman with gold canines and a poor complexion. Her hair was in curlers.

"This is the husband," Irwin said again.

"Irwin, this is Louis Lindenbauer—"

"I know."

"—and his mother, Mrs. Lindenbauer. Louis, would you give Irwin a chair?"

Wordlessly, warily, the delivery man pulled out a toy chair from underneath the table at which Carmela sat. Irwin glanced at Carmela and then sat down. "Go ahead," he said.

"Louis is a writer," she said.

"I thought he was a breadman."

"I earn my living with a delivery route," Lindenbauer said.

"Mother, sit down here next to me on the bench." When his mother had seated herself gingerly on his good side he went on, "I work to support my mother and me. Actually I'm—"

"You're a writer."

"I haven't been published yet, but I've been at work for a long time on an epic novel."

"An epic novel." Irwin gazed at the huddle around him.

Two crossed flags hung on the wall, somewhat askew, above an indistinct photograph of a man in uniform. His father? A tiny bookcase held a Webster-Merriam, a jar of peanut butter, some Red Seal paperbacks, a pile of back numbers of *Story* magazine, two loaves of the bread that he sold. The bench on which he and his mother sat apparently opened out into a bed. There was little else— a ceramic ashtray in the shape of a fish, a whale perhaps, in Carmela's taste, heaped with the butts of filter-tipped cigarettes. The room stank of smoke. Beyond the picture window lay other trailers, more or less like this one. It was like dying in a Pullman car going no place, dumped in a freightyard and forgotten.

"It's a great novel," Carmela said, patting the pile of second sheets. "It's all about the Gold Rush, and the building of an empire."

"Carmela has been very helpful," Lindenbauer said. He sat hunched, his hands on his knees, whether to give his mother more room or because he was used to cramped quarters, Irwin could not tell. "She and mother have been typing for me while I'm out on my route. It's a tremendous job."

"You come from Alaska?" Irwin asked.

He looked up, startled. "Oh no. I've always lived right here in western New York. I was born in a little town called Java, you know where that is? Then mother used to have a novelty store in Niagara Falls, but that didn't work out on account of the depression."

"Louis has always been a good son," his mother offered. Her voice was dry and distant, as though the trailer's bottle gas heat had dried out her nasal passages. "His daddy was killed in the Argonne fighting for his country when Louis was just a little thing, no more than five years old. And then later on Louis fell, trying to learn how to ice-skate, and his hip didn't mend right. But he's always been a good son."

"Carmela was sympathetic from the first time we met," Lindenbauer explained. His eyes, behind rimless glasses, turned gratefully in Carmela's direction. Irwin glanced away, out the window, as the man went on: "It's funny how those things are. I knew at once that she had a great feeling for art."

Irwin arose. "Carmela, get your coat."

"Dr. Metzger, I'm sorry if all this has upset you, about Carmela. She has a great deal to offer. She feels she was being stifled."

Carmela said, "I didn't ask you to come here, Irwin."

"Don't argue with me. It's late and I'm tired. Get your coat."

"She's an unhappy child," Mrs. Lindenbauer said. "I could see that the minute she walked in this door. Sometimes we have to learn to make adjustments, doctor. That's life. I'm an older woman and I know. It isn't easy."

Irwin walked to the curtain, it was only three steps, and pulled it back. To the right of the rounded cubbyhole in which Mrs. Lindenbauer lived, or rather lay, like an egg abandoned in the nest, was a toy closet. He yanked Carmela's coat off the hook and tossed it at her. "Put it on."

"Dr. Metzger, you can't force her. This isn't Arabia."

"Arabia?" Irwin said, puzzled. He reached out for Carmela's wrist, pulled her to her feet, and flung the coat over her shoulders.

"She's not your slave. There is a higher law. I appeal to your sense of decency."

"Bullshit," Irwin said. "Is this a place for her to live? To have a baby? I wouldn't let my dog have pups in here."

"That's her decision, not yours."

"She's my wife, not yours. And it's my baby, not—"

"What makes you think so?" Carmela cried. "What makes you so sure?"

Irwin raised his arm and swung at her backhanded, catching Mrs. Lindenbauer's curlers and knocking them askew. The old woman let out a faint yip like a dog that has been trod on, and fell back down on the bench. Her son made no move to stop Irwin from striking Carmela.

Irwin paused. Instead of bringing his arm forward across his wife's red mouth he gave her a shove toward the door. "Let's go," he said. "Move."

She moved, the coat half falling off her shoulders as she made her way down the narrow corridor, swaying drunkenly like a woman on a train.

"Why can't we act like adults?" Lindenbauer demanded. "Why

can't we sit down and discuss this man to man? Carmela found something here, you can't deny that."

"She sure did." At the door Irwin turned as he opened the door for his wife and nudged her outward. "You'd better get back to your book."

Lindenbauer stood beside his mother, wiping his hands up and down on the thighs of his whipcord bakery driver's pants, his pale eyes behind the rimless glasses swimming with tears. Irwin ducked his head and hastened out, prodding his wife ahead of him until they had reached the car. No sound came from the trailer behind them.

In the automobile Carmela's voice was indistinct behind the handkerchief that she held to her face. "I didn't ask you to come."

"You said that already."

"It's true. I was trying to find my own way. He didn't tell me what to think or how to vote. He was too busy creating a great work of his own."

"You knew I wouldn't let you stay there. You wanted me to show up, you wanted me to blow up, you wanted me to beat him up. Are you satisfied now? Or did you want me to beat you up instead, in front of him and his mother?"

"I don't know, I don't know what I wanted. I thought I knew, but it's all so crazy. Oh Irwin," she sobbed suddenly, tearing the handkerchief in two and pounding on the dashboard with her fists, "I'm the one that's crazy. Crazy! Crazy!" She slumped onto his shoulder and lay weeping as they drove home through the bitter wintry night.

4. SY

All the way to the post office, Sy was whistling. The weather was marvelous, it was early, and he had practically the whole day to be with Bernie before going to the plant. Ever since she had quit her job to work full time for the party things had been looking up. As long as he and Bernie had their days together he could not complain about being moved to the night shift. He parked the car behind the gloomy gray building and went on in to collect the branch's parcel post; if Vera had been able to stay home like Bernie, those last months on the night shift would not have been so trying for Norm.

Staggering a little under the weight of four bundles of *New Labor,* the heavy twine cutting into his hands, he wobbled back to his old car, dumped them on the sidewalk, and flipped up the trunk lid. Every week there were more. The paper was an eight-pager now, and the branch was distributing thirty-five hundred a week— not counting subscriptions. If things kept up at this rate they'd have to be delivered by truck. Capitalists.

When he got back to the flat he pitched the papers onto the driveway and carried them into the dining room—Bernie's office— where she was working assiduously on her accounts among notebooks, tally sheets, and papers.

Bernie made a face. "I wish Harry hadn't given me the job of writing our stories up for *New Labor.* I'm just not a good writer. It's hard for me."

"Read me what you've got."

A bit self-consciously, she started off, in her high girlish voice, holding the paper up to the light. Flowing through the open window at her back, the June sun struck her shoulders and touched her hair, which she had carelessly wound round and caught up with a pin on top of her head.

"Most of our bundle order is distributed every week at the gates of two UAW plants and one steel mill. Since this is traditional, we will point out only that our NL distributors are well received at each of the three concentration points, in fact many workers wait to congratulate them on one of Vito's cartoons, or to discuss some particular article." She paused and glanced up, expectantly.

"It would sound better if you said *a* particular article, instead of *some* particular article. And I think you ought to have a period after concentration points instead of a comma."

"I thought I'd add something about the Stalinists trying to get the CIO to ban our press."

"Explain how they don't dare attack our girl distributors—it'll probably hold good in other places too."

"Then I get to the main part."

"I'm listening."

"Most of our local subscriptions are obtained through house to house distribution, now up to seven hundred copies a week. Our usual concentration is a housing project, since a team can cover three to four hundred families in half an hour. After the project has been carefully mapped, each worker is assigned to a specific area, with the responsibility for every family getting the paper every week for four weeks in a row."

Now that Carmela had given birth, Bernie was the last one of the bunch without a baby. Except for Anne, whose husband was in North Africa. And Margaret, who had a profession.

"After four weeks, each worker begins a conversation—do you think that's clear?—with these families. Then he goes on, after his personal contacts, to leave papers at that portion of his particular area that he has not previously reached, so that by the time he does reach the end of his area, some of his prospective customers have been receiving *New Labor* for seven to eight weeks."

"That ought to impress some of those lazy people in New York."

"Then I thought of a separate paragraph on our special bundle orders for public events, like the eight thousand papers with the anti-Jim Crow banner headline that we placed on every seat at the NAACP-UAW rally."

"That ought to wrap it up."

"That's only the start. It's going to take me all day to process these subs, and get the contact list up to date, and break up those papers into distribution bundles. And you'll have to help me deliver the bundles to the newsstands too. After you go to work, I've got to get hold of Fred at the university to see if he's made any progress setting up the Dworkin debate."

The landlady's terrier began to yip. "That's the mail. I'll get it, you finish that report."

He threw a pebble for the dog, scooped up their mail, and brought it back into the apartment, tossing the letters on the table one by one. "Gas bill. Letter from my mother. Ad for victory tires —Bill says they make them out of skim milk. V-Mail, from Norm!"

"Read it to me. I read this junk to you."

Sy cleared his throat. He knew without looking how it would begin: Dear Boys. It was Norm's permanent greeting, his play on Bernice's nickname. *"Dear Boys: Long time no write. Two excuses, boredom and fright. Please don't pass this on to Vera and son, to whom I present a stiff upper lip. But boys, when I am not bored which is 90% of the time, I am so scared I need diapers worse than Marlen. We have just finished securing our third beachhead, and while I am no student of geography, I would be willing to guess that there are 500 more like it waiting for us between here, wherever the hell here is, and Tokyo. If you are expecting sociological analysis or travelog, read no further. I cannot tell these islands apart, partly because we do not stay long enough to acquire expertise. Well, why go on. It hardly seems worth while getting to know those around me—most don't live long enough. But my C.O., a nervy bastard known as D-Day Dick, insists that if I stick right close with him, he and I will be drinking plenty Jap beer together. A hero. Me, I haul ass because I can't stay on the beach, I fire a few bursts, flop again, try to make it off the sand and into the trees only because maybe I'll live a little longer there. In between, nothing but dirty words, warm beer, and stories I've heard a million times before. Even more boring than the industrial front. Does it pay to be restless, I ask you? Your rapidly aging old friend Norm. PS If the above seems a little runny-nosed, please forgive. The fact is nothing I ever did before seems to have any relevance to what is going on here. You know what I mean? Very unsettling. But things may change again when the shooting stops. If ever. N."*

Sy put the letter down without comment. Bernie was sitting staring at the table, her knuckles to her lips. Finally she looked across at him, desolate-eyed.

"We'll never see him again," she said.

"Don't say that. I don't believe it."

"Is there a chance he'll be relieved? Don't they send them back to Australia or someplace for relief after a while?"

A big bumblebee, plump and swollen with honey, rose from the rambler beneath the window at Bernie's back and buzzed against the screen, unsatisfied, searching for more. The still air was heavy.

"He has no belief in what he's doing there, that's what makes it seems so awful, to die like that . . ."

What she said would have startled their friends. If they thought of her at the dining-room table, it was with a pencil in her hand, crisply crossing their names off lists, exhorting them to surpass quotas.

"I think he'll make it. I think he really wants to get back to Vera."

"Wanting and being able to, those are two . . ."

I am different, he thought, and she knows it. Even if he had never told her how envious he had been of Norm and his mission to Mexico, of Joe and his voyages to the South Seas, she must have sensed it. And known too that if Norm or Joe had been classified 4F as he had been, they would have smashed things, yelled, gotten drunk, like Vito. They would never have been secretly pleased. And not because they wanted to kill, but only because they wanted . . .

He sighed. "Here, you read your letter and I'll read mine." His mother's sloping script crawled up the page like a schoolchild's, telling not of summer vacations but of yet more anguish. "The old man has had a setback. Mom wants me to come."

"Is it an emergency?"

"She wouldn't ask unless it was. Another small stroke, maybe. I can't call her at night from the plant. Maybe you could phone her this evening, when she's home?"

"Of course."

"Still," he said, "I have to write to her. Let me borrow the typewriter, it'll only take a couple of minutes."

When he had finished the cold-looking message of cheer, promising his mother that he would come whenever she wished, he pushed

back the machine. "I have to write to Norm too, but that's harder.
He doesn't want reassurances. I don't know exactly what he wants."
"News."
"You think so? Help me." Help me, he thought, to compose tips
on staying alive, reviews of movies he'll never see, tidbits about his
wife and son.

"I think you ought to tell him what Hoover learned from our
contacts in Pittsburgh during the miners' strike. Then when he reads
about the U.S. taking over the mines he'll have a little background
on it. And be sure to tell him about your three days at the Active
Workers' Conference in Chicago. It'll buck him up to know that
ninety per cent of our membership is in basic industry now. And
that we had two Negro delegates from the South there and that
the paper has hit forty thousand. You came back so excited!"

But maybe that wasn't the excitement that Norm craved. For me,
he thought, it was a break from the factory routine, a kick just to
meet strangers who by virtue of being my comrades renewed in me
the sense that I was in a *movement*. I came back like a kid returning from his first date positive that he is in love, all the self-doubting
and uneasiness washed away. But for Norm?

"All right," he said, "I'll try. But I don't think I'll write about the
riots in Detroit. It's too depressing."

"Do you think he's going to learn, unless we tell him, that all the
twenty-seven dead were Negroes? Do you think he's going to learn
about the victory for the Progressive slate in Bill's plant, about how
the Army got them fired—"

"He'll hear—from Vera."

"Still, he needs the details of how we got Bill reinstated. Damn it,
Bill did win."

"Should I play a drum roll while you give your speech?"

Bernie flushed.

"I was teasing. I'll write everything to Norm, but a little bit at a
time. And I'll tell him about the new slogan in our shop, 'Pay increase or job release.' He thought it was hopeless, and it's not."

No, it was not, he kept telling himself.

But how would it look on Norm's outcrop of coral, blasted and
bloody, lost in the blue Pacific? What could it mean out there?

Irrelevant. He had been pushing aside the Pacific warfare simply
because he had been taught to think of it as one more imperial conflict over useless real estate. What was relevant and what meaning-

less? Sitting in a darkened movie theatre while awaiting Lana Turner in WAC uniform, he gazed at lurching little men staggering forward, obscured by spume and smoke, then falling, some arising, some not, on an island called Guadalcanal, once known only to *National Geographic* subscribers and now the freakish point of collision between men told to hate each other. From there, from even more obscure islands, Norm was now crying back, *You* are not relevant to all this!

He was worried in the days that followed that perhaps he and Bernie were not being thoroughly frank with each other. Together they had organized a great picketline at the lying, slanderous movie *Mission to Moscow*. Dozens had joined to protest its cheap propaganda and its distortions of history. With chants and leaflets they had warned against the Stalin-Hollywood axis—but after their picketline had ended the movie continued to play, here and in a hundred other cities. Silently, without admitting to each other the implications of what they saw, he and Bernie watched the gum-chewing girls in slacks and wedgies sauntering in to the movie house, neither knowing nor caring that they and their husbands and boy friends were seeing a lie. If they had heard of the picketing, it might even have whetted their curiosity. Worst of all, how could you know, with people who had been brought up on cowboy movies but never learned to hate Indians, whether the whole matter wasn't simply irrelevant to them? The word that he dared not utter to his wife.

It was his responsibility to prepare the ground for a public talk that Dworkin was to give on his arrival in the city. He composed the leaflets, rented the auditorium (Harry had insisted on a shabby but very large fraternal hall on the fringes of the Negro neighborhood), had posters put in shop windows, leaflets distributed, releases sent to the press.

The day before the speech, Sy stopped in at the Smalls' to give them a bundle of leaflets and to see, as Harry had requested, whether they had done their share in getting word to their shopmates of Dworkin's forthcoming appearance. Albie Small was a lanky man in his thirties, vaguely from the Appalachians, with a sidelong smile and a nose thin as a knife blade. His eyes were slightly crossed. As he spoke, in a high, nasal drawl, hands stuffed into his hip pockets, his unhealthy chest sinking as if it would disap-

pear into his backbone, he seemed to be smiling to himself as if
something in your appearance amused or disgusted him.

Always a cigarette was stuck in the corner of his mouth, although
often it was unlit, and always within sound of his voice were the
two women with whom he had turned up one day, from nowhere,
in a clanking Chevy with Tennessee plates. Babe, presumably his
wife, lived in plaid slacks from which her blouse escaped here and
there over her massive haunches, and moccasins with heels worn
down to invisibility. Her hair was cropped short, her lower jaw
worked sideways on Dentyne gum, her eyes were tiny and reptilian.
Sometimes she wore a baseball cap; with her squashed nose she did
somewhat resemble Babe Ruth. Mildred, although supposedly her
sister, resembled her in no way. She was a starveling out of Erskine
Caldwell, her eyes vague, her twanging voice emaciated as her
frame, her dresses too long, as if she had been outfitted at the
Goodwill Industry.

The three of them lived in several disconnected rooms along the
narrow reeking hall of a roominghouse not far from the grim but
respectable pile of the Grosvenor Library on Franklin Street. It was
unlikely that any of the Smalls would ever venture inside of it, for
Babe and Mildred, at least, gave the impression that they could
not read at all.

Indeed, Sy was baffled by their nonchalant association with the
branch and had once ventured to remark to Harry that he could
not see what on earth the movement had to offer them—or vice
versa. Harry's reaction had been a nice mixture of indignation and
indulgence. "One of our troubles, Sy, is that we haven't succeeded
in attracting *enough* people like Albie Small. We radicals are going
to have to get rid of our ingrained favoritism toward immigrants
and intellectuals—it amounts to prejudice against native-born American workers."

"Small was no worker before he got here. God knows what he was
doing, but he wasn't in industry. He came into the shop on account
of the draft and the money."

"He came in because Comrade Lewis agreed with me that Small
would be useful in reaching certain workers whom you and Bill
couldn't. Therefore in building the Party."

Sy had suspected something like this. It only increased his ir-
ritation. "I think Bill and I know a little something about workers.

We both come from working-class families, we've both been in industry a lot longer than Small."

"But you went to college." The chemist smiled, but his tone announced that he was passing sentence. "You read books. Your family brought you up in a radical tradition. None of those things is true of Small."

"That's for sure."

"But his family has been here for the better part of three hundred years. Certain things about this country that we have to struggle to understand are second nature to him. Other workers accept him without giving it a thought. He had a rough time during the depression, riding the rods, living in boxcars, following the harvest." Harry extended his index finger. "He's like the *bezprizornyi*, the children of the revolution, the orphaned waifs whom the Bolsheviks found and nurtured. Small is a find, and we've got to nurture him."

When he thought of Small, Sy wondered what there was to nurture. If he was a hardy plant, it only meant that he would get along under any circumstances, and without encouragement. He gave you the impression that he would grow in the dark. Was he the vanguard of hundreds of thousands of his kind?

Small opened the door to his knock and stood leaning negligently against the casement, a cigarette butt in the corner of his mouth.

" 'Lo, Sy," he drawled. "What c'n I do f'you?"

"I've got some leaflets here. And I wanted to talk to you about the meeting."

"Well, c'mon in. Babe," he called across the hallway, "fix a cuppa coffee f'Sy."

"That's not necessary."

"Let her git it," Small said as he ushered him in. "She don' wiggle her ass a little, she's goin' look like a Mack truck."

Sy was taken aback to find Hunter sitting in a dark corner of the room, glum, silent, hands on his knees, shoes pointing dead ahead. He raised his head and muttered, "Hello," in his deep sepulchral voice.

"What are you doing here?" Sy asked. The question was rude but fair: "Aren't you working days any more?"

"Took the day off. Stopped in to see Small about precautions."

"Precautions?"

"Precautions have to be taken. Everything doesn't go our way. Forces are arrayed against us."

Sy glanced at Small, who grinned coldly around his cigarette. "Hunter uses fancy language. But I know what he means. Bunch of flag-wavers in his shop are givin' him a hard time. He's gotta lay a little low. There you go," he said, as Babe came in with a blue cup of coffee on a cracked white saucer. He slapped her on the rump. "Where's the sugar? Man takes sugar. 'f I can remember that, you can too."

"I'll tell Mildred." Meal-dread, she pronounced it. "She'll bring you some, Sy."

"Now you see," Small went on, "I got a problem somethin' like Hunter's in my department. With him it's the Legionnaires, with me it's the Commies. Adds up the same way, though—they both of them wraps theirselves up in the flag. Look what happened to Bill— got the whole U. S. *Army* on his tail, fin'ly threw him out."

"He got reinstated, didn't he?"

"Sure did, but he's got plenty of pull with the union."

"He's got rank and file support. That's what got him back in. And that's the only thing that'll protect any of us—not laying low."

Mildred shuffled in with the sugar bowl, slippers slapping on the linoleum.

"Thank you," he said to her, and spooned in sugar. He hit an obstruction, poked at it: it was the crusted sugar left by the last user. He put down the spoon and drank. Reheated, rank, bitter as witch's brew.

"You don' want to misunderstand," Small said. "Hunter an' me, we wanna build the Party. But you fellows been here a li'l longer. Bill's got himself some seniority, besides being chief steward. Ain't nobody knows us yet, 'cept the boys we eat lunch with."

It was hard to picture Hunter eating lunch with anyone. And yet he had found Small, and sat in his sour-smelling parlor on a lovely June afternoon. Talking about what? Conspiracy. "Well," he said, "you're going to have to get these leaflets out."

"Sure will. We got to git us a turnout for Dworkin. Man, he c'n pour it on. I'll git Babe an' Mildred to give me a hand. They're real good at that."

But when the night arrived there was no turnout for Dworkin. Sy had presentiments, but once again he went off to the night shift without uttering them to Bernie. She was waiting up for him in the kitchen when he came in, fagged after his sixth night on the line, opened his lunchbox, stuck his thermos under the hot water.

"How'd it go?" he asked.

Her face was bitter. "It was a nightmare. Nobody was there."

"What are you talking about?"

"Everything went wrong. The rain—"

"It didn't rain much tonight."

"Enough to ruin our last-minute literature distribution. And curl up the posters we nailed on telephone poles. And keep everybody in the bars. Or home."

"Now wait a minute. How many people did you count?"

"I'm trying to tell you, there was nobody to count. Fifteen? Sixteen?" Bernie's voice was almost shrill. She sat down at the kitchen table. "The location was a ghastly mistake. We found out at the last minute that no Negroes ever go in there, they've always regarded it as a white man's place. Norm would have known. Nobody even checked with Big Boy. Harry claims he tried, but he couldn't reach him all week, he was busy out in Lackawanna."

"How about our people?"

"Half of our people work nights, and they were on overtime tonight, like you. Some were tied up with union meetings or socials, like Big Boy. They couldn't even get the sympathizers out, much less the contacts. The aircraft workers live miles away. We really messed this up."

As he stood at the stove, stirring hot chocolate, he said, "Tell me what Dworkin did."

"Marty? He just laughed and said, 'The toiling masses are elsewhere tonight. Too bad, they'll miss me at my best.' And he went on with it as though he was addressing hundreds of people."

"Who listened?"

She shrugged. "Fred had a couple of students—Marty aimed at them, mostly. Then there were two Trotskyites. They sat there in the middle of all those rows of empty chairs, grinning. Oh, and there was an old man near me, with long hair and a long raincoat practically down to the ground. The kind that sits in the library reading about the War of 1812. I think he just drifted in out of the rain, he was all hunched over with our leaflet in one hand and the other hand cupping his ear. He even asked a question during the question period. It gave Dworkin the chance to talk for another fifteen minutes." Bernie smiled wanly. "And then Vito dropped by, with a new girl. He sat there sketching Marty and the deaf old man, as if he was working for the FBI." She snorted angrily. "I don't think we even rated an FBI man there!"

He poured the hot chocolate. "You might as well tell me what Dworkin said."

"The usual. Everything. He compared the coal miners to the fighting men. Then came the secret deals between FDR and Stalin. And the zoot suit riots in Los Angeles. And of course he went after the UAW's Equality of Sacrifice program . . ."

Bernie's voice trailed off. She sat holding the cup without drinking it. "I was just thinking, there wasn't one thing Dworkin said tonight that I could quarrel with. And yet, maybe because of all those empty seats, it all seemed so irrelevant." She looked at him anxiously. "Do you understand what I mean?"

Startled, he nodded.

"It sounds so disloyal. I don't mean that he'd be more right if he'd had a big crowd. Well, no, maybe I do! It was so ludicrous, that old man blowing his nose into a handkerchief, the spittoons in the corners, the old smell, you know the old smell those meeting halls have? Dirty drapes, yellow faded portraits of past presidents, banquet photographs with the faces all distorted. And those empty seats . . . What's the point, Sy?"

"The point is, somebody has to keep the idea alive. When we were in high school, it looked easy. There was a different demonstration every day. The Workers Alliance, the Unemployed Councils, the Bonus Marchers, the CIO. Now we've got to dig in. We're getting through. The paper is fantastic, twelve hundred subscriptions this month. They think about what we're saying, they *must.*" He held out his hand. "Come on, let's go to bed."

The next day he took the train to New York. He had to miss Dworkin's talk to the membership, but it was more important to travel on Sunday so as not to lose too much time off the job.

Making his way down the aisle of the last coach on the Empire State Express, hunting for a seat, Sy thought of Joe's classically simple comment on the war: "Everybody's moved up a notch." Privates had become corporals, corporals lieutenants, unemployables had become busboys, busboys waiters, waiters managers, managers—like Uncle Morris, Irwin's father—chain store operators, capitalists. And if those who formerly traveled by train were now flying, those who had formerly gone by bus or thumb, like him-

self, now could afford train tickets. A little something for everybody. A bonanza.

Suddenly he spotted a double space, near the ladies' room. Using
his battered laundry case as a wedge, he shoved past the hordes of
servicemen and fell into the seat as the train jerked forward. But at
Rochester a thin little teenager scrambled aboard, carrying a baby
in her arms and urging a toddler on before her. A soldier heaped
her luggage in the corner; she thanked him and turned to peer up
and down, frightened.

"Here," Sy said. "Take mine."

"I'll make some room," she said, as she settled herself. "I don't
take up much space."

"I guess you don't at that. Those kids both yours?"

She nodded. "Their papa's gone *over*seas. I been visiting his folks
over to Monroe, but we didn't want to outstay our welcome. Go
ahead, sit down."

"That's all right," he said. "Maybe I can give you a hand with
the older one. I'm not much on babies that small."

She proceeded to diaper the baby on the seat while he tried to
distract the older sister. The car was very close, the windows would
not open, and the ammoniac stench of the infant's diaper, unchanged
for far too long, made him a little faint. "Gettin' a rash," the girl
muttered. She could have been no more than eighteen. "I got to
find that ZBT powder before he starts to yell again."

When she had finished he stayed on, since she seemed hungry
for someone to talk to. But her talk was inane, her daughter squirmed
back and forth on his feet, and the baby began to shriek.

"Time to feed him," she said, looking about her distractedly, and
he took advantage of the occasion to leave.

He pulled open the door and stepped out between cars. But a
sailor was already there, pressed up against a young girl, one hand
supporting himself against the swaying train, the other hand up
her dress. The sailor's face was streaked with lipstick as though he
had been slashed in a duel.

"Hey, Four-F," he said, annoyed, "if you're not gettin' much, go
look someplace else. I got mine."

The next car was blue with smoke, and he could not go far;
six soldiers were deep in a poker game, and beyond them others
quarreled over a comic book. The overage had curled into foetal
positions, mouths agape, and begun to snore.

It was a long ride. As the train snaked its way across the state, searching out the Hudson and the drop down toward the sea, Sy swayed unseeing, seated on his laundry case, his mind's eye on the darkened room in which he and Bernice had made love on their first night, by the lake, someplace not far from here.

When he stepped out at Grand Central, it was as though he had never left home. Going downtown, the subway was an oven.

His mother had dinner ready. He smelled the stuffed cabbage in the hall; even before he banged on the door he knew that she would have tears in her eyes. She was heavier, he could feel it as they embraced. She sagged.

"How are you, ma?"

"Like always."

"Pa?"

She shook her head. "See for yourself. There's not so much to see. The doctor says he's going downhill, there's no way back up. You know what that means?" She shrugged. "It beats me."

But she knew. She didn't expect him to say much, she just wanted—he understood, without her having to say so—that he should stick around for awhile. Maybe until the end.

His father had the mark of death, yellow and greasy, but he behaved as though he expected to live forever. In the glow of his undimmed faith he grinned confidently, like those happy mystics who know despite the prick of every needle and the stab of every hot iron that nothing will hurt, nothing will wound.

He sat propped in his chair by the living-room window, encased in Sid's old Indian blanket from Pioneer Youth Camp like a mummy in a winding sheet, stains on the shredding lapels of his faded bathrobe, a clump of short white bristles at the corner of his mouth that his wife had not managed to reach with the razor. He seemed to be winking gaily at his son in greeting, but as Sy advanced he saw that the drooping eyelid was a souvenir, like a withering flower. By his side lay the *Daily Worker*.

Sy refrained from a physical embrace which he did not feel called upon to make. It would have been even more awkward to shake the palsied hand, so he stood for a moment unmoving, as though in the presence of royalty, unable to proceed until a command would be given.

From behind him his mother gave the command. "Go, sit down on the couch, you must be tired."

"How about you?"

"I'll sit for a minute, I don't want the cabbage should boil over."
From somewhere in his chest, his father produced sounds. The
voice emerged, slurred as a drunkard's, but understandable. "How's
Bernice? She likes it there?"

"Not bad, pa. She's a little lonesome for home, for the family,
but she's got friends. She works hard. She sends regards."

"Tell me about my sister, and Metzger," his mother urged. Her
hand made small caressing circles on his back, tentatively, almost
furtively.

"I don't see them much, since I work nights. They've had us over
to supper once or twice. They live very well."

"I bet."

"Oh yes," he said, "Uncle Morris is cleaning up. He's a big man
now, you see his name in the paper for the Bond Drives. Once
they even had his picture."

"You don't say."

"I'm surprised Aunt Minnie didn't send you a copy. But she was
upset about Irwin and his marriage for a long time."

"She had plenty *hartsesseniss* from him," his mother shouted at his
father. But he wasn't deaf, did she feel that she had to chase him,
to call after him as he faded away? "Remember? Minnie was all
broken up, her boy married a *shiksa.*"

"Who cares?" the old man demanded. "What's the difference?"
Relieved that he could agree with his father, Sy said quickly,
"You're right, I told her that myself. As long as Irwin is happy."

"She's a different generation," his mother said. "It's hard for her."

"Phooey. She's blind, your sister. Always was, always will be. She
went running to a rabbi to marry a bourgeois, a cloak and suiter."

"So what about Irwin?" his mother tried again.

"He's all right now. He had a hard time for a while, but once the
baby came they seem to have settled down. You know about the
little boy, Paul?"

"They sent us an announcement, we sent a present, a War
Bond." Sy lifted his eyebrows. His mother hurried on, "But tell
already, what does he look like? Did he have a *briss?*"

"Damn right. Irwin insisted. He dotes on him. The kid is dark, almost like an Indian, but beautiful. You know, Carmela's very dark
too."

"Looks like his mother, huh?" Her boys gone, without grand-

children, his mother beamed. And without malice; there was no
envy of her prosperous sister. "That must give Minnie *nachas*."

"Irwin's a captain, he gets home often from Fort Niagara. He's
got a partner, a nice fellow, running his office. I see him from time
to time."

A moment's silence. His father grimaced at him, one side of his
face pulled down. His mother's hand made circles on his back. The
cabbage simmered on the stove. Both of his parents were signaling
to him, but what? What message? Did they say anything to each
other, now, at the end of the road?

"What do you hear from Sid?" he asked.

His mother's hands came together. Released, he straightened up
and watched her fingers link and knot, as though she were sitting
in a classroom. Suddenly he remembered that he had seen her in a
classroom one evening many years ago when he had gone to his
own school to fetch her: she had sat in her citizenship class, her
large frame awkwardly wedged into the child's chair, her fingers
tensely linked on the child's desk as they were now. He looked
away.

"He's on a Liberty ship that carried blockbusters to the fliers.
He couldn't write me they were carrying bombs until they discharged them in London."

Sy gaped at his mother; at her age, he thought, to have to learn
the language of new ways of death from Sid's letters, from the
rotogravure section of the Sunday *Forward,* from the newsreels in
the Grand Street movie. Unaware of the effect of her vocabulary,
she went on: "His ship was in the coffin corner of the convoy, that's
what they call it when they're on the end of the outside lane, where
the subs can get at them easiest. Thanks God he got there safe."

"He's doing a good job," his father said thickly.

"Twice he was torpedoed already. If he would of been hit this
time with those bombs, you think he'd still be alive? How many
wars does he need? He wasn't satisfied with Spain, he got out with
his arm, now with the Merchant Marine."

"Ma, they say the worst is over with the submarines."

"The worst won't be over until he's safe. You think he's safe?
I don't. I can't sleep."

"Well," his father said, his death's head grinning, "what you got to
say about the Red Army now?"

"They're tremendously brave." He could almost feel his mother's warning glance upon his back as she rose and shuffled to the kitchen. "It looks like they're stopping the Germans."

"Stopping? The Germans are getting wiped out, worse than Napoleon. You know why? Because Stalin cleaned out the traitors. Tukhashevsky and all the rest, he stood them against the wall. I told you then, you laughed."

"I didn't laugh."

"You're laughing now, maybe?"

"If Stalin hadn't purged the army, the Nazis never would have gotten as far as they did. All those people slaughtered. The Jews."

"In Russia the Jews are safe. From Warsaw they could have gone east in 1939, who told them to stay?"

"Safe?" he shouted. "Who's safe? Where? What about Zygelboim?" He felt as if he had spat out a loose tooth that had been aching like a nail inside his skull, leaving a hole from which warm sweet blood leaked into his mouth.

His father sneered. "Whachu talking about? Zygelboim?"

"How would you know? If it's not in the *Worker,* it doesn't exist. Go ahead, tell me you never heard of Ehrlich and Alter."

"Social Democrats. Don't change the subject. What's with Zygelboim?"

"He committed suicide, in London. Because nobody would pay attention . . ." He really could not go on. This was what had been burning in his brain like an incurable infection, impossible to discuss even with his wife. He suspected now that it had been tormenting her too in the empty hall while she and the rheumy old man watched their leader's pointless virtuoso performance.

That very week Zygelboim had smuggled himself out of the Warsaw ghetto and come to London to make his plea. Ten thousand German prisoners, he asked for, in trade for ten thousand Jewish children. No one listened. No one was even aware of his plea until it had been cast aside and he had killed himself in his room, ashamed to be alive any longer.

Even now no one talked about his final plea, not even in whispers. Not even husbands and wives alone together, because it made everything irrelevant, their lives, their friends, their loves, their families, their support of the war, their opposition to it . . . He and Bernice had looked at each other, stricken, and then covered their nakedness with the garments of other concerns. As if there could be any other concerns.

"Who pays attention?" his father whispered. "You got to stop the killers. Period. You can't make business with them."

He had no heart to quarrel further with the dying man. And yet he could not let it alone. Late at night, while his mother tossed, groaning, in her high creaking bed and his father, unwilling to die in bed, lay stertorous on the couch, he crept into the living room and rifled the piles of *Daily Workers* stacked on the radiator, hunting for evidence to fling at the old man.

The next day he waited, crouched like a beast, waiting for his father to make the first move. As if he knew, as if he was eager to fire his son's fury, his father obliged.

"Well," the old man crowed, as soon as his wife was out of the house, on her way to the shop where she still worked to keep up the payments for the Workmens Circle doctor, the medicines, the burial plot, "did you see what Mike Gold says about the Russians? Same like I was saying."

"Don't mention his name to me."

"What's the matter with Mike Gold?"

He pulled out the *Daily Workers* he had torn into strips. *"I grieve to note,"* he read, his voice shaking uncontrollably, *"that even Jews have been drawn into the dirty work that Goebbels does in America. For many months the execution of two Polish Jewish social democrats by the Soviet courts has been known. They were guilty or they would not have been punished."*

"So?" his father grinned at him. "You can prove they weren't guilty?"

"Nothing is too slimy. Even Frank Hague is okay now."

The old man shrugged. "We got to have unity."

"With whom? When I was a kid you used to lecture Sid and me: Patriotism is for the bourgeois, our flag is the red flag."

"The red flag will fly in Berlin. Sid knows it, even if you don't."

"This lousy sheet, this so-called Communist paper, is offering an American flag and a cast of the American eagle for subscriptions. Listen: 'Show your pride in America by draping old glory in a corner of your home or office.'" He crumpled the paper into a ball and threw it on the floor. His father's face twisted into a knowing leer; Sy had not dared to throw it at him.

Worst of all, the old man refused to die. Several days later, Sy said heavily to his mother, "Ma, I have to go."

"I know. I shouldn't have made you come. We can talk on the telephone. That's enough, it's better than I can do with Sid."

"He'll be back soon."

"I got a hope . . . You saw Bernice's family today?"

He nodded dumbly.

"You'll give her my love? Sy, it's none of my business, don't be mad, but she ought to have a baby. Don't make her wait too long."

"You're right, ma. I'm not mad. If I was positive I wouldn't be reclassified . . . You sure you can take care of things here?"

"I took care before, I can take care now. My cousin Malkah looks in on Glantzman while I'm in the shop."

Beneath the soft, down-drooping flesh, she was granite. I wish I could be like you, he wanted to say to her, but he was not sure that she could understand. Instead he hugged her in silence, for a long time.

Before catching the train, he stopped in at the national office. Lewis was a little restless.

"The public meeting for Dworkin was a flop, I understand. You lead the country in press sales and distribution, and you can't even pull people to hear our best spokesman."

"Harry must have written you the reasons," Sy said. "The fact remains that we're doing very well in our concentration areas. Our guys are respected in the labor movement, our branch meetings—"

"I know, I know. But there is a contradiction. It gets around the country that one of the best branches, if not the best branch, with roots in the shops . . ."

Lewis was composed, but gave the impression that his mind was elsewhere; his plump hand jotted columns of figures.

In the cubbyhole next door Hoover was somewhat more searching. As he spoke he tucked a white handkerchief between his shirt collar and his neck, like a railroad conductor, to keep the collar from wilting. Hundreds of years ago, they said, Hoover had worked on the railroads, but as a Pullman porter, to put himself through Antioch.

"What kind of monkeyshines are going on up there?" he demanded.

"You mean the meeting?"

"I do *not* mean the meeting. Dworkin is used to spouting in empty halls. Next time you'll maybe use your heads before wasting your hard-earned money on the wrong hall and the wrong leaflets in the wrong neighborhood. I mean the factionalism, the *cry*baby politics of those infants."

"What infants?"

"That nincompoop Hull, that spook Hunter, those hillbillies. That's some prize collection Harry has got around him. I'd better get back up there and see if I can straighten things *out.*" He snapped off the last word as if it was a command.

"I wish you would." Small was up to something with Hunter, that he had seen for himself; but he had thought it nothing more than a sharing of their conservatism, springing from fear of sticking their necks out after the army had gone gunning for Bill. "What's about Big Boy?"

"He still thinks he's running those rednecks down in New Orleans. I had a feeling he'd get too big for his britches." Hoover's brown skull shone with sweat. "He's starting to think he's a theore*tician.* I blame Harry. He's stuffing the man's head with dialectical materialism and whatnot. I never believed Harry was clear on that stuff him*self,* much less capable of explaining it to someone like Hull."

"You're ahead of me. I don't know what's going on behind—"

"You're naive, that's what. Didn't you smell anything at the Active Workers Conference? They're making a bloc. They're going to present a document with a new conception of the Party. What a laugh." He shifted uncomfortably in his chair. "Too damn hot here. New York is no place to think, especially in the summer. The national office ought to be out where the workers are. Muste is a nut, but he had the right *i*dea about that. Except if we moved, how would Comrade Lewis be able to keep up with the market? He's got the future of the bourgeoisie pegged to the Wall Street Final." Hoover uttered his rare short barking laugh. His false teeth glinted. "How's things at home?"

"Not so good."

"Um. Okay, get going. I'll see you up there in a while."

Arrived in Buffalo, he was surprised to find Harry waiting for him at the station.

"I'm grateful, but you didn't have to bother. I'm used to the buses."

"Well, I gathered from Bernie that you've had a rough time this week. I thought I'd give you a lift straight to the branch office. Bernie will be there for the meeting when she comes back from a distribution. She's a marvel, Sy. You're a lucky man."

Harry announced this as though he were congratulating Sy on his car, or his record player. You never had to worry about leaving Harry with your wife while you were away.

"What's funny?"

He started guiltily. "I'm just pleased to be back. I didn't have many laughs in New York."

"Your father?"

"He's hanging on. I may have to ask Bernie to help my mother out, later on."

"That makes sense. See any of the boys in the national office?"

So that was it. Harry's casualness was marvelous, as artificial and "learned" as his manners. Was he simply uneasy that Lewis and the others would blame him for the Dworkin fiasco? No, more likely he was up to something with Hunter, perhaps even with Small, as Hoover had suggested.

Sy decided to temporize. Harry tried to pump him from more than one angle, but at last gave up, apparently persuaded that there was nothing to be learned from him.

"I've been immersing myself lately," Harry said, "in the history of the pre-revolutionary movement in Russia. What do you know about the Chaikovsky Circle?"

"Well, there was Kropotkin, I think," Sy said uneasily. Staring out the window as they approached the Lafayette Theatre and the turn to the Party office, he was beginning to wish that Harry would drive a little faster.

"Of course. But also Morozov, Tikhomirov, Shishko. Shishko!" Harry rapped enthusiastically on the steering wheel. "Talk about Hoover and Dworkin, and their insistence on our going into industry to become a really proletarian party—why, Shishko set up locksmith's shops for the Russian intellectuals, so they could learn a trade and sink roots in the people."

"You don't say. It would make an interesting topic for an educational, wouldn't it?"

"Take the Natanson Circle."

"It's vague in my mind. You say Bernie will be there?"

"It was a commune in the eighteen sixties, marvelous people. They tried to purify themselves of base material concerns. The men and the women lived together in comradeship, not in sensuality."

"A neat trick."

"Of course there were those who fell. Some became double agents, some became plain traitors, some even became big businessmen. But those who remained pure, what an example they set! They gave up selfish personal things, they gave up their lives with the greatest pleasure, they even pleaded with one another for the privilege. Sy, if we could have one tenth of their commitment . . ."

"Amen. Well, here we are. I'm much obliged, Harry."

Harry's protuberant eyes gleamed behind the glasses. "We really should try harder to understand each other."

But when they had mounted the steps to their headquarters, when he had hugged his wife and greeted all of his friends, Sy saw Harry revert in the twinkling of an eye to another of his roles.

He was addressing the branch on the German Question. Squeezing his wife's hand hard as Harry got underway, Sy surveyed the hall, searching among the rows of faces familiar and strange for some sign of the horror and helplessness that now possessed him— and, he was sure of it, he could feel it in her fingertips—his wife as well. Germany? Nazism? Of course it obsessed Anne Link, sitting alone with her long pianist's fingers knotted, half-crazed with loneliness and fear for her husband who faced the Germans in North Africa. No doubt it obsessed Fred too, more frightened than ferocious, hating Hitler but appealing the order to leave home and join the battle.

But what of the others? What did it mean to Big Boy, scowling and sullen among the troops he had brought with him from the steel mill? Or to Hunter, stone-faced and withdrawn, a twitching muscle in his jaw the only sign that something stirred within him? Or to Babe and Mildred, seated on either side of the mountaineer, staring curiously, open mouthed, at Harry, as though he were some creature in a science fiction movie?

Harry had started with the overthrow of the Hohenzollerns, the Kapp Putsch, Ebert and Scheidemann, the Treaty of Versailles. He moved majestically through the Weimar Republic and the disasters of the twenties (inflation, decadence) to the horrors of the thirties (refusal of Socialists and Communists to make common cause, corruption of Catholics, treason of Nationalists). Speaking of it as enthusiastically as though it were still alive, as though good Germans were still free to choose, he outlined Trotsky's rejected demand for a united front which could have afforded a fighting chance to keep Hitler from taking power, making the deal with Stalin, attacking the west, turning on his criminal partner.

Following on the indubitable historical truth that Harry set forth, men were broiled alive, trapped in their tanks on the African sands; they waded, blind and bloody, in the Italian mud; they blasted each other to bits high in the sky and deep in the ocean, soiling the sea with their greasy debris.

But what did any of it mean to those who sat stolidly waiting for the speaker to be through? Albie Small had been dredging in his ear with the sulfur tip of his match before placing the matchstick in his mouth once again. Sensing that a climax was approaching, he swung his arms out to embrace the chairs on which his two women reposed, the fat and the thin, the slattern and the drudge, relics of some sharecropper's shack, drowsing over the dialectics of the German Question.

"Social fascists!" cried Harry, his curved pipe descending through the smoky air in an unconscious mimicry of the tyrant whose polemical vocabulary he was mocking with heavy scorn.

Babe and Mildred, half adoze, jerked their heads up, prodded by Small's warning thumbs between their shoulder blades.

In the next row, beside Bill, one of his aircraft workers, eager for the beer that would follow the educational, licked his lips as thirstily as though he had been the speaker. A younger worker, hopeful of getting laid before the evening was over, stirred restlessly, eyeing Fred's girl students whom he had no doubt been assured were easy.

"Why didn't he say more about the Jews?" Sy whispered angrily.

His wife looked at him, her eyes bleak. "Do you think it would make any difference?"

He lowered his head, unable to return her gaze, unwilling for her to see what was in his own eyes. Was this what he had come back for? He muttered, "But we have an obligation . . . What's going to become of them all?"

"They're going to die, that's what. They're all going to die."

5.   BIG BOY

Coming off the shift after washing up, he decided to leave the mill by way of the yards. It was a good fifteen minutes out of the way, since the gin mill he was heading for was across from the north gate; but he had reasons for the detour. Harry would doubtless be late, coming all the way from Niagara Falls, and wasn't too familiar with the neighborhood anyway; Ham worked in the yards, in shipping, and it might be safer to see what he was up to there, to make sure that he wasn't moseying over to the north gate, in sight of that gin mill; and in any case it never did any harm to show your face now and then.

It did give him a boost to be greeted on all sides, waved to here and slapped on the back there as he made his way through the cavern, out the great doors into the nippy March air, around the obstructions, cutting across the thicket of crisscrossing railroad tracks, the cinders crunching like popcorn under his work shoes.

"Hey, Big Boy!"

"Howsa big man?"

"Committeeman, I mean Mista Committeeman, Boss Man!" This one went into his Stepin Fetchit routine every time he saw a union officer. It made no difference to the clown if there were whites around. "Y'all gwine ta' care o' mah grievance, Mista Committeeman?"

"What you know, Big Boy? Comin to the crap game tomorrow?"

"Don forget our stewards meetin, Big Boy. You got a promise to keep t'morrow, I ain letting you forget it!"

Slapping here, cuffing there, exchanging a right and a left—the

old one-two—with a longlegged shadowboxer almost his height,
Big Boy zigzagged to freight handling, his spirits rising as he left
the day's work behind, the taste of the beer ahead so strong that
it made him salivate, the shouts of his followers ringing out on
all sides. He was no longer just a new boy, fresh up from Dixie.
They were with him solid, they'd go along with the regional
director only when he said to, they'd walk out and take their chances
on getting fired, even drafted, when he gave the word. They were
his.

But his young cousin with the smooth lightskinned baby face
stood on a stack of rain-rusted ingots wired and tagged for ship-
ment, with a crowd of his own around him, serious, questioning,
intent. Catching sight of him, Ham took off his canvas glove and
waved it deferentially. His listeners swung around and called out,
"What's new, Big Boy?" "Seen your name in the paper, Big Boy!"
but it was all a little different. Maybe there was no basis for it,
but something indefinable in their attitude made him suspect that,
although they were among those who had voted him in, these men
were more Ham's than his.

Now he was certain that Ham was safely here and not heading
over to the other end of the yard where he might spot Harry, but
the knowledge hardly reassured him. Not when it meant seeing that
kid, hardly old enough to vote, gathering his own crowd, under-
cutting him. Innocent, sure he was innocent, he'd swear that he'd
been whipping the yard men into line, insisting that they come to
meetings, even pulling them out of the pool parlors to vote right so
the International would get the message that Big Boy was the man
to do business with.

But how could he be sure, he pondered as he hastened on, no
longer strolling because there was no one left to greet, whether Ham
hadn't been meeting on the side with Sy, or even with Hoover? You
couldn't put it past him. And if you confronted him with it, Ham
was just as likely to say, Sure, Hoover's got a lifetime of experience,
he can practically tell in advance what I'm going to say, he makes
everything clear to me.

When he thought how Ham used to say that not about Hoover,
but about him, how he used to trot after him, hero-worshipping,
how he paid more heed to him than to his own step-father, the
big-talking preacher . . . Uncertain, upset, he downed a rye, then
a short beer chaser instead of the slow lager he had been looking

forward to. He was humped over the bar, on his second boiler-
maker, when Harry strutted in with that Cagney walk, moving
cockily to conceal the news that he was not at home in a black
steelworker's bar. In fact he looked like he was stepping into a cathouse on a Saturday night. Big Boy raised his hand.

"Hey, man. I'm over here. What you drinkin?"

"I'll have a beer. Listen, is this private enough?"

"Grab that beer an I'll get us a table in the back. Nobody goin
bother us there, it's right in front of the kitchen an the john."

Harry had a little nervous habit of always looking nervous. Nevertheless he had always impressed Big Boy as the smartest man in the
Party. Certainly he was the best educated. And he wasn't the
organizer for nothing—he had an in with the national office, to
Comrade Lewis, no question.

After some little warm-up, Harry said confidentially, "If it wasn't
for the draft, we'd be in real shape to step out."

"Step out?"

"In front of the public, as a real party. But the draft is murder-
ing us. You think it's bad here with Joe gone, Norm gone, Fred
going, maybe even Vito, Ham—it's worse in New York and Chicago.
How do you stand?"

Big Boy laughed. "I got a bunch of women waiting for my pay
check. An not like you think. Got my mother an my grandmother
down in N'Orleans, an I pay part of the rent over to my aunt's
house too. I board there, with her an the preacher an Ham. Besides,
I don think they goin draft me out of the mill." He laughed again,
confidently. "Boys wouldn like that."

Harry was staring fixedly at him over his beer glass. "I'd like to
propose your name as a candidate member of the National Committee."

"You kiddin."

"I can't promise you, but I don't see why it won't go through."
Unwittingly, Harry debased the value of his offer by adding, "It's
miserable, every time we call an NC meeting, half of the members
have been picked off by the draft."

So it wasn't like getting named to the board of directors of the
steel company. Still, it was national. On the NC, he'd have a stake
in the Party. Nobody would lead him around by the nose—not even
Hoover. The Communists had given him rides in a Chevy convertible;
but even though he'd been young then, not too much older than

Ham was now, he'd known enough to resent being offered lolli-
pops instead of a real piece of the action.

Harry, he knew, wanted something in return. Harry had theories.
They were a little hard to follow, and Big Boy was not about to sit
down and bust his head over the books that Harry rattled off, whole
rows of them, like laundry lists or numbers for the runner; but
this was a party of men with ideas, and if you wanted to move in
it you had to have ideas, or at least the language to sell them
with. Big Boy had gotten far enough along so that when he took
the floor at a branch meeting he didn't have to feel that anybody
was laughing at him. And not just when he spoke about the mill,
the workers' mood, wildcats. They listened seriously to his opinions
on the kinds of agitation that would work, electoral campaigns versus
socialist propaganda, matters that he would have been afraid to open
his mouth about a year or two ago.

Harry's ideas for the future of the Party were based on those of
earlier revolutionists, Russians with names harder to pronounce than
the Bohunks' on the time cards at the mill. Most important, those
ideas were in opposition to Comrade Hoover's—and, so the story
went, to Comrade Dworkin's too. What Harry was shopping for now,
Big Boy realized perfectly well, was a deal.

"Well now," he said, "if you think I'm ready for it. I mean,
able to sit in there an vote on party policy. I got no background in
Marxism to speak of, except what I been able to pick up here an
there."

"People grow. Especially working-class leaders. You can grow,
Big Boy."

Grow to be like me, was what he meant. Well, why not? No
reason not to go along for the ride—part of the way, anyway.

What Harry wanted, Big Boy realized as he thought about it
during the days that followed, was not just a deal. If he really
needed Big Boy's support for a conception of the Party that
included running it as if it was as big as the Communists, with a
daily paper, candidates for Congress, names in the headlines, he
could start by running Big Boy for City Council. Not even Hoover
could object to a campaign right here in the city, with Margaret
Zivic attending to the petitions and the legal end, Harry raising
the money from his mysterious connections like that dentist, and
Ham calling out the troops to drag the voters from the gin mills.

But that wasn't exactly what Harry was after. It was all some big game to him, Big Boy was beginning to see it now, in which you won fifty points for getting people to string along, a hundred points if you conned them into doing what you wanted, all the lights lit up if you really won them over. A big game. It was funny that no one else in the branch was able to see this in Harry, even those who disagreed with him. Maybe it was a game for them too, a serious one for honest men like Joe Link, but a game just the same. An old timer who shuffled into his aunt's kitchen for coffee and crullers every so often, a Garveyite, still a black nationalist in his old age, just shook his head at Big Boy's involvement in union and leftwing politics and rubbed his gums together. "*They* ain in it for the same reason you are. You mebbe think so, but you in for a mighty big surprise."

A fool, Hoover had called the man, waving him aside with the back of his hand, an *id*iot. Still, wasn't it true that Harry could toss in his chips any time he felt like it, just be a chemist or whatever it was he did out at the Falls? And the rest of them too, for that matter. But I can't, he said to himself, for me there's nothing but the nigger work at the mill—and what I can build there with those lazy cowardly men.

The branch's Sunday educational was on the meaning of the second front slogan. Everyone was arguing about the Communists trying to pressure Washington, whether the invasion would succeed when it came off, what the chances were for revolution in Fortress Europe now that the Italians had led the way and partisans were fighting against fascism. Joe's wife Anne sat across from him, tense and pale, hands tight in her lap, not taking part in the discussion with all these amateur military experts. Joe was in training for the invasion, over in England. Big Boy tried to conjure it up— torpedoes whistling through the water, spray spouting to the sky, bombs crashing, craters forming as debris flew through the air, wood, stone, glass, bits of bodies, faceless goggled leather men on motorcycles roaring through ruined villages, tanks crunching across ditches, through waving grainfields and on into narrow cobbled streets that they filled to the curbing one after the other, unstoppable like endless columns of bloated ants taking over where humans once had been. But it was all secondhand, from pictures in magazines and newsreels at the occasional movies he went to with Coretta, who could not understand how he could sit there so stolidly.

It was not, he tried to explain to her, that he was indifferent to other people's troubles, but that he could not understand the strange languages of those who screamed or mumbled as they died. Nor could he see, despite Coretta's pleas, what the dying had to do with him or his people, the ones for whom he fought and schemed and took risks for, and yes would die for, if he had to. It was, he knew, one reason why he was attracted to the Party as Coretta was not. They alone assured him that he was right, it was not his war as the Communists and the patriots (and even Coretta) insisted, it was not being fought to defeat the bosses and the fascists. The Jew and the black man died just the same, war or no war. The Party was right about that, even though he could not always follow the details of the argument, just as it was right when it resisted those —like the old Garveyite in his aunt's kitchen or the wild hotheads in the corner saloon—who wanted to switch sides, to back the Japs because they were taking on the Ofay. All they were doing —and here Hoover was right in his weary contempt—was trading off one set of killers for another, even worse.

He could not imagine himself involved. While he read the letters from the drafted union men who sent back scrawled thanks for the razor blades and candy bars, he could not help feeling that it was all some vast annoyance in the way of what he was trying to do with the workers in the mill and the Negroes in the twelfth ward.

How did Joe's wife feel, with her long white fingers locked together? Did it hurt? Was she as far from it all, playing those pieces on the piano, as he was? Or did she secretly sweat over her good man?

The meeting broke up and he could not have been more surprised when Anne approached him. She said timidly, "Would you be able to give me a lift home? I just don't—"

"Why sure," he said. "I've got to take Ham back home, you know. You want to ride along with us, I'd be glad."

Her face changed, in some way that he could not define. "It's very nice of you. Can I meet you both downstairs? I just want to say good night to Margaret."

Ham was in a gay mood, and in no mind to go home. He took the steps three at a time and awaited Big Boy at the street level, the high school track team jacket that he still wore flopping about him as he hopped rhythmically over an imaginary skipping rope.

"You better calm down," Big Boy advised him. "No sense your callin attention to yourself right here on Main Street, branch office upstairs and all. Whyn't you wait till you get back on the turf, where people use to your monkeyshines?"

But Ham continued to jump up and down, arms swinging, until Anne Link appeared, hesitant, in the doorway. Then he stopped, somewhat abashed, and walked quietly to the car with them, a serious young man once again.

"Where you prefer to sit?" Ham asked her deferentially.

"If you don't mind, in the middle," she said. "I'm chilly, it's too cold alone in the back seat."

"Don feel like spring yet," Big Boy observed as he drove off. "But it's comin, any day now. Down home it's gettin hot already. Takes no time in Louisiana, all of a sudden the sun swell up an you're sweatin like it was July." He was talking, he knew, more than usual, unused to having a white woman pressed against his side. Even Joe Link's wife. She seemed distracted, nodding only to be polite. "Ham," he asked, "where you say you headin if you not going home?"

"Moonglo." Ham grinned. "I'm going to hear some jazz, have a couple beers. Maybe sit in on a couple sets."

Anne smiled at him. "Are you sure you haven't got a date? Nice looking boy like you?"

"Well . . . I just might meet somebody."

"You hope." Big Boy snorted as he swung the car around. "Guess I better drop you off first then, Moonglo's closer." He said to Anne, "You don mine if I do that?"

"Not at all. I'm in no hurry. But I think Ham is."

"You don mine, do you," Ham mimicked him, "if I want to have a little fun before I go on home?"

"Do what you want," Big Boy growled. "I ain your daddy, I'm just your cousin." He cut over to Ellicott Street, then cruised slowly up to Michigan, bringing the car to a halt in front of the vertical jumping neon sign. As always a knot of loungers blocked the sidewalk before the roaring night club. "Jus make sure you turn up for work tomorrow, is all. You got responsibilities, brother."

"I do thank you," Ham said politely, as he unfolded his long youthful body from the car. "Good night."

"Have fun!" Anne called after him. Easing herself a bit toward the door, sitting where Ham had sat, she said, "He's a nice boy.

And very bright too. He has a fantastic ear, you know. He could be a musician if he wanted to."

"He could be a bum too. No sense givin him a swelled head."

"Hamilton? That hardly seems likely. He does respect you."

"Well," he grunted as he turned the car around, "I'll get you home now. It's not too far."

"Don't hurry on my account. I'd just as soon ride around for a while, and talk. I don't think I could get to sleep now anyway."

Startled, he could not think of an expedient reply.

"I suppose," she said stumblingly, "you'd rather just turn in. I know how early you must have to get up, to drive all the way out to Lackawanna."

"That's all right," he said. He could not for the life of him figure out how to explain that he just wasn't used to this. In Louisiana you didn't go cruising with a white woman, not even the wife of a white friend—assuming you had one. He laughed shortly.

"What's the matter?" she asked a little uneasily.

"Jus thinkin how they'd take this, down home. You wouldn know about that."

"Oh."

"I'm not in a hurry. Where should I drive?"

"I don't know. I don't care, really. Delaware Park? As long as we can talk for a while. I seem to be all pent up."

They drove on in silence, out Delaware, heading for the park and the lake, hardly thawed yet from the winter's freeze. He would never have thought of starting up a conversation with her. He knew nothing about music and cared even less. What else could there be in her life that she would want to take up with him? Why him? Fiddling with the radio dial, trying to cover the silence between them, he turned past a quartet singing *Praise the Lord and Pass the Ammunition,* and found a Frank Sinatra record. But then that faded out, and the announcer came in. "And now we take pleasure in presenting Buffalo's own Professor Frederick Byrd, in another of his popular series on great voices from the past. For this evening's talk, Professor Byrd has chosen as his subject, Some English Poets of the Seventeenth Century."

"Now ain that some'n," he said. "I was wonderin why he took off so early tonight. Done change his name too."

"Fred's getting so successful with those broadcasts, he decided to pick a simpler name before he got too well known with the old one."

"I don follow that poetry. But I guess he's one smart man."

"So they say," she replied indifferently. But she reached out and switched off Fred's smooth persuasive voice. When she spoke again her voice was cool, like her face, but what she said wasn't.

"I've got a confession to make. I don't really care a damn about poetry. And what's more, I don't care a damn about politics."

He was startled, not so much by what she had said as by her calling it a confession. "Maybe," he said, "it's because you don *have* to."

She swung around, pleased. "I couldn't have said that to anyone else tonight. Not one of them would have understood, even my friends. They'd have thought I was unserious or plain spoiled. But you don't, do you?"

What he wanted to reply was that no one had ever spoken to him this way in his entire life. Instead he replied "No," since that was what she wanted him to say. But then he found himself going on. "I jus meant that our kind of politics is for people that got nothin else to make life worth livin. Or else for them that lives it and believes it, like a religion. Like Bill does. Or Joe."

"That's right! That's exactly right! Joe knew from the outset what music meant to me. So he made me understand that politics for him was what music was for me. It wasn't easy. But finally I swore to myself that I wouldn't ever, ever try to make him choose between it and me. And he knew better than to drag me into it, any more than he could drag me away from music."

"Then why'd you come to the meetin?"

"So I could write him about it. But the trouble is, his friends can do a better job of that than I can."

"You jus puttin yourself down."

She shook her head violently. "No. I'm trying to be honest. I try to write about everything to Joe, but I'm no good at it, even at describing my own problems. It doesn't come out right when I put it down on paper."

"Maybe if you was jus to tell it like you been tellin me—"

"I can't fake with Joe. I'd never fake with him."

"I ain sayin you should."

"But I'm a liar! Even now I'm a liar! Can't you see that?" She subsided, but after a moment, before he had recovered from the surprise of her outburst, she added, "I wasn't being truthful when I said I came tonight so I could write Joe about it. I came because I was so lonesome for him I'm sick, that's why."

"I don't blame you for that."

"I just wanted to be there, to do what he'd be doing if he was here. To close my eyes and feel him sitting next to me." She shuddered violently. "But it bores me stiff, you hear? What do I care about all that talk? I'd rather be in some movie."

"It's because you're lonesome."

"Have you ever been as lonesome for anybody as I am for Joe?" She swallowed. "It's killing me. Haven't you got a girl?"

He was silent for a time. Then, when they came in sight of the lake, cold and still in the moonlight, he said slowly, "No I guess I haven't." Why should she know about Coretta? "I keep movin so much, you know, I got to stay in there punchin, I don get the chance to think about people that way. But sometimes, when I'm layin on my back, late at night, say, looking up at nothin, I wish I was back home so bad . . . I can smell it . . . I can see that lil ol catboat, sun comin up over the tops of the oaks, me settin in the boat with a can of worms, fishin pole, couple bottles of Jax."

"Well that's something like it,'" she said. "Then you know what I mean."

"Funny thing. White folks up here, even in the Party, look at you like you out of your skull if you tell em you miss being down home. All they think about is lynchin, sheriffs, Jim Crow. They think I don know about that, better than them? But there's those other things they jus don know about. It's like you said—I can't put em into words. So I don even try, I keep em to myself."

Anne flung out her arm. "You see that lake? You talk about your river, that's where I grew up, summers in a canoe, winters on skates. You ever go ice skating?"

He laughed. "Miss'ippi ain never froze up. Least, not where I come from."

"I taught Joe last year. We used to come out kind of late at night. We'd cross hands and I'd pull him along, I'm pretty strong, until his feet got used to gliding. His ankles used to ache. You know, he's big like you, but I'd soak them in a pan of hot water. He was a good sport. He'd go back with me, even though it hurt and he'd rather have done other things, and he got very good. You know he's a natural athlete. After a while he could outrace me—

he'd cut clear across to those trees, and come zooming back with his hair sticking up half frozen in a clump, and grab me and twirl me, and I'd be screaming, the skates flashing in the moonlight, and everything going around . . ." She started to cry.

He wanted to touch her, to comfort her, but her tears frightened him. After a time they stopped, and when she spoke her voice was harsh. "I don't think I'm ever going to see him again."

"That ain right to say. If I *ever* see a man knew how to take care of himself, it was Joe. He'll be back, you'll see."

"It's kind of you to say it, even if you don't believe it." She blew her nose. "Tell me something. If you feel like it. How come you haven't gotten married?"

Oh no, he said to himself, she won't break me down. "Well now," he said, "I got three women to look after already. You think that ain enough, you better not tell my draf board."

"But haven't you ever—you know—"

"Like in the movies?"

"Like Joe and me."

"I guess maybe I scare em off—big, black, an ugly, an all I know about is organize. Organize an fight. That ain what they lookin for these days." Despite himself, he was saying things he hadn't intended to say. "What I want, it's not what mos women like to see in a man. Scares em."

"What do you want?" She was staring at him, her lips slightly parted.

"Power. An that's somethin they jus don hand out to black men —not even in the movement. I go jus so far in any direction, bam! Up against a stone wall. Can't even get my own people to follow me all the way. They go along jus so far, but then . . ." He gripped the wheel hard and pushed down on the gas pedal. "I guess I better take you home."

"Did you ever tell Joe?"

"What?"

"What you just told me."

"I didn't have to."

"You mean he understood."

"He knew more, that man, jus by feelin it, than any man I ever knew. I din have to tell him all those things. He din have to ask me. I din have to ask him why he in the movement. An I tell you one thing more. He had enough guts for ten."

"Don't speak about him in the past tense!" she cried. "Do you want to kill him off too?"

"I ain—I mean—"

"I'm sorry." She was clutching herself by the elbows. "He made it through Italy, he sent me such letters, I can't tell you. My God, he's such a man. They sent him to England and I said to myself, thank God, what can happen to him in England? He loves it there, he drinks in the pubs, he picks up little kids in the streets. It's home in a way, it's where his people come from. And they still care about politics there. He even got mixed up in a by-election, I'm not sure what that is, but he went knocking on doors with the ILP candidate, helped him with his speeches, it's a wonder he hasn't been court-martialed."

He was almost jealous. This kind of life he could understand; and Anne's pride in it was what he hoped for from Coretta. But then her tone changed.

"Here, though, they sit around talking about the second front this, the second front that, as if it was some kind of game. I know the people in the branch mean well, they're not brutal or unfeeling. Still, thousands are going to die, millions maybe, the way those landings go in the Pacific. Look what happens to men like Norm, wading ashore with bullets coming at them like snow, like hail. What chance has Joe got going in against the Nazis?"

"He's got a chance," Big Boy said doggedly. "As good as anybody else, maybe better, bein smarter and quicker than most. They ain stopped Norm yet, have they?"

"Once in your life," she muttered, "you find a man like Joe. Once in your life, that's all. I was sitting there, far away from home, minding my own business, playing Schubert, and he walked in the door. Do you think it'll happen to me again? Never!" She pounded her fists on her thighs. "What do I care about their God-damned war?"

He wondered if anyone else had ever seen her like this, unless it was her own husband. Then they were on her block, and he was drawing the car over to the curb under the streetlight, so that she could see to get out.

"Well," he said, suddenly bone-weary, "here we are."

She said nothing for a long moment. Then she leaned heavily on the door handle, almost as if she were falling on it, and twisted away from him as the door swung open. Halfway out of the car, one foot in the street, she fell back with a groan.

"What's the matter?" He leaned toward her, alarmed.

"I twisted my ankle." She tried to smile, panting a little. "If you'll just help me to get out—"

He ran around to the sidewalk and reached in for her. Leaning heavily on his arm, she made her way slowly up the walk.

"I'll be all right," she said, her breath coming a little jaggedly. "As soon as I get inside, I can lie down."

At the door she opened her purse, but her hands were shaking. "Oh I can't." She thrust the purse at him. "It's down in there someplace, hanging from the leather key ring."

Groping through Kleenex, lighter, lipstick, strange small hard objects that slipped away under his clumsy fingers, feminine fragrance that floated to his nostrils, he found the key at last. Anne was leaning against the wall, her mouth open, her breast rising and falling. "It goes in the lower lock," she said.

The door swung open into darkness. He reached out to guide her into the room with one arm, the other sweeping the wall within, feeling for the light switch. Before he could find it, she was inside the apartment, leaning against the door, breathing hard.

He said, "I'd better—" but then she was upon him, pulling his hand away from the wall with both arms. Thrown off balance, with his free hand he grasped the collar of her coat. She fell on him, the coat slipping from her shoulders.

"Don't go! Don't go!"

Frightened, he struggled in the darkness to free himself. They swung around awkwardly, his arm reached out desperately for the door, but encountered only air.

"Don't leave me!" Her voice was loud, almost a scream. She was pulling at him, tugging and tearing at his jacket as if he were some kind of doll. "Don't leave me!"

In terror, he clapped his hand over her mouth. His heart thudding, he held her tight, listening tensely for sounds from outside the apartment.

She relaxed, limp, almost falling from him. "I'm sorry," she whispered. "Forgive me." He released her. When it became clear that she was not going to move from her half-crouch, he backed to the door and let himself out. On the sidewalk he gulped air; then he was running for his car, desperate to get away.

6. BILL

"The place is in an uproar. Can you hear me?" Bill shouted into the telephone, glancing back over his shoulder into the plant cafeteria to see if he was being observed. "Tension's been building up ever since V-E day. One rumor after another—cutting back to one shift, cutting back production. Well, today it all came true. They've started passing out pink slips with the pay checks. It's mass layoffs."

"What do you want me to do?" Margaret's voice was cool and efficient. He could see her at her desk, pencil already poised.

"Call the regional office, tell them the shit hit the fan." He pulled his sweaty sport shirt loose from his chest. "We've been caucusing all over the shop. I've been running from group to group, it's like a lunatic asylum."

"Didn't the management foresee this?"

"Did the UAW? Did we? You can't foresee a mood. Even the foremen are asking me what they ought to do. The guys are talking strike, which doesn't make sense at this point. But it may happen before the shift lets out. Now you get on the ball and see what the International will do in case of a wildcat. Drop everything else, and do what a good little lawyer is supposed to do."

"I got you. Take care of yourself."

"Haven't got time. The Army is posting up notices reminding everybody that there's a war on yet. You ought to hear the guys— if we're still fighting Japs what are they firing us for? I have to hang up—I've got to stay one jump ahead of the workers and two jumps ahead of the Army."

"There's just one thing. Hunter called."

"At your office? What does *he* want?"

"Wouldn't say. He left a message for you to meet him at the back of the Waldorf Cafeteria on Pearl Street at six-thirty."

"Oh Christ. Well, I'll see you some time tonight. I'll try to ring you up later, if I can get to a phone again."

As it turned out, he could not. He found the president of the local in the wing department, surrounded by an excited group of low-seniority men and women waving their discharge slips at him angrily: "What are you going to do about it? What are you going to do about it?" The treasurer of the local he saw standing on top of a jig in the fuselage department, his feet tangled in hoses and wires, trying to explain to the riveters the union's program for reconversion, while inspectors and foremen stood by listening, not even attempting to get people back to work.

Hurrying from department to department, he managed to meet briefly with most of the key men in his rank and file caucus, scattered though they were throughout the plant, among the sections of half-finished airplanes. Talking fast, looking over their shoulders, peering around corners, hurrying into washrooms for quick discussions away from the roaring clatter, they agreed with him that the time had come to move, now. But to do what? Once the workers went home, talked it over with their wives, started looking for other jobs, their solidarity would melt like butter in the sun. The union would lose interest in fighting for temporary war workers, and the opportunity for mass action would be gone.

"I don't want to wait until we have to organize unemployed councils," he said. "We've got to move now, while we've got the workers together, right here in the shop."

"What do the officers say? How about the president? What'll the Reuther boys do?"

Bill took each question as it came, answered without hesitation, moved on to the next, pulling at his sticky shirt, emphasizing his words with his free hand. "The local officers see what has to be done but they're scared, they don't want the Army saying they started it. On the one hand they encourage us, they hint that they'll back us up as long as they won't be charged with responsibility for breaking the no-strike pledge. On the other hand, they're scared silly that if we pull this off, we'll win the next plant-wide election. So they want us to take the leadership and they don't."

A Trotskyite from maintenance, a big blond Finn with a mean self-confident grin, a very temporary ally, was eager to put him on the spot. "Where's your pals, the Reuther caucus? And where do you stand?"

"Look around you, Vaino. Here we are. I say, let's go. Let's pull the plug."

"What about Detroit?"

"They'll have to put up or shut up. There's no point in our calling for a walkout. Aside from the law, the workers know they can't force the company to go on making planes nobody needs."

"You don't want to walk out, but you say pull the plug. What do you—"

"I say we sit down. For one day. Today. Now." For a minute it was Akron all over again and he was a teenager once more, scared, looking for reassurance into his father's battle-hardened face. Wait till the old man heard about this! "It's not a strike, it's a stoppage. A protest against being dumped without provision for reconversion. We're not against work, we're for it. We don't want to lose our jobs, we want to keep them. What do you say?"

In minutes they had fanned out, section by section, department by department.

Clapping his hands above his head, he opened his arms in a V like Eisenhower greeting the troops. "Pull the power! Cut the juice! Stay at your bench! This is a demonstration!"

On to the next area, cutting around a pillar, jumping up on a ladder.

"We are not breaking our contract, we are not walking out, we are staying in! We are caucusing as a body, during working hours, for a plant-wide meeting. We are protesting mass layoffs. We are demonstrating for jobs. We want jobs not just for us, but for the boys who are already starting to come home!"

Chalk in one hand to scrawl these slogans on the shining slabs of half-riveted aluminum, half-eaten sandwich in the other, Bill ran down the long aisles, spitting wax paper, passing on the word, cutting in between planes. If he hadn't known every inch of the plant he would have been picked up, for Army and management, enraged at the spreading silence, began to move in parallel lines, trying to track him down, him and the other caucus leaders, some of whom he could hear shouting defiance as they were picked up not ten feet from him.

Twice the workers sheltered him, making him squat behind a jig, or a wall of heaped-up toolboxes. Once, after the searchers had gone through a washroom and left it angrily, he trotted in and sat down panting on a toilet seat, listening for the commands over the loud-speaker while he bit ravenous chunks from Margaret's salami sandwich.

The voices of authority urged, pleaded, cajoled, threatened. But the power stayed off and the rivet guns did not chatter. The workers milled about, pleased with themselves, exchanging overseas letters and snapshots. Women made up their faces, men started up games of catch, then collected in knots to argue whether it would cost a million men to invade Japan, whose fault it was that so many of them were being laid off, whether things would have been different if Roosevelt hadn't died. Some grew uneasy, claiming that they had made their point and that they ought to go back to work, mount their stations, man their guns, before they got into real trouble and were accused of being unpatriotic. Already they were saying, Do you think the union will get behind us? Don't make me laugh, they're all the same, they want the dues, they'll sell us down the river . . .

It was essential that the demonstration last through the entire working shift. Psychologically it would be bad for it to peter out, for them to drift back to work, embarrassed, feeling that they had been misled. If they stuck it out through quitting time they would know that they had accomplished something. Having learned a solidarity hard to explain to the passive, but palpable to the participants, they would be better prepared to go with those who presented a practical program and an idealistic goal.

So he had to stick like a burr, buttonholing his own guys to make sure that they'd hold out for the rest of the day, organizing discussion meetings that the stewards could run on an orderly basis. Once or twice he missed being picked up by a hair, feeling like a horse's ass as he stood on the toilet seats so the Army, peering through cracks, couldn't spot his feet on the floor, then running out to encourage another group like a cheerleader, but staying only a minute before trotting away lest he be betrayed by a stoolpigeon.

His luck held. Even at the end of the day, when the whistle blew to announce the end of the company's long frustration, and everyone lined up meekly to punch their time cards, he was exhilarated to see that the bosses had not thought—or dared—to pull the cards from the slots and thus force the workers to seek them individually and submit to questioning. Was it possible that they were only hoping that the workers would quietly punch out and disperse, go their separate ways, before something worse happened?

Before he could decide, he was intercepted at his clock-out station by a superintendent whom he knew slightly and a pudgy Army captain.

"There's no point in your sticking that card in there, Zivic. You've had it here."

Bill glanced up at the Army officer. A soft-faced punk with hard eyes. "You guys tried to fire me once and you couldn't make it stick. Better not try again."

"We've got the goods on you now." The captain talked like out of the movies. "We've got proof. What you did today was the next thing to treason. Seniority or no seniority—"

"Don't wave the flag at me, just because those captain's bars went to your head."

Already a crowd was gathering around the N-Z clockout bay. Even those anxious to get home and brag about what had happened today hung around to hear what he would say next. The superintendent stood quiet, uneasy, not commenting, now that he had fingered him to the Army.

"There isn't one of us hasn't got a brother or a husband in the service. And I mean overseas, not sitting at a desk and counting airplanes. They want jobs too when they get home, and we're going to fight to see that they get them. We're going to fight for a decent reconversion program, not just sit around and wait for another depression."

Some of the workers actually cheered. "Give him hell, Bill!" but they were safely hidden in the crowd.

"Now take your hand off my arm so I can check out."

It was an impressive exit after an exhausting and in some ways outlandish day. At the local office across the street, the leadership was already walking around in circles. The president was yelling on the phone long distance; as Bill closed the door behind him he was greeted with "You, you son of a bitch!" Grinning, he readied himself for a long session.

By the time he had talked himself out, it was late. Margaret was neither at her office nor at home but Vera said she had left word that she would see him later in the evening.

"Listen kid," he said to his sister-in-law, "get hold of Bernie on the phone and give her everything I've given you on this sit-down story. The quicker she types it up, the better our chances of getting it into the next issue of *New Labor*. That'll be a big help to us. But tell her not to write the lead or the last paragraph until she hears from me."

"I'll get hold of her. Are you all right?"

"A little tired. And probably fired. If not worse. Things move fast when you least expect them to."

"Imagine how Browder feels."

"Why?"

"The Communists have dumped him, didn't you hear?"

"Oh boy. That's all I need, is to have the Stalinist line change again. One more headache. Tell me, before I hang up, how's Marlen?"

Vera sounded surprised. "He's right here on the floor, playing with a coloring book. Say, good news. Letter from Norm today, it sounds like he's going to stay in the Philippines. No more landings. Isn't that wonderful?"

It was a miracle that Norm had survived all those island invasions, he seemed to lead a charmed life.

At the Waldorf, a men's restaurant that he did not care for, with its white-tiled walls and tired-looking help that made you feel you were in some kind of institution, he bought a plate of corned beef and cabbage and a cup of coffee and sat where he had been instructed. There was no sign of Hunter. He was finishing the coffee, thinking that maybe the message had been garbled, when Hunter marched past him as if he did not exist.

As he walked by, face closed and shoulders hunched, he dropped a napkin on the floor. For one moment Bill was going to call after him.

Instead he bent to retrieve the napkin. On the inside of it, Hunter had printed with a heavy pencil: *Meet me in my room. IMPORTANT*. He glanced up, but Hunter was already out of sight.

Cursing, he went out to his car. What was Hunter's address? At last it came to him. It was in the fruit belt, Plum Street, in the old German neighborhood, in an attic that had formerly been a maid's room.

He got there faster, he was sure, than Hunter could possibly have made it, and decided to sit in the car and wait for him. One last kid came down the somnolent street on his two wheeler, empty canvas bag over his shoulder, on the way home from his paper route for a late supper. I'll leave a note under his door, he thought tiredly, and be on my way.

He went round the side of the clapboard house and on up the rear entrance to the attic. Rapping on the door to make sure, he was fumbling in his pocket for paper and pencil when the door opened a crack. It was Hunter.

"Get in quick." Hunter stood panting in the middle of the darkened room. "They're after me."

"Who?" It was already twilight, the declining sun had gone round the corner, beyond the one window, and he could not even clearly discern the man before him.

"You know."

"Wait a second. How did you get up here so fast? I've been waiting out front for a quarter of an hour. I didn't see any sign of you."

"I took a cab from downtown to Peach Street. I went on through past the garage, jumped the fence, and cut across the backyard."

"Why?"

"I told you already. Don't you believe me?"

"You didn't say who."

"The FBI. They've been making inquiries about me, at work, where I eat, everywhere. If they come up here . . . if they find out what I've got in this room . . . You don't know what they could do to me. But then you don't know about what happened in New York."

"What made them suspicious of you? I want to make sure it isn't on account of me. Or Harry. Have you got any idea?"

"I've got an idea, all right." Hunter smiled unpleasantly, as though he was long out of practice, sitting hunched in this bleak room under the sloping eaves, with those unlikely photos of Einstein and Romain Rolland taped to the wall board. "It was the Nazis."

"Cut it out." What had gotten into Hunter?

"I warn you, don't laugh. You'll live to regret it. I used to work at Brewster, in Long Island City."

"It comes back to me. We had a good bunch there in Local 365."

"We still do. But it was honeycombed with Nazis. Honeycombed."

"I remember that too. They said you used to have to join the Bund to get a job there, the German toolmakers had the place sewed up. But that was a long time ago, Hunter, that was in the thirties."

"They were still there when I was hired. One day the Navy came in and took away twenty-one of them for setting jigs and dies a full thirty-second off. They'd been keeping production of the Brewster Buffalo at nothing, zero: One of them committed suicide afterward."

"What's that got to do with you?"

"They thought I turned them in. I was told in confidence they hated me for it, they swore to get me."

"How could they chase you all the way up here?" It sounded fishy. There had been Nazis at Brewster Aircraft all right, but why should they go after Hunter? Anyone could have turned them in —after Pearl Harbor the game was up.

Hunter stood his ground. In the shadow his figure grew more indistinct. "Vito and Fred have told me," he said hollowly, "how active the Bund used to be here. Did you know that they had close to four thousand members? Any one of those four thousand—"

"You mean you think—"

Hunter lifted his hand, a teacher quieting an overeager student. "I don't think. I know. There are ways. You of all people ought to know that there are ways."

"All right then. The question is what to do about it. Have you been interrogated yet?"

"They wouldn't do that."

"Why not? When they fired me the Army grilled me up and down. There's nothing to stop the FBI from pulling you in."

"They want me to make a slip. They watch me, day and night, like vultures waiting for me to die. Maybe they are, so they can come in here and pick my bones."

"We're going to have to have a meeting about this. Maybe that lousy union in your shop won't back you up, but then again they might. As soon as mine did, the Army let me alone. And we've got to brief Margaret. Why have we got a lawyer in the branch, if we don't make use of her?"

"No. That's exactly what you mustn't do. Don't you understand, you'll be falling into their trap?"

"Hunter, I don't see what harm—"

"They want to use me as their pigeon. You think they haven't infiltrated the Party already? There isn't anybody you can trust."

"I trust my wife." He said doggedly, "Aside from Margaret, whom have you got in mind?"

"If you don't believe me—"

He sighed. "I'm trying to, if you'll be specific."

"Small. He's been filing reports. How else would the FBI know every move I make, be at places where nobody knows I'm going to be, watch me even in the cafeteria where I eat breakfast, wait for me when I punch out, even sit in the next row when I go to the movies to see if I'm going to pass somebody something?"

In the gathering gloom it was now almost impossible to make out the man's features. "Let's turn on a light."

Hunter shook his head imperiously. "They'll see."

"We can pull down the shade."

"I don't want them to know I'm here. I shook them in the cab, but there's always a plant out front. If the light doesn't go on, he won't know I'm here. The room is bugged, I'm positive, but I think it works only when the lights go on."

"Wait a minute. What's your proof on Small? I thought he was one of the people you hung around with. Come on, Hunter, you've been in his faction, along with—"

"I don't hang around with him, he hangs around with me. I try to keep to myself. When he began inviting me over my suspicions were aroused. He wasn't really interested in obtaining my support. He tried to pump me, he even tried to use his wives."

"Wives? What do you mean, wives?"

"Babe and Mildred." Now it was Hunter's turn to be pitying. "You didn't really believe those two are sisters? He's been living with them both, you can ask Harry, he walked in one day and found the three of them in bed together."

"Cut it out!" He couldn't help laughing.

"If you don't believe me, ask Harry. But I've got more pressing problems. I've got to destroy my files without them knowing it. What I want you to do is take these two boxes." He nudged them with his foot; overcoat cartons from Irwin's father's clothing chain. "There are letters, diaries, things that should never fall into their hands. I've put rocks inside, and I've tied them well with heavy twine. As you can see." Hunter was a little pedantic. "Now if you can just take these to your car as though you were carrying off some laundry, and drive off slowly without turning on your lights until you round the corner, I don't think they'll follow you. They'll stay, waiting for me."

Bill looked at the boxes. "Why all this rigmarole?"

"Because there are names, addresses . . . Drive slowly to the foot of West Ferry, park as though you're waiting for the next boat to Fort Erie, and when the coast is clear, drop them both in the river. They'll sink. Even if they shouldn't, they'll wash over the Falls."

"I think this is nuts. I've got my hands full with an illegal sitdown, and you can't hole up here in the dark indefinitely."

Hunter smiled. "Your name and activities are in those files. It's to your advantage to get rid of them. As for me," you could see the faint gleam of his teeth in the darkness, "I've got another room."

"What?"

"When you're through with these, drive back here. I'll be watching from the window. Park in front of the house and blink your lights once before you cut them off. Then I'll leave the rest of my belongings just outside this door for you. I don't have too much, you needn't worry, everything'll be in two valises. I'll leave the way I came, over the fence. As long as I don't have to carry anything, I can shake them off. And we'll meet to go to my new room at the ice cream parlor on Northland Avenue."

"What ice cream parlor?"

"It's called the North Pole. A hangout for high school kids. You can't miss it, it's on the left as you drive out, the only store on the block."

The room smelled stale and already empty, as though no one had been living in it for some time. Even the pictures of Einstein and Romain Rolland looked left over, forgotten by a previous occupant.

"I guess there's no point in arguing with you," Bill said. "The quicker I go, the quicker I'll get it over with."

"I'll be waiting for you. Good luck."

Good luck? He needed strength, not luck. The weighted cartons were so heavy that he staggered under the burden, cursing as he stumbled down the stairs. Feeling his way, he kicked open the screen door and hurried to his car.

He opened the rear door of the Chevy, moved Marlen's canvas kiddy seat over to the other side, and put the cartons one atop the other on the back seat. As he backed out he straightened up too soon and fetched himself a mighty crack on the crown of his head —purple stars and planets whirled about, tears popped from his eyes. He fell to one knee, his palm mashing into what felt like apple pie. A fresh dog turd. Christ! He rubbed his hand on the scrubgrass, wiped it with his handkerchief, threw the handkerchief into the gutter. More cars were parked on the block by now, but he couldn't tell if any were occupied by men taking photos of him staggering back and clutching his head. Almost all of them looked empty, in fact, except for the car standing directly behind him, in which a boy and a girl were eating Popsicles, the unlikeliest-looking government agents ever staked out on any assignment.

Still, he was stuck with the cartons. So he drove off as Hunter had directed, not turning on his headlights until he had rounded the corner. After that he felt somewhat better, but just before he got to the foot of Ferry Street the sky opened in a Wagnerian burst, rain smashed like stones against the metal roof, and his head began to throb again. Anxious to get the thing over with, he slammed out into the street, but slipped in a new puddle, promptly soaking his leg to the knee, and dropping one of the cartons, which burst, scattering bricks, old copies of *Liberty* magazine, bundles of letters, onto the wet street. Scrambling after a loose letter, he reached into his hip pocket for his handkerchief to mop his steaming face and then remembered that he had already left it, covered with dog shit, in front of Hunter's house.

He glanced at the letter he had finally retrieved before consigning it to the Niagara River. *Dear Albert,* he read, *Your father and I are extremely . . .* He tore it into small pieces, feeling guilty, and dumped it with his first load. It was a job, getting the second carton out of the back seat without dropping it, for the rain was pelting now. Breathing heavily, he trotted to the ferry landing and hastily shoved it over the grill into the water, then hurried back to his car without waiting to see what had happened to it. He could scarcely hear any noise when it hit the water.

The rain let up as he headed back to Hunter's hideout, but he was scarcely any drier when he reached Plum Street for the second time.

Pulling over to the curb, he followed Hunter's instructions— blinked once, then turned off the lights. After a moment he got out of the car (the Popsicle kids, at least, had left) and trudged on up to the attic once again.

Two battered old suitcases stood outside Hunter's attic room. Both were heavy, but nothing like the clothing boxes. More bricks? Sweating, he made his way down the steep stairs with one bag tilted on his shoulder, the other banging against his thigh.

At the car, he was surprised to observe that one, an old Gladstone, still bore half-legible labels, browned and curling, legendary reminders of the good old days: Deauville, Karlsbad, Salzburg, Venice-Lido, Monaco, Biarritz, St. Jean de Luz, Pau. The watering spots of Dear Albert's parents?

And now where was the mysterious Comrade Hunter? Yawning, Bill slouched in the car across the way from the Northland ice cream parlor and awaited a sign. But none was forthcoming. Reluctantly, he got out of the car yet again and crossed the street.

An odd place for a rendezvous. Shadowless, garishly glowing under fluorescents, the ice cream parlor rang with Ray Eberly crooning *Amapola,* kids shooting the rumpled wrappers of soda straws like arrows, soda fountain-jockeys shouting orders.

Like somebody's father hunting for his wayward offspring, Bill pushed through awkwardly, staring into the booths while trying to appear as if he were not. As he passed each booth, the kids fell silent, and he was suddenly aware of his steamy eyeglasses, his stubbled cheeks, his sweaty sport shirt and stained khaki trousers. He felt like a little old man.

"Who d'ya want?" a gum-chewing waitress shrilled at him. "Lookin for somebody special?" She blew him a fat pink bubble, like a tumor.

He shook his head silently. Distracted by the thing growing out of her mouth, he backed into a boy carrying a double dip cone and almost took both scoops between the shoulder blades. The boy was yelling something, but Bill waved him away. He was halfway to the sanctuary of his car when he heard a short sharp whistle.

A figure stood in the dark alleyway to the left of the North Pole.

"Have you got the valises?"

"They're in the car. Did you want me to fill them with ice cream at the North Pole? Come on into the sleigh, Santa, I can't take much more."

Hunter was not about to apologize. "You can never be too sure. Say, you smell funny."

"Dog shit," he explained.

"Get into the car and watch me. I'm going to cross the street and walk around the corner. When I turn up the walk, you can drop off the bags in front of that house."

"Aren't you going to leave me a tip?"

"We're not out of the woods yet. Don't try to get in touch with me—I'll figure out a way."

"I'm sure." He shambled back to the car and started it up. He had the feeling that all the kids in the ice cream parlor were watching him, nudging, noses to the glass.

At last Hunter scooted off, his long black shadow enlarging and lengthening as he moved; Bill coasted behind him in low, and pulled up as he suddenly turned in to a two-family house no different from any of the others on the block. He went up the side entrance, he did not look back, he was gone. Sighing, Bill opened the rear door of the car and pitched the valises out onto the front lawn, then drove off.

When he reached home he was so tired that he could hardly get himself out of the driveway. Margaret and Vera were waiting up for him in the kitchen.

He raised his hand wearily. "Too tired to explain."

"You could have picked up a phone. After everything that went on in the shop today, to disappear that way! I was worried sick, I called the Local, I tried the boys, nobody could say. I didn't know, did the Army pick you up, or the FBI, or what, after your date with Hunter. And here I am, a lawyer. You put me in a hell of a bind."

"It's funny you should mention the FBI," he said. "It seems to be catching." Tired or no, he had to explain.

The two staring faces, both propped on their fists, gazed at him incredulously.

"You know what made me suspicious? Hunter's story about Small living with both of those women. Doesn't that sound crazy? Two wives? Two *homely* wives? We never had anything like that in Akron."

"Dear baby," Margaret reassured him, "you have just picked out what was probably the only reasonable statement Hunter made to you all evening."

"You mean it's true? How would you know?"

"Everybody does, except you."

"But that son of a bitch Small could endanger us all. Do you realize what it would mean if he'd be picked up? What's the law on bigamy?"

"Darling," his wife pointed out coolly, "it can't be bigamy. Not if none of them are married."

"Whatever it is. Why didn't somebody do something?"

"While you were in Grand Rapids last fall, fighting to get the

UAW to scrap the no-strike pledge and support a Labor Party, Harry was fighting for Babe and Mildred against Hoover. Misunderstood, he called them. The branch finally decided not to get involved, and I guess that's why I never talked to you about it. I assumed you knew."

"Well, I didn't. On top of all our other problems."

"Babe and Mildred will keep for a while. Hunter won't. He's a real time bomb. Billy, you'd better give me his new address."

"I haven't got it. If he was right about Small, what makes you so sure he wasn't telling the truth about the FBI?"

"Baby, baby, where's the evidence? In the river? The poor guy is sick in the head, and he caught you at the right moment, when you were exhausted."

Margaret was being kind. He saw it even more clearly the next morning. She managed it all with her usual efficiency, phoning the national office to find out about Hunter's relatives, commitment papers, formalities.

But where had he been more ridiculous, dumping old magazines into the Niagara River, or hiding in factory toilets? The workers' aggressiveness had melted overnight. More uneasy than militant, they returned meekly to the factory, still pleased with themselves but, like children after breaking a window, a little afraid of the consequences. He had been right in arguing against strike action. But what had been gained by the sitdown? Had they learned, if only in their glands, something of the potency of mass action as against the impotency of individual whining?

Perhaps. In the course of the day he was fired, with a certain formality, "for cause," as though he were being cashiered from a regiment, and in addition was notified that charges of disorderly conduct would be pressed against him. Still he was pleased with the waves, salutes, cheers, which greeted him as he strode firmly down the aisles.

Fired or not, he was going to run for president of the local. It was clear that he had the support of the rank and file, but the trick would be to keep in touch with them while he was denied access to the factory floor. He decided to talk it over with Harry. But there was no answer at Harry's apartment—odd because sooner or later the old man always picked it up—and finally he thought to try the Glantzmans.

Bernie sounded strained and distant, and not very interested.
"But what am I supposed to do," Bill complained, "send him a
letter asking for an appointment?"

"He had to send his father to the nursing home."

"Oh."

"There's something else. Sy just caught a plane to New York. We
got a telegram—his mother died this morning." She made an odd
noise, then stopped.

Bill said automatically, "You mean his father."

"No," she said, crying now, "that's the crazy part. His father is
still alive. His mother fell over, standing at the stove. Just like that."

"I'm terribly sorry." He felt stupid.

"I'm going to take a train tonight, for the funeral. I have things
to clear up here first. And listen, about Harry. He's in trouble at the
university. There's something queer about that course he gives."

That evening he drove out to the university. Harry had always
been very insistent that no one get in touch with him at the school
or the electro-chemical plant and it took a while to find the building,
and then the room. It was at the end of a long green corridor, waxy
and silent between semesters, like a half-empty hospital.

A tall husky boy was lounging outside Harry's office, leafing
through grade sheets tacked to the cork board by the door. He
glanced up. "You looking for Sturm too?"

"That's right."

"He's not home. His office-mate's in there, if that'll do you any
good. You want to sign up for summer session?"

"Well—"

"His course, inorganic chemical technology, isn't bad. I took it
spring semester. He's pretty sharp, I learned quite a bit, but man,
that final . . ." Lips puckered, the boy raised his eyebrows signifi-
cantly.

"What about it?"

"If you're not in industry, he gives you an open-book final, fair
enough. But most guys have got jobs, right?—that's why the course
is in the evening—so he lets you use your term paper as a final.
You have to describe in detail an industrial process, with diagrams,
taken from the place where you work, and related to the course
material." The boy winked. "He's no dope. I hear he's been doing
it for years."

Bill stared at him. "What for?"

"They say he cribs the stuff for his own Ph.D. Go know—
you can't prove it by me. Even if he does, his final is a lot better
than boning up and memorizing, like you have to do for every
other course in the department."

The door opened and another young man stepped out. "Let's
go, Murray."

The student turned to Bill. "If you do see Sturm, tell him for
Christ sake to post the grades—everybody else's are in already."

Bill poked his head in the office. A dull-looking man, his short-
cropped gray head glinting in the light of his desk lamp, was putting
a cigarette to his lips. "Well?" he asked.

"I'm an acquaintance of Mr. Sturm. Do you have any idea—"

"Last I heard his father had suffered some sort of stroke. There
hasn't been any word since." He added, gratuitously and rather
ominously, "The department would like to know what he has up his
sleeve, in case you see him first."

Bill returned to his car slowly. As far as he knew, Harry had
done no work on his Ph.D. for years. Something didn't add up.

By the end of the week he had been rehired—after pressure from
the International—but his civil case remained on the docket. Margaret
thought it quite possible that he would get thirty days for disorderly conduct. She was not happy about it, even though she said
good-naturedly, "Once you're in jail my conduct will not be
orderly." Harry was still out of sight, not answering his phone;
Bernie and Sy were still in New York. Vera took over Bernie's
duties and Bill had to take over the branch meeting.

Whether or not there was to be an invasion of Japan, he said,
the end of the war was in sight. The branch had hardly changed
the course of events, but it had kept alive the opposition to both
jingoism and Stalinism. "That's nothing to be ashamed of," he said.
"Without us, the unions in which we're active wouldn't have been
much more than extensions either of the Labor Department or of the
Communist Party. And we've managed to stay alive as an organization."

That was more than could be said of their European comrades.
He enumerated the people about whom Joe, recuperating from his
wounds, had written them: this one last heard from in a Spanish
camp, that one hanged, this one taken by the Gestapo and tortured,
that one dead of hunger. "As a movement," he said, "we no longer

exist in Europe. All we have are individuals—hungry and exhausted individuals. One of our basic responsibilities is to nurse them back to health, with money and food parcels."

As for the future, there was the virtual certainty of mass un-employment, the danger of a fascist movement arising among brutalized ex-GIs, the need to work in the American Veterans' Committee, and the prospects for growth within the labor movement.

He ended on what he hoped would be an optimistic note—the revolutionary wave, begun in Italy with the overthrow of Mussolini, was not yet finished. Here at home they could be the partners of people struggling to free themselves across the world.

There was a deafening silence. Finally Big Boy got slowly to his feet. Leaning his huge bulk against the wall behind him, he spoke in ominous tones.

"I din take the floor to argue with your summary. It was good. I got to criticize what you left out."

"Go ahead."

"You din devote any time to the struc-ture of the party. Or to the kine of party we got. Or to the com-position of this branch."

"This branch? Be specific."

"Comrade, *you* know. I mean the ones that are footin the bills. You think we ain aware that a non-party member is helpin to pay the rent for this hall?"

"We ought to be glad we've got sympathizers that can give us a hand."

"I ain glad, not when they're petty-boogewah. How do I know the kine of influence they got behine the scenes? I din join this party to see it run by a bunch of dentists."

Margaret said briskly, "You're out of order. This is not the time or the place for such a discussion."

"This is a workers party, ain it? Then it ought to be run by the workers."

The voice was Big Boy's, but the muddle of ideas was Harry's. Well, Hoover had warned them that Harry was stuffing Big Boy's head with a jumble of half-digested notions. Gazing reflectively at Big Boy's shining, discontented face, Bill suspected that he would never have pulled this if Ham Wright had been at his side; Ham was almost pathologically sensitive to that type of assault. But Ham's deferment had been reversed, and he had gone into the Navy—maybe on account of Big Boy? It was possible that Big Boy was simply bored, or worse, simply sick of everything, the branch, the movement, as he had been sick without reason of Ham's continued presence beside him at the mill.

As soon as Sy and Bernie returned Bill asked them to come over. They were understandably subdued, but gradually he began to feel that there was more to it than grief. They sat on the couch beside Margaret, who was playing with Marlen, ready for bed in his Dentons.

"Well," he asked bluntly, "how did it go?"

Sy stared down at his shoes. "I had the ceremonial dinner with my brother Sid."

"So he was home for the funeral?" Margaret asked. She handed the child to her sister with obvious reluctance, and sat as if bereft.

"His ship was in Panama. He flew up. He'd been on the West Coast. I get the feeling he might stay out there after the war ends, now that mom is gone. He's been changed by this war, more than he was by Spain. There's something alive beneath that political rigidity . . . Not just because he was torpedoed, but because of the suffering he's seen. And then to come home and find Browder discarded. I have the impression that he no longer considers himself a party member in good standing." Sy laughed shortly. "But of course he still considers my politics despicable."

"That reminds me," Bill said casually. "There's something I wanted to take up with you." He described Big Boy's flareup carefully, but when he finished he had the feeling that Sy had been attending to his words from a certain distance.

Sy frowned. "Why," he said, "I don't think Big Boy has any personal animosity toward Irwin. Unless . . . you know, Irwin's been very friendly with Ham, almost in a fatherly way. And Big Boy is very bitter about Ham, even though he denies it."

Encouraged, Bill went on, "You know something? It would make much more sense, in terms of his personality, for us to try to recruit Irwin's partner. He's less cynical than Irwin."

Sy tilted his head. He said, as if he had misunderstood, "Not Stuart?"

"Right. He's already sympathetic. Since you're the closest to Irwin, I think you ought to regard him as your contact."

Sy rose abruptly. He said over his shoulder, "I don't think I'd want to do that."

"But you know him better than the rest of us do."

"I don't want the responsibility."

What was he talking about? "Stuart doesn't have problems like Irwin did. Irwin was just getting started in practice, he had girl trouble, family trouble, war trouble. We need solid people to replace those who'll drift away." Or turn spooky like Hunter, he refrained from adding.

"I suppose that's all true."

"And if you're worried about Stu's being middle-class, there'll be less complaint from people like Big Boy than if he were just a sympathizer. After all, Stu's wife has very good connections among the liberals, in fact in the American Labor Party itself."

"I just don't know whether I want the responsibility of changing a man's life."

"That's the craziest thing I ever heard of. What do you think we've been doing all these years?"

Sy looked at him unblinkingly. "I'm not sure."

Bill turned to Bernie. She was mute, but her eyes were almost pleading. "Have you people gone sour on the—"

"If Stuart Kraft was working next to me in the shop, it would be different," Sy said. "But he's not stuck in a miserable factory. He's got other things to do, he's got season tickets for the symphony, he's got a nice house, he collects prints. Who am I to turn his life around?"

After a time Bill said slowly, "The way I was brought up, socialism was a way of life, not just something you felt over and held up to the light, as if it was a piece of goods in a store, before you decided whether or not to buy it." He gazed somberly at Sy. "Don't you feel like that any more?"

Sy said abruptly, "I have to go to the john."

As soon as he had closed the door Bernie said, "You mustn't press him too hard. He was crying last night." She went on quickly, her hands working as if she were speaking through them also. "We got a long letter from Joe yesterday, from Germany. He wrote us about the death camps."

Margaret was sitting stone-still on an arm of the couch. Something made him go over and join her there.

"He vomited. It was weeks before he could bring himself to write."

Margaret whispered, "We all knew. Sy knew. It's not as if he didn't."

"But what did we do? That's why Sy was crying, not just for his mother."

"We picketed, you remember the Bermuda Conference, we said Roosevelt and Churchill weren't lifting a finger. We did what we could. When Congressman Will Rogers went over to London to plead for the Jews, we—"

Bernie raised her hand. "Sy's mother had cousins in the camps. The last time she wrote us, she said that the Red Cross, HIAS, the Joint, told her that none were alive. None."

When Sy came back, Bill said hastily, "Let's forget about Kraft —that's really a matter for Harry. In fact, Harry is what I wanted to talk to you about. I know his father is deathly sick, but none of us has been able to get hold of him at all."

Sy and his wife exchanged glances. "Bernie, let me tell it," Sy said quite roughly. "I stopped in to see Hoover the other day. He's learned definitely that Harry has been questioned about his classes at the university."

"Questioned?" Margaret wrinkled her forehead. "By whom?"

"The district attorney."

"Now wait a minute. That sounds like poor Hunter all over again. Harry would surely have told us—"

"This is different. It's not political. And it's not in anybody's dream world. Harry's in real hot water."

I'm so thick, Bill said to himself, why didn't I see it before? He said slowly, "It has to do with the exams he gives, doesn't it?"

Sy blinked. "How did you know?"

"I bumped into one of his students. The boy told me Harry asks them to set down an industrial process for their final. It sounded a little funny, but I couldn't think that Harry . . . Besides, he's not working on his Ph.D., is he? So why should he want that data?"

"The students' employers went to the D.A. after comparing notes. They complained that secret processes were being revealed without permission. The investigation is trying to find what Harry's done with the information—apparently it's worth plenty."

"But that's crazy!" Margaret cried. "Who ever worked harder for the Party than he did? Who gave more time, or more money? Harry's an idealist. Do you know that he gave us twenty-five per-cent of his pay, week in and week out?"

"It sounds like a frame-up."

"Wait," Bernice said quietly. "Why hasn't he gotten in touch with us? Especially with you, Margaret? It sounds as though he's going to need a good lawyer."

They stared at each other.

"Well," Margaret said finally, "the first order of business is to find Harry. You people have had enough trouble for a while. And Bill may be going to jail himself for thirty days. So I guess I'm elected."

But before she succeeded, Harry himself phoned them. At the sound of his confident staccato voice, Bill felt all the pent-up resentment and frustration welling into his throat.

"Where in hell have you been?" he demanded. "Do you have any idea of what's been going on?"

"Bill, I know you've had troubles. I wouldn't want you to think I've been neglecting you. The fact is, my father has just died."

All the angry words withered on his lips. "Is there anything we can do?"

"Thank you. All the arrangements have been made. But we do have things to talk about. Do you think you could come to my apartment?"

"I'll be right over. Should I bring Sy?"

"Good idea." Was there a hint of amusement, even a chuckle, in Harry's voice?

What happened on the way stunned him so that by the time he arrived he had all but forgotten the reason for his errand: the excited voices on the auto radio, on one station after another, crying out the story of an immense bomb, an unimaginable bomb, dropped on Japan. Sy tumbled into the car and demanded, "Have you heard? It really sounds like the end—no more war, no more war!"

As they mounted the steps to the Sturm flat, Sy's elation faded. "I almost forgot about Harry's father. We seem to be walking into death everywhere. We didn't have to go overseas for it, did we?" He stood staring at his shoes, waiting for Harry to open the door.

Harry looked changed. He had bought a new suit, a handsome brown three-button model with a narrow stripe, and a green rep tie that went well with it. His cordovans wore a subtle glow, but then so did his freshly shaved cheeks. He regarded the two of them amiably, pipeless, his blue eyes darting, as if he were bursting with important news.

"Very good of you both to come. I was just packing up some final odds and ends."

"It looks"—Bill was not sure whether he was saying the right thing—"well, vacant. I was so used to seeing your father here."

"So was I," Harry observed dryly. "In fact, I regard this as his home, not mine."

"Where—" Sy began awkwardly.

"The body is at the railroad terminal. I'm going to take it to New York."

Bill lifted his hand to take in the barrels of books, the cardboard cartons stuffed, tied, and addressed. "But it really does look vacant. Aren't you going to stay on here when you come back?"

"I'm not coming back." Hands clasped behind him, Harry gazed at them both with benevolence, as though he had announced not death but birth, and awaited congratulations. Without giving them a chance to reply, he went on, "No doubt you've heard about the bomb.

"One bomb, and a city no longer exists. I've been expecting something like this, some harnessing of atomic energy. Too many physicists of my acquaintance had dropped out of sight. They had to be up to something, those boys." He laughed. "Well, they've finished off the war, they've made all our old ideas obsolete. No more of the old revolutions. From now on, new kinds of revolutions."

Sy's gentle eyes narrowed in fierce concentration. "This bomb: Can we be sure it means the finish of the war?"

Harry laughed shortly. "Forget about that war. Norm will be coming home to Vera and Marlen, Joe will be coming home to Anne without having to detour to the Pacific. No, we have to start thinking about the next war. The masters of this bomb are the masters of the world, do you see?"

"All this is very cosmic," Bill said. His head was aching. "But we've got a few little problems right here at home. And you've got a few explanations—"

"I have written a lengthy document which I want to give you before leaving. It summarizes my position better than I could, standing here in an empty apartment. It anticipates some of the developments we are going to have to cope with, starting with Hiroshima."

Sy's face was screwed up as though he were in pain. "Have you consulted with the National Office, if not with us, about pulling out of here? After all, you were the organizer."

"No longer. I've submitted my resignation. From the Party as well. I'm hoping this"—he picked up a manuscript—"will appear in the next issue of the Internal Bulletin as an extended statement of resignation."

"Have you got nerve!" Bill stared at the thick sheaf of legal-sized paper which Harry was extending to him; he made no move to accept it. "You didn't dream this up overnight."

"It's a crystallization." As if he liked the word, Harry repeated it, with a certain relish: "A crystallization. You know that I have been very dissatisfied with the Party's course. I have tried to press my point of view by every legitimate means—"

"And some illegitimate ones too."

Harry's smile broadened. "In a faction fight, things get rough. But even though I've been unable to make my view prevail, I have no complaint. Perhaps this document will help to alter a mistaken course. In any case, I wish you nothing but the very best of luck."

"Thanks," Sy said bitterly. "It's funny you don't mention the university and the law being on your tail."

Bill half-expected Harry to become enraged, but he remained bland.

"I assure you that didn't enter into my political calculations. Certain firms misunderstood my academic methods—just as the Party has misunderstood my political position. Period. But both have been clarified now, I think. My conscience is clear."

"That's just great. You walk out on us with no warning, no discussion, no nothing."

"Did Stimson and Truman give a warning when they dropped their bomb?"

"There's a little difference. We were your comrades—or we were supposed to be."

"It is my belief that there is no future for your kind of Party in this age. Our little sect died with that bomb, like the people of Hiroshima. We revolutionists are going to have to start afresh, to build a mass party that can compete with the old parties on a mass basis, through the mass media."

"You've sung that song already. But you couldn't sell it to us."

"And you posited your objections on minor irrelevancies, such as the fact that we were poor and few in numbers."

"Minor objections! Where's your magic formula for getting us millions of dollars and thousands of members, Mr. Scientist?"

"With millions of dollars you can get all the members you can handle. You can crack the mass media—even create new media."

"And where do we get the millions of dollars? From you?"

"I've already begun to address myself to that question." Harry placed the manuscript in Sy's palm. Then he brushed his hands with a gesture of finality. "I have no personal ambition, but I do have a personal responsibility—to use my skills to accumulate the wherewithal. Not to waste them on marginal political activity, as I did throughout the war years. I excuse myself only on the grounds of youth, primitive political interpretations, and an unreadiness to think things through to their logical conclusion."

"But now you know better."

"Do read my document. It's the product of careful thought as well as devotion to the cause. And now, if you'll excuse me . . ."

Bill and Sy stared at each other. In the silence the shock waves were rebounding across the empty room, wars ending, wars beginning, everything rocking, overturning, as they stood rooted to the bare floor.

PART FOUR

PART FOUR

1. NORM

Norm was hardly in the village when he sensed a change. It was not that anyone was unfriendly—after all, he had been coming for a number of weeks, ever since gaining the confidence of the Filipino who had admitted that he was—like practically everyone in his village—a supporter of the Hukbalahaps. They greeted him as always, grinning and nodding with the alacrity that always held, for him, a touch of unreality, as though they liked him because he was American (a madness, in view of the fact that the Americans were already persecuting them). Eager, lithe, little, trotting under the shelter of the *nipas* on thin legs spotted with beri-beri sores, they hastened to bid him welcome. Ignacio, Honofre, bandy-legged Jorge, and the others whom he knew by the wonderful new names they had chosen not so much to conceal themselves as to indicate their desire to be somebody new and different: Courage, Honor. And Ligaya—Happiness—the wide-mouthed, broad-nosed young man who had originally introduced him to his village.

"*Bilis!*" cried Ligaya. "Hurry! You come just in time for *merienda*."

"I'm not hungry."

"You never hungry," Ligaya laughed. "But maybe a little *cala-may*? Big man like you, you got to have strength. You don' like *tuyo,* you don' like fish, take a little *sorbetes*. Sugar give you strength." They went on past the nipa-thatched huts, to the village square where the chief awaited him. Ligaya was chuckling, but Courage and Honor were just subdued enough for him to sense that all was not exactly as usual.

"Ah, Kazama Vanderbilt!" the chief, a wrinkled little man with stained teeth, greeted him affably. "Welcome."

Squatting down in the midst of the circle that they automatically formed about him, Comrade Vanderbilt mopped at his neck. All this had started out more or less as a gag. Even after the initial cultural shock had worn off, he remained a character out of a Waugh novel, hunkered on his heels in a Pampanga village and explaining Marxism—at their request—to a scattering of half-naked peasants who regarded his enormous size, his short-cropped hair, his creased uniform, his glossy boots, with an intentness bordering on awe. But they loved him, that was what had happened in the course of these crazy sessions as he tried to explain the various Internationals, the labor theory of value, Lenin on the vanguard party, Trotsky on the permanent revolution. And now he loved them.

"Where did we leave off?" he demanded briskly. "I believe we were talking about the primitive accumulation of capital." They were fascinated by the bearded Marx and had insisted, despite the lack of a text (most of them couldn't read anyway) that he explain all of *Capital* to them.

This week however they had something else in mind. The two brothers, Courage and Honor, glistened with uneasiness. It was Honofre, an activist in the National Peasants' Union, who spoke up.

"We hear you go back to the States."

"One of these days."

"And the other GIs?"

"This is your country, not theirs." His answers were inadequate. "You look surprised."

The chief passed his hand slowly several times in a sweeping circle over the lateral wrinkles on his naked belly, as though the gesture were part of some incantation. He said deliberately, "They think maybe you don't want to stay."

Norm wiped his forehead. These charming little men had themselves been fighting the Japanese in the backwoods and the jungles. Within the year they had liberated the province and its capital. They had expected to be greeted as comrades in arms by the Yanks—who had promptly clapped their leaders into jail.

"Most GIs," he said, "have no interest in the Filipinos. They are homesick. In the States mothers, wives and girl friends agitate, Bring our boys home. This is important—it brings the troops into conflict with the military machine—and it makes possible mass action against American imperialism."

"Okay, okay," said Honofre. He had a way of speaking English from the throat so that it came out like the clever mimicry of a myna bird or a parrot. "We fight imperialism too. Why not together?"

Norm sucked on the sorbetes. "The guys who want to go home, and their folks who want them home, don't know anything about you. They're not mean. They think they did you a big favor by bombing the Japs out of the islands. If anybody told the GIs that they're the troops of an imperialist power, like Japan, they'd laugh. They don't know what the word means. They don't know who the compradores are—or what that word means. All they know is, the war's over. They want to go home."

"And us?"

"I think the best thing is to get them out of here. Those of us who lead demonstrations may be court-martialed. The Filipinos can't help us any more than we can help you—except by leaving. We have to count on the anger that's building up back home."

"We don't feel against you, Ka," Honofre said in his shrill voice. "We know you come to teach. We know you feel with us."

Norm traced a pattern in the dust. He wanted to explain not as Sergeant Miller, but rather as Comrade Vanderbilt. "They'd be shipping me out soon anyway. They count by how many points you earned in the fighting, like in school. I have plenty of points. Before I go I want to see that the others are sent home too. Then at least you'll have a chance to make your own future."

Their smiles were full of sympathy. He felt like an oaf. These weekly meetings were drawing to a close, and there remained for them what there had been before—the struggle to retain the weapons with which they had won their freedom, and without which they would be reduced to creatures without dignity or prospects. Even those few who had made their way to Manila to stumble, half dazed, along the neon-lit prospect of the Avenida Rizal, could hardly know that if he were to take up the profession at home of a radical organizer, no matter how obscure or harassed, his standard of living would still be stunning, dazzling, compared to theirs. And if they did know, would they still squat around him in the dust and attend to his learned lectures on Marxian economics?

Courage said wistfully, "Now you tell us about constant capital, okay?"

"Oh boy," Norm said.

"And variable capital," Honofre added, in his bird-like twang.

"Wow." Were they teasing him? Or was this their way of easing his departure?

Whichever, he decided to do it their way. But after he had finished and bade them farewell, the questions hung in his mind like the mites that hung in the air before his face, rising from the muddy ditches to torment him as he passed the small water buffaloes lying in the wet mud with only their heads exposed. Heedless that he was more exposed than the lolling beasts, he proceeded to cut across the flat fields that separated the village from his base. He was fairly certain that no one had noticed him leave the base, but someone could easily have observed him coming back.

He gave it no further thought, though, until Weiner came up to his cot while he was writing a letter to Vera. In a Bronx voice that rang harsh and whiny after the soft chatter of the Filipinos, he announced, "The Coynel wants you."

At the sound of Norm's heels the colonel cleared his throat. "Where've you been, Sergeant?"

"Writing a letter to my wife."

"That's not what I mean." The colonel tweaked his nose irritably. "You've been hanging out up in that Flip village. Now don't deny it, Norm, because there's two things I want to tell you. CIC knows about it, and they wanted to interrogate. I told them I'd take care of my own."

Norm cursed himself. He had gotten so involved in planning for the demobilization demonstration that he had grown careless about his auxiliary life as Comrade Vanderbilt. He said cautiously, "What was the second thing, Colonel?"

"That village is a hotbed of Huks. A hotbed. How do you think it looks when CIC tells me one of my men has been hanging out in a place like that?"

"You know the chief of that village, Colonel?"

Scott stared at him as if he were out of his mind. "How would *I* know him?"

"Too bad you don't. He's got the most fantastic daughter. You remember Anna May Wong, Colonel? This girl is more beautiful. I bring her old man stuff from the PX and old copies of *Esquire,* and he looks the other way."

Colonel Scott arose, his face alight. "Why didn't you say so, son? Why didn't you speak up?" For the first time, he looked Norm in the eye. He said with great relief, "I like to see a soldier with initiative. Nobody can blame you for trying." He added thoughtfully, "As long as you're honorable. A married man shouldn't promise things that he can't make good on."

"Amen, Colonel."

"I certainly am glad that nonsense about the Huks is cleared up. A man with your combat record! It always pays to look into things yourself, and not take the word of those Hawkshaws. How else can you stay close to your men? Now if you'd confided in me," the colonel chided, "this whole business could have been taken care of right from the start."

"Colonel, I honestly didn't think you'd be interested. And then, since you knew I was married . . ."

The colonel ducked his head shyly. "Well, I like to feel that all my men, especially my cadres, can feel free to walk into this office and unburden themselves. Just because I wasn't fortunate enough to be in combat with you fellows, I don't want you to look on me as a stranger. I'm proud of each of you, and if you level with me I'll stick up for you."

"I'm going to pass the word, Colonel."

"You do that. I want the morale of this outfit to be as high as it was last spring when you were storming those islands. Just because the war is over is no reason for us to let down." He did not sound convincing. "Dismissed, Sergeant."

On his cot sat an officer, nose in the letter that he had laid aside to answer the colonel's summons. His heart began to pound. Intelligence? But no, the captain leaped up guiltily, thrusting the letter aside awkwardly, and extended his hand in greeting. "Hello, Norm."

"Fred! Vera wrote that you were in Australia. I and E, isn't it?"

"I've been giving lectures to the troops—you know, English history, colonialism, stuff like that. Not very exciting, not like what I hear you've been through, but I got away with quite a lot." His face clouded. "But then I was sent up to Manila. Tokyo's next, unless I get my discharge. Been looking for you ever since I landed at Clark Field—is there someplace where we can talk?"

"We can have a beer at the PX, but we ought to be a little

discreet—the colonel has just been kind enough to inform me that CIC has had me under surveillance."

Fred looked frightened. "Maybe it wasn't such a good idea, my looking you up just now."

"Why not? There's no regulation against reunions. Besides, Dugout Doug signed the treaty with the Japs on September second last. The war's over."

"I know, I know. But we're not civilians yet. If they want to get nasty, they can really break it off." Fred glanced about nervously. "CIC must be watching you because of all this let's go home stuff. Do you think you're going to get away with demonstrations against the War Department's demobilization schedule? Against their occupation program in the hostile countries?"

"I think you've got it wrong." He led Fred to the washtub where the beer was kept iced and bought them a couple of bottles, then took him to a plank table set on sawhorses.

As he related his meetings with the Huk villagers, the outdoor classes on Marxism at the batalan of the chief's house to the noise of clanging kawali and caldero, Fred was frank in his envy and admiration.

"I thought I was doing something, lecturing on American imperialism, but you were the one who was taking the chances."

"They're the ones who take the chances. First they fought the Japs, then their own stooges in Manila. Now us. We'll be living like kings in the States while they're still sucking on mongo and carrying on their pakikibaka."

"What's that?"

"Struggle."

"I'm not so sure we'll be living like kings," Fred said. "The broken lives, the inability to go back to dull jobs and dull ways. Think of the couples who will have grown apart." He squeezed the beer bottle hard; there was a ring on his little finger that Norm could not remember having seen. "At least your villagers are on their home grounds, fighting for familiar things."

"Their problems are hellish. And they're all fucked up between nationalism and Stalinism. They admire us for the wrong reasons even when we disarm them and throw them into jail in their own country. What gets me is that they still believe in brotherhood, after all they've been through."

Fred squinted at him. "You must still believe in something, old boy, or you wouldn't be sticking your neck out, first with the Huks, now with that demonstration. You could get shipped home any day— you must have way over eighty-five points."

"It's not a personal or even a moral question," he said stubbornly. "It's political, man. When Wedemeyer says he needs more troops in China, besides the fifty thousand Marines that are stuck there already, it's got nothing to do with brotherhood or how many points I earned. If the mamas that are protesting at home don't understand it, they need us to tell them why."

"You think all our problems will be solved if we just get the troops home?"

"They'll just be starting. In the meantime I want to be where the action is."

"You haven't changed, have you, Norm?"

"Last year I was busy trying to stay alive. Now I'm on this committee with four other guys organizing protests like the Army never saw before. We may leave the Legion out in right field if we strike now. You ought to be in on this. When we march through Manila we're going to shake up the whole goddam island."

"You may wind up with a court-martial instead."

"If we sit on our duffs we'll have nothing. You do a lot of talking. Why not talk up the protests?"

"I can't see it as all that simple. Life is more complicated than it used to seem."

"Before you got drafted, or before you became an officer?"

Fred flushed. "They recognized my Ph.D. and my teaching experience. Was I wrong to try to help those boys get some education just because they were stuck in the Army like me? When they transferred me to I and E, was I supposed to let some hack lecture to the GIs instead of me?"

"No point in getting worked up. But why lose sight of the Army's real function?"

"I don't think I have. I still believe in—well, in socialism."

"Hooray for you. I don't know what I believe in any more. Too many dead bodies between me and those old days. But I'll tell you what I don't believe in, Captain—I don't believe in chickening out."

Fred made as if to rise, then seemed to think better of it. "You don't need to remind me that you were in combat and I wasn't."

"Screw that. I'm talking about today, Fred, not yesterday. You want to come to a committee meeting in Manila this Sunday? That's a straight question."

"I don't think I ought to commit myself without knowing who—"

"You know me. Come to the meeting and you'll know the rest. We're writing letters to the States, sending cables, setting up joint groups—"

"It's an enlisted man's show, isn't it?"

"If you're afraid you'll be out of your element, I'll vouch for you."

"I'm not sure what I'd have to contribute. Where's it going to be?"

"At the Blue Note Café right off the Plaza Miranda. Two o'clock."

"I'll do my best." Fred seemed eager to change the subject. "You haven't said anything about Vera and the baby."

"Marlen's a wild kid—active, inquisitive. Vera has her hands full. I think she'll be glad to have me back." He added, "Your daughter must be a big girl by now."

"She's in nursery school." To his astonishment Fred's face crumpled, his thin nose wrinkling, his eyes filling with tears. He pulled out a handkerchief and covered his face.

The best thing, Norm decided would be to say nothing and wait. After a moment Fred returned the handkerchief to his pocket. "I didn't mean to get overwrought. Do you think it's possible to be in love with two women at the same time?"

His first reaction was that Fred was pulling his leg. But Fred was gazing at him with hopeful seriousness.

"I suppose it's possible."

"It's happened to me." Fred unbuttoned his hip pocket and brought out his wallet. How many pictures did you have to look at in the Army? When the brass wanted to make an impression, they showed you color slides of syphilitic penises; when the ranks wanted to make an impression, they showed you pictures of pussy, or of wives in the backyard, knees knocking and eyes squinting shyly. "I met this girl in Brisbane, quite by chance."

Dutifully Norm studied the pocket photo. Better looking than Bea, that was clear. Younger, better features, not shrewish. "What's her name?"

"Sheila. Sheila Stickney."

"Very musical. Does she sing?"

Fred wriggled. "She does rehabilitation work. She wanted to do her part, her brother's in Italy. Actually, she's only nineteen."

"That's a little young, isn't it, Fred?"

"I didn't know her age when we met." He flushed. "She didn't tell me until after we'd become close. She's extremely mature." Balls. "So?"

"We've fallen in love. I've kept nothing from her—she knows all about Bea and Fernanda. I've even made it clear that Bea and I love each other. It's been a perfect torment to her. She pleaded with me not to see her any more, to the day I was shipped up here. Then she begged me to stop writing."

"Bet you haven't."

"I can't. Sheila says that what I feel for her isn't love at all, but that I'm simply lonely. But now I'm separated from Sheila as well, and I haven't stopped caring. It must be love, don't you think?"

In a twinkling Fred had transformed him from Comrade Vanderbilt into the kindly marriage counselor. Leaning his elbows on the greasy tabletop, he made a temple of his fingertips over the empty beer bottles, then kissed his fingers lightly with puckered thoughtful lips. Fred waited.

"First of all," he said gravely, "you do have a responsibility to your wife and child."

Fred groaned. "Every night I stare at their picture, and I cry. Maudlin, isn't it? I don't suppose you believe me capable of it."

But of course. "You may be overdramatizing. I believe in your suffering, but not necessarily in the genuineness of its origin."

Fred gazed at him with the faint beginnings of suspicion. "What do you mean?"

"As I recall, life wasn't always peachy with you and Bea."

"We had our troubles before the baby came. Who doesn't? Irwin and his wife had it rough before Paul was born."

"Those things don't end with babies. Do you really think a woman forgets her grievances once she's busy with formulas and diapers? Irwin is another story. If he hasn't found himself a little consolation in the Army, he couldn't have much initiative. And that goes for Carmela, in spades."

"But I wasn't looking for a girl in Australia, damn it. Bea and I had patched things up before I went into the Army, in fact before Fernanda was born. That's what's so awful, don't you see?"

Fred was enjoying his bad conscience. At the very least, the
affair would be more piquant if he could persuade himself that it
would kill his wife.

"The way I see it, you've got two alternatives."

This was the sort of thing Fred wanted. He leaned forward
eagerly. "Yes?"

"Either give up Sheila, at once, while you're separated from
her—"

"I can't do that, don't you understand! Why do you think I said
I wasn't sure about this Sunday? I've got a chance to bum an airplane ride down to Brisbane, and if it comes through Sunday I'll
grab it, even if I have to squat on a pile of mail sacks. I'm
thirty-two years old. I can't give her up. She means a whole new
life to me."

"Then you've got to tell Bea. You're not cut out to be a bigamist."

"What kind of a ruthless bastard do you take me for? After all
these years I can't just sit down and coldbloodedly tell her we're
through."

"Women do it all the time. In my outfit alone four guys have
gotten Dear John letters."

Fred shook his head. "No. I can't behave like that." He shook
his head a second time, more decisively.

The suave ones were the worst. When something hit, they could
only fall back on an artificial idea of how to react. They had so
firmly repressed the possibility of behaving naturally that even in
moments of pathos they could present their women with nothing
better than a collection of clichés, a nosegay of dandelions.

"You don't want advice," he said. "You want congratulations.
Having two broads is twice as good as the average joker does out
here."

"I don't want wisecracks," Fred said stiffly. "I thought you'd be
sympathetic."

Irresistibly Norm was reminded of the sickly grin that was all
Irwin Metzger could muster during his wife's idyll with that miserable deliveryman. Irwin was too honest for lies, even for indignation; when it hurt he bled. Despite her closeness to Carmela, Vera
had never succeeded in persuading him that the dentist was anything but an innocent suffering man.

Fred *thought* he was suffering. Maybe he thought he was innocent
too, but that was even more ridiculous.

"All you're doing," he said, "is making me sympathetic to Bea, and I wouldn't have said that was easy."

"She's a wonderful girl. I'd never utter one word against her."

"I would. She's a bore." Fred did not rise to this, so he went on. "Naturally, that's something you can't readily say to a wife even in a rage. But you owe her a nice letter. Tell her you've found somebody who interests you more. Chances are she'll be relieved. I think she was getting a little worn out, being the professor's wife. Or the commentator's—that was even worse, when she had to sit there and listen to you on the radio."

"You really think so?" Fred was so intrigued by the possibility of easing himself out from under that he did not even complain about the implications of these last remarks. "I keep telling myself that when I get my discharge I'll be able to sit down and have a civilized discussion with Bea."

"You mean you want her candid unbiased opinion of whether or not you should dump her?"

Fred was not amused. "I mean simply that we should be able to decide rationally, what's best for Fernanda as well as for us."

"Fred," he said, "if Bea is such a splendid woman and such a fine mother, it's unfair to make her do your deciding for you. Let her know as quickly as possible. Give her a chance to make plans."

This was the message Captain Byrd had hoped to receive. His face alight, he said once again, "You really think so?" and he enthused, "I feel that with Sheila there's no limit to what I can accomplish. There's a great deal I can do in education—I mean, beyond merely being a college professor. I want to think in larger terms."

"I'm sure you do."

"What about you?" Fred was genial now. "You're not really going back to the shop, are you?"

"There may not be any shop to go back to. Who's going to need fighter planes in 1947? I've been thinking about labor journalism. If there's a depression, maybe I'll wind up organizing the unemployed. At least I've got some training for that—and I may have a little more before I'm demobilized."

"It's marvelous, getting together with you like this. Let me buy us another beer."

Amiably they drank, amiably they parted. It was clear that Fred would not be coming to the committee meeting.

The others on the committee were: a skinny socialist intellectual
with khakis three sizes too large but with savvy and charm; a fat
UAW official from Detroit who looked soft but had seen combat in
three landings; and a couple of recent arrivals in the islands, delegates from a low-morale anti-aircraft battalion who were such committee types that Norm suspected them of being Stalinists. But
they represented warm bodies, not cold ideas, masses of men so
eager to get home that they were willing to march against their
officers. This alone ensured the committee a kind of security.

They waved off flies in the Manila bar, their rounded backs
sheltering them from eavesdroppers. Norm said, "Let's not worry
any more that we'll get picked off one by one by some provost
marshal or other. The rank and file are ahead of us. They want
action, and we've got to step out in front of them or drop out."

The UAW man shifted his cigar. Corporal's stripes aside, he
might have been sitting in on a strike strategy meeting in Flint or
Pontiac. "What's your proposition?"

"No more reliance on word of mouth. A mimeographed statement with demands. A coordinated line of march with representa-
tion from every possible outfit. A list of speakers, short and sweet,
strong and varied. One of them has to be you. We've got to break
down the barriers separating GIs from workers. There's been too
much horseshit about workers striking and sabotaging GIs. We have
to have a voice from the labor movement."

"And you?" asked the socialist. "Are you willing to speak?"

"Modest as I am," Norm said, "I insist on the privilege."

It was more than a privilege, it was a renewal. The thump of
thousands of boots down the streets of Manila freed him, for the
first time since those long ago days when he had strode with the
union ranks on Michigan Avenue and fought the scabs in the
streets of Lackawanna, from the sickening uncertainty that had
driven him out of the torpid defense plant existence into the terror
of jungle combat. Everything Dworkin and Hoover had taught him,
everything he had passed on to Sy and the others, was now stamped
and validated by the tramp of young men marching not to war or to
occupy others' soil, but toward their own soil, their own loves, their
own destinies.

The Filipinos in their chattering multitudes lined the curbs of
the old walled city and crowded the sidewalks of the bombed-out
port area. Even shy women with pandan baskets stared, then ap-

plauded as three, four, five thousand Amerikanos filed by, chanting "Let's-go-home, leave-them-alone!" It was a picnic, a real carnival, but for everybody this time, with barefoot brown kids waving sticks of sugar cane and GIs easing out of the bars, scrambling out of the jeepneys, gaping, then falling unasked into the line of march. One small half-naked boy, his belly so distended that his navel was turned inside out, like a flower, darted forth and slipped his sticky hand into Norm's. It was a gesture that sealed the day forever in his heart.

"Sergeant," the colonel said afterwards, "I am honestly pleased that you marched with our men in that parade. Maybe that surprises you. But it's one of my guiding principles that a good noncom will stick with his men through thick and thin. If these lads are going to act like a bunch of crybabies, if they are going to plead to go home to mama, at least let them count cadence and march with their heads up so as not to disgrace the uniform."

"Colonel," he had replied heartily, "in that respect I couldn't agree with you more. I believe in order and discipline, whether in combat or in protests."

"Combat veterans like you have a heavy responsibility. I know for a fact that many in the chairborne brigade look up to you as a model. Whatever example of pride you can set will be deeply appreciated by this command."

Now, standing on top of a half track at the corner of Clark Field with his arms outstretched to the multitude of upturned soldiers' faces, he shouted to the GIs before him, "We are not crybabies! We are citizens! Promises have been made to us and to our families, and we are here today to see that those promises will be fulfilled. Those who are planning the next war can count us out. Those who want a confrontation with our own allies can count us out. We are going home as veterans and citizens to take up the pursuits of peace!"

They were roaring, fighting to get at the petitions, jostling and laughing and bragging as they signed their names. They crowded around him. "Hey, Senator, what a filibuster! Wait till Harry hears about us!"

He was hardly surprised when Captain Marciniak blocked his way to the jeep the committee had commandeered. "You better get your ass over to Colonel Scott as quick as you can."

The colonel was pacing his office like a man in a cell. His neck

seemed to have thickened; it filled the gap behind the open neck
of his shirt. His thin sandy hair was disarrayed, his cheeks were dangerously flushed.

"By God," he burst out, "you really let me down. I treated you
like I would my own son." He wheeled dramatically. "You could
be court-martialed for what you said today. In fact I think you will
be. And I won't lift a finger for you, you hear? You made a
mockery of the uniform, you encouraged disobedience. That speech
was practically an incitement to riot. And if—"

The phone rang. It was fascinating to watch the colonel's face
alter, smooth itself into a new pattern, as the thin little voice of the
orderly drilled itself into his brain. He was even smiling as he cradled the phone. His anger abated, he turned expectantly toward the
door.

At the sound of Weiner's knuckles, he squared his shoulders. The
door opened and Weiner was ushering in a group of civilians, the
two oldest in Palm Beach suits, the other three in the baggy khakis
that apparently made them feel akin to their fellow citizens in uniform.

Norm stood to one side while the introductions were made. The
colonel, he was sure, would have wished him elsewhere, but had
no opportunity to say so. The five visitors were members of two
congressional subcommittees visiting the area—the oldest, a bald-
headed gobbler with wattles and a tremor, was a senator; all the
rest were congressmen—big, little, fat, skinny.

"Balance" was what they started to talk about, balancing international commitments against promises made to fighting men. The
colonel nodded knowingly, authoritatively. He snapped his fingers
at Weiner for tables of organization and point rating lists of those
scheduled for demobilization.

Eavesdropping furiously, forgotten by the colonel, Norm learned
that they had been on the fringes of the crowd at the demonstration. The second civilian, a stern Roman type with white hair cut
in a brush, said abruptly, "Colonel Scott, we were told we'd find one
of the committee in your office. Is this the man?"

The colonel nodded stiffly. "Sergeant Miller and I were just—"

"The American people are very disturbed that these boys are not
being processed and released more expeditiously. When you needed
troops out here, we got them to you, and fast. Now their families

need them, and they find it hard to understand why the return trip has to be so much slower."

A long drink of water with drooping earlobes even more pendulous than the colonel's and a Texas twang to boot, drawled, "And we can't sell them on that geopolitical jazz, you folla me, Colonel?"

Without waiting for an answer, he strode over to Norm, trousers flapping like furled flags about his long pole-like shanks. The congressman squeezed his hand, mumbling name and congressional district.

"Wanta tellya, Sarge, I heardya ram it home to those GIs. You're wastin your time if you don't go inta politics."

Norm laughed. The congressman drew him to one side, still clutching him in his immense paw. "Now let's be serious. What you figure on doing when you get home?"

"I used to be in the labor movement. But I don't take to discipline. I'm thinking about journalism."

"You write as good as you talk?"

"Better."

The congressman grinned a sad, pleased kind of grin. Across the room, the colonel was being desperately brisk and hospitable. Norm spoke up to the suddenly shrewd-eyed stranger towering between him and the others. "With me, talking is a means to an end, the way it is with you. If I'm any good, it's because I'm a salesman, not because I'm an actor."

"What do you want to be when you grow up?"

"Influential."

The congressman guffawed. "Me too." In the next breath he was asking, not angrily, but as if from simple curiosity, "What you selling? You a Communist?" The way he put it, he might have been asking what kind of Baptist he was.

Norm had been expecting the question, but not under these circumstances. "No," he said. "Sorry, but I'm not. I am a socialist of sorts, though. What difference does it make to you?"

The congressman cracked his knuckles and yawned hugely. "Reason I ask, I want you to look me up when you get home. No hurry. Whenever. Got a feeling you and I could do some business."

There was no opportunity for Norm to respond. The others were freeing themselves from the colonel and began to question Norm about the views of the ranks. They were not ranging themselves with him against the colonel as much as they were assuring him of their interest and sympathy. In that instant, as they gathered about him, nodding sagely, one even jotting figures in a spiral-bound notebook, Norm understood that what he had been engaged in had not been dangerous at all; it had not even been a radical gesture. All of the committee's work, even his own inflammatory speech, had been a kind of echo of the howling housewives back home, nothing more. It was not that the constitutents were more radical than he had imagined; they were merely reflecting a resurgence of the old isolationism, now that the war was over and done with. There were more boys at home ready to escape boredom with a year or two of occupation duty, and American imperial policy would go on undisturbed by the little ripple they had made today.

He should have known that his oratory would be received with a job offer from a southern New Dealer oozing savvy and cynicism. What did you expect, he asked himself as he made his departure— bread and water, the rockpile, a twenty-four hour armed guard? He was reminded of the tension in the faces of the Huks. If the march and the speechmaking had been for their benefit, how many Americans would have marched, listened, applauded? How many congressmen would have crowded about to assure him of their esteem?

Vera had written him, over several letters, of Bill's doing thirty days in the pen for leading a one-day strike, a comical classwar prisoner whose wife brought him borscht and pirogen prepared after the day's consultations in her law office. Bill didn't see it as funny, he was convinced simply that he had done what had to be done; he would never have conceded that his fellow-workers were as reactionary after his sacrifices as they had been before. At least he could point to history, he could reasonably believe that when you swayed workers at the point of production you laid claim to being a mover and a shaker.

At the screen door of his barracks he was brought up short by a pfc from Providence, an eyeglassed Irishman with a frightened scowl, a 4F dredged up in the closing days of the war to serve his country, or something, in the South Pacific. The Irishman, whom he scarcely knew, was gazing at him with admiration.

"I just wanted to say, sarge."

"Yes, what?"

"You really gave them hell today."

Norm paused, distracted. "Who?"

"You know. All those bastards back home that have been getting rich while we rot out here. Boy, if they could've heard you, they would've shit green."

Maybe Bill, the patient brother-in-law, was right after all. Buoyed up, he demanded, "Who?"

"The Jews." The man peered hollowly through his thick lenses. "All those Jews that sit home and clean up while we fight their wars for them."

Unable to muster up even hatred at the fag end of this confusing day, Norm stood silent, his hand on the latch of the screen door.

2. JOE

"Is Mrs. Link home?" Standing in the doorway of the apartment, flight bag in his hand, valise at his feet, Joe peered into the suppertime twilight from which came only the sound of very familiar Mozart. The Haffner Symphony?

The music stopped. Then her voice, as if he had never ceased to hear it. "Yes, who is it?"

"Come see."

Her bare feet slapped, then pattered more thinly on the linoleum as she began to run. He dropped the bag, thinking, she kicked off her shoes to cook supper, but thought stopped as she appeared before him, stunned, staring.

"Aren't you going to say hello?" he demanded. "Maybe put your arms around me?"

Seemingly she could not move. He stepped forward and took hold of her. She was so tall! He felt all of her, the softness pressed to him, the droop of her shoulder blades, fluttering like newly folded wings. She did not cry, but gripped the front of his shirt in her clenched fists as if to stop the world from rocking. He smoothed her hair with his hand and put his lips to the part, inhaling the fragrance of lilac, closing his eyes as the circles, worlds away, flashed and whirled dizzily.

At last she said, lips to his chest, pressing the words to him, "Why did you come without notice? Why didn't you tell me?"

He held her back from him and raised her face. "Sy picked me up at the airport. I wanted our reunion to be private. Right here."

"That's so like you! All these months and months and months, and you'd make me wait an extra hour."

"Isn't it worth it?"

"I don't know what to say first."

He knew what she meant. They were strangers once again, maybe more so than when they had first met, in British Columbia. Because her voice sounded strange to him, his own rang falsely, as if he were listening to himself in a record booth. If she would cry, perhaps, the way wives were supposed to—but that was not her way.

Stupidly he said, not having worked it out in his mind in advance, "Let's go to bed."

To his astonishment she did not demur. "All right," she said. Releasing herself from his grasp, she moved about in her bare feet, drawing the blinds, turning off the gas flame on the stove, switching off the record player, whose hum had suddenly grown loud in the darkened quiet apartment. Then she walked into the bedroom and drew her dress over her head.

There was something somnambulistic about it. Or coldblooded. They had not even kissed, and now, like a whore and her customer, they were disrobing in opposite corners of the room, without touching each other. In fact they were not even looking at each other, as if what they were doing was wrong, or illicit.

Joe saw just a flash of his wife's body as she bent over to pull back the coverlet, then slid swiftly between the sheets. He stepped out of his shorts, pulled off his T shirt, and slipped in beside her. She lay on her back, motionless; even her arms were not exposed. Her eyes were closed; as his became accustomed to the gloom, he saw that a pulse was beating in one of her lids. He began to tremble. He put his hand to her cheek.

"Anne," he said, "it's me."

She opened her eyes then, but said nothing.

"Let's push back the covers. It's warm, it's almost May."

"All right."

Her body was unfamiliar, distant. It might have been under glass. He began to sense, dimly, as one feels a small pain slowly grow and spread, bringing terror in its train, that he was in deep trouble. Whether or not she did, her body feared him. It diminished his desire, shriveling him, mocking his claim that their bodies must combine in order that their selves might, thereafter.

But how did you start, if words were unavailing? He was not ardent, it must be perfectly apparent to her, whether or not she understood that this was because of her own pudency. If he leaped on her in an awkward effort to convince them both, she might do almost anything—even laugh. He cringed.

Shyly he reached out to touch her knee. Flexed slightly, the kneecap glistened with a dull sheen that he could not remember, any more than he could remember the taut string of the tendon beneath her shaved shin. His palm rounded over her kneecap, slid down to hold the ball of her calf, then slid upward to caress the smoothness of her thigh. Her flesh crisped. She lifted her hands, which had been cupped over her groin, and let them fall, palm upward, at her sides.

He gazed with wonder at the blond hair that rose like new fern from the little mound. A steady thrumming began in his throat. He laid his cheek against the tight springy curls and drew circles on her belly. A million miles above him, high in some remote realm, her head began to turn slowly. Her eyelids fluttered.

Then she started to groan. It began deep within her, he could feel it far below her throat or her breast, in her belly really, under his outspread hand, as though something long buried in her were groping blindly for escape. At last she found her voice. It burst from her lips as if she were speaking in tongues, beyond her conscious will, and for a moment it was as unrecognizable to him as her opened body.

It welled from her uncontrolled, like a series of repeated sobs, gaining in clarity instant by instant until it seemed to him that he had never stopped hearing it from those lips, from that lonely soul, more solitary than he in his worst moments.

She wet her lips. Her arms rose. "Kiss me."

There were certain words his wife had never been able to say aloud, except in annoyance or anger, no matter how dearly he wished her to. Her whispered demand was the closest she could come to uttering the unutterable. Even as he lunged, seeking her mouth, her hand snaked out and curled around his cock, not caressing but urgent. The tense fear that he would be unable to perform was swept away. Her voice was hoarse, plaintive, then pleading. "Put it in. Put it in." In that last moment, before her parted thighs clenched him and her heels drummed him into a frenzy, he felt his pleasure heightened, guiltily, gleefully, by this mixture of familiarity and newness, as if Anne were Anne once again, and yet also strange pussy or even someone else's, yielding to him despite herself.

Afterwards, for a little while, he congratulated himself. Anne lay across him, kissing his knuckles with little kisses.

"I was dripping sweat all the way from the airport in Sy's car. All I could think of was what was going to happen when I got here."

"Did you know?"

"I had something in mind, you know, drastic action, because I was afraid we wouldn't know each other any more."

She leaned over him, brushing his face with her hair. "I have to go to the bathroom. I'll be right back."

She walked with the unself-conscious fluid grace that was his wife, his girl, not the frozen terrified stranger who had greeted him after years of absence. The groove of her spine swayed like a palm tree above the twin hearts of her buttocks, flushed where they had been pressed into the mattress; her long legs shone.

When she came back, she knelt beside him, her breasts hanging free like fruit. He clasped them in his hands as she spoke. "Do you want something to eat, my darling?"

"Later. I've got all I need here."

"I want you to have everything. Everything. When the war ended I couldn't believe it, I'd never expected to see you alive. And then when you stepped on that mine, just as I was getting ready for you to come home, I went crazy. I couldn't write you about it, but I went crazy." She pointed, not touching it, to the welt that ran, red and puckered, in an arc around the front of his body, from one side clear to the other. "Is it really all right?"

"Yes, it really is all right. I didn't lie to you. They did a fantastic job."

"There's so much that you can't say in a letter. How did I know what you were leaving out? I began to feel paranoid. They were picking on *me*, on *me*. My father died, and I was orphaned, and I didn't even have my husband to comfort me, even though the war was long over."

"I know how you must have felt."

"No. There are certain things we don't know about each other."

"We can try."

"That's what I wanted to hear. I have to know about you. I have to suffer what you suffered."

"I'd just soon you didn't."

"I won't torment you about the war, I promise I won't, but you are going to have to make me feel what it was like, your wound, everything."

When they awoke the next morning, tangled together after a long confused sleep better than any he'd had since leaving her, he became aware that it was going to be harder than he had reckoned. For no sooner had she opened her eyes than she went at him, pressing for revelations, driven to plague him by some urgency that he simply could not understand.

To look at the couples around them, one had no way of knowing which were going to make out and which weren't. Even their babies proved nothing beyond brute capability. Fred and Bea had been the first, Fernanda would be starting kindergarten next year, but daddy wouldn't be there to take her to school. He was already settled into a new life with a new wife in Ann Arbor. While he scrambled up the academic ladder, Bea stayed behind, her soured face embarrassing old friends: Pity me, I bore his child and he betrayed me.

No one could know. He found it hard to believe that there had been a moment when his own parents had been so sure of their love that they had conceived him. In his own case, he had converted Anne—if not to politics, then to the healing virtues of reasoned discourse. So now, while he tried to pick up the life he had left almost three years earlier, looking up shopmates, dropping in on union meetings, resuming his political responsibilities, Anne gave him back his own coin, pleading with him to reveal, to explain, to disclose.

"I have to *know*. Otherwise, it's like being married to someone with amnesia."

"What's wrong with going on the way we were?"

"You assume everything was fine then, you assume I was happy, you assume I'm going to want to stay here forever, even though my father's died and I've no family left. You assume I'm going to be content to give lessons here just the way I've been doing all these miserable years—while you go off to your branch meetings and caucus meetings and local meetings and mimeographing sessions and strategy sessions and literature distributions and all the rest of the nonsense." She took a deep breath.

"You granted a long time ago that it wasn't nonsense."

"All I ask is that you share more of your life with me than the

Party. You act as though you'd been away for the weekend, instead of for years."

What she wanted, apparently, was a confession. He broached it to Sy and Bernie, but they were more concerned with little Joey's congested nose than with Big Joe's problems. Having a baby, they hinted, was one way to resolve man and wife problems. But it seemed to him, hulking in an apartment that had shrunk since the arrival of crib, laundry rack, bathinette, and dirty diaper holder, that all it had done for these two was to keep them busy, broke and exhausted.

And when he brought up the question of Anne's restlessness, her reluctance to go on under conditions that had seemed agreeable before his departure, they grew evasive, muttering about the long-range effects of loneliness, and how people couldn't always be held accountable for changing.

He had the feeling that they were talking more about themselves than about Anne. He must understand that he couldn't expect simply to pick up where he had left off.

"I was disappointed that Norm didn't come back here." Even as he spoke, he was unsure whether Sy, bent over his baby while Bernie diapered, understood. He persisted: "Weren't you?"

"Of course. He's my oldest friend. But you know I voted to censure him." Sy straightened up. "I've learned a little since then. I don't think I'd do that any more. Norm wasn't selling us out. If he can't go on living under party discipline, it doesn't mean he's stopped believing in what we do. He wants to achieve it in another way. Maybe he's right. How do I know?" What he meant was, how do you know?

"Where does that leave the movement?" he asked.

"If we start to make it . . . he'll come back. The same holds true for Vito. We couldn't stop him from going to Paris, once the war was over."

"As long as you don't wind up making excuses for Harry. When I heard, it sounded to me as though he ran out on us."

"He did worse than that. He feathered his own nest. He's still defending a civil suit brought by some chemical companies. And yet all that time he worked like a dog for us. *He* doesn't think he did wrong—that's what fascinates me. The first person he conned was himself."

Joe was in no mood to argue about Harry Sturm. He had been

steered away from his unease about Anne, but he was daily more convinced that it would be necessary to put things right with her. Within the Party no one remained with whom he could discuss this; Norm perhaps would have understood, but Norm was in New York with his wife and son, out of it, on the GI Bill, writing articles about the Philippines and the future of guerrilla movements.

He decided to try Irwin. He felt a little lost, walking in the golden autumn sunlight under old elms still in leaf, while everyone else was at work, even his wife. And a little foolish, searching out someone to talk to about her, as if not he but she were the returned veteran.

As he approached the Metzger boy's nursery school, a converted mansion on Linwood Avenue, the children were already tumbling out. He recognized Paul at once. Dark, solemn, curlyheaded, he came onto the porch gravely, his hand clasped in his teacher's, not speaking. He moved with extraordinary solemnity, as if burdened with thoughts beyond his years; but when he saw his father on the walk, plump and smiling, his face lit up and he ran to him without saying goodbye to his teacher.

Joe cut diagonally across the street to place himself in the path of father and son. "Look who's here," he said. "Paul, can I walk along with you and your daddy?"

Like a minnow slithering out of gently grasping fingers, the little boy skittered on ahead when his father set him down.

"He's beautiful, Irwin," Joe said. "Almost like a girl."

"Every chance I get, I sneak out of the office to pick him up. What a marvel it is, watching him grow! Wouldn't you think my father would have told me that?" Irwin laughed his self-deprecatory laugh, partly at the ludicrousness of the idea, partly at himself.

"Maybe you didn't seem so beautiful to your father."

"That's for sure. But no, maybe I did, who can say? Only my father, and how can I ask him such a question?"

Joe did not enjoy talking about fathers. "You're happier now that you've got Paulie?"

"To me it's an irony. I'm doing fine, and those people are sitting in the DP camps."

"You can't feel responsible for all the misery in the world."

"Even if I wanted to forget it, Sy wouldn't let me. It eats at him. I send parcels, but I'm ashamed, when Carmie and I are building a house in Snyder, my name is near the top of the dealer's list for a new Mercury, and I'm going into orthodontics."

"What's that?"

"Shifting teeth, fixing the bite. They're doing fine things now with cleft palates, harelips."

"Sounds more interesting than straight dentistry."

Irwin nodded eagerly. "I'm back in school, under the GI bill. Stu and I will have a nice setup." He hesitated. "But Carmie doesn't think so. She thinks I'm a frustrated artist. We're just never going to see eye to eye on certain things."

"You sound . . . resigned."

"It's too late for things to be brand new."

They had reached the corner. Paul was already trained to heed a red light. Withdrawing his sandaled foot from the gutter, he perched at the curb before them, his narrow little shoulders hunched expectantly. Suddenly Joe felt Irwin's admonitory hand upon his bare arm; for a moment it felt oddly as though he were being restrained by his father.

"Have you been able to pick up where you left off?"

"Anne insists that it's not possible, at least not until I've taken her into my confidence. I guess what she wants is what I left out of my letters."

"She wants a confession, Joe."

How could he have known? Joe tagged along with father and son, scuffing at the sidewalk, his head down. "I've said it to myself already. But why should it be?"

Irwin shrugged. He said almost brusquely, "I don't understand women."

"You think they're that different from men?"

"I don't even know that. I don't know anything." Laughing, he turned his moon face to Joe, the sun striking the shaved glossy rondure of his cheeks. "That's one reason I never joined the Party. I mean, aside from cowardice."

They parted friends—better friends, perhaps, than ever before. Even Paul kissed him goodbye.

At the end of the day, after Anne's last student, Joe had two highballs ready.

"That's what I call service." Anne kicked off her shoes and tucked her feet beneath her on the couch.

"What else have I got to do?"

"You're getting tired of terminal leave, aren't you?"

"I can't deny that."

Her neck arched as she tilted her head for the fluid trapped beneath the ice. It was strong, sexual, that throat, the pathway to pleasure. For a moment he wanted to push aside the bottle and slide his hand inside her blouse. But then she said, "We haven't talked at all about the possibility of your going back to college. For the degree." In the face of his silence she plunged on, "Why not take advantage of the GI Bill?"

"What would you have me study?"

"Political science, labor, economics. You know better than I."

"Perhaps I don't. But I do know what wouldn't be right for me."

"Don't say No too quickly. If you're worried on my account, don't be. I'd be proud to go on teaching while you're in school. We could do it in California, UCLA, if you'd prefer that. You could still make the fall semester."

"You'd be willing to leave here?"

"Now that my father's dead? I was just waiting here for you to come back. I could have waited anywhere."

"You wanted children. I've got your letters saying so."

"I'm willing to wait. You come first."

Her goodness was too much for him. "Then why can't you understand that I'm not interested in joining the middle-class?"

"Surely there's nothing middle-class about going to school." She returned his gaze composedly. "Half the people you know are doing it. Look at Irwin."

"You think Irwin isn't middle-class?"

"You think Hamilton Wright is? He's matriculating at the university as a freshman. He's going to be a librarian. The Party isn't raising any objections."

He stared at her sullenly.

"How do you think Vito got to Paris? From his cartoons? He's enrolled at La Grande Chaumière, if that's the way you say it. Even Norm is signing up at Columbia. Or maybe it's NYU, what's the difference? He's not out for a degree, but it enables him to get on with his articles. So what's so awful about the idea?"

"It's not awful. It's just not for me. I don't want to be a scholar, I want to go into business. My business is organizing. And selling socialism. I've had several years of detours. I don't want any more."

"I fail to understand why you should look at college in that light."

When her back was up, Anne assumed a teacherly tone that grew progressively more maddening. "Won't it be easier for you to be influential—"

"Not there. Those GIs in college don't want to move things collectively—they just want to get ahead. Period."

"Could you go back to the airplane factory, as though nothing had happened?"

"No more planes. It's automobiles again. I think I could get taken on at the assembly plant."

"Why haven't you?" she asked coolly. "You seem to know what you want."

"Not without you." He slammed down his drink and reached for hers. "I'm going to make you another because I want you to drink it while I tell you something you've been dying to hear."

When he came back she was sitting where he had left her, composed but alert, as though she were visiting, waiting for him to put on a record.

As he handed her the glass he was tempted to say, "Drink this," but he bit the words off. "I learned not long ago," he said, "that it's still possible for someone to feel compassion for your predicament even on very brief acquaintance."

Almost imperceptibly, Anne's rather aristocratic lips had stiffened. She was very quick, she already suspected what was coming.

"I got to feeling sorry for myself in the hospital. The war was over, everybody was going home. There was I, cut practically in half by that mine, and not even able to write you how I felt.

"I panicked. I became convinced I was impotent. Could I write you about that?"

Anne waited watchfully, wary now as though he had turned into some kind of potentially dangerous animal. She took a long drink, but over the lip of the glass her eyes remained fastened to his.

"There was a nurse's aide, an English girl, a woman really, named Mavis. One evening she came in after they'd brought me back from PT, physical therapy, and I was feeling bushed and blue. She was a bit of a freak, people used to wonder why she kept coming when the English had their own worries and it wasn't even fashionable any more to look after the Americans.

"She sat down beside the bed and read me in one glance. 'Why so black, luv?' It was getting dark, and I was afraid I'd never get back home to you, and even more afraid of what would happen if I did. So, rather than break down and start to bawl, I told her.

"'You're going to make it,' she said. And then she told me about being stationed on Malta, where she made the mistake of falling for an RAF pilot who used to fly air cover for the incoming convoys. It was a mistake because the dogfights were ferocious. One day he was shot down in flames. By the time the Royal Navy fished him out of the sea he'd been swimming for an hour and forty-five minutes with sixty percent of his skin burned to a crisp. But he was a stubborn man. When Mavis went to see him he whispered to her, 'I'm going to make it.' She knew he couldn't, there wasn't enough left of him. He lasted six days.

"I said, 'Mavis, why complain to me about your romances? What good does old Roger do me? He's bloody well dead, but I can't even die.'

"She didn't get angry. She said, 'But you're going to make it. You're going home to your wife. Can't I envy her?' Then she lifted my gown and began to stroke my belly. No questions, no big discussions." Anne flinched, but he went on ruthlessly. "All of a sudden there he was, sticking up in the air, throbbing. She cried out 'Aha!' like a successful explorer, and without another word she went down on me."

Anne was on her feet, her pupils tremendous. The glass rattled in her clenched hand.

Joe reached out and grasped her by the wrist. "She blew me. Any one of a dozen people might have walked in, but she blew me. Afterward she wiped me all over with a warm washcloth, and then she covered me up and tucked me in like a baby. The next day she didn't show up. I never heard from her again."

Anne twisted free. "You bastard." She put down the glass and stepped into her shoes. "You filthy bastard."

"Is that going to be your attitude? After you pleaded for frankness?"

"Don't be self-satisfied with me. That bragging disgusts me. I'm getting out of here."

Drained, he watched wordlessly as she cast about in desperation for her purse. When at last she had found it she turned on him, livid.

"I suppose you expected I'd reciprocate. That's what you had in mind, wasn't it?"

"That's not so. I'd be just as pleased never to hear one word from you about anything that may have happened while I was away."

"You weren't saving up that choice little tidbit for nothing."

Now that he had done what she had been pleading with him to do, he stood irresolute as she swirled out of the apartment, cheeks flaming.

He decided to drink himself to sleep but realized with some surprise that he was already sleepy, as though he had done a hard day's work. He threw off his clothes and fell into an innocent slumber.

He was awakened by the smell of frying eggs and bacon. Struggling erect, he heard Anne singing in the kitchen. Good God, the Ode to Joy. She came to the archway, spatula in hand.

She said pleasantly, "You were sleeping like a rock."

"I went out more like a light."

"I'm sorry about last night," she went on, in the same tone. "I behaved like an idiot. We don't have to talk about it any more, do we?"

"We have to talk about what comes next."

"Oh sure, sure. Come drink your juice while I turn the eggs over."

Covertly surveying her as she mixed the coloring agent into the margarine, he felt a pang.

"You understand how I feel about college, don't you?" he asked.

"I guess so. But if you have to go into industry"—she placed her hands flat on the kitchen table—"does it have to be here?"

"Why," he closed his hand over hers, "I suppose not. But where—"

"Anywhere." She sagged suddenly. "Anywhere but here."

"All right."

"Joe," she whispered, "I want children. And if you're bent on going back to work, then . . ."

"Of course," he said. "Of course."

Things arranged themselves better than he could have hoped. Bill proposed him as a delegate (along with Big Boy and Sy) to the Party convention in New York.

"I'm going to ask for a transfer to the LA branch," he explained to Anne. "I could function just as well in the GM assembly plant out there as I could here."

Anne looked up from the book of preludes in which she had

been marking fingerings. Her lightly freckled face looked freshly washed, cleansed, scrubbed with new hope.

"Well, then," he wound up confidently, "we can ship the piano and store it until we find an apartment. We'll buy a secondhand car—"

"Ho ho!"

"No, I mean it, we'll drive leisurely out to the Coast. How does that strike you?"

Anne was pleased. The only sticking point for her was his suggestion that they drive to New York with Bill and Big Boy.

"That's no vacation for me," she said, "to be jammed into a car with you guys arguing politics all day and half the night. Couldn't we travel alone?"

"We'll take the coach. And we'll leave a couple of days before the others. Cancel your lessons and I'll take care of everything else."

He had the feeling that she was touched more by his willingness to change his life than by any strong conviction that the changes would really come about. But afterward, would she once again be the girl who had thrown herself into his arms crying out "What have I done? What have I let myself in for?"

Meanwhile she wrote to her former conservatory roommate, wangling an invitation for them to sleep on her studio couch.

So he met with the other members of his delegation, and with the cadres who were concerned that their point of view should prevail at the convention.

"We tend to overlook," Bill said in his rather owlish way, "that the other branches respect us for what we've built up, and for our influence among the workers. So we're in a position to swing other branches and other delegates."

What he meant was that those who, like himself and Sy, had stayed home, were deserving of credit for holding things together during the war years. Joe was uneasy only about committing this credit unreservedly to Dworkin. The Party secretary was involved in a faction fight on supporting the Reuther caucus in the UAW, on how to characterize Russia and on what kind of party to build in the postwar world.

It was this last problem that was for Joe neither arid nor theological but intensely practical. Crucial. Generations of socialists had floundered about and finally foundered. People drifted in, joined, dropped out—and aside from personal weariness or ambition, disagreement with this position or that, inability to make themselves heard (even among a handful) or lack of desire to do the dull dirty work, what drove most of them away was the perfectly obvious fact that the message was simply not getting through. Despite the sacrifices, the hours of labor, the meetings, the literature distributions, far fewer people were aware of their ideas than of the identity of the pop singer of the moment.

"I'm patient," he said to his friends, "I'm willing to spend my life talking socialism. But I can understand why people get tired, and why crazy ideas like Harry's get taken seriously. Radicals tend to want shortcuts."

"If we're ready to meet the depression," Sy said, "we'll be in business. If not, all bets are off."

But it wasn't only the coming depression that hypnotized them; it was the possibility of converting themselves from a sect into a force. "Let's be frank," Joe said. "There are guys who are in the Party now because we're small. If we really grew, if we really became an influence, they'd flee."

Bill stared. "You're crazy."

"One reason for the vicious circle is that we attract odd ones because we're off in a corner ourselves. We're safe and so we're self-defeating. If we ever got out in the open where we were accountable to millions of people, the odd ones would drop us—and the composition of the Party would change, the way the Bolshevik party changed."

"A tyrant took it over."

"It wasn't only tyranny. It was respectability."

Bernie ducked her head. She passed her hand back and forth swiftly before her face as though she were pushing away cigarette smoke. She was a quiet girl, a hard worker, but at night, when she and Sy were alone, what did the politics mean to her, what other chances did they discuss beyond this dull and tedious life?

Even before he got to the convention, Joe could sense that the Party was changing. Hoover's kind of discipline simply could not be enforced, not on grown men coming home from the war, not on the new generation.

In subtle ways, ways that they themselves could not quite see, they and their organization were being changed by the conditions of peace. Attempting to make history, they themselves were being made and remade, adapting like their fellow-Americans to the unforeseen new world and the flexibility of a social order which, evil though it might be, was less rigid than they had forecast.

Marty Dworkin spoke of Reuther and the UAW, of the tremendous possibilities for leftward movement among the auto workers, but his little son ran about the office in a sailor suit, the blue stars of his collar bobbing up and down on his narrow shoulders as he chased his paper plane among the mimeograph machines. And his father raised not so much as a murmur when Joe announced his intention to move to the Coast.

Nor did Comrade Lewis. Seated quietly in his accountant's cubbyhole, ten steps down from Dworkin's, he touched his white fingertips together while he listened to Joe. Behind him hung the same Rand McNally map of the United States, as wide as your outspread arms, a narrow sprinkling of red-topped pins speckling the country, with vast appalling emptiness in the interior, and no pins at all to mark any sign of life in the entire South. But now he had made space on the wall beside his desk for a small oil by Vito of a mythological figure, Sisyphus maybe? struggling and writhing against some unclear force.

The whole painting, done in thick wet swirls, was not clear to Joe; in fact its agitation and murkiness were disturbing.

Later on, he tried to explain it to Anne. "It struck me as an act of defiance. When I remarked on it, Lewis said something about impasto that I didn't understand.

"Today I didn't feel as though I was in a Leninist party any more. Nobody slammed his fist on the desk and said Vito, You can't run off to Paris. And nobody slammed his fist and said Joe, You can't take off for the Coast. Dworkin is grateful that Vito sends back an occasional cartoon, and Lewis was grateful that I agreed to visit the branches on the way out."

"You didn't tell me about that."

"You won't mind, will you, if the trip is a kind of tour? We'll be put up at people's homes en route, and they'll even pay for our gas and oil. Dworkin and Lewis are expecting me to push their position. They're not philanthropists."

But the convention sessions restored what his meetings with the leadership had eroded. The hall was full, all day and on into the night, with the hundred-odd delegates, with observers from other left-wing and student groups and foreign ones as well, and with curious sympathizers—here a sociologist, there a novelist and an art historian, there a film critic and his actress wife. They were eager, alive, argumentative, concerned. "And they're decent," he told Anne, "even when they disagree. One delegate after another gets up from Chicago, Ann Arbor, Seattle, Boulder, and speaks with real intelligence. Here I've been sitting and bitching!"

The following evening Anne came downtown after a performance at Carnegie Recital Hall and slipped into the seat beside him. One of the Pittsburgh members was arguing that they work harder among the miners, the most militant section of the entire working class throughout the war. "We're going to stay with him in Pittsburgh," Joe said.

It was then that he caught sight of Norm Miller. Taking Anne by the hand, he hurried to the back of the hall where Norm stood with Sy. He took Norm by surprise: "How's the war hero?"

"How's the leader of the toiling masses?" Laughing, Norm hugged him and Anne. "Come on up to Morningside Heights, you two, when this is over. I'm going to show off my kid to Sy."

Anne said, "I'd love to see Vera and the baby."

"Baby? He's bigger than Sy. Now Joe, if you want a real surprise, look over there."

In the corner of the hall, in the furthest niche, sat Harry Sturm. He was jotting in a notebook, glancing up occasionally to peer through his heavy glasses at the speaker.

"Man, has he got chutzpah. Taking notes yet."

"Nerve? He's filed countersuits against the firms that have been trying to regain the confidential formulas he hijacked. He says he's being libeled. He's also opened what he calls a consulting office, around Rockefeller Center." Norm looked happy about Harry's brass, as though it was all funny, like the plot of a Preston Sturges movie.

Later, on the way uptown, they talked about Harry.

"He looks so different," Anne said. "He used to be careless about himself, covered with pipe ashes, his shirt collar always sticking out. Now he seems—"

"Like an executive? But he is," Sy said. "He's sold himself, that's the best selling job of all, isn't it? Because it gives him warrant to go on and do anything he can get away with."

Vera, shy as ever, was waiting for them at the door of the apartment on Claremont Avenue.

"Could I see Marlen?" Anne asked.

"I'm staying in his room this week," Bill said, "and I'm here to tell you, that kid sleeps like a rock. Come on, let me show you." The boy lay on his back in the crib. Its side was already lowered, for he was firmly fixed in bed, the barrel chest that he had inherited from his father rising and falling in a smooth unhurried elemental rhythm, arms outflung, head tilted toward the door, enabling the visitors to observe his regular features, the eyelashes dusting the cheeks, the full almost sullen lips.

"Huge, isn't he?" Norm spoke as if he were describing a balloon. "Marlen's practically twice the size of the Metzgers' kid."

"He's six months older than Paul," Vera said. "More. And he was no picnic taking care of without a father. You can brag now. You didn't have the responsibility of keeping him from running out into the street."

Joe was struck with the memory of Irwin's little boy, thin-shouldered, aware, one sandaled toe poised over the curb as the light changed and he glanced over his shoulder to make sure that his father was there. Norman was pleased with his son, yes, but that was not what Irwin felt for the vulnerable child on the street corner. Suddenly, as he stood in the doorway, Anne slipped her hand into his.

The boy stirred. Abashed, they tiptoed back to the living room. Norm flung himself belly down on the carpet at his wife's feet.

Joe looked at them curiously. It was remarkable, how quickly a man could be domesticated after long months in combat, wading ashore with men dropping around him, bleeding, choking, drowning, bitten by poisonous insects while he hacked his way through rank vegetation in search of hidden figures firing down from treetops. And then, after the peace, to plot as he had, to lead his men in marches and demonstrations—for this? For pot roasts and scrambled eggs?

"I can tell what you're thinking, Joe." Norm made a funny face. "You're transparent. But wasn't that the whole point for us draftees, to get back to where we are now, home cooking and all?"

"And us radicals?"

Vera flushed, but Norm said easily, "Vera's still in the Party. Me, I'm going to make the fight in my own way. I think you'll approve of my article in *Partisan* on guerrillas."

"Norm, the Party no longer is what it was before the war," Sy said. "It has room for—all kinds of people."

Joe was morally bound to associate himself with Sy's plea. "I had a slow return from combat. When the war ended for us in Europe, when we saw the camps, that was it. We had no mass action, no demonstrations. Just cold and hunger and misery all around us. I'd have been home to mother's cooking too if I hadn't stepped on that mine. But I did, and it left me floating, suspended, half-drowned."

"And the Party is a lifeline."

"I would have grabbed hold even if it had been rotten, that's true. But I've been exhilarated by the convention. We haven't got many people, but the ones we've got are good. If anybody can do the trick, we can."

Bill said in his dry way, "I can't wait to get home and break that news to Margaret. There she is, stuck with a dull teamsters' contract case, and she doesn't even know socialism is practically around the corner."

"You're going to run for president of a local with close to ten thousand members. If a few hundred of our members—"

Norm rolled over and sat up. "That's where we part company. I don't think you've got much chance even in the UAW. You can't persuade people to do what you think they ought to simply because it's either moral or logical. Whether it's electing your boy as head of the Auto Workers, or making a socialist revolution, people are going to react from a whole series of motives—most of which will have no relation to logic."

"So history has become meaningless?"

"I didn't say that. Did I, anybody?" Norm shifted his massive torso. Suddenly they heard, very clearly, the Juilliard student in the next apartment practicing the Mozart variations, *Ah! Vous dirai-je Maman,* one of Anne's favorites. She smiled faintly, her attention drawn away from them and toward the music.

"All I claimed," Norm persisted, "was that vast decisions aren't usually made solely from rationality. That doesn't mean you shouldn't try to decipher history. It does mean that you can't expect people to follow you because you were right. It makes no difference now who said what about the war. It's over, that's all."

"So you've decided that it's all pointless."

"No I haven't." Norm laughed: "Oh hell, maybe I have. But

I'm not going to live my life as though it's pointless. If you can reach people your way, best of luck. Meantime I want to try my way. No intellectual constraints. I'm going to do battle, pal, because it's a constitutional thing with me. But on my terms."

When they were alone, Anne said sleepily, "Norman didn't sound unreasonable."

"Unreasonable? You mean he sounded right." Joe could not keep an edge from creeping into his voice. "It'd be more convenient if I had his attitude, wouldn't it?"

"Since you ask, yes. But I wouldn't love you any more than I do now."

Chastened, he took her in his arms.

It was very late by the time they left. His tour schedule took them across Pennsylvania to Pittsburgh, then through Ohio (in Akron they stayed with the elder Zivics), Michigan (where he took her to Ann Arbor to meet Fred's young Australian wife, and to Detroit to tour the Ford plant while he spoke to the branch, and to see where Bill and Norm had marched with the Ford strikers). After that the cheering hopefulness of Chicago's brave new branch headquarters, Iowa City, and then the great spaces where they knew no one and needed no one but each other, making love in the car at the side of the road, both of them straining together in the cold sunny silence, while the trailer trucks roared by and Anne's reserve dissolved like smoke drifting out the window. At night they kissed chastely and lay apart, zipped into their borrowed sleeping bags. From Denver and Boulder they drove on up to Salt Lake City to meet with some young Jack Mormon radicals, and to peer for fun at the shrunken Indian mummies and the odd trifles sent back to the Tabernacle museum by youthful Mormon missionaries. Somehow they managed the last desert crossing and the wheezing ascent of the last range in the old Buick, and in Seattle they parted, for the first time since their reunion.

Anne wanted to visit her aunt in Canada for what was likely the last time, and he had to check in on the little clusters of *New Labor* subscribers, mostly old timers no longer active, pensioned railroad workers, retired lumberjacks, men sitting on motel steps, their eyes wrinkled from straining to recall the roistering days of their radical youth. Seattle down to Portland, Port Angeles on the way, then Coos Bay and Gold Creek and the other dying towns, old Wobbly ports where once you needed a red card and now needed only a credit card.

Anne flew on down to San Francisco; he was waiting for her at the airport. "Darling," she said. "Darling. It seems as though it's been forever."

Arms around each other's waists, they walked on out to the parking lot.

"The Bronsons are expecting you," he explained. "They've got one of those big old Berkeley houses. We'll leave first thing in the morning for Los Angeles."

But when they got there, Molly Bronson was too excited for hospitality. "I told you before about the Retail Clerks' strike in Oakland, where the girls at Kahn and Hastings' walked out. While you were at the airport, somebody called from Oakland. All hell has broken loose. A bunch of scab truckers up from LA have been roughing up the girl pickets, elbowing them, showering them with glass from the windows on the upper floors. People were getting sore, they went to appeal to the central labor council, but the official labor leadership disappeared. So they've begun forming independent committees on all the street corners. It sounds like the whole town is going to walk out."

"Come on, no time to waste."

The motor of his jalop was still warm. In a moment they were barreling up El Camino Real toward San Francisco. "We'll take the Bay Bridge across, and I'll park somewhere down by the front, if I can. Nervous?"

"Not if you aren't."

"I have a feeling we're arriving at the psychological moment."

Later he would never be able to recall those days without remembering the tense moments of expectancy just before the reality of the general strike.

The streets and even the sidewalks of Oakland were crowded, and the downtown area, a few blocks from where they parked, was aswarm, as though something remarkable was afoot.

"We'd better not get caught in the mob before we find out what's up. Let's check at the SIU hall."

Practically the first person he ran into there, like meeting your fate, was the old man himself, the hulk, Harry Lundberg, older but still the only man in the hall bigger than Joe himself. The six foot four Norsky was surrounded by a jabbering bunch of sailors half his size, mostly Hawaiians—mixed-up Portugee, Chinese, Puerto Rican—all trying to talk at once, white caps bobbing above their brown flat faces. When he spotted Joe, he spoke as if it had been only yesterday that they'd last met.

"Hi kid. Grab a button and get out on the street instead of plugging up the hall."

Some button! Big as a saucer, it said boldly: SIU SUP— BROTHERHOOD OF THE SEA. Joe pinned it on. "Now what?"

"Now you're a policeman. It's your identification. The cops have all disappeared—kaput, see? We got maybe forty sailors here we're putting at the disposition of the strike committee."

"This is my wife." He produced Anne. The union leader merely grunted. "We were heading for LA but I heard about the action here. Where can we put her to work?"

"You remember Bob Ash? Makes no never mind. He's from the Retail Clerks. It's their show, that's the strike headquarters"—his English faltered, as it tended to when he was excited—"dey can use her over dere, on de phone or somet'ing. You guys all get over dere, go on, clear out, I got to get to work."

Caught up in the crowd of sailors, Joe recognized a wall-eyed Hawaiian AB with whom he'd made one coastwise voyage. "Remember me, Steve, from the *Yankee Importer?* This is my wife. Fill us in, will you?"

"The whole town's out. Looks like everybody got tired of working, all at the same time."

Anne laughed excitedly, but Joe was a little exasperated. "Come on, how did it get started? Who organized it?"

"Nobody. Talk about spontaneous job action, this is it. Near as I can figure, it's the streetcar conductors and motormen, and the bus drivers, that pulled the trigger."

"You're kidding."

"You asked me, didn't you?" demanded the sailor, aggrieved. "Five o'clock this morning, the cops were stopping cross traffic for a long caravan coming right through the center of town like a line of ghosts. The first bus driver that was held up climbed out in order to see what was going on. It looked suspicious to him, maybe scabs sneaking in. After he talked to the cops he passed the word back to the buses that were starting to back up behind him. The other bus drivers got out, and their passengers too, and they never made their transfers out to their shops, see? They got out and stayed out."

"Wait a minute. What about all the people who were driving to work in their cars?"

"The main reason this thing could happen is the car shortage. People been coming in to work by public transportation. They take a bus into the middle of town, then they get a transfer out to wherever they work. Two rides. When the buses and the streetcars started to pile up, and the word got out that they were being held up to let a bunch of scab trucks through—that was it, man. Come on, here's the headquarters."

In the Retail Clerks' hall two girls were yelling into telephones, trying to make themselves heard above the arguing, and a group singing "All or Nothing at All," Sinatra's ballad that they were trying to adapt to the strike. At the sight of the white-capped sailors surging through the door, plate-like buttons pinned to their chests, someone shouted "Yay!" and a little bandy-legged man jumped up on a folding chair.

"All right, you guys!" he cried. "You're detailed to find evidence of any attempt to molest our girls, any attempt to interfere with striking workers. Clear?"

"How about the traffic?"

"Take care of traffic. You know who should get through and who shouldn't." Someone laughed. "We already have some teamsters at the intersections—check with them. You may run into trouble. As policemen deputized by the strike committee you have the right to defend yourselves. Clear?"

"Damn right!"

Joe took Anne aside. "There may be trouble on the streets. Stay here till I get back. Ask this guy to give you something to do. They need help in here too."

Out on the sidewalk, Joe and his crew decided to fan out. "I'm itching for it," said one with a nervous mouth. "I tell you I'm itching for it. Them scabs gonna be sorry they was ever born."

They were all spoiling for it. Even me, he had to admit to himself. But they found no scabs, they found no fascists. Eager to fight, they found no one who would fight, not even the young businessmen who obeyed them with alacrity. So they moved from one block to another, shutting down businesses which had not yet closed, locking up small factories, looking for scab trucks.

For an hour, Joe and his wall-eyed buddy took over a busy intersection and checked all incoming traffic. "Park your car here. Just leave it here and walk the rest of the way. You'll have to pick it up later. If you've got a union card, brother, you can come on through."

The Oakland Teamsters' Local, the largest west of the Mississippi, with maybe six thousand members, had gone out on strike, even though their leaders had gone into hiding. Ex-GIs in Eisenhower jackets, hash marks still on the sleeves, the seats of their pants shiny from jockeying buses and trucks, were taking over all of the downtown area. They closed down stores and retail shops, but allowed bars to stay open—on condition that they bring their jukeboxes out onto the sidewalks. Joe stood by while one of them explained patiently to a perspiring bartender, "We want to give our folks some entertainment and relaxation."

He hoped that Anne was hanging out the window like all the others, applauding the holidaying workers. Okies and Arkies danced in the streets to the songs blasting from the jukeboxes. Leaning over their women awkwardly as if they were still square dancing, they shagged and lindyed awkwardly in the high-top boots they had put on this morning to go to work, they snapped their fingers and sang: "Pistol Packin Mama."

Back at strike headquarters he found Anne typing envelopes with her left hand and taking notes with her right. The bandy-legged little man was trying to engage the Oakland Auditorium for a mass meeting in the evening, but the Teamsters' leaders were still in hiding and across the Bay the CIO, controlled by Harry Bridges, still clung to its wartime no-strike pledge. Word was getting around that this was a genuinely popular movement, a holiday more than an insurrection, and the Teamsters' second-string leaders were starting to turn up to take over the direction of their striking membership and arrange for renting the auditorium.

"I'll tell you why the auditorium is so important," Joe said to Anne, as they squatted before a camp chair on which one of the girls had spilled a sackful of ham sandwiches and half a dozen containers of coffee. "The weather is turning bad. Rain will take people off the streets, make them blue. If they have to sit home, alone, and hear nothing but slanted reports on the radio, the whole thing may evaporate. This is one of the moments when people have to be held together."

He was right about this but not about the weather. By the time they made their way to the auditorium, a raw cold rain was skimming the streets, but they were packed anew with crowds of laughing jostling thousands still buoyant with the holiday spirit. Among them all was a kind of letting-go, a reaction to all the petty tribulations they had had to undergo during the war years without being able to fight back. If he had not still been wearing his magic talisman, the SIU-SUP button, he and Anne could hardly have squeezed inside among the fifteen thousand in the hall.

More than ten thousand others stood outside in the cold rain listening on the public address system.

"It's beautiful." Anne turned to him, radiant. "No one here is mean or hateful. Nobody wants to kill or burn or destroy. I'm not sure what they do want, maybe they don't know it themselves, but I hope it's what you want for them."

Lundberg, the huge Norsky, dominated the stage and mastered the audience despite his awkwardness and his accent—"De City Council is not just finks, but superfinks!"—or maybe because of them. Row after row, thousands of men and women moved to cheers, to laughter, even to tears—they wept unashamedly as Lundberg hammered on—not so much at what was said as at their shaken awareness of the latent strength that coursed in them. The power to bring into being a world distinct from the drab daily routine that was known as ordinary life. To take command, to make decisions, to work for their pleasure rather than to stay alive, for once to be human instead of simply to exist!

On the way out Anne held on to him tightly. He felt vindicated, and not because she had yielded to his arguments, his entreaties, his domination—but because she had shared with him the simple moment necessary to prove to her that he was not demented or foolishly obsessed.

The next day it was apparent that there would soon be a settlement. There was no further need for Joe—if indeed anyone had ever needed him as anything more than a witness in that brief period of euphoria and street dancing.

That afternoon they picnicked outside a Sonoma winery in Marin County on Tillamook cheese, sourdough bread, and a bottle of cabernet sauvignon.

Leaning against the sunny side of an old barn, he asked his wife: "Are you happy?"

"I'll never be happier."

"Don't say that!"

"I don't care. I know that it's true."

All the way across this country that would never cease to astonish him, he had kept to the schedules of both his political itinerary and his private voyage of rediscovery. Now it was done. He headed the old car for US 1 and wound around the curves slowly, the sun blazing into his eyes as he swung around the rim of a chasm.

They stopped at Carmel, at Monterey, they camped at Point Lobos and sat on a jut of rock in the bay, feet in the froth, shaded by a twisted Japanese pine. They scrambled up the cliffsides of Big Sur, they thumbed their noses at San Simeon, and after Santa Barbara the sun turned tropical and he knew he was coming home.

At the door of his mother's house Pauline stood with a fly swatter, her arm drooping. Joe sat in the worn-out Buick, halfway up the drive, unable to leave the car. "Pauline, Pauline," he said. "Pauline!" he cried loudly, and half-tumbled out of the car.

His sister turned, the swatter dangling from her hand, her head tilted as if with mild curiosity. Then a smile of such sweetness came into her plain simple face that Joe, stumbling over the flagstones, thought he would never be able to reach her; he seemed to be drifting toward her as in a slow-motion film, but actually he was running, panting for breath.

"Pauline!" he cried, clutching her. "It's Joe, your big brother. Did you miss me? Did you miss me at all?"

His mother was at the door then, her hair falling loose over her brow, graying as he had not remembered it. "She missed you, Joey," she said. "The war didn't end for any of us until today."

"Never mind," he said. Holding onto them both, he swung about. "All right, Anne," he said. "Come meet the family."

She was swinging up the walk, face pink, arms outflung.

"Come on in, Anne," his mother was saying. "We'll unpack your stuff when Uncle Jerry gets back. Anne, you might as well call me Lettie, since Joe does. I thought I'd never get to see you. Do you realize it's practically Christmas?"

"Wait," Anne said. "Just a minute." Her voice was commanding, she stood like a queen, a tall freckled queen. "I want to tell you something, I want you always to remember how it was, the very first moment we met."

Lettie stared at her, puzzled. The fly swatter was dangling by its loop from Pauline's hand. Joe was going to speak, but his wife raised her arm imperiously.

"I want you to know," Anne said, "that I'm going to have a baby."

3. VITO

The two lines in the tourist class saloon before the immigration and health officers were not terribly long. During the off season most Americans came home by plane. Vito slipped out on deck for one quick glance at the city.

New York lay below him, one big fifty-foot jump. Gray-black slush churned into a filthy foam by the grinding wheels of trucks turning into Twelfth Avenue, stinking steam rising like the vapors of hell from sewer grates, hoarse voices shouting obscenities, unheeded pleas for taxis—and behind everything a dull steady roar, as if you were hearing the hidden gears that moved all the massive machinery. It was wonderful.

Very early that morning, at dawn, Vito had bundled up for a first look at the country to which he was gratefully returning. Seen from afar, as you sliced through the black icy water, the new capital of the world earned the murmurs that it received from those huddled at the rail. The skyscrapers grew heavenward like precious stalactites, each reflecting from a thousand windows a brilliant fragment of the rising sun. It was almost too stunning, too theatrical, too remote. How could an immigrant ever cope with the country, after such an introduction to it? My poor father and mother, he thought, from Calabria to this—did they ever recover?

Now he took his place on line, presented his credentials, and was surprised to hear the man who stamped and returned his passport say, "Welcome home." Touched by the courtesy, which did not go with the clamor and the squalor, Vito ducked his head in gratitude and went on down the gangway to the raw scarred pier. Shivering inside his worn overcoat, he made for the big letter B and seated himself on the wicker basket that held his few belongings, beside the canvases that he'd crated himself in Paris, and awaited the arrival of a customs inspector. Above him the ship, baggage still issuing from its guts on steel rollers, was already a stranger, a big metallic hulk that had nothing to do with him. It was as if he had never set foot on it.

It had been a strange voyage. Worn out, frustrated, even a little homesick after his Paris year, he had scrambled aboard at Le Havre, overcome with a sense of relief at having escaped from the city that he had entered with the timorous passion of an uneasy young lover, and was leaving before he should be trapped into a fore-doomed marriage. Paris had been everything he had dreamed, had given him everything he had hoped to find—except himself. Freezing in his rotten room on the rue d'Assas, he had burned everything he could lay hands on, he had huddled up to Giacometti's skinny shanks at the Café Flore and stared spellbound at Sartre, warmed by the awareness that he, Vito, was accepted as a man and an artist. Rationed to a liter of alcohol a month, he had leaped into the black market-survival game with the same alacrity with which he engorged the museums and galleries and cafés and clubs. They stunned him with their pulsating vitality, they stimulated him to dream and to live as he had never done before—but in the end they made him flee, back to a homeland which was cold and un-hospitable, neutral or contemptuous of his aspirations—but where he would be able to find himself, undazzled by the gifts, the skills, the culture of those around him, and most of all unhampered by that terrifyingly insecure inferiority that was paralyzing his good right arm.

Well, he was home now. Passed by the customs inspector, he confronted a city that was freezing and unfriendly, but only on the outside. The meanest coffee joint was warm inside, friendly too, and for that matter served real coffee. He was glad to be home, at first for the most selfish of reasons. How easy it was to get set up, to find the things you needed!

Before the day was out he had himself a loft on Broome Street near Rivington, four steep flights up but perfectly enormous, ten times the size of anything in Paris, and with enough junk lying around to provide a good living for a whole family in the Flea Market.

It lacked only basic necessities. But the super, a limping Sicilian with a runny nose, sold him a two-burner hotplate for a buck and a half after telling him that it was a violation to use the loft as a dwelling place, and sent him over to Park Row to case the Army-Navy stores. Most of their stock was pre-war Boy Scout stuff, but the folding cots were so cheap he bought two, with roll-up mattresses, in case someone should want his hospitality; and he bought three reprocessed wool Navy blankets meant for a ship that would never be built, some sweat socks, paratroop boots.

Over on Canal he found a floor heater, rusty but reasonable, a set of fittings, some reducers, seventy-five feet of rubber tubing. Back at the loft he ran the tubing along the baseboard, chiseled a rathole through the wall to slide the tubing through and hook it up to the main gas line, which he tapped off just the other side of the gas meter.

It was only a matter of time before the super would spot the tubing. He came pounding on the door, black in the face. "You crazy?" he demanded. "This what I get for fixing you up?"

"Now look, Bruno," Vito said, "let me tell you about it." It was a very sweaty hour, the super was unimpressed with the truth, that he was broke with no references and in no shape to open accounts with the public utilities. But he cried a little, he showed Bruno that he could pull the tubing back inside his loft when the meter reader came and that the meter reader couldn't get into the building without Bruno letting him in and therefore having time to tip Vito off. Finally he promised to do a pastel of Bruno's daughter in her communion dress.

"I don' want my daughter coming up here," Bruno said warily.

"I don't blame you. Ask your wife when is the best time, and I'll come to your place."

With all his economies he was running very low, even after he'd sold a Sixth Avenue picture framer the few cheesy prints he'd brought back. The one thing he knew was that he was not going to paint signs any more. Fortunately he made a connection, in a Grand Street coffeehouse, with a couple of guys who were looking for a trumpet player to make a trio for Italian weddings and fiestas.

"I used to blow a horn," he said hopefully.

"You got one?"

"I could get one."

"We don't make scale."

"I wasn't figuring on that. What do you say, you want to try it?"

"You get the horn."

He gambled virtually the last of his dough on a tarnished trumpet in the window of a Bowery hock shop. It wasn't much of a gamble. He didn't blow good but he blew loud and he knew the old songs, everything from *Funiculi* to *Sorrento* and back again. Playing weekends he made enough to pay the rent and stock up on staples.

Now he was painting all the time, with a concentration and a lack of inhibition that had been beyond him in Paris. He had no idea how it was coming out. But for the first time he really didn't care, it was enough that nothing was getting in the way of his attack on the canvas. It was frightening; but all of his life he had been tiptoeing, and now he was running.

One day, coming back from buying supplies, he ran into a guy he had known in the WPA days; they had a beer and met two others, a painter from Chicago and his intense wife, thin as a knife, who lived on Attorney Street. There was a whole nest of them, on Attorney and Stanton and Ridge, holed up in the old tenements, some of them on the GI Bill, all of them working like crazy. All these birds had flown in, like himself, because somebody had passed on the word. They listened to Byrd, they argued about highbrow articles that Vito had to borrow and burrow his way through, they tramped through the Museum of Modern Art and the Whitney and knew in the wink of an eye what was right and what was wrong, they even started up some coop galleries so they could show together. Here he drew the line—he didn't mind their coming up and looking at his stuff, but he wasn't ready to show.

After looking at their work, some of it exciting, he felt that he was off in left field somewhere. They saw what was painterly in his canvases, they appreciated his color values—but as far as what he was *up to,* he had only his nerve and his imagination. Sometimes he was even frightened that he was going off his rocker: horror stories, fairy tales of princesses remembered from childhood and Henry James stories about American girls in Europe. All of this lay behind the series of canvases that he was working on, sometimes four and five at a time, clamped up against the walls of the loft like nightmares in progress.

He couldn't tell anyone, it would have been pretentious. But when people, young artists, came and stared hard, and walked out silent, he began to think about showing after all.

Winter wore off. He hardly felt it go, even though the heater only warmed one corner of the loft at a time and he could scarcely go through the ordinary motions without freezing solid. But one day a freshening wind blew through a broken pane, and he smelled spring as if it had come for the first time in his life. He threw on his old jacket and went for a walk. He hadn't done any walking since Paris.

At Seward Park he sat down on a bench and picked up a discarded *Post*. 111 DIE IN ILL. BLAST, it said. When had he last read a newspaper? The headline about the mine disaster made him think of his father's brother the sulfur miner who had lost a leg in the old country.

The story from Centralia was horrible. Rage and despair were intermixed. Someone was to blame for those deaths but no one would be punished. Men still went down into the mines, and were trapped and gassed and drowned, even though he had put them out of his mind. He found himself composing in his mind a Centralia cartoon, like those he used to do for *New Labor* not so long ago.

Suddenly he felt an alien presence beside him on the bench. He looked up into the calm calculating eyes of Comrade Lewis.

"It gets you, doesn't it, that story?" Lewis demanded. "I imagine it gives you a twinge."

"I couldn't have saved those men," he said defensively. "Neither could you."

"True." Lewis crossed his legs—he was neatly creased, as always —and offered him a cigarette. "But we could use one of your cartoons, Vito."

"I haven't done anything like that in a long time."

"How well I know. It's as if you'd been swallowed up."

"I've been concentrating on my painting. I suppose I should ask how things are going."

Lewis grinned. "I suppose I should reply that the organization is making excellent progress in auto, and with the veterans. But the unhappy truth is that the paper is going to have to be cut back to four pages."

"I enjoyed getting it in Paris. But I just couldn't go on doing cartoons from there. It made me feel like a hypocrite. And I couldn't write to explain. It seemed better for me just to fade out."

"Believe it or not, I understand. You know I've always admired your work. How's chances of my seeing what you've been up to?"

"Why . . . I haven't shown it to anybody, except a couple of painters."

"You don't have a gallery?"

"No reason for it. I don't like what I was doing before, or when I was in Paris. What I'm doing now, it's like my own mythology. It's hard to describe, you probably wouldn't even like it."

"Why not let me decide? If you don't mind, I'd like to bring Feinstein with me. You know Feinstein."

"I know the name." It was one of the names, along with Shapiro and Greenberg, that mattered these days on the Lower East Side. It stood for a passionate concern with problems of the new painting on the part of people who had formerly been political and now brought to his world their polemical commitment. They exhilarated him, but they frightened him too. He said cautiously, "Are you a friend of his?"

"From the old days." Lewis smiled that narrow smile. "The paper has been sponsoring a Sunday night series of discussions on culture and politics. We've had people talking on film, on fiction, on sociology. You really should be coming, they're very lively sessions."

"I'd feel kind of funny . . ."

"No one is going to come up to you and say, Deserter! Feinstein is speaking this coming Sunday—why don't you come? Afterward we can go on down to your place." Lewis arose and added: "No strings. I promise you that."

This last remark was almost enough to make Vito decide against going—it was a little too cute, it assumed a little too much—but in the end, after they had parted, and he had turned it over in his mind, wandering around the loft and staring at his stuff as though he'd never seen it before, he knew that he would go.

Sitting in a rear row of the stuffy hall off Union Square, packed with a new generation of combative young people, he discovered that Feinstein knew how to put his own convictions into words. It wasn't what he said about this or that painter as much as it was his attitude. The man was able to demonstrate the relevance—more than that, the importance, although it was a word Vito shied away from—of what he and his friends were trying to do.

Feinstein was a small man with a large bald head and an unlit cigarette that bobbed up and down between fleshy lips. "I'm trying to give up smoking," he explained, when Lewis introduced him. "I used to enjoy your cartoons in the paper."

"They weren't so great," Vito said. "No particularly original line."

"I guess that's true," Feinstein said equably. "It was the political line that I liked. I can count on one hand the socially minded artists who weren't patsies for Stalinism."

"I was one of those once," he said, as they walked to Feinstein's car. When they had scrambled in he added, "But I lost interest."

Feinstein held his bald dome somewhat bent forward, peering through the misted windshield, his king-size cigarette jutting forward like a little baton. "You mean you got more interested in your own work. Which means more interested in yourself than in others."

"It sounds pretty selfish when you put it that way."

"All good artists are selfish. It doesn't mean they don't care."

Arrived at Broome, they parked the car and climbed all the flights in a silence that grew increasingly grim. Vito had long since forgotten how high up he was, but these two, both fat and soft, sighed openly at each landing.

He took out his key ring, opened the big lock he'd bought against burglars on those rare occasions when he wasn't around, and threw the main switch. "Well, this is it. The lighting's not the best, but . . ."

Feinstein had lost his cigarette on the way up. He stuffed a new one into his mouth, wiped his alarming head, and said with surprise, jabbing his thumb at a canvas taller than he that leaned against the wall before him, "You didn't size this."

"That's right. I stained it first directly."

"Why?"

"I wanted to see what can happen. You get sick of the rules. And I got some delicate effects, see?"

"Pure chance. You couldn't control that stain, Vito."

"That's not the whole canvas, the stain," he said, more irritably than he had intended. "The rest of it is controlled. What I'm trying to do is work one against the other. I mean, the control and the freedom." Oh Christ, he said to himself, I never should have done this.

Feinstein was sniffing about now. "Can we see those stacked against that wall?"

"Hold on, I'll move them. I do this all the time. I'm always looking at them in one sequence or another."

After a while Feinstein said, around the cigarette, "I can see that. It's almost like an extended commentary on Europa and the Bull, not a rendition but a commentary."

"It's not really Europa, it's America—the female aspect of this country. I can't put it into words much better than that." He laughed tensely, as he shunted the paintings about. "I've got my hands full with the work without talking about it. You can see just from looking how I'm all tied up in knots."

"But then the whole country is. It's the tension between the two, between the dream and the reality, between the chance occurrence and the conscious gesture, that makes your work so exciting. And you work big."

"The thing is, I'm never sure in any particular canvas whether I've got it in balance. That's why I keep a whole batch of them going."

"Instead of working on one canvas over a long period and trying to create a traditional work of art. Of course that's gone, that's finished."

"That's why I got so restless in Paris. I didn't have to find the past there, I had to lose myself here."

Lewis had said practically nothing. Now he said softly, "What do you think, Feinstein?"

"I already said," Feinstein replied, almost angrily. "He's trying to reconcile the irreconcilable. But that's all right. Another six months, another year . . ." He gestured about the loft. "You're on your own," he said, "but you're not alone."

"Oh sure. They come and look, I go and look. You couldn't pry me out of New York with a crowbar."

"Well, I want to thank you," Lewis said formally and rather abruptly. "Vito, we'll be in touch."

"I've got no phone, but they take messages at Colletta's Grocery, I'm here all the time, trying to catch up."

"You're doing it," Feinstein said. "You may even be getting out in front."

In the days that followed he was warmed by the memory of Feinstein's roving eyes. Lewis had ulterior motives, but since it wasn't quite clear what they would be, Vito decided to return to the *New Labor* symposium. Not only was Lewis not presiding this time, he wasn't even present. Vito sat alone, but toward the end of the evening, the couple to his right slipped away, and the empty chair beside him was taken by a girl in a suede jacket.

He felt her eyes on him. After a while she touched his arm and said, "Excuse me, aren't you Vito the artist? The one that used to do the cartoons for the paper?"

"That's right."

She gave him a big grin. "It's a shame you don't do them any more." She added emphatically, her coarse brown hair bobbing on her shoulders, "They were great."

"Thanks. I'm painting full time. I've got a studio down on Broome Street."

"Oh." After a moment she said, "I should have introduced myself. I'm Sandra, I'm in the uptown branch, I live in Washington Heights. My girl friend and her new husband had to leave early tonight, that's why I'm alone." She hesitated. "You don't mind—"

"As matter of fact," he said, "I was going to ask you, would you like to have a cup of coffee?"

"I love it." As she stood up he saw that she was not merely a tall girl but a big one—buxom and sturdy—and was no more than twenty or twenty-one. She cinched the belt on her jacket. "Where to?"

"Feel like walking? We could go on down to Grand Street and get some cappucino."

"That sounds swell!"

On the way down they congratulated each other on avoiding the usual cafeteria hangouts, and they paused in front of a radio appliance store, with a crowd which was silently watching a wrestling match on TV, but once she was seated across from him she leaned forward and said with great eagerness, "You know, what you did has always been my big dream."

"What did I do?"

"Go to Europe." She took a deep breath, her bosom straining the buttons of her pink wool cardigan. "You don't know how I envy you."

"Europe is still pretty miserable."

"I'm not talking about the hunger and the armies and the destruction. Doing what you were doing—getting up in the morning and going where you wanted, walking along the Seine if you felt like it, or taking a train to Rome or Florence, being creative . . . Gee! I suppose I sound infantile, but . . . Did you live on the Left Bank?"

He was touched. "I lived in three or four different places, mostly wherever I heard it was warm. But it never was."

"You can't tell me you didn't like it." She gazed at him archly. "I wouldn't believe you."

"I liked Paris." He finished his coffee. "It's everything they say."

"Then what's the matter, didn't you have a girl?"

"I had one or two." How different Minette, the concierge's daughter, had been! Slight, small breasted, sallow, vivacious in her own sharp way, she never let him figure out whether she went to bed with him to get away from her mother, because she liked him, or because she wanted his Hershey bars. Maybe all three? Those girls of Paris, he thought as he looked at Sandra, they've forgotten things that you'll never know.

"You're a funny one," she was saying. "You're not married, are you?"

"Never have been, either."

"No responsibilities, living an artist's life—I can't see why you'd come back here. New York's so ordinary."

"I don't think so. Especially not tonight."

She flushed with pleasure, and he felt like a fool, making sex talk in this sappy way with someone almost young enough to be his daughter. No more. He said sharply, "For my work, this is the livest city in the world right now. Would you like to see some of my work?"

"I'd just love it."

"I'm practically around the corner."

When they got to his door she was panting. "No wonder you're so thin! How often do you go up and down these steps?"

"Whenever I have to." He reached in and flicked on the light. "Come in."

She entered uncertainly—not timidly, but hesitating, as if unsure of what she would find. But as the lights went on, she turned, first this way, then that. "Wow!" she said "They're wild!"

"Do you like any of them?"

"How can I say, so fast? I never saw any paintings like this before."

"At least you're honest."

"I didn't mean it in a bad way, Vito. I'm just not equipped . . ."

"You're equipped. Let me have your coat."

She loosened the belt of the suede jacket and turned her back to him. Instead of removing it, he slipped his hands under her arms and covered her breasts with his palms.

She breathed in sharply, shudderingly, but instead of moving to free herself took a step backward, fitting herself more tightly into his embrace. Her soft buttocks collided with his thighs and he caught fire at once, pulling her to him and burying his face in her neck. Her breath came fast, swelling her breasts under his hands; swiftly he worked open the buttons of the cardigan and slid his hands all the way inside her brassiere. After the memory of Minette, these breasts felt absolutely enormous. The nipples wrinkled between his fingers. The more he pressed the greater they seemed to grow.

Suddenly she placed her hands over his. "Sweetheart," she said, "at least let me take off my jacket."

He turned out the light. When he reached for her, she was already tossing her sweater over the back of the chair and shrugging out of her brassiere. He sat down on the cot to slip off his moccasins, but before he could work his shirt free she was kneeling before him, half in shadow. She was holding her breasts in her hands like twin offerings.

"Are they too big?" she asked anxiously. "Do you think they're too big?"

"No no no."

"Then bite them, go ahead, bite them." She groaned as he bent forward and took her breast in his mouth, feeling the nipple swell astonishingly beneath his tongue until it was pointing at him like a child's finger. "Don't be afraid, do it harder."

Feeding on all that abundance, he took gratefully what she so bountifully offered. This was the end of the longest period of continence in his life. How could I have done it, he marveled, how did I live without it? Sandra's coarse brown hair tumbled forward over his face. I'll never marry, he was tempted to say it aloud as he bore the girl back with him onto the cot, I'll never never marry.

Three days later, when he stopped in at the grocery for coffee beans, sugar and rolls, Mrs. Colletta handed him a piece of paper from an order form. "There was somebody called for you, yesterday just before we close up. I wrote it down."

"Induscon? What the hell is that? I never heard of it."

"Tell Vito Mr. Lorch called, he said. He expects you, four o'clock today. Doesn't it say there, didn't I write that down too?"

The elevator deposited him directly in front of it on the third floor of the newish office building on Madison Avenue. Here at least the pebbled glass doors were more informative: Induscon Ltd. no less, Consultants to Industrial Management, Dr. Harry Sturm, Director.

He felt in some obscure way as though he had been had. It had been years since he'd given a thought to Harry Sturm. Inside a vast main room, desks scattered at random, men at phones. An attractive girl with braids and hornrims was at the first desk. Behind her, some partitioned cubicles, and several private offices.

Before he could say anything she glanced at him, then up at the wall clock. "You must be Mr. Brigante."

"You're one up on me."

"They're expecting you. Do you want to go into Dr. Sturm's office?" She indicated the first door behind her. "Just go right in."

Vito looked about the big room before moving on. It was full of a sense of business, of money being made. Charts hung from the walls, two young men argued at a desk, a third consulted a slide rule, talking into a phone clamped to his shoulder. Holed up in his grimy loft, peering from paint table to canvases day after day, month after month, he'd forgotten about the existence of offices like this, where people figured, schemed, and connived over pieces of paper and sweating-dripping telephones. He shoved the office door open and walked in on Harry Sturm and Comrade Lewis.

They were standing by the window that looked down on the Avenue, chatting, their backs to him. Harry's shoulders were somewhat rounded, but Vito recognized his figure at once. His foot was up on a chair; a length of argyle sock was exposed, and a burnished cordovan shoe. He was dressing better. He and Lewis—or Lorch, of course, that was his right name, Lewis Lorch—might have been two executives discussing a merger.

Harry turned at the sound of his entrance. "Well, well," he said, smiling fiercely, eyes popping in the old familiar way, "my friend the artist."

"What are you up to?" Vito said. "Believe me, whatever it is, I don't think I'll fit in."

Lewis stared at him solemnly, almost disapprovingly, but Harry burst out laughing. He extended his hand. "Vito, you march in here like a surly old bohemian. Admit it, you like my office, don't you?"

"It's a step up from Niagara Falls. Is it all yours?"

"You haven't seen it all. I have a little research lab out in Forest Hills, nothing elaborate, just a quiet place for me to think while the

boys in there get on with day to day matters. If they weren't out
there functioning, I wouldn't be able to sit in my lab."

"Functioning at what?"

"Induscon is a service for small technical firms. You know how
those people used to operate in Washington during the war, bringing
the visiting fireman together with the right bureaucrat, telling him
whom to meet, making the appointments and the introductions—"

"Showing them where the body is buried?"

"Upon occasion." Harry laughed again. "Sometimes it's a simple
technological problem, checking data, making processes available.
But I don't want to bore you with all that."

Lewis said, "It was Harry's suggestion that I invite you up. Certainly it's a more suitable place than the national office."

"Suitable for what?"

"Suppose we show you."

As they went into the main office, Harry paused at the girl's desk
to pick up a key. He leaned forward, his hand on her back as if to
balance himself, and murmured something into her ear. How do
you like that, Vito thought, old Harry is sleeping with her! Confused at this further alteration in the fortunes of his former friend,
he hastened after him and Lewis.

He caught up with them at the end of the business office. Harry
unlocked a door and waved them on in. "Adjoining suite."

"You like it?" Lewis asked.

Vito looked about curiously. He was in a large, white-walled
room, well lit. A smaller room and an office cubicle lay beyond. But
it was completely empty. Bare. "I don't get it."

"Harry is going to sublet it—to the Lorch Gallery."

"Congratulations."

"I'd like to open this fall with your work."

"A one-man show?"

"That's right."

Harry smiled intensely. "It's quite simple, Vito. Lorch has persuaded me that there's yet another new life in the process of being
brought into the world. And that we ought to join forces—if not in
political life, then in this one."

"Harry has a knack for obfuscation." Lewis Lorch smiled thinly.
"He thinks it's the secret of his peculiar success. He rented all this
space, he overextended himself, now he wants to sublet this suite
to me. That's all. Period."

"Not period. Semicolon." Harry raised his arm. His cuff shot out of his coat sleeve, revealing a small glittering stone. "I have to lose some money this year and next because of Induscon's overrapid success. True. The perils of capitalism. Comrade Lewis has a good head for figures—he's promised that if I back him in the Lorch Gallery, I can show a tax loss."

"With a very substantial profit possibility for the years ahead," Lorch added. "I happen to believe in what I am doing."

"You make it sound as though you believe in profit instead of art," Vito said.

Harry flung his arm about Vito's shoulder. "He believes in you, old boy. That's what's important."

"Well," he said slowly, "I'm flattered. I'll tell you frankly, I thought I was being asked up here to talk about political activity. So I'm taken aback too."

"The very first time we met," Harry said, "you were working away in your studio—painting the girl, in fact, that Irwin Metzger was later to marry. Irwin and Fred Vogel and I barged in on you, and it was through you that I managed to get underway so quickly. And it would make me very happy to be able to reciprocate now. Lewis believes that your work deserves a fine home and I believe that the Lorch Gallery ought to be that home."

"Nobody knows about my work except some painters. It would probably look good here, but it wouldn't do you any particular good. They'd come in and sign the book and drink your punch, and that would be it."

"Suppose you let me worry about that part of it," Lorch said. "I'm not exactly going into this blind, you know. I believe there's a public waiting to be developed for important new work. Feinstein thinks you're important. When you show here, I'm sure he'll say it in print."

"You mean he wouldn't if I showed somewhere else?"

Lorch lowered his lids for a moment. Vito could not tell whether this retreat was a sign of modesty or of annoyance. When he opened his eyes he said, "I'm prepared to draw up an agreement with you, Vito. The terms will be comparable to those you'd get from the most select dealer on 57th Street. I'm referring to percentages, commitment to purchase, all of it. In addition, I'm prepared to make an additional commitment, contingent say on a minimal success for your show, of a small stipend to enable you to continue to paint without worrying from week to week about living expenses."

"So that's where all those big party dues have been going."

Lorch looked a bit grim, as though he was going to close his eyes again, but Harry said, laughing, "I'm the guy who should complain about that, if anyone. I paid enough in dues during the war years to liquidate the national debt."

"You had enough left in 1945," Lorch said quietly, "to set you up in this business, didn't you?"

"Thanks to my sobriety and initative. I just want to make clear to Vito that the Lorch Gallery will have nothing more to do with the New Party than Induscon does."

"And how much is that?"

Harry grinned his maniacal grin. "Nothing. Dworkin has a marble skull. I cannot get past it to the brain. But that's another story." He popped his eyes. "Before you leave, tell me what you hear from Fred?"

"Not very much. He's too busy with his radio show and his professorship. He wrote me that he may be on television soon, if things work out."

"I have a soft spot for Fred. I think I understand him. Well, we mustn't bore Comrade Lewis with our reminiscences. Vito, I hope I become your landlord this fall, in a manner of speaking."

When he and Lorch were out on the sidewalk, Lorch said to him, "I suppose you're a little curious about Harry."

"You sprang this on me all at once."

"You're heading downtown? Let's walk for a way." Lorch adjusted his hat and fell into step. "Once the path was clear I thought you might as well know everything. This is my own undertaking. It has nothing at all to do with my political life or convictions. I went to Harry because he had kept in touch. He has his own political ax to grind."

"I remember, there was some long essay he wrote when he left. I never read it."

"A pity. In its crazy way it's a masterpiece."

"Wait a minute. What the hell do all those guys do upstairs? How do you know the sheriff isn't going to padlock that joint while you're hanging pictures?"

Lorch looked at him quite seriously. "I've gone into it with a lawyer. He assures me that Harry's earlier troubles are quite distinct from what he's doing here, which is essentially a service operation for technical firms. Apparently there's been an out-of-court settlement. In any case it won't affect Lorch Galleries."

"I understood up there that he was backing you. Where's Lorch Galleries going to get the dough to keep me on the payroll, if not from Harry Sturm?"

"You certainly look every gift horse in the mouth, don't you, Vito?"

"I might just as well. Right now I'm eating every day and painting every day. What else do I need?"

"Recognition. Let me worry about the money—I've been doing that for the Party ever since it was founded."

"And look where the Party—"

Lorch laughed abruptly. "Don't say it. I just may be able to do better with you than with the Party." He halted at the kiosk and extended his hand. "I'm going to grab a subway here. Thanks for coming, and think about it."

Vito found it difficult to think of much else. It brought him face to face with a problem he had been putting off. When Sandra came in panting, lugging a heavy sack full of groceries, he said to her, "Baby, I want you to give me some dirt about the Party leadership."

"Let me put the potatoes up first, they take the longest. Then we can talk. I got us lamb chops, isn't that scrumptious?"

Vito already knew from nocturnal confidences that Sandra had just recently recovered from an involvement with the New York organizer of the Party, an ex-GI who went by the name of James Russell Lowell and was reputedly a powerful soapboxer, but a versifier of petty bourgeois origin. He stood in well with Dworkin and had passed on to Sandra (in their exchange of data) certain details about the lives of her leaders which she might never have gotten to know in Washington Heights.

When the potatoes were on the boil and the vegetables were under way on the illegal gas burner Sandra wiped her hands and plumped herself down on his lap. "Okay, *bubala.*"

Vito restrained himself from clutching that succulent flesh. She made him feel, as no girl had for a long time, like an adolescent with a permanent hard-on. Nor could he conceal it, not when she could just reach down, as she often did, and take hold of the evidence with a pleased grin, like a kid finding a lollypop. "I was saying before," he said determinedly. "About the leadership."

"I thought you gave up on politics." She gazed at him solemnly. "Why should you start pumping me now, what are you, a spy or something?"

"A fucking spy, that's what I am." When she had stopped laughing, he added, "I'll tell you why later. You just tell me what the people in the national office live on."

"They get paid every week, depending on how much is coming in. During the war, I heard Dworkin was getting as much as eighty bucks a week. It's nothing like that now. Still, he lives a very middle-class life, they say." By they she meant James Russell Lowell. "His wife is a fitter or something like that in a dress shop, she comes out of the garment industry. I understand when you walk into their apartment, except for the library—he's got a *fabulous* library—you'd think you were in some lawyer's home instead of a revolutionist's."

"What about the others?"

"Hoover you can imagine, just by looking at him. His wife sits and knits while he reads his articles out loud, so she can correct his grammar. She teaches English in a junior high, otherwise he'd starve to death."

"What about Lewis?"

"The mystery man. He's the only one whose wife isn't in the Party. In fact nobody's even sure that he's *got* a wife. What always struck me funny about him in particular was how he kept his private life separate from the Party. With the rest of us, between meetings and assignments and caucuses, everybody knows exactly how you spend your time. But when you get up to the top it's different. Nobody knows what the people on the Political Committee do when they're not in the office or on tour, where they go, who they associate with—"

"You were talking about Lewis."

"Well, I still am. I don't think even Dworkin knows what Lewis does with himself when he's not working on the Party finances, or arranging tours or transportation. He's always been such a whiz at that stuff that everyone takes it for granted that they can count on him forever."

"You sound like you wouldn't."

"What do I know? Anybody so jealous of his privacy, it must be he leads another kind of life away from the office."

"Could you visualize him leaving the Party?"

"Yes I could. Does that surprise you? I know he's been Dworkin's right hand man forever, like his shadow in a way."

"But?"

"But there's got to be another side to him. Dworkin couldn't live without the movement. If you stop and think of it, he's the only one never bothered to take a Party name. But I never once heard Lewis talk with passion about the movement. If he ever decides, you know, coldly, that we're not going to make it, he'll do something else. Don't ask me what, but something else."

"How about opening an art gallery?"

She got up from his lap. "You must be kidding, Vito."

"As a matter of fact, no. I just found out that Lewis Lorch is going to open the Lorch Gallery."

"There, you see?" she said triumphantly, hands on hips. "I'm not so dumb."

"Who ever said you were? Do you think he'll be able to do it and stay in the Party?"

Sandra shook her head. "It's got to be one thing or the other. The leadership don't just take outside jobs like you or me. It's either the movement or another life."

"Then it looks like he's got himself a new movement. Come on, kid, either we screw or we eat."

The following Sunday, the last of the *New Labor* symposiums for the season, Sandra had to spend the evening at a family function. Vito decided to go on alone. When the program turned out to be one that did not interest him particularly, he made up his mind to go down to the Cedar Bar where he might find his friends.

His way out was blocked, however, by a couple who turned out to be the Metzgers. After hugs and handclasps they tiptoed out together. Irwin and Carmela were both very well dressed, Irwin smelling of bourbon in a three button glen plaid as though the suit had been doused with it, Carmie smelling of Arpège and hair spray in a New Look dress that came down to near her ankles. She'd put on weight; but then so had Irwin.

"You both look stylish and prosperous," he said. "In fact, you look like you're slumming."

Irwin blushed. "We're on vacation for a few days. I thought the discussion might be interesting."

"The Marshall Plan may be good for the Europeans, but it doesn't do much for me. Care to join me for a beer?"

"Love it. You're one of the reasons we came here tonight."

"It's true, Vito," Carmela put in. "I've got regards for you from your family, and from the old gang down on Niagara Street."

"Who would have thought it?"

"As a matter of fact," Irwin persisted, "everyone in the branch asked to be remembered. They all heard you were back from Europe. Especially Sy. He led a big picket line downtown, must have been a hundred people, protesting the British trying to keep the Jews out of Palestine. You must have read about it in *New Labor.*"

Vito shook his head.

"But you're hard to locate—we couldn't find you in the phone book, and nobody seemed to know—"

"I never have had a phone. If you've got time now, let's head downtown."

Irwin said eagerly, "We can take my car."

He had a hunch that Irwin would be thrilled to meet some of the painters down on the Lower East Side. On the way, Carmie chattered on about a play they'd been to see, Boyer in *Red Gloves.* She seemed more struck by Boyer's baldness than by Sartre's philosophy.

In the bar, Irwin tried hard to catch up with the painters' conversation. But Carmie was uneasy, not just because she was wildly overdressed, and she drew him aside.

"Don't kid me, Vito," she demanded. "Are these the real thing?"

"I guarantee you."

"How do they stack up with those artists in Paris?"

"There's no comparison."

"Well, that's what I figured. I mean, these people are nice enough, they're all right, but they don't seem like real artists."

"You'll just have to take my word for it."

"Any chance of our seeing some of your work this evening?" Irwin asked.

"Why not? Finish your drink, and we'll go."

As they walked around the block, he said to Carmela, "Who's looking after Paul?"

"My mother, thank God. She takes him to school every morning and then takes him back to her house. For her it's a treat, for us it's a blessing. A real vacation."

Irwin was pulling out his wallet. He stopped under a street lamp. "Don't listen to her. He's beautiful. This will give you a vague idea; I took it myself."

Vito gazed at the photo of the swarthy, gypsy-like little boy on the tricycle. Thoughtful, almost stern, he stared darkly into the camera with his brilliant piercing eyes.

"I took up photography on account of him. I was afraid I'd forget those moments when he looks at the world like an explorer."

"Good enough reason." Vito circled the trash barrels that guarded his stoop. "I'll go first. The stairs aren't very cheerful."

He seemed always to be bringing people in and then standing back, hopelessly awaiting the right reaction. But Irwin, plump and puffing, his receding hair standing up a bit around his ears as if from the exertion of climbing, was smiling excitedly.

"A wonderful loft. So much room!"

"Good place to work. These I'm not satisfied with yet. And over here"—he began to tug and haul—"are some of the more recent ones."

Carmela threw herself down on the army cot and kicked off her pumps. Her legs, in black sheer hose, were as good as ever; her glance as avid as ever—if not at the paintings then at the shadeless windows, the odds and ends on the cork board, the gas heater, the socks stuffed into the paratroop boots.

"Living alone, Vito?"

"More or less."

"Same old Vito."

"I've been trying to change my style, Carmie."

"I can see that," Irwin said seriously. "All of these seem to have the same central theme, the big swirly stuff, I don't know quite how to put it. In fact," he admitted frankly, "it's kind of ugly. But it's terrifically disturbing."

"So's the loft," Carmela said. "I thought by now you'd go for something a little more . . ."

"Classy, right?" Vito laughed. "Same old Carmela!"

"If things are going so good, you ought to have something to show for it! And if—" She stopped, her eyes sliding away from him.

He turned. Sandra, as dressed up as Carmela, had pulled her

key from the lock and was staring at the Metzgers in embarrassed
surprise.

"I'm sorry, Vito," she said. "I didn't know you were expecting
company."

"I wasn't expecting you either. I thought you'd be tied up with
that family party till all hours."

"It was in Brooklyn Heights," she said, as if that explained
everything. "At the St. George, don't ask me why." She was groping
for small talk, to give everyone a chance to cope with a new situation. "I got dropped off, I thought I'd stop in and say hello before
I went home."

It was too transparent. "Well, meet Dr. and Mrs. Metzger from
Buffalo. Carmie used to model for me in the old days. Irwin is a
good friend of the Buffalo branch."

Sandra nodded jerkily. She was trying to ward off Carmela's
appraisal—of her hemline (awkwardly lowered) her hairdo (piled
up but starting to work loose here and there), and of the key in
her hand. Finally she stuffed the key into her purse with a kind of
bravado.

"I hope you're having a good time in New York."

"We had a hard time finding Vito," Irwin said. "We bumped
into him at the *New Labor* Symposium."

"I guess if we'd known where to find *you*," Carmela said, without
moving from her catlike snuggle on the cot, "that would have
solved our problem."

Sandra giggled tensely. "As a matter of fact, Vito and I first met
at the symposium."

"Sounds like everybody picks up old Vito there. I never knew
he was so interested in intellectual stuff."

Sandra was clutching her purse as though it were a life belt.
She stood silently chewing on her lower lip.

"Let me take your wrap," Vito said. "I'm going to make a pot of
coffee."

"No, thanks, really, I just stopped in for a minute to see if you
were all right."

"Has he been sick?" Carmela asked interestedly. "Or do you
bring him some special kind of medicine?"

"The fact of the matter is," Irwin said hastily, "Carmie and I
have been hoping to buy a painting from Vito."

Vito was so angered by Carmie's common snottiness that he

hardly heard what Irwin was saying. Who gave her the right to come up here and toss insults around? The worst of it was that he couldn't even tell her off without wounding Irwin. What nerve, to flounce in with the airs of a frigid suburban matron!

You bitch, he wanted to say, nobody ever threw your behavior up to you. Even after she had started going with Irwin, teasing him all the way to the altar with a hard-on, she had continued to drop in for a little last-minute jazzing. She was too hysterically unsure of herself to make a good piece of ass anyway. And if she didn't even know that about herself, she didn't know anything.

She stared him down defiantly, almost angrily. It struck him with a shock that perhaps she was jealous. But he hadn't even thought of her in years; she had herself a husband and a child and a house in Snyder, all of which she'd gotten by taking her clothes off for him and giving poor Irwin a thrill. Sheer luck—or maybe now she thought it was skill.

"I'm very serious," Irwin was saying. "I want to own one."

"Irwin, I wouldn't even know what to charge you."

"Well, whatever your going price is." Irwin was embarrassed. "I wouldn't want any special consideration. I'm not broke any more, Vito. My mother died some months ago and left me a little something."

Vito was not sure whether condolences or congratulations were in order. He tried to remember what Irwin's mother had been like, and could not. "I'd rather not put it in money terms. If you were here in Manhattan, you could just fix my teeth for me, for an even swap."

"Irwin's going into orthodontics," Carmela said. "He could wire up your jaw and make you look like a new man, Vito. Sandra's too."

He should have wired hers closed. "Irwin, let's say a hundred bucks. Would that be all right? If you still like the painting next year, I'll charge you two, three times as much for another one."

"That's ridiculously cheap."

"It'll buy me some art supplies."

"I really don't know which one . . . I'd prefer one of those, really." Irwin pointed to the opposite wall. "Like that one with all the reds."

Without thinking Vito said, "I did that in Paris. I don't like it myself. The only reason I keep it is to see what I did wrong."

Irwin flushed. Nothing for him to do but insist, "Just the same, that's the one I'd like to own, if it's okay with you."

"And with me?" Carmela put in.

"Well, naturally—"

"I think we ought to ask Sandra." Carmela swung her feet to the floor and sat up. "As long as we're lucky enough to have her here, we can get an expert opinion on what Vito's really good at."

"Jesus Christ, Carmie," Vito said.

"I think that's about enough," Irwin said to his wife. "I really do."

"Never mind," Sandra said. She was fighting back tears. She looked no more than her nineteen years, and utterly incapable of meeting such crummy competition. When Vito moved to her side, she twisted free. He saw with dismay that she was furious with him too. "I'll just say good night now."

Irwin hastened to hold the door open for her. She blinked an attempted farewell smile at him and hurried out.

In the silence her footsteps clattering rapidly down the empty hallway.

"God damn it," Irwin said, "that was a rotten way to act."

"God damn it yourself." Carmie slipped her feet into her pumps. "I don't have to put on the dog for Vito. I've known him since I was sixteen."

"That's no excuse."

"For what? Not wanting to sit around and bullshit with his chippies? That's not what I came to New York for."

"Irwin," Vito said, "you take that painting."

"Really, I feel—"

"Forget it. I want you to have it. Here," he slid it away from the wall, "I think it'll fit in your trunk. Then I won't have to bother about crating it for you. A load off my mind. Honestly."

If Irwin had not reached out for it Vito would have let go. Irwin had to take it if he did not want to let it fall. He stammered apologies.

"Next time," Vito said, "bring the kid."

Irwin looked at him gratefully over the painting. "You'll like him, Vito. He's a wonderful boy."

"Better than his mother, is what he means," Carmela said.

Now that it was all over, Vito felt a little calmer. "You don't have to act so tough with me, Carmie," he said. "I know you from way back. You're not as mean as you make out."

She gave him an uncertain glance. "Wouldn't it be funny," she said, "if you turned out to be a great artist after all? You know, like in the movies."

"Vito," Irwin extended his hand, "I can't tell you how grateful I am. We'll be in touch, I'll mail you a check."

"No rush."

When he had closed the door on them he paced the loft, trying to see it as it must have seemed to them. Impossible. All he could see was that he was alone again. He picked up a length of wood and wedged open the window. Fresh air drifted in, and the voices of the Metzgers, subdued, almost unrecognizable, as they arranged his painting in the trunk of their car, down on the street below.

He picked up a handful of brushes and turned to face his work.

4. HAM

There were five of them in the seminar room that Ham had reserved for the program committee as chapter chairman of the AVC: the Markowitzes, diehard Stalinists both, Jerry the liberal law student, and Conrad Something, a crew-cut Polack ex-Marine whose commitment to AVC rather than to the American Legion nobody had as yet succeeded in explaining.

"In accordance with your instructions," Ham said, "I went ahead and had the posters lettered up." He drew one from his briefcase and held it away from him for the others to see. It fluttered, caught by the coolish April breeze that blew through the open casement window.

Libby Markowitz read aloud, *"Students and Veterans, Which Way in '48?"* She drew her mouth down suspiciously. "I thought we agreed that we were going to have a panel on third party possibilities." She was a heavy, rather sullen girl who had joined the WACs when the line had changed; even four long years of military discipline hadn't diminished her ardor for marching orders. Her husband, a long-headed psychology major, hastened to fall in behind her.

"I'm sorry," Ham said to them, "but that isn't the way it was. It's in the minutes—we decided to include third party spokesmen in our election panel discussion, but not until fall. If we want to sponsor separate meetings for individual candidates or their representatives, there'll be time for that in the fall, after summer session."

"That's right," Conrad said unexpectedly, in his Black Rock

accent. "Dat's right." He was going to be a physical education teacher and he had to be handled with care: in this committee, he was the swing man, and if the Markowitzes could get at him, they'd have it their way. He added innocently, "All we got to decide on is the speakers. I'll get a Democrat if Jerry contacts a Republican."

"I don't know any," Jerry laughed, "but it's time I met some."

"Then Jack and Libby can get a Progressive, a Henry Wallace man. And Hamilton can round up any other minority parties, like the Socialists, or that fellow Hull's Workmen's Party."

Conrad was as subtle as a kick in the ass. Jerry was grinning openly, but the Markowitzes had sense enough not to be outraged. They didn't control the chapter, not yet. So they took their quota of posters, and after some discussion about obtaining a law professor to chair the election panel, the meeting broke up.

"I think we'll have a good turnout," Ham observed, as he gathered up his belongings. "Now that midterms are over, interest is starting to build up in the elections."

"Peace is going to be the issue," Libby said stubbornly. Her big shoulder-strap purse snapped shut like the jaws of an alligator. "It ought to be our special responsibility as veterans. Come on, Jack."

Conrad said amiably, "Going over to the lounge? I'll buy you a Coke."

When the three had closed the door behind them Jerry said, "That's the most warlike woman I ever saw."

"I bumped into her on Main Street last month, right after the Communists took over Czechoslovakia. I couldn't help but say, 'Isn't it awful about Masaryk jumping out the window?' She said it was probably a fascist provocation."

"I'd hate to think how long we'd last if she was running this city."

"The sad thing is, she doesn't want to hurt people, she wants to do good. She's going to be a social worker, for the same reason that she's a Communist. If only she wasn't so humorless." As he uttered these last words, Ham observed that Jerry lowered his heavy lids for just an instant. Why? Was he disbelieving? Or was he thinking that Ham himself didn't have any saving humor?

But Jerry said quietly, "Libby and Jack think I'm just another dumb liberal. Maybe I am. You're the one they're afraid of. Let's face it, the only thing that inhibits them from going after you is that you're colored."

"You don't think I'm taking advantage of it, do you?"

"I bet they think so. That's all I'm saying."

Was that all Jerry was saying? He could not be sure.

"Come on," he said abruptly, "Let's get these posters up."

They made their way through the hallways, posting and tacking from building to building, then cutting around the tennis courts to the big sweep of lawn where students were lying around, chatting, reading. White, all of them. Not a black face in sight. It was like the Navy—except that he had hated the Navy and he loved the university.

As they reached the walk that led to Main Street and the trolley, Jerry said tentatively, "Say Ham, I've been wondering how you came to get interested in library science."

"What's wrong with it?"

"Nothing. I like books myself, or I wouldn't be going into law. But there isn't much money in being a librarian."

"I'm not out to get rich. I'm out to learn."

"Well, I guess I envy your attitude. Just like I envy you working for a good lawyer like Margaret Zivic."

Suddenly put on the defensive, he said with a sullenness that he could not suppress, "All I do is clean wastebaskets and ashtrays for her."

"Do you mind if I envy you?"

"I'm sorry. The old chip on the shoulder. The more I talk, the more confused I get."

"Who isn't? It's not just Communists like the Markowitzes that call me a dumb liberal, your friends do too. Don't deny it."

"They can talk for themselves. As for me, the war finished everything I believed when I went in. After what I saw in the Navy, I decided to go to college and try to find out what was wrong with my old ideas. When I was a kid my father taught me non-violence, but after I went to work militancy—and Marxism—made a lot more sense to me than my father's preaching." They had reached the street where they would be parting. "And when I got into the Navy none of it did me any good."

"I had the impression you were pretty close to the New Party. The Markowitzes seem to think you are. Why else would they be so afraid of you?"

"Because the one thing I learned from the New Party is not to trust fanatics. The Markowitzes would like to attack me publicly, but they're inhibited on account of my being colored. Compared to them, the New Party people are very open-minded on questions that they used to take for granted."

Jerry glanced at him skeptically. "Like what?"

"Centralization. Or arguing out differences within the organization."

"To me they still behave as if they got the word from on high. Maybe not like the Markowitzes, but I feel Bill Zivic looks down on the likes of me. Margaret's a sharp lawyer, but I wouldn't say she's exactly tolerant."

This was true, but no one could know how good the Zivics had been to him. He had to defend them, even though he had drifted away from them. What they stood for—socialism, racial equality, an end to colonialism—he did too; but more and more they seemed to him to be dated, and out of touch with the deeper realities.

When he said goodbye to Jerry at the trolley stop, he was already withdrawn into reverie. Seating himself on a hard straw bench for the long straight ride downtown to Margaret's office, he was unable to open a textbook and concentrate on his studies. Staring out the window at the dull commercial prospect that succeeded the campus as the trolley rattled downtown, he could think only that today he was going to have to decide whether his first loyalty lay with Big Boy or with Margaret.

The story of my life, he thought—one impossible choice after another. First had been the question of whether to become a preacher or a laborer in the mill. Then whether to go into the Navy. Then whether to settle for being a messman like all the other niggers or to struggle to become a gunner's mate. Then whether to return to the mill where Big Boy needed him, or to go to college on the GI Bill.

Really, it was the war that had turned everything around. Buoyed up, kept from drowning in misery and anguish by the notes painfully scrawled in Big Boy's massive fist and by the packages from Margaret and Bernie and Anne, he had gained the courage to fight for the right not to be a servant and stooge to college boy officers looking, in their summer whites, like characters in the musical comedy movies he used to see for a nickel on Saturday afternoons at the Jewel. He had virtually gone on a one-man strike, he had

memorized and recited the President's Executive Order against
discrimination. Finally he had won, one of the first black men in
the Navy to be trained as anything other than a scullery boy.

His step-father, miserable minister of the Gospel who had died
of asphyxiation, choked by his own verbiage, while Ham was at
boot camp, would have been appalled at the sight of his adopted
son, Hamilton, psalm-singer and pianist, calling off the parts of an
Oerlikon gun to a cracker instructor and winding up as loader on
a three-inch gun, member of the naval armed guard on a Merchant
Marine tanker. For that first year in uniform Ham was more faithful
to the prescripts of the comrades he had left behind than to those
of his late father. "Be the best man in your outfit," they had urged
him, according to the dictum by which he would emerge as a worthy
revolutionist when his fellow servicemen were ready to forsake their
officers and seek new leadership.

"I told my Chief yesterday that I'm a socialist," he had written
Bill and Margaret, ignoring the thin smile, the wide yawn with
which Lieutenant (jg) Wirtz would read the news while censoring his
mail. "He's got me down for a nigger troublemaker anyway, so I
figured I had nothing to lose. You know what he said? 'Hambone,
I don't give a damn what your religion is, you're in the Navy
now.'"

And as month followed month on the SS *Rainbow Ridge,* floating
like a sliver on the endless reaches of the flat Pacific, Ham began
to see how pointless, in terms of anything other than his own stiff
and stubborn pride, his violent effort had been; for he remained
a black boy among whites, with no hope of influencing them in
any significant way. Gradually he became convinced that what Big
Boy, Bill, and the others had persuaded him to believe had little to
do with his daily life.

The *Rainbow Ridge* was off Ulithi Atoll, in the far reaches of
the Pacific, waiting to take on stores for the run up to Okinawa,
when Sparks tacked up the wireless report that President Roosevelt
was dead. While he was still asking, 'Who's the Vice-President
again?' half the crew was making it clear that they expected him to
be the chief mourner aboard ship because of all he owed to the
nigger-lovin First Lady and her cripple husband. While the flag was
lowered to half-mast, the officers of the black gang were drinking
toasts in denatured alcohol and pineapple juice to the son of a
bitch who was good and dead at last.

"You'd think we were on a goddam yacht," muttered Sam Polonsky, his eyes full of tears. Polonsky, a draftee seaman first class, a former needle trades worker from Lower Manhattan, had attached himself to Ham from the day he had joined the ship's company, apparently on the theory that they were natural allies. When he learned that Ham had known Sy Glantzman, a friend of the Polonsky family, he regarded this as cement to their lonely alliance. "I haven't heard this kind of hate talk since I used to sell Good Humors down on Wall Street."

As a pacifist, Polonsky himself hated not FDR but his beloved Navy. As a sunworshiper, he took fanatical advantage of being afloat in the South Seas. Blackening in the sun until he took on the tint of some cordovan-colored Aztec, he hung out his wash in his shower clogs and then lay naked in the noon blaze, turning from time to time like a side of mutton on a spit, disregarding the nickname of Nig which the others automatically bestowed upon him. He became much darker than Ham, leathery like an old man, his deep-sunk eyes glowing passionately on either side of a hawklike Indian nose, his mop of thick kinky hair, resistant to its brush cut, growing low and thicketlike on his polished brown forehead. When he smiled, nervously, twistedly, as if ashamed of any betrayal of his customary solemnity, his teeth shone, white as bone, between his heavy lips.

Ham resented the automatic claim to kinship that Polonsky made upon him, as well as the fact that they were thrown together by their common ostracism and their common opposition to the war. The man's preachy pacifism served only to arouse guilt feelings about his dead father.

On the other hand, what could he say for his own little baggage of Leninist notions? The more irrelevant it looked, the more receptive he became to a pacifist opposition to the way the world went, for it had at least the virtue of virtuousness, if not of relevance. Ironically, Polonsky himself was growing uncertain, just as shaken up as he by what living with their shipmates had done to his preconceptions; and he too was guilt-ridden, having compromised his own principles by going into the Navy.

"My old man—he's a presser—he's mixed up too," Polonsky explained apologetically. "He's a pacifist, he didn't want me to go into the service, but he loved Roozvelt."

"How about you?"

"To me Roozvelt was just another capitalist politician, and I didn't want to shoot anybody just to make him happy. But on the other hand, go and explain that to Adolf Hitler, you know what I mean? You follow me?"

Seated on the hot iron deck, backs to the bulkhead, pitching their orange peelings through the scupper into the sea, they talked of how the war had shaken their convictions.

"If it was only the Japs," Polonsky confided, "I would have maybe been a conchie. The Japs never did me anything—it's one more imperialist war, Pearl Harbor or no Pearl Harbor. But with Hitler, the *momser,* you got a horse of a different color. I'll tell you something else." Polonsky leaned over, as was his way when he waxed confidential, and put his head close to Ham's bare arm, resting the great beak of a nose almost on Ham's shoulder, pursing his heavy lips as if he was going to whisper confidences into Ham's ear. "I didn't have the guts to go CO. I was afraid to face the folks on my block. And how about my mother's landsmanschaft, that was sending gifts to all the boys fighting Hitler? And the older workers in my shop?"

Ham was bemused. He had admired Big Boy because he was tough, stood up to the boss, took on whitey, even in the south. So he had gone into Big Boy's militant socialist organization because it prized those who were willing to struggle and bleed; he had gone on into the Navy because he had been told to stick with the workers, fight where they fought, and prepare himself to lead them to something better. Never had he confronted the proposition that it might be more courageous to refuse to join this mob that hated its allies, admired its enemies—for exactly the traits that it was supposedly combating—and cheered when its own leader fell dead.

What he had gotten from the hodgepodge of party meetings and educationals simply would not carry him through the war. It was ludicrous to think of propagandizing the armed guard crew—For what? Against what? To turn their arms against their officers, in the person of Lieutenant (jg) Woodrow Wirtz, who asked for nothing better himself than to be back in Wichita in his father's wholesale plumbing supply house? It was obviously wiser not merely to stay clear of their primitive arguments, but to avoid revealing to them what he believed—or had believed as a civilian.

By early summer of 1945 he was no longer sure just what that was. And he began to wonder, as they changed course and headed for Panama and a layover for refitting and repairs, what would have become of him had he himself said no to the whole thing, and gone off to jail instead of fighting for the right to be a part of a group that continued to despise him—and to couple him with "Nig" Polonsky as the twin objects of their contempt.

Apparently the pacifists kept their own consciences clear at the price of isolating themselves from the volunteers and conscripts whom they might otherwise have influenced. Well, he hadn't isolated himself, he had fought his way into the midst of these so-called fighting men—and had won only the opportunity to become a visible butt for their crude jokes instead of an invisible black sambo. (If some of them occasionally accorded him a grudging respect he suspected it would wear off under more traditional pressures once they were separated.) At best you could say that, regardless of race creed or color, they would all be glad to see the last of each other. Big deal. As for Polonsky's conscience being further confused by going through the senselessly repetitive drills with a gun that they had never fired in anger, the pacifist seemed to have no case; even if he had to fire at a fleeting enemy, it would hardly have scarred him as much as enforced association with his shipmates was marking him.

None of this really crystallized in Ham's mind until well after the landfall signaling the end of the long slow voyage across the Pacific. Everyone was keyed up by the approaching liberty in a port town filled with real bars, cheap rum, and good-natured whores. Ham liked Panama too. Once you got out of the Zone, which was just one more southern town, color bar and all, you were in the Latin world, lively, musical, with every color under the tropical sun, where no one eyed your skin with misgiving or hate.

The streets of Panama City were aswarm, as they had not been eight months earlier, with roving gangs of GIs. It took no longer than the first bar to learn that the soldiers had been released from a troop transport, a converted cruise ship which had just brought them from a Channel port, and would be ferrying them across the Pacific for duty on the other side of the world.

As they poured ashore, the soldiers were at first exuberant, for they had been under the impression that they were being sent home. When they were informed of their ultimate destination, they began to smash things in blind fury at having been tricked.

"The sons of bitches!" a gangling thin-wristed corporal cried out to Ham and Polonsky. "They tried to sneak us right through the Canal without an hour on dry land. The bastards! First they lied to us and then they tried to sneak us through."

"What did they take us for, morons or something?"

"They treated POWs better, for Christ sake! Am I right or wrong?"

"Back where I come from we wouldn't treat a dog like that. First we win their goddam war and then they ship us out to take on the gooks. Let them use the fuckin draft dodgers back home."

Polonsky leaned forward, rum and Coke in hand, his sun-blackened countenance with the hawk nose in profile oddly resembling a tropical bird. "So what happened on your ship?"

"What happened? We busted all their fuckin crockery. Then we pried everything loose on that fuckin ship and threw it over the fuckin side."

"After that they announce a change in plans." The corporal finished his Panamanian beer and slammed the bottle down on the bar with a crash. He waved angrily at the barmaid. "Hey, chiquita, shake your ass! A little service here! The colonel gets on the PA and says, All qualified personnel will be given shore leave upon making port in Panama. You think they was gonna do it until we raised unqualified hell? Not on your ass. They was going to snow us. But we smoked them out."

As they drank they turned mean. Not just the men in the bar, but others all over town, turning up by twos, by threes, in larger clusters, with sidearms and the will to use them. Far from fading, their outrage grew, fed upon the fact that while this was land it was not their homeland. They egged each other on, bluster became brutality; they turned their hatred on everyone not of their company.

A shot rang out. Then a second. After that the firing broke into rapid bursts, like the chattering of angered wildlife. The intervals of silence were ominous, broken only by the hoarse cries of men no longer under constraint and clotting into roving bands.

Suddenly four of them came pounding around a corner, kicking with their heavy boots at a stalled chiva, an ancient Chevy panel truck converted into a five-cent bus. "Get the fuck out of the way!" they cried. "Here comes Patton's Third Army, get the fuck out of the way!" An arm waved drunkenly, a sidearm flashed; a globe shattered. Ham and Polonsky ducked into a doorway. A red-faced quartet of Shore Patrol and Military Police pounded up to them. "Take off. All shore leave canceled. Take off."

Across the street high hysterical voices shrieked like tropical birds: "Get the fuck out of the way, here comes Patton's Third Army!"

Safely back aboard the liberty boat, Ham turned in relief to his shipmate. But Polonsky the pacifist was in no mood to talk. Even after he had regained the ship, trembling so that he sloshed coffee from the urn all over his hand, Sam could only mumble, "Those nuts, they could of killed us."

Ham had been frightened himself, but once it was over he found himself far more concerned with what had been killed in those men, and with the contrast between the stillness of the waters of the Chagres in Gatun Lake and the miserable howling of the wretched soldiers on the streets of Panama City. If that had been insurrection, even protest, he wanted none of it. What he had wanted in its stead was simply not going to happen.

And now, nearly three years after the war, it had still not happened, despite the brave gestures of partisans, maquis, and guerrillas— and the weak echo that their sacrifices had brought forth on this side of the sea. Knowing this in his bones as he knew the blackness of the skin that covered his bones, he had still temporized, unable to deny not only Big Boy, but all the others who were still more devoted to him and to what mattered to him than any other people he knew.

Their revolution was not going to happen, any more than the post-war years had brought the depression they had predicted with such certainty. But other revolutions were coming, of that he felt sure, just as he felt sure that he would play a part in them. He could only hope that the others would too.

The trolley had made its way downtown. He picked up his book-bag and alighted, then walked slowly over to the Rand Building, dreading the decision he was still putting off even as he took the elevator to the eleventh floor and the offices of Kuralsky, Schopfel and Zivic.

The receptionist nodded. He stowed his bookbag in the bottom drawer of her desk, put on the gray poplin jacket that hung on the coat rack, and set to work at once stuffing and licking the envelopes that lay in a snowy heap beside her typewriter. If he was going to get at Margaret's personal file, it had better be soon, before she came back. To make sure he asked Wanda, "Mrs. Zivic in?"

"She's having lunch with a client." Wanda twisted her heavy neck. "She said for you just to go on with what you always do."

His heart pounding, Ham walked casually into Margaret's office and paused at her desk, piled high as always with papers for him to file. Beneath them, in the middle drawer, in the pencil tray, lay the duplicate key to her personal file. Margaret was not the kind of person to hide it away. In fact, if he were to take the key and open her file now and dig through it for material on Big Boy, and if she were to walk in on him, she would probably say, "All you would have had to do was ask, Ham. I'd have opened the file for you."

It was that more than anything else which made up his mind finally. He did not touch the middle drawer, but took up the stack of correspondence and carbons and began filing them in the main cabinet. Perhaps there would be something in them on Big Boy's case. But there was not; when he had finished, he thumbed the file until he came to Hull, and began to read through the two-year-old folder on the felonious assault case. He was just finishing it when Margaret came in, swinging her purse, a cigarette sticking out of her mouth.

"Hi," she said. "What's new, Ham?"

"Been getting ready for the AVC's election forum."

"I suppose the Stalinists are still giving you a hard time."

"When their line is peace instead of cold war, it's attractive to a lot of people."

Margaret said rather sharply, "And if Stalin changes his mind, the line will change. Since when are you against peace?"

"If I'm not for it more strongly than they, then they can make honest people believe that I'm sabotaging a worthwhile effort."

"What do you suggest, turning pacifist?" She punched out her cigarette, not angrily, but absently, as if ready to drop the matter and get down to her own work.

"Plenty of people are frightened of a confrontation with Russia. They're going to be attracted to Wallace's Progressives, not to a Marxist group that simply says it's against Washington and Moscow."

"There aren't enough pacifists in the whole damn country to crowd this office. The American working class never was pacifist and never will be."

"I guess that's true. There's one thing sure, Big Boy won't turn pacifist."

"That'd be the day, wouldn't it?" She glanced at him shrewdly. "He's not exactly satisfied with the way I've been handling his case, is he?"

She sat down at the desk, pushed up the sleeves of her cardigan, and began to scribble on a large yellow pad. The backs of her forearms were shadowed with dark hair; her small hands were supple and muscular, like those of a woman golfer. Her rather pushed-in face was undisturbed, businesslike, friendly.

"You're right," he said. "He's very unsettled. In fact . . ."

"In fact what?"

"He thinks you're shafting him."

Margaret's voice was casual. "How?"

"He suspects all sorts of things—that you made a deal with the union, maybe even with the company, to get rid of him. To have him sent up the river for a year or two to get him out of the way."

"If Big Boy's jealous of his reputation, I'm jealous of mine too. If I sold him out in collusion with the D.A. or the union bureaucrats or whoever, my name would be mud. And he knows it. He may be a nut, but he's no fool."

"I'm just telling you how he interprets all this delay."

"I've told him a million times that the delay is a deliberate tactic. He's harder to deal with than my husband. The '46 strike was a rough one, and the assault charge was a rough one to beat— especially with the local press like it is, and with the pictures of the strike that they ran. The further in the past it is, the more people are apt to forget, at least to be lenient. It was the prosecution that wanted to nail him right away, as an object lesson."

"He doesn't see it that way." He rubbed his palms with a handkerchief. "Big Boy thinks you've been cooking up a deal behind his back. He's convinced that ever since he pulled his group out of the Party you and Bill, and the others too, have been out to get him— first to isolate him and then to get him."

"I've told him before: If he doesn't like the way I'm handling his case, he's perfectly free to engage other counsel. He knows that as well as you do. Why does he keep harping on it without doing anything about it?"

"Because he's really not that sure of himself. He's afraid if he gets a new lawyer and you have all the documents and affidavits, you'll be in a position to mess him up."

"How vindictive does he think I am?"

"He's had reason to be mistrustful. Especially of whites."

"I'm well aware of that. What does he want out of you, Ham?"

Swallowing, he hesitated. It was one thing not to betray Margaret. Did it follow that he had to betray Big Boy? "Well," he said slowly, "he doesn't approve of what I'm doing. Going to school, working for you."

"I know that too."

"Yes. Well, he figures the least I can do, for old times' sake, is to be helpful to him. You know, with the AVC, the Labor Vets—"

"And with me."

"Hell," he said crossly, goaded at last by her calm anticipation of everything he had to say, "if you know why do you keep asking?"

"I just wanted to hear you say it. I haven't got any secrets from you any more than I do from Big Boy himself." She pulled open the drawer before her and took out the key to her personal file. "Here, take a look. There isn't a damn thing about him that isn't in the office file." She stretched out her arm, swinging the key between thumb and index finger. "Go ahead."

He shook his head dumbly.

"Believe me," she said, dropping the key onto her blotter, "I haven't got anything hidden away at home. All I've got in our basement is Bill's UAW stuff, plus our old leaflets and back files of *New Labor.* You can tell Big Boy that I'm going to do my goddamndest to get him off, regardless of what kind of adventurist line he follows in his union or with his nutty political group. And if you don't believe me, you shouldn't be working for me."

"I do believe you."

"Okay then, let's get going before we shoot the whole afternoon. On your way out, tell Wanda to come in here, will you?"

Even though he worked for her, Margaret no longer demanded that he see the world as she and Willie did. That was more than you could say for Big Boy, who was forever demanding allegiance from his troops—and foreswearing his old allegiances to those whom he saw as betraying him. But Margaret had all the advantages, and Big Boy had none, beyond guts, integrity, and a kind of animal cunning. What gives me the right, he thought, to choose up sides when both of them have been good to me, even if in such different ways?

By quitting time, he was firm in his mind. He left the office more decisively than he had entered it, and struck off on foot through the hurrying crowds of business people and shoppers, around the battlements of the grim old Public Library, on down through the black belt to Mary Lou's Diner, where he had a date with Big Boy for a dinner of pigs' feet among their own people. Coretta, he knew from experience, would have welcomed him to their flat, would gladly have cooked him dinner—but Big Boy kept his wife to himself, preferring to meet even his closest friends on neutral ground.

It was worth it to be reminded, no matter how many hours he spent on the campus or on the quiet eleventh floor of an office building, no matter how neatly he dressed in sport jacket, slacks and tasteful tie, that he was still tiptoeing through white man's country, liable at any moment to have his passport torn from him and ripped to shreds. You could clutch that briefcase and smile until your jaws ached, but in a flash the lowest of the low could strip you to the buff and leave you naked, standing there shivering in your black skin.

It was good to be among your own kind, yes, he thought, his nostrils flaring to the odors of fat old Mary Lou's greasy greens and chitlins, wafted to the sidewalk by the lazy fan in her transom; but damn, it was too easy to be brown among the blacks, just as it was too hard to be black among the whites.

Pushing open the door, he saw Big Boy at the table nearest the kitchen, but facing the door and dominating the room as he dominated every room, bigger and blacker than anyone. He was wearing a plaid shirt, open at the throat, and heavy work shoes that scraped on the sloping sawdust floor when he slid them beneath him. Fork in his fist, he raised an arm in salute.

"Sorry I couldn't get here any earlier." Ham slipped into the vacant chair.

"That's all right. I know you don get off work till late." Big Boy wiped his chin with the back of his hand and dug into his dinner.

From behind the counter big-busted Mary Lou, moonfaced imitation Aunt Jemima, called out in her musical soprano, "What you like tonight, Mist' Wright?"

"Same as Big Boy. Looks good enough for me any time."

"Mist' Wright," Big Boy mumbled sardonically, between mouthfuls. "That's hot stuff. Knows you since you was a runny-nose kid, don she? But soon's you come on in with that white shirt an tie she's misterin you all over the store."

"Never mind that. What's new?"

"I ought to ask you that. Ain that why we're here? You really want to hear what the president of the Local said to me? Or what I said to the International Rep? Who you kiddin?"

"Let up, Big Boy. If you don't take that wild hair out of your ass I can take my appetite someplace else."

"Like where? Laube's Old Spain? Or maybe the main dinin room of the Statler Ho-tel?"

"What's biting you, anyway?"

"Man if you don know now you never will. I'm sittin here waitin for some news about my so-called lawyer, remember? If I wanted to be a social butterfly I could take Coretta to the church supper at the AME Zion backyard. Now what you got to tell me about Margaret Zivic?"

Ham sighed from sheer relief. When Big Boy decided to lay it on the line, he didn't beat around the bush. "Is it all right with you," he asked, "if I eat a little something first? My stomach feels like my throat's cut."

"Can't understand why you always so hungry, jus from pushin papers aroun. If you was back in the mill I could see it."

"Maybe I get the appetite from studying."

"That's a laugh. Is that all you been doing, studyin, all these years? I thought you was messin aroun with college boy politics."

"You want to be on a panel discussion AVC is going to have on the labor movement?" He threw it out as a challenge. "You can say anything you damn please. But don't treat them like college boys—some of them are combat veterans."

"How can I go up there an talk if I'm sittin in jail? Now are you goin tell me what you found out or not?"

Mary Lou set the steaming plate before him and he fell to. With his mouth full, chewing hard, he mumbled, "I didn't look in her private file."

"What's the matter—lose your nerve?"

Ham clenched his knife and fork. "I don't think so. I simply decided I wasn't going to do that behind her back."

"You know somethin? I had a feelin I wouldn be able to count on you."

"I told you I'd find out whatever I could. Well, I did."

"You did not. All you did was take her word for it that she's fighting for me."

"I went through the office files. I went through every single item, starting with the memo of your phone call to the office from the precinct house when you were booked. As a matter of fact, I still had it in my hand when Margaret walked in."

"You had it in your hand all right." Big Boy leaned on one hip, pulled out an enormous red polka-dot bandanna handkerchief and wiped the sweat from his glistening chin and forehead. "It's a wonder you didn't wave it at her, yoo-hoo, like one of those goddam night-club fairies."

For a moment he was outraged. But the insult was so wild, so far in excess of any imagined grievance, that the only thing you could do was laugh. To his relief—and a little bit to his surprise too, although he figured he knew Big Boy about as well as anybody— Big Boy grinned, slyly at first, then more broadly. "I s'pose you think I'm kiddin."

"You got a mighty big mouth, cousin, that's what I think. Now let me tell you what happened. Margaret swore to me there wasn't another piece of paper about you but what was in the firm's files. She offered me the key to her own file so I could see for myself. What was I supposed to do, make it look like I was calling her bluff, or suspicioning that she was a liar? For Christ sake, Big Boy, I work for her."

"Doesn mean you have to take her part." Big Boy's voice was sullen. But he was sipping quietly at his coffee, and Ham was encouraged to think that he might yet be reasonable about the whole thing. "Got chicory in it," Big Boy said, holding up his mug of coffee. "Onliest place in town you can be sure of getting chicory in your coffee."

"I'm not taking one person's part against another. I don't want you to get clipped with a felonious assault rap. I'd serve the time myself if it'd get you off the hook. And it isn't just that I owe it to you on account of all you did for me when I was a kid."

"Then what is it?"

"It's because what you're doing is more important than what I'm doing."

"You talk one way, you act another. I get the feelin you're lookin down your nose at me."

"What would you like me to do, get down and kiss your ass?"

Again Big Boy grinned. But coldly this time. "I don b'lieve you ever got over that stretch you did in the Navy. War's over, boy. Done been over better part of three years already."

"I don't hear you kicking about what I've been doing in the AVC or the Labor Vets. You don't complain when I invite you out to the university."

"Talk's cheap. Action is my religion. You know somethin? I think you're ashamed of me for bustin that scab, for tippin over that car back in forty-six."

"That's not true."

"An I'll tell you somethin else. I think you still blame me for dumpin your ass in the Navy." Big Boy bit down hard on a cruller.

So it still sat on his conscience, after all this time. "Not only don't I still blame you, I never did. If you don't believe me, all I can tell you is that the Navy turned me around. It jarred me loose from my old ideas. Besides, if I hadn't been eligible for the GI Bill, I never would have had the chance to go to college."

"Then you might as well thank me for it."

"Boy, are you something!"

"I ain afraid of takin responsibility for your goin in the Navy. I din cross the street an say, he's yours, you can have him. Maybe you figure I threw you to the dogs because I was pissed off at you. I was dealin then, like always. You know what that means? I was fightin grievances for at least a couple hundred men. Sometimes I had to give up on one guy's beef if I was gonna get somethin for forty-five other guys. That's the way it goes. That's what they call the facts of life."

"What you're doing, even when you put it the best way, is making a virtue out of necessity."

"I'm talkin facts, you're talkin college talk. Say it in English."

"I mean you're arguing that just because you had to do something, it was good. How about the times you had to do something when you knew it was wrong? Didn't you say to yourself, maybe I have to do it, but it's no damn good?"

"I din say—"

"That's one reason why I didn't come back to the mill after the war, aside from the fact that I wanted to go to school. I didn't want to get mixed up in your kind of horse trading, selling off one guy's beef in order to get a better shake for some other guys."

"Now you soun like a preacher," Big Boy said bitterly. "You don get your hands dirty at that college, do you? Who you think stans between those sweatin black men an all the miseries?" He beat his plaid-covered chest with his huge fist. "Me, that's who. An it was me that stood up for you when you was workin."

"I know that."

"What I believe, there's always got to be somebody willin to take on the boss. Onliest way you can get the men to follow you is to be ready to lead them. Sometimes you got to sacrifice one in order to save the others. But you're too good for that, right? Well, you go ahead an be a preacher or a librarian—just don stick your nose up at the leaders of the working class."

Maybe Big Boy was pompous. Nevertheless he had the capacity to make you feel ashamed of yourself, to play on your innermost uncertainties. "I'm not criticizing you for doing what you figure you've got to do. All I say is, I see the world differently from you. I couldn't do what you do."

But he seemed doomed to be misunderstood by this aggressive, brooding, prickly man. "You couldn a tipped that scab's car, is what you mean. It's too goddam bad if that makes you sick to your stomach. If you got no solidarity you got no nothin. You think different, up at the college? Then go peddle your pacifist bullshit to the white boys. You ain ever goin sell that to black workers, sonny. Not to men who been beaten an kicked an smelled their own daddies' skin fryin."

A thought struck him. "We don't know our own history. Let me read you something." He delved into his bookbag and came out with the volume he'd been studying. "It's called *The Conscientious Objector in America.*"

"Who write that?" Big Boy demanded suspiciously.

"Norman Thomas, after the first war."

"You think I'm goin hold still for that right-wing crap?"

"Come on, don't talk like a Stalinist. Just listen for a minute."

Big Boy drank from the mug and looked at him coldly over the fine thread of steam.

He cleared his throat. "The humor and persistence of the Negro objectors stands out in their comrades' memory. At Camp Upton a devoutly religious colored brother was interviewed by a number of psychiatrists who tried to combat his conviction against war. The argument ran somewhat thus: Major Rossanoff—'Collier, were you ever tempted by the devil?' Collier—'Yes, sah, just like you all is temptin me now.' Another Negro used to walk up to the officers one after the other, put his arm familiarly on their shoulders and say: 'Now look here, brother, how do you suppose the good Lord Jesus feels when he sees you gettin' ready to fight with yo' brothers? Repent, brother, repent, before it's too late.' One of the objectors adds: 'He was so sincere and pleasant that he used to get everybody's goat.'"

"Where did it get him?"

"Who?"

"That black brother. For all I know he's still sittin in jail. Did he turn anybody aroun?"

"Don't you see what I'm trying to tell you?"

"That you got a new hero. Well, those pacifists ain no heroes of mine. Ain goin keep me out of jail. Ain goin keep my enemies from bustin me." Determinedly, Big Boy bent over his cruller, his massive jaws grinding.

Ham sighed and began to gather his things together. He had studying to do. It was no longer possible to talk with the very people who had first opened his eyes. Neither Margaret Zivic nor Big Boy wanted to be disturbed in their own certainties, even when it was a matter of his confronting them not with new answers, but only with new questions.

Suddenly the announcer broke into the sugar-sweet music that had been coming from the table radio on Mary Lou's pie shelf. "Detroit," he pronounced in a voice of doom, as if the place were Golgotha or Gehenna. "UAW President Walter Reuther has just been shot by an unknown assailant. The labor leader, who had been standing in the kitchen of his home, received a shotgun blast at the hands of the would-be assassin. It is speculated that the shooting may have resulted from union rivalries, Communist infiltration, or gangland efforts to maintain profitable control over in-plant gambling."

Ham looked up, the roof of his mouth dry, his tongue metallic. Big Boy was staring at him with a kind of cold pride. "Pacifism, huh?" he said. "Maybe you better tell it to Walter. It sure could comfort him now, couldn't it?" Chewing coolly, he stared him down; and Ham, feeling not so much disturbed as frozen behind a wall of ice, isolated from the world of passion and retribution, pain and punishment, arose and left the older man to his bitter satisfaction.

5. FRED

Small as Martha's Vineyard was, Fred and Sheila might have spent their entire two weeks on the island without running into the Millers if not for Fernanda, who liked to stare at the Indians of Gay Head, but was afraid of the surf. Sheila, who had grown up on Bondi Beach, suggested that they take Fernie to the quiet waters of Tisbury Pond.

There they found Norm and Vera, also intent on teaching Marlen to swim. It was going to be easier for Marlen than for Fernie: poised and self-confident, he was well-coordinated like his father. Norm still looked like a beach god—brown, hard-bellied, fit, tough as when he had been a combat infantryman. He was as fanatical as ever about keeping in shape, and determined to see that his son took after him.

Norm made Fred all too aware of his own pale-pink skin and the little pot he had developed; but he seemed more interested in talking than in teasing.

"We're running away from my father," he explained. "When I got back from my last freelance writing job, he wanted us to be his guests at Grossinger's. He's afraid of islands. Who goes to islands, he says? So I figure we're safe here."

"My parents are still not up to posh hotels. Fortunately they see Fernie as often as they like, so I'm not under any pressure."

"Lucky man. But then you always were lucky, weren't you?"

Fred glanced at him uncomfortably, but Norm's smile was almost benevolent; and Vera betrayed nothing. Norm went on, "My old man has been on an emotional binge ever since May. I'm supposed to dance the hora with him to celebrate the birth of Israel. And why don't I write about it instead of doing articles about unimportant things like the United Auto Workers? I tell him nobody asked me to, but he can't believe that."

Sheila was trying hard with Vera, but finding it difficult to penetrate her reserve. The children got on well together, though, and they agreed to meet there again; they shared a baby-sitter for a trip to the movies in Edgartown; and when it turned out that they were leaving the island on the same day, he urged Norm and Vera to take the same ferry. "I do have a station wagon," he pointed out, "and there'll be room for both kids, so why not drive to Boston with us?"

Norm accepted amiably. His increasing success apparently had smoothed out some of his prickliness. He was vociferous as ever about his independent radicalism, which had in it an element of fanatic self-absorption like his determination to keep his football player's frame in the trim that it had been at twenty; but he seemed to have given up measuring people for traitor's togas and dunce caps.

He insisted on their playing several singles sets at the Chilmark Tennis Club when he surely knew beforehand that he would win so easily as to make it rather dull; on the other hand, he was curious in a nice way, not condescending or superior, about the academic life and the business of popular education through the mass media.

It was a profound relief to be able to talk about matters which were not only beyond Sheila, but sometimes tricky to take up with colleagues who had not been in the radical movement themselves or who looked upon his involvement with radio as at best a spooky aberration, like fox-hunting or collecting old comic books, and at worst, evidence of intellectual incapacity.

"You know," he said to Norm, "the movement made us a present that we can't get rid of—a way of looking at the world that's our own, and that's not easily shed in favor of some newer fashion. I've drifted away from them as you have, but just the same—"

"Are you sure you didn't drift away because you didn't want to be labeled as a red? Or some kind of a nut?"

"I wouldn't like that, why should I lie? But I honestly don't think that was in front of my mind. All I'm saying now is what I couldn't explain to many others—that I do feel different for having been involved, even though it wasn't for terribly long."

"Grateful, maybe?" Norm glanced up from the racquet which he had been fixing in its press. He tightened the screws and said deliberately, "My trouble is that the Party isn't radical enough for me. They're too narrow. I spent some days with my brother-in-law Bill, researching my UAW article, and he never once threw up to me that I've dropped out and taken Vera with me, so to speak. But his life is bound by his shop, his local, his union, and everything else matters only if it relates in some way to his narrow interests. I'm not saying he doesn't care about Israel, say, or the bomb, but he doesn't have anything valuable to *say* about them. And the same holds true for the whole branch. Last spring, Sy and Bernie led a picket line in front of the British consulate to protest Palestine policy. They drew in all sorts of middle-class types, they got publicity. But what's innovative about that? What's radical? And what's it got to do with what goes on in Washington or London or Jerusalem?"

"Maybe we're asking too much of them."

"Nothing I wouldn't ask of myself. New times, new politics. The big trouble with the New Party is it isn't new enough."

"What is?"

"There you have me. One thing is sure, it isn't the Progressive Party. They're a bunch of rubes, stage-managed by the Communists. It's pathetic, and yet Wallace is a kind of inspirational figure. I've seen the poor guy at 3 A.M. stretched out on an airport bench to catch a half hour's sleep between planes. Even if he knows he's being used, in his heart he still feels innocent."

"To me the whole thing is dismal."

"Politics is dismal. So's being a college professor, isn't it? Otherwise why would you knock yourself out with your radio show? You want to touch a lot of people. Don't knock Henry for trying to do that too. It's what you touch them for that matters."

He felt uneasy all over again. Always he had the feeling that people like Norm, no matter how polite, teetered on the verge of scorn.

"There's going to be a big Wallace rally in Boston tomorrow night," Norm said. "You want to take a look, come on along with me."

In the end, after they had driven from Woods Hole to Boston together, men in front, women behind, children playing in the back among the valises and souvenirs, he wound up doing just that.

He hadn't intended to. Sheila wanted to get to New York City,

where he had network business before driving Fernanda home to
Bea, but Norm posed it as a kind of challenge: I listen to your
silly radio show, I look in on your world, now look in on mine.

Well, maybe it wasn't quite like that, since he was tolerably aware
of what the Wallace backers were up to; but it was different, seeing
the show with Norm, almost through his eyes, with the aid of press
passes. Before, he had considered the campaign as an outsider,
and one peculiarly influenced (as he had explained to Norm) by
his earlier political commitment. The commitment no longer held
him, but the attitude persisted, he could feel it in his bones as he
and Norm pushed through the milling crowd: a suspicious mistrust
of Stalinism in any incarnation, a fear of being taken in by sharp
operators with ulterior motives.

Norm felt all this too, and yet he had managed to surpass it. He
was amused, fascinated, saddened—and as Fred gazed about him
at the withered old couples, at the transfigured, once more hopeful
middle-aging radicals lifted out of themselves for at least an evening,
and at the chanting kids, he too sensed the pathos of the occasion,
of these collective hopes for a smoothed-out world that they would
never be permitted to realize.

"You know what's wrong with these types?" Norm demanded
with a certain brutality. "They're losers, and they don't even know
it."

"Isn't that what defines a loser, a lack of self-awareness?"

"They're aware that Henry isn't going to get elected, but they
haven't got a clue as to why the Progressives have no future."

"What makes you so sure they don't?"

"November is going to be a disaster for them. Who'll be going
for Henry and that idiot guitar player from Idaho? The Jews? Not
with Truman rushing to recognize Israel. The Negroes? Not with
FDR still alive in their memories. The trade unionists? Certainly
not the UAW—I've just written an article on those boys. And not
even the Communist-controlled CIO outfits. The Communists' big
weakness in the labor movement has always been that they could
control from the top but not from the bottom. They can't make the
ranks vote right. If John L. Lewis couldn't make the ranks vote his
way back in 1940, why should the Communists be able to now?"

On the platform just above them mikes were being set up, en-
tertainers and program managers were huddling in last-minute con-
ferences. Suddenly his heart skipped. He grasped Norm's forearm.

"Look at that man carrying chairs up there. The one with the narrow eyes and the cigarette hanging out of his mouth."

"Kind of familiar, isn't he?" Norm was grinning.

"Am I crazy? He looks exactly like that guy that drifted into the Buffalo branch not long before we went into the service. Small, that was his name, Small, the hillbilly with the two women."

"You're not crazy. There he is."

"It can't be."

"It is. I've seen him at a couple of other Wallace rallies, and his wives too, Babe and Mildred. If we hunt around, we'll spot them in the crowd, eating peanuts together. They're very big on peanuts."

"Quit clowning, Norm. How could anyone in our movement have turned to this kind of outfit? If we got nothing else out of it, we learned not to trust—"

"We, we." Norm's tone was almost scornful. "Don't equate me with Small. He wasn't in the movement to learn. He was in it to get something. Whatever it was, we couldn't offer it to him. This kind of half-ass desperation circus is just right for him and his guitar and his wives."

Small, with his selfish grin and calculating eyes, stood before him as a kind of reproach for his own wasted hours and misdirected loyalties. If he had been depressed before, squeezing his way through the last-ditch crowd, he now felt despairing.

"Don't look so down in the mouth. That guy wasn't in the movement for the reasons we were. And he isn't in this because Wallace loves peace, or because he's got illusions about Russia. Don't you see, it's something to give him the illusion that he's alive."

"That may be true, but I don't want to spend the evening looking at him."

Norm shrugged. "We'll leave early. If you saw half the things I do in my business, Small would bother you a lot less . . ."

Even if it had a kernel of truth, this journalist's tough talk was hardly worthy of Norm. Who didn't think that he really saw the world in his business? More or less the same brag was standard among cab drivers, doctors, waitresses, bartenders. The difference, of course, was that Norm knew how to organize his experience and set it down so that it made life coherent. Nonetheless, when it came time for them to part Fred no longer felt defensive. What I am doing, he thought as they said goodbye, has as much social utility as what he is doing; what I am going to do I don't have to apologize for.

What he was going to do, he had made up his mind, was to explore further certain advances that had been made to him in New York.

When they got to the city and checked in to a motor hotel Sheila, not without making a moue, took Fernanda to the Central Park Zoo while he hurried on to the appointment for which he was already overdue. At the network offices he found the two producers whom he already knew were waiting for him. They hailed a cab for a five-minute ride to the expense account restaurant on 56th Street where an ad agency man, tall, tanned, and somberly enthusiastic (like a mortician, Fred thought, selling expensive caskets), awaited them at the bar, glass in hand.

"I'm one ahead," he announced. "Order up. Thirsty conversation lies ahead."

They had three screwdrivers apiece, and when the captain led them to their table, one more with their steak sandwiches.

"Howsa steak?" the second producer demanded. He was small, compact, eager to be taken for an intellectual. "Rare enough?"

"I can't taste it after all the booze. I've been living a clean dry life on Martha's Vineyard."

"Then you're in shape for high level conversation. Fred, may I call you professor?"

"You're picking up the check."

"Professor, now is the time to get in on the ground floor, if I may coin the expression, of a brand new medium. Not everyone in radio will be able to cross into the promised land. Romantic tenors like Dennis Day will fall by the wayside. One thinks of John Gilbert. Sad. You however are not dependent solely on your baritone, or even on your good looks. You have a treasurehouse up here." He tapped his skull. "You follow?"

"Is intellect going to be a prerequisite? I don't have exactly that impression from the wrestling shows I've seen on barroom television."

The second producer leaned forward and tapped on Fred's plate with the tines of his fork. "You have touched on the crux of the matter, perhaps inadvertently. TV wrestling is on the ropes." Smiling at his own wit, he demanded rhetorically, "What looms over the horizon?"

The agency man cracked his knuckles. His hands were very dark and elegant below the starched French cuffs. "We have visions," he said.

What they were planning was an entire series of programs, so many that his head, already expanded by the liquor, began to buzz alarmingly. After awhile what they had in mind for him, Professor Frederic Byrd, fell into place inevitably, almost soothingly, as part of a grand scheme, a rainbow of programs appealing to every aspect of the American taste. His would be on the upper arch, and would draw to it, by the force of his personality and the substantial following he had already attracted, a great new audience. His was not only an opportunity (to reach uncounted millions, to be compensated with unheard of sums), but, when you stopped to think of it, an obligation.

"You must understand, however," said the first producer, "that the production of television programs is vastly more complicated than radio, particularly one-man shows or panel shows. Radio can be piped from anywhere. Television . . ."

"Wait a minute," Fred said. "Let's, let's hold it a minute. I have obligations at the university. I can't just—"

"There are airplanes," the ad agency man said hollowly, as if they were flying coffins. "New York is reachable from Detroit."

"Every week?"

"Oftener if need be."

He felt at once exhilarated and dismayed. "But I'm not a traveling salesman."

"How about a salesman of ideas?"

"That's not exactly the way they define me in Ann Arbor." But, he thought, how do they? How will they? "And I'm not sure that they . . ."

"It may be," the first producer observed, his mouth full of steak, "that you'll want to consider a major shift. There are worse places to live than New York."

When he laughed, it sounded shrill in his own ears. "You're not seriously suggesting that I pull up stakes for something like a thirteen-week contract."

"We have much bigger things in mind than thirteen weeks. And besides, professor, Michigan may be a great university, but there are others, aren't there? Closer to here? No one is urging you to leave the teaching profession."

It was a question that revolved in his mind as he moved somewhat unsteadily through the warm September sunshine to pick up Sheila and his daughter. Sheila had been rather bored, it was plain, but she revived.

"Good Lord," she said, "you smell as though you've been boozing it up."

"I have. But with good reason. Big things are afoot."

But when he spoke of certain contingencies Sheila stiffened. If he had wanted to be cruel, he could have observed that her uneasiness only showed that she was caught between greed and insecurity. But that was unfair; he himself was uncertain about what to do next, how to manage things; and he had only to recall Bea's recoil from anything non-academic to be reminded of how women seemed at bottom creatures of habit and routine, more eager to be secure than to challenge the unknown.

When he suggested, though, that she stay on in New York for two or three days while he drove Fernanda to Buffalo, she was overjoyed.

"It's not that I don't want to see your parents."

"Of course. They'll understand. Why shouldn't you have a little vacation on your own? You can fly out to Ann Arbor—it's reachable from here—and have the house fixed up by the time I get home. If you have a roast in the oven I won't object."

"Actually I think it might be just the thing for you and Fernanda to be alone for a bit."

But in the event, Fernanda, a docile if somewhat spoiled child, spent most of her time on the day-long ride either twisting the radio dial or dozing with her head in his lap and a lollipop dangling from her lax fingers. When he delivered her to her mother she seemed not only happy to be home but glad that the vacation with daddy was over.

"She'll be more than ready for school tomorrow," Bea assured him after she had put her to bed. She was being very decent, trying to distract him from the possible hurt of Fernanda's having gone off to bed with scarcely a thank you for the weeks on the Vineyard and in New York. "She's simply exhausted—summers are too long for kids—they need the discipline of school."

"Me too."

She glanced at him casually. "You like Ann Arbor, don't you?"

"Well, I'm not married to it." He could have bitten off his tongue, but it was too late.

Bea's face grew a bit more pinched. Two vertical lines seemed to be descending from the sides of her nose. He could not remember their being there before. "Does that mean," she asked, "that you haven't got tenure yet? Or shouldn't I ask? I don't mean to be nosy."

"Oh that's all right," he said. "I'm up for reappointment this winter, and that'll be it. And there's a television possibility . . ."

"That's wonderful! Nothing like getting in on the ground floor."

He looked across at her over the rim of his coffee cup to see if she were up to her old tricks. But no, she appeared honestly pleased.

"We'll see," he said. "I'll keep in touch. Anyway I'll be in town for a while visiting with the folks, before I drive on out to Ann Arbor. You don't mind if I look in on Fernie after you've got her settled in school, will you?"

"Just give us a ring beforehand."

"I was thinking . . ." actually it hadn't entered his mind until this minute, ". . . she might like to see those Indian dioramas at the museum."

"I'm sure she would."

"Don't say anything to her until I've phoned, all right?"

"Of course."

"I never even asked you if you enjoyed the freedom from motherhood while she was away."

"I went to New York, got an air-conditioned room, slept late every morning, saw some shows, did whatever I felt like."

To his genuine regret, he discovered that the thought of her familiar if already half-forgotten body at someone else's disposal, sprawled naked across a hotel room bed, did not give him so much as a twinge. She could arouse his ugly passions, it seemed, only on those rare occasions when they quarreled over Fernanda.

"I'm glad," he said to her. "I enjoyed having Fernie. She's easy to be with. And thanks for the coffee."

He was tired, but his parents were still waiting up for him. He drove automatically from his former apartment to his former home. Since his last visit, the neighborhood had gone downhill some more. It wasn't just that Negro families had moved onto the block. Half the lawns had gone to weeds, and the others were overgrown, uncut and uncared for. The houses behind them were flaked, checked and peeling, their porches sagging like jowls on the faces of the old and weary. Rubbish lay uncollected in the gutter, papers blew along the walk. He went up the steps.

Without knocking, he pushed open the door with his overnight bag. Beyond the hallway, in the living room, he could see his parents in the pool of light cast by the floor lamp. His mother lay on the sofa, his father sat beside her in the matching club chair, sharply illuminated as if on stage. Motionless in the shade, he was as remote from them as a single spectator in a darkened theatre.

The console radio was tuned to the news, something about Truman and Dewey. His father listened, his balding head cocked, the *Evening News* folded lengthwise, neglected, in his lap. His mother lay with two cushions under her head and the embroidered sewing basket—he remembered it from the earliest days of his childhood, playing trains while she darned—beside her on the carpet. She looked like some cumbrous object dumped on the already sagging sofa. He stepped forward.

His mother struggled upwards, his father peered into the darkness over the top of his glasses.

"Hi," he said, "it's me."

At first glance his mother appeared unchanged, while his father, as if moved by some contrary principle, had shrunk down into himself. "Welcome home, Fred," he said. "We weren't sure just when you'd be getting in."

"I had to tuck Fernie in. Don't get up, mother." He hastened to her side and bent over for the maternal embrace. He was going to add some jocular remark when he suddenly realized that she was enfeebled, and sick. Turning, he saw with a thrill of terror that behind the heavy glasses, his father's eyes were glittering in the lamplight like a cornered animal's.

"I'm sure you'll want a cup of tea," his father said. "Come on in the kitchen with me while I put up the kettle."

"What is it?" he asked, as soon as they were out of his mother's earshot. "What is it? Mother looks heavier than ever. But—"

"She has an enlarged spleen."

"Is that bad?"

"It's . . . not good."

"The spleen can be removed, can't it? I've heard of people getting along without their spleens."

His father smiled sorrowfully; it was not clear whether he was reacting to his son's ignorance or to his wife's illness. "The inflammation is symptomatic. The trouble isn't in the spleen. The spleen is a lymphatic gland, right? It serves as a kind of filter; when there's an infection in the bloodstream, it swells. Other glands do too."

"So it's the blood." He was going to say, Can't you do something, but just in time he caught himself. He asked: "What's the treatment?"

"I'm beating around the bush," his father said. "She is suffering from chronic lymphatic leukemia. It's only a matter of how many months she's got left."

"How long have you—"

"Not so long. I kick myself that I didn't spot it earlier, when she first complained. But it wouldn't have done her any good, you see what I mean? I can look after her pretty well, so far."

So far. He gazed at his father, who stood flatfootedly at the stove, waiting with great patience for the water to boil. "Listen," he demanded urgently, "why didn't you at least let me know earlier?"

"What could you have done? I wanted you to have a nice quiet holiday with Fernie. That was more important."

"Well, you're very . . ." Very what? Thoughtful, or kind, or sweet? He simply could not go on. He turned away blindly from his father, who began to measure out water and tea meticulously, just as he used to compound his own prescriptions in his office.

Now that he knew, he could not pick up his bag and go. He had intended to stay on for one night, perhaps two, but the days stretched out and he could not bring himself to turn his back. The scene—he thought of this place from time to time not as the home of his childhood, but rather as the stage setting of a miserable naturalistic drama—had a kind of awful fascination. Even if his mother had not been hopelessly ill, it would have been far more difficult to tear himself away than it had ever been.

The most obvious reason for this, as he had to confess to Irwin, was that he did want to flee, that he hated it here for every possible reason, and that in consequence he felt himself guilty of a certain treason to the parents who had always been good to him, and could think of no other way to punish himself but to stay on, lingeringly, as his mother persisted in staying on.

"Frankly," Irwin remarked, "I can't see it. You help nobody by sticking around. Sooner or later you'll have to . . ."

To what? Not just to leave, but to make decisions about his future, one in which his parents would have no place. What lay before his father was not just more of the genteel poverty to which he had grown so used that he seemed to enjoy it, but loneliness as well. No more Polish hams, no more pails of soapy water on the steps, no more darned socks in the drawer. The contrast between Dr. Metzger on the way up and Dr. Vogel on the way down was all the more painful because he could not speak of it to either man; and because Irwin seemed to have made his peace with his wife while Dr. Vogel, who had always lived at peace with his, could not come to terms with losing her.

So he shuttled from his house to Irwin's, from dark to light, pulled now in one direction, then in another. If his father was not to blame for being a failure, it was hardly Irwin's fault that he was doing so well, with a new speciality that he found engrossing and a new home that his wife was furiously decorating. And a son who filled him with pride and wonder.

Certainly, he reflected, if my father has pride in me, it is not unalloyed; after two marriages and a series of accommodations, including giving up his name, I am nothing for him to wonder or marvel at.

Grinding his teeth, he fled his swollen mother, beached on the couch like a stranded whale washed up against its will (soon, soon she would begin to shrink and shrivel), and went out with his father making calls. He had not accompanied his father on his rounds for many years. What came back to him as he made conversation while they drove, and tried to focus on the new Hutchinson biography of Henry Vaughan while his father went off with his little black satchel, was the earliest days, sitting on his father's lap and helping him steer.

"Do you remember," he asked his father, "when I was a little kid how I'd have to go when mother and I waited for you? And she'd lift up the carpeting and take out the piece of floorboard that covered the battery, and let me pee down onto the street?"

"Maybe you didn't learn to like medicine, but you learned patience, sitting out in the cold."

He saw himself as another person, lost and gone now, a little boy in a lumberjacket and scarf, sheepskin mittens and buckle-up galoshes, corduroy knickers and knee-length woolen stockings, stomping his feet on the floorboards, scratching on the icy windows of the Chevy, hugging himself to keep warm. What had happened to that boy? For his father such a question would have seemed foolish—he sat beside him now, and that was all.

Dr. Vogel moved more slowly, his step was less springy, but he lifted his bag out of the back seat with the same automatic gesture that he had made twenty years earlier, he drove to the same neighborhoods, more rundown and seedy now than they had been in the nineteen twenties, he clumped up and down the steps on the same errands and with the same bagful of remedies. For him it was all one experience, a seamless whole.

Maybe this was best, maybe it would protect him for the transition to a solitary old age, but for himself it was unutterably painful. Casting about for excuses to get away for an hour or two, he remembered that he had promised to deliver the carbon of Norm's UAW article to his brother-in-law.

Bill Zivic was in the rather bleak office of the local of which he had been elected president the year before. He rose from behind the desk at which he had been seated, a smile creasing his ordinarily owlish face. "This is an honor, Fred," he said in the Ohio twang that he would never lose.

"Well, that's a little extreme. I'm just an errand boy for Norm." He passed over the manila envelope.

"Oh boy, I look forward to reading this. He wrote that he was done but I don't know what his specific approach is. We had some long sessions while Margaret was playing with Marlen—she's really crazy about that kid. Norm wanted to join me here, just to get an idea of the mechanics of running a local. He's very conscientious, sat here next to me for two days, watching while I answered mail, made calls, met with the grievance committee, saw stewards, argued with management. You know, the whole thing."

"Did you argue politics?"

Bill shrugged. "We're a family. We try to steer clear of personal bickering. At least Norm has kept a radical perspective. Look at how he gives me this carbon for my opinion." He smiled proudly. "Maybe he won't agree with my criticisms, but he'll take them into account."

"But tell me, how long can you carry on as the leader of five thousand men who don't follow your politics?"

Bill looked unhappy. "Not long. I knew that when I ran and

the caucus knew where I stood. I'm not desperate for this job, not to the point of compromising my principles."

"You mean you'd go back to work in the shop? You really would?"

"I may have to. I'll go wherever I can be most effective."

In anyone else's mouth the words would have sounded stilted. But coming from Bill, in his dry matter-of-fact tone, they were touching.

Behind him the long venetian blind had been raised some inches to permit the late summer sun to play on the sill, on which stood, oddly out of place in the barren, dusty, paper-stacked union office, a group of cactuses in glazed pots. Apparently Bill noticed that his gaze had strayed, for he half-swivelled about and picked up two of the plants. "You like these? This here is a Christmas cactus, Zygocactus is the real name for it. And this other one, the pincushion, is a Mammillaria. I like the Latin names better myself."

"When did you get them?"

"One of our shop committeemen has a beautiful collection. We were over at his house one night, and when Margaret and I saw some of them flowering, we decided that was for us. We've got about a dozen better ones at home. These are just to spruce up the office a little."

Bill went on to explain how gorgeous they were under a magnifying glass, where you could see all sorts of hidden delicacy and orderliness. Finally he put them back reluctantly on the windowsill.

"Norm hinted to me that you served as a go-between for certain private talks between the union leadership and Dworkin." He added quickly, "He thought it wasn't betraying a confidence, since the talks never came to anything and it's all past history now."

"It wouldn't be past history if we'd had the forces." For the first time bitterness crept into Bill's voice. "We've got remarkable people, and the union leadership knows it."

"People like yourself."

"Never mind me. There's Sy. There's Joe, who's working in Buick-Olds-Pontiac, out in Los Angeles. He was elected to the CIO council not long ago. If we had some more, if professionals like Norm hadn't dropped out, we could be the greatest single force in the UAW."

Always if, if, if. Doggedly Bill went on dreaming. But how much longer would Sy and the others stick it out? "What's Joe doing, out in that auto plant?"

"Sy's the one that hears from him. He says Joe's working on the trim line, putting on stop lights."

"Now look. How much longer do you think a sharp guy like Joe is going to go on doing something like that?"

"You sound like Norm all over again. I guess he did a job on you, all right."

What Bill was on the verge of saying was, If all you people hadn't turned away from us after the war . . .

"Never mind Norm," he said. "I don't see how you can deny that Joe has nowhere to go. The Stalinists are very strong in California. Between them and the union bureaucrats, what kind of a chance will he have?"

"If he gets clobbered, we'll all get clobbered." Bill added stubbornly, "We've got roots in the most militant and most democratic union in the country. Dworkin is going on a national tour this fall. When he comes here I can promise you that we'll draw the biggest crowd in our history."

"I wish you luck." No doubt they would have a big crowd—in a political year Dworkin could be reasonably sure of attracting an audience—but then what? Regardless of how the election turned out there was no practical possibility that the New Party could become a force. Good and devoted people it did have, but most of them were concentrated in one industry, and even there they would wind up, in their isolation, turning sourly on people like himself.

"I had a feeling I'd be reproached," he said later to Irwin. "But I guess that's what I get for returning to the scene of my early crimes."

"Bill means well." Irwin added feelingly, "If he had a son he'd be a happier man."

"What makes you so sure?"

"My own experience. But I must admit, I'd like to get away like you did. I never did leave the scene of my crimes, not even during the war. I've always dreamt of going to Europe, like Vito."

"He didn't get all that much out of it."

"He was looking for something else. I'd be satisfied just to look around." Irwin laughed shyly. "Just to *be* there. I've promised Carmie a trip in a few years, when the new practice is running smoothly. I'd love to go to Israel, but Israel doesn't mean all that much to her."

"You'll get there. And with Carmela too."

"And Paul. I wouldn't go anyplace without Paul."

That was their farewell. When he got home to his mother, she told him that Sheila had called, just to have a chat.

"She's very nice," his mother mumbled. "I just can't get used to her accent. But I guess she thinks mine is pretty funny too."

His father took him aside. "I think your wife misses you."

"That's good news."

"Don't joke. She didn't say so, I say so. It's time for you to go. You can't accomplish anything here. You've got responsibilities, you've got to prepare your lectures—"

"I did that first thing this summer."

"And your radio program?" His father held up his hand to ward off protestations. "Never mind. Go. You've got your life to lead. I'll keep you posted."

In the end he did what he might have done some days earlier. He said goodbye to Fernanda, no longer so eager to see him now that she was involved with school, and he set off for the drive across Canada to Windsor and Detroit.

Arrived in Ann Arbor, he drove straight out Washtenaw to their house without stopping off at his office. He was greeted by Sheila with a kiss and a message.

"Watson wants to see you. He asked for you to call him as soon as you got settled."

"What does getting settled mean? Does it include getting laid?"

She gave him a little push. "You know Watson. Give him a ring."

"Later." But he was in no mood to pursue her, not after these last days, and Sheila too seemed to sense that his physical presence did not mean that he had really come back to her.

"Go on, get along," she said. "You might as well get it over with."

"The story of my life." But he rang up his department chairman at home, no answer, and then at his office, where his secretary said that he could probably be found at the coffee shop across from Angell Hall, or else at the Michigan Union, downstairs.

He drove back downtown and found the graying Watson, who always combined gravity and cheeriness, as if he were a small-town lawyer with a new client, sipping coffee. He was sitting alone at a small table, and gestured to him to draw up a chair.

They spoke of the election campaign, then of the offer to undertake a new television series.

"I'm glad you told me of that," the chairman said. "As you know, Fred, you're due to be notified of your status here by Christmas."

"That's the system."

"Under ordinary circumstances, I wouldn't have spoken before then, and before final consultations, but I thought it only fair to give you an extra few months' notice, and in fact to let you know at the earliest possible moment." He laughed uneasily. "If you were just an average academic I suppose you'd look on me as a bringer of sad tidings. But with your television opportunity, I don't imagine you'll be too surprised to learn that the decision has been not to grant you tenure. Next year will be the terminal year of your appointment. Between you and me, if you do want to leave earlier, I think it could be arranged. There wouldn't be any hard feelings."

He felt the blood rising to his face. "What about me? What about hard feelings on my part?"

"I'm awfully sorry, if you take it personally. I've enjoyed having you here."

"Aren't you going to tell me what I did wrong? Did I screw somebody's wife? Was I a lousy teacher?"

"Not at all. But classroom proficiency isn't everything, you know. My colleagues insist on other guidelines . . . work within one's field . . . publication . . ."

He shoved back his chair. "It boils down to jealousy."

"That's possible. It's always possible, when a man gets the attention you've been receiving. But"—Watson glanced up, his eyes suddenly cold—"it's also possible, isn't it, that your colleagues wouldn't want to do what you're doing, that they see it as demeaning and unworthy of a scholar?"

"I'm not a scholar. I'm an educator."

"Maybe we'd better leave it at that. I do wish you all the best of luck. But somehow I don't feel you're going to need it."

"Thank you." He added bitterly, "Now at least I know what I have to do. And what I ought to do."

"Well, it's best that way, isn't it? Not to be encumbered by compunctions?"

With the chairman's words ringing in his ears, he walked out blindly, thinking only of how he would explain it all to Sheila. Suddenly he wanted her very badly, he wanted to pull off her clothes and screw her on the bedspread, in the sunlight. After that he would be able to explain everything.

6. SY

Standing near the open grave of Maurice Metzger, one hand clutching at the borrowed yarmulka which kept slipping off the back of his head, Sy glanced beyond the chanting rabbi to his cousin Irwin, who teetered, eyes closed, before the raw wound in the earth, wife on his right, son on his left. Bernie had offered to take care of Paul for the day, but Irwin had refused almost curtly. "Paul is almost seven," he had said. "There's no reason why he shouldn't be at his grandfather's funeral."

There were reasons, of course; but his cousin could be stubborn about the boy. His own two, Joey and little Serena, were digging happily in the sandpile behind the apartment house while Bernie figured their future on the clipboard in her lap. Sy wondered how much Paul could understand of all this. The fact of death? Maybe, but surely not the confused mixture of guilt, relief, remorse surging through his father's mind. Or the purgative quality of the three ceremonials—the stifled greetings and farewells in the wildly artificial funeral parlor, whispering of walnut, velvet, and unburied bodies, the lugubrious procession through city and country in which passersby measured the unknown deceased's status by the number and vintage of the automobiles in the parade, and this final leavetaking over the gaping grave, ancient as the shawled and hatted people who *davened* jerkily from the waist over the gaping grave.

It was disquieting to look at the boy. He clutched his father's limply hanging hand, his large soft eyes fixed wide open on the incomprehensible rabbi, then on the hole in the ground and the box in which his grandpa lay, neatly folded like a present ready to be given to God. He did not look once at his mother, grimly elegant in a little black dress one size too small, black hose and pumps, and a tiny pillbox hat with net veil that halted just beneath her own huge dark eyes. She looked Semitic, like a member of the family, but restless, her fingers drumming against the patent-leather purse that she clasped in her free hand. With the other she allowed herself to be held by her husband.

Incredibly, two tears formed at the outer corners of Irwin's eyes and coursed slowly down his glistening, freshly shaved cheekbones. Irwin released his hold on his wife and child and groped for his breastpocket handkerchief. The rabbi concluded the insistent, almost bewitching prayer for the dead, earth rattled on the grave everything was finished.

Why was Irwin crying? Sy dug about for reasons while the grave-diggers spaded shovelfuls of earth onto Maurice Metzger. True, Irwin had not despised his father as Sy still despised his, half-senile but still possessed by love—dated as a silent screen romance —for a stainless Soviet Union. But the elder Metzger had been dominated by his petty shrewish wife, and with a view of life bounded by the plateglass windows of his men's furnishing store and its incoming customers. Self-satisfied and vain, unaware of his own limitations, he had attempted to shrink his little grandson's self-esteem as he had damaged his son's. What was there to weep over? The reluctance with which he had quitted a world which never acknowledged his existence with anything more than a nod? The will, in which he had left both vulgar advice and common stock to a son already well-fixed in both departments?

It was Irwin himself who provided the answer. As he waved Sy into the first limousine, insisting that he accompany him and Car-mela and Paul back to town, he said, wonderingly, "I may as well admit it, I was crying for myself." He drew Sy aside so that the boy would not overhear. "All of a sudden, during the *kaddish,* it hit me: Irwin, you're an orphan." He giggled. "I mean, it's ridiculous, isn't it? I'm thirty-six years old, I'm losing my hair, and all I could think was, Irwin, you're an orphan."

Sitting on the jump seat with the unsmiling little boy, in front of Irwin and Carmela, Sy made the decision to go to California to see his father. Even as he tried unsuccessfully to interest the somber child beside him in the homely details of passing traffic, he knew that he was going to have to make the trip. Alone. Without the children or Bernice.

Their big voyage lay ahead, but in the other direction. Like two exhausted explorers who stare at each other one day, lost and freezing, stopped in their tracks, entranced and released by the realization that they cannot go on, he and Bernice had finally agreed that they were at the end of the road on which they had set out from Lower Manhattan nearly a decade earlier.

Once they had decided that this city and the political camp which they had staked out in it held nothing more for them, the next step—however ill-considered and even wild it would seem to others —was inevitable. It was a matter of saving, at least until they had enough for their fares, the hard-earned money they had so prodigally contributed to the movement.

Israel was after all, at least in the kibbutzim, as hospitable to frustrated but unrepentant socialists as any other place; his trade of sheet metal worker would likely be as useful as Bernie's adolescent experience on her uncle's Lakewood chicken farm. And the time to move the children was now. Bernie threw herself into the planning with the same passion she had given to the movement. She went to the library, she wrote away for information, she began to teach herself basic Hebrew.

Irwin was happy to share his little Hebrew with them. He had been troubled, he admitted, by their increasing isolation. "Boy, if I had the nerve," he cried, "I'd go with you! I'm not that much older than you guys, it would be the greatest thing for Paul, it would be the making of him."

Carmela in a kibbutz? That was too funny. But they were touched none the less. Whatever his reasons, Irwin was practically the only one to approve.

The others conceded that things had been going downhill ever since the Wallace fiasco, and that the working class was not immune to the rising anti-Communist fever. But they could not see any sense in what Bill called "running off to the end of the earth." He was perhaps the most outspoken. His resentment was really the expression of a hurt at being left in a foundering craft.

"I had the feeling years ago," he said, biting into an apple with his little feral teeth, then staring into it as if it might disclose certain secrets about human behavior, "that one day you'd pull out. Like Norm and Harry and all the rest."

"Not like Harry," Bernie replied gently. "We're not leaving to get rich, or because people have been complaining about us to the district attorney."

"So you're leaving because the odds are against us. But the ball game isn't over, not by a long shot. And you'll never know, out there in the middle of noplace. I could see it, if you were dropping out because you wanted to make it in the middle-class. But Christ, to stick yourselves and your kids on some rockpile with a bunch of religious fanatics . . . I just can't see doing it to the kids, that's all."

"Do you think this is such a wonderful atmosphere for kids? Don't you think they'd be better off growing up on a collective farm?"

Bill shook his head. He was baffled by the phenomenon of Zionism. He had no trace or taint of anti-Semitism; in fact, he had never been able to understand what all the fuss was about, on one side or on the other. The sick notion of Jews as exploiting parasites was ludicrous to him, a transparent capitalist dodge, especially since so many of his comrades were Jews. So was the parallel absurdity that radicalism was the creation and property of Jews, when his own father and grandfather had been soaked in a tradition of mountaineers' rebelliousness. But the Zionist response to racism was no more reasonable to him than were any of the other nationalist delusions that he had been taught in his Marxist study groups to regard as simply expressions of frustration and impotence.

And didn't Norm have essentially the same reaction?

Joe Link was a bit more guarded. "I suspected this was going to happen," he wrote from California. He added ambiguously, "I didn't think you'd travel so far, though."

"I think he might have been more blunt," Bernie observed with a touch of maliciousness, "if it wasn't that we named Joey for him."

Somewhere deep within her she had been shocked by Sy's insistence on this—it violated the canon that the child should be named after a deceased member of the family. It seemed to have awakened in her too a suspicion of Joe as a rival. Ever since, she had regarded him with a certain odd mistrust.

"After all," he said defensively, "I did recruit Joe."

"Can't he let you forget it? We're in for a long period of reaction. In a way we predicted it, we said it would happen if there wouldn't be a labor party. It's nothing to take any satisfaction in, but on the other hand, why be ashamed?"

"I'm not ashamed. But people like Joe are going to have to suffer for it."

That had closed the discussion, for the time; but now that he had decided to go to California before leaving the country, he was excited to think that he would be seeing not only his father, but Joe also; at the same time he wondered guiltily if he were not using his father as an excuse for this. Bernie would not say it, but she too would have to wonder.

She did say, when he broached it to her after the funeral, "Couldn't you talk to your father on the phone?"

"One of these days," he said, with what he feared sounded like a crazy levity, "I'm going to be an orphan, like Irwin."

"Very funny. And I won't?"

"You'll see your family in New York before we sail."

Bernie was fighting to contain herself. "You want to spend hundreds and hundreds of dollars to see two people who despise you?"

She had never concealed her relief that Sid, settled down in San Francisco and married at last, had taken the old man along with him. No matter how logical this had been, Sy could not rid himself of the guilty feeling that it simply added one more to his brother's list of grievances.

"I want to go to say goodbye," he said stubbornly. "It's important to me."

Stonily restrained, she desisted from reminding him that they had been desperately saving for the big move, economizing in petty and exhausting ways. She herself had even begun to take in neighbors' children to look after with her own, baby-sitting for a price while he continued to work these last weeks, up until the very last minute before leaving, at a stultifying job.

He was fabricating brake linings in a shop that was very small compared to the aircraft factories where he had worked during the war years. Now that he was committed to leaving he had given up the horseplay that you had to indulge in to be accepted, in order to establish a foothold in the union. He had gained such a foothold, of sorts, but it had led only to compulsory participation in countless dull meetings and a suspicion on the part of his shopmates that he was a pushy Jewboy.

So now he delivered himself over (as many of them did, after

all) to fantasy. The strangest part was that the planned voyage to
Israel was growing so matter of fact that it was entering the realm
of practical possibility, like a vacation or a new job; while the un-
planned trip across the country, unencumbered by family, baggage,
or even expectations, was by contrast so impractical, so rebellious,
that it came to serve as an excuse for daydreaming, like Joe's old
letters to him from the Fiji Islands.

And why not, he demanded of himself furiously, wiping his oily
hands on his stained work apron; why shouldn't he have the chance,
just once, to go off on his own? The more he was met by Bernie's
grim silence, the more determined he became. If she was going to
look on his trip as akin to sleeping with another woman, then she'd
damn well get what she was looking for.

I'll take a few bucks out of the bank, he thought, just enough
to hit the road, and I won't even draw a line on the map to show
where I'm going, I'll just go.

But one evening, after she had put the kids to bed and was
bowed with needle and thread over a pair of Joey's torn pajamas
(they were hand me downs from Paul, all of whose clothes were
saved for Joey), Bernie said quietly, "You're really bent on going
out there, aren't you?"

Struck dumb, he could only nod.

"Why couldn't you drive one of those new cars to the Coast?
They're always advertising for bonded drivers. They even pay for
your gas and oil."

"How will I get back?" A stupid question, but how else could he
respond?

"You'll probably go down to visit Joe and Anne, won't you? As
long as you're there?" she asked coolly.

"Well, I . . . I might as well."

"Then Joe will find a way for you to get back. He must know
people who drive East. In any case I think you ought to go. You
deserve a vacation."

"I'll have one on the ship," he mumbled.

"With the children? No, you should go. And I shouldn't have
made that crack about your father and your brother."

"Oh, they're . . ." he wanted to say, They're just an excuse, but
she knew that. The words stuck in his throat. He passed his hand
through the air between them, arose, and kissed her on the back

of the neck, where she had gathered up her hair and piled it loosely on the top of her head.

She murmured absently, "I'm going to have to cut my hair before we leave. You might as well get used to the idea."

It was that simple. He hitchhiked to Detroit in one ride, and before the day was out made arrangements for the car. With a zipper handbag and the money Bernie had withdrawn from their savings account in his wallet, he settled down behind the wheel, driving a new car for the first time in his life, and headed west.

It was not real until he had crossed the Mississippi into Davenport, Iowa. Then suddenly the country exploded for him. It was not merely a country, it was a world, lost and unknown to him and to all those who drudged every day at their workbenches with milky strips of glass tubing serving for daylight and gaping metal ducts serving for fresh air, with parking lots for landscape and traffic lines for marking the passage of time. Alone on the endless ribbon, he rolled on and on through the endless cornfields, exultantly. "I'm free!"

No one had told him truly how huge, how enormous, the land really was. He had read Wolfe in college, but those rhapsodies had been far more exotic to him than the burning arguments about the Chinese question, Kronstad, Vienna 1934. It was frightening to think how their lives had been forced and bent by arguments treating this country as a series of problems that could be resolved in New York, Detroit, Washington.

Now he knew what he had barely suspected as a youthful hitchhiker. It made him uneasy, fearful almost, that it would go on forever and he would never reach California, much less make his way back to his wife and children.

At Iowa City he paused to take on supplies: gas, oil, water, bologna, mustard, bread, Drake's Cakes, and his first hitchhiker, a long-necked college student en route from the university to Des Moines for an aunt's funeral.

"How did she die?"

"Carelessness. My uncle was running a thresher and she drove out with his lunch because he didn't want to take time off to eat. He's a fanatic. She got too close to the machine and whomp, it chewed her up."

"That's terrible."

"Those things happen." His bony fingers drummed on his jutting kneecaps, his white wrists protruded like great knobby celery hearts. After a while he said thoughtfully, "She was a little queer, was what my father always said about her."

"How do you mean?"

"She used to go all the way to Chicago to see a play. Sometimes an opera. There wasn't a damn thing my uncle could do. It was her farm and her land. Her money, you might say."

After about ten miles Sy asked, "What are you going to do when you graduate? What are you studying?"

"Wholesaling." All conversational possibilities now exhausted, he demanded, "Mind if I turn on the radio?"

A blast of country music filled the car, interrupted only by the commercials of men's furnishing shops and feed warehouses, all the way to the outskirts of Des Moines, where his passenger roused himself and disembarked.

"Have a good time at the funeral."

Unsmiling, the student waved him on his way. Forgetting for another ten miles to turn off the radio, he pressed on toward Nebraska in a sea of noise. When night fell he pulled over to the side of the road, loosened his belt buckle and dozed off, his fitful sleep punctuated by the whoosh of the semis and the high steady whine of their multiple tandem tires burning down the arrow-straight road at a steady sixty miles an hour.

At dawn he struggled erect. An amiable truckdriver, high in the cab of his lordly vehicle, raised an arm in salute, and he came awake in Nebraska. With the motor idling, he peed on the lee side of the Plymouth, then eased himself back onto Route 6 and headed onward.

It was full daylight when he pulled up at an all night truckers' stop on the edge of Fairmont. While the attendant changed the oil, he took his zipper bag into the men's room, changed his shorts and socks, brushed his teeth, and shaved. Then he drove slowly up the yawning boulevard, wide enough for triumphal processionals of chariots, elephants, and massed ranks of captives, but empty as the plains on either side of it, until he found an open grocery store among the row of shuttered stores. The farmer's widow who stood behind the counter, her hand self-consciously hovering over her goitre, explained that she was plain used to getting up early. Deliberately she placed the container of rich milk, the pasty bread and brilliant orange cheese, and the box of Oreos in a paper bag.

She counted out the change into his hand coin by coin, prolonging
the encounter until he felt guilty at sidling out of her store. "Have
a good trip!" she called after him.

In the great treacherous stillness of the undulating wheatfields,
he sat enclosed, virtually alone on this black line bisecting the sea
of grain. He felt annihilated, deprived of his faculties by what
sprung up all about him, for as far as his eye could see, without
pause or surcease.

When he came to Minden he was almost weak with relief at the
sight of two teenage girls, standing at the traffic light with a traveling
bag between them, their thumbs outstretched. He leaned over and
pushed open the door on their side.

"Hi," he said. "If you put the bag in the back you can both sit
up front."

"Okay," said the more forward of the two. "Come on," she nudged
the other, who seemed to be hanging back, "pass it in. Man," she
laughed, squeezing in beside him, "it's a lucky thing you came along.
Folks were beginning to stare at us cross-eyed."

"You come from Minden?"

She shook her head vigorously, as though he had blundered.
"Oh no! We're both from Holstein. It's only a few miles down the
road, south of here. You wouldn't know it," she added, "unless you
lived around here. Most everybody there knows Alice and me,
and I'll just bet that they were saying, There go the wild McConnell
girls. But I don't see why we should buy bus tickets if we can travel
for nothing," she laughed. "Do you?"

"Depends on where you're going."

"Up to Elsie."

"Where's she?"

The girl turned her impudent face to him. "Elsie's a town, where
my sister lives, up near Madrid. And if you don't know where
Madrid is, you can let us off at Imperial, and we can make it up
from Route 6 without much trouble. Imperial's over near the Colorado line."

"I'm glad it's not over the line," he remarked. Bill had kidded him
about not transporting young girls across state boundaries, "You
kids look young enough to get me in trouble."

"And you look old enough to make trouble," the stocky girl retorted. Perhaps fearing she had offended, she added reassuringly,
"Don't worry, we can take care of ourselves."

"I'm sure you can," he said lamely. How long was it since anyone had talked to him like this? Forever. "What's your name?" he asked.

"Scottie. What's yours?"

"Seymour. People call me Sy."

"Then I will too. I bet you thought Alice and me were sisters. Well, we're not, we're cousins, but we live together and everybody takes us for sisters. Boy, this is some sharp car." She leaned over to peer at the odometer, and her plump breast pressed against his elbow. "Gee, it's practically brand new."

"It is new. I'm driving it out to the Coast."

"To California?"

"Los Angeles, by way of San Francisco."

"How's about taking us along?"

Her silent cousin, the prettier one, emitted a sudden giggle. "Scottie, you're crazy."

"Alice is right. What would your sister say, up in Elsie?"

"Oh, we could write to her. Or send her a telegram." Scottie tapped his knee with her pink-painted fingernails. "She'd be just as glad."

"Well, I doubt if I'd be. I don't remember inviting you."

"You asked us in. You wouldn't throw us out, would you?"

As Scottie's archness increased, so did her cousin's hilarity; each egged the other on. Was this what he had missed as an undergraduate, marrying his first girl? Their chatter was so inane, their flirtatiousness so secondhand, derived from Ann Sheridan movies and cheap paperbacks, that he was embarrassed by his own complicity and his inability to remind them that he was twice their age and beyond their badinage. The things that single men had to put up with in order not to have to sleep alone!

And yet the pressure of Scottie's thigh against his own, all the way from hip to knee, was neither funny nor childish. As she kidded him, she increased the pressure, presumably to give her cousin a bit more room. The heat of her flesh was a potent reminder of the solitary state in which he had been making his way across the United States. He pressed down harder on the accelerator.

"Wowie!" Scottie cried, her pressure relentless. "Look at us go, Alice! Sy, you're a regular cowboy. How fast do you think we can go?"

"Not too fast." He raised his foot a trifle. He itched to wipe his perspiring neck, but feared ridicule. "This car isn't fully broken in yet."

"Neither are we."

Alice leaned across Scottie, wedging her even more tightly against him. "Say, how about you, are you married?"

"Why should you—"

"He hasn't got a ring on." They both shrieked at this, apparently sharing an obscure joke. "You *look* married. Don't married men wear rings back East?"

"Not always."

"That proves what my sister says."

"What does your sister say?"

"That married men are the worst kind. Do you think that's true?"

"I haven't the faintest idea." He added severely, "Don't you kids realize you could get in trouble, horsing around like this?"

This only provoked them both to new outbursts of hilarity. Hoping to shut off further conversation, he turned on the radio to a guitar-playing yodeler. At once both girls broke into song, swaying to the beat; Scottie tapped out time against his kneecap, and he clenched the steering wheel tight, perspiring freely as he breathed in the odor of their mingled body scents. When he came to the signs announcing the fraternal orders' weekly luncheon meetings in Imperial, he wanted to shout Hallelujah.

"I guess you girls want off at the junction."

"Last chance, Sy! When I think of the lonesome traveling salesmen that would jump at our offer . . ."

"I'm not a traveling salesman."

"Well, what are you? Would a normal guy turn down a special two for one gift offer?"

Their laughter was taunting, but when he stopped the car, they shook hands with him demurely, and as they backed out onto the sidewalk with the valise their parting was small-town and schoolgirlish. "Goodbye, and thanks!" they cried. "Thanks a million!"

He was laughing when he crossed over into Colorado, but somewhat ruefully: Maybe this was what they meant when they said traveling was broadening; but he was unsure that Bernie would laugh too. Then he gained the foothills of the Rockies, the scene exploded for him, and from that moment on he was a captive of the landscape, so staggered by it that he was freed from the guilt of unwritten letters.

He reached San Francisco exhausted, during rush hour, after the hardest driving he had ever done in his life. Staring hopelessly at the strung-out lines of one-way traffic, all of it seemingly traveling in the wrong direction, he finally extricated himself, found a side street and a bar, and telephoned his brother to ask for directions to his house in Mill Valley.

Sid was brusque and commanding as ever, ordering him to take pencil and paper and write down the exact instructions for after he had crossed over the Golden Gate Bridge.

"How's pa?"

"You'll see."

"Well, I'll be there in an hour or two. I'll have a bite and get washed up first."

"Nonsense. Didn't I always use to buy you dinner, once a year?" Sid demanded gruffly. "The year is more than up, so get your ass on over here."

"Well . . ." He was irresolute. "I hate to barge in . . ."

"Mimi'll be very sore if you don't show up."

He yielded at last, just as he always had, half anxious to be with those he had always known, half reluctant to invite their renewed scorn.

Sid lived on a half-rural, half-shabby lane not far from the towers and traffic of the city, but with the feel of the small town about its unpaved driveways and dead end streets in which kids could still play ball and ride their bikes undisturbed. The houses were extremely modest, some looking as though they had been thrown together by their occupants, others separated by vacant lots in which eucalyptus trees towered, gloomy and dripping. He parked in Sid's driveway behind a beat-up pre-war Pontiac and tapped at the sagging screen door.

A strong-looking, extremely handsome young woman with shell-rim glasses, wearing an apron embroidered Visit The Empire State! held open the screen door and extended her hand.

"I'm Mimi, come on in."

He followed her into the kitchen, past something that was crackling in a frying pan.

"Where's your luggage?"

"I've got a bag in the car. Here's a bottle of wine."

"You shouldn't have bothered."

"It's more for christening your house. From my wife and me."

"Why don't you go on into the living room? Sid's been waiting for you there, with your father. I'll bring your bag in meanwhile, I've got a bed all made up for you."

He had not bargained for this, but after asserting twice that he could not, he did not know how to argue further; and so he went on in to confront his father and his brother, his throat tight as though he were entering a classroom, utterly unprepared, for an examination.

The old man was seated in a creaking rocker, his back to the light. At first it was difficult to make out his features. Then he saw that his father was indeed awake and conscious. The memory of that frozen countenance, with its down-drooping eye and stroke-twisted mouth, had mercifully blurred with the passage of the years. But here it was again, peering at him aslant, as though he were entering the room at an angle and had to be sized up the bias. The old man was hideous, hideous—but amazingly he had not grown any older. All but moribund six years ago, he seemed now to be dying no longer, but instead to be calcifying into some grotesque caricature of old age.

"Hello pa," he said. He cleared his throat. "How do you like California?"

"It's a place." His father made a strange sound, high, congested —a laugh. "Like any other place." Sy was suddenly reminded of Harry Sturm's father, exiled to Buffalo to die in his bachelor son's flat. The old man said thickly, from the side of his mouth, "Sid likes it, I got to like it."

"Pa's a pretty good sport." Sid stepped forward from the mantelpiece where he had been winding a clock. He held out his hand. "Have a good trip?"

"Tiring, but educational."

Sid laughed indulgently. "It's a big country." As he spoke, the light from the half-open window caught the side of his face. He had gotten heavier in the jaw, but in addition he bore a scar, wrinkled and red, that ran from his left temple to the side of his mouth. It looked almost like a birthmark, borne from the womb as a reminder of a heritage of burning and suffering. Sid must have noticed his shocked stare, for he touched his fingertips to the scar briefly. He remarked calmly, "I forgot, you never saw my souvenir. It's been a long time between dinners, hasn't it?"

"I didn't mean to stare."

Sid shrugged. "I'm used to that. Mimi tells me it makes me look rugged."

Sid was sardonic but not exactly mellow. Bulky in his plaid sport shirt and slacks, no longer young, he had the look of a man still struggling against coming to terms with life.

"What did you do," their father was asking in his slurred voice, "you drove out?"

"That's right. I thought I'd come visit you before leaving. Did Sid tell you we're leaving?"

The old man's head wobbled on his neck as though it were suspended on the end of a stick. "You're taking the whole family?"

"The kids are small, we couldn't leave them. Besides"—he hesitated momentarily, then plunged on—"we're going for good."

"What's for good? I give you six months in that desert, you'll be home."

"Maybe. We'll see, pa."

"You got some pictures of the kids?"

He knelt beside the rocker in which his father slumped, blanketed to the toes like a sea-voyager in a deck chair. As he reached for the wallet in his hip pocket, he leaned against the rocker, and the bad smell of the old man stung his nostrils, acrid and sour like ammonia. The good hand emerged from under the blanket, wrinkled and freckled with liver spots. For one shameful moment Sy was afraid that his father was going to reach out for his head, his cheek, or his hand, caress him; and he shrank away. But all the old man wanted was the photos.

"That's Bernie with the children in the yard." He tapped the first photo.

"I can see, I can see. You think I'm blind already? She looks good, your wife—she should have had babies years ago. That's what I tell Sid, he shouldn't wait, he's getting to be an alte cocker. What can I do? He's waiting for me to die."

Behind them Sid said nothing, and did not seem to so much as breathe, but Sy could have sworn that he grew rigid down to his very toes.

"Who's this?" The swollen-jointed index finger wavered over the second picture.

"That's Irwin's boy, Paul, in the middle. We took them to the zoo in Delaware Park—they were leaning over the seal pond."

"Irwin?" The voice was quavering now, like the finger.

"You know, Aunt Sadie's son, the dentist."

"Oh yeah, sure."

Sid bent forward, tapped Sy on the shoulder, and jerked his head slightly toward the front door. He took the pictures from the old man's hand. "Let me give these to Mimi, pa. You take it easy for a while, I want to show Sy around the grounds before it gets dark."

Out on the squatty front porch, with its tipsy glider, tied-up bundles of old newspapers, and sagging screening, Sid said, "That's a nice family you got."

"Thanks."

"The kids look healthy."

"Knock wood, as ma used to say. The little one, Serena, we named after her."

"I figured that. Well, you can see how it is with pa. He's not so very old, you know, compared to the King of Sweden. But it's a little different, being royalty and being a member of the working class."

"Ma always worked a hell of a lot harder than he did. And he's still here and she's not."

"The point is, he's all used up, there's no juice left. He sleeps a lot."

They stepped down onto the scraggly front lawn and began to pace off the small lot. Sy said, "I didn't know how to write to you about pa, Sid. It makes more sense for him to stay with you than with us. You always got along better, politically and in every other way. But it's a lousy miserable burden for you both."

Sid shrugged. "It's one of those things. Can we help it if he's lost his marbles? He's still our father."

"How do you look out for him during the day?"

"Mimi stays home now. She used to work in the shipyards, she was one of the real militants, but he has to have someone here all day. Evenings I'm always here, and she gets out a lot."

"But if you were both working you'd be so much more comfortable."

Sid replied rather sharply, "I'm doing all right on the front as a warehouseman. I'm in the best damn union in the country."

"Just the same, I want to chip in."

"For what, his milk and soda crackers? That's his menu, Nabiscos and graham crackers, soaked in warm milk. He doesn't take up

much space either. So forget it. You worry about your kids and I'll
worry about pa, OK?"

"You make me feel guilty."

Sid showed the old twisted grin. "Maybe that's what I want."

"But your wife . . . Mimi . . . she must think I'm a rat. After all,
she's the one with the biggest burden."

"I'll tell her you said so. Is that what you want, for her to know
that you're sorry about the whole thing?"

"You know what I mean."

"And I know Mimi. She knew the score when she married me. She
was married before—her husband was killed on Iwo Jima, leading
his platoon. He was one of my comrades, just as tough as her in his
own way."

"She didn't need the extra headache of me staying over."

"She wouldn't have it any other way."

When Mimi called them back inside for supper, he said to her,
"I think it's fantastic, what you're doing for my father."

Mimi simply said, "Nonsense," and proceeded to carve the roast,
standing up to brandish the flashing steel blade. "I don't mind in the
least. It's a part of marriage."

Her attitude was admirably free of self-pity or the whining about
degradation and waste that soured the conversation of educated
housewives; still there was something bone-chilling about her matter
of factness.

Her conversation with Sid was very political: union business, neighborhood organizations, the Independent Progressive Party, which
apparently still lingered on in California. Their talk was spiced
with code words: "progressive," "militant," "friend of the Soviet
Union." What had brought them together in the first place had been
their common loyalty to a now-eclipsed faction of the Communist
Party.

They belonged to a society within a society, a little world which
as it shrank forced them closer and closer together. One of the few
avenues left for them to travel on together was Harry Bridges' union,
a haven for men like Sid.

Sheltered and strengthened by a woman who was supremely confident about everything, Sid now began to rail at him, genially but
with some of the old venom.

"I suppose you're going to bring up the children Orthodox once
you have them in the Holy Land."

"Not as orthodox as you, Sid," he replied sharply. "I've never been able to adapt myself to a rigid faith. But I do want my kids to grow up in an atmosphere of fraternity, even if they miss a few of the conveniences."

"It isn't the conveniences they'll miss out on. It's the struggle against fascism. But then I guess you aren't interested in that any more—if you ever were."

Mimi sat very still, the light from the white kitchen globe winking on her eyeglasses, a fixed smile on her clear smooth countenance. Sy said patiently, "I've come a long way to say goodbye, Sid. There's no need for these cracks. Not when you've been asking yourself at least as many questions about your politics as I've been asking myself about mine."

The scar on the left side of his brother's face, which he had been trying all along not to stare at, darkened perceptibly. "You're right," he said. "I'm sorry. Let's drop it."

After dinner they rejoined the old man in the dark and rather bleak living room. The bookcases on either side of the fireplace were lined with the volumes that he remembered from the old days in their bedroom on Senator Street—*Proletarian Literature in the U.S.,* Gorky's *Mother,* Gladkov's *Cement Factory,* Barbusse's *Under Fire,* the *Little Lenin Library,* Plekhanov, three volumes of *Capital,* together with piles of back issues of the *Western Worker,* the *Pilot,* and the *Dispatcher.*

But he was struck anew by the gentleness and patience with which his brother and his wife handled the old man. Opening a card table at his side, they jollied him along, one slipping him cod liver oil while the other helped him with his bowl of milk and crackers. It was so tender that he was plagued with contradictory feelings. What right did he have, he thought, watching Sid trundle pa off to bed in his arms, to look down his nose at him? Had he done any better in the years he had exhausted himself and his wife for an even smaller sect, itself nothing more than a footnote to a footnote?

When Sid returned he said to him abruptly, "Sid, I'm glad I came out. Not just to ease my conscience—I'll always feel guilty about pa—but to have things on a better footing between us. Somehow I felt that it was possible."

"Me too, me too," Sid muttered. He brought out a bottle of Scotch. For the first time, while they drank together, his brother talked with a certain humility of his political life and of the terrible mistake his party had made in expelling his leader and revealing itself as hopelessly tied to the Kremlin. He still spoke with contempt of Sy's friends—but at least he no longer referred to them as fascists. Progress.

In the morning Sy awoke to the dripping of the gloomy eucalyptus. The old man did not recognize him at first. When at last he did, he was confused, and under the impression that they were all on Senator Street, and that Mimi was ma. It was painful. Bag in hand, Sy shifted from one foot to another until at last pa got clear and gave him his withered hand in farewell. His eyes swimming, he quitted his brother's house and drove off.

For a long time he had been looking forward to the spectacular winding road along the Pacific Coast from San Francisco to Los Angeles, but now that he had completed the first part of his mission he was anxious to get rid of the car, and even more anxious to see Joe. Suddenly too he was terribly lonely for Bernice, and eager to be back. So he took the fast straight road south through the interior, expecting nothing but what he found at first: small towns, vegetable farms, desert.

When he stopped not too far south of Stockton for a Coke at a crossroads café, he was astonished to discover that he had fallen into a hillbilly hangout. Surrounded by baying hound-dogs, he glanced around in wonderment at the saturnine tobacco-chewing loungers, lean, gnarled, and drawling, and at their calico wives and barefoot kids. The Mexicans he had half-expected, but these people? Half-deafened by the dogs, he made his way to a tree on which was posted a handbill.

COON DOG FIELD TRIAL. All Special Events Run On Saturday. SPEED RACE—HEAT MONEY—WATER RACE.

"Got a dog, mister?" A long-jawed stump-jumper spat tobacco juice at his feet. He shook his head; the countryman shrugged and turned away. He put the Coke bottle to his lips and read on.

"We have plenty of coon for all special events—Please leave your bottle and fowl language at home—Bring the family and enjoy the race's National rules with few exceptions—Dog must be barking up for tree. Land owners or sponsors not responsible for loss or accident."

I'll be a son of a bitch, he said to himself.

"Gate Donation $1—Children Under 14 Free—All Tracks Layed

So Starter Will Beat Dogs Back to Tree. Also a Coon Dog Field Trial Last Sun. In Each Month. Sponsored by Stockton Houndsmen."

He dropped the empty bottle back into the rack and made his way to the Plymouth. He eased it through the hangers-on and their lolling, colorless hounds, then pressed hard on the accelerator. The further he traveled, the less he knew about his country.

Later it came to him that those people must have been Okies or more likely Arkies, Joads, come out in the thirties in their tin lizzies, bringing with them not just hunger but traditions as exotic as bagpiping or skirling.

It was very late when he arrived in Los Angeles, and made his way to Joe's house on Morton Street, in the Echo Park district. He was exhausted not from the driving alone but from the reunion, but Joe turned him away from all that. "Christ," he said, clasping him by the shoulders with both hard strong hands, "it's been so long. You can't imagine what it means to me, your coming out here."

Joe made it clear that although he had to be at work the next morning, he had no intention of going to sleep before they had talked themselves out. Anne, worn out by the demands of her two tiny boys, had been unable to wait up, but had left sandwiches. Joe set them out on the kitchen table, along with some beer. "I have to tell you. Your pulling out is an awful blow to me."

"You too?"

"You were the one who indoctrinated me with the long view. Never mind that the work of making a revolution might take longer than our own life span." To cover a certain embarrassment Joe bit deeply into the cold chicken sandwich. "You know what I'm talking about," he said, his mouth full. "Now you act as though none of it was true. None of it."

"I could have said the same thing to Norm, when he left. After all, Norm was the one who recruited me. And Harry Sturm——"

"Different types," Joe said in his old decisive way. "Neither of them committed to the long haul. I can't even conceive of Harry working in some of those crummy shops you and I have been stuck in recently. And there's something else about Norm. He got out when our hopes were still high, when we had a cadre in the shops and fresh troops coming back from overseas. But you . . ."

"I know," he said slowly. "I'm just deserting a sinking ship."

"I didn't say that."

"But you imply it. Bernie and I have no fancy excuses. We're just tired."

"And us?"

Maybe it comes down to a difference in our personalities."

"That's all? Nothing else? What about that interpretation of history you used to drum into me?"

"Maybe I just don't believe the workers will turn to us when they see that we've been right and all the others wrong. For one thing, we haven't always been right, not about the war bringing a military dictatorship, or a depression afterward. For another thing, there aren't enough of us. And maybe I am getting impatient, but I just don't think the country is going in our direction."

"One of the things that has sustained me these last couple of years was the idea that you were in the same boat."

"It's been accumulating. It's not something you can write about in letters. I became morally hesitant to involve people who had something to lose. Especially in a cause I was no longer sure I believed in myself."

"You quit believing in socialism."

"No. In sacrificing my family, much less anyone else's, to a shrinking group. Maybe revolutionists shouldn't marry, like priests."

"I'm still making it with Anne," Joe observed belligerently.

For how long? He did not have the heart to ask. Instead he tried to keep the talk on his own plans. "And I'm still a socialist," he said. "In fact, I want to live like one for a while. Not necessarily forever. But long enough to see if it's another way."

Joe did not answer. Finally he said, without looking up, "Well, I'm not quitting. I've signed up for the duration."

Out of politeness, Sy asked tiredly, "How are things with your branch?"

Joe glanced up and grinned his old grin. "Schlecht," he said honestly. "When I got back, toward Christmas of forty-six, they had a store-front office on West Pico, not far from here, in the central core. They were having a spurt when I showed up—you know, the postwar boom. We managed to keep the office going through forty-seven, but by the time of the Wallace campaign we were back to meeting in people's homes. We sat around and looked at each other and agreed that ideas were all we had to peddle."

"And now?"

Joe laughed shortly. "I've been trying to hold the branch together. They're all busy buying tract houses and appliances. The automatic dishwasher is the big thing this season. I can understand it, I'd like to make things easier for Anne. But I can't very well, on sixty-five bucks a week. Meanwhile the literature distribution is falling off. They're starting to say to me, 'Look, Joe, you keep the bundle orders of *New Labor* in your house, not in mine, it makes a mess.' They have the same attitude as my mother—she calls me the snobbish factory worker. I make the comrades uncomfortable—they're getting ahead in the world, and just because I'm not they think I'm looking down my nose at them. At least my mother's got a good excuse," he wound up bitterly. "She never even pretended to be a radical."

Sy could not find it in himself to comment. At length Joe said, "I know what you're thinking: I've just made your case for you. But I don't care how many black years we've got ahead, I'm not giving up. Maybe it is a question of personality."

Sy ate the last of his sandwich. "What about your own work?"

"When I first got here, it was pretty good. I was working nights at B.O.P. in South Gate, which is an enclave of LA, just west of Watts. Maybe you passed the plant on the way up here. The union was run by a right wing-Stalinist coalition. But it wasn't too bad, I survived politically because there was—there still is—a straight trade unionist pro-Reuther element that I fitted into. About five thousand guys worked there, a couple thousand that started at four twelve when I did, and got off just before 1 A.M. Anne didn't mind the hours, she was pregnant for the first time, and excited about it. Another beer?"

Sy was past the point of exhaustion. Drowsily he extended his glass.

"It had its points. I got to work easily, and home in a hurry, down Sunset Boulevard and across on Alameda Street. Fast and straight. And pleasant, not like grinding through ice and sleet. One afternoon I was going down Alameda to work and I saw this little Dago across the way, in Watts, attaching some junk to a rickety old tower that I heard he'd put up himself. Next day I leave home early and turn off to get a better look. I introduce myself, he turns out to be easy to get along with. Name of Simon Rodia. We're pretty good friends now. He's got another tower going up now, some people in the neighborhood say he's nuts, but to me he's just one of those rare people who enjoys what he's doing. People can't stand that, you know—it's like being queer, or communistic, to do what you want instead of what other people want you to do."

"What about the men at the auto plant? You were starting to tell me."

"I think I wrote you, I worked on the trim line. The plant was 50 percent Okie, say 20 percent Negro, most of the rest Mexican-American. I bumped into fellows I went to school with—one of the committeemen used to be on the basketball team with me in high school. A very good-natured bunch, the Mexicans. We'd often trade sandwiches. They knew how to eat—they'd bring burritos in their lunch pails—beef, chili, refried beans, cheese, chorizos. They'd wrap a tortilla around all this stuff and fold it up at the end— man! It was a picnic, they'd bring them in hot towels to keep them warm." Joe shook his head reminiscently. "Let's have some more beer."

"So why did you leave? They elected you a delegate to the State CIO Convention."

"True, but after that it was all downhill. I was boxed in. I refused to hide my party membership. At the time I thought that showed my integrity, but now that I think back, it was just damnfoolishness, given the fact that the Party was so small it was almost invisible. I got crowded from all sides, and I couldn't recruit from among those guys and build even a minimal group to protect myself. I got labeled like old Simon with his towers, you see what I mean? There goes Joe, not a bad guy except that he's got a screw loose. That's the best that was said about me. You can imagine the worst, from the Stalinists and the careerists. So I pulled out, not too long before the election. I smelled that Wallace was going to be shellacked but it wouldn't have made any difference."

"Then what?"

"You know what had to come next, you went through it yourself. Odd jobs. I had to stay working, partly because Anne got pregnant as fast as she could after David was born. I couldn't blame her for wanting to get caught up. I drove a truck for the Teamsters for a while, which I liked. You know how I love being outdoors. But it didn't last, so I bullshit my way into this job I've got now, painting houses."

"Now you're ahead of me."

"Not any more I'm not. You're all caught up. I turn to at eight-thirty, work top speed seven hours a day, half hour for lunch, off at four. The hours are fine, otherwise it's a bitch. I told you how much I make."

Sy propped his cheek on his hand. He felt blurry, wobbly. "What do you paint?"

"Private houses. I work with a partner, an old guy, a fifty-seven-year-old bachelor. A lush, name of Rheingold, like the beer. We use two forty-foot extension ladders, a jack, and a plank that we bring up rung by rung. Hoist up the paint cans with a line and a clothes-hanger hook. The two of us paint and talk. The usual—gash, beer joints, baseball."

"Sounds fascinating."

"Rheingold is pathetic. The work is monotonous, insecure—seven months a year at best. If I stuck at it I'd be an alcoholic too. He kept talking to me about his beautiful girl friend, this fantastic broad, until one night I saw him with her—a dumpy middle-aged woman who runs his boardinghouse . . ."

"Tell me something." He leaned forward, bringing down on the floor the front legs of the metal kitchen chair on which he had been teetering. "What has all this got to do with socialism?"

Joe scowled. His long face, already wrinkled at the corners of the eyes from exposure to the elements, tensed. "This is a bad time," he said. "And I know it's going to get worse. The craving for commodities is bound to increase, like any other appetite, from being fed. But that doesn't mean to me that socialism is dead," he said, looking across the table with a kind of blind stubbornness. "You can't kill idealism with washing machines."

"Maybe not. But in the meantime?"

"I'm not going to stand on that plank with Rheingold for the rest of my life. But I do have to bring in some money—Anne can't give lessons now—while I gather myself together and figure things out. Don't worry, Sy, I've got some ideas. I've still got a connection with the Teamsters from when I was driving that truck. I'm trying to get fixed up through the Teamsters' warehousemen's local with a job in a paint factory. It won't be outside work, but what the hell"—he grinned suddenly—"you can't have everything, can you?"

In the silence that followed the clock in the hall struck four times, and then, startlingly, an infant's voice could be heard through a bedroom door, half a sigh, half a moan.

"Jesus, the kids'll be up in a couple of hours. I'll tell you what. You sleep late, and after work I'll scout around the Teamsters and see if there's anything cooking in the way of rides heading east."

Anne had made up a studio bed for him in the little boys' bedroom. Groping toward it in the dark, Sy stumbled over a terrifying bulky object. It turned out to be a teddy bear. He slipped out of his clothes, stretched out, groggy with fatigue, and knew nothing more until late the next morning, when he was awakened by the homely rumble of a washing machine and the familiar sound of a mother shushing her child.

Her hair falling across her face as she leaned over the sink, Anne laughed as he stumbled into the kitchen. She wiped her hands on her apron and extended them. "You did look a little incongruous, sleeping with a teddy bear."

He followed her about the house as she worked, holding one child, comforting another so that they could talk together.

"You've got it rough now," he said. "Like Bernie. Little money and few satisfactions."

Anne shook her head vehemently. "Not true. I wanted these children desperately."

And you'll want things for them, too, he thought.

"Joe has given me more than I can measure. He's made sacrifices not just for the movement but for me. I can make a few for him." She smiled, and swept her hair out of her face with her long bony fingers. "It won't kill me."

That was the image of her that he conserved all the way back home, and presented to Bernie. "Anne looks tired," he said, "but not tense the way she used to. Even though she's got no time for the piano, she has the record player going while she looks after the kids, Schubert and Beethoven all day long—they'll grow up with it ringing in their ears." He hesitated. "I have a funny feeling that she enjoys the hole Joe is in. It seems to strengthen her to know that she's got three boys to look after."

He had had time to ponder this, bouncing along in the cab of the produce truck from LA over the pass and across the desert to Boulder Dam, and then on across the southwest to Oklahoma and Missouri. From there, after bidding farewell to the saturnine driver, he'd had to buy a Trailways ticket to Buffalo, and as he stared out the tinted window, speckled brown with dried spray, he thought about his friend. Across the aisle a pretty girl in a frock that was too light for the season, her face shaded by an incongruous picture hat that looked out of style, began to weep and then could not stop. Silently she wept, hour after hour, fist clutching a wet ball of handkerchief pressed to her nose. She brushed aside his efforts to enter her life, even to comfort her with a Kleenex, and continued to cry. Why?

"I don't know anything about anybody," he confessed to his wife. "Not the first little thing." It was soothing to admit it, folded in her arms.

"That's not true! You know more about more things than any man I know. You're going to turn Israel upside down, wait till they get a load of you!"

It was Bernie though who turned things upside down in these final days. They could not believe how much they had collected over the years, like pack rats: note pads, scrapbooks, unanswered letters and answered ones from half-forgotten relatives, three by five cards with notations for unwritten articles, baby souvenirs, used-up clothing. He could have mulled over it all for weeks; frightened that he might be losing something precious, he lost himself in indecisive contemplation of memorabilia, ignoring the packing, the children playing at his feet, bills to be paid and farewells to be uttered.

Bernie gathered them together, got them on the train, retrieved the secondhand footlockers and steamer trucks at the pier, herded them onto the ship, pushed through the crowds of travelers and goodbye-sayers, and found them their dark stateroom with its two uppers and two lowers, deep in D deck.

Oblivious, Joey and Serena sat down on the floor beneath the wash basin and began to play train. Train! He felt a wild desire to laugh, but he was afraid that, like the girl on the bus, he would not be able to stop. He asked his wife: "You don't have any aspirin, do you?"

Of course she did, in her raincoat pocket. Now that they had parted from her family, who could not take a holiday from their little shop to see them off, the sudden emptiness was frightening. He dared not look his wife in the eye, he wanted to run away, from this hideous little rat trap, from the kids yelling "tchuk tchuktchuk tchuk kazoom!" From the ship itself.

Someone knocked on the open door. A man in uniform said

stiffly, "You people were supposed to have turned in your passports."

"I told the guy when we came aboard that they're in my wife's purse."

The official turned to Bernie. She shook her head. Her compressed lips were beginning to turn white.

"You'll have to leave the ship with those who are going ashore if your documents aren't in order."

"That's ridiculous. I don't need a passport to leave the United States. We'll find it later, when we unpack."

"Those are my orders. We must have all passports before the ship sails."

The children began to fight. "Cut it out!" Sy yelled. Serena began to cry.

"That won't help." Bernie knelt down to her children.

"What will? Where the hell did you put those things?"

"If you'll give me the keys, I'll open this footlocker. We tagged it Stateroom, so I must have put all the things we'd need aboard ship in it."

"That one has no key. Christ, don't you remember? The kids slammed it shut, the goddam lousy secondhand piece of crap. We decided to break it open later."

The official said, "Listen here," and Bernie began to tear at the rusty footlocker with her bare hands. Now both children were crying. He picked them both up. Everything was working in his throat, he wanted to cry himself.

Bernie had pulled a hairpin from her braid and was picking at the lock with one hand and tugging at it wildly with the other. What are we doing here, he thought, clutching his two little children and staring from the cold bleached countenance of the officer to his frantic wife, her usually composed features distorted with rage, her hair uncoiling where she had pulled out the pins, all of them squeezed in with the tin trains, the toidy seat, the boxes of disposable diapers, the valises, the battered footlocker that Bernie was frantically trying to yank open.

"Jesus, Mary and Joseph," a voice called out from the companionway, "it looks like out of a Marx Brothers movie. Got room for two more?"

He turned with the kids wriggling in his arms to stare at the long, dour, broken-nosed mug in the doorway.

"Vito!" he cried. "For God's sake, Vito!"

"The same." He was carrying a bucket. "Nothing in this except ice. The one behind me has got what goes in it."

"Surprise, my friends, surprise!" Harry Sturm was crowding in behind him. Popping his blue eyes, he raised aloft two bottles of champagne and began to swing them slowly like censers through the stifled air. "I bring a liquid sendoff!"

"Now listen," the officer said. "Now wait a minute."

"Aren't you going to give me a kiss?" Vito demanded of Bernie. "You gonna stay down there on the floor all morning?"

"I'm trying to break open this footlocker," she replied with dangerous calmness. "Our passports are in it."

"Why didn't you say so?" Vito took a bone-handled pocket knife from his trousers and lifted her to her feet. "Let me at it." He inserted the can-opener blade behind the hasp, whacked at it smartly with the horny heel of his powerful hand, then reared back and kicked it hard with the heel of his cowboy boot. With a rusty squeal, it popped.

Bernie flung herself at the open footlocker.

"We seem to have stumbled," Harry said as he twirled the champagne bottles about in the ice bucket, "into a dramatic scene."

"It's not worth explaining." The children had suddenly stopped crying.

"Everything is worth explaining."

Bernie extended the passport case. "Here."

The officer said, "Thank you," and started to back out the door.

"Don't you want a drink, Mac?" Vito asked.

"Thank you, no."

Vito closed the door on him. "The truth is that one of these bottles is Norm's. So's the whole idea. He wanted to drink a toast to you. So did Vera, but she had to get their kid from camp, and Norm left town for some article about the hydrogen bomb. Will we do?"

Harry was pressing Necco wafers and jujubes on the kids, Vito was rinsing the toothbrush glasses, and next thing they knew the first cork went off with a bang, foam flew through the air, the children shrieked with delight, everyone was rushing to drink before it all fizzled away. Bernie sat on the footlocker, hugged by Vito, Harry stretched out full-length on a lower bunk, the kids were on the chair. All that was left for him was the upended waste basket.

Vito was insisting that the whole scene was uncanny, like something he'd lived through on the ship coming back from Paris, Harry was insisting that they should look up a friend of his in Tel Aviv, a manufacturer of menorahs who shared his views on achieving socialism through infiltration and capture of the mass media. "You're making a good move," he shouted, "if you go to learn. If you go simply to till the soil, you'll be bitterly disappointed. You have to look upon it as a stage in your education."

"We do, Harry!" Bernie assured him, laughing. "We do!"

The second bottle began to go. "This is crazy," Sy said, "this is preposterous! Who comes to see us off? This terrific painter that I thought wouldn't even know us any more, and my poor old comrade who must have a million bucks by now in Swiss banks. It's crazy!"

"You're repeating yourself," Vito pointed out, and began to sing. He interrupted himself. "That's opera," he explained. "Grand opera."

"I want you to read this. Promise me." Harry was pressing a folder on Bernie. "An original document on new roads to socialism, written by one of the German comrades."

"I've got no German comrades," Bernie said. "They're all dead. Kids, turn off the faucets before the management complains."

A boy in a white jacket was coming down the aisle tapping on a gong, the ship's whistle was blasting, Vito was dragging Harry out of the stateroom. "They ain't getting me back to Europe again," Vito said. "You can stay if you want, Harry."

But then Harry was gone too, the kids wanted to go out on deck and watch people throwing confetti, the cabin had no porthole, and they were closed in it once again.

Another rap at the door. "Now what did we do?" A young steward was holding out a telegram.

"Who's it from?" Bernie asked. "What does it say?"

He opened it and read aloud, "Pa died last night in his sleep. Best of luck. Sid."

PART FIVE

1. VITO

Vito was hard at work when he heard the knock. It might have been the second or even the third knock, trying to make itself heard over the noise of his radio. The super knew better than to bother him. Then who? With a sigh he dropped his brushes into the mason jar filled with turps and wiped his hands down the front of his jeans.

Not one, but two men stood in his doorway. Youngish, serious, like junior executives in their dark suits and starched white shirts. Even before they had introduced themselves as agents of the Federal Bureau of Investigation he knew what they were after.

"Now look," he said, "I'm right in the middle of my work."

"If you prefer, Mr. Brigante," said the one named Kelly, a snubnosed young man with wavy hair, "you can make an appointment for a meeting in the district office. We're assuming that you wish to cooperate with your government."

"That all depends," he said. "As long as you climbed this far, you might as well come on in. You already interrupted me."

They looked around curiously as he waved them over to the canvas director's chair and the camp stool. He flung himself down on one of the Army cots and waited.

"This is certainly very interesting," Kelly said. "I don't profess to know anything about art, but this is certainly interesting. Mr. Brigante, you were once a cartoonist, weren't you?"

"I used to do a political cartoon for a weekly paper called *New Labor*. Signed Vito, no secret about it, don't tell me you haven't seen some of them. Are you going to tell me it was illegal?"

"*New Labor* was the organ of the New Party, which has been listed by the attorney general's office as a subversive organization."

"You guys can do better than that. That outfit isn't even in business any more."

"The New Party was succeeded after its dissolution"—Kelly consulted his notes—"by the New Socialist League. The personnel and the publications have remained the same, and it too has been placed on the list."

"That's tough. But I haven't had anything to do with them for a long time. I get the impression they're just a talking society now, and I'm too busy doing what you see here. It takes up all my time."

"I'm sure it does. No one would question that, Mr. Brigante. But when it comes to subversion and to conspiracy, sometimes seemingly minor facts can be useful. Now while you may have severed your connections with the New Party group, you did maintain contacts with certain individuals, so whatever you can—"

"Like who? What individuals?"

"A Miss Sandra Leibowitz, to name one."

"She used to be my girl, but that was years ago, back in the forties. I heard she married an accountant, then I lost track. Anyway we didn't use to talk politics. That was a nice healthy girl, about as subversive as J. Edgar Hoover. Who else have you got on your little list?"

"These things may seem amusing to you. But information available to the authorities puts things in a different light. Would you care to tell us what you know of the business operations of your dealer?"

"Who, Lorch?"

"You wouldn't say that you're unaware of his background."

"He used to be a functionary in the New Party. Everybody knows that—that's how I met him. But he only came after me when he was ready to quit politics and open a gallery. As far as his opinions nowadays, I haven't got any idea. From what I can see, he's all caught up in the art world."

"And what about his relationship with Harry Sturm?"

"Now wait a minute," he said. "Once you start in with questions like that, you can leave me out. That's snoop stuff. You can go to their accountants or subpoena their books. I never asked either of them, but even if I had, I wouldn't tell you."

This made Kelly's junior partner blink. "Mr. Brigante, the New

Party and its propaganda organs weren't your first involvement in subversive movements, were they?"

He got up off the cot. "Are you asking me or threatening me?"

"It's our responsibility to determine whether you wish to cooperate with a federal agency."

"Depends on what you're after. If you want to find out about me and my beliefs, such as they are, I'll tell you anything you want to know. But when you ask me about other people I want to know whether you're really after spies or whether you're just fishing around for dirt. Where'd you get your legal training?"

A bit taken aback, the young man put his hand to the knot of his tie. But he answered readily: "Fordham Law."

"How about you, Mr. Kelly?"

Kelly smiled politely. "Georgetown. Now may we—"

"When you were kids playing stickball in The Bronx, I was working as an assistant on a WPA mural for a post office. I never joined the Communists but I worked with them, I did posters for the New Theater League and for the Unemployed Councils, stuff like that."

"Would you care to tell us about some of the people you worked with?"

"I certainly would not. You guys have got the advantage on me. I don't know my rights, but I do know I'm not going to name people I knew fifteen, twenty years ago. How do I know what they're doing now?"

"Why not let us worry about that?"

"Why should I? It's my conscience, Kelly, not yours. And if you keep after me I'm going out and hire myself a lawyer so I can talk to you on equal terms."

"There's no need for that at the moment. Your cooperation is entirely voluntary."

"Yeah sure. Until I get called up before some committee. Then what's voluntary?"

"That's not within our province."

"Neither are my former friends. Or even my former enemies. You get the point?"

When they had left he could not get back to work. No more today. He stripped off his blue jeans, put on a pair of slacks, and nosed around among the bills, clippings, and gallery notices scattered over his paint table until he found the letter from Margaret

Zivic. He stuffed it in the pocket of his corduroy jacket, slammed the door behind him, and clattered down the stairs to the street.

Better not phone from Colletta's. Turning up the collar of his sport jacket, he continued on up the street to the cigar store. In a booth he pulled out Margaret's letter and read off her office number to the operator. "And make it collect."

In a minute Margaret herself was at the other end of the line. "Vito, how are you?"

"Mad at myself. I'm sorry about making this collect, but I'm in a Schulte's and I wanted to get you in a hurry without finding out how much change I'd need."

"You mean a big shot artist like you still hasn't got a telephone?"

"That's why I'm a big shot. Listen, I put off answering your letter because I was working so hard. But that's a crummy excuse, like telling myself that I wouldn't be of any use to a kid like Ham Wright. If you still want me to testify for him—if it's not too late —I'll come up."

"Great. Can you possibly make it tomorrow?"

"Why not?"

"Harry Sturm is flying up then to testify too. You might be able to travel with him."

"Harry? You're kidding."

"Life is full of surprises. I've been trying to line up all the support for Ham I could, people like Norm and Fred. But Norm is overseas on an assignment, or he's have come through, of course. And I got a turn-down from Fred."

"I'll be a son of a bitch."

"You won't need to be prepared, not to be a character witness. Vito, if you're definite, I'll schedule you as a witness for tomorrow."

"It's definite all right. Where should I meet you?"

"I'd gladly come out to the airport to pick you up, but I'm going to be terribly busy. Would you come straight up to the Federal Building, you remember where it is, Ellicott Square."

"Sure."

"Harry will give you the details, what floor we'll be on, and all the rest of it."

Happy was happy to see him. In recent months he had not been around his offices much, to say nothing of the Lorch Gallery next door. There was talk that he was becoming interested in the theatre, more as a backer than a participant. He had a hard sincere smile now, and a firm manly handclasp.

"Since we met on the pier to see the Glantzman family off," Harry said sorrowfully, "I bet I can count on the fingers of one hand the number of times we've met, in the last couple of years."

"Not my fault. I try to keep up with you in Leonard Lyons."

Harry's smile broadened. "Don't try to pretend that *you're* not successful. I read about you too. You're getting some fancy prices nowadays—and your overhead is lower than mine."

"Well, maybe, but I haven't got any idea how you're making all that dough."

"You think I understand what you're doing? I look at those paintings and I say to myself, Well, at least they're enormous, there's value for the investment."

Vito couldn't keep from laughing. "You're more honest than most. I was surprised when Margaret Zivic told me you're going up to Buffalo to testify for Ham Wright."

Harry glanced up innocently. "Why shouldn't I?"

That made him a little uncomfortable. "Seems to me the D.A. was after you at the end of the war."

Harry waved his hands. "Trumped up, the whole thing. The case was nolle prossed. Do you think Margaret would have invited me if she didn't think I'd make an eminently respectable witness?"

"Supposing it comes out about you once upon a time being the New Party organizer there?"

"Don't you think I have principles?" Harry was indignant. "I can't just think of myself. If I can do that boy any good, it's worth taking a chance."

"I have to admit, I wasn't going to do anything about it until I got a visit from the FBI this afternoon. They tried to pump me about Lewis and you, among other things. It pissed me off, so I called Margaret and told her I'd go up tomorrow."

"Good man. Stout fellow."

"Don't you want to know what I told them about you?"

"Not particularly. For one thing, you don't know all that much about me. But maybe you should tell Lewis—he scares more easily than I do."

Nervy little bastard. "I intend to," he said. "It's one reason I came uptown."

"Now I'll tell my secretary to get us two seats on the 8 A.M.

flight. And I'll pick you up at your studio at a quarter to seven. Don't say no."

But if Harry took him aback, Lorch positively threw him. "Why Vito," he said, as he sipped his tea reflectively in his cozy office behind the gallery, "I'm only surprised that they've never called on you before. They may not be the brightest people, but they're extremely thorough."

"They asked me about you."

"Cross filing. I've already had a number of fairly lengthy sessions at the district office. There's nothing more they can possibly learn about me—they were simply trying my name for size."

Vito stared at his dealer. "You mean you talked?"

"Didn't you?"

"I threw the bastards out, after a while."

"They'll put it down to artistic temperament. But I'm a businessman—I can hardly go in for such luxuries as intransigence. Besides, they're not much interested in the likes of us, except insofar as we can help to identify clandestine Stalinists."

"Why should I help them? Most of the Communists I knew in the old days were plain stupid. That's no crime. Anyway, chasing spies is the cops' job, not mine."

"But they've suddenly discovered, Vito, that we can be useful. Not only have we got memories for little matters like betrayals, we're gifted with more sensitive nostrils than they. We can smell the real thing a mile off. These days that can be useful."

"What's so special about these days? Why is everybody so Goddamn scared?"

Lorch poured himself some more tea. "If we didn't have the bomb, it would be held alone by the greatest tyrant in history. How long do you think we'd last?"

"How the hell should I know? If you know so much, why are they running around and picking on people who never were Communists?"

"I think that's been exaggerated. No one has been threatening me."

"They didn't have to. You talked without it."

Lorch had the grace to flush, though ever so slightly. "So you didn't. But they didn't threaten you, did they? I gather that they put on their hats and walked out of your studio as quietly as they came."

"We'll see. Besides, I'm not the average guy. I've got no family, I don't give a shit."

"No one is stopping anyone from behaving exactly as you did. I do think all this talk about a climate of fear is grossly exaggerated."

"As long as you're talking about that, I want to tell you something else." Lorch's imperturbability was beginning to get on his nerves. "Margaret Zivic has asked me to come testify at a hearing for Hamilton Wright. He was one of Big Boy's crowd out at Bethlehem Steel, when he was still just a kid."

"I recall."

"He was in the branch before he went into the Navy. He went to the University on the GI Bill when the war was over. He left the movement and became a librarian, but he got canned. They claim he concealed past membership in a subversive organization."

"That's too bad."

He stood up. "You guys sat here in New York and indoctrinated people like Ham. Then when they get in trouble for peddling your papers all you can say is, That's too bad."

"They were peddling your cartoons too, Vito."

"Why do you think I'm going up to Buffalo?"

"If you can help, I think that's fine. But I haven't been asked, I suppose because I could testify neither as a spokesman for the movement or a friend of the boy."

"Two minutes ago you were talking about exaggerations and Communist spies. You think I'm exaggerating about Ham? You think he was a Communist spy?"

"Hardly. But he is getting a hearing, isn't he? It's not as if he were being shipped off to Siberia."

"Why bring up Siberia? Will that feed a guy that you and I helped to recruit? Or pay his legal bills?"

"I'm not sure just why you're so outraged by one unfortunate incident. Do you honestly think it demonstrates the country is going fascist?"

"I didn't say anything about fascism. I'm talking about responsibility. I want a check from you that I can take up there with me."

"I can't remember when I've been solicited so graciously." Lorch took a three-tier checkbook from a side drawer and managed to smile as he glanced up. "How much would you suggest?"

"That's between you and your conscience."

"I don't suppose your conscience will rebel if I make it out to Cash?"

"As long as it doesn't bounce, Lewis, as long as it doesn't bounce." He took the check from his dealer's outstretched hand and stuffed it into his pocket without glancing at it. "I don't suppose your conscience wants a receipt."

"Not from you, Vito, not from you," Lorch imitated his tone. "Berner was very disappointed that you didn't come to his opening. Did you look at his work as you came in?"

"I tried not to."

"Oh come on." Lorch arose and tried to ease him into the central room where the long slablike Berners hung from their hooks like bloodless, bleached-out sides of beef.

He twisted free. He said fiercely, "I don't have to like everybody that you show. Some I do, some I don't. But Berner says nothing to me. He's making decorations for rich farts on Central Park West so they can brag about how they had to hoist his pictures in through the terrace, like their Steinway Grands. If that's painting, I hate painting."

Lorch puckered his lips as if to whistle, then shrugged. "No one asks you to admire all of my artists. But I do like to think that they're esthetically compatible. And after all, those rich farts, as you so elegantly characterize them, are buying your outsize paintings too."

"This year."

"Let's hope next year too. Which reminds me, speaking of collectors, I trust you haven't forgotten that Willis Cohen is expecting us for dinner. I'm going to have to leave shortly to dress."

"Well, I'm not changing."

Lorch shrugged. "I imagine Susan Cohen is used to your corduroys. They live at the Carlyle, in case you're trying to put that out of your mind too, and we're supposed to be there at seven-thirty. So you do have time to buy a shirt if you don't own another one, and if you'll excuse me—"

"I'll go like I am. In the meantime I think I'll drop in on Beverly."

Beverly was one of the better young painters, which was not surprising, since Vito had taught her practically everything she knew. What was more, she was tall, good-looking, and expert in bed. But all she knew about politics was names, like ballplayers or movie stars: Truman, Dewey, Impelliteri; and when he walked into her studio and started trying to explain why he wouldn't be able to see her tomorrow, as they had planned, her reaction set his teeth on edge.

"You're going up to Buffalo with this crazy tycoon," she demanded, "just to testify for some colored librarian you hardly ever knew?"

"You make me sound like a horse's ass."

"That's the last thing in the world I'd want to do," she laughed. Actually she seemed to want to do it a little too often for his comfort, particularly now that her work was beginning to get some attention. "But it does seem to me that for someone who resents interruptions, you go out of your way to find them. I know it'll make you feel virtuous, but wouldn't it be more sensible to feel guilty and get on with your work?"

"Oh, shove it," he said rudely. He was begining to realize something that she didn't—that maybe it was time for their goodbyes to be permanent instead of provisional.

Susan Cohen was something else. She was a willowy blonde with a gentile maiden name and a degree from Bennington: the Winslows had money and she had married buckets more. Willis Cohen was an amiable real estate man who flew around the country building shopping centers, but it was his wife who had the taste and the collector's ambitions. Vito had a hunch that she would have liked to lay him, except that her husband kept coming home; but maybe it was just her way of assuring him that she liked him not just as a painter. It was entirely possible that she and Willis joked about it—and about the painters they had to dinner—late at night when they had kicked off their shoes and were sprawled out on the couch, chewing over the artists whose work—none of it more than two years old—lined the walls of their duplex.

It was one thing to be hung there; but in order to have made it you have to have nibbled at the lobster tails and squab at one of Willis and Susan's little dinners for ten. I am too old to be flattered, Vito told himself; but he did not honestly mind sitting on Susan's right and having her press his knee from time to time.

The other guests were creeps. A bald businessman in a boiled shirt with a squiggly vein in his temple and a pouting wife with blue hair and fat hands were too much like the squabs that they picked at. The others were younger but not better, noisy namedroppers who chatted through drinks and dinner about Bernstein and Thomson, Tennessee Williams and Arthur Miller. Their chatter was as obscure to him as the inadequately lit paintings behind them. Why did rich people buy paintings and then let them hang in the dark—were they afraid of being thought ostentatious?

He was on the point of asking Willis Cohen how he could ever expect people to see what was in his painting, when somebody said something about Truman and MacArthur. Lewis Lorch shot him a warning glance, but he was in no mood to keep his trap shut.

"I saw Dugout Doug waving from his limousine," he said, "the day of his triumphal return. I was coming out of the Art Students' League on 57th Street. It made me sick to my stomach, a parade for that Mussolini type. He should have got a court-martial instead."

Lewis needn't have worried; the rich were more liberal than those guys down on Broome Street who stood around in the bars cussing out the President for trying to dump a great general. When you were secure you could afford to be bold. He was not surprised that the Cohens themselves, as well as their guests, were a lot more opposed to Joe McCarthy than the downtown barflies.

Over their brandy these comfortable unfrightened people were indignant about the discomfort and fright of others. They argued among themselves about McCarthy's attacks on the State Department, and while they took it all more seriously than Lewis Lorch, who sat quietly examining his hands, for them it was really just one more thing to talk about, like the new show at the Museum of Modern Art.

He was glad of the excuse to say goodbye early. After you'd had your little moment, after these people proved that they recognized your name and your work, it was a waste of time listening to them rattle on. You're a far worse snob than they, Lorch would have said; he had already as much as demanded, What world do you think you belong in, Vito? Maybe the answer was that he didn't belong in any.

Next morning he was up early, ready for Harry, who arrived meticulously turned out for what he referred to as his "performance." "I've rearranged my schedule," he explained, "in order to go on to several more places before coming back to New York. So if there's a choice when we get there, would you mind if I went on first?"

"I couldn't care less. For me the day's shot anyway."

Grateful, Harry proceeded to lecture him about the mass media as a tool for social change. His nonstop performance lasted to the airport, through coffee on the plane, and all the way on into Buffalo.

"You're trying to prove something," he said to Harry, "but I'm not sure what."

Harry laughed indulgently. "When I've succeeded, you'll see. The concept is terribly simple—those committed to changing the world must move in on the media."

"Fred used to talk like that, but if he hasn't even got the guts to come up here and give somebody a hand, who needs him?"

"Maybe he thinks he can do more by not jeopardizing his position. But that's not the point either. He's just a performer. I'm talking about taking over the media themselves, not just a few minutes of air time."

"Man, you're talking about hundreds of millions of dollars."

Harry grinned. "Maybe just a few million, properly employed."

When they got to the federal building the hearing was already underway. They were stuck in an anteroom whose only advantage was that it kept Harry from lecturing him any further. Bored stiff, he took out his sketch pad and was just starting to sharpen a pencil when Margaret stuck her head out from around the frosted-glass door.

"Hi," she said. "Delighted you're both here."

"Harry goes first."

"You make it sound like a barber shop. It's pretty informal. I'll take you each through a number of obvious questions on Ham and you can say whatever would impress the board that he's a decent person. Then they may want to question you about this or that. But they're not in the least inquisitorial—this isn't one of those congressional hearings. After Harry, I'm going to have Marty Dworkin testify on the New Party's politics, and if I know him that will take us up to lunch. Vito, do you mind—"

"Don't worry about me. I'll go see my cousins, better than sitting here."

When he came back, a little frayed from explaining to Zia Concetta's kids that he could only say hello and goodbye to them, the session was just breaking up. Margaret emerged with Dworkin. He had lost most of his hair but maintained his quizzical mocking expression, an odd one for a professional revolutionist, a man who

had never held down a nine to five job, but had spent his entire
life speech making, article writing, plotting, joining parties, splitting
old ones, forming new ones. It struck Vito that he looked something like Sy's late father the clothing salesman, in his neat worsted
and neat striped tie, his neatly combed receding hair, grinning to
show those teeth with the little gaps between them.

Marty said easily, "It's been a number of years, Vito. Do you
still get a twinge?"

"Only from my own cooking."

"There I can't help you. But if you ever feel like getting involved in politics again . . . Well, I've already talked too much this
morning. My only vice. I must run."

When the elevator had closed on him, Margaret was laughing.
"He sure wasn't kidding. He was eager for the chance to put his
position on the record—he's anxious to get off the attorney general's subversive list—so he gave them an hour on force and violence, and half an hour on why the Communists are deforming
Marxism. I think he's as effective as ever, even when he's propagandizing three middle-class gentlemen and a stenotypist."

The other elevator opened, and Hamilton Wright stepped out.
The boy whom he had known early in the war was a man now.
He seemed changed in temperament, too, more sober and more
restrained. Some of his old vivacity returned when he hurried
forward. "It certainly was nice of you to come. Especially since
you don't even know what I believe any more."

"Blame Margaret if I screw things up for you. She's responsible
for my coming."

"Come on," she said, "we can talk in the restaurant."

While they ate she went rapidly over the portrait she was attempting to build of Ham. "With Marty, we wanted to show that
this was a legitimate socialist organization, with a history of opposition not only to capitalism but to totalitarianism. Ham had a perfect
right to associate himself with it. We're claiming further that Ham's
views have since changed, and that he has a right to those views
too, whatever they are, without his job being yanked out from
under him."

"Well, what are they?" Vito demanded. "I don't mean to be
nosey, but suppose they ask me this afternoon?"

"The thing is," Ham said, "that I've become a pacifist."

Vito paused with a forkful of omelet midway to his mouth. He realized that he was thinking of Ham as a Negro instead of as a man who had the right to believe what he wanted. To cover his embarrassment he said, "You say it as though it was some kind of crime."

"My Marxist friends regard pacifism as weak-kneed bourgeois avoidance of the class struggle. Practically everybody else thinks I'm unrealistic, like vegetarians."

"And the library board thinks you're a menace."

Ham smiled faintly. "The papers are talking about the gooks in Korea, and about Operation Meat Grinder." His skin glistened, Vito noted with some fascination, as though he had been running for a great distance; a pulse beat inside his temple as if it struggled to burst out. "But I wouldn't go back to the library anyway. I want to go on working through the Fellowship of Reconciliation, for CORE."

"What are we knocking ourselves out for, if you don't even want the job?"

"For a matter of principle. I hope that doesn't disappoint you."

If he said, No, he'd be a liar; if he said Yes, he'd be a fool. He temporized. "What's CORE?"

"The Congress of Racial Equality. I didn't know much about it until I went out to St. Louis on a visit. The chapter there has been fighting against lunch-counter discrimination since forty-nine. There wasn't one eating place in the whole city, outside of the railroad station and the ghetto itself, where a Negro could sit down and eat. They started in on the downtown dime stores, with sit-ins at the lunch counters."

"Now I remember. I read about that."

"I became involved, I sat in a few times. The staff was all volunteers, they had no salaried employees, so I decided to do what I could while I had my job. Eventually I hoped to switch over to full-time field work. Now the decision has been made for me."

"Make a living at it?"

Ham smiled wryly. "I don't need much. But I do need my self-respect. And I want that hearing board to acknowledge that I have my right to my opinions—and my right to fight for them."

"His opinions," Margaret said, "include opposition to the war in Korea."

"That's all right with me. I haven't been painting recruiting posters."

"I simply wanted you to get the picture straight. You're an object of civic pride. You're coming back as a local boy who went off to the big city and became a famous artist. You heard that an injustice was being done to this fellow whom you knew as a teenager, and you're here to speak up for him."

Well, he thought, as he settled himself after lunch into the chair that Margaret indicated in the hearing room (Ham was not permitted to sit in), the men facing him around the glass-topped table before the long rows of dusty venetian blinds did not look as eager to meet him as the Cohens' guests had been the night before. The spinsterly stenotypist sat frigidly poised over the machine above her virginal thighs, not reacting to the introductions.

All three men wore vests, two of them with chains across the front. These were the ones who never got dumped themselves, but at best murmured regretfully when someone like Ham had to be pried loose from his grasp on the lifeboat and kicked adrift. They were much more polite than he expected, even the one with jowls and a belly like a southern sheriff. It struck him suddenly with terrific force that they accepted him; he was in. His paintings were bought for cold cash by people smarter and richer than they, and therefore he belonged.

Feeling this, it was hard to keep it from affecting his testimony. Yes, he had gone to Hutchinson High; yes, he had played football and been a prizefighter afterwards. Yes, he had done the post-office mural and gone on to teach at the art school. Yes, he had had dealings with the Communists in those days and had become disillusioned with their manipulation of impractical artists.

"You wouldn't have had any way of knowing, I suppose, that after Wright was hired as a librarian, he openly attacked our boys in Korea?" This was the middle one, the kindly looking one with rimless glasses.

"No."

"Doesn't that sound like the Communist line to you? He's giving aid and comfort to the enemy."

"He's got no more use for the Communists than I do. You can't tell me he supports their side. He's a pacifist. That means to me that he's against the war, not that he's for the other side."

"This is a time of great danger for our country. They're shooting at us over there."

"To me the danger is that fear could make us take people's basic rights away from them. That boy's got the right to think what he wants and say what he wants without getting fired for it—or even being afraid of getting fired. I'm no pacifist, but I'm here to defend his right to be one. Even if he was a Communist, I'd defend his right to be one. I'd fight his ideas, but I wouldn't do it by taking his job away from him. As long as he does his work, he's entitled to that job. You take it away, and you're cheating him out of his rights as an American. You're doing worse: you're proving to him that as a member of a minority group—*two* minority groups—he can't get a fair shake in his own country."

When it was over, they shook hands all around. The board thanked him for his time and trouble; and when they were out in the anteroom at last, Margaret was enthusiastic.

"I couldn't have improved on what you said if I'd sat down and written out a speech for you."

"I'm dripping."

"You poor guy. Listen, Irwin Metzger is terribly anxious to see you. I didn't want you to get involved with people here, but I had to tell Irwin you were coming up—he came through for Ham just as I knew he would. And his office is just up the street."

"I remember. I'll drop in and say hello."

He was reluctant. But when he saw how pleased Irwin was, how he shushed his youthful patients in the waiting room with comic books and drew him eagerly into his office, he forgot his reluctance.

Irwin was heavier, his brow was pale, but the middle of his face was flushed, like a target. "I knew Margaret would persuade you to stop by. And I know what it meant for you to break off your work. Not many guys would have done it."

"Balls. Margaret told me that you came through for Ham."

"He's been good to Paul. He was like a big brother to him at the library. Besides, it was just money. What's money?" Irwin leaned forward. "You know something, Vito? I really don't give a good God damn about money. That's not what keeps me up nights."

"What does?"

"The cold war, and all this hysteria. My Paul is eight years old. I can buy him all sorts of stuff—but not a good life."

"You're not the first one to say that."

"Oh, I know. Everything I say is secondhand. I've never had an original thought in my life. Carmie says I have intellectual pretensions without intellectual distinction."

"Who the hell is she to talk?"

"She has native shrewdness. She can go for my weak spots like a tiger for the jugular."

"So what else is new, man? How's business?"

Irwin laughed. "If you really want to know, it's fine. This is only going to be our downtown office. Stu and I are setting up shop out in Williamsville. We'll just be here by appointment for some of our old patients. Everybody's moving out to the suburbs. The Germans, the Jews, even some of the Poles. And there's a whole new population, young engineers from out of town with wives and kids."

"With bad teeth."

"Right! But come on into my lab so I can show you what I've been doing."

Irwin had built up a little museum of plaster jaws along the walls of his lab. Almost all were "before" and "after," sometimes in three or four stages, a triumphal procession of cosmetic progress.

Some of the original malocclusions were amusing—Bugs Bunny uppers, underslung jaws—but others were pathetic, even terrifying.

Irwin lifted one from the shelf and tapped at it with a pencil. It was truly repellent, the teeth twisted to one side, overlapping in a crazy patternless grin. "You should have seen this girl. Dropped out of school, hiding in her bedroom. I felt like crying for her. But I knew that I would be able to help. When I told her so she looked at me like I was tormenting her. But here's the way she looked after six months. And here, after a year. Not bad, hey?"

"Irwin, you're all right. I don't know many guys who get as much kick out of their work as you do. And no wonder."

Irwin caught him by the arm. "You're an inspiration to me, Vito. You're not taken in by any of this crap around us, the house in the country, the appliances. You just go ahead and do what you want to do. You're the one person that Carmie and I can agree on."

"You make me sound like a cross between Dr. Schweitzer and Errol Flynn."

"I'm serious. I'd like to devote myself to something bigger than myself, but where is it? For a while my cousin tempted me with the movement, but it's dead, right? Maybe Sy's fulfilling himself, emptying latrines in the desert, but I had in mind something that would

make use of the best that's in me. Now I think it's too late. I like
to help people, I'll always do that, but I can't help myself."

Vito put his thumb against a photo of Paul tacked to the wall of
the lab. "Remarkable eyes that kid has. Like some kind of innocent
animal."

"Do you think Carmie appreciates him? I think she wanted some
big ideal, too. I've offered her everything, I mean not just material
things, but whatever is in me. It's not enough for her. Social problems she never cared about—she's always tried to get away from
that—for her it's art! I'm sorry, Vito, but she'll never know what
art is."

"I would have figured having a baby would do the trick."

"I was so sure of that . . . all it did was make her more restless.
She wants all the things that ordinary women do—in spades—but
she wants something else too, and neither Paul nor I can provide
that for her. So there's no point in our having any more, is there?"

Christ, what a misery. He was tempted to console Irwin by
pointing out that he was doing beautiful things right here for
people who needed him badly. Do you think, he wanted to say,
that the people who buy my paintings really *need* them? When
they say they do, they sound like polite liars. I'm the only one that
needs them, and even I don't when they stop challenging me, when
there's nothing left to be done but crate them and cart them out
of the studio and turn them over in despair to Lorch to be disposed
of for money. So I can't win either, can I? Until this moment he had
not thought of Irwin as anything much more than the good-natured
slob that Carmie had hooked. But he could not trust himself to
speak.

He looked up. Carmela was standing in the doorway, smiling,
voluptuous. "What's going on in here?"

"We're admiring your son's picture."

"That's typical Irwin. Meantime his patients sit and wait." She
stepped forward and embraced him. She didn't look as though
she had put on weight, but she felt it; and she smelled of good
living. "I know Paul is beautiful, Vito. Too much so for his own
good. He'd be better off if he could mix it up with the kids in the
neighborhood."

"Can't he?"

"It isn't that he's a coward. He can't stand violence, or physical
force. Like a girl. It makes him sick to his stomach."

"He must see plenty of it on TV."

"He doesn't watch those shows. He sits and reads."

"Well, it's good to see you, Carmie, but I really have to get out to the airport, and Irwin's got those patients waiting."

"Carmie can drive you out."

"Sure I can. I just stopped in from my shopping to check up on Irwin."

So he sat next to her in the car while she spoke to him of her husband and her son. "Maybe the difference in background was too much to overcome. I suppose he made sure to tell you, we're always fighting. It never ends."

"You could have gone a long way without finding a nicer guy."

"I didn't say he's not nice. But he's got no understanding of my inner needs."

"Have you?"

"Have I what? Come on, Vito, you know what I mean. What does a woman get married for? I thought, him being a Jew and all, he'd be artistic, or at least sympathetic. But all he ever thought about was his goddam left wing friends and his folk songs about the coal miners and the starving peasants. And teeth, for God's sake. Now he's all wrapped up in the kid. It's sick. He watches him like a hawk, he reads to him seven nights a week before the kid goes to sleep. Seven nights a week. I'm not exaggerating. And not kiddie books either. Grown-up books he reads to him. He fastened onto him like a leech, and he's turning him into a little old man. So where does that leave me?"

"Maybe if you tried to take some interest in his work, he'd be more interested in your concerns."

"Now you sound like a marriage counselor."

And she sounded as though they had already been to one. "You know what I think, Carmie? I think you don't know what you want. You never did."

"Maybe that's true." She threw back her head defiantly. "But my husband should have been the one to show me, or to teach me. Right? Maybe I'm all mixed up, but I'm not a goddam vegetable. You remember from when I was a kid, Vito—I was always interested in the finer things, wasn't I? I didn't have much chance, or maybe much sense, but I wanted to learn, didn't I?"

She was close to tears. Baffled, he held out his arms. It was the only way he had ever known how to comfort a woman; but then it was time to go, and he had to unclasp her hands from their frantic hold on his neck.

On the plane he glanced at his watch. It would still not be too late to get hold of Beverly. But then he thought of their parting and he said to himself, The hell with her, and he leaned back and told himself to relax.

The stewardess brought him coffee and a bun, each neatly clamped to the molded indentation in the plastic platter that she placed carefully on a little pillow on his lap as though it were a sleeping infant. Far from being precious, the bun was as tasteless and uninteresting as the stewardess herself, with her standard hairdo, standard smile, standard girdle beneath her standard uniform.

Sipping the coffee, he tried to read the paper. One column after another on the roundup of second-string Communist leaders, the retrial of William Remington, the results of a Midwest poll showing that only one person of one hundred and twelve was willing to sign a petition consisting of word for word excerpts from the Declaration of Independence and the Bill of Rights.

Shit. He threw down the paper and began to sketch the cloud patterns now visible from the window at his left side. Absorbed in his drawing, he hardly noticed the arrival of the stewardess. Her task finished, she had slipped out of her bolero jacket and was reaching up to place it in the rack over his head. As she strained upwards, her white blouse slipped loose from its moorings, displaying a bit of her underwear. Her full breasts pushed sharply against the fabric of her blouse, and two little perspiration half-moons came out through the cloudy fabric as she raised her arms.

Encouraged by these evidences of reality, Vito sniffed hopefully when she plopped down onto the vacant seat beside him. He did not speak to her, but continued to sketch, feeling her eyes on his hand as it moved back and forth across the pad.

She could not contain herself. "Are you an artist?"

"Why, are you a model?"

Disconcerted, she smiled her real smile. "Gee, that's one thing I've never done."

She was hoping that her luck would change. "You may be due," he said. "What's your name?"

"Millicent Ryan. What's yours?"

"Vito Brigante. I suppose they call you Millie."

"Not if I can help it. Where is your studio, Mr. Brigante?"

"Vito. In Lower Manhattan. But nobody gets in without a commitment to model, not if I can help it. Where do you live, Millie?"

She laughed, shaking her head back and forth. "You're impossible. In Jackson Heights."

When he alighted from the plane at La Guardia, whistling, he nodded coolly in response to her professional farewell smile at the foot of the ladder; but he had her phone number in her own eager handwriting across the back of the sketch pad that was warm in the pocket of his corduroy jacket.

2. IRWIN

When the news came on the radio that Julius and Ethel Rosenberg had been electrocuted, he canceled his evening appointments and locked up the office. For a minute he stood in the familiar but empty green hallway irresolute, actually trembling. He was drawn by some perverse feeling of solidarity to show himself at a shul or a synagogue, but where? Which one? It was almost four years since he had last shown his face, following the death of his father, and if he turned up now they'd start nagging him about Paul, and the need for a Jewish education if he wanted Paul to be bar mitzvah . . . In the end he went instead to his bar.

Rapidly he downed a couple of doubles. Jack Daniel's solace instead of Rabbi Lookstein's sermon; would the good rabbi try to explain why the Supreme Court had turned them down? Why the Eisenhower crowd had moved up the execution date in order to kill them on shabbos? Or why they themselves had made such a big thing at the very end out of being good Jews when it was obvious that they had been no such thing, but simply a couple of small-time fanatics who were first tormented and then burned to death for nothing more than believing in another religion?

Irwin found that he was crying, and he was grateful to the bartender for leaving him alone with the bottle. It was more than the rabbi would have done. Sy had been shaken up by the prolonged travail of the Rosenbergs, particularly after the Communists had belatedly taken up the cause and sponsored international protest demonstrations even in Tel Aviv. He had been stirred to write a long letter, his first since the arrest of the Jewish doctors in Mos-

cow for allegedly plotting against Stalin. He was excited about
Irwin coming for a visit, and anxious to learn about the American
political scene. But what would there be to tell him, now that the
Rosenbergs were dead?

Irwin had never believed that it would happen. As with a
threatening war, he had been irrationally certain that something
would intervene at the last minute. If they had been noble, like
Vanzetti, or defiant, like Mooney, the whole thing might have been
epical, and therefore bearable; but they were so *ordinary* . . . Sy
had been a couple of years behind Rosenberg at City College, but
wrote that he remembered him well as an engineering student
Stalinist who always turned up at Student Union meetings in the
guise of an innocent liberal, or "progressive." Now he had deluded
himself and his wife into the grave, thanks to an hysterical country
and a judge anxious to prove that Jews could be superpatriots. Irwin
wept into his hand.

The kids, the orphaned kids. They wouldn't even have the comfort that their parents had been heroes or martyrs. They had chosen
to die as "simple Jews," a pose as false as their earlier claim to
be "simple progressives," ignored almost until the end by the very
movement for which they were sacrificing themselves—and being
sacrificed.

It was all cruel, mean, and stupid. And he had not even known
how to protest effectively. The country was designed to make you
wallow in impotence—and live well while you wallowed.

"Put it on my bill," he said, pushing back the bottle to the bartender. His prayer for the dead. He straightened up and dusted
imaginary ashes from his sackcloth.

When he walked in the front door Carmie sniffed. "Bourbon as
usual. You know the Zivics are coming over to say goodbye."

"I know, I'm sorry," he said humbly, only to forestall her predictable follow-up: "They're your friends, not mine." If he had asked,
"Don't you know that the Rosenbergs are dead?" she would probably
have replied, "They're your friends, not mine."

He picked his way through her new matching airplane luggage,
lying open here and there like so many obstacles on the road to the
bathroom. He fumbled around among the sliding glass doors and
rinsed with mouthwash. But when he went into Paul's room and
bent forward to kiss him, his son turned his head away.

Wincing, Irwin withdrew his hand from above the dark tousled curls. "How was school?"

"Boring."

"Two more days left. It's always a letdown, after exams." He tried to peer over Paul's shoulder to see what he was doing, but the boy sat hunched over his desk. "Are you excited about the trip?"

"Sure."

Uncertain, Irwin waited.

"Daddy."

"Yes?"

"Do you think the Rosenbergs were spies?"

Irwin started. "Why . . . I don't think it's important. If they were, it was only to help the cause they believed in. I don't think they should have been punished the way they were."

"But why didn't they confess?"

"Some people confess to things they didn't do, some people don't confess to things they did do. Maybe they were innocent. I think they were just foolish, and I think this country has been terribly cruel to them. And to their children."

Paul did not seem to wish to pursue, it, so he retreated to the kitchen and fished out some cold chicken that Carmie had left him. Gnawing on a wing, he returned to the bedroom, where he found her squatting before her closet, mulling over rows of shoes. "Stick to flats," he suggested.

"I wish you hadn't promised to take Paul along. We should have found him a good camp."

"A camp?" The very idea was preposterous. Appalling. "He's barely ten years old."

"They're putting him in seventh grade in the fall. He was mature enough to be skipped."

"He was smart enough. Which is why we're taking him along. He'll appreciate it more than us."

"Everybody that I know, when they go to Europe they put their kids in camp. What can a ten-year-old get out of art galleries, or museums, or—"

"Or what?"

"You know what I mean."

He did, but he was saved from the temptation to argue by the arrival of Margaret and Bill with going-away presents. It was a little hard for him to understand how a childless couple could be in such good spirits, particularly when their faith in the American working class and in progress itself was being called into question. Dumped from his presidency, Bill had gone off to the UAW convention in Atlantic City as a delegate and come back with a staff job as international rep. Freed of daily pressure from the ranks, he had begun to take comfort from the cracks in the Communist wall rather than from his union brothers. The death of Stalin had renewed his hope for the realization of their dreams; and now he was inclined to push aside the dead subject of the dead Rosenbergs.

The workers were on the march in East Berlin, and Bill's forehead was shiny with the perspiration of excitement. "Isn't it great, the news from East Germany?"

"I guess so," Irwin said. "I doubt that those strikers and anti-Stalinists ever raised a finger against Hitler or the concentration camps."

"Berlin was a center of anti-Hitler resistance."

"What resistance?"

"The Berlin working class never voted for Hitler."

"I'm trying to think what they ever did to stop him."

"You're pretty cool about it, when they finally do stand up against tyranny. After all, it is the biggest single event in Europe since the war."

"I guess that's true too. But it's like the economic miracle. You just can't expect me to get whipped up about the Germans, is all."

Bill turned persuasive, in his best political manner. "All the intellectuals who gave up on radicalism have been busy creating a bogeyman, a monolithic society peopled with faceless hordes. And here we are, a handful who insisted that you couldn't freeze class antagonisms forever, you couldn't change people into automatons simply by treating them as automatons. Who was right?" he demanded triumphantly. "Who predicted that the workers would rise again?"

There was something infinitely depressing about racking up a score when you had no real opponents, or weren't even in the game. What difference does it make whether you were right or wrong? he wanted to ask, except for your own satisfaction?

Margaret seemed to sense that he was restive, and she turned the talk to Ham Wright, from whom she and Bill had just received a letter. After he had won reinstatement to his library post, Ham had gone to work for the Fellowship of Reconciliation, which had sent him south.

"Myself I think," she said, "that Ham won't marry. Not while he's living in Mississippi. He's dead serious about bringing the message of non-violence to the Negroes. To him it's his wife and his mistress, just like the movement used to be for us."

In an instant Irwin forgot his annoyance. Did Margaret realize what she had let slip—or was that "used to be" something she and Bill had already conceded to each other? Bill looked suddenly older, his eyes no longer sparkled behind the rimless glasses. In the silence that followed Margaret's seemingly casual remark it was borne in upon Irwin that Bill's decision to take the union staff job must have been as important as marrying, or moving away from his birthplace—a crossing of the bridge, a burning of it maybe, an acknowledgment of everything that his wife's words implied.

Two days later they were on the plane to New York. As soon as he had learned of their trip, Fred had insisted that all three of them sleep over at his apartment. Carmela was uneasy—for her half the fun of a vacation was staying in a fancy hotel—but then there was the comfort of knowing how impressed people would be when she said that they had stayed with Fred Byrd.

Fred had become a culture hero. To millions he was living proof that intellectuals could be regarded not just as freaks or foreigners, but as real Americans. Even the new word egghead, applied to someone like Fred, implied a kind of pleased indulgence, more envious than mocking. He was in everyone's living room every Thursday evening, as much a part of their lives as Kukla, Fran and Ollie were of their children's; he even managed an occasional review for *The New Yorker*. During all of this he had not left teaching, and was now a living example of what Irwin began to see was a very new breed: the rich professor.

Fred's apartment building, just north of Washington Square, roughly resembled the bow of the Queen Mary; the doorman looked like its chief navigating officer and the elevator operator the chief steward. He was deferential. "Professor Byrd left word for you to make yourselves at home. He'll be along later."

Carmela was impressed. "What floor is he on?"

"Fourteen, Mrs. Metzger."

Paul had been studying the touch buttons on the elevator wall.
"I don't see any thirteen."

"There isn't any on a lot of New York buildings, sonny."

"Why not?"

The elevator operator smiled with the indulgence of the wise adult.
"Even the ones that claim they're not superstitious figure, why buy
an apartment on the thirteenth floor?"

"But thirteen comes after twelve. And if Fred's apartment is on
the floor after the twelfth, then—"

The operator's smile was beginning to fade. He opened the door
for them and took the master key from the pocket of his striped
pants. "This way, please. Is this your only bag?"

"We checked our other bags at the airport." Carmela added
proudly, "We're flying to London tomorrow."

The snow-white living room into which they stepped could have
held the entire apartment in which Fred and Bea had begun their
married life. The chrome-legged black leather chairs and couches
stood discreetly here and there alongside the glass cabinets in which
Fred and Sheila had mounted, very severely, their collection of pre-
Columbian pottery. The very size of the room—Fred had knocked
out a wall—was somewhat intimidating, and gave Irwin rather the
feeling that he had dropped into an unguarded museum.

Irwin too had been reluctant to come here, but there had been an
insistent quality to Fred's voice when he phoned from New York
that had made Irwin cancel the sentimental reservation for their
honeymoon suite at the Taft. "Now is when I need you!" Fred had
cried, in an unnaturally loud and high voice, and Irwin, surprised
and flattered, had yielded.

Gratified, Fred had explained, "You and Carmela will have the
second bedroom. It's Fernie's, when she visits. And Paul can sleep
in the library."

The library had not been noticeably raided by Sheila before she
walked out. It was not one of those spare bedroom-second TV
cubicles that middle-class America liked to christen "The Library,"
or "The Study," where Dad could make out his income tax or write
to mother in an atmosphere of literature and learning. Water-stained
first editions stood beside shelf after crystalline shelf of mint condition rarities.

"Here's a good way to spend your dough."

"Yes, isn't it?"

He turned. Fred stood in the doorway, freckled hands outstretched.

"You look fine," Irwin said. "I was a little worried about how the separation would affect you."

Fred leaned back against the door. "I am determined to survive."

"I suppose the primary thing is not to lose your balance."

"For a while I was a little lopsided. I felt that I had given up a lot for Sheila. A home, a wife, a daughter. She pointed out that she'd given up an entire country. The whole process is degrading, you know what I mean, Irwin? She was willing to let me keep the pre-Columbian stuff, but not these books. It's to laugh. She got it into her head that Americans had no right to be specialists in English literature. An eccentric fixation. So to fix my little red wagon she enrolled in graduate school in order to claim a share of my library."

"That sounds a little raw."

"Carmie is a tempestuous girl, but you don't know what women are capable of when they are really vindictive. Sheila wasn't above mocking me in public. A show-business professor was what she called me."

"That must be one of the hazards of success."

"You know something? The more idealistic women claim to be, the more crass they are. Sheila will tie up everything I make for the next twenty-five years, I promise you."

Once he had said this, Fred seemed much relieved. "Now," he said, "let's get your family together. I'd like you all to be my guests at the studio for my show."

They drove straight up Sixth Avenue in a cab, Carmie squeezed between him and Fred, Paulie upright in the jump seat and staring out the windows. At Radio City, Fred helped Carmie out and tipped the driver with what struck Irwin as wild generosity. "Thanks, Professor," the hackie said.

"Don't mention it, Harry."

"Gee," Paul said, "he knew who you were."

"I knew who he was too."

"But he had his name and picture in that little frame."

"Smart boy. We were both practicing public relations."

He led them through the tourist queues and past uniformed guards, to an elevator that whisked them up so fast that their ears popped. They were grinning at each other when Fred took them swiftly

down the corridor to a paneled room furnished with potted plants,
two huge television sets, and a dozen comfortable chairs. A cluster
of well-dressed men and women did not glance up from their
drinks.

"This is a VIP room. Admen, time buyers, sponsors, girl friends.
Just ask the waiter for anything you'd like. I'm going to have to go
and get made up. When we're ready they'll show you to the front
rows of spectator seats, before they open the doors for the outside
audience."

"You run along," Carmie said.

"I'll see you here right after the show. There's going to be a little
supper."

Irwin caught the white-jacketed waiter's eye. "One Jack Daniel's
and two ginger ales."

"That didn't take you long." Carmie was annoyed, but it hardly
seemed worth the effort to explain that he was nervous for Fred
and needed the sustenance.

A tanned young man with bright teeth and tasseled moccasins
clapped his hands together. "This way, please." They filed obedi-
ently into the studio. "I know who he is," Carmela whispered. "He's
an announcer!"

"Whatever he is," Irwin replied as they sat down, "he paid a lot
of money to have those teeth capped."

Then the doors at the other end of the studio opened to admit
those who had been queued up down below. "The second class
passengers," he explained to Paul.

"Is that why they make them sit behind us?"

"Tomorrow it'll be our turn on the airplane."

"They're noisier than the people we came in with."

"It's more of an event to them."

The announcer with the moccasins and the teeth wove his way
nimbly through a dense tangle of creeping cables overlapping across
the floor like some proliferant tropical growth. "While the panel is
preparing for tonight's show, we're going to be entertained by that
famous funny man, Jack Jacobs."

"I never heard of him."

"He's a night club comic."

His son's explanation fell heavily on Irwin's heart. It hurt to
hear him glibly repeating the patter words of the entertainment
industry.

It hurt doubly when Jacobs came trotting out, buttocks quivering inside the flapping striped trousers, fat little hands clasped over his head in token of what? self-admiration?

"I've got to keep the yokels awake," he cried, "until the intellectuals come on. After that, all hell breaks loose."

The audience, not yet settled in, puzzled perhaps, waited expectantly.

"Oy veh," Jacobs complained, "a bunch of stiffs I'm stuck with. This is going to be worse than Yom Kippur at Kutscher's. What do you want from my life, a strip?" Lifting the wings of his jacket, prancing, mincing, he shook the wire at the end of his portable microphone as if it were a whip with which to beat the spectators.

Now they were beginning to respond. Emboldened, Jacobs began to taunt the weakest among them. "What are you laughing at, Curly?" he demanded of a bald man on the aisle. "You think you'd look any better than me out here?"

Vulgar and quick, he jabbed at the audience as if it were some great dumb beast. His own bulk, the fat that made him mortal, was only a mask, like his comedian's smile. From beneath it he exuded ruthless cunning.

And as he bent to his task, Irwin felt himself shrinking, ashamed for Fred and uneasy for Paul.

Suddenly he realized that Jacobs was staring directly at him.

"Hey, skinny," Jacobs wiggled the microphone menacingly, obscenely, "why so sour? Maybe you don't appreciate what I've done for fat people? Maybe you're jealous because I get paid for being fat and you don't?"

He went hot and cold. Flushing, he opened his mouth. But before he could say anything, the tanned announcer bounded out.

"Thanks, Jack! Super as always!"

Having fulfilled his function, like an artillery barrage before an infantry advance, Jacobs moved off with the grace of a ballerina, his absurdly tiny feet twinkling, his magic wand waving farewell maliciously, it seemed, at Irwin himself. If he hadn't run off, Irwin wondered, would I have been betrayed into some angry retort that would have embarrassed my family and my friend—or would I have played the suburban masochist like all the others?

He mopped his face and neck. Fred was coming on with his panelists: an aging second-string actress whom he had once seen in Buffalo in a road-show production of *Life With Father,* a pre-war catcher with huge misshapen hands which he waved aggressively like a beggar displaying his wounds, and a former congressman with a long humorous nose, like a sausage. They were all knowledgeable in unexpected areas. The actress was a walking handbook of batting averages; the catcher knew the cast and notices of every opening night for a generation; the western politician was full of minutiae on Chinese pottery, particularly of the T'ang Dynasty.

It was like watching a seal blow a horn or a bear bounce a basketball. In order to jazz things up the producers had devised other viewer-catching devices, including a tiny isolation booth (it made Irwin think of a Reichian orgone box), blindfolds tied round the contestants' heads by inane girls in leotards, opera hose, and pumps, and blackboards that glowed in the dark. With all the claptrap, it was sadder and stupider played out before your eyes than when it was diminished on a screen. He was uneasy about what to say to Fred; but he might have spared himself the worry.

The very important people were herded back into the room from which they had been ushered and then were whisked up to the sixty-fifth floor, where several banquet rooms had been prepared for them and for the performers.

The view of the metropolis below Radio City, sparkling like so many jewels flung at its feet, was breathtaking; the smorgasbord laid out for the guests scarcely less so. But he was depressed to observe that Fred now looked ten years older. Taut and trembly, he smiled haggardly, his freckles standing out like blotches; you would have thought he had been lecturing to savants instead of asking those seated on either side of him the dates of the T'ang Dynasty or of *Arsenic and Old Lace,* or the three winningest southpaws in the American League.

"Having fun?" he asked Irwin.

"Sure."

"I'm so glad that you all could come today. I couldn't tell you before, but tonight was a kind of audition. A sponsor is interested in a new format featuring our panelists plus people from all walks of life selected for native intelligence and ability to talk intelligently about a specific topic."

"They must have liked it."

"There's going to have to be discussion. One idea is to make the cash prizes big enough to catch not just middlebrows, but ordinary viewers." He dropped his arm about Irwin's shoulder. "I'm going to have to stick around and thrash some of this out. You won't mind going back to the apartment without me?"

The next morning the door of Fred's bedroom did not open as they tiptoed out. It was easier to leave a note than to face him at such an hour, after such an evening.

But Fred's drained countenance faded from his mind as he sat strapped to his seat on the airliner with his wife and child, lifting off the ground, away from his native land for the first time in his life. "Let's admit it, Carmie," he said, clasping her tense fingers. "This is exciting."

Her smile still had the power to shake him. "It's great . . . I just wish I'd known there was going to be a party last night."

"Why?"

"I could have worn the pearls you gave me for our tenth anniversary."

After that, London was a blur. Carmela disliked the weather and Paul was more interested in simply staring at strollers in the parks than in visiting landmarks. He had to remind himself not to make too many demands on the boy.

Paris was different. Carmela was very happy there, the shop windows on the Faubourg St. Honoré glittering in the early summer sun were just what she had dreamed of. She was so seduced by the glamor of the golden city that she became very ardent every night, after Paul had finally fallen asleep (or maybe she was just acting out what she had been reading about in the *Kinsey Report*). During the day she willingly tramped up to Sacre Coeur and through all the quarters that he assured her were historic, asking in return only that Paul photograph them in this corner or that. She was excited at seeing famous people sipping drinks at sidewalk cafés, and was grateful when he took her to what she called an "existentialist night club."

She loved Paris so much, in fact, that their disagreement about Israel started up all over again. At home it always began with arguments about Paul ("You think I'm such a dope I can't see that you're trying to turn him against me with all this Jewish stuff? You think you'll save him from the Church by dragging us off to Jerusalem?"). Here it became a charge that Irwin wanted to ruin their vacation by imposing his crazy neuroses on her desire to live a little in Paris.

Carmela was not without weapons. Aside from the fact that

half the travelers' checks bore her signature, she knew that a sitdown strike at a café table could ruin his holiday.

So he resorted for the second time to the kind of compromise that would appeal to her as a recognition of her reasonableness. At home, he had made Israel palatable by promising her Rome and the Vatican. In Paris, he made it palatable by booking a stopover on the Riviera.

Carmie was more than appeased. She was thrilled with the huge cactuses and salmon-pink geraniums at the Nice Airport, with the outlandishly uniformed attendants at that living wedding cake, the Hotel Negresco, with their expensive rooms overlooking the Promenade des Anglais, with the Bay of Angels, over which the gulls circled ceaselessly, wings gleaming in the dazzle as they flashed downward.

Irwin had been trying to fraternize, but the language barrier and his own shyness were as nothing compared with the assault of those Europeans who wanted to hold him personally responsible for Senator McCarthy. Stung into a reflex patriotism that he felt was demeaning, he found it easier to relax into tourism, to take pictures of Carmela and Paul on the Croisette at Cannes, on the beach at Juan les Pins, in front of the chateaux at Antibes and Cagnes. Time after time he posed them, poking them into place, his plump wife beside the slight, serious boy, the one pouting, the other blinking sternly in the neutral sunlight.

Then they drove east, to the doll world of Monaco, a playcountry of plumed guards in candy-striped sentry boxes before a fairy castle. They rolled down beyond the green flower-bordered mall before the Casino that he knew so well from the E. Phillips Oppenheim mysteries of his childhood and parked near the entrance to the Hotel de Paris.

Paul waited outside patiently, licking at a *cornet,* while Irwin led Carmie through the Casino's vast dowdy rooms with their faded tapestries of nymphs and goddesses and their equally faded clientele, elderly pensioners poring over the little spiral-bound copybooks in which they had penciled, in private shorthand, winning systems for chemin de fer or roulette. Carmie lost twenty-five hundred francs betting on the red numbers, and was content to leave.

Paul had finished his cone and was standing on the sidewalk before the Casino, gazing across at the entrance to the Hotel de

Paris. "I never saw any place so fancy. See that Rolls-Royce? It's the third one since we got here."

"Let's go look in the lobby, Irwin," Carmela said eagerly. "Just to look."

"Maybe we can have a drink inside."

As they crossed the street to the hotel, the occupant of the Rolls opened the car door and backed directly into them.

"Oops!" he cried. *"Pardon!"* He used the French pronunciation, but it was Harry Sturm, escorting a strawberry blonde. When he recognized them, he embraced them all in turn.

"Did you track me down?" he demanded. "Is it possible that this handsome lad is your little baby?"

"We're staying in Nice. We're more or less on our way to Israel to see Sy."

"Splendid. Let's go upstairs, I'm staying here, I have much to tell you." Carmela and the blonde were eyeing each other warily. "My secretary Denise—she does everything for me."

I'll bet, Carmela whispered. Harry brought forward the driver of the Rolls, a slim and wary young man of dark, rather Indian complexion. "Sirani, my all around man."

It was all too crazy. Harry didn't just have a room, he had a suite. When they entered, the phone was ringing—it made you feel that it rang all day.

Sirani picked it up and listened briefly. Then he murmured, "It's Leydoux."

Harry waved his hand. "Later, later. Take messages, I must talk with Dr. Metzger. Denise, would you show Carmela and Paul the sea view from the bedroom balcony?" He went to the bar, which had a bowl of pink and dark red roses on it. "As I remember, you like bourbon."

"What the hell are you up to, Harry? Last I heard you were in New York."

"Harry proposes, but the D.A. disposes. I'm on the lam, Irwin."

"Cut it out."

Harry laughed, that short sharp bark that would always be associated in Irwin's mind with the war years, locked in his memory along with dull meetings, rationing, A stamps, bars jammed with soldiers, the whole scene. It was not what you expected to hear in Monte Carlo.

Harry poured the Jack Daniel's liberally. "I got wind of something too good to pass up. It's a matter—I can be frank, you won't give it away—of trade mark registrations."

"You mean scientific patents?"

"Not at all. This has nothing to do with technology. It's simply taking advantage of a loophole. The only connection it has with science"—Harry grinned like a boy, his rubicund cheeks glowing—"is that, like most first-class scientific discoveries, it's so simple you wonder why no one ever thought of it before."

"I don't suppose you can tell me about it yet."

"I shouldn't, but I will—for a very good reason." He lowered his voice, although they were now alone save for Sirani, murmuring in the far corner into the phone.

"You know the expressions that have been drummed into us since childhood, so that they're as much a part of us as Shakespeare? I'd walk a mile, not a cough in a carload, ask the man who owns one, ninety-nine and forty-four one hundredths percent pure? OK. You know the special script signature of Ford, of Coca-Cola? The anagrams, the acronyms, all the little tricks dreamed up to make a product stick in the mind? OK. Not long ago, in the course of doing something very different both in Andorra and in Lichtenstein, I learned that this little principality has a loophole. It will be closed very soon, but at the moment it exists."

Irwin found himself leaning forward too, straining for Harry's sibilant whisper. Suppose the rococo mirror was bugged? Suppose the lissome Denise, the curve of whose corseted ass he could just discern leaning out over the balcony with his wife and kid, was in reality a spy for Harry's enemies?

"None of the giant trademarks, not one, is covered here by patent or by copyright. For a laughable consideration I am registering an entire list of names, slogans, marketing titles, devices, all quite legally in the name of a business organization incorporated by certain associates in an office building just up the hill."

"What's in it for you?"

"It costs my organization, Protection des Marques, a thousand francs for each trademark we file with the Monaco Registry Office. That pittance confers on Promarq certain rights no longer enjoyed by those companies which have ignored their deadline. It's a bit complicated," he said delicately, "but perhaps you have the drift?"

"Without your permission none of those firms will be able to do business here?"

"Or in all of France."

"But that's—"

"They will have to resign themselves to negotiations with my associates. Meanwhile, I shall be back with my first love—after all, I am a man of science, not of business. The Rolls, all the rest, has nothing to do with what goes on here." He rapped the monogram on the breast pocket of his shirt, in the proximate region of his heart. "I intend to set up a lab in Switzerland, in very pleasant surroundings. European firms are beginning to recognize the need for sophisticated research and consultation."

"But what about your outfit in New York?"

Harry waved his arm negligently. "We'll speak of that another time. Tell me, do you share my opinion that the political situation in the States is unhealthy?"

"You shouldn't have to ask."

Harry put his hands on his knees and prepared to preach. Irwin felt the years slipping away. "It is part of the price for our not getting our program across. We are just as responsible for McCarthyism as the right wingers."

"That's what all the Europeans keep telling me. But why should I feel guilty for McCarthy?"

"None of us did enough. I was an organizer, and I consider that I failed miserably. McCarthyism is simply a gauge of the extent of our failure." Harry put his hand on Irwin's knee; it was a preparatory gesture that Irwin knew well. "Every serious American socialist should be ready to acknowledge that failure. You will be going home shortly?"

"After Italy and Israel."

"*Bon.* You have the respect of Dworkin and the rest because you have no ax to grind. I will be grateful if you inform him on your return that I am renewing my offer—this time with substantial practical assistance. At the moment I'm not free to return to the States, and even my correspondence may be monitored." Harry's eyes popped. "You can be the honest broker."

The notion could only have occurred to Harry in the last five minutes, but he spoke of it as though it were a part of a grand master plan. Harry must have read skepticism in his eyes, for he drew himself up.

"Why else do you think I'm struggling with these big corporations? For my health? My bank account?" He waved at the shadow of

Denise that fell in a pleasantly curved pattern across the carpet.
"There are other ways of affording that."

Irwin gazed at him with a certain awe. He said slowly, "You know
something, Harry? I think you're nuts."

Harry laughed. "Nobody could ever accuse you of not being
forthright. But you are afflicted with the ignorance of the liberal.
I've done my damnedest to make a dent in that complacent liberal
ignorance, but it's like trying to push Boulder Dam with your nose.
I don't suppose you remember who Parvus was?"

Irwin shook his head humbly. "But I'll look him up when I get
home."

"Do so. And while you are catching up on your reading, inform
the comrades that Parvus is ready to cut them in on a percentage
of the Monaco operation. The details will have to be worked out
over here when and if Dworkin receives a passport—I understand
the McCarthyites have denied him one."

"You make me feel like an international courier."

"Good for the soul."

"Like giving money to a lost cause? If I had all the dough I used
to give you and Sy for the Party, I could have bought this whole
hotel."

"Never mind. Our cause is not lost. If you show the people
that you have it in you to be not a bad joke, a little sect, but a
great power, capable of great things—"

"Then you can change the world?"

"Why not?"

It was too much to comprehend, relaxed on a down-filled couch,
with the Mediterranean sun streaming in through the open floor-
length windows. Irwin said, "Maybe you've been away too long.
The Gallup polls show that the American people admire McCarthy,
that they'd vote down the Bill of Rights and the whole Constitution."

"Are you telling me that the American people are all fascists?"

"It took me years to be persuaded that most Germans—the
workers included—loved Hitler."

"You speak as if you'd never attended my course on the German
Question. How little effect our educationals had on the middle-class
mind!"

"And on the working-class mind?" he couldn't resist asking.

Harry sighed. "We oughtn't to go on in this fruitless way. You

must take Paul to the Oceanographic Museum. It will do him
worlds of good."

"That's what I want to do him."

"Before we separate, I want your promise that you'll be my
guests at dinner. I know a really first-class restaurant not too far
from here—Sirani can drive us all there if we meet here, say at
seven."

"Who would have thought," Carmela asked, snuggling up to him
next day as they flew over Corsica en route to Rome, "that Harry
would turn out like that?"

"Not me. I always pictured him sitting in jail, writing like mad
on problems of science or politics. I guess circumstances alter cases,
although I was never exactly sure what that meant. Now the
question in my mind is, do Rolls-Royces alter passengers?"

They landed in Rome happy. Unfazed by a dank hotel and a
leaky bidet, they photographed Paul before the Arch of Titus (Paul's
eyes filled alarmingly when he saw the bas relief of the Jews being
led off into slavery) and prepared themselves for the audience with
the Pope. For Irwin it was worthwhile just to be able to gaze down
through the showcases at the precious old Bibles in the Vatican
Library, but he grew uneasy at Paul's dilated pupils when it came
time for them to join the throng of nervously excited tourists in the
high-ceilinged chamber.

"I don't forget," he whispered to his son, "that he didn't lift a
finger for the Jews during all those awful years."

Carmela flashed him an angry look. Despite her own upbringing,
she had retained no interest in Catholicism. For her the papal audience was simply a "feature" of their vacation, like seeing the Mona
Lisa through glass or the Grand Corniche through Harry's Rolls
window, but she wanted Paulie to have "respect."

Eyeglasses glinting in the beams of sunlight descending from
above, the Pope made his little remarks in half a dozen languages
(a trick, as Harry had observed, that was in the standard repertory
of all the concierges of Venice). For Carmela the best and greatest
part of the trip was over.

For Irwin it was yet to come. He had not enjoyed Rome, and
it had cost him an effort of will not to say so. In the waiting area
of the Rome Airport, vast, echoing, and pompously phony like the
city itself, he took Paulie off to the *Uomini* to make pipi.

There they waited their turn behind a flock of elderly British clergymen in black turned-down felt hats and black turned-up shoes rocking at the white urinals. Chafing each other while they paid their tribute to the vitreous china, they called out comments.

"Take your airsick pill yet, Philip?"

"Was busy with my last will, Roger."

Paulie, staring gravely at the black wiggling behinds while their owners shook their dongs before taking to the air, forgot to be impatient.

Irwin was only relieved that the clerics would not be crowding onto the Tel Aviv plane as they had crowded into this john. When he told Carmie about them she got the giggles and forgot to sulk about having to leave Europe for Israel.

They were holding hands when the pilot tilted his wings over Cyprus, its crisp shoreline, like the edges of some giant pancake, crumbling away into the rich blue sea. Trying to remember who lived in its ancient cities, ruin built upon ruin—Greeks mostly, and some Turks, always at each other's throats, forever locked in insular combat?—he could remember sharply only the Jewish remnant thrust ashore and penned in by the British in one last ferocious effort to keep them from finding their way to freedom.

When they approached the Palestine coastline moments later he was trembling. His wife asked in some puzzlement, "Are you scared?"

"Yes," he said, "I certainly am."

But not when they touched down. The Hebrew signs lacked the diacritical points of his *Chumesh,* and so were unintelligible, but they had the homey quality of the word Kosher hanging, always twice, in American butcher shop windows. So for that matter did the guards, immigration and health officers, customs inspectors, money changers, and shoulder-shrugging cab drivers. Sloppy and ill-dressed, bearded or plain unshaven, they babbled away in half a dozen tongues, including his grandparents' Yiddish.

"For Christ's sake," Carmela grumbled, as they settled into a taxi for the ride to their hotel, "we might as well be in Williamsburg. Or on William Street."

She was so right that he was outraged with her. At the side of the road lay the rusting bodies of Army vehicles. Annoyed, he leaned forward and asked the driver why.

"From the War of Independence. Those are our statues."

That was more like it. But Tel Aviv only depressed him all over again. Grubby and unlovely, it sprawled away from the shore, a series of hastily thrown-up clusters of cell block apartment houses, a little Brooklyn, some Eastern Europe, a half-hearted touch of Nice-Côte d'Azur. He tried to take pride in the blue and white flags, the sea of Jewish faces on street corners and buses, the sidewalk cafés where old folks drowsed in the sun over tea or *gazoz,* secure at last, dying in peace like Norm's father in Miami Beach, unmolested, fearing only the ineluctable, the thin sheets of the Roumanian, Hungarian, Hebrew newspapers rumpled in their wrinkled laps like large grimy napkins.

He rented a car for the visit to Sy and Bernice. South of the city, on the edge of the desert, the Glantzmans' kibbutz did not announce itself in advance with a signboard or a row of Rotary and Kiwanis invitations to the weekly luncheon meetings. They almost missed it; the road along which they drove was flanked with a hedge of young poplars, planted to conceal the bleakness of a landscape bitten down to bed rock by countless generations of goats. It was Paul who noticed the little black and white English and Hebrew sign, hardly bigger than the name on a mailbox, at the intersection of a dirt road seemingly running into no place.

The dirt road too was bordered with trees, but more irregularly, almost halfheartedly, as though the job had been done once, but after the desert sun had burned out half the struggling saplings, not a second time. In the intervals someone had planted shrubs, but again only here and there; as the road went on, becoming somewhat rutted, for a good quarter of a mile or more, the immediate surroundings beyond the gaps became rather more noticeable than along the highway.

"I hear voices," Paul said.

"Me too, but I don't see anybody." He was looking hard, but not enjoying what he saw: some old kerosene drums, a pile of hay half tumbled over and greenish-white with mold, a split wagon tongue leaning forgotten against a fruit tree, several coffee cans full of tenpenny nails red with rust, a split-open box of shingles, a tangle of half-deflated inner tubes of monstrous size, for an absent truck. And beyond it all, the urgent ugly cries of scrabbling chickens.

At last they came to a clearing, a dusty courtyard enclosed on three sides by long low buildings on the order of quonset huts, oblong, with curving corrugated roofs and cinder block sidings. Between two of them hung a long laundry line festooned with symmetrically pinned diapers. A lanky man in sandals and ballooning trousers emerged, shirtless, from the middle building, pipe and paper in hand. He waved amiably.

"Shalom."

"I am looking for my cousin," Irwin said. "Seymour Glantzman."

"Why don't you park just there? And I'll go fetch him for you."

They were scarcely out of the car when Sy came running, skinny in khaki army shorts, socks rolled down to his ankles, hair standing on end. He was adjusting the tortoise shell templet of his glasses over his left ear, awkwardly, as he ran. When he caught sight of them he burst into tears.

Choking with embarrassment, Irwin allowed himself to be caught up in his cousin's embrace. As he yielded to Carmela and Paul, he said, "You've lost weight, Sy."

"Outdoor life." Sy blew his nose and smiled, abashed. "Bernie's jealous—she's put it on instead."

"Where is she?"

"She works in the nursery school—Serena's one of her twenty-seven brats. Joey's in school of course, and the baby is napping. Want to go see Bernie? Come on, we can peek in at Serena at the same time. Remember her, Paulie? She wouldn't know you, you're so big."

As they trudged up a weedy lane past temporary shacks and outbuildings now all too plainly permanent, it struck him that the kibbutz was not unlike Aunt Bessie's chicken farm in Lakewood, New Jersey. Sy glanced back at him over his shoulder.

"Well, what do you think of Israel so far, Irwin?"

"Remember Aunt Bessie?"

Sy's grin was wry. "It wasn't until I settled here that I understood what that farm meant to her—it was a lot better than Russia."

"But is this better than America?"

"You bet your sweet ass."

Irwin burst into laughter, the American expression sounded so incongruous here.

Twine had been strung along the side of the one-story nursery; morning glories bloomed up and down the wall. Gravel was freshly raked on the path to the front door; on either side petunias winked, crisp and pink. They peered through the windows, pasted up with cutouts of flowerpots, ghosts, goblins, toyland fairies; between the parted petals of a tulip they could glimpse Bernie, seated in the middle of the floor with a double row of children ringed about her.

"Serena is the dark one with the dimples."

Bernie caught sight of them then and came running out. Like Sy, she was adjusting her glasses—it was as if after all these years of marriage they suffered from the same shortness at the bridge of the nose; but she was more contained than he, and did not cry.

Now that they saw the children, Sy's and Bernie's and all the rest, for whom the flowers had been planted and the gravel paths raked, Irwin began for the first time to feel that Israel existed for him. The children were a new breed, self-assured and free of their parents' qualms; and their land was beautiful because it was being recreated with human hands, like something painfully carved in remembrance of a vanished primordial model. Bitterly beautiful as the desert was, its blasted wildness was challenging, for beneath it lay something that demanded release.

The desert rolled out blindly under the blaze of sun to meet the metallic sky. But no longer uninterruptedly: it was stunning to see it beaten back with half-inch pipes, drums leaking water, men and women breaking the intractable ground to bring up green rows of leafy living plants, food for the children they cherished and nurtured like the lettuce, the cucumbers, the cabbages that glistened defiantly in their long parallel lines.

"What difference does it make that the work is not for me? or that we came too late? Or that"—here Sy hesitated—"what we're used to isn't to be had here?"

"I should think that would make all the difference."

"Well, it doesn't."

"Are you doing it for the kids? That's what our parents used to say."

"For the first time I appreciate what they meant. For them we were their lives. It does make sense to live for the next generation. I don't mean for an unborn generation, I mean for the children that you can see growing up around you. But weren't you ever glad you simply did something, even though you didn't enjoy doing it? That's how Bernie and I feel." Sy removed his glasses, blew on them, wiped them on his shirt tail; without them he looked frail. "In a way, it's like the years I put in the shops. I wasn't meant to be a factory worker—who is?—and I wasn't even good at it, but I can't regret those years. We didn't come here as refugees,

like some of the American Communists. We came here to participate in something. For the kids, it's almost all they know—and
that makes us uneasy. Shouldn't they know the United States too?
Do we wipe all that out? If we should decide one day to go back,
I won't feel that we've wasted our time here."

Sy had to go to Jerusalem on business for the kibbutz, so he
would be able to drive on with them, as they had already checked
out of the hotel in Tel Aviv.

Irwin was particularly pleased because there had been hovering
over him the shadow of his fortieth year, and his birthday would
fall in the course of their visit to Jerusalem. It had become a running joke; but now that it was really upon him, he had suddenly
become obscurely frightened, and had stopped joking about it. He
was glad to have Sy at his side during the drive into Jerusalem.

Modern Jerusalem was grubby too, but even at its seediest it had
a kind of glory. Surprise swung in upon him at every hilly corner,
with a road falling away or rising steeply. The signs pointing to the
Holy Places, leading back to a scarcely imaginable antiquity of
awesome sages and slippered women balancing jugs, stood beside
those warning of the Mandelbaum Gate or the Nablus Road,
guarded by Jordanian soldiers with plainly visible red shoulder pips,
black moustaches, and poised rifles. The mixture was unsettling;
the modern clinics and the grizzled beggars turned him now this
way, now that. And yet the sense of dislocation, the juxtaposition
of disparate elements from his life and past, produced a sensation
that was oddly voluptuous.

Returning to the hotel, he found that Carmie, whom he had
thought to be shopping on her own for Yemenite handcrafts, had
been conspiring with the chef. She had not acknowledged with
even one word this morning the actual finality of his fortieth birthday; but she had had a cake baked, and mounted in plain view of
everyone in the dining room of the King David.

Standing at the entrance to the long narrow salon in full view of
the visiting Hadassah ladies and UJA big givers, Irwin felt his nose
prickle dangerously. Only the realization that it would be misunderstood prevented him from bursting into tears as his cousin had.

"Please," he said miserably, "don't sing Happy Birthday. Don't
make me blow out any candles."

"He's such a crab," Carmie complained.

"Come on, Irwin," Sy said. "Relax."

"It hurts too much. You think I'm kidding? For you forty is still a long way off. I only hope it'll hurt you less than it does me." He was trying to make another joke, but panic had been building up in him for a long time now. How could he possibly explain that his life was slipping away without his ever having done anything but screw his wife and move people's teeth around? How could he say that he wished, he wished, to change careers, change women, change languages, change countries, not necessarily shovel chicken shit in shorts and sandals, but dive into the Mediterranean and come up with ancient amphorae, put his tongue to new words, his hands to new curves—before it was too late for anything but more of what he had already done . . .

He looked up from the cake knife, his eyes swimming dangerously, and discovered that his son was not there. He said stupidly, "Paulie's gone."

"He excused himself. Maybe he had to go to the toilet."

"With that huge hunk of cake?"

"What's the difference?" Sy asked. "Dinner's over, why should he waste his time with us? He's probably in the lobby, or out on the sidewalk."

Carmela's eyes rolled impatiently as she and Sy went with him to the lobby. But Paul was not there, nor had he gone up to his room, and the doorman at the porte-cochère could only gesture off to his right, down the street, when Irwin asked whether he had seen the boy go out.

"You stay here, in case he comes back," he ordered Carmela. "Come on, Sy."

As they set off along the Jaffa Road, peering into the windows of antique and curio shops catering to tourists, Sy said amiably, "I wouldn't worry about him. This city may be right on the border, but it's still safer than New York. Believe me, you don't have to be afraid that Paulie will get mugged here."

In an instant he was filled with hatred for his cousin, hatred so pure that it tasted sweet, like an essence. What did this man know, with his three fat little kids chattering away in Hebrew, safe, happy, innocent on their communal farm? What would he say if he had only one, what would he say if that one were his only accomplishment, his only solace, his only protection against the horror of no longer being young?

Sy asked a passerby something in Hebrew and received a shake of the head and an impatient *"Lo, lo."*

"God damn it," Irwin said in a strangled voice, raging in his dependence, "we've got to find him."

No longer smiling, Sy replied, "I promise you, we'll find him." He darted into this store, stuck his head into that one, his hands moving, vertically describing the boy's height, horizontally shaping the huge slab of cake that perhaps he still carried. A gray-bearded paperboy, grunting with annoyance, pulled free of them and struggled off with the papers held against his breast, crying out their red banner headlines in hoarse unintelligible Hebrew. A walleyed man in a business suit, briefcase in one hand, shopping bag with a live duck in the other, was more polite, but no more helpful, shaking his head back and forth forcefully. How could he have seen Paulie?

The sky had turned lavender, night was drawing in on the mauve Judean hills. The last reflections of the disappearing sun glittered on the Dome of the Rock, the marvelous Mosque of Omar in the Old City; on the darkening Mount of Olives above and beyond it the first faint lights of the Arab Legionnaires encamped on the remains of the ancient Hebrew cemetery were winking on. In this light the city was staggeringly beautiful. Irwin felt as if his entire chest cavity were occupied by his swollen heart, expanded to the bursting point with joy and fear so intermingled that he could no longer tell which was causing it to pound with such force.

"Here we go, Irwin," his cousin said confidently. He took him by the arm. "This lady says she saw him turn off to the left across the street, going downhill."

Irwin groped his way around the blue and white metal barriers erected to prevent jaywalking. Dumbly, he followed his cousin across the broad street to the narrower one down which his son had supposedly preceded them.

"Apparently he's heading for the Mea Shearim quarter," Sy said.

"What for? We visited it already."

"Maybe it made more of an impression on him than on you."

They were passing men and boys whom he had seen earlier in the day, as he had once or twice encountered them on visits to Brooklyn. But never as now, garbed to greet the incoming Sabbath: freed from the encumbrance of their womenfolk, they strolled in pairs and occasionally in larger groups, some clasping their sons by the hand, gorgeously gowned and so self-assured that it was difficult to understand why they had chosen to enclose themselves in this dark ghetto.

Huge-brimmed brown fur hats sat on their leonine heads like the crowns of arrogant rulers. With noble stride they made their way to the synagogue, some bearing loosely draped over their broad shoulders, as though they wore ermine, black and white striped *talesim,* the hand-threaded fringes hanging over their forearms and along their thighs; others carried the prayer shawls folded in their hands, the more regally to disclose the splendor of their calf-length figured satin gowns, belted at the waist with the silk *gartel* that symbolically separated head and heart from the lower regions. Fingering their beards, they discoursed broadly on the way to prayer; a few hastened at a half-run, gowns parting to reveal white pantaloons, white stockings, the black pumps of eighteenth-century courtiers.

Two blocks farther down, a group of chasidic boys had gathered in a cluster at the corner, heads together, black hats touching, their *peyot* still visible in the gathering darkness, the ringlets either tucked back behind their ears or allowed to fall from otherwise shaven temples all the way to the shoulders; their high-top shoes scraped on the paving, their knickers rustled, as they drew closer.

As he approached them, Irwin saw that his son was in their midst, seated on the curbing, head bent forward intently on what he held in his lap. Irwin hastened to part the group and retrieve his boy; but he had not proceeded more than a few steps when his cousin's fingers closed on his arm.

"Wait."

And as Irwin stood there with his mouth open, reaching for breath, Paul unfolded the hotel napkin on his lap, disclosing the birthday cake still adorned with four candles, and with the pocket knife that he had been given for his tenth birthday proceeded meticulously to cut it into measured portions, extending each as he finished to the silent staring boys who surrounded him.

3. JOE

Joe and Anne seldom looked at TV. Occasionally at his mother's, perhaps, and then only to humor her. At night, Anne was tired and wanted only to listen to music. She rationed the boys strictly, limiting them to Captain Kangaroo only when they had finished the major part of their two hours each at the piano.

Tonight however was the premiere of Fred Byrd's new show. "I'm curious," she had explained, after reading about it on the entertainment page of the LA *Times*.

The color rose in her cheeks as she sat on the edge of the couch, straightbacked as always, her two blond boys on either side of her. "Look!" she cried. "Look, Gene, David!"

Unfolding his leg from the arm of the threadbare easy chair, Joe followed the rapt gaze of his kids. Fred looked back at them in his familiar pose, arms before him on the table, one hand loosely cupped inside the other, his freckled face creased in the rather rueful smile assuring you that he shared with you a private joke—perhaps the mutual knowledge that what he was doing, and you were watching, was less foolish and more engaging than it appeared.

"What's his name?" David demanded. "What's his name?"

"Fred." She could not resist adding, "He's an old old friend of ours. We knew him long before he became famous. Joe, doesn't he look wonderful?"

"I never thought Fred looked wonderful."

He could not bring himself to rhapsodize over someone about whom he had never been enthusiastic to start with. Now Fred was starting on what was apparently going to be his biggest success, presenting

men who combined humble origins with specialized learning. Tonight's hero was a truck driver with an encyclopedic knowledge of
Italian opera. For all of Fred's emphasis on the richness of the teamo's
inner life it was perfectly obvious that the appeal was to man's
hunger not for culture but for dough: the truck driver stood to make
a fortune if he could dredge up the answers to questions posed by
Fred's panel.

Actually, Joe reflected, Anne's enthusiasm was perfectly understandable—and he was a shit to be so short with her. If their life
had gone sour, it was because he was out of work and seemingly
unemployable, not because of his dedication to the revolutionary
movement. There was no more revolutionary movement, and for
him there had not even been any labor movement since '53, when he
had been thrown out of the paint factory.

He was not smitten with nostalgia for those years as a teamster
warehouseman, stocking paint cans on shelves and making up orders
for outgoing trucks. Still the factory had been a base, a happy change
from the lonely months on the painter's scaffold with Rheingold.
The sixty workers, mostly Mexicans, respected him. They belonged
to a Teamsters' local of over a thousand men, composed of workers
in some hundred small plants like their own. Once their urgent postwar wants had been satisfied, they resented the union's giving up a
dozen paid holidays simply for another dime an hour, and that
barely to keep up with the rising cost of living. They started to
rebel, and once he had made connection with the half dozen men
who were the guts of the rebellion, he met with them weekly to
coordinate plans and map strategy.

While it lasted, it was good not just for their morale but for his.
Dave Beck had his roving goon squads operating from Seattle to
Pedro, determined to crush his rank and file, and in the space of
two years it was all over. Joe woke up fired on a trumped-up
charge, with the connivance of the union. Only gradually, as one
job after another melted away, did it become painfully evident
that he had been blackballed up and down the coast. In 1953, with
blacklists far more effective than protests against them, and with
his income approaching the vanishing point, he had taken a job as
a spray painter in a scab shop, figuring that a non-union employer
wouldn't be subject to union pressure, or would ignore it. He had
lasted two weeks.

Crawling home beaten, pink slip in his pocket, he had found Anne at the piano with the boys. She was showing them how to practice scales: two octaves at a time, then four; left hand following right, then left hand opposing right. For the first time the noise made his teeth ache.

The mail was in the hall on top of Anne's little Leopold Mozart book of studies. Two bills and an envelope of photos from Israel, with love and good cheer from Irwin and Carmela and Paul, visiting with Sy and his wife and kids. He crumpled the bills in his fist and then he was on the couch, his face pressed into a pillow.

The next thing he knew, Anne had his head in her lap and was stroking his hair. "I've really screwed it up." He gave her the pink slip. "I really have."

"I wouldn't have wanted you to go against your principles."

"What principles? If they took me off the blacklist and just let me make a living for us, I wouldn't even to be a threat to the mailman."

"They're afraid of your organizing ability. Why else do they hound you?"

It was almost all she had left, the myth that he was a menace. "Anyway," she said defiantly, "I'm amazed you stuck it out there for the two weeks. There are a million better things you can do, a man with your background and your experience. A million."

"Name one."

She was biting down hard on both lips while she continued to stroke his hair. He wanted to tell her that he didn't mean it, he was only kidding. But she had heard that before too, so he decided to keep his mouth shut and work it out by himself.

Next day he tacked up a three by five on the bulletin board of the neighborhood supermarket, announcing his availability for household repairs and auto engine work. No job too large, no job too small. While he waited for the phone to ring, he put a new float in the water closet, new washers on the shower faucets, a new spring on the screen door.

After a while the odd jobs started coming through—bracing a sagging porch, a ring job on a neighbor's car, installing a metal cellar door. Some weeks he was kept busy, and even had to put people off, tell them they would go on his waiting list. But when the waiting list melted and the phone did not ring he was nothing more than an unemployed handyman, the only man on the block at home, terribly present when parents drove up with children for piano lessons.

Not daring to ask Anne for the money she would have been glad to stuff into his pocket, he registered for unemployment comp and started going for walks in order to get out of her way while she gave the lessons that fed them.

When you were young you could say to the girl, tight-lipped, Bogart-style: I've got a lonely road to travel, baby. And she could answer what you hoped she would: I don't want the things other girls do, I'll be happy to do without everything just to be with you.

But now? He could no longer make the claims that had been his right when they were young and childless. Now they had two boys with perfect pitch. Anne was positive that David was a musical phenomenon and had prevailed upon old Bertini, the distinguished Lisztian pianist in semi-retirement, to take on David. There was even a prospect that the old master would teach Gene too. Could he ask her to throw this away, crate the piano, leave town, simply because he was unable to make a living here?

Maybe the best thing he could do for her would be to leave. Hands in his pockets, he would walk down Morton Avenue away from their eighty-five a month house, to the Echo Park district, and drop into Baby Arizmendi's bar for a beer to help him on his way. He liked the atmosphere in bars run by former champs—flyblown fight pictures, tarnished silver cups, arguments about which city and which year it had been, when Abe Attell and . . . But it was almost too easy to become a regular. And there was the matter of buying an occasional round so as not to be labeled sponger. It made no sense, not when Anne was sitting home beating time with a pencil on the edge of the piano.

So he would wander down around the nutty relic of an earlier day, Aimee Semple McPherson's Angelus Temple, and cut back to Stuart Boulevard, up to Skid Row, not far from City Hall. He could not help remembering how Anne used to tease him about what a natural bum he would have made if not for her. "But I'm fastidious," he would protest, "even if I took to booze, I'd want to shave and put on a fresh shirt every day." And she would laugh, "Not after a while you wouldn't—not if you didn't have anyone to shave and dress for."

Gazing at the wheedling, meek, and broken bums, it struck him that it had been a long time since Anne had teased him about becoming a bum. As long as he was neat and clean—which meant as long as his wife continued to tap on the piano with her pencil at three fifty a half hour—he was in one world and the derelicts in another. But who knew? Could he go on indefinitely shaving every morning and putting on a freshly laundered shirt as if it really made a difference, when all that faced him was the question of which direction to walk?

Then, just when he wanted most to prove that he was capable of being a real husband, he discovered that once again he could not get it up. It was worse than the convalescent hospital, for here he was with his family—smiling, alert . . . and jobless. What terrified him most was that Anne did not seem to care one way or another. He began to have the feeling that if he were to tumble down to Skid Row, she would not weep for him, but would simply set one less place at table.

He became meticulous with the kids about arriving on time for dinner, he lectured them on table manners, and he urged them to eat heartily. "Second helpings all around," he would say cheerily, meat platter in one hand and serving fork in the other, and Anne would smile at everyone like a TV housewife.

He took to sitting in the sun, persuading himself that he had been too long confined in the paint factory and under his neighbors' cars. The odd citizens whom he encountered—meter readers, paper boys, salesmen—congratulated him on his healthy color. For the first time since the war he was putting on weight, and he began to take an interest in the only problem that was disturbingly real to his fellow Americans: losing ugly fat.

Fred's new show, that Anne was insistent on watching, was sponsored by the manufacturer of a soluble crystal which you drank to dissolve the fat of prosperity—or unemployment. The commercials were far more interesting than Fred's party game, for they presented real live fat people first in all their miserable ordinariness, and then, transformed by Fizz-Off, glamorously slim at beach parties and fun gatherings.

Anne was both artless and unimaginative, literal in the way of women who reject the extravagant and the fantastic but cannot deny themselves the privilege of daydreaming. She jeered at the commercials and used the intervals to put away the dishes; but she gazed on the opera-wise teamster with her chin in her hand and her eyes glazed, nameless visions drifting through her mind.

He had half-decided that once the show was over and the boys were put to bed, he would take up with Anne what he was beginning to think of as a possible last chance to redeem what he had been and perhaps still might be. Buick-Oldsmobile-Pontiac, which he had left in disgust in the summer of '48, was hiring again. The biggest season in automotive history couldn't last indefinitely, sooner or later the pipeline would get clogged with cars, but if they were as indiscriminate in their hiring as they seemed—he had driven out Alameda Street, casing things, and found the South Gate parking lot jammed with the cars of new employees—they just might be more impressed by his experience than by his name being on a black list.

When David and Gene were tucked into their trundle beds Anne took his hand. "You know something?" she asked. "You'd do fantastically well on Fred's program. You could make a fortune."

"I don't know what you're talking about."

"That truck driver isn't just a plain truck driver, any more than you're a plain factory worker. If you went on the show people would be bowled over, just bowled over, by how much you know."

His mind was still on the auto plant, and he answered her absently. "I don't think Fizz-Off or Fred would be interested in my kind of concern."

"Oh Joe," she cried, twisting around, squeezing his hand, "do it! Do it!"

"Do what?"

"Write to Fred. What have you got to lose? I bet he'll think it's a terrific idea."

"You must be joking."

"Didn't you ever feel anything in your bones? That's the way I feel now. If you were to call Fred, long distance, you know, just to congratulate him, then you could more or less casually add that you'd be willing to go on his show. It'd be a holiday for you, they'd fly you east, they'd put you up—"

"I could never do anything like that."

She misunderstood. "If you're shy, I'll do it for you. I'll sit down and write to Fred. You just tell me what subject you want to compete in and I'll do the rest, I'll—"

"If you ever did that," he interrupted coldly, fully aware at last of her intent, "I'd never forgive you for it."

Anne did not recoil. Instead she turned wistful. "It's just that you're so good-looking, you photograph so well. And you're so persuasive."

"I never persuaded you."

"Oh yes you did. Your day is going to come. I keep trying to explain to your mother, it's just that we're in a period of reaction."

He turned away, his eyes smarting. Anne made a final try. "I only wanted you to have the chance to tell millions of Americans what's wrong, and to show them a better way."

"Shades of Harry Sturm. One hour of prime time and we can sell socialism to thirty million Americans."

"You mean you'd pass up the chance even to try?"

She was so patently dishonest, and at the same time so ingenuous and naive, so much the girl he had fallen in love with in British Columbia, that he was ashamed of himself for being angry with her. He began to stroke her cheek. She slid back slowly on the couch, sighing, her eyes closing as she drew him down with her.

His anger was transformed into passion, and he tore impatiently at her clothing, excited by her movements, here instead of in bed. She groped blindly for his belt and opened his trousers, and there was no problem at all. He was poundingly ready, and he threw her down, his excitement mounting as he felt the grip of her legs, slippery in their nylons, and the embroidery of her garter belt still girdling her belly. They bounded together in a frenzy of haste, pounding as if their excitement was heightened by fear of interruption.

When they had finished, Anne arose, seemingly unconcerned that his resurgence might have been triggered by resentment. She wiped him sweetly, even kissed it for him, then took him by the hand and led him upstairs into bed, where she fell asleep almost at once in the crook of his arm.

He was glad that he had not spoken of the factory to her at a moment when she was daydreaming over him like a teenager. It might have plunged her into something even worse than what he had been sinking into. Supposing he were turned down for employment because he was too old, or too prominently engraved in the blacklist? Then she would know what he already did—that he had reached the end of the line . . .

He awoke at dawn and ate a quick furtive breakfast, like an eager hunter on the first day of the season, with a family opposed to bringing down birds. He arrived at South Gate early enough to be able to look across briefly at Watts and be cheered by old Rodia getting in his licks, pushing a little bit closer to heaven with his tilting spires.

He eased himself into one of the booths at the employment office, unzipped his nylon jacket, indicated Yes he had worked there before and Yes he would be willing to work swing shift, and the recruiter was incurious about why he'd left in '48, or why he wanted to come back at his age. Stepping out of his moccasins, stripped to the waist, the little bulge of the prosperous hanging over his beltline, he met the surprised gaze of the examining doctor.

"That's quite a tan you've got there."

"I've been in the sun a lot."

"I can see that," the doctor said sharply. "That's what I was commenting on."

"I hope you don't mind, doctor," he replied, stung at being patronized. "I understand you don't provide much sun inside."

He was to be notified by telegram to report for work. It was like waiting for labor pains; Anne canceled her evening lessons, got a sitter, and they went out every evening until the telegram should come. Anne spoke of it, when she had to, as a temporary expedient —Joe's return for a sociological survey of the new working class.

For her it was not really that; it was rather a cruel disappointment. For him it was pure hell. Physically, morally, he felt tested, taunted, and tormented by the starting bell. They put him on as a polisher, and as the cars came out of the oven after the second spray coat, he buffed half the roof (a Mexican kid did the other half) and sometimes a door panel too. Within a week his fist was like a claw from gripping the brush in the effort to keep up with the endless procession of swaying auto bodies; every muscle ached from the constant scrambling; the oven ventilators roared in his ears long after he had left the plant, the hot acrid paint smell stung him between the eyes, up to the sinus, and he had lost eleven pounds.

Like a weak-willed woman on a diet, he ate furtively but ravenously, raiding the refrigerator at one o'clock in the morning, digging at the ice cream with a tablespoon, gorging, while he crammed potato chips into his mouth with his left hand.

Anne was matter of fact. And he, once it was clear that the blacklist did not reach into the assembly plant, took a hard pleasure in having escaped from the morass of self-pity. He got rid of the waistline flab, and if he could not scrub away the paint smell, which soaked through his work gloves like a poison gas, he felt like a man again nonetheless.

There was a brief wildcat, which ended as suddenly as it had started, but through it all the hiring went on, the recruiting station was jammed with money-hungry youngsters, signing up to be chewed up on the line even while others were gunning their jalops out of the blacktop lots, quitting in droves before the end of the pay period, taking off to look for other less killing work.

"For the first time," he wrote Sy, "I find myself in the shop simply as an observer. It's almost as if I were there specifically to report to someone like you on the mood of the workers."

He had no political base in the factory from which to operate. The New Socialist League attempted to keep alive, mainly among college students, the idea of a socialism independent of both Moscow and Washington, but it had given up hope of influencing factory workers in any significant way. As for the union, he had gone to two swing shift meetings. Pointless: wildcat or no wildcat, the attendance had been about fifty each time—out of a work force of five thousand.

Rank and file militants existed, but they scorned the union as they detested the management; in a sense they were, as he wrote to Sy, a bunch of saboteurs. And so he became one too, fighting grievances for the men immediately around him, fighting union committeemen as he fought foremen and supervisors, and gumming things up if only because that was the only way you had of reminding yourself that you were not simply an extension of the assembly line. The thousands who poured in and out, buttons pinned to their plaid shirts, sullenly holding their lunch boxes ajar for plant police inspection, were more a mob than a disciplined work force. They had no sense that what they did might serve as a bond; all they seemed to hold in common was a contempt for the work and a desire to do something else—anything else.

In these circumstances he found it hard to play-act that he was once again a noble proletarian, not simply feeding his family by the sweat of his brow (that part of it was true enough) but also bringing the workers news of a better tomorrow. He simply rode along with them in the slough of the great wave, cursing as they cursed, working as they worked, living—more or less—as they lived. "One day all this will change," he wrote to Sy. "It has to. For now, I'm doing what they are—punching in and out, keeping an eye open for a good break, keeping up the car and the house, buying things for the wife and kids . . ."

One night when he came home he found a letter from Sy waiting for him on the kitchen table. The familiar Israeli stamps cheered him. He opened it quickly, reading while he gobbled ice cream.

Sy's brother Sid was going to be in Pedro for a longshore union convention. Would Joe have a cup of coffee with him and say hello? It was an odd request but he sensed beneath Sy's offhand boldness an urgency and an embarrassment. Sy added two other pieces of news: Norm had been at the kibbutz for several days, in the course of researching an article on the Israel-Egypt situation. And he had given Hoover, who had more or less retired to Southern California, Joe's address.

He was uncertain whether he was less eager to see Sy's brother or Hoover. "But that's not quite right either," he said to Anne. "It's just that I dread seeing that tough old bastard put to pasture in Southern California. I'm afraid of old people," he blurted. Then he added, "Especially old agitators."

"You don't mean you're not going to look up Sy's brother?"

"Oh, I'll look him up. But I'm sure he's one of those types that still regards me as an enemy of the working class."

He had the opportunity to find out in a few days. The longshore delegates were meeting in a moderate-sized hall; Sid Glantzman was seated in a corner with a group from the Bay Area.

He was half a head taller than his brother, bulkier too, with a wide hard belly that jutted over his belt and a shock of graying hair that arose angrily from his scalp. His heavy, sad, swarthy face was scarred lengthwise; so was his arm, which he raised to emphasize what he was saying, and then let fall heavily on the cloth-covered table before him. Only around the mouth, with its full and almost delicately carved lips, was there any indication that he could be the brother of Sy, or the cousin of Irwin Metzger.

Joe went over and introduced himself.

Sid's voice was so New York-accented that it gave him a twinge; ever since he could remember he had associated that singsong drawl with intellect, radicals, excitement, Jews; he had never been able to tell Sy, since it would have embarrassed them both, that it was one of the things that had made him worth listening to when they had first met. Now his brother was saying, "Sy mentioned you last time he wrote. You're working out at BOP."

"That's right. I thought we might get together—"

Sid scraped back his chair. "Ya wanna getta cuppa coffee?"

At a formica table for two in the corner drug store Sid was scarcely less forbidding. He drank his coffee black, frowning at its heat while he sipped, disinclined to open even a neutral conversation.

"Your brother's family is getting very Israeli," Joe said. "But I think that's the very reason they'll be coming back."

Sid looked up, surprised.

"You have to reach a certain point, living abroad, when you know that you can't stay away any longer or you'll never come back."

"To me that sounds metaphysical." Sid used the word almost contemptuously.

"The moment of decision comes, when you know you have to go back. Sy is too curious about what's going on over here. Why else would he ask me to look you up?"

"I've been wondering about that myself."

"Because he knows he'll hear from me quicker than from you."

Sid flushed. "We've never been close. We've had political differences."

"But people mellow, right? Just having children changes you."

Sid's heavy face tightened in some indefinable way. "I never took exactly that view of politics. Maybe we better steer clear of politics."

"If you're got a list of subjects that you want to put off limits, why don't we say goodbye right now?"

At this Sid smiled slowly. "All I meant was that by bourgeois custom you don't pick a fight during a courtesy call."

After that they got along better than he had expected. Over their second cup of coffee Sid conceded that while he had been out of the CP for years he still retained a certain stuffiness about discussions with anti-Communist leftists. "It's an automatic defense." He gestured upward with his closed fist. "I suppose it keeps me from feeling that I'm selling out to the enemy just because I'm not under party discipline. Even with my own brother."

Grateful for employment and shelter as a dissident Communist in a union that was still dominated by Stalinist attitudes, Sid remained hesitant to grant independent leftists the right to function freely. "Smash" was the word he had learned twenty years earlier, and he found it hard to unlearn it. But if he had been able to come this far, one day he might go further.

So Joe spoke of family rather than politics, and to his own surprise found himself reminiscing.

"When my sister was little, we found she was retarded. My father couldn't take it, and he walked out. My mother had to raise the two of us by herself."

"Your father must have been a pip."

"A prick is what I'd call him. I haven't seen him in sixteen years."

"Sy wrote me that you were blacklisted."

"It looked that way for a couple of years."

"I never thought . . ." Sid stopped, and tried again. "I used to think only people on my side of the fence had that kind of trouble."

"And I used to think that your people took care of each other. Do you have any idea how many guys like me got frozen out because they were tagged as anti-Stalin?"

Sid drew himself up tight and folded his arms against his breast. At length he said, "Listen, if you're sick of that assembly line—"

"I miss being out of doors."

"It occurred to me, you might be interested in working on the front." Unfrivolous, he tried to be light: "Fresh air, and all that."

What Sid was offering was extraordinary. The least he could do was to warn, "Your politics—or even Harry Bridges' politics—still aren't mine."

"We've got all kinds up in the Bay Area. You name them, we've got them." Sid was stretching himself further than ever.

"I've got ties here. Not just my sister and my mother. My older boy is a kind of prodigy. He's studying with a concert pianist, a great old man." He repeated Anne's words: "That's not the kind of thing you throw away."

Sid shrugged slightly. "Keep in touch anyway."

He was still turning this over in his mind several days later when he got home from a trip downtown to buy valve seats for the Pontiac. Staring without seeing it at his dandelion-infested plot of grass (he gave the boys a penny a weed when they came out with a basket and dug away), he could hear David inside, playing a Schubert impromptu, his own particular favorite; Davey was to perform it at a recital in a week or two.

He stuffed his hands into his pockets and strode into the house. Under the Spanish archway leading to the living room he stopped short. A straight-backed man was seated in the good chair, hands on his knees, attending to little Davey at the piano. For a crazy moment he was sure that it was his father, who had searched him out, moved into his house, and installed himself in his favorite chair.

The man turned. It was Comrade Hoover. Impassive, unsurprised, he put his index finger to his pursed mouth in token of silence, almost of reproof.

"He came in while David was practicing," Anne murmured. Her hand on his shoulder blades was cool and steadying. "He's really very sweet."

An odd word for Hoover. He went on in and seated himself. When Davey had finished the old man clapped gravely four times.

"That was very good," he said. "I used to play the violin when I was your age. But I was a *lazy* boy, and I never did get very far."

The vision of a little Hoover, in curls, sailor suit, and fiddle under the chin, was almost too much. Davey and Gene, who had been half-hidden at the tail of the piano, were staring at him in fascination, mouths half-open, as if he were a creature from another planet.

Joe felt in turn that he was looking at his own boys as a witness, almost a stranger, as though they existed apart from his design or control, with their own secret thoughts, unrelated to a father who disappeared every afternoon to do something in a factory.

Davey had been pleased by Hoover's praise. His face, still rounded as a baby's, was still knitted with the concentration he had brought to his music. "How long did you take violin lessons?" he asked.

"Only four years. It was a long time ago. I certainly do thank you for letting me listen."

As Anne led the boys out of the room he gripped Hoover's hand. "It's been a long time. What are you up to?"

"I'm on the shelf. At least, that's where they *think* they put me. I'm on social security."

Was this what happened to overage revolutionists? He had seen them in his mind's eye as tough old exiles, plotting and planning to the last breadth. But never standing in line with quavering oldsters, anxiously holding the registered postcard, or awaiting the postman and the green government check.

Hoover smiled, a frosty grin that still breathed defiance. "You haven't heard the worst. I've moved in with my married daughter in San Bernardino. I'm a babysitter."

"And the Party . . ."

"What party? You think we're back in wartime, when we had guys

like you in the factories, paying dues every week? To say nothing
of professionals, sympathizers, writing us out checks month in and
month out? Now there's nothing but a bunch of *clubs,"* he said
scornfully, "kaffee klatsches for schoolteachers and lawyers that
like to sit around their living rooms and com*plain."*

"You voted to dissolve the Party."

"Damn straight. Why de*lude* yourself, with no more than half a
dozen people like you and Bill? Without cadres you got no influence
in the shops. Without influence you're not a party, you're a *talk*ing
society. That's all right, it's nice, it keeps people out of mischief,
maybe it even keeps socialist ideas alive in certain circles. But it's
a middle-class activity. It's not for me."

"Wait a minute." He raised his arm, and almost knocked into
Anne, who was bringing in a tray of coffee and sandwiches. "You
had fifty years in the movement. What do you do now? What do
I do now? Concentrate on getting rich like Lewis Lorch and Harry
Sturm?"

"Harry is a *freak.* Lewis, or Lorch, is a *fink."*

"How come we attracted so many freaks and finks?"

Hoover held up his hand. It rose from his starched cuff like some
formal agency of authority. "Now you just *wait* a minute." He
accepted a sandwich from Anne. "You want to know about me? I'll
tell you about me."

"Go ahead."

"You think I'm going to commit suicide because the Party did?
You lived through your war, I lived through mine in the Argonne
forest. And plenty more—depressions, race riots, even a lynching,
that we don't have to go into. But I'm not about to lay down and
die."

"I'm waiting to hear."

Hoover grinned foxily. "Anybody wants to listen to me, I'll talk.
That so-called New Socialist League has got a youth group at
Berkeley, asked me up there to talk last week. Not a bad bunch—
considering how *ig*norant they are. No traditions, no militant labor
movement around them. They like to weep and wail about The
Bomb."

"Can you blame them?"

"I told them, no use to cry together, you might as well cry alone, it's
more dignified. If you get together, get together to hammer out a
*pro*gram. In a period of reaction, you learn, study, prepare yourself

for leadership when the tide turns." Hoover smiled reminiscently.
"That's what I said at their public rally at Sather Gate. Couple
hundred people there, no booing, no heckling, lots of intelligent
questions. You'd be sur*prise*d how people respond to a little common
sense."

"The workers don't. Not right now, anyway."

"That's because they've been fed so much baloney for so long.
Maybe if we'd just shut up for a while, I mean all of us, and let
them go to work and buy their groceries, they'd be in a mood to
listen after a while. Myself I'm taking advantage of the times, and
my so-*called* retirement, to do some research."

Anne asked curiously, "What's that?"

"I'm corresponding with people in Ohio, also in Virginia, for
information on my forebears. And I'm applying my bottom to a
library chair, going through old records and documents. I intend
to write my autobiography, not because I'm any more vain than the
next man, but because the story of how I came to be a class
conscious socialist may be useful to the next generation."

It was not clear to Joe whether Hoover's program of library
work represented a rational calculation or a rationalization.

"Do you think I'm wasting my life?" he asked abruptly.

Hoover regarded him impassively. "That's like asking a friend
if you should marry his sister."

"But I know what I think. I want to know what *you* think."

At this Anne rose abruptly and went into the kitchen.

"Within limits," Hoover said, "you're doing what you want to do.
So why ask me? To get me to back you up in front of your wife?"

He winced. "You're one of those that got me to commit myself
to the working class."

"Do you know of any other class with the power to make a new
society?"

"I don't even try to sell that line to Anne any more. She knows
as well as I that the men I work with aren't interested in making
a new society. They're not even interested in the AFL-CIO merger."

"Why should they be? Sooner or later the conditions of life will
lead them to organize into unions or sometimes even against unions,
right? Their own interests lead them to struggle, to *collec*tive struggle.
When they start to fight again, their fight will be inevitably a*gainst*
reaction and toward progress."

"The question is when. After being blacklisted, and without

prospects, and now finding that the guys in the shop don't care about collective action, I'm not so sure I still have the right to ask Anne to be patient with me."

"She hasn't done too badly by you."

"You don't know the half of it."

"I wasn't referring just to her. I was thinking of your boys." Hoover was regarding him somberly, hands folded across his dark conservative vest. "That's right, your boys. They are not ordinary boys. And if you ask yourself whether you're wasting your life, think of them first. If I were you I'd think of those boys before *any*thing. You know what I mean? Before *any*thing."

Two nights later he came home to find Anne waiting up for him, white-faced with fatigue.

"Why do you stay up till three A.M.?"

"I wanted to talk to you. I was reading this new novel, *Out Went the Candle.*"

He knelt on the bed beside her and took off her reading glasses so that he might kiss her eyelids. "You'll be dead tomorrow."

"I'll catch up. Listen, Joe, Bertini is going to San Francisco."

Why should he care about Davey's piano teacher taking a trip? He said wearily, "So the kid'll miss a lesson."

"He's leaving for good, for the San Francisco Conservatory. Where does that leave us? Or Davey?"

The rising note of hysteria in her voice made him uneasy. "We'll have to consider alternatives."

"You're not at a meeting. I'm talking about your children."

"Take it easy."

The worst retort he could have made. She sat up, glaring, her pupils dilated. "What do you think I've been doing while you sat in the sun, or passed the time of day with bartenders and crazy Italians building towers out of Coke bottles?"

"I know what you've been doing."

"I've been sitting with those children two hours a day, seven days a week, giving them good practice habits, making them learn what discipline is. You felt it was a threat, didn't you, my devoting so much time to them when I could have been holding your hand."

"If I had reservations, it wasn't on my account. Your sitting with them doesn't hurt me and it won't kill you. But I've never been convinced that it was good for the boys."

"When did you offer any better ideas?"

"Would you have listened? You would have told me that I don't know anything about music, which I never denied."

Groping for a Kleenex, she demanded, "Then why are you starting now? Have I cheated you out of something while I worked with the boys?"

"You've become obsessed. I don't want you to be like those Jewish mamas that beat their kids to make them play the fiddle."

"Very funny."

"Even if they're as good as you say, what right do you have to commit them to the piano?"

"You make it sound like committing them to prison. Is it un-American not to let them play baseball? Their fingers are precious. There are other games."

"I don't give a shit if they never pick up a ball. But I do care if you force them into something they may resent later on. Why can't they make up their own minds?"

"You can't decide to become a pianist when you're twenty-one, the way you decide to become a lawyer. They have to work at it now. I practically went on my knees to get Bertini to listen to Davey, and now he's going to San Francisco. And if you don't want to help me then I'll go ahead and resolve it on my own"— she concluded coldly—"just the way I've had to resolve other problems, these last few years."

What was he supposed to do? Fly Davey to San Francisco every week? Fly me to the moon. Or—something opened and closed in his head—suggest that they move to the Bay Area?

Next day he drove out to South Gate sick with the knowledge that nothing had been, to use her word, resolved. It was bad enough going to work in the afternoon, to see the day men heading for home, family, and relaxation; but then he had to tie on his stained apron and pick up the stupid bucket and brush with nothing ahead of him but another job coming at him, another car, another one, another one, until the relief man showed up to give him the lousy twelve minutes off so that he could sit down on a crate and think about the situation at home.

The foreman came around shortly after eleven to ask if he wanted to stay on for overtime. He shook his head grimly. With his teeth clamped he said, "Got to get home to my wife."

When he did get home Anne was asleep; she had not stayed

up two nights in a row. From their darkened bedroom he could hear her even breathing. He moved on to the boys' room and listened to them too, their sighs mingling, one a little strangled by swollen adenoids, the other interrupted now and then by a word spoken in sleep: "I said no . . . we flew all the way . . . why? I don't . . . He played too loud, he hurt . . ."

His heart swelling, he bent over each in turn and smoothed out the pillowcases moist from their mouths, the twisted knit cuffs of their pajamas. The frowns faded from their freckled foreheads. Gene reached up for a hug, but he was hardly awake, and would not remember anything in the morning.

In the kitchen he took out the ice cream and picked up Anne's memo pad. *Call Long Distance at 7 A.M. and ask for New York Operator 73. Have set alarm.* He fell asleep almost at once, too tired even to wonder who it could be. But in the morning, shuffling out to the phone without enough sleep, he was irrationally uneasy, as if he were waiting for someone to read him a telegram.

The girl who answered sounded like a secretary, but she was prepared for him. "We'd like to know, Mr. Link, if you'd be interested in auditioning for the Fizz-Off show."

"I think you've got the wrong party."

"Joseph Link, Morton Street, LA?"

"Yes, but I'm not in show business."

The girl laughed. "Professor Byrd warned me that you'd be difficult. He just wants a tape to make certain of how you sound on mike. After that he'll call you himself."

"He wants me to go on his show?"

"Hard to believe? The worst you can do is not make it through the first round, but even at that a contestant is guaranteed, you know, a minimum of—"

"What makes you think I'd be interested?"

"Why . . ." She was suddenly at a loss. "Dr. Byrd said . . . We've never had anyone . . ."

"Well now you have," he said. "Tell Fred no."

"I'm sure he'll want to talk to you when he gets in."

"I'm not interested."

He slammed down the receiver and ran into the bedroom. Anne sat up, blinking, hand over her eyes.

"What is it, Joe? Is something wrong?" She was wide-awake now. "That phone call—"

"Yes, that phone call." He was on her now, shaking her by the upper arms, her flesh bed-warm under his hands. "Didn't I tell you not to put my name in? Didn't I?"

"What are you talking about?"

"Don't play those games with me."

She twisted under his grip. "You must be crazy."

"You betrayed me. I never thought the day would come that my own wife would betray me."

"What did I do?" Her voice was whistling in his ear as he pressed her back to the rumpled pillow from which she had risen. "Tell me what I did!"

"You asked Fred to turn me in to a whore. What did I tell you when you brought it up? I said if you did it I'd never forgive you. And I swear to Christ I never will."

"I never called him, I never wrote him, I never did anything!"

Behind him he heard the sound of his children's feet, swift but furtive in the hallway. They were hiding behind the door jamb, just out of sight. He turned back to his wife, his breath rasping in his throat, his paint-discolored hands still gripping her reddened shoulders. He had to blink to get her in focus—she kept sliding in front of his eyes, multiplying, blurring.

"You bastard," she whispered, falling away as he released her, "you bastard."

4. HAM

For a long time, too long, they sang Gospel songs, harmonizing across the prison corridor. The music that Ham had rejected in his teens had become a part of his life once again, but although it drew him back to his earliest childhood just as it did those with whom he had been arrested, he knew other kinds of music, as they did not. After a while the chanting and the exhortations to the Lord made his head ache; it made him feel like a snob, but there it was, and after some time he simply sat silently on his cot, jotting notes on an envelope while the others in his cell and across the corridor continued to chant, one starting a new song when the others had trailed off.

At last Leonard Foley, in the opposite bunk, drawled, "What's the mattah, Ham, getting restless?"

He shrugged. "Isn't anything we can do at this end."

"Except sing."

"I wish they'd get up the bail money. We can't accomplish much just sitting here."

"That's why they're holding us."

"Oh, I know why they picked us up. I didn't run that red light, and you didn't talk back, and Fred's registration wasn't expired. But if all of us miss the meeting—"

"Like you said, isn't anything we can do at this end. Don't fret about the meeting—they can't stop that, unless they lock up every black man, woman, and child in Montgomery. And that's fifty thousand souls."

Ham slid off the bunk so that he could stretch. His toes shrank from the cold cement floor. "What I worry about is whether they can organize the meeting around our absence, so it could serve some point. But Frank has the key to the room with the mimeograph paper right on his car key ring. And you were going to make up the list for Audrey to telephone. And I had those press releases to write—"

The minister's smile was so patient, so benevolent, in this gloomy Lysol-smelling black man's jail, Saturday night haven for sleeping-it-off knife wielders, that it was irritating. "If we weren't making them a whole lot of botheration, you think they'd mess with us? You think they'd take a chance on stirring things up even more?"

Always the bright side. How I wish, he thought, that I could play Pollyanna; Big Boy brought me up wrong. All of these God-infected persons, from his dead step-father to Leonard Foley, pleased themselves by taking the long view of the black man's troubles. Big Boy had taught him—and so well that he could never believe otherwise—that nothing you tried was any damn good unless the people you worked with could measure the result in larger pay envelopes, fewer aching muscles, or at least greater solidarity. But the parsons were the people with whom he had to work. Among them he now found not only Leonard Foleys but the sharpest organizers he had ever encountered. Thanks to their mixing traditional faith with bold improvisation, the bus boycott was not simply an expression of solidarity. It was a success, a harbinger of great deeds.

The jailer arrived, hand groping in his mouth for a morsel wedged between his teeth. "You," he mumbled around his hand, nodding at Ham, "you got a visitor. You're gittin out anyway, soon's the bondsman's money goes through. If I was you," he added in what he apparently intended as a not unkindly suggestion, "I'd git my tail back to Jackson, or wherever it is you come from, jes as fas as I could. Nex time they jes might forget where the key is at. Or maybe you'll wish you was settin here." He pointed his toothpick at Leonard Foley. "You too, reverend. Who'da thought you'd disgrace your flock by winding up in the drunk tank?"

Smiling benignly, Leonard declined to rise to the bait. He contented himself with motioning to Ham to precede him. Striding fast, anxious to get back to things, Ham reached the desk first and saw the great bulk of the man standing beyond it and turned sideways, massive arms folded so that his blue serge suit coat was pulled taut across his broad back.

"Big Boy!" he cried. "Big Boy!"

His old mentor turned deliberately, unfolded his arms, extended his hand. It was less than three years since they had last met; Big Boy could only be in his early forties; but his nappy head was sprinkled with white, and the grooves on either side of his big firm mouth were deeply engraved.

"Surprised?" Big Boy smiled faintly.

"That's not the half of it. What are you doing here?"

"Later. Now come on, sign your name for the man and let's go— I got my car sittin outside. Your bail's taken care of."

On their release, he introduced Big Boy to Leonard Foley. "I want you to meet my cousin, Clarence Hull. He just about brought me up. Big Boy, this is Reverend Foley, one of our leaders."

"Already heard about you," Big Boy said.

Not to be outdone, Leonard Foley inclined his head. "You were a splendid influence on Hamilton. Outstanding."

"Little early to say." Big Boy shoved them both out the jailhouse door.

Ham breathed deeply. Sharper than the fresh air of freedom and the return to the boycott was the exhilaration of having Big Boy, dry and cutting as ever, once again at his side after their years of estrangement. His heart leaped when Big Boy, who had been so bitterly contemptuous of his commitment to non-violence, said briefly, "Went huntin for you, looked up E. D. Nixon, from the Sleeping Car Porters."

"He started the whole protest. When he heard from his wife at the Brotherhood office that Rosa Parks had been arrested, he lined up the ministers—"

"I know all that." Big Boy gestured across the street to the mud-spattered black Olds parked at the opposite curb, its New York plates crusted, its windshield clear only in the arcs described by the wipers. "Let's get away from the jailhouse. I don like the crowd that hangs aroun here."

Leonard asked eagerly, as they drove off, "Did you get to the mass meeting?"

"Sure did. Nixon took me to the church."

"Did it go well?"

Big Boy pushed out his heavy lower lip. "That Reverend King

talks up a storm. An when they sang 'My Feet Is Tired, But My Soul Is Rested,' they really raised the roof."

"You'll come to our strategy meeting tonight," Ham said. "I was afraid we were going to miss it."

"Well, I don know."

"You'll be more than welcome, Mr. Hull," Leonard assured him. "If you'll just drop me off at that second corner, I'll be able to rejoin my wife before she worries any more. I know you two must have plenty to talk about."

When Big Boy had dropped off Reverend Foley Ham said to him, "It's the preachers who've kept us going. We've got a lot of rivalry between Baptists and Methodists, but we decided from the start to rotate the mass meetings, a different church every week. And when you've got seventeen thousand rank and file bus riders, the prima donnas can't get away with much. Besides, those Baptists know Roberts' Rules of Order like my step-father knew Deuteronomy, inside out and sideways. Makes for discipline."

"Yeah, I guess. You hungry?"

"I could eat," he admitted. He was about to suggest that they go on to Mrs. Barrow's, where he had been boarding ever since his arrival in Montgomery, but something in Big Boy's tone said that he wanted privacy. "We can get some pigs' feet, and a table to ourselves, at a place I know, just turn right and park."

Big Boy followed directions in silence, then walked heavily alongside him into the small restaurant. It was not until they had been served that he spoke up at last. "My ma jus died, in N'Orleans."

Ham looked up from his plate startled. "Why didn't you tell me right away?"

Big Boy shrugged. "It's no news for the jailhouse."

"I certainly am sorry to hear it."

"She was gettin pretty old. I got a long distance call she was failin, so I got in the car an took off." He chewed stolidly. "Got there too late."

"What a rotten shame."

"Woulda wanted to go for the funeral anyway. She was laid out nice, but I got no pleasure from it. She didn live easy, she didn die easy."

"But it would have pleased her to know that you were there, at the end."

"Maybe so. Didn work out that way. Took care of the in-surance, saw some of the brothers from the Warehousemen, first time in maybe fifteen years, an that was that. Nothin else to keep me there. So I headed north by way of Mobile an figured, why not see what kind of hell Ham's raising in Montgomery."

"Well, now you know. I told you years ago, I swore to you that I wasn't quitting, I just wanted to fight in another way. We have a bus boycott going in Tallahassee too, I was there last week."

"I heard." Big Boy would not comment further.

Stung, he found it hard to keep from bragging. "I don't know if you heard the way we got it organized. We picked out thirty-five key locations on a city map. Every morning at seven-thirty sharp we've got a hundred and fifty cars waiting there. By nine-thirty we've transported three thousand people to their jobs."

"What do the rest of them do?"

"Five thousand people walk to work every day. You'd be surprised how many whites are sympathetic, even pick our people up. It helps make up for the terrorist gangs. Meanwhile they're hurting every day. Don't forget, 75 per cent of the bus riders were black. All our people have to do to keep up their spirits is to look at those buses rolling by empty."

"Sounds like you got things under control." Big Boy's tone was not so much commendatory as grudging. He gestured curtly with the knife and fork that looked small in his big fists.

"It's a model set-up."

"Then they don't need you too bad. I was thinkin you might want a ride up north. You could spell me with the drivin."

He kicked himself. How quickly he had fallen into the trap! Would Big Boy always be one step ahead? "I'd like to do that," he said, "but I've got responsibilities here. It isn't as easy as it looks from the outside."

"They got along without you while you was sittin in the jailhouse."

"Nobody's indispensable. But I feel an obligation. You wouldn't ask me to walk out in the middle of a strike, would you?"

"Depends on whether you could do more good someplace else. Like gettin support for the boycott."

Had Big Boy already been talking to Nixon about finances? It never paid to underestimate him.

"I'm no fund-raiser."

"What are you?" Big Boy asked coldly.

"An organizer, I guess."

"It's all organized, way you tell it. Ain gonna fall apart to-morrow, is it?"

"The Montgomery Improvement Association is in good shape. You'll see at the steering committee meeting tonight. But it's complicated. The original three-point program didn't ask for an end to segregated seating, only for fair treatment and Negro drivers for Negro neighborhoods, so the NAACP refused to support the boy-cott."

"But they're fightin a court case."

"When we broadened our demands to attack segregation they came in."

"Takes money, don it? Means a lot when money comes in from outside."

By the time they arrived at the hall, most of the hundred-odd members of the steering committee were already there. After they had been called to order Big Boy was presented to the full com-mittee as a guest bearing greetings from his steelworkers local.

Massive and grim in his mourning clothes, he used none of the tricks from the old days, but spoke to these middle-class people with respect and even admiration. No sarcasm, no epithets. He talked of the new Negro American Labor Committee. "We want to unite black workers in the industrial north in support of their struggling brethren down here."

"Amen!"

"I will tell them about your solidarity in this holy struggle."

Gravely he acknowledged the shouts and fervent prayers that greeted these final words. His English was more accurate and gram-matical when he spoke to a hundred people than when he spoke to one. Much as he would hate to admit it he had learned plenty from Hoover—just as, Ham thought, I've learned plenty from him.

After he and Reverend Foley had been officially welcomed back from jail, the committee reports were encouraging—except for that of the finance committee.

"The NAACP, which is deeply committed in the arguments that will be heard before the Federal District Court, can't be expected to turn aside one precious dollar from the expensive legal battle. We can't expect CORE, which has terrific demands upon it, to finance our fight." The speaker was a well-to-do insurance agent who had been goaded into involvement, Ham knew, by the sight of his sister-in-law rising at dawn to walk to work, and coming home at night to soak her swollen feet in a basin. "Brothers and sisters, we are going to have to dig deeper ourselves."

"We will!"

An elderly woman jumped up in the second row. "We have walked in cold, we have walked in rain!" she cried. "Well, it's spring now! You mean we can't do in spring what we did in winter?"

From the platform one of the ministers' voices rose above the chanting chorus that greeted Mrs. Jones's rhetorical question. "The fact remains. We have heavy expenses. We have bills to pay and more debts coming up. I will entertain practical suggestions for fund-raising."

"Let's hear from Brother Hull."

Big Boy rose again. Without moving to the front of the crowded hall, he spoke unhesitatingly. "You've been carrying a heavy burden. But pride is no reason to carry the whole burden alone. When we have a strike, we appeal to our trade union brothers. Why not appeal to your black brothers and sisters? I am going to take your message to four thousand black steelworkers, and I promise you they will respond." He held up his hand to still the scattered cries. "Send Ham Wright with me. Let him speak for you to the workers who still remember him. Let him carry your story to the white folks who know him. If they're not stirred up by him like I've been stirred up by you, I'll come back here with him and walk with you for the rest of the year."

It had all been worked out, it was clear, while he had been sitting in jail biting his nails. They didn't need him here to mediate, not the way they needed money. As for Big Boy, he had his own motives—there would be time to discover them on the long ride north.

At dawn they were on their way, with his few belongings crammed into a bag flung beside Big Boy's on the back seat. Suddenly overcome with euphoria, he punched Big Boy on his right biceps. "Chattanooga, here we come!"

"I know that song. But you know how far it is from there to Cincinnati? To say nothin of Cleveland?"

"Doesn't worry me. Not with all the horses you got under that hood."

"You wanna drive this wagon, remember where you at. You jus got outa one jailhouse, don go sit in another. We ain breakin no laws, not in this part of the country."

Big Boy's carefulness was not confined to his driving. By nature
he was violent and explosive, impatient of both rationality and
book learning, which he associated with the old or the fearful. He
had not chosen caution, but was pushed to it by the successive
failures of two movements.

"It's a good spirit, that bus boycott," he admitted. "But how far
you expect to get with a bunch of preachers an domestics?"

"A lot farther than anyone would have guessed a year ago."

"You ain answerin my question."

That was the old Big Boy, the aggressive counterpuncher.

"We underestimated the ability of the new generation of religious
leaders. We've got to go with them as far as they'll go. If they cop
out—"

"Then what?"

"I don't know yet."

Big Boy fell silent. They drove all through the day, the night, the
next day, as though fleeing pursuers, in the way that black people
had always had to move through their own land. And yet it was
different now, something elemental was stirring behind them, and it
lent exhilaration to their trip.

Even Big Boy's spirits rose as they rolled onwards. He spoke less
of the stagnation in his home parish outside New Orleans, less of
being stymied and trapped at the mill, and more of the effect on his
own people of what was happening in the South.

When they arrived at last they were like Greeks returning with
news of distant victory. And when he awoke from ten hours of dream-
less sleep, Coretta had long since left for her teaching job and Big
Boy was in the kitchen, coffee mug in one hand, newspaper in the
other.

"Now listen. I got to be back in the mill tomorrow. Gonna get
on the phone today an start roundin up some of the guys. I'll set up
maybe two, three meetings before we try an get you officially on the
agenda of the next local meeting as an invited guest. It's got to be
official, because then you can get up an make a pitch for the local to
vote up a contribution."

"I'm ready."

"Meanwhile get on over to the UAW an talk to Bill Zivic."

"You and Bill on good terms again?"

"Bill ain so tight-ass now that he's an international rep. He got no
more New Party, he don have to worry about winnin no more

elections. I like him better that way. And he tries to give us a hand with the Negro American Labor Council."

"He's got to do something to keep the franchise."

"You got to appeal to his bad conscience."

"I'm on my way."

"Then what you standin around for with your face hangin out?"

He took a bus downtown to the UAW regional office. He walked past a girl cutting a stencil on the typewriter and on into the tacky office in which Bill Zivic sat humped over the same morning paper that Big Boy had been reading, his small eyes screwed up with concentration behind new eyeglasses. "Hey, I thought you were sitting in the pokey in Montgomery!"

"Bailed out. Big Boy drove me up, on the way back from his mother's funeral."

"Everybody's dying. Last year we lost my father, the other day it was Margaret's mother. She and Vera are in Akron now, winding things up. But she'll be back in a day. You'll be here for a while, won't you?"

"Depends. I need help."

"Shoot."

Always ready to get down to business, Bill doodled on a yellow pad of legal-size paper while he listened, occasionally jotting down a phrase, a number, a name.

"Now listen," Bill said when he had finished. "I'm going to get to work on the UAW like Big Boy is on the Steel Workers. If you can stay long enough, I'll get you scheduled for a pitch in a couple locals with substantial Negro memberships. In the meantime let's get hold of Irwin. He's doing fantastically well in the money department and he's got a bad conscience."

Just what Big Boy had said about Bill. And hadn't he himself thought the same about Big Boy? It was not funny, having to depend on the collective bad consciences of all the old radicals. On the other hand, it was a lot better than having to deal with people without consciences.

". . . That's right," Bill was saying to Irwin on the phone, "our wandering boy."

Bill hung up, pleased. "We're started. How's nine o'clock tonight, right after Irwin's office hours? He was so excited he started to stutter."

"I have to see his kid. I'm very fond of that boy."

"You will—I made the date for their house. Paul has been giving Irwin a certain amount of heartache. Not that he's mean, in fact he's always been more responsible than Vera's boy Marlen, who can charm the pants off you in order to make you forget how willful he is."

Remembering the Zivics' blind devotion to their only nephew, he could hardly accept without reservation Bill's appraisal of the next generation. How could a boy like Paul, who virtually trembled with sincerity in his extraordinarily mature letters, give his father heartache?

Bill insisted with finality, "Irwin has been too wrapped up in that boy. That's a dangerous business. It can only lead to disillusion."

Somewhat impatiently, he demanded, "But what's wrong?"

"Nothing too terrible. The kid got bit by the religion bug, and he almost drove his parents out of their minds. Irwin had to get him a Hebrew teacher, and he spends all his spare time after school studying the Bible, memorizing stuff, or whatever it is you have to do to be bar mitzvah."

"I suppose his mother is annoyed about it."

"Guess again. Carmie's having a ball—Irwin says she's planning the biggest vulgarest bar mitzvah of the decade. The only thing that bothers her is the idea of her son putting on spiritual airs and making her feel like a bum."

"Poor Paul."

"And poor Irwin. You might bear this in mind tonight."

Bear it in mind? He couldn't get it out of his mind, even though he was preoccupied with Montgomery. What he wanted from Irwin, from all of them, was neither blood nor sweat, but just money—as though money was ever just.

When he and Bill pulled into the Metzgers' driveway shortly after dark, the house was ablaze, although Irwin was still busy in his office. Carmela greeted them in pants and sweater. She was wearing harlequin glasses with a pencil tucked under one temple. She led them down the shallow steps into the dropped living room, its carpet scattered with sheets of paper.

"I've been trying to make up a guest list for the bar mitzvah. What a job. If you ask people from out of town, they get mad because they think all you want is a present. If you don't ask them, they're hurt. Jesus."

"Paul isn't here?"

"The only time I can work on it is when he's not around. If he had his way we wouldn't invite anybody. He's practicing his maftir with the rabbi. That's the thing they have to do in Hebrew. Ever been to a bar mitzvah, Hamilton?"

"They didn't go in for them in my end of town."

"Mine either." Carmela laughed nervously. "I hope you'll come to Paul's. You can make it interracial, not just interfaith."

"If I'm still here."

"You don't have to bring a present." She grinned. "Listen, I know you still correspond with Paul. I was just wondering whether he's said much about his getting so involved in Judaism."

"He only writes me about his reading. I doubt that he can understand Sartre. On the other hand, maybe he got something out of *Anti-Semite and Jew,* who knows?"

"It scares me. I mean, don't misunderstand, better that than those crummy teenagers who don't believe in anything. But he's got no sense of proportion."

"At that age—"

"I don't mean I tease him. I swear to you, I never once did. But supposing he grows a long beard and puts on one of those black coats and fur hats, you know, like the guys that come to the door asking for handouts for some poorhouse in Israel?" She laughed nervously. "Irwin himself says that half those damn poorhouses don't even exist, it's just a racket."

"Irwin says more than that."

The dentist was standing at the head of the living room steps, coatless, his hat pushed back on his head. When he took it off and threw it on the hall table behind him, he revealed a raw red stripe around his bald forehead. His stomach hung over the belt of his trousers. "Irwin says he's sorry he couldn't cancel those appointments."

"We've been talking about Paul."

"Well, you might as well know." He shoved his hands into his pockets. "I've got more bad news. At least for you, Carmela."

"Now what?" she asked nastily.

"Paul says if we insist on a big bar mitzvah it'll have to be without him."

"Paul says, Paul says. When did this announcement take place?"

"Before I dropped him off on the way to my office. From his point of view I think he's justified."

"Naturally. Now tell me, wise guy, how do you have a bar mitzvah without a leading man?"

"For once, he's in the driver's seat, and you'd better believe it."

"Don't give me that crap. It's your dough that's tied up in this production, and you'd better remember it. Who put down the deposit?"

"I don't care about the money. Why not respect his wishes? For him it's not a chance to show off. It's a moment in his spiritual life."

"In his . . ." Carmela's lips were trembling. She drew herself up almost physically, with a pushing movement of her palms against her hips. She said, smiling mechanically, "I'm a lousy hostess. Excuse me while I go make us some coffee."

Irwin was at the liquor cabinet. "How about a little bourbon while the coffee's perking?"

Bill shook his head. Ham said, "No, thanks. But you go right ahead."

"Don't worry." The whiskey sloshed high in Irwin's glass. "Those things go on in this house all the time. They're not in the same world as your problem. If there's anything, anything at all, that I can do to help, I want to hear about it."

He began to explain. The meetings, the calls, the cars, the gas, the oil, the mimeograph paper, the dinners, the appeals, the arrests, the bail. Carmela came in silently with coffee and cake on a tray.

"It's a movement that none of us would have been able to predict ten years ago. It's not being led by radicals, and it's not being carried out by workers or peasants. The roots are Christian, the inspiration is Christian, and it's more radical than anything we could have dreamt of."

Irwin's eyes had wavered. He turned his head. Paul was standing quietly at the head of the shallow steps, hands clasped before him. He had shot up, yet seemed only on the verge of his true growth.

"Paulie," his father said, "I wish you could have gotten here earlier. You missed everything."

"No I didn't. I've been listening back here in the hall, by the mirror. I didn't want to interrupt Ham."

"Now come on down and say hello properly," his mother ordered.

Paul shook hands with him and Bill and said, "Please go ahead. I really wanted to wait up there until you were all through."

"I'll never be all through. I was just trying to fill in your folks a little. When you need money you have to explain why in a way that will make people want to go out and help you get it."

"I had an idea about that. It has to do with my bar mitzvah." Paul glanced uneasily at his mother. "I know you want to make a big splash—"

"Not a *splash,* honey. It's something that comes once in a lifetime, like getting married."

"Anyway I was just thinking," Paul hurried on, "why not specify that the guests should give money to Ham instead of to me? For the bus boycott, and what they need down there, instead of giving me defense bonds or gift certificates."

For a moment no one said anything. Then just as suddenly everyone was talking at once—Carmela, her hands flying palms up, as though she had reverted to Italian instead of English, Irwin in his tenor stutter, even Bill, his eagerness overcoming his customary solemnity.

"You *can't* make people—" Carmela pleaded.

"We've got to discuss this," Irwin urged, "it's a whole new concept!"

"Why not check it out with your rabbi?" Bill asked.

"It's my bar mitzvah, isn't it? If I say that all the gifts will go to Montgomery instead of to me, wouldn't that be the same thing as asking people to give the money directly to Ham?"

"That's like blackmail," Carmela said. "And you complain about me!"

Bill interposed himself. "I don't know anything more about the religious angle than you do, Carmela. But there is a precedent for Paul's idea, at least among the Jewish trade unionists. Remember that mass meeting in Union Square last year? They had twenty thousand people on the street. Needle trades, garment workers, clothing workers, hatters, most of them Jewish, protesting the murder of that Negro boy down South, Emmett Till."

Bill had hit upon the argument that Irwin needed. He said enthusiastically, "That's absolutely right, Carmie. That demonstration was in the real Jewish tradition. I was proud of the Jews when they turned out to protest the lynching."

"I read about it," Paul said. "I saw the pictures too." He added frankly, "That's where I got the idea."

"I don't see why you have to involve Ham," Carmela complained. "This family has a talent for lousing things up."

Frustrated and uncomprehending as she was she understood one thing better than Irwin. Paul did lack a sense of proportion. But if that made him somewhat humorless, it would also make him capable, one day, of great things.

His notion of Paul clarified as the days passed, even though he was too busy to go out to the suburbs to see the boy. His task took him in the opposite direction, to the working-class areas where he could keep his appointments.

He was shaken by his return to the steelworkers hall where he had first learned about organizing, getting people to do what you felt was in their interests. Big Boy moved among faces more often black than white with the stolid assurance of a district leader in an area that voted right. His impatience with those slow to understand had only deepened and hardened with his own aching realization that his primacy would never extend beyond these walls, or beyond the mill which squatted across the way, begrimed, smoking, and sending its flames into the sky in token of the mastery which it claimed over leaders and led alike.

The hall filled Ham not at all with a sense of nostalgia (as Big Boy had perhaps hoped), but rather with relief at his escape. The battered cuspidors rancid with floating butts and unraveling matches, the long-unwashed windows crisscrossed with battered metal venetian blinds, the Sunday-supplement photos of Franklin D. Roosevelt and Philip Murray yellowing beneath streaked glass, the charter under crossed flags won with such pain and now gathering dust like the portraits of dead leaders, the ranks of folding chairs whose wooden slats were scarred and broken like the men who slouched on them or sat uncomfortably erect, caps on their laps, the odor of sweat-stained cotton undershirts and woollen socks in ankle-top work shoes—the shabbiness and the lack of glory in it all aroused in him finally shame at his own pride in having fled to another kind of weary endeavor.

The Metzgers' synagogue was an elegant entryway into that other endeavor. Built of dun-colored stone on a sloping grassy plot, its divided approach scooped out in the shape of the Mosaic tablets of the law, it was for Ham at once impressive and depressing. The steelworkers were entitled to this, but it was only their absent employers—and their elected leaders also sitting far away in Washington—who had the resources to put up such edifices.

There were three other black faces in the assemblage, a classmate of Paul's and his parents, a psychiatrist and a college instructor, imported as living proof of the tolerance and good neighborliness of the suburban community into which they had been accepted. Gazing at their well-scrubbed black faces and well-laundered garments in the bleached-wood pew across the carpeted aisle, he had the feeling that, in their flight from the steeltown ghettoes, they were as distant emotionally as they were geographically from those whom he represented here.

This Saturday morning service was his first exposure to the rituals of a people whom he had come to feel were if not his closest allies among whites, anyway the least prejudiced of the other world. He sat with his hands in his lap, no more able than most of the others to follow the rapid zigzags of rabbi and cantor through the prayer book, listening to the strange ancient words, looking at the ordinary business faces of the congregation, and trying to discern the connection between the two. Could these dentists, merchants, lawyers, and their corseted wives and pudgy complacent children be stirred inwardly by the singing, the droning, the rapid incantation of words whose meaning they did not know and in any case could hardly believe in anyway? They could have been embarrassed to nervous laughter if they were asked to prostrate themselves, kneel, or kiss the ring on someone's fat finger. But what did they—any more than he—have to do with the shawled mumbling, the whispered mutters and rapid outbusts, the passionate chants to his ears more Moorish than Jewish, the flipping of pages as though they were nuisances rather than sacred texts, the jerky genuflections from the waist that looked more like a nervous tic than a yielding to the divine spirit? How much more our religion means to us, he thought, we children of slaves, when we shout together, weep together, sing together! Could it be that these people, in scrambling and clawing their way out of the ghetto, had lost their way? Was it possible to be holy only when you were poor and oppressed?

Paul was called forward to read his portion of the prayer, and everything that Ham had been constructing in his mind came tumbling down, leaving him defenseless before the pale-faced boy in the blue skull cap whose gold thread glowed above the dark curls that lay damp on his forehead. His body engulfed in the blue-edged prayer shawl, his eyes burning with a fervor that was passionately familiar, his still unchanged voice rising high and clear in the pure accents of childhood, he intoned the sounds that bound him to his ancestors and to their fearful and grandiose concept of creation.

After the service Paul was formally introduced to address the congregation. This part of the ceremony was supposedly closest to pure comedy, this and the inky flood of fountain pens that rained down as gifts—for its unsurpassed banality customarily consisted of assurances of undying affection and gratitude to the self-sacrificing parents and rabbi-coach.

Paul stared directly at Irwin, who was very red in the face, and sat, his knuckles knotted, beside his wife, who appeared stunned, fingers to her mouth as if she were listening to an announcement of a great cataclysm. As he spoke his voice seemed to grow older, to leave childhood behind, even as he stood, quite tall, pale, composed in his silken prayer shawl.

"At this time," he said, "it is supposed to be incumbent on the bar mitzvah boy to thank his parents for having helped him to grow up and become a man. I am uncertain as to how much I really have grown up, but I do know how much I owe my parents—particularly for having allowed me to make this bar mitzvah a special kind of occasion."

Ducking his head to consult his notes, Paul went on, "I just want to thank them from the bottom of my heart for allowing me to dedicate this day to others whom I admire and want to help. I hope you will all join us downstairs for some refreshments and for the pleasure of meeting our family friend, Mr. Hamilton Wright, who is my special bar mitzvah guest."

At the reception Ham felt clear in his own mind that if he had any obligation at all to anyone other than those who had sent him, it was to Paul. Irwin was urging toasts on the celebrants with a whiskey bottle in one hand and a shot glass in the other. *"L'chayim, l'chayim!"* he cried, pressing glasses on those who complained weakly that they never drank before lunch. "Today you drink! If you want to eat, you have to drink!"

Fortified, his guests strolled alongside the linen-covered table that bore sliced chicken, turkey, and tongue, garnished with plump green olives and wrinkled black olives, glossy twists and nut-brown pumpernickels, smoked whitefish and sturgeon and pink slabs of Nova Scotia belly lox, alps of potato salad and vats of baked beans, Danish pastry and petits fours, salted nuts and sweet halvah. Grazing like cattle, ruminating, jostling, they foraged at leisure, forking up a morsel here, rejecting one there. This was not like a barbecue or a church supper, but the intensity of the concentration on meat and drink was hauntingly familiar. Ham's determination to speak was strengthened.

Irwin tapped on a glass with a fork and called them to order. Paul stood quietly at Ham's side, his ordinarily pale face flushed as though he too had been drinking.

"I am sure," Ham began, "that you were shaken as Paul was, as all of us were, by the bombing of Martin Luther King's home. Let me tell you how our people reacted. Many of them have been storing up arms. No one has been eager to publicize this, but there has been a strong sentiment for violent retaliation. It isn't just the single instance of the bombing. There have been other incidents, provocations, insults, that don't get into the papers."

He reached into his breast pocket and drew forth a leaflet. "This was distributed at a White Citizens Council rally in Montgomery not long ago. 'When in the course of human events it becomes necessary to abolish the Negro race, proper methods should be used. Among these are guns, bows and arrows, slingshots and knives. In every stage of the bus boycott we have been oppressed and degraded because of black, slimy, juicy, unbearably stinking niggers.'"

The silence was broken by a high nervous laugh. Before he should lose them he drove on, explaining both the ethical and the practical necessity of responding to sick fearful hatred with non-violence. It was a commitment which was religious in the broadest sense, just as it was social, just as it was—in its revolutionary implications—political.

When he had finished, he outwaited everyone in order to be alone with Paul for a moment.

"I want to thank you now," he said. "You've made my whole trip worthwhile."

Paul shook his head nervously. The prayer shawl was slipping off his shoulders. He removed it with a quick tug, then stood folding it into smaller and smaller squares until it fitted into the little blue velvet sack that he held in his hands. "You don't have to be so polite with me. I'm the one that has to thank you, but I'm not good at that. I haven't mixed with people enough to do it right."

"Well, you sure are learning."

"But that was on account of . . ." Paul hesitated, then blurted, "Listen, could I come down and visit you this summer?"

Ham gazed into the desperate eyes of Irwin and Carmela, side by side behind their son. Beseechingly, silently, they appealed to him, but for what? Against what? To what end?

Now he wasn't uttering appeals for support, but simply, as he might have known all along, equivocating. "We'll see," he said to the boy. "Let's keep in touch and see how things work out before we commit ourselves."

And even as he spoke the words and watched the faces of the parents dissolve behind their son as in some dream, Paul's eyes veiled, then closed; he removed his skull cap, tucked it gently into the sack with the prayer shawl, and turned slowly away from them all.

5. NORM

It was no fun, going back to Little Rock after the fortnight in Washington. He had stayed there long enough on his first visit, early in September, to talk not only to the worried school superintendent Virgil Blossom and the anxious editor Harry Ashmore in their downtown offices, and to the professional people, embarrassed and humiliated by the antics of their governor; he had also met those who stood behind Orval Faubus and egged him on. The haters, emboldened by their successes, were paralyzing the schools, destroying the hopes of the Negroes, building hatred with the same cool pleasure others derived from building a useful object. He had seen them in action, the Mothers League of Central High, speaking "as a group of Christian mothers in a Christianlike way," warning that "a nigger in your school is a potential Communist in your school," and now he would have to watch them again. He had listened in the antique shop of Amis Guthridge, who ran the Capital Citizens' Council, while the racist lawyer passed his hand over his thin hair and grinned at him patronizingly through his glasses; now he would see him triumphant. All so that he could write about it for people convinced that they understood anyway—that it was simply a matter of the President trying to take the easy way out, temporizing in his Newport summer retreat while Faubus made a fool of him and of their country in the eyes of the entire world.

And yet he was driven back by the same compulsion that had made him go to Budapest the year before; and then to the New York convention of the confused and half-repentant American Communists; and then to the indictment of Jimmy Hoffa. He was afraid to define it too closely, since that might raise the question of whether he was running toward something—or away from it.

Peering down through the plane's curtained window at Tennessee, or maybe it was still Kentucky below the patchy cloud formations, Norm felt that he had aged far more than a year in the course of the eleven months that had brought him from Budapest to Little Rock. The quiet years with Vera in New York, their move to Mamaroneck with Marlen, appeared in retrospect hardly more than an interlude between the island invasions in the South Pacific and the battles he had been witnessing in the fifties. The fighters were younger and he was older. Now the front-line troops were children, the crusades were children's crusades, and he was their middle-aging chronicler.

What stuck in the mind, what drew him back now, was not the agonized middle-aged liberals, nor even the fighting Negroes like Daisy Bates, but the memory of fifteen-year-old Elizabeth Eckford coming to the corner of Fourteenth and Park on that quiet Wednesday morning. A thin girl with sunglasses, she had gotten all dressed up for school registration. Her shield against the Arkansas National Guardsmen's rifles was her armload of schoolbooks—the weapon that filled everyone with terror at her appearance. Closing ranks, the troops blocked her path. Elizabeth turned and headed for the front of the school, but the Guardsmen were there too, a solid line. She walked along that line, thin and dark in her starched and ironed white dress, searching for an opening that did not exist. The crowd of whites across the way caught sight of her a moment after Norm did, and made for her shouting and cursing, "Nigger! Nigger!"

He was baffled, awed almost, by the girl's inhuman poise. The Guardsmen shoved back the yelling crowd; but after he had waved his press card and slipped through he discovered that the girl was trembling.

She crossed the street and sat down at a bus stop bench, her knees pressed together. As he moved to join her, a white woman came up to pat her back. The child's eyes filled with tears and he found that he was trembling too. Then, before anything else could happen, she had boarded a passing bus and the first of the confrontations was over.

But Elizabeth had not been the first of the children that he had seen present themselves during this last year as blood sacrifices.

That had come in Budapest not long after his arrival there, late last October. Like football fans in Ann Arbor tearing down the goal posts, the Hungarian kids had set upon the twenty-four foot statue of Stalin in City Park, across from the Yugoslav Embassy, melting the old bastard's knees with blowtorches; they had marched, singing and laughing, to the radio station on Sandor Brody Street; and then their blood had started to course through the streets. By early November the insurrection looked like a success in a blasted city dominated by the young—kids with clotted blood sticking to the bandages wound around their arms and heads, kids with bandoliers over their shoulders and hand grenades stuck in their belts trotting out of buildings draped with black mourning flags, kids carrying the tommy guns they called "guitars" picking their way through the tangled spaghetti loops of dangling telephone and high tension wires, their shoes crackling as they crunched over the crystals of broken glass. And the boy who, when he saw the American flag on Norm's car, shoved his arm through the window, his face contorted, waving a rusty razor blade and crying, "This is my only weapon! When are you going to help?"

At the Chain Bridge, smashed tanks, kids firing from behind a barricade of trolleys, 85 millimeters zeroing in on them, two boys hit and killed before his eyes. At the hospital where they brought in the wounded from the Kilian Barracks a thirteen-year-old boy named Jancsis, not wounded, simply bloodless with exhaustion after holding an intersection for four days and nights, leaving his post only to fetch food and ammunition for his comrades. The overpowering stench (like that on the atolls where his buddies had been cut down around him, their bodies stinking on the beach in the swelling sun); the doctors like busy butchers in their bloodstained white aprons; the truck pulling away with a huge sign in Hungarian: DEAD BODIES. A ten-year-old carting a rifle as big as he, a staring-eyed fifteen-year-old girl in a forage cap cradling the submachine gun with which she had fought for five days with no sleep. The tanks crunching off Bela Bantok Avenue, past the chalked signs *Nem Kel Kommunismus!* and *Ruszki Haza!* ignoring the appeal that they go home, tried instead to escape the narrow streets and the Molotov cocktails, tried to crush the kids. Sixteen-year old Sandor, youngest of his group, waited for the tanks to pass, then ran out of a doorway, throwing his grenades at a tank platform and when they rolled off climbed aboard the lumbering mon-

ster and tossed them all onto its turret, his eyes glistening with
tears in the frozen instant before the explosion blew him up with his
target.

For Norm the climactic episode of the wild ten days came shortly
before that sickening Sunday morning when the Russians flowed
back like some giant flood, catching the kids on Lajos Kossuth
Street while they were wrenching paving blocks from the gutters for
their final barricades. The new regime had installed itself, people
actually smiled at each other as they picked their way through the
litter, peering cautiously around corners, avoiding the uncollected
bodies of lynched AVO assassins, folding into their pockets the
thin newspapers that had begun to appear from nowhere along with
the instant posters and the defiant slogans chalked on the walls.

He drove gingerly through the rubble to the Margaret Bridge,
turned off halfway to Buda onto Margaret's Island that lay like a
great lozenge in the widest part of the Danube, and continued the
length of the island past the amusement parks and the casino,
through the last of the autumn foliage to the elegant bulk of the St.
Margaret Palace Hotel, set like some pre-war spa in the midst of
sculptured gardens and gravel walks.

In its immense, cool, luxurious lobby, he came upon a crowd of
laughing young people, caps on the backs of their heads, the inevitable hand grenades hooked to their belts. He counted several
dozen, perhaps thirty, seated at their ease in the deep lounge chairs,
or perched on the arms of the chairs with their legs folded beneath
them, discussing the future of mankind, no less, with a group of
poets and actresses.

"A stirring tableau, isn't it?"

The voice behind him made him whirl about. Harry Sturm stood
smiling, puffing on a pipe, plump, genial.

After the initial shock, he had to ask, "What are you doing here?"

"I have a room here." Harry's smile broadened. "I find it one of
the most charming hotels in Europe, and quite unspoiled by Stalinism. I have the most delightful balcony, with huge marble
columns, looking down on the bandstand of the outdoor dining
area. Grandiose, but still comfortable."

"Are you here as a Wordsworth of the revolution?"

"I leave that to you. But I must say, it's gratifying to be vindicated.
They laughed at me, as the ads used to say. You remember that,
no doubt?"

"I hadn't realized that that's what these kids were doing—vindicating you."

"You mock me. Well, perhaps I deserve it." Harry smiled, as if to show how little he believed his own words.

"You still haven't told me why you're here."

"My father was born not twenty miles from here. He knew Anna Kethly personally. He'd be a proud man today. I'm going to leave with great reluctance." As usual, Harry was being blandly unresponsive.

"I'm not as certain as you that they've won. I smell something in the air."

"What would you call it?"

"Anguish." He added, "I can't believe that Russia is simply going to let them bow out of the Warsaw Pact. With the west distracted, the Russians can still make a move."

"Distracted? What a brilliant euphemism for the attack on Suez. You writers! Well, I'm on my way to Tel Aviv to see for myself. No doubt the Israelis are very self-righteous, but an invasion is an invasion. And if they could see how these people have been abandoned as a result—"

"So you're going to tell the Israelis they should be ashamed."

Harry chose, as in the old days, to respond in all solemnity. "Not exactly. I have pressing business there."

When he got home, it was not mysterious Harry whom he tried to describe to Marlen, thirteen and car crazy, but rather the Hungarian boys of Marlen's age who had known nothing but Communism and died fighting it in the streets after a few days of romantic freedom. But his son, his appetite for vicarious adventure quickly sated, listened only briefly. Sick with the inability to convey to his own the crazed courage of other children who were perhaps senseless—no one could testify as to that—but had entered history on the side of the heroic, Norm had turned to his typewriter, and after that from Europe to America.

Covering the convention of the Communist Party, their first attempt at legitimacy since the advent of McCarthyism, he felt as though he were peering down one of the long corridors of history, its walls splashed with blood and stained with the handprints of those who in attempting to move mankind forward had themselves slipped and fallen, pulling others down with them into the bloody welter. Muste, that Christ-like man, was right to remind the independent radicals that the handful of Communists desperately trying to salvage something from the wreckage of their politics and their lives were not monsters but simply confused and floundering men. Nevertheless, with Budapest still festering in him like some ulcer that would not heal, he could not rid himself of the suspicion that given the power they (and by extension their opponents on the left too, his own former comrades and leaders) could very well have killed. Worse than that—for all sorts of good Americans from Washington to Lincoln to Roosevelt had killed. Tortured as well, all in the name of humanity. And then been tortured and killed themselves, all in the name of purity or progress.

It was a relief to be drawn back into the finagling life of the labor movement. A long piece on the teamsters' union not only introduced him to Jimmy Hoffa, fighting against his first indictment, but gave him the excuse to pay a quick visit to Joe, moved from Los Angeles to San Francisco, to a house on Kansas Street in the Potrero Hill district.

Joe claimed to be happy, working intermittently as a casual longshoreman and living among working people. Even in his home it was the young—whether or not they themselves willed it—who fixed the course of the household. Everything was subordinated to the boys' need for frequent lessons, practice time—and an expensive Steinway that Joe was not going to be able to buy unless he got out of the working class once and for all.

Norm knew a politically liberal but very tough young builder who was putting up high-rises in the central city and tract houses on the peninsula. The builder was looking for a trustworthy guy with enough savvy about mechanical equipment to be a purchasing agent. Anne was excited, Joe was interested; and he filled the bill. In short order he was charged with buying trench-diggers for foundations, spray equipment for painters, circular and hand saws for carpenters, cat tractors and fork lift trucks and back hoes for drivers; he bought pickup trucks for the foremen and worked out amortization schemes to sell them off later to farmers. He spent his lunch hours with the skilled workers and the operating engineers; quickly, he began to make a lot more money than he had as a casual on the waterfront. Rewarded by Anne's cheaply won gratitude, Norm took off for home.

He found Vera tense, after a visit to Marlen at summer camp in

Vermont. The Quaker couple who ran the camp were uneasy about Marlen: he was not socializing properly.

"Socializing?" he demanded of his wife. "What the hell does that mean? Those social worker types always come up with cant words."

Her hand went nervously to her graying hair. "It's not what you think. According to them he's almost too self-possessed for a boy his age."

"That's supposed to be bad? If they don't like Cary Grant, would they prefer him to imitate Bogart?"

But Vera had been shaken. She seemed to think there was something to it, despite his belief that they had been confused by a highly sophisticated only son, exposed since childhood to older people.

If he had to be caught up in the problems of the young, he preferred that it be in more objectively definable areas, like school integration. In Little Rock at least the issues seemed clearcut, the moral determinants inescapable. Except that it hurt to watch Elizabeth Eckford running in her carefully ironed white dress. Behind her, Terrance Roberts, also rebuffed and driven off. And after that, the hysteria growing as the crowds gathered outside the school to sing *Dixie,* the FBI "investigated" endlessly, and Faubus surrounded not only the school but the governor's mansion with his National Guardsmen.

The mayor called this "a political farce," so they burned a cross on his front lawn. Six Negro kids, accompanied by their ministers, tried to enroll at North Little Rock High School: "Go back where you belong!" the crowd shouted at Norm and the other journalists and photographers from New York. President Eisenhower announced from Newport that "Patience is the important thing," Faubus went on up there to talk with him, and Norm packed his bag. Maybe there would be other answers in Washington.

In the capitol he sought the congressional liberals, latter-day New Dealer types, for clues as to their intentions and their prospects. Shrewd, tough-talking, more naive than he would have thought beforehand, they were eager to be liked and understood, and they insisted that he come to their parties.

At one of these parties, not long before his return to Little Rock, a sad-eyed psychiatrist insisted on quizzing him. He wanted to know what Norm guessed the deadlock might do to the minds of the children, those held off at bayonet point and those being schooled behind a wall of armed soldiers.

The doctor had read his articles on Budapest. "I was particularly impressed by your perception that these revolutions have been given over to the children, or have fallen into their hands."

"Why should that interest you particularly?"

Despite his worn and mournful air the doctor was youngish still, with tousled hair which he combed with his bony fingers. "I work primarily with psychotic children. I have a kind of clinic not far from here, in Maryland."

He had published a book, which Norm had not read, about experimental work with autistic and schizophrenic children. "I have a particular affinity. When I was younger," he said bluntly, "I was crazy myself."

Norm checked an automatic smile when he saw that the doctor was serious.

"When did you recover your sanity?"

"I'm not sure that I ever have. At times I feel I am in the keenest rapport with the everyday life. At other times the connection is as tenuous as it was in my painful teens, when I lived with a set of very complex delusions."

"How can you treat kids when you're so unsure of your own mental health?"

"Young people mistrust the aggressively healthy nuts who try to rule their lives. Why don't you come out and see for yourself?"

"Would you be willing for me to write about it? If it hit me right—"

"I wouldn't be eager for you to publish anything, not unless we had first talked together for a long time. My colleagues already look at me crosseyed. They don't need any more ammunition." The doctor grinned suddenly. "Of course, I was looking forward to meeting you tonight. Ordinarily I'm not a partygoer, and my tolerance for senatorial speechwriters is low. You were the bait to get me here tonight."

Next day Norm canceled his appointments and drove on out to Pine Grove. Set in a clearing at the end of a winding gravel road, the turreted stone monstrosity had the conspicuously wasteful look of a minor robber baron's castle.

Before the day was out he was stunned and shaken. The doctor entered completely into the dream lives of his patients, sitting motionless with a catatonic boy, getting down on all fours with a barking girl, becoming Mozart for a smiling lad who insisted that he was Beethoven.

"I don't understand," he said later to the doctor. "How can you invest so much energy, all of yourself, in another human being?"

"I believe in him."

"Have you any evidence that it works?"

"Read my book."

"Just the same, what it comes down to is a clinic for sick rich kids."

"Wrong. It is a place where love and recognition can happen. If you know of a way for me to keep it alive without the checks of guilty fathers or grandfathers, let me know—and I'll gladly throw the doors open to kids in pain even if they haven't got a dime. You want to help the children of Little Rock by writing about them —maybe you can help these kids too?"

The doctor was a fanatic, and he mistrusted fanatics; still, he thought as he left Washington for Arkansas, it was better to be fanatical about love and survival than about hate and destruction. He stared out of the plane unseeing. There arose before him, along with Sandor's wet glittering eyes as he crouched on the tank turret in the moment before his death, the haunted slanty eyes of the girl at Pine Grove who barked hello and went about on all fours. Shaking his head impatiently, he got into a cab at the Little Rock airport and drove in to the Marion Hotel.

Judge Davies had issued an injunction against Governor Faubus. The crowds were bigger than before; they passed segregationist and anti-semitic literature from hand to hand. In front of Central High School, a beer parlor waitress named Louise whom everyone seemed to know became the cheerleader of a mob of hundreds. She shouted at a local reporter, "Hey nigga lova, why you writin for those papers up north?"

Early Monday morning, September twenty-third, more than a thousand of them formed up on the fringes of the barricades. A little before nine Norm saw, with a premonitory thrill of danger, a Negro boy walking toward the school, accompanied by an adult.

"Here they come!"

"Go home, ya fuckin nigga!"

The boy ran away, but they clubbed the adult to the ground and kicked him in the face as the cameras clicked. Then they turned on the newsmen, grabbing two who were Negroes, beating, pummeling.

"Let's hang them. Get a rope."

At that moment the mob's attention was distracted by the arrival of a caravan of cars at the south entrance to the school. The eight Negro students had gotten in safely.

Infuriated, they shoved at the barricades, pushing the cops back to the school sidewalk. Gene Smith, the hefty assistant chief of police, was grabbed by the collar. "There was no niggas when you went to this school, Gene. Why should we let them in now?"

"The hell with Gene. Les jus go in an get the niggas." A beefy redneck charged the police line, but Smith's men knocked him off his feet.

Gradually the police contained the crowd, but in its frustration it turned on the newsmen. To his shame Norm had to turn and run even while men around him were being slugged and kicked. At the far corner the cops maneuvered some squad cars up to them, and as they scrambled in and slammed the doors the rednecks showered the police cars with rocks. When he had caught his breath, Norm insisted that they let him out so that he could get back to the scene. He walked back, unnoticed, toward the cacophony that filled the air. Each time a white kid marched righteously out of the school building the rubes cheered raggedly. Above the cheers rose the wails of their women, keyed up to a kind of sexual hysteria that reached a climax when a pair of white girls hurried out of the building in tears, sobbing like the women who waited for them, and crying, "They're in, they're in!"

Norm went to the homes of the Negro children who had gotten into the school and gotten through the morning (at noon they were sneaked home by the back door), and he learned from them that the liberals' articles of faith had not been wholly breached. Most of the white children had received them decently; the hours had been bearable; only a very tiny minority had baited, shoved or slapped them.

The next day they didn't go back. Daisy Bates said they wouldn't until they were assured of protection, and the mayor asked the President for federal troops. Eisenhower federalized the National Guardsmen and then flew in a detachment of the 101st Airborne Division.

On Wednesday morning Norm felt as though he was back in

Budapest, except that everything was inside out and he stood on the side of the invaders, troops from outside, some of them with walkie-talkies up on the roof of the five-story school building. Overhead an Army helicopter circled slowly.

An Army station wagon followed by a jeep brought the nine Negro kids to the door. They walked in quietly with an armed guard of twenty-two soldiers. On the sidewalk the paratroopers, bayonets fixed, prodded back the crowd, arresting one here, knocking over another there with a rifle butt. By noon it was all over, for the time anyway, until the haters could decide whether to stick it out or go home.

That was his problem too, but it was taken out of his hands. As he walked through the lobby of his hotel on the way to the elevator he was intercepted by a call from the desk.

"Your wife has been trying to reach you for hours, ever since early this morning."

His first feeling was of annoyance. He had been phoning Vera every night at the same time, checking in, reassuring her. It was trying when he had evening appointments too, but Vera sat up and waited for his ring. "It's different when you can't. I sweated out Budapest. But when you can, you should."

Now her voice breathed into his ear, low, abrupt.

"Marlen has been in an accident."

He swallowed, wiped his free hand, shifted the phone. "An accident?"

"He wrecked the VW."

"Is he hurt?"

"He's home. Upstairs. The Schatz girl was with him. She went through the windshield." Vera made a strange sound. "You have to come back. I hate to ask you, but you have to come back."

"I'll take the next plane. I'll wire you from the airport when I find out what's leaving. My best bet is probably to get to St. Louis. Vera, will you be all right?"

"I'll be waiting for you with the station wagon." She hung up as if she were slamming a door.

On the airplanes, and in between them, pacing the plastic lounges, he found that he was sweating with terror, as though he had just been awakened from a nightmare by the noise of his own moaning. His father, at seventy-one still womanizing and still moralizing, would assail him as if he were a son who had failed at his assigned task. "How the hell did you bring that kid up? Did I let you run wild? Drive somebody's car, a fourteen-year-old? Did I warn you or didn't I, you weren't giving him any kind of discipline?"

Why should he now sweat with fear of what Milton Miller would say? Why couldn't he concentrate on Marlen Miller? Or Doreen Schatz? But he couldn't concentrate on anything as he neared New York; he couldn't even distract himself by trying to think up answers for his father. Nothing worked; nothing was going to work. When he stumbled to the lavatory to wash his face the plane was already in the landing pattern; he had to hold onto the wall grip with one hand while he swabbed his eyes with the other.

Vera was waiting for him. She looked old. They embraced briefly but did not kiss, and it was Vera who released herself.

In the parking lot he took the car keys from her. "How's Doreen?"

Vera closed her eyes. She leaned against the door. He drew her back so that he could open it for her and ease her onto the front seat. Then she said, "She died this afternoon."

Automatically he got into the driver's seat of the station wagon, mechanically he headed for home. Finally he found words.

"Have you spoken to her parents?"

"They were in San Francisco. Doreen's older sister was supposed to be keeping an eye on her. They're flying back." She crushed her hands together with a clapping hollow sound. "I couldn't face them without you."

"Well, I'm here," he said dully. "Is Marlen home alone?"

"They came and took him."

"Took him?"

"Into custody. When they found out how young he was, and after Doreen . . . He claims she put him up to taking the car, it was all her idea."

He pounded on the steering wheel. "You mean first he kills her and then he tries to blame her?"

"He didn't know exactly what happened. He was in shock at first, and then they just told him that she was in the hospital."

"I suppose now the argument is that he was too young to take responsibility. But if he was old enough to know how to drive and how to steal . . ."

"The responsibility is mine. No one else's."

"Bullshit. I'm not going to accept that."

"See him first. Just see him and then let me talk to you." Something in her voice frightened him all over again. He felt suddenly as if, once she had introduced him to catastrophe, she intended to open a door on fresh horrors. "Promise me."

They stopped at the house to drop off his bags. There was no hurry. Vera moved with a somnambulistic calm that was unnerving. She made him a drink the way he liked it, with one piece of ice, and they sat together on the couch talking about Little Rock and the high school kids. He could almost have put his feet up on the coffee table and pretended that Marlen was at Mamaroneck High playing soccer. But then Vera arose and smoothed out her skirt with her wind-roughened hands. He earned a lot of money, but she looked as though she had been working very hard all her life.

"I guess we'd better go," she said. "If you're ready. You're sure you don't want something to eat first."

"I told you, I ate on one of the planes. Maybe twice. I forget."

They found Marlen at the detention center. "Hi, dad," he said. "Welcome back." He was in slacks and a V-necked sweater pulled over a button-down shirt open at the collar; casual but correct. Preppy. Away from him, you tended to forget how handsome he was.

"I was worried about you, dad," Marlen added. "I was afraid some of those crackers might gang up on you."

Vera stood to one side, gazing at her son in silent fascination, almost transfixed. She might have been admiring his serene self-assurance. Rage rose in Norm's breast.

"Never mind that crap. You'd better start worrying about yourself."

"It was just one of those things. I should have said No when Doreen begged me to borrow mom's car, but you know how girls are. And if she hadn't grabbed at the wheel—"

"Stop it, Marlen." Choking, he mumbled, "She's dead."

Marlen's eyes widened. "Gee, that's a shame," he said. "She was one of the nicest girls I've ever known."

"What's the matter with you?" he shouted. "What's the matter with you?"

"Dad, it was unintentional. I never meant to hurt anyone." Marlen smiled, slyly. "You don't have to get all worked up. After all, I am only fourteen. I mean, what can they do to me? Doreen was a year and a half older than me. She was sixteen. She pushed me into it, she—"

He swung. Marlen ducked. Norm reached out, grabbed hold of

his sweater and twisted hard until he had brought his son's grinning face close to his: it revealed nothing but pleased anticipation. His ears were still ringing with the chanting voices of the boys at the doors of Central High School, having fun. "Nigger nigger. Nigger nigger."

When he let go, Marlen fell back, but his expression did not change.

Vera said quietly, "He doesn't understand."

Turning, he stumbled to the doorway. With Vera at his side he made his way somehow to the station wagon that sat alone out on the blacktop.

"I'll drive," she said.

"No, never mind. I'm sorry I did that."

Vera did not answer. They drove in silence.

When they got back to their house he threw himself heavily on the couch. Vera loosened his tie and unbuttoned the collar of his shirt. Then she undid his laces and pulled off his shoes.

"I wish I could have told you beforehand," she said. "I didn't know how."

"What's wrong with him?"

"He doesn't feel any guilt. None at all."

"Maybe he hit his head when they crashed."

Vera shook her head slowly. She stood facing him, her hands knotted. "They suspected something at the camp. They tried to tell us. But you were distracted by all those things you've been living through. As for me, I didn't want to admit it. Now I'm ready. I have to tell you. Marlen is my punishment."

"That kind of talk isn't going to help us."

"You promised to listen to me."

Something new had entered her face. He felt a premonitory chill at the remote fixed quality of her gaze. "All right. Go ahead."

"You don't believe you can kill a baby by rejecting it. I believe it because I did it. They told me mine was born wrong, but I never believed that, not for a minute, even though Margaret tried to talk me into it."

"Those things do happen."

"I didn't acknowledge my sin, for years I hid it from you." She said pitifully, "Don't you remember before we were married how I said I wasn't worthy of you? And you just laughed?"

"Once I knew, it didn't make any difference to me."

"But that's the way you are. You're very upright, you're always concerned with the way people suffer and struggle to make their life better. You're so good!"

He had absolutely no idea whether she was being sincere or bitterly ironic. In either case it was profoundly humiliating. He knew all about the far-off things, the places where she had never been, but he didn't know the places where she had been, the hells where she had burned. He didn't know her at all.

"So now you can stop thinking of me as that simple working-class girl. Marlen is my responsibility. He's my punishment for my sin."

"You keep talking about sin. I don't believe in sin."

"What do you call what Marlen did?"

"He's a sick boy."

"Then tell me how to make him well, and I'll do it. And tell me what to say to Doreen's parents."

"What are you asking of me?"

"I never asked the impossible of you before. All I did was ruin things for you."

"That's not true."

"Tomorrow you'll think different. Because that's when the real trouble starts, tomorrow. And I want you to go away before then. There's nothing for you here any more. No marriage, no child."

"Stop it."

"You've had enough. You had a terrible war. And you've seen so much suffering this year. Now it's my turn. It's not your guilt, it's mine."

"Guilt, guilt . . ."

"Yes. And I won't have you punished for it."

Oh, he thought, as he tumbled off the couch and knelt before her rigid body, it's too late for that. Even if everything was as she imagined it to be, there was nowhere for anyone to escape to. His son sat smiling on his cot, his wife pierced herself with fantasies of murdered infants, and he had to arise, make calls, present himself to mourners, write about the suffering of others, earn the money that would pay their way through purgatory. Closing his eyes, he felt the warm tears flow from them as he reached out for his wife's cold hands and clasped them tightly about his head.

6. FRED

Third Avenue was a maze, so it looked from the twelfth floor, with young men and women scurrying into each other's arms, then to drink, see a Bergman movie, shop for a dry sink or a Tiffany lamp. When he had bought the apartment in the new building, Fred had been charmed with the prospect, and hopeful that the sight of crowds of bright and hopeful people at the outset of their adult lives would cleanse the bitter taste of a second failed marriage and distract him from its oppressive memories.

Now, amazingly, he scarcely thought of Sheila. It was not that it no longer rankled, the shabbiness with which she had treated him, forcing him to give her the apartment on Fifth Avenue and the better part of his library as the price of freedom from her gnawing ambition. But new pains always tended to drive out the old.

Devoted to him as Evie was, he could only be grateful that she was out in Chicago, singing at the Pump Room, sweetly unaware of his torment. Without her, without even the cleaning woman whom he had notified not to come until further notice, he was more alone here than he would have thought possible before the rumors had begun to circulate like a noxious gas through the corridors of the television studios.

As the rumors grew stronger his associates evaporated. Producers, directors, lawyers, accountants, executives even, were called to the bedsides of sick in-laws, developed heart murmurs themselves, discovered urgent commitments in Toronto or London. Those who remained, and who were nervously willing or suspiciously anxious to talk, Fred was afraid to talk to; this week he had even felt that his phone was being tapped. He heard strange noises on his line, like the squeaks the ex-Communists were so paranoid about, and who could say for sure that some investigator was not tapped in, waiting for him to quote a figure or drop a name?

Prowling the apartment, he paused at the long birch table in his study on which lay the galleys of his new anthology, *Poems of Courage and Fortitude,* together with some of the place-marked volumes against which they had yet to be checked. He had no stomach for the task, although the publishers were pressing for a prompt return. In their innocence, they had plans for issuing it as a Christmas gift book. He cringed at the mental image of all the Doubleday windows stacked with the bloated volume, packaged (with a big red ribbon) in tandem with his forthcoming long-playing record of a selection of readings from the book. Worse than a textbook, he could hear the high-brows already, unworthy of review. The publishers themselves referred to it as PCF, as though it were patented with a guarantee to eliminate knocks or end wash-day worries.

On one wall, alone and unadorned, hung the Albers for which he had paid the greater part of his publisher's advance. And gladly, for whenever he looked up from his desk, peevish or confused, he found great peace in the gently floating concentric squares, so delicate, so pale, so powerful, so stirring. Now he found it merely annoying and empty; he turned from it in exasperation and confronted the vast canvas of Vito Brigante which consumed the other wall as if, smoldering, it had charred the very plaster and studs to which it was fastened. Raw, hideous, beautiful, it mocked everything else in the apartment, the shelves, the books of verse, the remnants of his pre-Columbian collection.

He wondered briefly if he should call Vito. Hadn't he gone up to Buffalo, years ago, to testify for that Negro boy who had been charged with membership in the New Party? That's all I'd need, he thought, for them to work me over for my political past— as if I haven't got enough on my hands. How easy it had been, he reflected with a sudden access of self-pity, for all those people assaulted by the McCarthyites. How good it would feel to stand up to an inquisitor on a straightforward matter of principle! But all that was rot. The trouble was that Vito probably had less respect for him than for Ham Wright. Never mind that he had scrupulously insisted on paying the gallery price for that monstrous canvas. To

Vito he was what, one more show biz type? All right, fine. The real question was, how could such an ignorant man have anything useful to suggest?

The phone rang. Evie? He glanced at his watch. No. He hesitated, his hand hovering over the instrument. It could only be more bad news. Only a miracle so far had kept the columnists from laying siege to him. They were bound to be after him soon, unlisted phone or no, and what was there to say to them beyond the set phrase dictated by the network lawyers, hideously like a gangster's monotonous response to investigators' questions?

The phone continued to ring. Only his intimates knew of his reluctance to answer before the eighth or tenth ring. He picked it up at last, hoping that maybe in his last second of indecision the other end had given up and disconnected.

"Fred, this is Bea."

He cursed to himself. Direct, no nonsense, she was more impersonal than his tax lawyer. And more predictable. Fernie's clothing bills. Fernie's school payments. Fernie's camp expenses. Now that the orthodontics were finished and Irwin was a few thousand richer, adolescence was upon her and skin treatments had begun at the fanciest dermatologist that Bea could lay hands on. Do you think she should cry herself to sleep, Bea had demanded, if she doesn't *have* to?

"Yes, Bea," he said wearily, wincing at her familiar manner, her way of taking it for granted that he would always be at home to her on the long-distance phone.

"I'm afraid I have a little bad news for you." She paused, as if savoring his uneasiness and waiting for him to throw himself at her feet.

He stood in obstinate silence, leaning forward with his fist on the galleys of his book.

"Fred?"

"Yes."

"I thought maybe we were cut off. Fernie has had an accident. She broke her leg, ice skating."

"Ice skating? At this time of year?"

"It sounds foolish, doesn't it? She was at an indoor rink with Artie Tannenbaum, you remember the Tannenbaums from the sociology department?"

It was only the beginning. After all, she was not yet sixteen.

There were bound to be skiing accidents, and in more fashionable areas than western New York. Gstaad? Megève? She was reasonably clumsy; no doubt she would be falling off donkeys in Mexico and camels in Egypt while carrying on the search for an eligible young man.

"Is she in pain?" he asked.

"Fortunately, no. It was a clean break. She caught the blade in a fissure and went right over. She might have fractured her skull. It was inexcusable of them to have the ice in that condition. I really think we ought to sue."

"Is she in the hospital?"

"No, she's here, home. Artie had enough presence of mind to call an ambulance, and Dr. Spector set her leg in the emergency room, then he had her brought back here. I'm so furious at the—"

"Let me talk to her for a minute."

"Oh, that's impossible. She has this great huge cast, and she's just lying there and crying. It's really pathetic."

"What's she crying for?"

"She's afraid she'll miss out on her finals. Her first Regents. She was worried enough before this about getting through. Now, well, maybe with crutches . . ."

He surprised himself by saying, "I'll fly up first thing in the morning. Do you think she'd like that?"

"Why, that's very nice of you. She'd be just delighted. I hope it won't interfere with your schedule."

"I'll work things out. Tell her I'll be by right after breakfast."

After he had hung up he poured himself some Scotch. If Fernie was crying now at the prospect of dropping back, what would she do, faced with the prospect of dropping out? Supposing he were to sit down beside his daughter and break it to her that the party was over, that her mother's money tree had withered and died, how would she take it? He did not know her well enough. Perhaps she was ready to grow up, perhaps a core of her grandmother's peasant toughness lay beneath the schoolgirl chubbiness and the crush on famous daddy, who came home just often enough to renew the franchise. His own father, he knew, would not have been tough enough to live with what was going to happen. For the first time he was really glad that his father had died so soon after his mother.

If only he had someone to turn to. While he phoned the airline for a seat on the first morning plane he stepped out of his moccasins and stripped off his socks, shifting from one foot to the other as he shifted the phone from one hand to the other. Then he lay down on the bed in his shorts to finish the Scotch. I'm forty-five, he thought, I can think for myself.

But everything seemed to buzz around just over his head, like a squadron of menacing invisible mosquitoes. He wanted to sit at his desk, push aside the galleys, organize his thoughts, set down alternatives, regard the matter dispassionately. But he was tired, tired—and besides he was afraid that he would be unable to, that instead he would slowly petrify, turn to stone in the paralyzing effort to make a nightmare rational.

Not Vito, that crazy lone wolf, but Sy Glantzman or Joe Link, someone like that was what he needed now. Someone who had not only been in the movement back in the old days but had kept faith with his old ideals, even while coping with the job of being married and raising children.

Norm, there was a possibility. He was the most sophisticated of all, he made it his business to know what was going on. But that was the catch. Once Norm knew, based in Washington as he was, how long would it be before everyone did? No, Norm already was friends with too many of the new Democratic congressmen, and a cluster of senators as well; and it was his profession to expose, not to be discreet. Suddenly he remembered, with something like relief, that anyway Norm was off on a South American junket with the Nixon party, watching the vice president being stoned by Latin students. Who the hell needed him, anyway? When you think how cutting, how snotty, how patronizing and condescending he had been throughout their encounter in the Philippines . . . I must be out of my mind, Fred thought, to think of trying to confide once again in somebody like that.

The others were just as well out of reach too. Joe Link was off in California, raising prodigies and building tract houses. And Sy was wallowing around on the high seas on a Zim Lines ship, finally bringing his Israeli brood back to New York. What on earth could he possibly have in the way of advice, a man who had been planting beets and hoeing potatoes, and had never even looked at television? It would be like asking a Nigerian tribesman for advice on taking the fifth amendment.

What's the matter with me, he asked himself, why can't I stand on my own two feet? Why can't I just take a stand and see it through? His mind kept spinning around like a crippled glider out of control, heading for a crash in the darkness. He groped his way to the bathroom, afraid that if he turned on the lights he would become wide awake and incapable of escaping into sleep; he swallowed three aspirins and a Librium and flung himself down once again on the bed.

In the morning it was no better. But at least it was morning and he had things to do. He dressed hurriedly but with care, thinking of his daughter, and phoned down to the lobby for the doorman to whistle him up a cab to the airport. On the plane he had coffee and a roll, and by the time he had borrowed a razor from the stewardess and scraped his face in the john, he was in Buffalo.

Bea had a second breakfast waiting for him. She still made good coffee and she still had enough sense to leave him alone with Fernanda, who was stretched out on her back with the big bulky cast and *Catcher in the Rye.*

"So that's how you spend your time," he said.

"Oh daddy. You're not going to tell me that I'm too young for this book."

"Certainly not. I leave that to your English teacher. But I do think you're too young to break your leg."

So he had her laughing, and they got along fine. She complained to him about her teachers, and he complained to her about the cool kids, his students whom he found so distasteful in their acquiescent uninvolved complacency. Fernie was pleased that he had come specially to see her, and he was pleased that he could talk to her man to man and pretend that she was as fascinated by his literature courses as she was by his show biz anecdotes. It helped to push back the queer emptiness of no longer having a father and mother to visit.

But no sooner had he kissed her goodbye, extracted a promise of long letters, and rejoined Bea in the living room, than everything that he had suppressed came boiling to the surface. Bea still thought he was interested in faculty gossip about former colleagues who had finally become her closest friends, just as they had once been the people among whom she felt most inadequate. As her monologue went on, he felt the sweat of unease oozing up through his pores, covering his skin with a fine film as slippery and greasy as sin. He had gained nothing by coming here other than the momentary delusion that he would still be an influence for good, when what mattered was not at all what he said to his daughter but what she was going to hear about him and how she would react.

Bea had stopped and was staring at him, her small eyes tightening on either side of her long thin accusing nose.

"I'm sorry," he said. "What was that?"

"I was saying, I suppose you've heard about Irwin."

"Heard what?"

"About Carmela's leaving him."

He arose and brushed off his slacks carefully. "No," he said, "I hadn't heard anything about that."

"I'd have thought surely . . . Well, what did you expect? I know he's your friend and all that, but how long can a woman put up with a drunk?"

"Irwin is not a drunk."

"Why not, because he's Jewish? I'd hate to tell you how many patients he's lost because of his boozing. It's lucky for him most of them are children who don't know the difference."

She went on with a certain ugly gusto, not telling him anything that he really wanted to know; he was extremely anxious to learn at least about Paul, but he could not bring himself to fuel the licking flame of her spiteful talk. At last he was able to excuse himself.

He drove to the nearest drugstore and phoned Irwin. The nurse was reluctant to put Dr. Metzger on, and he had to identify himself, which was uncomfortably like pulling rank. But Irwin sounded excited and pleased, and in an instant the warmth of old friendship had melted the icy fear and loneliness which oppressed him.

"What are you doing here?"

"Fernie broke her leg ice skating, and I've just been commiserating with her. Any chance of our getting together before I head back to New York? I've got a rented car here, so—"

"So come on out to Snyder and have lunch with me. I won't take no for an answer."

Irwin was anxious to talk. He had ordered a table in a corner of the fake-Spanish restaurant in the shopping center around the corner from his office, and they had barely settled in, with a mutual toast, when he began to explain.

"I guess you've heard about Carmie."

"Just. Bea was bursting to pass on the news."

Irwin made a face. Even without the gesture of distaste, his features were distorted, a gross caricature of what they once had been. His cheeks were swollen, his eyes seemed smaller, his nose bloated. Even his hair, which had been growing sparser for some time, now looked as though he had torn out handfuls: the remnants stood up here and there defiantly, pitifully, as though he could not even accept baldness as other men did.

"I don't care about the gossip, Fred," he said. "Really I don't. I told Carmie, all that matters is how this will affect Paul." Irwin downed his double and called for another without a glance at the menu. "I can't tell you how anxious I was to talk to you about this. You've been through it all."

"Several times."

"I mean, with a child."

"Fernanda hardly remembered who I was supposed to be when I came back, and since then she's always taken the situation for granted. Come on, Irwin, let's eat something."

"I'll have a steak," Irwin said absently to the waiter. He explained, "That's all I have for lunch, a small steak. I'm trying to lose some weight."

He needed to. His white shirt bulged over the belt. "Anyway, Carmie doesn't want a divorce. At least, not right now. She just wants to be on her own, so I said all right, why not?"

"Where is she?"

"Mexico. A place called San Miguel Allende. You know it? She said she has to live a creative life before it's too late. Don't ask me what she wants to do. Whatever it is, I felt that I didn't have the right to deny her."

"Oh, Irwin!"

"I mean it. I give her credit for sticking it out this long. I guess I do drink too much. I'll tell you something else, maybe you think I'm crazy, but why should she just stay here and vegetate? She's still beautiful and high-spirited, and . . ."

"You mean she walked out, she's banging around in Mexico, and you're footing the bill?"

Irwin glanced up briefly from the steak with which he had been toying. "She left Paulie with me, Fred."

What kind of life could they be leading, the two of them? He said angrily, "You make it sound as though she deserves a merit badge for not dragging him along."

"I'm only trying to explain."

"Go ahead."

"No one else's life is easy to understand, right? I've never been able to sort out my own. The thing is, she felt she was exercising a bad influence on Paul. She was right. She's just never been able to understand his commitment to a spiritual way of life."

"Have you?" He did not mean to be abrupt, but he could not hold back.

"No, but I've tried. At least he'll come to me, as long as we're under the same roof, and discuss things that he knows are hard for me to accept. But Carmie thinks he's a zombie, she even calls him that . . . The irony is that he's turned away from Judaism. Lately he's been exploring Catholicism. The last thing in the world she wanted for him."

"I really don't understand."

Irwin laughed painfully. "Do you think I do? Only fifteen, and in the fall he starts his last year of high school already. Without even studying. Orthodox Judaism he felt wasn't humane enough, that much I got out of him, it's too stern. So he began reading up on Catholicism. I was scared, but what could I do?"

"And Carmela didn't like that."

"It was the last straw. For her the Church was that old dump on Niagara Street smelling of mold and candle drippings, and having to drag her tail out of bed for early Mass, and the priest putting his hand up her skirt when she was twelve years old. She'd never even heard of the Catholic Worker movement. There she was, hardly finished explaining to her paisanos about bar mitzvah, and Paulie was reading Maritain. It was too much, you see?"

"I guess so."

"If there was any kind of politics for him to attach himself to, he'd be a socialist. Sy wrote me that when I described the situation to him, and I think he was right. But this isn't the thirties, it's the fifties, and all he sees around him are the kids bucking for Yale and Harvard. When I try to explain that to Carmie, her reaction is, what's wrong with Yale and Harvard? From her point of view she's perfectly right. Maybe later on, when Paulie's gotten over his adolescence, and Carmie's gotten over the urge to roam . . . Well, all I can do is hope. And sort of be around the house as much as I can in case he needs me."

Fred stirred uneasily. "I really have to get back to the airport and catch a plane."

As soon as he had spoken he wished he had not. His friend's face reddened slowly, all the way up to the forehead. Beneath the thin strands of hair, even his skull was flushed. It was obvious that Irwin was struggling not to apologize, not to say, I'm sorry I burdened you with my troubles.

Suddenly, before he realized what he was doing, he said, "Listen Irwin, I'm in awful trouble." He spoke rapidly, unable to stop himself. "That's why I said I ought to be back in New York. I ran away from it."

Irwin's high color faded. "Is it about your program?"

He felt his heart bump, a real knock, as if it were a motor momentarily insulted with low-grade fuel. "Wait a minute," he said. "What makes you ask that?"

Irwin said uncomfortably, "The stories about those rigged quiz shows, you know, people get so cynical. Especially after the college basketball players started shaving points and taking payoffs. Even the West Point cadets."

"What's all that got to do with me?"

"Not you, Fred. Your show. There's so much dough involved, the rumors start floating around, not just about one quiz program, but about all of them. I hope you don't think I was—"

"We don't have to be polite with each other. Any day, maybe any minute, they'll be moving on to me. With those other shows, it was just plain ugly. I had no idea. My program as you know appealed to a more mature audience—at least it was always my hope that the intellectual content was such that, that . . ." he felt himself beginning to stutter and stopped. He pressed his palms together and was surprised to feel that they were soaking.

"I know what you mean," Irwin encouraged him.

"The lower the level the other shows sunk to, the higher their ratings went. It's a very competitive business—I'm sure I'm not telling you anything you don't know."

"Go on."

"The way it was put to me, we would be forced off the air if we didn't liven up our program, make it more suspenseful. I agreed only on condition that the intellectual content shouldn't be vulgarized like those other stupid shows. And they said fine, what was uppermost in their minds was to keep a program of our standards and our quality before the public. What I didn't know, I suppose I should have, was that all this implied my acquiescence . . ."

He really could not go on. Groping for the pitcher, he poured himself some ice water.

After a while Irwin said quietly, "Acquiescence in what?"

"Well, keeping certain of the more popular personalities on the program. As long as they were the ones that kept our rating competitive."

"Even if they flunked the questions?"

"But they didn't flunk them."

"That was lucky."

"It wasn't. It was planned. I wasn't involved, Irwin, believe me." He hated himself for using those two words. "At least, not until I went to the producers and said, 'Hey, what's up?' And they said, 'Well look, what did you expect us to do, die?'"

Irwin pressed him no further. They sat for some time in silence, and at last his friend said, "Fred, whatever I can do . . ."

"I've been trying to figure out what I ought to do myself, and I can't seem to come up with any answers. Isn't that ridiculous?"

"I know that feeling."

"Those sharpies, those shrewdies. They kept telling me, Stay cool, deny everything. I have the feeling they've said it for the last time."

"What does your lawyer say?"

"Which one? I've got a roomful. They argue among themselves. They like the word 'tactics' a lot. What does that have to do with me? They're all working for someone else, not just for me."

Irwin snapped his fingers. "I know who you ought to talk to."

"I've talked too much already."

"You want to get through this business, don't you?" Already Irwin was looking better. The color was back in his plump cheeks, and his eyes were shining. "You've got to sit down with Margaret Zivic."

"What are you trying to shove me into?"

"That girl is the hottest lawyer in town. She doesn't just do labor law, you know. Ever since the time she got Ham Wright off, when they tried to hang the New Party around his neck, she's handled one civil rights case after another."

"Is that my problem, doctor?"

"You tell me. Where does it hurt, in the pocketbook? In the heart?"

"If I knew, maybe I could figure out what to do. I took aspirin last night and it didn't help. I guess I'm scared, like before an operation."

"Yes, but what's the operation?"

"What will people think of me when I'm up there in front of that senate committee, that's what I worry about." He was tempted to go on and tell about Evie, but then he thought of Carmela. "Anyway," he said, swallowing hard, "when Margaret asked me to testify for Ham, I said I was too busy."

"So you sent a check. Margaret holds no hard feelings. She's counseled a whole bunch of people who've been called before committees. She's sympathetic, she's smart—at least let me phone her. It won't have to go beyond us—even Bill's away, he's off in Detroit at some UAW conference."

He allowed himself to lapse into acquiescence as readily as he would have eased himself into a warm tub. All at once it seemed not only logical but simple. Clapping his hat on his head, Irwin signed the check, led the way to the parking lot, and bade Fred follow him in the rented car.

He drove as in a dream, pulled into the driveway behind Irwin, tagged after him into his home. They entered by way of the kitchen, an appalling mess—crusted pots soaking in the sink, empty cans on the counter tops, the dishwasher ajar (apparently Irwin served himself from it, then re-stacked it every few days), stains on the floor, muddy moccasins in the doorway.

"The woman'll be in to clean soon," Irwin remarked. The messiness extended to the newspaper-strewn living room and the record-strewn music alcove. Fluff-balls rolled along before them. Irwin flipped open the liquor cabinet, a jumble of sticky glasses and open bottles. "Make yourself a drink while I ring up Margaret."

In all his years of executives' and producers' luncheons, Fred had never been able to learn the midday drinking exercise. But Irwin did not demand that he drink, or do anything more than stretch out on the couch.

The next thing he knew the slam of a door awoke him with a start. He blinked at Irwin, regarding him from his easy chair, glass in hand.

"Forgive me," he said. "I took a pill last night and here I am messing up your office hours."

"Forget it. Here's Paul to say hello."

Fred pulled himself erect and stared at the boy in the doorway.
Paul was holding his schoolbooks under one arm, his right hand
already extended in greeting.

"Hello, Mr. Byrd," he said in a deep and resonant voice. "Welcome back again." He was a young man, almost, with an intense,
almost piercing gaze and a hard handclasp.

"You're not going to call me Mr. Byrd, are you, Paul?" He tried
to be jocular. "After all these years?"

"I'm sorry," Paul replied, but did not add his first name. He was
polite, but despite his attentiveness he seemed at bottom terribly
remote.

It was unsettling. Although he tried to tell himself that there was
no basis for it, Fred had the feeling that Paul was not only not interested in him (and why should he be?) but did not even like him.
Am I imagining it, he wondered, or is the boy actually contemptuous
of me? What have I ever done to him? What does he know about
me?

But by now many people, maybe millions, thought that they knew
something about him from watching him one evening a week for
less than an hour, while he chatted with contestants and tried to
instill in those watching him some feeling for literature, for the history of drama and the drama of history, for . . . He could almost
see the faint smile which would widen Paul's ascetic lips if he were
to say something of the sort. Damn it, he wanted to demand of the
boy, who sat with his hands clasped about one knee and talked
gravely about the problem of southern school integration and the
prayer pilgrimage to Washington, how do you know what I really
am? What I really am up against?

He was relieved when Paul excused himself.

"What do you think of him?" Irwin asked.

"He's remarkably mature. Sensitive too." Irwin seemed to want
more. He added, "I'm really struck by the gap between him and
Fernanda. Girls are supposed to mature faster than boys, aren't
they? And I guess she's quite ready physically to bear children and
all the rest of it. But she seemed such a child when I sat and
talked with her this morning. When I contrast that with Paul, who's
almost a year younger . . ."

"I tried to steer the conversation onto his track, but I didn't
really succeed. I guess he feels he doesn't know you well enough
any more to talk about personal things."

"Apparently."

"Listen, I made a date for you with Margaret. She'll be waiting for you at her house whenever you feel like ringing the bell. You remember where they live, don't you?"

"You shouldn't have done that."

"Among friends, why sit in an office like a stranger? It was Margaret's suggestion, in fact, since I said that Paulie might inhibit a discussion here."

"Irwin, I don't know how to thank you."

"Stop it. I just gave her the bare outlines, I said you wanted a private talk with her. And I'm not going along—I'd just be in the way anyway—so we can say goodbye here whenever you want to take off."

In the driveway he clasped Irwin's hands. "I hope you can work things out with Carmela."

"Keep in touch, will you?"

"Never fear."

Never fear? What a stupid way to say goodbye. They were both driven by fear, he and Irwin, to protect a daughter, a son, from nameless perils. Why else would he be on his way now to the Zivic house?

Once in Margaret's living room, gazing over her shoulder at the sun parlor that had been converted into a greenhouse for Bill's cactus collection, he recounted the situation somewhat more consecutively and connectedly than he had to Irwin. It came easier the second time around. He even began to suppose, drinking Margaret's tea and eating her homemade cookies ("My hobby," she explained, "I like to bake late at night to relax, while Bill fusses with his succulents"), that it might even be bearable to go through it all in a senate committee room.

Margaret had not changed much. He didn't remember that she had worn glasses before, but she was still petite and trim. And still methodical, jotting notes in a minute hand, almost without taking her eyes from his face, or altering the expression of interested concern—more than professional and a little less than maternal—on her rather ordinary but not quite homely countenance.

When he had finished she was not smiling at all. Chewing on the inside of her lips, she remarked, "I can understand why you're upset. It's a mess."

This was not exactly the response he had hoped to elicit. The

old uneasiness began to creep up, destroying the simple release
he thought he had gained. He said nothing.

After a moment she asked, "You want my opinion?"

Laughing nervously, he tried to be jocular. "Well, that seems to
be the idea."

"All right. I won't even try to make a guess as to how things will
wind up within the industry. Anyway I'm sure you're better informed on that than I. As far as legal complications are concerned
—possible prosecution for fraud, or even complicity—they seem to
me unlikely. Of course one can never be *certain* when there are
such intangibles as the public temper, and the possibility of a D.A.
or a federal attorney wanting to make a name for himself."

His blood froze. This was not what he had had in mind. Wasn't
this backhanded reassurance a way of saying that his position was
as every bit as bad as he had feared? Was this all that lawyers,
friends even, could offer you? Where the hell was the reassurance?

Then she went on, "I feel very strongly that you shouldn't just sit
and wait. Whatever action will be taken, whatever the public response will be, it's up to you to take the initiative. At least that will
show how much you care, both about your good name and about
your commitment to"—she smiled slightly—"public education. If
you move first, it may discourage anyone from attempting to include
you in whatever prosecution may follow the public hearings."

"I'm not sure that I understand," he said, "exactly what it is that
you think I ought to do."

"Issue a statement, the sooner the better. Don't let the businessmen or the lawyers do it for you, Fred. Sit down and write out in
your own words what you've been telling me. Say what's in your
heart." She looked at him frankly. "Don't be afraid to admit mistakes in judgment. Didn't we use to say that if we told the truth
to people—the masses, we used to call them, in our innocence—
sooner or later they'd listen to us?"

"Oh, as for that," he said lightly, already heartened by the
prospect that she had opened for him, "time has proved how ridiculous we were. The best you can say about those days is that we
were unrealistic."

Her mouth tightened. "It's up to you how you want to state your
case. I've told you what I think you might do in general terms."

"But I agree."

"Then the specifics are up to you. The quicker the better, though."

"You're right, I can see that." He had the feeling that now she was anxious for him to go. He arose. "I've been kind of paralyzed. I'm just not used to being in this kind of situation. But then everybody must say that to you, right?"

"Sometimes."

"I'm going to follow your advice," he said. "I'm going right back to New York and get at it. Do you want to see my statement when I'm through?"

"If you think I ought to."

That was a delicate way, he supposed, of asking him if he wanted her to represent him. "Well look," he said, "I want you in my corner."

"As counsel?"

"That's right." Before he could stop himself, he added, "And also, you know, in other ways. I mean you and Bill, and Irwin too, and Sy when he gets back. Even Norm—"

"Let's take one thing at a time," she said. "Suppose you get in touch with me, either at my office or here, when you're ready. As for Washington, I have an associate there, if it should come to that."

But when he arrived back in the apartment the official invitation from the committee counsel was already waiting for him, on the very top of all the mail. Courteous, inquiring if the proposed date would accord with his no doubt heavy schedule, it turned him hot and cold. Panicky, he grabbed up the phone and called Margaret.

"Listen," he said, "I was too slow. They sent me a telegram. They're baying at my heels, like in some goddam movie."

"Let me call Washington, the committee counsel as well as ours. I'll tell them that you'll be delighted to appear—"

"Yes, that's a good word. Delighted."

"—and that you're grateful for the opportunity to clarify the picture. Meantime, just sit down and do what you said you were going to do."

"Is that all?"

"That's all." She did not seem susceptible to irony by long distance. "And Fred—"

"Yes?"

"I'll be there too, waiting for you."

There was nothing for it now. He called the operator and had her disconnect his phone until further notice. Then he sent out to the delicatessen over on Second Avenue for a case of beer, a roast

chicken, and enough cold cuts and sliced rye to last him for a prolonged siege. After that he pushed aside the galleys and set to work.

When he was through at last—he had never worked so hard on
anything in all his life—he was not only grateful to Margaret but
rather pleased with himself as well. It was good to know that you
could still work around the clock, draft after draft after draft,
changing and polishing until you had made the words on paper
do exactly what you wanted them to. And he had done it on his
own; no one would be able to say that the words, the style, the tone,
were anyone else's but his own.

He typed up an immaculate copy on bond with three onion-
skin carbons. Then he showered, shaved, and called down to the
lobby for a taxi.

On the shuttle to Washington he was somewhat tense—people
recognized him, the requests for autographs made him wonder
whether the same thing would happen on the way back—but once
he had checked into the Wardman Park he felt better. He treated
himself to a tranquilizer along with a bottle of vichy water from room
service and a throat spray, and told himself that when you came
down to it it was just another performance. The nerves were the
same old butterflies that still persisted, after all these years, when the
director held up his fingers behind the cameras and the red lights
began to blink.

Margaret picked him up at his room. She wore the same detached
expression with which she had shaken his hand in farewell in
Buffalo. From a purse that matched her suit she took out her
eyeglasses.

"Well," she said, "I guess we'd better have a look at your statement."

"You want to check over my script?"

It got no rise out of her. She had no sense of humor, he should
have remembered that from the old days. On the other hand, who
needed a lawyer with a funnybone?

He handed her the sheets over which he had worked so hard. "No
one else has seen this," he said. "Not a living soul. I typed it up
myself, with some carbons."

She nodded casually. "You'd better let me have those too." Then
she settled down in the easy chair and began to read, her face as
devoid of expression as though she were scanning a real estate
transfer.

He turned away and walked to the window, hands clasped behind his back. Everything was very silent behind him while he gazed down at the pleasant leafy scene below. This was a nice hotel; it was almost like being in the country, or at least in a well-kept resort. Certainly you didn't feel that you were in the nation's capitol. Why did everyone say that this was a terrible place to live? Why did people commute from here to New York? There was a relaxed quality here, even a freshness in the air, that you simply couldn't find in Manhattan.

He glanced at his watch. Margaret was taking an awfully long time. He turned back to her and discovered that she had already put his statement down on the little table at her side. She was sitting quietly, hands in her lap, looking at him quizzically, her lips drawn together.

"Well?" he asked.

"It's not exactly what I had in mind."

He fought back the little fluttering that was starting up. "I don't think I follow."

"You gave me to understand that you were going to be utterly frank."

"Haven't I been?"

"I had the impression that you were going to explain how you were led into this situation. That you were going to admit your mistakes."

"Haven't I done that?"

"Let's say that you've put the emphasis on your good-will and your innocence. And the onus elsewhere—on the rating system, the competitiveness, the greed of the networks."

He put his hands to his cheeks. They felt hot. "Now look. You couldn't expect me to abase myself. This thing has gotten out of control, granted. But we meant well, those of us who have tried to use the medium to raise cultural standards."

She held up her hands, palms out, as if to close out the discussion. "Okay."

"Weren't you the one who was saying that people would eventually follow us if we showed them we were trying to make their lives better?"

Margaret dropped her hands and put his statement into a folder in her briefcase. "By getting rich in the process? By trafficking with slobs and cynics? Or with the kind of greedy vulgarians you yourself describe here?"

"Oh, it must be nice to be able to maintain your purity," he said bitterly. "But name me anyone who's succeeded since the war. Didn't you ever defend a guilty client? What did you expect of me? To settle for being a lousy English professor? Do you think the program would have been better without my efforts? Do you think I would have achieved more by concentrating on my seminars and ignoring twenty million viewers?"

"I think your statement is excellent," she replied flatly. Then she added, as she arose. "Of its kind."

"Christ," he protested, "here I've been all tied up in knots, I thought you were going to support me and sustain me. Instead you look down your nose—"

"That wasn't my intention. I'm really sorry. One thing I'm sure of—you know far better than I what will appeal to large numbers of people. If I have any personal reservations, they have nothing to do with your legal rights or your appearance today. So put that out of your mind."

"You don't want to withdraw?"

"Not as your counsel. Unless you feel that you don't want me."

"All right," he said decisively, "then let's go."

In the taxi Margaret said, "These hearings are usually kind of haphazard, I mean if you think of them as spectacles. Senators come and go, you're never certain how many will be there. The same goes for spectators. Sometimes the committee room is half empty, sometimes it's jammed. And you shouldn't be disconcerted if people push in while you're testifying, or get up and walk out."

"As long as they don't throw tomatoes. Or give me the hook."

"I imagine that you'll have a full house, since word has leaked out about your testifying. Senators like to be seen with celebrities as much as anyone else does."

"Don't lawyers?"

"Not always, not always. My Washington associate has already been making arrangements with committee counsel. You'll be free to confer with us, but I don't anticipate any special problems. There is one thing: will you have any objections to microphones? To newsreel and TV cameras? Because if you do, we have the right to obtain certain—"

"No no," he said. "I'm ready in my own mind for the works. And if I asked for special dispensation, it would look as though I had something I wanted to keep from the public."

"Nobody's going to think that after they've heard your statement, are they?"

He was not sure whether she was needling him; her face showed nothing. "There is the matter of my contract," he said. "I'm not supposed to be seen on any other network or program—"

"We take care of the waivers and that whole end of it. In any case"—she smiled for the first time all morning—"this isn't a sponsored show."

If it wasn't it had the air of an event. They had to push through a substantial crowd at the taxi entrance to the senate office building. Inside, the corridor was lined with reporters, and technicians were busily hooking up cables and carrying heavy black boxes of equipment on their backs. The familiar tension before show time, the bustling, the scraping of metal on linoleum and cement, the hoarse rude cries, the long looping cables coiling across the floor like rubbery snakes, gave him, surprisingly, a sense of security.

Squeezed rather tightly to his side, Margaret glanced up at him. "Are you all right?"

"I'm ready," he said confidently.

He could feel the adrenalin coursing through his system as he introduced himself and was introduced to counsel, assistant counsel, senators, administrative assistants, committee staff. Everyone was extremely polite. The chairman, his long graying hair wonderfully brushed back behind his ears in the style of a symphony conductor, was as courtly as if they were about to enjoy after-dinner cigars on the terrace.

"I understand, Professor Byrd," the committee counsel said to him after he had been sworn, "that you have a statement you wish to read into the record."

"If I may."

The chairman inclined his head.

Fred took the sheets from his breast pocket, smoothed them out before him, and waited for silence. His moment of patience, almost of resignation to the will of the camera and the crowd, was more effective than he could have anticipated. The silence was absolute. He began to read.

As he detailed the origins of his program and his connection with it, glancing up from time to time into the eye of the camera, and also directly into those of the committee chairman, it seemed to him that they were coming around. I've got them, he thought exultantly, I've got them, and as he warmed to his task he decided not to be bound by the text to the very end, but to try to anticipate in his own way some of the questions that might be put to him at the conclusion of his statement. As he scanned the last paragraphs of the explanation on which he had labored so painfully, he came to the decision that the moment had arrived.

Very carefully he turned over the page, like—it flickered through his mind—like turning over a new leaf, and with the slow movement of his hand made it clear that he was not quite done, that he wished to say something else, something which he had been unable to commit to paper before this moment. Everyone in the hearing room, from the senators in their single row to the spectators and the press table, remained utterly quiet as he folded his hands over the pages and spoke.

"I have endeavored to sketch a history of this entertainment, oddly American in its mixture of striving for material gain and admiration for expertise in many areas. At this point some will persist in asking—and with justification—why did they do it? Why did some fool us, why did others pretend to knowledge that they did not possess, why did you yourself not seek out the truth and verify your suspicions, now that you yourself have told us that you were in fact suspicious?"

Fred allowed himself to smile slightly as he shook his head. "In the name of those who are not here today, but may speak subsequently, I ask for your pity. More than that, for your compassion. Before you cast the stone, ask yourselves whether you would have declined the opportunity to provide for your families, to assure the education of your children—remember the scholarships which my program offered, in addition to the monetary rewards—and to become a figure of consequence in the community. As for the executives of the industry, who are perhaps better qualified to speak for themselves, I would ask for your recognition of their typicality. Impelled by that spirit of competitiveness and enterprise which has been the mainspring of our progress—and perhaps of some of our failings—as a capitalist society, they have striven for the maximum possible exposure of their wares. They have simply acted according to the rules of the game which we all play, and I would suggest that if we do not like the outcome of this particular game, we change the rules instead of crucifying the players.

"As for myself"—he spread his hands deprecatingly—"I would ask only for your understanding. It may be that the prepared statement to which you have listened so patiently has already achieved that. It was my hope, by utilizing this extraordinary new medium, to stimulate as many as possible of my fellow-citizens, indeed to excite them, with the potential of the human mind. I do not feel that this was a mean objective. Nor do I feel, despite the unpleasant disclosures of recent days, that I have completely failed. If I have sinned, if I have allowed enthusiasm for the continuation of this program to overrule my rational compunctions, it was because I had the interests of my country at heart. For this I would beg your indulgence, but I would still insist: We must all of us try to aid the mass media in making the mental athlete as glamorous as the physical athlete. I see this as one facet of our national purpose, if we are to succeed in the international competition with a science-minded antagonist. May I close by saying that I pledge my continuing efforts to this end. I hope to be able to go on using whatever I as an intellectual may have learned from this saddening but fascinating experience, to contribute my small share to the advancement of our people and our way of life."

The room remained quiet for a measurable moment. Then his eardrums seemed to contract and expand, to deflate and then swell, as if there was a roaring going on within his brain. But it was not within, it was out there, in the room, and as he blinked in the glare of the flashbulbs he realized that they were applauding.

The chairman was rapping with has gavel. "Have you finished, Professor Byrd?"

Fred nodded.

"Then I thank you for your very interesting statement. I believe counsel had some questions to put to you on behalf of this committee?"

The thin, intense young man who had shaken Fred's hand at the outset now smiled with the uneasy bravado of a graduate student being asked by a senior department member to proceed to the defense of his thesis. Instead of proceeding, he bent over the senators' table and whispered to the chairman, who covered the microphone with his hand to muffle their discussion. Uncertain,

Fred glanced over at Margaret, who had also been conferring in murmurs with her associate. She made the slightest sit-tight gesture, her face expressionless. Screw you, sister, he said to himself, as he folded his arms and awaited the next move.

The chairman banged his gavel once again. Passing one hand affectionately along his silvered temple, he asked, "In relation to your very stirring statement, professor, I wonder if you have any specific recommendations that you would care to pass along to this committee. I am thinking of suggestions as to how we can in future avoid affronts to the public conscience, or at least the weakening of public confidence in the media."

He sighed. How easy it had all turned out to be! "I'll be glad to set forth my suggestions, senator, for the guidance of this committee. But I'd prefer to do it deliberately rather than impulsively, on the spur of the moment. I'm sure you understand."

"Of course. Let me add my thanks for your coming here and being so frank with us." He rapped one final time with his gavel. "Thirty minutes' recess. Will that do, professor?"

Then they were all gathering around him, sticking microphones under his nose. Margaret stood to one side, but before he could say anything to her in triumph he was being hugged fervently by Evie herself.

"Darling," she cried, "I was so proud! I didn't get in touch beforehand, I didn't even want to let you know I was in town. I was afraid it might throw you."

"I was a bit nervous beforehand. But now I feel fine."

"You should. You were wonderful!"

"I'm just a ham at heart," he said. "As long as I've got those faces out there to lecture to, somehow I can rise to the occasion. But I could use a cup of coffee. Are you free now?"

"Why do you think I flew in?" Evie laughed and linked her arm through his.

They were practically at his lawyers' side when he realized who the third person was, chatting with Margaret and her associate. He hardly needed to turn that leonine graying head.

"Norm!" he said. "I didn't know that you were back from South America."

"Oh, I wouldn't have missed this for anything." Norm's grin was so wide, so wholehearted, that for one wonderful heart-stopping moment Fred believed he had won him too—the greatest conquest of all! Then Norm held out his square powerful hand. "Let me say to you what I was just telling Margaret. You have just given one of the truly great performances of the Eisenhower Era."

PART SIX

PART SIX

1. SY

"Listen gang," Sy announced, "I think I've got a deal going. How many of you would like to go to the inauguration?"

The room erupted. Save for those asprawl, heads on their desks, the kids began to babble. Two boys slapped hands, in the back of the class someone applauded. The girls he called The Terrible Trio started to giggle wildly.

"I have to find out how many of you actually will go. Once you say Yes, you can't back out, remember that. Come on now, let me count hands."

"Where is it at?"

"It's in Washington, Jimmy." The class clown. He blinked at the grinning boy in the front row. Since you could never be sure whether he was putting you on, the only way was to take him straight. "Where'd you think it was, at the Apollo?"

"Man, if it was there, I'd know."

"Quit bragging. Who can tell Jimmy about the inauguration?"

The faithful duo, Uretta and Maria Luisa, raised their hands eagerly. Reluctantly he ignored the frantic waving of both the dark and the pale hand. Nothing would be gained, no one would be impressed, by their giving the explanation. They always did their homework, they always knew the answers, they were always on time, they even knew what they would do after they graduated—go to nursing school. By now they did not excite either hilarity or envy among their classmates, but only the same sullen incomprehension with which such knowingness on the part of white students

—had there been any in this ninth grade—would have been greeted.

Hesitantly Ronnie Thomas, who had been poring over a comic book, gestured with his elbow, as if he were blocking rather than volunteering. Sy knew the meaning of the gesture. Pleased, he nodded at the slow and somber boy.

"Well, that's when the doctor sticks you with something so as you won't get sick."

Shrieks, howls. Angel bayed like a wolf. "He sticks it into you!"

"How far in does it go?"

"Does it hurt good?"

Two big buxom girls, Jayna and Clara, encouraged each other to near hysteria. He walked over to them and snapped his fingers. At least they would stop on command.

"If you think that's so funny, Jayna, you tell Jimmy what the inauguration is."

"I don know, Mr. Glantzman."

"Then why laugh at Ronnie?"

"Cause he mean nockilation, what the nurse gives you."

"Okay. Now we're halfway there. How about the other half?" Resolutely he ignored the imploring arms of Uretta and Maria Luisa. "Billy, who was elected last month?"

Billy the athlete shuffled his Keds uneasily. "Elected where?"

"All over the United States. From Harlem all the way to California."

Billy rolled his eyes. Fascinated, shamed, Sy thought of a frightened horse, rearing and plunging. He wished there were some way to relieve Billy of his momentary misery. Uneasily, hopefully, Billy asked: "Eisenhower?"

Angel hooted.

"All right, Angel. What's wrong with Billy's answer?"

"Ike, he's been President since the war."

"Not that long."

"Anyway, he didn't get elected on account he didn't run this time." He laughed. "He ran Treeky Deeky instead. And bam! Deeky lost."

"Now tell us," he asked, "who did win?"

"Kennedy, he's some kind of senator or something."

"Hooray for the Democrats!" called out Sebastian.

"Is Kennedy a Republican or a Democrat, Sebastian?"

"He's a Democrat, they're the best, they stick up for the poor people."

"And what happens to him next month?"

Sebastian's face lit up. "I got you. He gets inau-hurated!"

"Bravo! Like pulling a tooth, but we finally got to it. Now. Right after the Christmas holidays, President Eisenhower turns over the government to Senator Kennedy. He takes the oath of office from the Chief Justice of the Supreme Court, and then he becomes President Kennedy. It's a very solemn ceremony, and it takes place—"

Uretta could restrain herself no longer. "Every four years!"

"That's why I said it's a special deal for us to go to Washington to watch the inauguration."

Gloom. "They got any music there?"

"Nothing that rocks. They have bands, you know, for the parade, and then they'll have inauguration balls. But let's face it, they won't invite people like you and me."

"Why not? Why not you, Teach?"

"It's for important people."

"Like who?"

"Politicians, people who gave a lot of money to the cause—"

"What cause?"

"The party. The winning side."

"Didn't you?"

"Very funny. This is a kind of victory celebration, like when a school team wins the big game. Only they have business leaders, union leaders, movie stars—"

That broke it open. "Like who? Frank Sinatra?"

"I'm sure. And Dean Martin, probably, and Shirley MacLaine, and Sammy Davis . . ."

"They goin have a nigger in the White House?"

"You want to find out," he urged, "you all come along to Washington."

They were not to be sucked in that easily. One more crowd scene was not for them. When he tried cajoling they turned sullen. The more he went on about the historic sights and the rare opportunity to see them at a historic moment, the more they resisted. The President and the President-elect were only names, and as for the Smithsonian and the mint, they were on the other side of the moon; one more supervised bus trip to the other side of the moon was not for them. So what was he knocking himself out for?

Only Uretta and Maria Luisa, faithful to the end, held up their hands.

"I can't make arrangements for a bus for just three of us. If I can squeeze us into the bus from another grade, I'll do that. Otherwise . . ."

The two strivers were cast down. The plump, scrubbed Puerto Rican girl and her tiny, black, eager girl friend were too young to conceal their disappointment, even though it was only the latest of a long series. He cursed himself for having muffed the entire idea of the excursion. If thirty of them scorned it why should he have dangled it before the only ones for whom it was exciting, and then snatched it away?

"Otherwise I'll tell you what," he wound up, looking into the soulful eyes of the two girls who sought excuses to follow him, holding hands, down the corridor from one classroom to the next, pleading for his opinion of Sidney Poitier, James Baldwin, Little Richard. "Those of us that want to go are going to get there together, by hook or by crook."

He was all too readily recompensed by their shining gratitude. As for their expectations, he would find some way of fulfilling them if he had to carry them to Washington on his shoulders. That gave him an idea, but before he could think about it, at the end of school he was shaken by the folded square of ruled paper that he found on his desk next to the briefcase into which he stuffed lesson plans, texts, and student papers to take home.

He looked at the block-lettered message as if it informed him of a kidnapping or a murder.

Dear Mr G, How would you like to fuck me. I will wait for you outside the men teachers toilet at haf past four. Guess Who. P.S. I think your cute.

He shoved the note into his briefcase, buckled it, tucked into his jacket the ends of the scarf that Bernie and Serena had collaborated in knitting, and shouldered into the biting winter wind that swept petrified paper bags and frozen sheets of newspaper stiff with frost, like fragments of cadavers taken with rigor mortis, down the Harlem streets.

On the subway grinding across to Queens, Sy asked himself who could have written it. Unbidden, the image of surly Rita, lolling in her chair in the second row, leaped to his eye, complete and fully fleshed as if she now sat opposite him in the train: chewing slowly, pouting lower lip working sensually, she filed her long coral fingernails with an emery board, blowing the fine dust negligently across her blank writing tablet, swinging one long leg sibilantly over the other, offering from one rhythmic moment to the next glimpses of a bronze-gold thigh. Arising, she responded to the call to the blackboard by rotating her hips as if she were swaying down a burlesque runway, flaunting her rocklike rump, rubbing it on the edge of his desk as she flared her nostrils, breathing deeply to urge upon him the two treasures that swelled in her sweater like the carvings of a sex-mad sculptor.

Fourteen years old. If he were to charge her with having written the invitation she would be capable of laughing in his face, or of responding to the accusation with ladylike hauteur.

What was worse, he had no way of knowing that some other girl, primly in place behind her social studies text, had not composed the note. Or even a boy, grinning and nudging, proud of his jocular ingenuity. And here he was at forty, swaying in the smoggy-windowed subway, staring vacantly at the black puddles of melting heelprints on the foul floor of the squealing car, thinking of Rita. Who was the guiltier?

When he entered the apartment, he found Serena already making a glass of chocolate milk and a peanut butter sandwich for her eight-year-old brother. He kissed her and Mitch and sat down at the kitchen table to join them in a glass of milk.

"Didn't Joey come home with you?" he asked Serena.

"He plays soccer today."

"In this weather?"

"You know he's a fanatic."

What she meant was that her big brother had brought back the skill from Israel and used it to make his way in his school. Why not? Serena herself had slipped into Queens as if she had never been away; she had no need to fight her way to security. What she had brought with her was an unquestioning sense of responsibility, an acceptance of her role in the family, that had permitted Bernie to go back to school for a master's and now to take up another life as a case worker. Small, sweet, and dark like her mother, Serena at thirteen took it for granted that in her mother's absence it fell to her to run the house, blow Mitch's nose, bandage the scraped knees and kiss away the tears—and share with him the Silvercup sliced bread and Skippy peanut butter that had so quickly replaced *hummus* and *pitta* for all of the children.

He blew on his eyeglasses, then wiped them on the tail of his tie in the habitual gesture that always delighted his children. "I need the table for my homework. Serena, you go to your room and do yours. Mitch, you can watch Captain Kangaroo."

He was sitting hunched over the formica marking up his students' scrawls when Bernie let herself in.

"Hi, sweetie." She stripped off woollen gloves and kerchief. "Have a decent day?"

"Normal," he said, "normal. And you?"

"Misery." But she wrinkled her nose, taking away the sting. She was not dismayed by what she had rediscovered in the city. In a sense she had merely readjusted the focus of her idealism, narrowing it down somewhat so that instead of exhorting the bottom dogs to turn on their masters at a time when they were unwilling and unable, she helped them at least to understand their rights to live, to eat, to guard their young against the depredations of neighbors and the exploitation of the top dogs. He could not say it to her, but in a way her life among the poor was easier than his.

Except, he thought, watching her steal an anxious glimpse at her pink-nosed countenance in the dull reflection of the chromed bread box, that she feared the stealthy unstoppable approach of middle age. When Irwin had visited them in Israel he had been in a panic because of his fortieth year. Bernie had tried to sympathize but had been baffled by what she could only regard as self-indulgence. "Who cares?" she had asked. "Who cares as long as you're doing your work, living your life? Would it be better to be a permanent teenager? What's wrong with being forty?"

That had been in Israel, where she worked for the next generation but did not prostrate herself before them. Here, hurrying past the mannekins in the windows of Bonwit's and Bendel's, catching sight of herself in the glass, she was unprotected by amused self-deprecation and unable to escape the infection of the age. The more she worried about the crowsfeet and the neck muscles, the more she asked, after twenty years, "Sy, do you still love me?" the older she looked, and the more he had to deny the evidence of her mirror, and to insist that he, lover-boy, had no interest in other women.

She had not yet gotten around to asking him about fourteen-year-olds.

"Let me get your slippers."

She had already stepped out of shoes and galoshes and was moving about in her stockinged feet. "Sit still and finish up. I'm going to need that table soon. I have to get dinner ready."

Bernie did not raise the question that had hung between them ever since the great machine of the Board of Education had turned up his name as eligible for the assistant principal's exam. After a suitable period he would become eligible in turn for a principalship.

"That's not why I went into teaching," he had said to Bernie. "Granted, I had no dreams of being the beloved Mr. Chips of Harlem. I'm not even that crazy about teaching in an impossible situation. But I didn't come back to the States to be a boss." Her silence made him uneasy. "Well, did I?"

"Then don't do it. We can get along without the extra money. I'll be on permanent staff myself as soon as I get the academic credits."

It hadn't been just a question of money, much as they needed it for music lessons, camp, all of the American expenses which had never been a part of kibbutz life. It was rather that the exams opened a door, allowing him to flee the frustrations of a classroom in which he could disclose the pleasures of English prose only by reading *Photoplay* to kids who would listen to nothing else. And to enter a realm in which—it was at least conceivable—he might one day be able to try out certain notions about how to teach and not just baby-sit the children of the poor.

It would mean leaving the teachers' union, which was just beginning to reconstitute itself after long years of dead-end Stalinist isolation.

"At last," he wrote to Joe, "a chance to function in a union that's coming to life. It isn't shocked by radical proposals. It's going to be increasingly interracial and concerned not only with salaries and conditions, but with the quality of education in the ghetto. Do you think I'm bragging if I say that the union needs me? So you can imagine how hard it would be for me to go into supervision and kiss the union goodbye."

He was also reluctant to move up from the teaching job precisely because it was poorly paid, tedious, and frustrating. He was still oppressed by the ascetic morality which he himself had inculcated in Joe: stay in the ranks, resist personal advancement no matter if it was disguised as assuming new responsibility or being rewarded for acquired skills, go where the workers went, turn your back on the escape routes to the middle class, including the union bureaucracy.

Joe's reply had surprised him: "If it was me I'd go with the union. On the other hand you have to decide whether in the course of the next five years or so you'll be more effective in the union or in the administration."

Bernie had been pleased by Joe's comment, and so they had slipped into passive acceptance of a compromise. He would take the exam without committing himself beforehand to taking an assistant principalship. Maybe Norm would have some idea on this.

Before Joey should come in, starving and noisy, he said to her, "Do you think Norm and Vera would put us up if we went to Washington for the inauguration?"

"We've got a standing invitation."

He had also made commitments to Uretta and Maria Luisa. "I won't drag the other students against their will. It occurred to me that we might go ourselves, just us, the family, with those two girls."

She could not get away, really; and she thought Mitch was too young to absorb much from it. "What you ought to do," she said, "is ask Norman and Vera if you can bring Joey and Serena and your two students. Then maybe you can borrow a car for the trip."

In the end he did obtain the loan of a cousin's second car, a jalop shakier than the pickups he used to tool through the rutted roads of the kibbutz. With wheels assured and the kids steamed up about the trip, he rang up Vera.

She was delighted. The three girls could sleep in the guest room with a cot added, and Sy and Joey would stay in Marlen's room.

All four kids loved the trip. Wrapped in the blankets Bernie had provided as substitute for the Chevy's broken heater, they sang their way down through the Jersey flats, counting new cars and leaving him to his thoughts.

When they got to Georgetown, they were awed into silence. Even the leafless trees lent a somber grace to the severe federal homes, their cool front doors surmounted by glowing fanlights. He was almost ashamed to park the brokendown jalop on such a street.

Arms crossed over her bosom against the icy wind, Vera stood smiling on the front steps. His kids ran to embrace her and to introduce Uretta and Maria Luisa. Five minutes later they were in the kitchen with hot cocoa and Margaret's cookies.

"Marlen is at boarding school," Vera said to the kids. "He'll be here after dinner though, and in the morning he's coming back to take you sight-seeing and to watch the inauguration. Now you can go off and explore if you want."

Vera had aged. She was no older than Bernie, but her hair, which she had chopped off short, was quite gray, and she had allowed her body to thicken. She was anxious to talk about Marlen; maybe that was why she was so disappointed that Bernie hadn't come along. "I wasn't sure," she said, "just what you'd told your kids about him."

"Nothing much. I figured why shouldn't they simply get to know each other on their own terms, since Norm says he's doing all right."

"You'll see when he comes in. Things have been going very well. Dr. Goldsand says he's very pleased. Actually Marlen does quite brilliantly in classes. But he has to come straight here and go straight back."

"Why is he still so closely supervised?"

Vera linked her fingers and pulled on them. It was not easy for her to reply; even small talk had always been difficult for her. "The thing is that people like Marlen usually don't change. They look pleasant and all that, but they don't develop, they never feel anything deeply. Only Dr. Goldsand thinks maybe Marlen will, some day." She added quietly, "That's the problem, you see. We never know. We just hope."

"It must be horribly expensive."

Vera's laugh was harsh. "You could put all of your three children through college and then some, on what Norm has spent." She said Norm, he noticed, rather than we, as though the money were something utterly beyond her. "You know I come from poor people. We never even dreamt of such sums. There isn't even any assurance that it'll do Marlen a single bit of good. But Norm was determined. As soon as he managed to get Marlen released he insisted on packing us up and moving here."

"He's very strong willed."

"You mean stubborn. People make jokes about his being a

writing machine, but they don't know how he's up every morning
at four-thirty, working to pay for all this. Or that he's gotten big
advances from several publishers for book ideas that I can't see
him ever completing."

"Oh, I'm sure—"

"Don't be. The money has long since gone to Pine Grove. Meanwhile he keeps taking on other commitments, like setting up shop
as a consultant. Why else are we in this house? Do you think I'd
pick such a fancy neighborhood? Do you have any idea what our
mortgage is?"

He felt embarrassed. To change the subject he asked, "What's a
consultant?"

"It's one of those Washington words. He advises policy bodies,
international unions, liberal groups like that. He shows them and
their lobbyists how to make presentations, and sometimes he intro-
duces them to people—he knows a lot of politicians by now. All I
know is, he works eighteen hours a day."

"How does he find time to keep in shape?"

"You don't think he'd ever neglect that, do you?" A certain
bitterness in her voice made him think of Bernie stealthily peering
at her image in the mirror. "After he writes for two hours, he
goes out and plays tennis before breakfast, how do you like that?"

"He sounds as though he's thriving."

"He likes challenges. He had to prove he could go into a shop
and organize, or go into the Army and be a hero, or go into
journalism and make people listen to him. Once he decided on
Pine Grove, he had to show that he could make it in Washington,
even with the Republicans in power. He sets us up on the same
street with a Supreme Court justice, when his father comes up
from Florida he's impressed, but what's the good?" She looked
down at her hands. "His own son can't sleep here, except on special
occasions. Nobody else knows what it means not to be able to
trust your own son."

To this he had no reply.

She forced a smile. "Your children are beautiful," she said.
"Simply beautiful."

"I'm afraid Serena's too fat."

"She'll lose that."

He was showing her his wallet photos of Bernie and Mitch when
a taxi discharged Norm, who was returning from the airport, eager

to eat quickly so that he could drive to Pine Grove and pick up Marlen.

They all ate together, adults and the four kids, and then he went off with Norm in the white Thunderbird. "The three of us can squeeze together on the ride back. Come on, we'll talk on the way."

In the car he said, "You look well, Norm."

"Why shouldn't I? Got a big house, loyal wife, sharp car, handsome boy."

"How's he doing?"

"You'd never know. There's a system of rewards, and he's doing brilliant schoolwork. He hasn't lost a single semester. I suppose Vera's filled you in."

"A little."

"I can tell you one thing. Your own kids are going to be utterly charmed by him. Everyone is. They'll find him gracious, amusing, a good listener, the works. Strangers compliment us." He said, as if he were reciting, "You've done wonders with an only child. Nowadays adolescents are so restless, they're willful and cynical, our own children are always nagging at us. You can be proud."

Sy said nothing. For a moment he wished that he had not come.

Norm turned businesslike. "Now bring me up to date. I want to know about Harlem. Don't tell me the girls you brought are typical."

"They were the only ones who were interested in coming. Does that answer your question?"

"Tell me more."

"I read them movie magazines to get them interested in reading." Suddenly he remembered the anonymous note. He took it from his pocket and passed it to Norm when they stopped for a red light. "Just to give you an idea. It's sinking lower every term."

Norm made a face as he read. "I've got to show this to our company tonight. Two freshmen congressmen are coming, and a senator's administrative assistant. They're trying to see how the new congress will shape up, and they're receptive to all kinds of ideas. From people who have been in the movement—in the labor movement—in a kibbutz—in the front lines in the civil rights fight—in the ghetto. They're ready to listen. We're in a whole new ball game, kid."

Then they were cruising up a gravel drive and Marlen was trotting out to meet them, bright-eyed, ruddy-cheeked, everything his father had said. He bent over the car, stuck his arm in for a handshake, and demanded of his father: "I don't suppose you'd let me drive home, dad?"

"Come on, wise guy, squeeze in. Sy's got a bunch of kids waiting at the house for you. When Goldsand says you can drive, you'll drive."

Marlen's poise was impressive at first, but after the first few minutes Sy felt disquieted. Shouldn't the boy display some signs of uneasiness, some of the tremors of adolescence already beginning to manifest themselves in Joey?

His own kids and his two pupils had organized an assembly line clean-up of the dinner dishes from the dining room to the kitchen dishwasher. When Marlen joined them, they happily accepted his leadership for the evening.

The doorbell began to ring and the guests to unburden themselves of coats and scarves. They had nothing but the highest intentions, about which they spoke with the zealot enthusiasm of football fans. They believed that great things were about to happen, that the incoming administration would possess determination and vision, and that the country would be uplifted.

During the years of tractor driving and beet-digging Sy had been remote from American concerns. He would always feel uncomfortable among those at ease with the mighty. Still he was convinced of something that seemed to escape these earnest liberals, who put their faith not in the slow forward press of the people but in the benevolent dispositions of great men. Just as his own daily behavior grew from the constant love of his wife and children, so he was sure that in the larger world only pressure from below could inspire movement at the top. Only the manifest desire of a brutalized working class to better itself, spurred on by its rank and file leaders, had impelled Roosevelt to grant the charter of labor's rights. Only the profound stirring of oppressed Negro fieldhands and urban drudges could wring concessions from the whites who ran things; only a profound desire for peace abroad and progress at home made manifest by ordinary people could spur even the leaders of the well-intentioned to jeopardize their newly won positions by acting out what they dearly loved to talk about.

Even the oldest of the trio of men (by now their wives had been impelled like iron filings into Vera's corner, in that sexual polarization typical of middle-class gatherings) revealed in his speech the liberal characteristic of reverent respect for the powerful mixed with sympathetic contempt for the unlettered. This man was the senator's assistant, a high-strung, hard-driving Jewish lawyer from Upper Manhattan who had probably served an apprenticeship in a Stalinist-oriented student group before trading in his youthful radicalism (adulation of far-off despotic power) for an adult liberalism (adulation of domestic power) better suited to the long haul. Sy had met men like him before—you found them in courthouses, in the upper reaches of the Board of Education, in the communications industry—and he was more interested in the congressmen.

The thin-faced young man with the brush cut had been an assistant professor of political science at a state university in the midwest; his plump and energetic colleague from California had taken advantage of the GI Bill to go into the lumber business, had been active in AVC, ADA, CLU, PAC, and now felt that, as he put it, "I've got this great chance to put my principles to the test."

All of these people, Sy was startled to see, were younger than he. Ever since college he had been the youngest—in his class, on the soapbox, on the picket line, in the caucus. Even in the kibbutz he and Bernie had been adopted by the older settlers, who liked their kids and referred to them as "the young Americans." He had always thought of congressmen as old farts with drawls and string ties. But here were these earnest young men deferring to him not only because of what Norm had told them about him, but simply because he had lived longer than they.

They spoke of what the next day would bring, of the difficulty of finding decent apartments, of the high prices, the school problems of their kids who had been so happy back home. They sounded scared but excited, and anxious to take from people like himself what nourishment they could. In that sense Norm was right— they were honestly concerned and wildly hopeful. Deferential, even. To me, he thought, of all people!

But they were impressed by the wrong things. It disturbed him —as it did not seem to disturb Norm—that they were more impressed by his bringing two Negro girls to the inauguration than by his reasons for it, or even for continuing to teach in Harlem. They were more impressed by his having raised his family in a kibbutz than by his reasons for it. They were impressed more by his having worked in factories than by what he had hoped to achieve there, or what he had learned.

Still, even though he could hardly bring himself to believe that people like this would change his life, or the lives of those listening to Ray Charles down in the playroom, it was flattering to hear them assure him that his life mattered, and his opinions too.

Norm himself was not unaffected by this admiration. When they had left he undertook to explain how he intended to turn it to the advantage of the programs he wanted enacted. He lifted his feet to the coffee table. "You're very quiet, Sy."

"I can't share your expectations. You haven't even got a Socialist coming in tomorrow, like Blum or Attlee. What you do have is a Boston Irish politician, plus a handful of eager beavers. The first time you ask them to vote their conscience on something really tough, they'll run out on you."

"Old boy," Norm said pleasantly, kicking off his shoes and wiggling his toes, "I'm not counting on those youngsters to make the revolution. When I said this was a whole new ball game, my model was the old one. You have no idea what it's been like here. You don't know Washington."

"I know Harlem."

"Fair enough. But aside from some jazz and an occasional riot, that's not where the action is. This is. Right here."

From the basement came the steady low pulse of rock, like the beating of some caged monster's heart beneath their feet. Vera murmured something indistinguishable as she stacked dirty ashtrays and coffee cups on a tray and carried it out of the room.

"I thought you lived here only because you had to."

"Have to? Yes I have to. I have to keep a commitment. But why not make the most of it? I'd do the same if it was a jail. That's the way I took the Army, so it wouldn't take me."

"And you're going to make the most of it here too."

Norm set his feet on the floor. His smile faded. "You sound like you're comparing me to Fred. Is that the way I look to you?"

"Fred sold out. At least that's the language we used to use. No one could say that about you."

"But you're saying that I'm becoming part of the scene here the way that Fred is part of the TV scene."

"You're saying it, not me. How do you know what I think unless I say it?"

"I can tell. You've got that humble look. Listen, don't you think I couldn't have found myself a cushy spot here in the last couple of years?"

That was begging the question, which was not whether he had resisted the old order but whether he would be able to resist the new. In a few hours they would be witnessing the inauguration (as Norm himself did not tire of observing) of the first President to have been born in the twentieth century.

"I suppose you're thinking," Norm observed shrewdly, "that the new administration is going to smooth out my compunctions for me. Maybe you figure that because I've known the next vice-president, a crazy, fascinating, awful guy, now I'll be able to cash in. I've got news for you—being known as his friend is a hindrance from here on out. Aside from that, whatever reputation I have is based on my independence. What would I have to gain by taking a job for a year or two, say even for four years, if in the long run it destroys my main asset?" He sat back and grinned. "Well, what do you say to the argument from self-interest?"

Sy felt himself groping, as if he were in a familiar but very dark room, reaching out blindly and helplessly for the light switch. "Believe me, I'm the last one to be righteous. I wasn't asking you to sign a pledge."

"But I will, I will! What do you think of that? I hereby promise not to go on the payroll of the new administration. I promise something else too. I am going to do my damnedest to cultivate those guys. Not only the freshmen, but the whole new wave. I'd be a fool if I didn't. That goes for all of us who want new programs for the cities, dough for the Negroes. You can go on believing if you feel like it that the motor force of progress is the people and not their rulers—"

If I feel like it, he thought in dismay, if I feel like it?

"—still, you wouldn't turn down a federal program of aid to Harlem schools, would you?"

He laughed dutifully.

Encouraged, Norm went on expansively, "I've got it all figured out, what finished us off as a movement. For a little eccentric group, we were too reasonable. Take somebody like my brother-in-law. The most reasonable guy in the world. What could Bill Zivic have to offer to nuts like Comrade Hunter or Comrade Drang? We attracted the nuts all right—we were small enough and freakish enough— but we had no demons to hold them with, no monkey-like Jewish conspiracy, no terrifying Trotskyist reptiles. Even the capitalists in Vito's cartoons weren't as scary as the fat bankers that the fascists and the Stalinists used to scare people. We didn't even have folk singers or salutes to go with them."

Vera said quietly from the doorway, "You make our past sound like some kind of keystone cops routine."

"It's the only way I can look back on all the madness without seeing myself purely and simply as an asshole."

"To me it was more than one big laugh," Sy said stubbornly. "It was a matter of respecting the potential of ordinary people. We were wrong about plenty, but that was partly because we were powerless."

"And if we'd gotten power? Then what? When I said we were too reasonable I didn't mean that we weren't deluded too—about the power of reason, among other things. I hope to Christ I've learned something in the last twenty years. Could you see yourself now in the shop, trying to sneak the Little Lenin Library across to the workers bit by bit? Could you see yourself arguing now about arming the workers, or about whether the thirty hour week was an immediate or an ultimate demand? Maybe we were crazy enough for Hunter and Drang, but we were too reasonable about reason."

Vera said to her husband, "You'd better get Marlen back before he's overdue. And I'll show Sy and the children to their rooms."

Exhausted though he was, sleep did not come readily. Unlike Norm, he was unused to traveling, especially without his wife. His thoughts circled in upon themselves; was it possible that this very morning he had seriously considered discussing his dilemma with Norm?

He lay still in the dark listening to Norm drive off with Marlen. It was not until after Norm had returned that he himself dropped off at last.

At breakfast the kids were bouncing with anticipation. Norm had already done several hours' work. "I was just wondering if your principles would allow you to accept some box seats that I wangled for your gang."

"Political connections?"

"Disgusting, isn't it?"

"I don't want to do you out of them."

"I've got press passes too. Let's all go in the station wagon. Marlen wants to show the kids around afterward."

Norm and Vera were going on that evening to one of the presidential balls; they urged him to stay on. Ashamed of himself for being uneasy, he pointed out that he had promised the girls' mothers that he would have them home in Harlem late that night. He really did not want to see Norm with any more politicians.

Norm seemed to understand. He made a funny little gesture with his hand, as if to dismiss the matter, and took over the task of getting them to the parade and the ceremony.

Neither the old President nor the younger man at his side had the look of politicians. The general, grave and abstracted, a zigzag vein beating in his temple, was gentle and forlorn. If he did not resemble the dimwitted golfer he had been made out to be, neither did he seem at that moment a leader of men; as for his successor, he appeared so absurdly young that Sy had to remind himself: he's older than I am. Only when he removed the ridiculous shiny top hat and stepped forward to take the oath of office, his hair tumbled by the cold breeze, did he become a different person.

Sy turned to observe the girls whom he had brought to witness this moment. Stocky Uretta, nose wet from the wind, black face set and serious, stood squarely on her heels, a mittened knuckle between her teeth. Beside her Maria Luisa, pale and pretty, gaped, her hand in Serena's. Next to them the boys stood somewhat apart, sharing a pair of binoculars. Joey was not as tall as the Miller boy, and his pug dog face was now too grim. But Marlen's cool perfection was terrifying, and Joey's homeliness infinitely reassuring.

After the ceremony Marlen took them for a cold tour of the festive city. They all parted finally with reluctance, the adults perhaps with a certain relief. With the three girls bundled together in the back seat, and his son beside him, Sy reached out to Norm for a final handshake.

Winter darkness fell swiftly. In the interior of the old car the three girls sang the songs of the young, their innocent voices rising in the night as they challenged each other to remember. Joey, more serious, his tough-boy features half-illuminated by the dashboard light, sat up front, arms folded on his breast. Sy trod harder on the accelerator, eager to rejoin his wife, pleased not just with the children's excursion but with himself as well. He knew now what he wanted to do, although he was not sure exactly how he had arrived at it. As he gripped the steering wheel and peered out into the night, it seemed to him as inevitable as all the other decisions he and Bernice had made.

2. VITO

When Lorch phoned and asked him to come into town to dinner, Vito was hesitant. The dealer was persistent. "It's going to be your fifty-second birthday."

"Christ, who wants to be reminded of that?" He would have been pleased, except that since the big blowout Lorch had thrown for him on the occasion of his fiftieth, they had seen very damned little of each other. So he added, "Besides, I've been off my feed lately. I got stomach trouble."

"Too much dago red," Lorch laughed. He hurried on, to take any sting out of it, "It won't be a party or anything that ambitious." He wound up ambiguously, "Just a couple of the old-timers."

For the last couple of years, Vito had been feeling increasingly antipathetic to Lorch. He had reason for it—his dealer's growing indifference, the difficulty he had in finding dates that would be "suitable" for a retrospective—but it annoyed him that he could not master his annoyance. Instead it grew, irrationally, malignantly, like the hatred of a husband for a wife who cannot conceal her boredom with his aspirations, but who remains (he knows in his heart) the same person whom he had fallen in love with and married. If Lorch was now more interested in hard-edge types and comic strip characters who dressed like the figures they blew up, that was his business—particularly if it was good business. Why should I let it get to me, Vito asked himself, why should I let it affect my work?

But it did, it did. He found himself cursing Lorch, and hating himself for allowing the grievance to fester while he worked alone in the big Easthampton studio. If he'd had someone to complain to the whole thing might have blown out of his mind like a musty smell released by opening windows to the spring air; but when you went around talking to yourself you could only strengthen the poison instead of expelling it.

He still had friends on the Lower East Side and whenever he went back to the studio on Broome Street the old-timers were ready to stand him a drink. But after all these years he had the Long Island studio set up just the way he had always wanted, and it seemed a waste to work there only in the hot summer months. When people asked why he stayed on out of season he'd explain, "I like the sea air—it clears my head."

Beyond all that he wanted to avoid Esther. If he stayed in town he was bound to run into her at one of the galleries, at somebody's apartment, or even just at a movie. And he didn't want her to see him alone, not at any of those places, not after the look she had given him that last day.

She had been good to him, he would be the last one to deny it; when he had a bellyache she had made him chicken soup like a yiddishe mama; and she screwed like a mink, without inhibition, yelling her head off for sheer joy regardless of who might be on the other side of the wall. But he had made her what she was, who could deny that? He had taught her every single thing she knew about art starting from the letter A, making her unlearn all the bullshit they had shoveled at her in college, standing behind her for hours on end while she worked, encouraging her, guiding her arm. When she got her own gallery and her own following by running with the new crowd, she had repaid him by turning her back on everything that he had stood for since the earliest days.

No, he was better off alone, even if it meant talking to himself and giving way to bitterness now and then. I'm my own boss, he said to himself, I'll go on painting the way I want and fuck them all, from Esther to Lewis Lorch.

Nevertheless when the letter came from the National Institute his immediate reaction was to call Esther, then Lorch. Esther was out of the question. He was ashamed of himself for the impulse, because it wasn't to share his pleasure with her but to throw it in her teeth. As for Lorch, time enough to show him the letter when he went into town for the dinner. Or even just to mention it casually. "By the way, I got an invite from the National Institute of Arts and Letters to their annual shindig. They want to give me a bronze medal. No mileage in refusing it, is there? You can't make a splash by being a bad boy any more."

The more he turned it over in his mind, however, the more he was convinced that he ought to let Lorch make the first move. It was hardly possible that Lorch wouldn't learn of the award independently; certainly he knew every goddamned little bit of gossip about all the other artists in his stable, and sometimes even before anything had happened. And if Lorch wanted to pass this off as a minor event hardly worth comment, much less congratulations, why risk humiliation by bringing it up?

So he tacked the engraved invitation to the bulletin board below an old snapshot of Zia Concetta with the hairy mole on her chin.

Eventually he replied to the invitation, pecking out an acceptance on the rusting old Underwood that he had nailed to a stepstool more as a curiosity than a useful machine. But he left it on the bulletin board when he backed the Jag out of the barn for the drive into the city for his birthday celebration.

He tuned in the radio to keep him company on the way. It was the only thing on the dash that worked right. In order to get some music he had to sit through the headlines, which always seemed to be about who Jackie was having to dinner, what the Negro kids were doing to get a cup of coffee, how the Cubans were piling up Russian missiles. He half listened, just in case somebody in the course of the evening should ask for his opinion of a story in the news. It didn't seem possible that he had once been able to produce topical cartoons to order, as quick as a lightning artist sketching heads at a carnival. He could still do an acceptable caricature of Khrushchev or Castro, but that was no trick—to put horns on them as he had done with Hitler or Stalin, that was what he could no longer manage, the evocation of an emotional rather than an esthetic reaction.

Lorch lived in the East Seventies, walking distance from his gallery, although he had a silver-gray Mercedes 220 for getting out to his own place in Easthampton and visiting his stable of painters, now rich enough, most of them, to be scattered all over upstate New York and New Jersey. He himself was loaded too. At least he lived in luxurious sin with a rich freckled Catholic lady who (so people said) was unable to secure a divorce from her husband. Vito was not particularly interested in Lorch's domestic arrangements, for Lorch to him was a man who approached incomprehensibility. Although he was a mine of information on art and artists as he had once been on socialism and socialists, he left you with the distinct impression that neither area really meant anything to him. Despite the seeming intensity of his commitment in each case maybe nothing mattered except his own well-being, and who could care about that?

He put the car in a Second Avenue garage so as not to find the tires slashed when he came out, and went up the street to Lorch's. Generally you could tell what kind of gathering he was having by the housekeeper's greeting. Tonight Louise was poker-faced, so stiff that he didn't even try to kid her along.

In the living room, at ease in the Eames chairs lined up facing each other across the glass and onyx coffee table, he found Maureen, Lorch's lady companion, with Marty Dworkin and Sarah Franckenstein who, it appeared, had married the old leader of the New Party. She had been a kind of gray eminence in the old days, with money, mind, and international connections that went back to her philosopher father. She threw her support to those splinter leaders like Dworkin who struck her as the most pure carriers of the Marxist tradition. She was frankly gray-haired and dumpy now, but the king-sized cigarette still dangled between the thin lips from which still poured a stream of obscenity.

She greeted Vito without removing the cigarette from her mouth. It made him feel like turning around and going home. Dworkin was friendly enough in his sly way. He had aged spookily. He arose to say hello, shrunken and hunched. His once wavy hair was gone, leaving him with a naked head of skin that looked fake, like the bald wigs used by movie actors playing monks. He was chipper, but very slow in his movements, and when he spoke, even his harsh penetrating unforgettable falsetto was slurred. Hadn't he had a stroke a while ago?

"Well, well," Marty said, grinning, "if it isn't our home-grown Daumier."

"If I was that good," Vito said, "I never would have quit drawing cartoons. The truth is, I never had much political savvy."

"The beginning of wisdom," Dworkin laughed. "Would that more socialists had your modesty, isn't it so, Sarah? Still, Vito, if you recognize your weakness, perhaps you should be less free with the use of your name."

"I don't get it."

"I refer to your inimitable signature, your famous signature."

What was all this? Was Dworkin knocking his work? His last show, maybe? Dworkin had always been shrewd enough to avoid areas in which he lacked basic competence. He refused to elaborate, but reached for the peanut bowl and turned back to his hostess.

Still confused, Vito responded automatically to Lorch's polite questions about the progress of his current work. He was used to being needled by the old politicos about his retreat from public concerns, but Dworkin was up to something else. At that moment Irwin and Carmela Metzger came in.

"Hey, what are you doing here?" Too late he realized that he sounded rude rather than relieved.

"I invited them." Lorch took Carmela by the elbow to introduce her to the women. "I hope you don't mind."

"Come on, they're my home town gang!" He meant it too. With Carmie and her husband here, he could relax a little.

"I was aware of that." Lorch was trying, in his involuted way, to be gracious. Kind, even. He didn't know that whatever he said grated. "As soon as I learned that they were going to be in town for a couple of days, I insisted that they help us celebrate your birthday."

Irwin and Carmie looked good together if not separately. The dentist, always plump, was now gross; his small eyes were now half-buried behind puffy lids and when he sat down he had to put his legs apart to make room for the vast width of thighs that stretched his trousers tight; yet he bore himself with a dignity, almost a gravity, that Vito could not remember. He was reminded of those great Etruscan tomb sculptures of massive old men with sustantial breasts and large bellies half draped in togas, reclining on their funerary stones and staring off profoundly into eternity. If Irwin were draped in such a winding sheet he would look more impressive and less ludicrous than he did now in his white shirt with the curling points, the twisted tie lying on his girth like a colored rag, the lightweight suit vainly trying to contain him.

Carmie hugged him hard, crushing her still marvelous breasts against him and enveloping him with the over-heavy perfume she had always loved ever since she was a kid.

He held her off to examine her until her lowered eyes, pained at what he might see at close range, moved him to release her. She was voluptuous like some great piece of fruit bursting with juice but with a skin just starting to crease, a flesh just beginning to speckle. From a reasonable distance, in an elegantly lit room, in a hand-knit dress and sheer black hose that glistened on her first-class legs, she still looked stunning. It was as much as she could reasonably hope for.

"What are you doing in New York?" he asked.

Carmela smiled secretively. "A little private expedition."

He persisted. "I heard you were in Mexico."

"It was fabulous. They took me for Spanish until I opened my mouth. But I couldn't cope with it, Vito, it was too much for me. I'll explain what I mean some day."

"And Paul. What's with Paul?"

Irwin looked up from his chair. "In six weeks he finishes his junior year. One more year and he graduates."

"Already? What's he going to do?"

"He's majoring in philosophy. Ethics. What can you do with that, run for President?"

"Maybe he'll be a lawyer, something like that?"

"I had to plead with him last week to go ahead with his senior year. I promised him that he could take off a year, after getting his BA. He talks about going full-time into the civil rights movement. You think I like the idea of his getting his head cracked open by some redneck sheriff's deputy?"

"He'll be all right, that kid."

Louise announced dinner then, and at the table the conversation turned to the old days while Vito picked at the dry slabs of roast veal and the gluey potatoes.

Far from coming up with stories of the New York painters and the old downtown crowd, Lorch seemed determined to avoid any mention of the art world. Vito began to suspect that this was a part of his dealer's "kindness," his promise that the dinner party would be unbusinesslike, friendly, intimate.

The intimacy seemed to consist, all the way through to the dessert, of anecdotes about the national office of the New Party. Although their involvement in radical politics went back to the twenties, both Lorch and Dworkin agreed that the real period of glory had been during the war years. It was then that all of the infighting of the thirties and the struggle to build a party had looked as though they were paying off.

"Fifty thousand circulation, *New Labor* had in those days." Dworkin announced the figure as if he himself could scarcely believe it.

"Vito's cartoons didn't hurt." Lorch tilted his head.

"And the money that was pouring in from all over?" Dworkin gestured with knife and fork. His voice had a quality that went with rubbing his hands together. "We had GIs who signed over their allotment checks to us, and workers in the shops like Sy who paid dues of up to twenty per cent of their pay checks."

"Listen," Irwin grumbled, "if I had half the dough that I gave Harry during the war I'd be a bloody millionaire today."

"What would you have done with it?" Sarah Franckenstein laughed. "Thrown it away on groceries? It was much more practical to help Harry play at revolution."

Vito was jarred by this cynicism. But Irwin seemed less offended than reflective.

"That Harry," he said admiringly, as if he were recalling a great athlete. "He was really something, from the day I picked him up at the railroad station to the last time I saw him in Monte Carlo. Budapest, I suppose you heard about Budapest?"

Carmela was barely toying with her food. Vito couldn't blame her, and she'd already announced that she was on a diet—women like her always were—but she was also bored, and probably still regretting money that Irwin had thrown away.

Dworkin grinned secretively. "Indeed I have. I've been afflicted with some harebrained nuts during my long years of selfless service to the movement, but Harry topped them all. When I think of the man-hours we wasted in mimeographing his maniacal, unreadable polemics! He was my prize cross, wouldn't you agree, Lewis?"

Lorch chuckled. "I suppose he would merit pride of place." He was so thoroughly at ease with Dworkin that it was hard to recall how angry Dworkin had been with him for deserting politics in favor of art. Who deserted who? Who joined who? Dworkin seemed to get more fun out of reminiscing as if he were with his old Legion buddies at a convention party.

Dworkin raised his hands in his familiar attention-commanding gesture. "For years that mad scientist used me—me!—as a cover for his international swindles. It wasn't enough that the FBI tapped my phone so assiduously that I developed ear trouble. I also had to play host to a gentleman from Interpol asking about my relationship with Harry in his incarnation as dangerous revolutionary. I assured them that I spurned his indecent advances."

Lorch was benign. "The most elegant thing about his operation was that no one ever knew—including Harry himself, I am fairly sure—whether he was embezzling for the cause of international socialism, as you say, Marty, or using the cause as a cover. In any case"—he turned to Irwin—"when the matter of extradition finally came to a head, Harry transferred his base of operations to Rio de Janeiro. Life has gotten more difficult for him, at least in the sense that he seems to have broken with the Posadaites in Montevideo." To his wife he explained, "That's an ultra-left tendency that calls for a Russian pre-emptive nuclear strike before the U.S. can wipe out the so-called socialist states. Well," he sighed, "Harry's an enterprising man."

"That is true," Dworkin said. "I would not want to take away from that conspirator his wartime achievements. All I have to do is glance around this table to be reminded of his persuasive powers."

He raised his wineglass. "To those stirring times, comrades. And maybe even to Harry—a little bit. He is going to need our best wishes in the difficult days ahead. This afternoon I arrived at the airport from a conference at MIT, and who should bob up in the lobby but our old friend."

"Harry?" Lorch asked. "But the authorities—"

"Harry has turned himself in. No doubt we'll be reading about it in tomorrow's *Times*. He wore no tie, he needed a shave, he was lugging a Panagra flight bag and a brown paper sack as though he had all his wordly goods in them. Very uncharacteristic. Two familiar-looking types were keeping him company. Federal marshals, no doubt."

"Did you talk to him?"

Dworkin was in no hurry to come to the climax of his story. He touched his lips with his napkin. "Harry stood there blinking for a moment when he caught sight of me. Then he smiled—I must give him credit for savoir-faire in highly unfavorable circumstances. 'Marty!' he cried. 'A friendly face! We must get together on a more favorable occasion.' And then they led him away."

To Dworkin, and apparently to Lorch as well, all of this was good clean fun, with a dash of nostalgia. To me, Vito thought, it's horseshit. As the older people remorselessly pillaged the past in search of amusement and a peculiar kind of self-justification, he became convinced that Lorch—too calculating not to know exactly what he was up to—had invited him not just to salute an anniversary better left unnoticed, but as a subtle way of letting him know that this was where he placed him. Not with his own favorites, who were swinging in a new way, but with the relics of an entertaining but definitely dead past.

His heart sinking in him along with the food, Vito listened silently as they reminisced down through the years to a present in which Lorch tooled around in his Mercedes from one artist's elegant pad to another and Dworkin earned his per-diem as consultant on the social structure of the Communist bloc.

"Hoover?" Dworkin intoned amiably, responding to an interchange between his wife and Irwin. "Hoover? There was a tower of strength. A rock of a man, a veritable boulder. A shame that his head was made of the same material. Absolutely impenetrable. Not one new idea ever succeeded in piercing it."

"I respected him." Irwin hauled himself erect as they adjourned to the living room for brandy. "And I liked him, too. It's true I was only a kibitzer, but as far as I was concerned, he did a lot more for the movement than some of the orators."

Not at all taken aback, Dworkin bowed and saluted. "Your loyalty is admirable. Nevertheless, brains are always in shorter supply than bullheadedness. Look at where we are now! Look at how some of the self-styled socialists are collapsing into ecstasy over the revolutionary fervor of Doctor Castro!"

"Better that," Irwin said stubbornly, "than conniving to put the Havana Yacht Club back on Varadero Beach with the pimps and the hoods."

"Your eloquence does you more credit than your analytical powers."

"Why do you suppose I paid the rent for your party headquarters? It was because I hoped for something positive, not because I read your original contributions to Marxist theory."

"Ah, and what you lost out on! My deathless prose might have saved you from falling into the trap that lies in wait for those who refuse to learn from history. Because the Bay of Pigs was a fiasco, does it follow that artists should lend their names to the front organizations of blockheads eager to excuse any kind of tyranny in the sacred name of socialism?"

So that was why Dworkin had been needling him.

"Now wait a minute," Vito said. "I signed the Fair Play thing because a bunch of young artists asked me to. Later on, when I found out who was running it, I asked them to take my name off. But they came to me in the first place because they remembered that I used to draw bloated capitalists for you, and I'm glad they did. I'm not ashamed of that, but I am ashamed of what this country has been trying to do to Cuba."

Dworkin pounced, grinning. "So you don't feel we should try to save the honest socialists whom Castro has thrown into prison? We shouldn't try to stop a terrorist dictatorship from strangling the Cuban working class—to say nothing of the artists?"

Ah fuck it, he thought; and at that moment he was struck in the gut by that same stabbing pain, that same wrenching agony, as if someone had stuck him with a rusty knife and was slowly withdrawing it. Excusing himself, he stumbled to the bathroom. Sitting on the edge of the square sunken tub with a glass in his hand, he chewed up two Gelusils, flushed them down with water, and waited for the pain to subside. It was the ulcer, there was no getting away from it, and if he went to a doctor he would be taken off booze and cigarettes and coffee and everything else, except ass, that made it possible to go on living and working.

"Are you all right?" Lorch inquired solicitously when he rejoined them.

"Sure, why?"

"You looked a little under the weather."

"I told you before, I've been having stomach trouble."

"Maybe you should see a doctor."

"I've been through all that. Listen, I hope I won't break things up if I sneak out. I've got a long drive out to Easthampton."

"At this hour? Why not stay in town?"

"Because the air is better out there." And if you don't like that, he thought with satisfaction, it's too damned bad. He turned to Maureen and took her hand. "Thanks for a smashing evening."

"We have to leave too," Irwin said. "Vito, maybe you'll walk us to the cab stand?"

"I'll do better than that. I'll drive you to your hotel." In the elevator he said, "Let's stop someplace and have a nightcap first."

Irwin brightened. But on the sidewalk he paused, irresolute. "You were the one who said you've got a long ride home."

"I just wanted to get the hell out of there. Come on, let's go up Second Avenue, we'll find a bar near the garage."

Spreading himself over a stool in a nearly pitch-black imitation of an English pub, Irwin raised his glass gratefully. "Now I can really drink to you, Vito. That wasn't much of a celebration."

He shrugged. Carmie sat quietly, swirling her stick around in the glass which she was not going to empty.

"Well," he said, "I had you two. So it wasn't a total bust."

"Don't be so polite, Vito." Carmela turned on him angrily. "You're a famous man now. Was that the best they could offer you, all that boring crap about the old days?"

"Come on, Carmie," Irwin said. "Don't exaggerate."

"I thought, in homes like that, where artists get together, well, shouldn't it be more interesting? More exciting? Even the food was lousy!"

"You're right about that. Why should we make excuses for them? We can let our hair down better without them."

But if they could, it led to nothing much, to no real intimacy. In the bar, later in the Jag on the way downtown to their hotel, finally saying goodbye while he double-parked before their marquee, all that came out was that Carmie and the husband to whom she kept returning like a bird weary of its senseless circling flights had only just succeeded in struggling to a painfully limited understanding of what his target had been all these years.

What an irony! For the ones who made a profession out of keeping score, for the critics, he wasn't even in the game any more.

Maybe it's me that's wrong? Vito asked himself, maybe I'm as square as the Metzgers who don't even know that I'm out of style, and as hopeless as Carmie's dreams of becoming a ceramicist or a señorita or whatever the hell curdles her life and torments her husband?

The next day he stared around him at the half-finished work on every side of his solitary studio. Some of it cried for more effort, more intensity, more application. The rest—maybe all of it, how was he to know, was he really in a blind alley?—demanded to be destroyed.

He prowled the planks from one canvas to the other, hunting for a clue like a dog sniffing out a bone, a brush in each hand and another between his teeth. One day he painted for fourteen hours, not eating, prompted by the rain drumming on the roof to piss in a pail, knocking off for a sandwich and a beer only when the pain in his gut brought him back to himself; another day he got rid of eleven canvases, putting his foot through those which he could not otherwise put out of his sight or his mind.

At last the day of the presentations, his moment of recognition. He took from the closet his good spring suit, the one Esther had taken him to her tailor uncle to have specially made to disguise the unequal length of his arms, and was annoyed to discover the trousers were way too big, they hung on him baggily. Muttering, he punched a new notch in his belt and took up the slack, then knotted his tie carefully and brushed down his neglected hair. When he pulled out of the barn and drove to the road he stuck his hand into the mailbox half expecting a telegram. GREETINGS FROM MEXICO CITY STOP SORRY CANT BE WITH YOU ON THIS GLAD DAY, or something of the sort, whimsical and Lorchlike. But no. Only bills and a request for the use of his name from a so-called artists' committee. He stuffed everything back in the box and drove on.

He arrived in Manhattan at eleven-thirty, early enough to find a parking space on 154th Street past Broadway, and hurried on for the pre-lunch drinks. He was confused by all the impressive old buildings in the middle of this half-slummy area. For one crazy moment he found himself staring at Sioux dioramas in the Museum of the American Indian, and wondering what this had to do with anything. But a schoolteacher with a mob of colored kids steered him out. He went past the Hispanic Society to the proper entrance for artists and prize winners.

On the sidewalk he bumped into old Bukoff and his wife, also just heading for the entrance. Bukoff pulled off the beret that he still affected and exposed his yellowing hair as he extended his hand. "Jesus Christ, Brigante!" he said. "Shades of the artists' project!"

Despite the fact that he had always regarded Bukoff primarily as a poster artist and hardly worthy of membership in the National Institute, he was glad to see him. He had been uneasy about marching in here alone, having to prove his right to enter by flashing the invitation, so he took hold of Fanny Bukoff's arm with a certain alacrity.

"I guess for you people," he said, "this place is practically a second home, like Ratner's or the Royale."

"Not exactly." Pleased nevertheless, Bukoff added, "We come in maybe two, three times a year, like for their big group show and for this annual ceremony. They're giving you a bronze medal, right?"

"Don't ask me why. I never thought I'd be their cup of tea."

"You can't tell with those things. You could have knocked me over when they elected me to membership. Me, with those *alte cockers.*"

Despite his eagerness to point out that he was on the inside Bukoff was pleasant, leading him through the doors and introducing him to two, three, four ladies and gentlemen before excusing himself and disappearing with his wife.

As the booze warmed his belly Vito began to enjoy the occasion. It was nice to be congratulated by people whose faces were familiar from book jackets, to be clapped on the back by people who had remembered that he had served on the jury of the Biennale. Large as they were the reception rooms were crowded and stuffy, so he went out onto the small balcony that overlooked the street where he had parked his car. A good breeze was blowing from the Hudson but warmish already—New York would have summer before it had fully recovered from the winter—and even here a lady touched his arm. "You're receiving an award today, aren't you?"

"Yes," he replied, and she smiled.

"I just wanted you to know how richly I think you deserve it."

On this happy note he answered the luncheon gong and went inside to the dining hall, in which several dozen round tables had been set, each for eight guests. It was festive and grand, but still intimate. Excited, he made his way through the cheerfully chattering groups until he came to the one at which his own place card was propped behind the inevitable cherry-tipped half-grapefruit.

The others introduced themselves to him: a tottering architect with a marvelous mop of white curls and an asthmatic wife; a wrinkled composer with a hearing aid and a stout wife gripping a businesslike cane; and a pouchy-eyed literary critic whose left hand trembled uncontrollably, thumb rubbing against index finger with the horrible regularity of a metronome. The critic's companion, an aristocratic lady with blue hair piled up high, took Vito's hand and drew him down beside her in a friendly fashion.

"Where's your wife?" she demanded peremptorily as if she had known him for years.

"I haven't got any."

The critic's wife indicated one last empty chair on his left. "Weren't you bringing a guest? There's a place being held."

Vito looked at the place setting. Blank but accusatory, the red eye of the grapefruit gazed back at him. Who did they think he was going to bring, Esther? Had she expected to be invited? Would she be in the audience afterward, maybe with Lorch?

The critic's wife was calling a waiter. "We won't be using this, could you take it away? Or seat someone else here, if you need room?"

But the seat remained empty throughout the meal, nudging him, the odd man with the three distinguished old couples. They all seemed to know each other. In fact he had the feeling that they had known each other, and argued about the food here, and the institutionalization of culture, ever since he had been a kid delivering papers on West Ferry Street. They were all famous but they were nice, taking him into their talk as much as possible, even trying to make him feel that he belonged.

After dessert and coffee they had to file through a narrow corridor to get to the auditorium where the awards were to be given out. The aged architect first led him into the john, where he had trouble with his fly, and then escorted him down the picture-lined passageway, pointing out this or that dead Academician and enlivening their slow walk with anecdotes about those he had known in their time. Vito had no way of knowing whether the old boy was trying to put him at ease or was just talkative. In the auditorium the architect gave him a final clap on the back.

Bleachers had been installed on the stage for the new inductees and for those who like himself were to receive awards. The auditorium was already filled with guests. Conspicuous, sweating, Vito took his place in the third row, furtively pulled up his socks, and studied the elaborate program. Speech by the outgoing president, induction of the incoming president, presentations (thank God he was at the beginning of the alphabet), reception on the terrace.

Throughout the preliminaries, Vito scanned the main floor and the balcony in search of a grin, a suppressed wave, some sign that someone he knew was watching, waiting to greet him. When the new president turned to him from the lectern and said, "Vito Brigante," he arose, stumbled because he had been looking out at the audience rather than at his feet, and made his way forward to the center of the stage.

He stood there clenching his knuckles, listening to the tall bald man, a former ambassador and college professor with rounded shoulders and nose glasses.

"For his lonely search, for his quiet but passionate years of dedication, for his discovery of beauty in anguish and form in flux." Then he held out the little box, while all those people out there, whoever they were, applauded, making a sound like splattering rain.

He made his way back to his seat without stumbling, although his eyelids were swelling and he was in terror that tears would start to trickle out. I should have sent Zia Concetta a ticket, he thought, fumbling for a handkerchief to dry his hands; she wouldn't have understood but she would have been proud to come just the same, it would have meant more to her than, but what am I saying, he thought in terror, Zia Concetta is dead, she's long since dead . . .

At the end they filed out of the auditorium and onto the sunny terrace in the handsome open square, more European than American in its leisurely urban spaciousness. The canvas canopy of an outdoor bar fluttered in the breeze. On either side were tables with snacks for the audience that was now coming out to greet the guests of honor.

Vito took a glass of punch, to have something to hold, and stationed himself in the middle of the terrace in the grateful sunshine. Two or three elderly ladies took his hand and congratulated him but then he was left alone. For a few moments he stood there without moving, persuading himself that it was good to expose himself to the sun after the fidgety hours in the dark artificially lit auditorium. But it wasn't true, he knew it wasn't. He stood bareheaded in the sun with the stupid glass in his hand. He was exposing himself not to the sun but to the strangers in the vain hope that someone whom he knew and wanted to come, Esther, Lorch, Feinstein, would emerge from the clustered groups of strangers to assure him that this day was not what his heart told him.

What a laugh! The only ones in this crowd who weren't already on social security were the children and grandchildren of the academic architects and portrait painters, the retired writers of unread novels and composers of unperformed symphonies.

What was he doing here in this forest of canes and crutches, this thicket of support hose, bifocals, and ear trumpets? Look at me, he was saying, I'm practically in the club, I'm on the waiting list for the hasbeens and I'm even grateful for it.

No I'm not, I'm not, I'm not, he cried to himself. Maybe I was sucked in for an hour or two, maybe I was kidding myself a little, who doesn't do that at least once in his life? What mattered wasn't here, never had been, never would be, not among all this politeness and good cheer, among all this kindness to those who had done their work, good or bad, and were ready to call it a day and lean back, tremblingly grateful for the little awards and the little medals.

What mattered was in his studio, propped against the walls, staring at him, glaring at him, daring him to attack it once again. He swallowed the punch, set down the glass, and made for the exit. Halfway there, he was hit in the belly, stabbed by the same familiar devil driving the air out of his gut with the force of a pneumatic hammer and filling it with a pain so exquisite that his eyeballs started. He would not double up before all these people, he could not let himself, he wanted no pity, he wanted only to greet his destiny alone. Striding toward the street, one hand to his stomach, pressing as if to keep it from falling out, he heard himself swearing in Italian, and when that did no good, praying to the God in whom he did not believe in a Latin he thought had gone the way of the fiestas and the fears of his forgotten childhood.

3. HAM

Hour after hour the kids sang, rocking in the bus as it rolled north. Straining the seats of their crackling new bib overalls, those who could sit still squatted in the aisle to harmonize with the others. Ham was tense about Gloria and excused himself from participating. The kids had left him alone; maybe it seemed funny to them that an old guy like him should be on the verge of fatherhood for the first time. Loving Glory, they knew what it would have meant to her to go along on this March after her months of work on it and her years leading sit-ins and picket lines. It was out of the question; but she raged nonetheless, furious at having to stay behind in Atlanta.

"Promise me," she'd insisted, "that you'll tell me every single thing about Washington first chance you get."

Chatting with Paul Metzger in the midst of the singing, he wished that he could be as cool as his companion, at twenty more self-assured than he himself at forty. Paul gestured at Joey Glantzman, the only other white on the bus, squeezed in up front with Royal and Daisy. His pinkish cheeks puffed out, he was blowing on a harmonica while the other two were attempting to sing in two-part harmony. Joey was just seventeen but he towered over the black high-school kids, his broad shoulders filling out the blue denim shirt.

"You were wrong to worry about him," Paul said. "He worked out fine."

"I'll be gladder than you can guess to deliver him to his folks.

He did more than fine, he did great, but what if something had happened? How could I ever have faced his folks?"

"You sound like big daddy."

"Easy for you to talk. All you had to worry about was yourself."

Paul's long face darkened. "That worry goes deep. Deeper than objective facts like jail."

"You think parents shouldn't worry about little objective facts like jail? You think the parents of these black kids weren't worried like the Metzgers about their nice respectable children being thrown in jail like a bunch of falling down drunks? Wait till you're a father."

Paul smiled sadly. Whenever that smile appeared, it struck Ham not just with its sweetness but with how little he understood what lay behind it. At this moment it seemed to be saying, Oh I know more than you think. Or did it mean something more strange than that?

Ham let his head fall back. He had not foreseen this summer, or that he would assume responsibility for the grown children of his friends. Much less that they would all spend the summer on Big Boy's native soil. The long-ago names that Big Boy had reeled off to him when he had been a boy Paul's age—St. Helena, West Feliciana and East Feliciana, Iberville, East Baton Rouge and West Baton Rouge, Point Coupée, Tangipaho—were no longer mythical. They were solid political realities, parishes of a congressional district in which this busload of kids had been working on voter registration.

Starting with Iberville, where they had spent orientation week in a beat-up hotel presided over by a motherly fifty-year old Negro lady (and where they had picked up some local high-school recruits, including Royal and Daisy), they had fanned out across Plaquemines. The Negro kindergarten teacher from Brooklyn, the romantic Irish poet, the dogmatic graduate students, the college kids Ham himself had brought in—all of them quickly learned the complex differences in racial attitudes between Louisiana towns which until then had been for most of them simply "The South." How could they have known that Iberville was a prosperous friendly area, civilized, complete with a biracial commission, but that West Feliciana did not have one Negro registered voter? Or that Bogalusa, in George Washington Parish only sixty miles to the east, was Klan territory, a completely lawless wilderness?

For the first few weeks Joey and Paul had been assigned to

Iberville itself, which Joey found boring, too "safe" for a seventeen-year-old, but where Ham at least could feel that he was fulfilling his pledge to the Glantzmans that he'd safeguard their oldest child. But then the boys had been assigned to different parishes, with Joey going off to Point Coupée. He was good at voter registration, rang doorbells indefatigably, falling asleep dead exhausted on one of the six cots in the living room of the middle-class Negro couple with whom his group was billeted.

One Sunday, addressing a crowded church after prayer meeting, Joey had allowed his rhetoric to get the better of him. Ham could not resist the temptation to write it to the Glantzmans.

"You would have been proud of your boy, standing up tall and pounding the pulpit about the effect of voter registration on local issues. Until he got carried away by his kibbutz background and demanded—after explaining the need for drainage ditches—'How many of you *like* mosquitoes?' Some soul in the back was overcome by Joey's oratory. 'Me!' he yelled. 'I do!' and poor Joey almost passed out."

Some Sundays they went off to New Orleans for fun, and on one such Sunday several dozen of them had driven their cars onto the ferry in order to reach the highway that ran down to New Orleans on the far side of the Mississippi. Friendly at last with his group leader, a big dark skinny cat who affected a vaguely racist rhetoric and always referred to the white volunteers as "you colorless ones," Joey had mounted with him and the others to the cheesy little lounge where they all disposed themselves along the metal benches.

As soon as the group leader and the kindergarten teacher went to the drinking fountain the ferryboat captain came storming out. "You can't drink out of that fountain!" he yelled. They stared at him in silence until he had slammed the door behind him. Then all twenty-six of them lined up and started to drink.

The squatty captain erupted once again. This time he had a gun strapped below his bulging waist and a billy club clenched in his fist. "Didn't you hear what I said?"

It was the little kindergarten teacher who spoke up before any of them, even the group leader. "You've got a problem, Captain. If this fountain is just for whites, where do *you* drink? Look at you, you're pink!"

Worse than pink, mottled with rage, the captain trotted back into the wheelhouse, put the boat about and phoned ashore in bull-like tones. Four squad cars were waiting at the pier when they headed back into the slip. Cool, pleased, Joey led the way into the police cars. At the station house he was one of the first to lock arms and begin the singing when the police attempted to take them in one by one to be booked.

The cops got them in at last, but they had to drag them after breaking them up into four groups, white females, white males, black females, black males. For Ham it was an old story; but he did not like being separated from the two boys whose safety he had guaranteed.

He need not have worried. For Joey and Paul even more than for the others, it was a triumphal experience. During the five days they sat in jail they were neither isolated nor alone. Five hundred others had marched in Iberville not merely in sympathy but with a firm deadline for the release of those behind bars. The sheriff was running for re-election, and the authorities yielded to the deadline with what you could almost call meekness.

A week later things did get rough, with Jim Farmer arrested, then hiding out, then fleeing the area in a coffin. But by then Ham had seen Joey safely settled with his group in Tangipaho, going ahead with the canvassing and the voter registration clinics.

Now, except for the March on Washington itself, it was all over for Joey and Paul. Joey would be returning to Queens, where his father had been busy recruiting and organizing teachers for the March, and then maybe the Glantzmans would be off for a week's vacation on the Cape before school started again.

As for Paul, he sat in silence beside Ham, his chin in his palm. "Yes," he remarked ruminatively, "this summer has been a natural for Joey. Remember how worried you were about his adapting, with his foreign background? For a kibbutznik like him, the rural South was a cinch. So were the rural Negroes. Even the bigots were simply a fact of life, like terrorist infiltrators in Israel."

Paul felt that he himself had been less prepared than Joey to enter naturally into the lives of Negro farmers and laborers. Not that he ever referred to his comparative physical inferiority, or contrasted his stooped shoulders with Joey's exuberant ruggedness.

Paul's malaise went deeper than simple envy. He cherished Joey as if he were his brother, and he admired the younger boy's un-hesitant quickness in talking turkey with tenant farmers or simple artisans. For Joey the message of political liberation was at bottom no different from the message of intensive cultivation, crop rotation, grafting, fertilizing. Freedom and scientific farming—Joey had grown up assuming that these were only two sides of the same coin.

What troubled Paul was the fear that unlike Joey he would always be looked on as an outsider who had not earned the right to tell others what to do—especially when his advice did not grow from the soil of his own experience. Not only was Ham uncertain of how he might allay this fear; it made him feel emotionally shallow beside this intense unashamed spirituality, just as Paul accounted himself false and patronizing when he regarded the artlessness with which Joey, blowing on his harmonica, became quite simply one of the crowd.

"Joey did great, it's true," Ham said. "And so did you, in a different way. He didn't have your stability. But then we didn't expect him to, not at his age. By next summer he'll be much more mature, if he comes back."

"Oh, he'll be back. It's just right for him."

"And you?"

Paul's face came alight with the smile that was all the more beautiful for its rarity. "If you'll have me," he replied.

"Can you doubt it?"

"I doubt myself."

"Why?"

"I have to laugh every time I think of me, me! with thonged sandals and a knobbly stick, bringing the croppers the gospel according to Jaspers. It's a wonder they didn't stone me as a false prophet. And I don't mean the whites, I mean the blacks."

"You did your job."

"Not to my satisfaction. I'm no good with people who can tell that I don't belong. I want to stay with the people that I'm going to talk to. I want to work with them, not just visit or sleep on a cot in someone's living room for a few weeks. I think I belong in the city, I'm more at ease with city people. Now that I have my degree, I've fulfilled my obligations at home. Home isn't . . ." Paul hesitated. "I spoke to my father on the phone the other night. They've split up again. For the millionth time."

"Where is your mother?"

"New York, I think. But I'm not sure. Dad says she wants to take a course in photography. Sooner or later she'll tell me all about it. She's always so enthusiastic, it's contagious, I get all caught up in her dreams of a new career."

He spoke without malice but with a certain weariness that would have been suspicious in any other twenty-year-old. Although he loved his parents and they loved him, each was incomplete in some way that was not easy to define. Even when they were together they did not fulfill each other—and Paul, aching to be himself, could not begin to realize himself in the presence of his contesting parents.

The bus was approaching the suburban area of the District. Ham blew the whistle that hung from his neck by a knotted sneaker shoelace.

"Let's shape up, gang," he said. "When we pull into the lot, there'll be another bus to take us to Union Station. Let's not horse around, let's get right into the other bus so we can fall into the line of march. I want us to make a first-class impression, and we can only do that if we stick together and behave."

"Okay, Pops!" Royal called back. "We hear you talkin, Pops!"

All summer they had been teasing him about his impending fatherhood. Nevertheless they did listen to him. And although they were dying to wrestle around in the fresh air after the thousand weary miles grinding along in the bus, they formed up and hopped aboard the shuttle bus that awaited them, its motor already turning over.

At Union Station they climbed off and began to fall in line. In their staging area, only one of many, the District policemen, natty in powder blue, were not the only ones maintaining order. Big black men in business suits, their starched shirts unwrinkled by the summer heat, herded them into line.

Ham passed the word. "They're the Guardians."

"What's that, man?"

"Negro patrolmen from the New York Police Department. They all volunteered."

"You mean we got our own cops? *Black* cops? Wowie!"

"Hey Pops, which way is downtown? Where's the White House? You know where the President is hiding at? Where does the March begin?"

He adjusted his dark glasses and made a quick head count to ensure that he had everyone. Considering that they had slept in the bus in their clothes, on each other's shoulders and laps, they looked remarkably neat.

Only when he glanced behind them and saw other groups, stout women in white uniforms and red satin capes, marching eight abreast, their tasseled fezzes embroidered *Int'l Masons* teetering above black faces shiny with sweat, did he begin to realize that they were already marching. This was it, at last, decades after Randolph, and his own dead step-father, had planned for the first abortive march.

He broke free and trotted to the curb to gaze ahead for a moment, standing on tiptoe. The line of march stretched forward as far as he could see, block after block, glittering in the hot August sun—ordinary men looking like office workers in shirt sleeves, jackets slung over their shoulders; straight-line marchers moving in cadence, the overseas caps of their union locals tilted rakishly over their brows, black and white intermingled; high school kids in sweat-shirts lettered CORE. He could not see the beginning, nor the last of the marchers either. It was endless.

"Hey," he called out as he rejoined his group, "this is it! We're really on our way!"

But they had sensed this already. They began—tentatively at first but with increasing confidence—to sing *We Shall Overcome*. As they stepped along past the Washington Monument, there loomed up before them, growing from the base of a gleaming truck, the giant glittering yellow crane of a television camera. Cupped in its claw like someone in a science fiction film, the cameraman regarded them all intently through the eye of the machine while it lowered him smoothly to a point just above them in order that he might stare them in the face.

"Smile, you're on TV!" yelled Royal.

Ham glanced back at the group for which he had been responsible throughout two tense months. For them this was the culmination of the summer—for him, more like fifteen years. They nudged each other delightedly as they caught sight of a bearded Sikh in a freshly wound pink turban shinnying up a light pole before the Pan American Union building. Scrambling up, gripping with the soles of his highly polished black shoes, the bearded dark man was pointing his movie machine at them, recording them for some future private showing half a world away.

"Hey Ham, what street is this?"

"Constitution Avenue, and you better believe it!"

No one could know how much it meant to each of them, after a summer's doorbell-ringing, pleading, preaching, praying, singing and jail-sitting, to be inspected as they moved on down the avenue of the nation's capital, under the leafy bower of the great old trees, by government workers standing with folded arms on the steps of their office buildings, by cameramen, journalists, startled passersby, and the seemingly uncommitted thousands who stared in silence.

Paul slipped into line beside him as they approached the turnoff for the Lincoln Memorial. He had been struck, he said, by the expressionlessness of the local Negroes who watched them quietly, not smiling, not waving, not even blinking in the strong sun.

"What do you suppose they're thinking?"

"I don't know. I don't imagine anybody does. One thing is sure. They never saw anything like this, or even dreamed of it—a hundred thousand of us, maybe two hundred thousand, taking over the city in their name."

"You think that's enough?"

Paul was always puzzling.

"I think we're doing pretty good. What more do you want?"

"To reach those city Negroes standing there. In this town alone there must be more of them than there are of us marchers from the whole country. Why don't they fall in with us? Why don't we ask them to?"

He shook his head. Paul's utopianism could make you feel like shaking him. "Washington has one of the most lethargic Negro populations in the country," he said patiently. "They're notoriously unorganizable. Today they're bound to get a sense of our power and our purpose, isn't that something?"

"Not enough." Paul switched tracks, with that always startling mixture of practicality and prophecy of which he was capable just at the moment when you despaired of him. "The people among whom we've been working are either trapped and terrorized, or ready to flee the South. When they turn up in a city like this, lost and uprooted, all they do is stare at us and our songs and signs. How do you know that they aren't saying to themselves, God, what fools?"

"Well . . ." He hesitated. "No one can be sure. But I've been on the phone with the March people for several weeks. The response has been fantastic in cities all over the country. And if the ones who didn't come were skeptical before, they won't be after today."

"You really think so?" Paul smiled slightly. "I think that depends on what happens after this parade, not on the parade itself. Meanwhile, look at those blank black faces." He pointed at the Negroes who lined the curb, staring. "I think they're skeptical. They got out of the rural misery but they found the urban slum. "And that's where the issue will be decided, for good or for ill."

For good or for ill. Paul had a talent for chilling you, for shaking the beliefs that you had come to take for granted and leaving you uncertain of your course.

But they were off the avenue now, making their way across the grass toward the reflecting pool where tired marchers who had gotten there first were already seated at the water's edge with their pants rolled up, soaking their bare feet in the pool.

"Let's get as close to the platform as we can!" Royal cried. From here on it would be all but hopeless to keep them together.

"Remember," he called out to those who could hear him, "pass the word, we'll meet back at the bus tonight." He grabbed hold of Joey Glantzman, who would be going on up to New York with his parents, if they could be found. "Stick with me."

Crushed together, he and Joey and three or four others pressed on through the endless crowd, adrift in the biggest picnic grounds in the whole world. Here black and white clergymen of the Episcopal Diocese of Newark posed with arms linked, in their shirtsleeves, clerical collars sticking up oddly, blinking for a snapshot. They picked their way past a fraternal club that lolled on the grass sharing chicken wings and poking into box lunches, their shoes and shirts scattered about them.

When the speeches began he and Joey and the others were still not close enough to see the platform before the Memorial, much less to watch those whose amplified voices boomed out over the lawn, over the water of the pond, through the trees, on and on for acre after acre to the furthest ranks of the massed thousands. The famous and the important were probably on the platform or in the press section.

Even if they could see what he could not, even if they had a view all the way across to the Washington Monument, to the Capitol, perhaps even to the White House where the President was supposedly watching it all on television, he wondered whether they or the President could see what he did, from the very middle of the mass, one among the nameless thousands.

Middle-aged men and women stood with their arms linked, captured, frozen, almost as if they had simply been out for a stroll when they were stopped short by an unexpected event. Young men squatted on their haunches, moving only a forefinger to draw lines in the dust as they listened. Some stood with arms akimbo or enfolding wives or girl friends, quietly supporting them. Schoolboys hung high in the forks of trees or straddled heavy branches, watching a trembling speech by John Lewis, with whom Ham had spent more than one night in jail.

"We will march through the South, through the streets of Jackson, through the streets of Danville, through the streets of Cambridge, through the streets of Birmingham." Lewis's voice rose, and almost broke. "But we will march with the spirit of love, and with the spirit of dignity that we have shown here today."

In front of Ham, a heavy-set man, a solitary figure in a wrinkled white shirt, hands clasped prayerfully before him, murmured to himself half-aloud. "Yes, yes." As if picked up by the wind that sighed through the trees, the murmur swelled, issuing from the lips of thousands. Mesmerized, Ham felt the ground shake beneath his feet as the murmur rose to a roar.

When it had subsided, when the speechmaking was over, they were once again simply tired people, strolling back in the direction whence they had come, some barefoot with shoes laced together and slung across a shoulder, others with arms linked about each other's waists, their signs and banners drooping. But they retained the sweetness that had been so overwhelming earlier in the day, at the crowded Good Humor trucks and at the overburdened temporary latrines. Young deferred to old, old were kind to young, and all were color blind in a way that he could never have foreseen. Had the man with folded hands who sighed his assent been black or white? For a moment Ham, astonished, could not remember.

In the midst of the returning marchers, the grave black doctor with the sign saying simply MD above a neatly drawn caduceus, the fairhaired college student with a placard mysteriously lettered, CALIFORNIA FEDERATION OF MINERAL SOCIETIES, LAND OF PLEASANT ROCKHUNTING, the Crusade for Voters, the Savannah Freedom Now Movement, the Shreveport NAACP, among all of the singers and the footsore, he caught sight of Bill and Margaret Zivic. They bore no signs or placards. Hand in hand, munching on ice cream suckers, they strolled like one more middle-aged couple.

Bill was calm as always. He scratched the grizzle at his temple with the dry end of his ice cream stick. "We thought we'd run into you people sooner or later. Big Boy's been looking for you."

"Is he here with a group?"

"Big Boy? What else?" Margaret had her arms around Joey.

"I'd like to see him," Ham said, "but it's more important for me to make sure that Joey gets together with his folks."

"You don't have to worry about me," Joey protested.

"Who's worrying?" Margaret said. "Your folks will turn up later at my sister's. Norm is going to have a big open house. That includes you and your gang, Ham."

"I don't think Vera would appreciate an entire busload."

"Never mind. You know how Norm loves young people."

Ham glanced about. There weren't many left of his busload. Six, seven maybe, counting Joey. And where was Paul? "That reminds me," he said. "Was Irwin with you?"

"He was coming separately. He was dying to see Paul here. We haven't bumped into him, but we'll all connect at Vera's."

"Come on," Bill said impatiently, "let's go see what's happening up there."

A fracas had started at the angle of the street and the park. A knot of forty or fifty homeward-bound marchers had gathered in a rather loose circle, some of them lifting their hands above their heads in excitement, perhaps in anger. Paul, he was relieved to see, was standing there quietly, his hands in his pockets. He hurried over with Bill and the others.

In the center of the circle a small group of scruffy young men stood at bay. Nervous, hunched, sweating in their brass-studded leather jackets, they shook their heads tensely, pomaded pompadours flopping over their ears.

"Who invited the niggers to Washington?" One of them jutted his jaw aggressively. "We Americans got just as much right here as you."

"Who are they?" Ham asked.

"Hell's Angels. They came a long ways but they're all alone— Rockwell and his Nazis already been arrested."

How strange to be in the majority! If the boys in the leather jackets had been entirely alone he might even have felt almost sorry for them. But they had allies—a shorthaired female with a squashed nose, and a baseball cap pulled over her forehead; an emaciated woman in a drooping flowered dress; next to the two women, a tall skinny hillbilly who stood slouching, his pelvis jutting insolently, hands crammed into the hip pockets of his levis. The neck of a guitar leaned against his legs, an unlit cigarette dangled from his thin lips.

"What's eatin you," he drawled, "why you pickin on these guys? You think it's wrong to be proud that you're white? You got something against Americans?"

"Ah," a college boy turned away in disgust, "let the street cleaners sweep them up with the rest of the garbage."

One of the motorcycle jockeys made an obscene gesture at the boy's back, but the crowd was already breaking up. Ham turned to Bill and was startled to see that his old friend had turned pale.

"What's the matter?" he asked. "You look sick."

"Don't you recognize that guy?"

"I was thinking he looks familiar."

"Albie Small. And his women."

As soon as he heard the name the memories of twenty years ago and more came flooding back—Sunday evenings early in the war at the New Party headquarters. Sy's educationals, Bernie's discussions about "literature" sales, and that one tilted in a chair between his women, gum working, cigarette drooping. He could not bring himself to look at the little group. It was as if they were doing something dirty, simply by standing there.

Bill said shortly, "I knew them well. But maybe not well enough. Last I heard he went over to the Stalinists in the Wallace campaign. But to become a racist? Is that what all our work was for?"

Margaret had been standing by quietly with Joey, who was angry and puzzled. She said, "It's understandable. He was a loser. Where did he have to go? He was always looking for something so he could get over the feeling that he was out of it. How long could you expect him to stick with the left? When you think of it, it's only logical."

Maybe, Ham thought, maybe; the hillbilly gravitating at last toward the outcast Californians, children of the Okies. Old Americans lost and bewildered, huddling together, putting a surly face on their fear that the new America overwhelming them was not that of their fathers or their families.

He turned for the one last look at the defiant ones, adorned with the chains, iron crosses, swastikas, *NEVER* buttons that they had brought all the way to their miserable little counterdemonstration. The paraphernalia of hatred. Small, plucking at his guitar, had begun to sing once again, in his whiny rusting voice: "Move them Niggers North, Move them Niggers North, If they don't like our Southern ways, Move them Niggers North."

A horrible doubt began to creep through him. What if they were not the last ragtag remnant of rural ignorance, kicking against the inevitable? Suppose that they stood for something as unyielding as the hatred in the hearts of those who burned down churches and blew up little girls in their Sunday school dresses? Suppose that in their confused rancor they represented the only momentarily outnumbered waiting to strike back?

Today such a notion seemed ludicrous. But maybe that was wrong. Maybe the happy thousands who had captured everyone's attention were still the ineffective minority. It was in the cities, Paul had said, that the issue would be decided for good or for ill. He had been referring to the Negroes, the silent thousands chopped off from their roots in a way peculiarly like those deracinated clots of cyclists—and bottled up, unlike the Californians, in urban ghettoes. He had pointed to the impassive faces of the uninvolved blacks; but couldn't he just as well have pointed to these? Couldn't he have asked whether they were the vanguard of the others in the cities, the Poles, the Irish, the Italians, who had not as yet been heard from?

And there was something else. Why should he share the idiot optimism of those who believed that freedom *now* would come *now?* Was it even thinkable when you looked into Albie Small's green eyes, still smoking with hate two hundred years after his ancestors had fought for freedom and twenty years after he himself, poring over the Communist Manifesto, had pledged equality for all mankind?

No wonder Bill had turned so pale. Maybe he too had whiffed the smoke that stung Paul's nostrils.

No matter. He had to get on with it. Lifting his head, he drew a deep breath.

"I have to make a call." He snapped his fingers. "Glory is waiting to hear from me. And I'm anxious to hear from her." He linked arms with his friends and led them up the avenue. "If it's a boy, we're going to name it for Paul."

4. JOE

On the way in to La Guardia from Washington, last leg of a trip east that had taken him to Chicago, Detroit, Buffalo, Joe worked the stewardess for three fast cups of coffee. He was uncertain whether they left him stimulated or depressed. The sedatives and the stimulants that other people took either from habit or to persuade themselves that they were soothed, stoned, grooving, flying, whatever, never did anything to him but intensify what he had been feeling beforehand.

He himself was still not sure how he felt, after all these thousands of miles, all these meetings, all these notes that jammed his briefcase. Embarked on something he had never undertaken before, he couldn't tell as yet whether he was a damn fool or was really on to something. Now that his savings had leaked away on what could be his biggest gamble, he could not be certain that the manila folders stuffed with notes would actually become the book he had imagined.

Early in sixty-two, when the boss had decided to toss in his cards, he had sat him down for a long private talk.

"Joe, I'm overextended. It's no secret to you, I'm sure. As far as tract houses go, we're fresh out of land. And the high-rises just aren't fully enough rented to provide expansion capital. The quicker I disengage the better."

Ruddy, in fine trim, he was hardly the picture of the defeated enterpriser or the busted speculator. "I'm going into consulting. I've got some ideas about land use, and that's the best way I can think of to push them. Now what about you?"

It was good of him to ask. After five years he knew most of what there was to know about the Links. He had ordered a whole block of seats for David's Gershwin program at Hollywood Bowl, and then flown down a planeload of people from Oakland for the concert. He knew too that Joe was restless, gritting his teeth at the squabbles among the aging radicals and on the prowl for workers and students who would be receptive to his ideas.

Joe said coolly, as if it were something he had been carefully considering for a long time, "I want to write a book."

The builder was neither incredulous nor patronizing. A book? "That's just great. What's it going to be about?"

He heard himself saying things that had been, until the moment he uttered them, nothing more than half-formed notions. "I want to do an analysis of the state of the labor movement. I want to relate it on the one hand to the radical movement—the past—and on the other hand to the Negro revolution—the future. It would point toward what I think will happen next."

"Why, that's marvelous."

Encouraged, he went on, "With my own background, I can look at the unions from the bottom up, instead of the way professors do. I think I can show the new generation that militancy hasn't died, it's just been dormant. And it's going to come to life under new kinds of pressures, especially on the Negroes."

"I believe you've got your mitts into something. Let's see what we can do to get it going."

He lined up appointments with West Coast academics and labor people; he suggested areas of exploration; he checked out possible means of help in research and publication. Best of all, he made out a generous severance check and then fired Joe so that he could collect unemployment compensation while he was getting under way.

Committed almost before he was ready, Joe rang up Norm in Washington and arranged to meet him there after visiting a list of former comrades and local union leaders in industrial centers on the way east.

By the time he got to Washington, he was dismayed by how much there was to learn, how little he knew about specific factory problems, and how much he had spent—not just in energy but in cold cash.

When he tried to explain this, Norm brushed it aside. "Listen, pal," he said, "nowadays money is the least of our problems."

"Maybe for you."

Norm laughed. "You're looking at somebody that's deeper and more permanently in debt than Balzac. And with a little less talent. But I've got the key to some of the best vaults."

Joe looked up uncomprehendingly.

"Book publishers. They're just starting to clean up. The high schools are jammed with the kids us GIs made, in a year or so the colleges will be jammed too, and textbooks are going to make it big."

"You've got a name. But who cares what I've got to say about rank and file revolts?"

Norm waved this away. "Any half-ass idea is good for a sizeable advance. Not that yours isn't a natural," he added quickly. "All we have to do is show them you're the natural guy to do it. I'm going to phone some editors so that when you get to New York they'll be salivating."

Generous Norm was; in fact when he spoke of their one-time comrades who had made it as labor bureaucrats he was inclined to be overly forgiving. "What did you expect?" he demanded, after listening to a description of this or that former militant now more anxious about his golf score than about speedup, more concerned about zoning around his summer bungalow than about the slums, more worried about his son's getting into the right school than about Negroes getting into the skilled trades. "They're not traitors, they're just tired. The old jism isn't there, that's all. Of course Meany and Company copped out on the March on Washington, but the UAW came through, didn't they? Look at Bill—he brought out the troops, didn't he?"

"That's true. But you know how he spends his time. He not only showed me through that hothouse he built for his cactuses, he gave me a lecture on the mammillaria and the echinopsis."

"He can't be too bad as a lecturer. The names seem to have stuck in your mind."

"Ten per cent did." As soon as he had said it, he knew that he had gone too far.

"What you don't dig, Joe," Norm said, "is that the cactuses aren't taking the place of politics. They're taking the place of kids."

"I'm sorry."

"Bill at least used to have the pleasure of Marlen's visits. Margaret

always had the guest room made up for him, they wanted him to
feel it was his own. Well . . . they had to find other interests."

"Where I grew up cactus wasn't an interest, it was a weed. But I
was in his office for a couple of hours. Christ, it's like an annex to
the Democratic Party. Campaign literature all over the place, the
phones going all the time to hustle up votes for some God-damned
judge—"

"—who is probably a liberal. If they don't work to put him back in,
who will?"

"We were supposed to be socialists, remember?"

"You think Bill has sold out because his office girls are doing
Jimmy Higgins work for some judge?"

"It isn't just some judge. Bill's up to his neck in Democratic Party
politics. Six months from now he'll be banging on doors to get
Kennedy re-elected."

"None too soon. The election's only a year off."

It was easy for Norm to bait him. He had benefited from his connections with the liberal lawmakers, the White House professors,
even the Vice-President. It made Joe uncomfortable about accepting his aid, and uneasy about whether the book could withstand
the pressure Norm intended to impose upon it.

"Look here," Norm said. "You want to write about the rank and
file radicals and the forgotten underdogs. Great. But if all you want
to prove is that the Gospel of the thirties is still Gospel now, who's
going to listen?"

What he wanted, apparently, was a book that—if it had to have
a thesis—would validate his own biases. He was insatiably curious
about dissident longshoremen, rebellious steelworkers, miners, auto
workers, but he refused to entertain the possibility that the sounds
to which Joe had been listening were the early warning signals of
a generalized revolt.

"It isn't just that the working class is shrinking. What you haven't
grasped, Joe, is that no matter how much rank and file belligerence
increases in the years ahead—and you know I'm constitutionally
in favor of that—the welfare state has a whole box of tricks to
contain discontent."

For Norm socialism was as dead as God. If you argued that the
prospect was very different viewed from an Indiana smelter, a
Michigan assemblyline, a Pennsylvania doghole, or a Chicago slum
than from Georgetown, Norm would agree. He read it, though, only

as additional evidence that ordinary people had not become robot-
ized. Nothing more. His years based in Washington he now felt
had placed him at the center of things. He did not confine himself
to the view from the drawing-room window, he still got out to see
for himself, but increasingly his attitude was shaped by the opinions
of editors, legislators, television reporters, columnists and commentators like himself—many of them, like him, former socialists.

He was unselfishly ready to promote the project even though he
suspected it to be wrongheaded. But he failed to see, Joe thought as
he reflected on their final discussion on the way to the National
Airport, that it was a questionable help to be of assistance—whether
from kindness, nostalgia, or personal guilt—if you made it clear
that you did not believe in the thesis itself.

Leaving the plane, laboring through the maze of Queens buses
from La Guardia to Sy's apartment in Long Island City, he told himself that the book would not be for Norm but rather for younger
people scarcely aware of the problems that had agitated an earlier
movement.

Why shouldn't the postwar babies whom Norm had spoken of as
textbook consumers be the consumers of his view of reality? It could
work if he avoided coming on as a parent or an uncle full of good
boozy memories. They didn't even have an antiquarian interest in
the fact that he and Norm and the others had repeated during the
dead years, in the dead of the night: Kilroy Lives. All they wanted to
know was, What help can Kilroy give us? Have you got anything to
offer?

He gazed around at the red brick wasteland in which the Glantzmans had been living ever since their return from Israel. Kids in
snowsuits scrambled on cold concrete. Black mothers gossiped on
one bench, white on another. How could they remember which of
the identical rectangles was home?

"Building G?" he asked a dark broad-faced woman.

Without hesitation she jerked her thumb up over her left shoulder. "Across the playground."

The key had been left for him with the lady in 8B. He went up in
an elevator soaked and seasoned with the smells of those it serv-
iced. Like the stairway of a creaking rooming house stinking of
clandestine cooking, it reeked of canned soup, fried potatoes, cheap
fish, sauerkraut, hot grease.

The neighbor lady, a middle-class Negro girl, wife of a city em-

ployee, peered through the prism peephole. She kept the door on
the chain while she passed him the key, holding the infant that was
not yet ready to be let loose on the blacktop playground.

He was telephoning the people on the list Norm had made up
when the youngest of the Glantzmans came in, an outgoing kid
with a zipper wool jacket and a grin.

"I'm Mitch," he said.

"I bet you don't know who I am."

"I bet I do. You're the one Joey was named for."

"Actually I was named for him."

He laughed. "I bet you can't guess what grade I'm in."

"Fifth?"

"Sixth!"

"Listen, I'm hungry. You want to have some lunch with me?"

"How come you didn't eat in school?"

"We're on split session. There's three different times, some kids
in sixth grade don't go to school until afternoon, but I go real early."

Serena and Joey, arriving from high school, filled him with long-
ing for his boys. He had hardly missed them during these weeks
of separation. Now however, looking at this gentle sad-eyed girl with
the long dark hair and the soft, almost secretive smile, and her
pug-nosed stocky brother, he yearned to see his own.

"We saw part of David's Hollywood Bowl concert on TV," Serena
said shyly. "It was really wonderful."

"He works hard at it, five or six hours a day. But I still want
him to go on to college. He's got an engagement to play Gershwin
at Lewisohn Stadium next summer."

"I wish I could be there," Joey said, "but I'm committed to Mississippi for next summer."

"They say you did a great job in Louisiana."

Joey flushed. "All I did was ring a bunch of doorbells. But I'd
like to go into politics. I mean, I'm not a hot-shot student like Serena,
but to me people is politics."

"I suppose your father told you about how we met in the student
movement."

"Take him with a grain of salt, kid," Sy said from the hallway,
where he stood with his key in his hand. "We trickle in," he explained to Joe. "Bernie will be along in an hour or so. Serena
will you please put up the potatoes and get the roast ready? Mitch,

set the table. Joey, get your homework out of the way so you can do the dishes afterward."

"You've got this place organized like a commune."

"If everyone didn't pitch in, it would be pure hell. Now tell me about your trip."

Sy was a good listener. His responsiveness arose naturally from his daily life. You could say this about Bill too, but despite his help to Big Boy, Bill seemed tired in a way that Sy would never be.

"I'll introduce you to the right people in my union," Sy said. "You really should fill yourself in on the white-collar unionists. Take the growing split between parents and teachers. I'm afraid of real strains, maybe some day even hatred, between teachers and parents. Negro mothers, militants, are going to want the same kinds of controls over the schools as suburban parents have. I don't know if that's going to fit in with your thesis. Maybe it will contradict it. Then what?"

"I had my dogmatism knocked out of me during the fifties."

Sy asked, with painful casualness, "What's with my brother? His letters are warmer than they used to be. And it's because of you."

"Sid learned, once he broke the mold of discipline. Nobody taught him compassion and solidarity, he tried to stifle them, that's all. But our kids are less bound by worn-out prejudices. That's why Gene and Sid have become such good friends."

Sy stared at him unbelievingly.

"It's not easy for me to admit that I messed things up. Gene rebelled against the piano. I couldn't reach him. I didn't want him to know how close Anne and I came to breaking up over her pushing him and David to the piano. He didn't hear the arguments, so he didn't think there were any. He thought I was an even worse fink than Anne, on account of all my crap about being liberated from bourgeois morality."

Sy sat with his palm supporting his forehead. "If my mother had tried to tell me how hard it is to be a parent I'd have said Sure, sure. But what would it have meant to me?"

"Gene took up the guitar, which was like thumbing his nose at Anne, then he let his hair grow down his back. He's too young for a license, but he started cruising over to Sid's on his illegal hot-rod."

"Sid, of all people."

"It's not so crazy. I named Gene for Debs, didn't I? Sid was the kind of workingman I'd always held up to him as a model."

"But you have the scars too."

"Mine don't show. Sid welcomed him, no questions asked. For Sid and Mimi all that ear-splitting unmusical noise is the good old days all over again, Josh White and Pete Seeger and all the party-line benefits. They really love him." He hesitated. "Maybe Anne isn't grateful, but I am."

"But Sid's never written me a word about Gene. Not one word."

"You still don't give Sid much credit for sensitivity, do you?"

Sy flushed.

"Well, I go over there and work with them on Gene's heap. It's got a good engine, and I know more about tuning it than Sid, that's one thing in my favor. So the three of us lay on our backs in the driveway. We don't talk much, we just pass parts back and forth."

"You and Anne haven't had it so bad these last few years, have you?"

"Not until my job folded and Gene turned on us. I can't blame Anne for looking on this trip—and the whole idea of the book—as one more example of my incurable adolescent radicalism. Or for thinking that when I go over to Sid's to work on the car, I'm poisoning Gene against her. Sometimes I think we've passed the point of no return."

Bernie came in then, and Joe could feel only relief. The territory they had been exploring was treacherous.

"Greetings." She put down her shopping bag and shook out her hair.

He took her in his arms and felt the sigh that passed through her body. It was like a wind that touched him too, leaving behind a quick shudder like an uncontrollable nervous reaction. She patted his cheek and slipped free. "Forgive me, Joe. I've had a miserable day."

"Tell me."

"I've just been to see Vito at the hospital."

"Bill told me he was sick."

"He's not just sick. He's dying."

"Are you sure?"

"He's got stomach cancer. They did a laparotomy but it was inoperable. I see suffering all day, you'd think I'd be tough by now." Suddenly she reached for her husband's handkerchief and pressed it to her face. Her voice was muffled. "It's so awful. He's all alone. No family, no relatives."

"Maybe I ought to go and see him."

"He's ashamed of the way he looks, but I think he'd be glad to see you. He's at St. Vincent's, down in the Village. He was pleading with me to get him out. What could I say?"

"Does he know?"

"He must suspect. If you go you'll see for yourself."

"I'll go."

He was not sure why. As you grew older there seemed to be more and more *tsourros*. After supper, after he had reported on his talk with Norm, he said, "Vera asked me to look up Carmela and see how she's doing. I half-promised, but I don't know that I'd have much more to say to her than to Vito."

Sy said, "All I can tell you is, she's trying to do something with American primitive art. I think it's weathervanes this time, little old hand-painted weathervanes. Hex signs too."

"There's always been a funny bond between her and Vera," he observed. "But what about Paul?"

"Joey never really got close to him. Paul is living in Harlem by himself. He came to dinner a few weeks ago and we all had a good time. At least I thought we did. But I don't pretend to understand him. Neither does his mother."

"Does he see her?"

"They have lunch together occasionally. You can guess what that's like."

That night he was tempted to creep off the Glantzmans' convertible couch and whisper a collect call into the phone. But he had no assurance, none at all, that his family would be eager to hear his voice. Every time he had phoned he had hung up frustrated, as if he had failed to make it clear that he loved them. Oppressed, uneasy, he lay on his back and waited for the dawn.

In the morning he arose determined to get on with what he had started. Emerging into Manhattan at Union Square, he walked west on 14th Street, a little like the rotting center of Los Angeles, but seedier here, dirtier, sadder; colder too, the wind reddening the noses of the shabby men already drifting eastward to the Third Avenue bars and the cheeks of the scarfed Latin women pulling their children into fake auctions and fraudulent fire sales in grubby

novelty shops. Pocket transistors tuned to clattering rock, chrome
replicas of the Statue of Liberty, clock radios, five-dollar wrist
watches that glowed in the dark, Jack and Jackie pillow cases in
red and purple velour, opera glasses in imitation mother of pearl
for people who never went to the opera, pocket knives with fish-
hooks and scale scrapers for men who never went fishing, beaded
purses for women who never went to balls, Pope John in sunset
colors to bless them all. And transparent shopping bags to display
the junk they had been conned into buying with their hard-won
dollars.

He quickened his pace and turned off at Seventh Avenue. The
lobby of the hospital was a momentary haven of dark calm peace-
fulness. But when the stout sister, panting silently, led him to the
room in which Vito lay alone with his fate, he stopped motionless
in the doorway, stunned into an irresolute silence.

"You can go on in," the sister said encouragingly. She coaxed
him to examine the merchandise more closely. "Our friend is up,
he's all shaved and ready for company."

Vito lay on his back beneath a small crucifix of slightly better
quality than those on 14th Street. A drain led from one wing of
his hawk's nose to a bottle on a metal stand at the bedside. His
gray dried-out hair lay behind him on the pillow, no longer a part
of him, more like an ugly bouquet of bleached moss draped by a
well-meaning visitor over his liverish skull. His head was like some
caricature, sinister and morbid, that he himself might have sketched
in a fascinated, prophetic moment of repellent self-examination.
The cheeks were gone, collapsed into the hollows of the skull, but
the chin like the nose jutted forth in an angular expression of
defiance. Or was it despair? His hands, those horny powerful extensions of a personality once combative and creative, were now
reduced to veined claws, spotted and speckled. They picked vaguely
at the hospital sheet that covered what was left of him. The smell
alone was enough to make you weep for all this reduction.

Driven forward by shame, he said, "Hey Vito, it's Joe Link."

The sunken eyes squinted, then lighted as if the failing current
within had once again been summoned forth. "Word gets around,
doesn't it?"

It was startling to hear the familiar voice issuing from this
wasted sack of bones. Unable to speak, he nodded.

"Sit down, Joe. I wish I looked as good to you as you do to me."

"Same old Vito."

"Not any more. What are you doing here?"

By here, he decided, Vito meant not in the hospital but in the East; at least it was easier to speak of the book idea than of the medical reality.

"I'm glad you're still in there punching. Don't quit." Vito's voice trailed off. Then he roused himself. "Even if you don't get it done, it's the trying that counts, follow me?"

"I follow." He could only take refuge in banality. "How are they treating you here?"

"They do their best. But I'll tell you something." Vito paused again. "There's one thing these people just don't know."

"What's that?"

"How awful dying is."

In the silence the little squeal of a medication cart being wheeled into the next room was like a cry of pain.

Vito went on as if he had been talking about the weather. "Bernie asked me if she could do anything. I told her, but she didn't listen. She smiled but she didn't listen."

"I'm listening."

"Maybe." Vito beckoned to him with his finger. He whispered, "Get me out of here. I want to go home to Broome Street. I've got all my paintings back there."

"But—"

"It's the last favor I'll ask of you."

"Vito, I swear to you, I'll do what I can."

Angry with himself, he backed out of the room and stood for a moment in the corridor, gulping air. It was seventeen years since he had lain in the hospital, impotent, staring, while others turned over on their sides and died. He wheeled about and made for the duty nurse at the end of the corridor.

She listened to him, surprised. "But you're not a member of the family. It ought to be a family member. Or his doctor."

"I'd better talk to the doctor."

He was a youngish man in tweeds, slim, quick, rather nervous. "Ordinarily," he explained, "it makes good sense for terminal cases to return home. At its best, a hospital stinks."

"I know. I've served my time. What about Vito?"

"He has no real home. No facilities in his studio. How can I let him go in such circumstances? Even here, under sedation, his pain is severe. If he left . . ." The doctor paused, then added earnestly, "I've always admired him."

He shook the doctor's hand and went out to catch the uptown Seventh Avenue express.

At 96th and Broadway he emerged once again, into yet another of New York's worlds. On the benches in the tiny square, all but engulfed by the Santini moving vans that belched gaseous exhaust into their upturned faces, old women in ratty furs, stockings rolled at the knee, smoked cigarettes and presented their withered cheeks to the feeble rays of the autumn sun. Squeezed hip to flank, Negro junkies dozed and actors on unemployment comp exchanged the *Village Voice* and the *Times* crossword puzzle. An elderly unshaven Jew, too poor or too neglected by his children to winter in Florida, moved his lips silently over the *Forward* beside a blondined fairy in stovepipe pants who teetered on one buttock, filing his nails meticulously, extending his hand from time to time to admire the effect.

Joe crossed with the light, heading toward the Hudson. At West End Avenue he paused for a moment to survey the numbers, then hurried on to Carmela's apartment house.

He leaned on the button marked Metzger for some seconds. The response was not long in coming. Carmela's breathy, nervous voice inquired through the tube, "Who is it? Who's there?"

"Hi, Carmela," he said. He added, "It's Joe Link."

Her exclamation was stifled. After a moment she asked, "Are you alone? You are? My God, this place is such a mess. Well, come on up."

When she opened the door cautiously to his buzz, she already wore fresh lipstick, but she was still in a dressing gown.

"What a surprise," she said. "You're just in time for some coffee, if you can stand the disorder."

The place did not look that bad, nor did she. Uncorseted, she was opulent but not sloppy; her dark eyes still snapped. But she was ill at ease. She talked too much and too fast as she bustled about, buttering bread and perking coffee.

"I haven't been here too long, it's just a sublet, I haven't had the chance to fix it up properly. But from that corner window you can see the river, and when it's nice out you can see the bridge, you know, the George Washington. Say, how did you find me? I'm not even in the book yet."

"I visited with Norm and Vera in Georgetown. I've been traveling around doing some research."

"Oh." Vera's name brought some color to her cheeks. "How's Vera?"

"Fine. Considering."

"I know what you mean." She sipped at her coffee. "How about your wife and kids?"

"Anne is still teaching. She's in big demand now, what with Davey's publicity."

"It must be something, having a boy like that, a genius."

"I don't think he's a genius."

"Never mind. I heard about his playing in Hollywood Bowl. What about the little one?"

"Little? Gene's my size, almost. He's what they call fucked up, Carmie."

"Come on, I don't believe you."

He shrugged. "I myself think he'll be all right, but it kills Anne that he doesn't cut his hair. And skips school."

"Ah, he's one of those."

"I don't blame him, I'd cut loose too if my big brother was the star of the family."

"Christ," she burst out, "who would have guessed what kind of trouble we were borrowing, back in those early days? If you have two kids, one is jealous of the other. If you have one, you're a selfish parent, you're bringing up a spoiled one, or a neurotic. Look at poor Vera. Or Irwin and me."

"But Paul's all right, isn't he?"

The coffee cup shook in her hand as she set it down on the saucer. "He says it's not safe for me to go uptown, it's dangerous in Harlem these days, not like when I was his age. Okay, I said, you come here. But he works during the day, and at night he's busy with his social work with those colored kids, whatever he does."

"What does he do for a living?"

"He runs errands for some garment firm. For that he studied philosophy. The value of a college education. When we were kids, if you had a college education you were like a god or something."

"At least he's doing what he wants."

"How does he know what he wants? He can't even explain it so I can understand. Irwin claims he does, but I'll tell you something, he's as much in the dark as me. I just couldn't stand it, watching him hit the bottle, kidding himself that he's proud of his college boy. You don't think I'm selfish, do you, Joe? Believe me, if I could have helped him, I would have. But I've got a life to live too. I'm sick of having people mumble about feeling sorry for me on account of Irwin. And now Paul."

"I don't think you're selfish. In fact one reason I'm here is that I was hoping you could help me. Have you heard about Vito?"

"I heard he was sick." She added wistfully, "In the old days we were close, before he got famous. I don't want to take advantage, just because we're living in the same town again. I mean, why should he want to hear about my troubles? Or if I told him I'm interested in primitive art, what's that to him?"

"He's not just sick."

She heard him out in silence, her hands tightening around the cooling coffee cup. When he had finished she said simply, "Can you wait till I get some clothes on?"

He was startled. "Sure."

Carmela did not pause to explain, but hurried into her bedroom, leaving him to stare at the Americana strewn about the room—old ads for chewing tobacco and liniment tacked up on the walls, rusted coffee mills, an outsized tricycle, a weathervane in the form of a bearded farmer in Uncle Sam silhouette.

When she came out, dressed and ready for the street, even to a raincoat and scarf, she said, "I'm ready. Let's go."

He looked at her stupidly. "What do you want to do, Carmela? Do you want to go to the hospital?"

"I'm going to get him out of there."

He felt like a fool. This was what he had wanted, but when she said it, as though it was the most ordinary thing in the world, a thousand objections came to his mind.

"Wait a minute," he said.

"We'll talk on the way."

When they were seated in the subway he turned to her. "The doctor won't let him go without an assurance of twenty-four-hour care."

"At the hospital we'll pick up the keys to Vito's studio and I'll start cleaning it. If I know him, it's as messy as ever. And while I'm doing that you can make arrangements for a nurse. Don't worry about the dough, Vito must still be loaded. If his money is socked away I'll hit up Irwin for it. That's one thing about Irwin, he'll come through."

It took him a while to understand how rapidly Carmela had responded without balancing, reflecting, weighing. What he had thought of as almost insuperable obstacles she disposed of as easily as so many dishes to be washed, wiped, and put away.

"I'm moving in," she said, as they stood staring about the huge dust-laden studio. Against two of the walls, the huge canvases that Vito had trucked in from Long Island leaned blankly, their frames draped with brown wrapping paper. "You sit tight here," she ordered. "Just wait for the ambulance while I go back uptown and pack a bag. I'll bring some sweaters and slacks, and pick up some junk to clean the place with."

He could not just wait. He found a rag on the paint table, wiped away the worst of the dirt, and had the bed made up when the ambulance arrived bearing Vito back to his home.

For a moment he was frightened. What would he do, how could he handle the responsibility? The driver and the attendant panted up the rickety stairs with their frail burden, and he could only stand with folded arms.

But when they placed Vito gently on the bed that he had made, he knew that his impulse had been as right as Carmela's. Vito did not appear to be conscious, but as he felt the covers being rearranged he opened his eyes. It was amazing that lids could move so slowly, like the raising of a curtain. He stared up for a moment, unblinking. Then he whispered, "Thanks."

After that Carmela took over. She slept on the tattered chaise in the corner that Vito had been accustomed to throw himself down on, brush in hand, when he took a break. Between herself and Vito she stood a paneled screen on which he had tacked postcards from friends, from the Tate, the Uffizi, the Prado. It separated them by sight but not by sound. She could never sleep for more than an hour or two without being aroused by the low moans that escaped from the artist's lips, welling up despite himself.

She was busy. She cooked for herself and an occasional broth or bouillon for Vito on the two-burner that he had hooked to the gas line with a loop of discolored rubber tubing. She gave him his medication, consulted with the doctor when he came by, and in short order fired the nurse. In consequence she took over the washing, the shaving, the emptying of Vito's urinal and chamber pot. Bending over his naked yellowing frame, its shrunken skin covered here and there with tufts of graying hair, she laved his flesh with the devotion that he had once, years ago, lavished on hers.

Her spirit, it seemed to Joe each time he arrived at the studio, communicated itself to Vito. After several days he experienced a remission. The mask of pain faded from his hollowed-out face as if it had been washed away by her gentle hands. He asked to be propped up into a sitting position. Carmela plumped up two pillows and slipped them behind his back.

"Joe, bring me my sketch pad," he said. "It's on the rack under the paint table."

"Sounds like you're getting ready to go back to work." He handed Vito a pot of sharpened pencils while Carmela was getting the pad.

Vito stared at him with the enlarged eyes that dominated his waxen countenance. He insisted huskily, "I'm always working. You understand me? Always."

It occurred to him that maybe the artist was wandering. But Vito's gaze was unblinking. "I mean it, Joe," he said. "Don't think just because I'm laying here like a lox, that I'm not working. Now I'm going to try to get something down."

Dismissed, he backed off to the corner where Carmela was stirring soup, but Vito's voice followed him: "That's what it's all about."

He turned around. "What?"

"Work. That's all there is."

He shouldered into his topcoat and stumbled out of the studio. He could not bear the sight of Vito's hand trembling over the pad, or of Carmela, her head bent over the soup that she was stirring around and around.

Vito's words echoed in his ears as he listened to others, questioned them, took notes. The young editors whom Norm had suggested were pleasant, sometimes even eager. "There's a book there!" one of them exclaimed. "There really is!" Instead of being encouraged he felt somehow that he had been completely misunderstood. He was so anxious to regain the studio that he flagged a cab the moment he parted from the last editor.

A thumping scraping noise was coming from the head of the stairs. Alarmed, he took the hollowed steps two at a time. Carmela was staggering behind a huge canvas, trying to turn it about so that Vito could see it from his bed.

"Here," he said, "let me do that."

"Thank God," she muttered. "He wants to look at some of his pictures." Her hair was disarranged, her perspiration-ringed sweater had hiked above her slacks. She had been ranging the canvases along the wall facing the bed.

When they were done they turned and saw that Vito, supine, no longer able to draw, was gazing not at his paintings but at Carmie. He motioned her to him with a crooked finger. He could not speak aloud. Carmela hurried to the bedside and bent over.

When she straightened up and turned away, her eyes were filled.

"What it it?" Joe took her aside. "What did he say?"

"He said, 'Kid, you're the greatest piece of ass I ever had in my life.'" She stared at him defiantly, her bosom rising, her eyes almost wild. "I don't care, I'll tell you something else. He meant it."

5. PAUL

It was still pitch dark when his Little Ben went off. Staggering out of bed, Paul crashed into the edge of the desk chair with his knee before he managed to punch the clock into silence and find the switch on the desk lamp. Shocked into wakefulness, he hobbled back to the bed and slumped down, rubbing at his leg and blinking while his pupils adjusted themselves to the artificial light.

From the wall across from the bed, his heroes gazed at him benignly. Camus with a cigarette, Russell with a pipe, Pope John with a twinkle, thick peasant finger upraised as if in warning against the sin of pride. Quarter to seven. From the bureau top two couples surveyed him with a personal regard: His father and mother side by side in backyard butterfly chairs, stiffly relaxed in the effort to persuade the world and themselves of their unity, and the Wrights in Atlanta in that same summer, Ham frowning into the sun like his mother, Glory presenting her belly to the camera like his father.

When he was halfway dressed he pulled up the blind and peered out the alleyway to 119th Street. The darkness was fading, but the satellite moon of the streetlamp was still blue-white. In its ghastly glow a line of working women, hands to their throats against the November chill, were already hurrying to their mops and pails, to the dishes piled in the sinks of white women. Behind him the bathroom door clicked. Rufus Rogers, Miss Rockwell's other tenant, a burly brown-faced bachelor who drove a postal truck for the government, had finished.

Paul hastened to take his turn in the john before Miss Rockwell should have need of the facilities. She was very nice. She had even pleaded with him not to be so shy about using her kitchen, but he preferred not to be obligated or involved. Miss Rockwell was a bird-like black woman, a retired kindergarten teacher who seemed to have shrunk with the years to the size of her former charges, and was now so humped and so tiny that she seemed lost between Paul and Rufus. But she carried herself like the mistress of a grand menage in the narrow three-room apartment that she shared with them by sleeping on her living room couch. She had three interests: her teeth, her church, and the doings of the Kennedy family. It was a pattern already familiar to Paul from his experiences with the genteel Negro women of small-town Louisiana, but he still felt there were more valuable ways for him to spend his evenings than watching Jackie rearrange the White House furniture while Miss Rockwell demonstrated to him, the dentist's knowledgeable son, the deficiencies of the dental mechanic who had misfitted her upper partial.

He had stayed up too late the night before, sitting on a stoop down the block with several boys who had noplace to go, talking with them about everything from sex to the Supremes. One lived with a wino aunt who entertained callers when the welfare check ran out, another had been beaten by his father and thrown out for swearing, a third could not claim his bed before midnight, when the roomer who occupied it vacated it for his night-shift job. It had taken him a long time to gain their confidence. They had been justly suspicious that he wanted to peddle something—junk, queer sex, whatever. Once it was clear that they trusted him he was reluctant to leave them, even though he knew that the next morning it would be hard to drag himself out of bed.

He soaked his head with cold water from Miss Rockwell's rusty tap and combed down his curling hair into a semblance of neatness. Then he zipped up his jacket, slipped the paperback of Baldwin's *Fire Next Time* into his hip pocket against those moments during the day when he might be able to read a few pages, and left the house quietly.

Five minutes later he was in a White Tower having coffee and a bowtie before pushing into the subway for the ride down to Penn Station. The morning he had first come in, the only white at the counter, the atmosphere had been very different from the friendly curiosity of the little Negro restaurants of rural Louisiana. He had felt himself the object of a scrutiny that was almost menacing. Not one soul, not even the grease-spattered counterman, spatula in hand, had given him the benefit of the doubt or the courtesy of a greeting.

Now, some months later, he was a regular, if not an old-timer. That was progress, as he had written his father. To walk in feeling not like an interloper, or even a man with a message, but simply a customer with a quarter, who drank his coffee and dunked his cruller in silence, was all that he wanted for now. Whatever else he might some day want, as with the kids on his block, would come only when he had earned it.

The Seventh Avenue subway was so jammed all the way to Times Square that he did not even try to pull out his paperback from his pocket. The brief respite after the mass exodus just gave him time to catch his breath, and then at Penn Station he was off, up the steps, out with the crowd, and shuffling along with the garment workers who streamed off chattering in Spanish, Italian, Yiddish. English was practically the exclusive property of the Negroes for whom it became, slurred and softened, almost a secret code that allowed them to move unheard as well as unseen among all the others.

Paul worked for a dress house on the fifth floor of a 33rd Street loft. For fifty dollars a week he served Jackie Jumpers as a delivery and errand boy. No questions were asked when he first came in, but after they realized that—unlike his predecessors—he was not going to disappear after the first week everyone, from the well-corseted switchboard girl to the fattish young boss, burned with curiosity. What was he trying to prove, an obviously educated fellow, throwing his life away as if he was some dumb Puerto Rican, content to jockey his four-wheeled pipe rack among the trucks of the West Side streets?

The answer was so ridiculously simple that they would not have believed it—and so painfully complex that he would not have known where to begin. So he held his peace, aware that they were surrounding him with an air of mystery. Maybe it was silly, but he preferred having them speculate aloud as to whether he was a runaway rich boy, a fugitive from the narcotics squad, or a poet gathering material about the poor, leaving him free to concentrate his affections and his energies on those who might in the long run want something more from him than banter.

During the course of the morning he took orders for the coffee break, unloaded trucks as they backed onto the sidewalk, ran dollies on and off the freight elevator, trotted out to Walgreen's for the boss's Antony y Cleopatras, and accepted as if it were a tip the kidding about his glasses and his hair.

He ate lunch with two of the other delivery boys from his building at the Moe-Jan Delly. Adam Clayton Smith was a big husky Harlem kid whose god was not his namesake but Willie Mays; he wore ankle-high sneakers and sweat socks. He had dropped out of school because he hated math the way some people hate loud noises or cigarette smoke but he could compute Mays's batting and fielding averages to four places, and he could calculate without a pencil the number of years and the number of homers Willie needed to close in on the Babe. He loved to sprint, to charge, to dash, and the boss referred to him as the lazy *schvartse.*

Adam's friend Angel, a slight and sallow Puerto Rican who suffered from adolescent acne and acute shyness, was also known as a lazy goof-off, more often sick than on the job. He had attached himself to Adam because Adam took him as he was, scared, unathletic, and desperate to do something better—although he could not quite imagine what—then pushing clothes racks up and down 33rd Street. He too had dropped out of school, but he was unable to articulate even the ostensible reasons with Adam's quick readiness. "It don't add up," was the most he could say.

He blamed himself for its not adding up and dreamed aloud of other escapes, other schools. "I bet if I was in one of them schools like you see pictures of, all glass, I'd study like crazy."

"Don't give me that." Adam blew across the top of his Pepsi bottle for the foghorn effect. "You'd be right here jockeying them garments around. Who's goin give you fifty bucks a week to sit in one of them glass schools?"

By now Angel's mother did depend on his pay check to help keep the family afloat; but it had not always been so. Now he was caught feeling one way and looking the other. Licking mustard from his finger, then gazing at the finger as though it were a curiosity, he said, "What I was thinking about was night school."

"You crazy," Adam said bluntly. "I had a cousin did that once, he fell asleep every night till they threw him out. You ain got the jism to wrestle the racks all day and study the books all night."

Paul did not want to antagonize Adam. He said only, "Why not?"

Adam stared at them both with a certain defiance. He had no use
for any of it. His hero could hardly read and write. Willie didn't
have to. He was so great, so unique, that he could live all by himself
in a hundred thousand dollar house with his world records and his
phonograph records. If you went for anything else you were a sucker.
Next thing to a deserter.

Adam's mistrust could swell like some poisonous mushroom into
hatred—of Paul for reverting to type, color, and class; of Angel for
trying to make it in whitey's world. If Willie had done just that,
Adam did not see it that way. But was it fair to turn Angel off, to
tell him that a diploma would earn him nothing but more discrimination? To offer him instead the prospect of becoming the
Fidel of the Lower East Side, when he couldn't run, couldn't hit,
couldn't field, and worried about his complexion?

There was really no choice. You had to offer what you were able
to offer, not what you weren't.

Angel raised his half-defeated, half-hopeful brown eyes and demanded of Paul, "If I did it, would you help me?"

He nodded slowly.

Adam rose abruptly from the tiny formica table over which they
had been crouched. He reached up to the chrome coat hook for his
baseball cap and clapped it on his head backwards like a catcher.
"Going to warm up with Walleye before we go back to work," he
said. "See you."

Paul said, "Angel, if I say I'll do it, I'll do it. It's going to be up
to you to get started."

He would be spreading himself a little thin. But once again he
had no option, if only because he hadn't yet put down roots in his
neighborhood or his job. Last night it had been the kids on his
block; the night before, some young addicts who hung around near
the East Harlem Protestant Parish. Tonight it would be the men
at Hospitality House down on the Bowery, and if tomorrow night
Angel asked him to come down to East 5th Street to tutor him, he
would have to do that.

What mattered, he thought with a certain jubilation, was that
they were coming to him, slowly, surely, as he had known that they
would, and that they would let him come to them, if only he were
not false to them or to himself.

He took up the afternoon's work. Maybe the secret of being adult
was to put aside impatience and prepare yourself for a long life.

The orders came, a dozen size twelve, powder blue, two dozen size ten, cherry pink, he hustled them onto his rack, gave a Gesundheit to sneezing old Schmulke on the freight elevator, and shoved his loaded rack out into the street.

The first few days on the job he had felt as conspicuous pushing the Jackie Jumpers cart as if he were weaving naked through the dense crosstown traffic. Gradually he came to know that for the motorists and the truckdrivers he was invisible. He did not exist for them independently of the wheeled pipe rack which they cursed. He might almost have turned black.

The discovery was liberating. In a way, this was what he had sought and not found in Louisiana. In itself nothing, it freed him to do what he wanted, to become what he hoped. To fail if necessary, to succeed if possible. Even in Harlem there were those who knew —some had actually seen him—that he was a garment district delivery boy; it helped to certify him.

Working his way uptown to 39th, he crossed over, then was totally blocked on the left flank of the rusty-red hulk of the condemned Metropolitan Opera House. Horns blew, drivers cursed. He stuck his head through the size twelves to peer up the street, his nose emerging inches away from the side window of a silver-gray Mercedes driven by an impassive chauffeur. The sole occupant of the back seat, an elegant puffy man with bags under his eyes, held a portfolio open on his lap. He gazed out pensively, apparently bored by what he held on his knees. The sudden appearance of a head through the powder blue Jackie Jumpers caused his forehead to furrow. He stared hard at Paul, as if trying to decide whether the apparition was real.

Now that he had become visible, Paul locked eyes with the older man, who put his hand to his mouth in a considering gesture. He might have been musing to himself on the other side of the glass, Yes, you are real, but do I know you?

Paul was pleased that the scrutiny of the man in the Mercedes did not disconcert him as it once might have done. No more middle-class shame. The jam broke and he was on his way.

The afternoon wore on swiftly, the life of the streets absorbed his attention; when he clocked out at five, he was physically tired. He would have liked to relax with a beer, but it was more important to get downtown.

The Sixth Avenue subway was as packed as the Seventh Avenue

had been in the morning, and more unpleasantly, for it smelled now of weariness and worn bodies. He was happy to leave it, and hurried over to the Catholic Worker building on Chrystie Street. The last of the derelicts were tottering out of the anteroom on whose benches they had been sitting over their lunch meal, picking their teeth, arguing desultorily, mumbling to themselves, dozing. A few remained upstairs in the TV room, having carried with them the odor of decay and capitulation; but they were served only one meal a day here, and would shortly be on their way to wipe the windshields of traffic-stalled cars, hoping for the guilty dimes of the uneasy affluent like the man in the Mercedes.

Several of these broken beings recognized him. They waved cracked hands scored with the stigmata of scabs, cuts, bruises, the fingernails blackened and split, and stretched their chapped lips in greeting to expose missing teeth, their mouths gaping.

He could scarcely bring himself to reply. He had already discovered that he lacked the final element of faith that would enable him not only to join hands with the busy young men on the third floor, but to believe that the forsaken whom they fed as a matter of course, with no expectation of reward, were as worthy of succor as any other of God's creatures. For him these blasted men, doped with wine, cigarette butts, and incoherent memories of the days before disaster had sawed away their props and dropped them out of society, were far down the desperate scale of priorities. Maybe this had to do with his own background and the guilt that continued to arise from it like gas escaping from a badly capped sewer, but now that he had to decide whether to work with the vanquished or with the resentful, he was choosing the latter. Or being chosen by them.

If he continued to come to the community of the Catholic Workers not as a member entitled to quarrel over policy but as a respectful outsider, it was mainly to persuade himself that he was doing the right thing, by occasionally participating after the shared evening meal in the sessions devoted to what they liked to call clarification of thought.

This evening's meeting, in the kitchen-dining room on the first floor, was attended by the upstairs editorial staff of the paper, some people vaguely like himself, some anarchists, some pacifists. Most attractive was their determination to combine activist radicalism with commitment. Their bias against what they called sociological first-aid was one he had leaned toward in college and become convinced of in Louisiana.

They were willing, as he was, to argue anarchism; they were eager, as he was no longer, to argue doctrine and the connection between religious theory and church practice. But they did accept as natural to the point of ordinariness his own life of voluntary poverty. To be able to discuss the kids on the stoop, or Angel versus Adam, without having to parry praise for his courage or amusement at his naiveté was important to him.

What they did not have—no, that was not fair—what he did not have was a sense that his life was *necessarily* bound up with theirs. Loving Jesus, they loved the lowest of the low and saw themselves as only the first of all those who would one day refuse to kill for the state or exploit for the supposed sake of their families. They believed with all their hearts that they were the vanguard of a new breed of Americans—a generation not of Marxist-Leninists but of God-loving anarchists pledged to replace exploitation with love and patriotism with brotherhood.

Believing this too, why couldn't he take the last step? If it were a matter of the draft, or refusing to accept just the one more war that would no doubt be asked of his as it seemed to be of every generation, he would link hands with them. But something in his spirit, perhaps that little grain of skeptic rationalism that had kept his father from submitting to the discipline of the New Party, prevented him from uttering the Credo.

Maybe it had to do with his being more of a Jew than a Catholic. In any case, it was with regret, almost with a sense of poignancy, that he said goodbye to his friends for what might be the last time in a long while. "I'm busy uptown when I'm through working," he said, when they urged him to come back soon. "The more involved I get there the less opportunity I'll have to come down here." Something made him add, "But I'll be thinking of you. I get a great feeling here, it makes me wish I could be less of a lone wolf. But I'm afraid I can't have it both ways."

In the subway for the long ride uptown he was half-drunk with weariness. He bought a city edition of the *Times* when he changed at 14th Street, but was too tired for anything more than a glance at the weather forecast: brisk and chilly tomorrow. Fair enough.

At 116th he folded the paper under his arm and left the train with a sighing charwoman and two gum-cracking teenagers who had

gotten on at Times Square. But when he turned uptown and
headed toward Miss Rockwell's, he was alone once again.

He was surprised to be suddenly crowded by three boys who
seemed to have come from nowhere. Approaching soundlessly from
the rear, two of them grasped his elbows from both sides while the
third jostled him in the small of the back with something that felt
sharp.

Startled, he glanced about. Was it a gag, was it the kids from
the stoop? "All right, you guys," he said. "You can have the paper.
Just let me keep the crossword puzzle."

Their answer was a shove that sent him sprawling against an
overloaded garbage can. Then they yanked him to his feet, and he
saw that they were strangers. He had been conditioned by Louisiana
to guarding not against blacks but against whites; with each succeeding day here he had given less thought to how he might react to
a situation like this.

"Wassamatta, whitey," the tallest drawled, "white pussy ain good
enough for you? You gotta come uptown after black stuff?"

"I live here. I live on the next block."

Standing on the stoop so that they could look down on him, the
other two burst out laughing, their voices shrill and raucous. The
tall one, gripping him just above the elbow, began to punch him
staccato fashion on the biceps, rap rap rap, the blows seemingly
light but increasing in intensity. "Who you shittin, boy? Who you
think you shittin?"

"I can prove it to you." With his free hand he reached toward his
hip pocket, but one of the two on the stoop leaned forward to
restrain him.

"I'll get that." With his switchblade he snicked open Paul's hip
pocket, catching the wallet before it hit the ground. The big one resumed the rhythmic punching. His arm was beginning to swell, the
pain was growing unbearable. He bit back a groan.

The one with the knife was leafing through the wallet. "Hey,
how about that. He wasn't shittin us after all."

Paul's heart jumped. Even the agonizing rapping on his upper arm
stopped. But before he could say anything the tall one snapped his
fingers. "Now I know who he is. He's the four-eyed beatnik, sits
on the stoop tellin fairy tales to the kids."

With one sweep, he knocked off Paul's glasses, then raised his
booted foot and deliberately ground them against the pavement.

"Ok, beatnik, done you a favor. Now you ain't no four-eyes. Now you don't have to read no more fairy books."

The one with the switchblade pointed it at him. "I think he got the hots for nigger boys."

"If you give me a chance," Paul said, "I'll tell you what—"

"You'll tell me shit. I'll find out for myself." He began to pull everything out of the wallet systematically. "Ain much bread, like nine bucks." He stuffed the bills in his pocket and ripped everything else into tiny shreds one by one. Draft card, social security card, driver's license, pay envelope. "Look at this, he work for Mr. Goldberg. Maybe he Mr. Goldberg's son." He paused over a snapshot.

Everything was blurry, but he knew what the snapshot was. All at once it was desperately important to get it back, a matter of life and death.

"Let me have the picture," he pleaded. "Just let me keep that, you're welcome to everything else."

"You're welcome, you're welcome. First you move in on my turf, mothafucka, then you think you givin me orders too?" He turned over the photo and read the inscription. "For Paul from Paul with love from us all. How about that, you think this mothafucka done gone and got hisself a nigger baby?" He spread his legs and shoved the photo between his buttocks. "I gonna wipe my ass with this Paul-shit."

Paul leaped forward. As he grappled for the taunting hand a tremendous blow in the back staggered him. He fell forward and a boot flashed at his head. He could not avoid it, it caught him on the temple and spun him down half a flight of steps to a black cellar areaway.

Groping, he gripped the concrete steps with his fingertips and began to work his way up. One, two, if he could reach the sidewalk he would make his way to the streetlamps, to life. But then, with the sound of high shrill laughter and fleeing footsteps fading as he strained to lift his ear from the concrete, something gigantic, overwhelming, a huge wave-like force, arose within him. He opened his mouth to release it and blood came gushing forth as he slid back down the steps into darkness.

6. NORM

Sy had said over the phone that he should go directly to the Taft. Jolting into the morning rush hour, Norm squirmed painfully on the torn taxi seat. A broken spring. When he did get to the hotel they would first have to go on up to Harlem.

As soon as she could pull herself together, Vera had hurried to New York to be with Carmela; he had been the one to tell Marlen about Paul. Marlen had been concerned and grave. But once he had demonstrated that he could look gravely concerned with the best of them, he had allowed himself a pitying smile, the kind that seemed to say, Well, we all have to go sometime.

Norm leaned forward. "Hey driver, maybe you ought to go up to 57th and then cut across."

"Just relax and worry about your business, friend," the driver said over his shoulder, "while I relax and worry about mine. We'll both live longer that way."

Gnawing on a nail, he tried to contain himself; but in the end the creeping traffic, the memory of his son's little smile, and the anticipation of what lay ahead were too much.

"Let me off here," he said, thrusting several bills at the hackie. "I'll walk the rest of the way."

The city was heedless of the catastrophe that made him shudder for his bereft friend. Even if, instead of one innocent boy struck down, two miles away, there were to be a hundred such only two blocks away, the stream of city life would continue to flow.

At the Taft he went straight to a house phone and asked for Dr. Metzger.

The voice that answered was not Irwin's. It took him a moment to identify it. It was Sy speaking rather abruptly over a barrage of noise. "Come on up."

"Is Vera there yet?"

The reply was muffled, and then they were disconnected. Muttering, he hurried to the elevator. On the seventh floor he followed the arrow and turned right. Not fifteen feet in front of him stood his wife and Carmela, black-clad and clinging to each other.

Their dresses were terribly new, their make-up desperately fresh, but they seemed like two figures in some ancient frieze, his wife angular, her drawn-back coarse gray hair pulling her cheekbones into relief, her friend's olive skin sallow and bloodless.

Before he could think of what he might say to her Carmela had thrown herself at him, teetering forward into his arms on absurd stiletto heels that could hardly support her solid flesh. He accepted the burden, enfolding her and gazing over her head into the shadowed eyes of his wife, who was trying to signal a message that he could not read.

"You've got to get me in there." Carmela's voice was muffled by his lapel. ". . . want to do something for me, make him let me in."

"Who?" he asked. "Irwin?"

She nodded against his chest. Then she raised her head, drew breath, and said more clearly, "He doesn't realize what he's doing to me."

Vera explained flatly: "He's drunk. He won't let her in. And she won't go to the services by herself."

"Isn't he going?"

"If they can pull him together."

"I can. That's why I came." Carmela started to cry. "Once he lets me apologize . . ."

"For what?"

"For everything I've done to him."

"Maybe he can't face that, Carmie."

"How about me? Am I supposed to face what he's doing to me? Why did he have to insult me by moving into this hotel? We spent our honeymoon here. I told him, stay with me, it's your apartment as much as mine, you're paying the rent."

Why had Irwin done it? Norm had the feeling that he would never know—and that he never should, any more than he should see his friends unclothed together. He released Carmela to his wife, went on to the door beyond them, and pressed the buzzer.

He waited, patient now. The door opened a crack. The chain was dropped and Joe Link waved him on in silently.

"How about the women?"

Joe said matter of factly, "Irwin says if we let Carmie in, he'll jump out the window."

"Where is he?"

Joe jerked his thumb up and over his shoulder in the direction of the bathroom, like an umpire signalling a man out. Not speaking, stepping swiftly over the unbuckled valise and scattered clothes, Joe led the way to the bathroom and pushed open the door.

Sy sat facing them on the edge of the sunken tub. He was in his shirtsleeves, his tie yanked open and the lenses of his glasses so smeared that it hardly seemed possible he could see out of them. He glanced up and nodded curtly.

Irwin was on the floor in his shorts next to the toilet bowl. The seat was up, and he was resting his cheek directly against the china; occasionally he raised his head to spit into the water, and Sy would reach over him to flush it. Joe stepped across Irwin's legs, naked except for incongruous socks and garters and shiny black shoes, and tapped him on his fat freckled shoulder.

"Norm is here."

Irwin glanced up, eyeballs rolling whitely in his blotched countenance. He released his hold on the toilet bowl, which he had been embracing as if someone were trying to take it away from him, and passed his hand across his scalp to smooth back the long thin strands that had fallen forward across his bald head. His breasts, hairless and square as a buddha's, creased above his swollen belly.

"Join the party." He belched deeply. "This john is jumping like the stateroom in that Marx Brothers movie." He twisted around to look at his cousin. "Which one was it?"

Sy was impassive. "It's getting late, Irwin."

"Sy has never approved of my drinking. How about you, Norm? What's your feeling? Does it bother you to see me like a swine, a porker, swilling at the trough?"

"You're entitled to be drunk. In fact I wish I was."

"Oh you do, do you? Well, go meet my best friend, Jack Daniel. He's in the bedroom, if Sy hasn't thrown him out. Do you think

Groucho could pull one that good at his son's funeral? Tell me honestly, muscle man, wouldn't Paul be proud of me if he could see me now?"

"I don't think he'd be ashamed."

"What do *you* know?"

He felt himself turning cold. He said stonily, "I know."

"I'm sorry. You're right." Irwin began to cry. "Paul understood better than anybody. He understood and he forgave. That's why they had to kill. The bastards. Why should I go up there and look at those faces?"

"For him."

"Don't give me that shit. There's nothing I can do for him any more. I just wish it was me instead of him, that's all."

"Wouldn't that be easy? The trick is to go on living even after you've found out what kind of world it really is."

Irwin's nose was running; a string of colorless snot hung down to his lip. Eyes closed, tears leaking from the lids, he extended his arm feebly. Joe tore off a length of toilet paper and handed it to him. He blew his nose and wiped his eyes.

"I found out a long time ago," he said, "what kind of world it is. You're the ones who never knew. Goddam Pollyannas."

"So now we know," Sy muttered. "What does it change? We still have to go to the services."

"You were the guys that tried to sell me on the brotherhood of man. You and Ham worked on my boy, you got him to throw his life away. For what? For nothing."

"That's not true."

"For less than nothing."

Norm felt the sweat exuding in his armpits. "Listen." He squatted down next to Irwin. "I won't accept that, you hear?"

"Too bad about you. You and your optimism. But it didn't happen to your boy, it happened to mine."

"You think I haven't suffered?" Suddenly he wanted to hit, to slam. "How do you know what Vera and I have gone through?" He reached out for Irwin, but Joe grabbed him and shoved him against the wall.

Irwin began to weep again. "I'm sorry, I'm sorry! I didn't mean it. We're all in the soup. We struggled, we knocked ourselves out, for what? I don't care what you say, it was for nothing. Paul never had a chance to live a life, to become a father." He was howling like a dog. "What do you think I got drunk for? If he died fighting against the bigots, like we fought against Hitler, I would have been sober, I would have gone up to their services with my head in the air. But they didn't even want him, they stabbed him in the back after I warned him, I begged—"

Joe cut him short by pushing him in the chest with the toe of his shoe. When he spoke his voice was cold and measured. "I'll be goddamned if I'll stand here and let you spit on his grave. How do you know how many people were changed by him? Ham told me that wherever Paul walked in Louisiana people's faces lighted up. He did more in three months than most men do in three years."

"And this fall?"

"This fall too. Because he didn't finish his work? Who does finish?"

"Don't kid me. He was like everybody who tries to bring people what they don't even want. Look at you." Irwin flung out his arms to include them all. "Twenty years you blew, no, twenty-five. A lifetime. On something so laughable, so comical, all the survivors can do now is to make jokes about it."

"They can talk for themselves," Sy said. "Not for Paul."

"You know what you are? You know what all of us are? Not even a footnote." Irwin struggled to his feet. "Roosevelt and the war that you were against, Truman and the war that you were against, Eisenhower and the McCarthyism that you were against, Kennedy and the Bay of Pigs that you were against . . . Who cared what you thought? Nobody but a handful of cranks and psychopaths. Nuts, freaks, unhappy slobs like me. And kids like my son that you had no right to—"

"I don't hold myself responsible for Paul's death. I don't hold Ham responsible for it. Or you for that matter."

"Go ahead, cousin. Give me a Marxist interpretation. I used to enjoy hearing that stuff from you. It was so impressive. Tell me how capitalism brutalized the Negroes. Maybe you can mix in a little Freud. Tell me they weren't savage, those killers, they were just sick, they were acting out hostilities against their absent fathers."

"I have nothing that fancy to say. One way or another, we tried to keep an idea alive. There weren't enough of us, there never are. We were ridiculously wrong about a lot of things but who wasn't? And what idea did they keep alive, the others?"

Irwin stared at him. For the first time he did not attempt to reply, but stared at them uncertainly.

"Don't tell me," Sy persisted, "that Bernie and I wasted the years in Israel. That's not what you said at our kibbutz. And don't tell Joe that he wasted the years in California during the blacklist."

Irwin turned on Joe. "All right. Was it worth it?"

"What kind of a place is this to—"

"Are you going to answer me or not? You said I had something to show for my life. What about yours?"

"You want me to say that I've got two sons and you haven't got any. Right?"

"You're saying it, not me."

"I am not. One day I'll lose them, one way or another. Everybody does. I'm not saying that to be kind. Maybe I've lost them already. And Anne too. The one thing I haven't lost is my pride. Maybe that'll mean something to them yet."

"What's your pride got to do?"

"I had to keep the idea alive in myself before I could get anybody else to believe in it. So did Paul. You think I'm going to stand here and let you say that it's all been meaningless? That Paul's life was meaningless? Instead of standing there with your nose running put on your goddamn shirt and pants and let's get out of here."

Norm waited until his friends had helped Irwin into his clothes. Then he stepped forward.

"Vera is out in the hall with Carmela. I think they should be with us when we leave here."

Irwin had gotten himself together amazingly well. Maybe it was the water glass of bourbon that Joe had given him. His eyes were swollen, but clear.

"Vera has had enough," he said. "Why should she have to be involved in this?"

"Because she loves Carmie."

"Don't you think I do? Do you know how many times I stood knocking at the door, begging to be let in?" He set the glass down and clasped his fingers. "I just can't stand the thought of seeing her. All those terrible fights, those stupid separations, those useless reconciliations. There's nothing left, the only decent thing we ever managed to do together has been . . ." He stopped.

For the first time Sy and Joe seemed to hesitate, uneasily. Norm felt a sudden access of surety. "Let's find out."

With one hand on Irwin's arm, he extended the other and opened the door. Carmela stood in the doorway, half-leaning on Vera, the grief of middle age rendering her desperately uncertain.

He said, "We're about to leave."

"I just wanted to say, Irwin . . ." Carmela began. She moistened her lips. She reached out, to touch Irwin's tautly clasped hands. She said rapidly, "He was yours. All those times I taunted you, it wasn't true. It wasn't true, what I said."

"I know it," Irwin muttered.

She did not seem to have heard. "I thought that if you wouldn't be sure, you'd never be sure of me either. It was childish, but you always came for me. But I was a liar. He wouldn't have lived like he did if he hadn't been yours."

"I know it," Irwin repeated. "You don't think it was senseless, what he did?"

She opened her eyes wide. "Nobody could be as proud of their kid as I am of him."

"We're going to be late," Sy said.

There was no question of who would get in which taxi. It seemed taken for granted that the first one would be for Irwin and Carmela, and Vera, who glanced back over her shoulder at him with a quick, rather twisted smile before she clambered in after them.

He squeezed in with the two men. Sy raised his voice to the driver. "Go up to 59th and drive through Central Park to 110th. We might as well go by way of the park and relax for a minute, right?"

"I don't know about you guys," Joe said heavily, "but out on the Coast I seem to spend half my time going to funerals."

"When you hit forty," Sy observed, "you start losing parents, uncles, aunts. I guess when you get old yourself, it's your brothers' and sisters' funerals that you drag yourself to."

The day seemed more sharply etched than any he had ever lived through since—since when? The return from Little Rock to the ruin of his family? As they rolled northward past the zoo and the playing fields, deserted on this sunny but frosty Friday morning, he was uneasy that the keenness with which his senses reacted even to the wind ruffling the uncut grass at the edge of the parkway might be nothing more than cold professional opportunism. Was he salting everything away like a pack rat against the day when he would write of the burial of his friend's only child? If so it was as shameful as the fact that the three of them were alive to horrify Irwin with the physical proofs of their comfortable existence while his son, who had tried far harder than they, lay wretchedly dead.

Maybe, though, it was simply a defense against the pain. Not the life, but the waste, was more abstract than the sweat staining the back of the bicyclist whom they drew abreast of and then passed at a bend in the parkway.

Deliberately, he turned back to his friends.

Just as Vera had hastened to New York to comfort Carmela, so Sy had taken over the task of which Irwin had been incapable—reclaiming the body from the morgue where it had lain for twenty-four hours as Unidentified White Male, until the Reverend Bankhead of the Adventist Church had gone downtown and made the identification of the white boy known to him and his parishioners only as Paul.

"I'm still not sure how they ever came to me," Sy said. "When they traced him to that garment manufacturer they must have gotten his social security number. And that must have led them to Irwin."

"Maybe Irwin asked them to get hold of you," Joe suggested. "How did you get him to agree to the services this morning?"

"It wasn't easy. He wanted an Orthodox Jewish burial, out of respect for Paul's faith. I said to him, let the neighborhood people where he lived say goodbye in their own way. After that, he can take him home for an Orthodox interment."

"Except, why drag out the agony?"

"Because it may help him and Carmela to cope with the fact that the boy is dead."

But everyone was selfish; even while Vera sat huddled in the taxi with the shattered couple, he himself was torn between guilt that his own son was alive and envy of Irwin and Carmela's security —the memory of a stainless son, theirs forever and ever. Amen.

Sy was directing the driver to the Adventist Church, but when they got there they found the street blocked by a green and white squad car. The two policemen, one white and the other Negro, would not permit the taxi to enter.

"I'll pay the fare," Norm said. "You guys go ahead and find out what's up."

By the time he caught up with them, he could see for himself. A huge crowd was milling about before the small church in which the services were to be held. It parted for the three of them, the only whites, almost as a matter of course, closing in after them as they entered the building.

Engulfed in the flood, his nostrils assailed by the smell of massed bodies, his ears by the high-pitched whine of predominantly female voices, he searched for his wife in those standing against the walls on either side, and in the early arrivals, squeezed onto folding chairs with their hands pressed between their cramped thighs. Here and there among the women mourners was a scattering of men, some of them white and very young. Friends? Classmates?

Then he caught sight of Vera, her arm raised in the front row, where she had brought Irwin and Carmela. On either side of them were the upturned faces of his young manhood.

Fred the eager young college instructor, now professionally wry and locked into an eternally smiling middle age, wore his label like a name tag. He had come not with his divorced wife but with his grown daughter, who sat in the crook of her father's arm, a handkerchief pressed to her face. Beyond her Ham Wright, thin, distraught, and Big Boy, his hair gone white, his black granitic countenance seamed and set. Next to them his sister-in-law Margaret clutched her husband's hand. The Zivics hid behind sun glasses as if ashamed to show their swollen eyes, the childless come to console the childless.

"Many voices heard," he whispered to Vera.

She was gazing at the preacher's lectern, on which stood a cheap glass vase bearing a single red rose.

"Hoover sent it from California."

"I didn't even know he was still alive."

Staring at the rose that seemed to grow out of the Reverend Bankhead's cupped hands as the packed mass quieted, he had a vision of the bald and saturnine organizer, retired from the revolution but straight-backed and grim, marching into a florist's with his social security check to telegraph a rose, a blood-red flower with a thorn, the symbol of radical bereavement. Extended not only across the country but across an age, from the hounded anti-war

Wobblies of his youth to the young rebels offering their love to the oppressed.

The simplicity of Hoover's gesture pricked him now as the meaninglessness of the event had not, as even Irwin's collapse and his friends' lacerating struggle to bring him here had not. Tears filled his eyes; he covered his face with his hand. Vera reached out to touch him.

"Doesn't all this remind you of something?"

He remembered at once what she remembered, their evenings —before Marlen, before marriage, before the war—in the storefront church of Reverend Matthews, where they had barged in with their cocksure doctrine, smiling at the sweaty rhetoric of the black preacher. What had they learned in the course of all these used-up years—that now the tables were turned? Groping, he found Vera's hand.

"This young man," the minister was saying, "came to us like a missionary, with nothing to offer but a loving heart and helping hands. He was struck down by those whom he might have helped, if they had only listened. But many did listen, more than he could ever know. The children whom he took to the movies on Saturday afternoons. The girls whom he comforted when they offered themselves to him for the price of a fix. The boys whom he helped with their lessons and gave the hope that they could awaken from the nightmare. Those like myself, whom he simply asked, Is there anything I can do, a bench I can repair, a boy I can sit with on the curbstone for an hour?

"For all of us who will never be the same, I want to give thanks for the brief period that he was loaned to us. Would that it had been longer. Thanks that it was at all."

Others, younger, less fluent, took turns bearing witness. Then they were on their feet, all of them. Among the general weeping a path was made for Irwin and Carmela. Tearless, they led the way up the aisle, arm in arm.

Crushed together on the sidewalk, everyone clasped those they had only just left as well as those whom they had not seen in long months and years. They embraced in the near-exultant relief that exhilarates survivors even while it shames. They spoke of everything, it seemed, but Paul.

He drew Vera aside. "It's as if all of us were in a hurry to get him out of our minds."

"For the time being, we probably are," she conceded. "After all, Paul isn't an easy figure to confront for too long at a time."

A figure? Already not a person? But Vera was right, he had been seduced by the red rose and by his own feelings into taking the preacher's promises literally. The boy had changed many lives, maybe including their own, but he had been too demanding, and those who lived on would not wear the change in their faces.

An auto radio squawked. The crowd broke, reformed; the car was suddenly surrounded; someone shouted hoarsely.

"What is it? What?"

"They shot Kennedy. Somebody shot Kennedy."

"Man you crazy."

"Ain crazy, somebody plugged him down in Dallas."

"Dallas? Dallas? What he want to go there for?"

He grabbed Vera by the wrist and plunged with her down the street, weaving around the parked cars, through the clots of radio listeners and the women weeping anew. They ran, without calling back to their friends, without shaking hands, without saying good-bye. They had to get home.

In the cab that they finally flagged down on the corner of Seventh Avenue the Negro driver did not wait for them to catch their breath. "You folks hear about it?"

"We heard. We want to get to La Guardia as quick as possible."

"The way I figure," he went on imperturbably, "it's all the violence in the air." He held up his hands, encased in a woollen glove from which the fingers had been cut off. "All that killing, it had to come back to haunt us."

Who was haunted? On the shuttle back to Washington, after the pilot announced that the President had died and a killer had been apprehended, two middle-aged Americans across the aisle began to argue about whether the Sunday football games would be or ought to be canceled. Vera sat beside him without saying a single word, her fingers digging into his arm as though she were waiting for their plane to crash.

When they landed at the National Airport Vera turned to him as if she were honestly surprised that they were still alive.

"Now what?"

"Home."

He had feared that she was in shock. Now he saw that she was not. She had simply refrained, as he had, from uttering their son's name. She had known from the very first moment that she would have to go to him, but she had not looked forward to it. That was because she persisted in supposing herself guilty. She did not see that everyone who had survived all of these deaths would be forever oppressed by the guilt of his own survival. They paused, irresolute, in the swirling lobby, as if awaiting a sign.

"Come," he said to Vera, who was standing with her gloved hand to her mouth. "There'll be a radio in the cab."

The announcer seemed to be repeating over and over lines that were being fed to him on an endless roll. Air Force One, he said finally, was flying the slain President and his successor back to the nation's capital. The absent cabinet members were returning from the Pacific. Everyone was converging on Washington.

In Georgetown they left the cab and walked sedately to their door as if they were returing from a walk in the park. Before they could buzz, the maid, her face swollen, opened the door and handed him a message.

Far from being surprised, he felt at once that this was why he had hurried back, not to get home but to get the message asking him to meet Air Force One. He handed it to his wife without comment.

"I suppose you want to go," she said. "Go ahead. I'll take care of everything here."

Backing the car out of the garage, he realized that he had not kissed her goodbye. Well, it was too late to turn around. Without his noticing it, night had drawn down. The lights were winking on as he drove; the radio was reporting the flight path of the plane. Once out of the District he hit Suitland Drive, and Westover Drive, and let himself be guided by the red and white water towers to Andrews Air Force Base. It was noisy, floodlit, already crowded, but beyond the wire fence thousands stood waiting, silently.

Was it possible, he wondered, to die for others, when you did not want to die? Or did not know that you were supposed to be dying for others? Could you live for others when they did not know or care whether you lived or died? Earlier in the day his friends had tried to rescue, to bind up and set on his painful path, one wounded man who must have asked himself such questions. What would they think now if they were to stand here, where he stood? In the extremity of their isolation, would they see him simply as one of whom the best you could say was that he had held out a little longer than most?

The crowd sighed. Blinking steadily, the plane was coming down, bringing its burden to earth with the heavy grace of an aging mother. He took a deep breath and stepped forward.

DATE DUE